Annisa
Daughter of Afghanistan

By

Kathleen MacArthur

eBookstand Books
www.ebookstand.com
www.cyberread.com

Published by
eBookstand Books
Division of CyberRead, Inc.
1877_6

Copyright © 2004 by Kathleen MacArthur
All rights reserved. No part of this publication may be reproduced or transmitted in any form or by any means, electronic or mechanical, including photocopy, recording, or any information storage and retrieval system, without permission in writing from the copyright owner.

ISBN 1-58909-202-3

Printed in the United States of America

Acknowledgments

I wish to thank Malcolm MacArthur, Max Trautman, Karl Trautman, Samantha Soper, Debra Trautman, Marty Vinograd, Hayes Gorey, Nancy Tatlock, Mary Sargent, Mary Clayton and Joe Griffin for their efforts in helping me to tell Annisa's story.

Dedication

For Mary Anne Bowen, teacher extraordinaire

1980

CHAPTER 1

The sound was born high in the mountains and traveled in a zigzag fashion down the steep granite slopes until it reached the deserted streets of Kabul far below. *"Allah e Akbar,"* the bearded man on horseback shouted as he galloped towards Jad-i-miwand, the street that parallels the Kabul River.

One by one the shuttered windows flew open to the moonless night and the Afghan people answered back: God is great. *Allah e Akbar!*

The machine gun on a Russian tank ripped out a volley and the horse and its rider fell, but there was no stopping the sound. Men on rooftops took it up. *"Allah e Akbar"* undulated in and out of the winding bazaar and surged across the river from Bagemerdan, hitting the army barracks near Dilkusha Palace. Afghan soldiers threw down their guns and rushed into the street shouting at their startled Soviet advisors. "God is great."

The chanting now swept towards the residential section of Shar-i-Nau, wafting over the high whitewashed walls, which sheltered the city's beautiful private gardens.

Annisa, the adolescent daughter of the eminent Afghan poet, Professor Sulaiman Aziz, threw back the coverlet from her bed and raced to the door of her bedroom balcony. The protest had begun! Barefoot in her flannel nightdress, she stepped outside. Patches of snow on the balcony numbed her toes. A frigid wind from the mountains whipped her long dark hair and flattened her gown against her. Yet Annisa felt as though her limbs were on fire, fueled by her defiance.

A Soviet tank turned the corner on quiet treads and passed swiftly along the street beneath her.

"Allah e Akbar," Annisa challenged, leaning over the railing to shake her fist at the disappearing tank. Cowards! Afraid to walk the street at night like men. Cowering inside their armored shells. Hiding like faceless turtles behind the menacing guns that never differentiate a target.

She raised her arms in exultation. *"Allah e Akbar."*

"Allah e Akbar," a young man's voice answered back from the rooftop across the street. She could not see him because of the blackness that canopied the dim street below, but she knew it was Kassim. Kassim with the soulful eyes and the dark hair that curled

at the nape of his neck. Kassim, whom she watched in the early evenings from her upstairs window as he kicked a soccer ball inside the compound of his father's house. Kassim, who once had handed her a ripe peach as he passed her on his way to school. Annisa blushed at the memory. She had not refused his offering and had boldly thanked him with her eyes. For two days the peach had sat on her windowsill until its ripeness brought a swarm of flies and she had been forced to eat it, the sweet juice trickling down her chin and staining the collar of her school uniform.

The door of Annisa's bedroom opened from behind her and Panna, the girl's aged Indian ayah, shuffled in. "Child, come inside. You will catch your death."

"At last. We show our true feelings to the puppets. Look! Below!"

The street was beginning to fill with men who defied the curfew and rushed out from behind the high walls to shout their allegiance to God. Fifteen-year-old Kassim had left the rooftop to join his brothers who were gathered under the street lights. Annisa heard the garden gate open below. She saw her father hurry into the street, still buttoning his jacket, his karakul hat askew. Behind him, Sultan followed. Annisa had never seen their ancient gardener without his turban and she laughed at his baldness. There was also laughter in the street and the shaking of hands, and the chant of "God is Great" grew even louder.

Annisa could not restrain herself; she had to join them. Determined, she re-entered her room and scurried to her closet. A poster of the American rock singer Elvis Presley was tacked inside, a gift from her brother's best friend, Najib Duranni. She idolized Najib who was always bringing her gifts and who defended her in her frequent spats with her brother, Rahmin. It made her anxious that there had been no word from either of them since the Soviet invasion.

"And where do you think you are going?" Panna asked, as she watched Annisa pull her nightdress over her head and in her haste toss it on the floor. The old woman could not help staring at the sweet promise of the girl's young body. Annisa would enter her womanhood and soon. What a pity there was no mother to guide her. Panna was much too reticent to discuss such delicate matters. "Answer me. Where are you going?"

"To join my father."

"You'll do nothing of the kind. Have you not heard the machine guns!"

"The Russians are only trying to scare us." Annisa was dressing in frantic haste. "Tonight no harm will come. Allah is with us."

"Lord God Shiva loves without motives," Panna muttered under her breath. Hers was a different god but gods were all the same. They never took sides. Panna leaned over and picked up the fallen nightdress from the floor. With uncustomary firmness, she said: "I forbid you to go outside."

"You are a non-believer. You do not understand."

"I understand too much." Panna shuddered, remembering the days of partition in India and the blood splatters on the windows in the train station of Lahore. A Moslem mob had slaughtered her family as they waited for the train to Delhi. She had never burdened Annisa with her story. It was not a story to repeat to an impressionable young girl. "Your father pays me to look after you. You are not to leave this room."

Annisa snatched her shoes from the closet floor. There was a petulant set to her full mouth and her jaw was rigid. But there was also a pliant, almost pleading look in her eyes. This, too, Panna understood. Annisa's mother had died giving her life and this motherless and defiant child before her was forever at war with her own nature. Dutiful and devoted, Annisa was at the same time entrapped by the overwhelming forces of a very strong will. Her desire to be conventional often collided full force with an untamed bubbling spirit. It was a terrible worry to Panna, watching Annisa fight for control of her feelings in a world that was rapidly spinning out of control.

"Panna, please. I want to be a part of it."

"No, Annisa. It's not proper. The protest is no place for a girl."

Annisa smiled inwardly at how easy it was to fool Panna. For two nights in a row she had slipped out of the house—defying the curfew to distribute pamphlets for the Resistance.

"Allah e Akbar." The chanting outside swelled upwards and filled the room. Men's voices resounded like thunderclaps.

"Hear that? How can you deny . . ?"

The spray of bullets, which struck the center gate, littered the garden of Professor Aziz with flying splinters. Shouting and a woman's scream followed an eerie silence; a machine gun belched another round and another and another.

Panna pushed past Annisa and hurried to the balcony. When she saw the bloody carnage below, she attempted to shut the door on Annisa, who fought her to open it.

"No! Don't come out here," Panna pleaded. "No child, don't look down."

Annisa turned and raced into the hall, bounding down the wooden staircase past the darkened living room where embers still glowed in the fireplace. "Father! Father!" she wailed. But before she could reach the front gate it opened, and her father entered, staggering under the weight of Sultan, the gardener whom he carried over his shoulder. Sultan's bloody entrails hung from an open hole in his side. With his right hand Sultan was desperately trying to stuff his own insides back into the wound.

"No, no," Annisa sobbed, pushing past her father and into the street littered with men who lay at her feet like discarded rag dolls. Under the street light where she had last seen him, she found Kassim on his back in the shallow water of the *juie,* the open drainage ditch that ran in front of the houses. Poor people bathed there and watered their livestock. Now blood oozed from behind Kassim's head, turning the water pink. His eyes were closed, but he opened them to her. A soft smile began on his lips before his eyes closed once again.

Annisa tried to speak his name. But the words would not come. Dry mouthed, she stood there and watched as the water in the juie turned from pink to a brilliant red.

"Get back!" Panna was at her side, tugging on her arm as she pulled Annisa away from the edge of the ditch.

High above their heads, a whirling bird of prey swooped downward, flashing its lights on them, hovering, harassing. Those who would dare tried to remove their loved ones from the streets.

Stunned, Annisa followed Panna past the frightened faces of the wounded. They groaned in terror as the Russian helicopter shone its lights on them. Then the helicopter lifted and was gone. The only noises left in the night were the moans of the dying.

In the morning light, Russian Migs flew low over Kabul, zooming back and forth, their bright silver wings cutting like razors into the peaceful blue of a cloudless sky. But the chant *"Allah e Akbar"* refused to die and could be heard in different quarters of the city. "Oh Russians, get out of our land!" Towards midday the sounds of heavy bombs exploding shook Khushal Maina and rockets were fired from low-flying helicopters. *"Allah e Akbar"* echoed from street corner to street corner amidst the sobbing for the dead.

Miraculously, Sultan the gardener lived through the day and into another night, but young Kassim had died before they could pull him from the drainage ditch.

Annisa took to her room and refused to come out on this auspicious day—a day neither she nor her country would ever forget. It was the third of Hoot 1358 (22 February 1980), a day when the Afghan people from every tribe spontaneously demonstrated together; a people united under God.

Kassim's body, swathed in white, lay in his father's house where a steady stream of mourners came to pay their respects.

Annisa did not go. She remained secluded behind her bedroom door, her hands folded lifeless across the prayer rug on her lap. A crumpled piece of paper, a clandestine leaflet she had helped Kassim and his brothers distribute before the protest, was on the floor at her feet. Annisa knew every word by heart:

"The Moslem people and the Mujahideen of Afghanistan, with the sublime cry of '*Allah e Akbar*,' will bring down their iron fist on the brainless head of the infidel and Communist government. Our weapons are the weapons of faith."

When the time came for the brothers of Kassim to carry his coffin on their shoulders into the hills of Shuda-e-Saleheen, Annisa watched the procession from behind the shutters of her upstairs window. Remembering the dawn of Holy Day she made a solemn vow. She would not go to school. She would fast until death.

"It is shock," her father said.

"I think she is being overdramatic and that we have given in to her theatrics too long," Panna answered.

Panna had good reason to worry for the girl. Annisa always retreated from pain into a fantasy world. When her brother Rahmin first left to study in America, Annisa had gone without food for days. She was a lonely child and her father's reaction was to indulge her. In Panna's view of the world, this was exactly the wrong thing to do. "These are times of crisis, Dr. Aziz. Annisa had better learn to cope."

Upstairs, in the shadows of late afternoon, Annisa wrapped herself in a blanket and pulled a chair near the window. Soon it would be dark and the streets would empty for curfew. She knew that Panna and her father had good intentions. But being with them only made her feel more lost. Everything seemed so trivial now and Panna's platitudes meant nothing. In fact, they grated on her nerves. 'Life is an endurance, child. . .be free from birth and death. Do not let suffering agitate you.' Worst of all was Panna's constant prattle about karma. Annisa refused to believe that Kassim's violent death was his punishment for something terrible he had done in a past life. Ridiculous! Kassim was only the good. Just like the angel everyone said her mother had been.

"You killed her," Rahmin had accused her on the day Annisa was six years old. "You just had to be born and you tore out our mother's insides." Later, there were tears and apologies from her brother but Annisa could not erase his words. They stalked her dreams. And she knew that no matter how hard she tried she could never justify her birth. They said her mother had been gentle in contrast to her own hot tempered and willful ways. Even her father said so.

"It's in the blood. Annisa is like her Uncle Omar in Mazar—-full of fire and passion and grandiose ideas." Annisa did not know her mother's family; they were Tajicks and considered a lesser tribe. Her father was said to have married beneath him.

Annisa had never met her uncles who lived in the north and Rahmin had lauded this over her. Before she was born Rahmin had journeyed with their mother every spring to Mazar-i-Sharif to visit with her family and to see her younger brother, Abdul, play the great game of *buzkashi*. Abdul was a famous *chapandaz*.

"Why don't I know my uncles? Why doesn't father ever take me to visit?" Annisa would complain.

"They don't want to see father anymore than he wants to see them. What use could they have for a man like him?" Annisa had never understood exactly what Rahmin meant by this. True, their father did not like to ride or shoot but he was kind and loving and he needed a family as much as anyone else. An only child, her father had no living relatives. So he had filled their house with his university colleagues and writers and artists from the outside world. Yet, despite all the comings and goings, she sensed her father was lonely too. They never spoke of it; it was just something they both knew they shared.

Tonight Annisa ached for her mother. She needed her there. She needed her mother to tell her how to "be." So often Rahmin had accused her of not knowing how to be a girl. He had railed against their father when he had agreed to give her horseback lessons. "Annisa acts too much like a boy as it is," Rahmin argued. "She is forever stealing my slingshot and practicing with it in the garden against the birds. What kind of a girl would do a thing like this? Panna teaches her nothing. She is Hindu and illiterate and allows Annisa to boss her around. Annisa has no sense of direction—never ever knows what she wants."

Annisa dug her fingernails into her palm at the memories. Rahmin was wrong. She knew what she wanted. She wanted to avenge Kassim. If she were a boy she would run away into the mountains and fight with the Mujahideen. But she was only a stupid girl. It was all so hopeless. If only she could cry, but the tears refused to come. Her heart felt empty. Like the deserted streets below.

CHAPTER 2

Darkly handsome, Captain Najib Duranni of the Afghan army was not unaware of the female heads that turned as he walked through terminal B in New York's JFK airport. An old fencing scar, visible on his right cheekbone, hinted he might be a bit dangerous—a danger which he quickly disarmed with a friendly, laid-back grin. He was certainly not a man one would suspect was a double agent—a fact Captain Duranni himself found it hard to believe. The spy trade went against his nature. In his opinion the only real asset he brought to the task was his ability to detach—to view life with a rather amused indifference. Humor always had been his best defense against an autocratic father.

His father, General Abdullah Duranni, had foolishly thought he could play off the two superpowers. 'Let the Americans build an airport in Kandahar and send their agricultural experts to the Helmand Valley. The Soviets can train and equip our army. If trouble comes it will be from the Paks.' The General had arrogantly pushed his half-baked theory that the Russians would never invade Afghanistan because there was not a single bridge across the rivers between their borders. 'My son, when you ride a good horse, do you care in which country it was born?' Najib did care.

Near the baggage claim Najib stopped to retrieve a newspaper that had been left on a chair. He was debating whether he should give Claire a call. It would be after midnight in London. 'Better not,' he thought. It was not good strategy to appear too eager with the elegant and elusive Claire, a woman who absorbed him. No woman had ever owned his thoughts and desires so completely--certainly, not his wife. In hindsight he knew he had paid too big a price for the privilege to study abroad. It was either marry the empty-headed Margahalia, his father's choice, or give up going to Sandhurst, Britain's prestigious military academy. Najib had chosen Sandhurst—not because he coveted a military career but because he wanted out of Kabul—to taste the Western world.

Always the gentleman, Najib stopped to help a middle-aged lady retrieve her luggage from the moving carousel before reaching for his own. For the first time since the Soviet invasion he felt he had something concrete to do. His meeting with CIA operatives in Washington had gone well. It was also good to be back in New York, if only for a night. The city was always a tonic to his spirits and he was looking forward to seeing his childhood friend, Rahmin. Rahmin Aziz was like a brother despite the fact they were polar opposites. On some strange level this had made them both feel more secure in their growing up years--drawing on each other's strengths. Najib headed for a bank of public phones to inform Rahmin he had arrived on an earlier flight.

Rahmin sounded exhausted. "I need to crash for an hour before we go out. I've been on duty for over 72 hours. Let me warn you, my place is not exactly the Ritz Carlton."

"I'm disappointed," Najib teased. "I thought you were living the American dream."

"Your dream, not mine."

Najib shook his head as he scribbled down the home address. It was so like Rahmin. His original excitement over his acceptance to Columbia University's teaching hospital gradually had faded into a laundry list of petty complaints. Rahmin was convinced that as a Moslem he was not really accepted in the States but then, Rahmin had felt the same way in Kabul because his mother was a Tajik.

The change in their friendship had been gradual and subtle and Najib was sad about the growing rift. He was fond of Rahmin despite his crotchety ways and his intolerance of others when he was in his "devout" mood. Rahmin had this habit of hiding behind his religion in order to curb his passionate nature. He was always so sure of his path—his direction in life. Rahmin's rigidity gave Najib a freedom of sorts --the luxury to explore. It also amused him to see how much Rahmin enjoyed pointing out his errant ways. It wasn't until Najib returned to Kabul from special training exercises at Ft. Benning, Georgia that things began to change. It was obvious Rahmin suspected him of being CIA. No accusation was ever made but when Adolph Dobbs, the American ambassador, was murdered in Kabul, Rahmin had quipped, "Sounds like something big is about to come down with the Russians. You'd better sleep with one eye open, my brother."

Outside the airport terminal Najib faced a long queue for a taxi and surprisingly enough he savored it. It gave him time to study the impatient faces waiting in line. He loved the tempo of New York, the raw and naked push and shove of everyday life. In contrast, his life in Kabul was drab and subdued. Working for the KHAD, the Soviet controlled Afghan secret police, had plunged him into a humorless world filled with anonymous shadows. He missed the easy camaraderie of his old tank division and it annoyed him that the puppet government had seen him as malleable as his father. Half of the official world of Kabul was friends of his father and the other half were disgustingly unctuous because of his well-connected wife. The acid tongued Margahalia was a first cousin to Barbak Karmal, the new president of the Afghan puppet government. Flaunting her new status, Margahalia was almost a comic figure to him now.

The sky was overcast and from his slow moving taxi Najib could see the outline of New York skyscrapers emerging through the mist like an improbable mirage. God, what a different world it was from Kabul.

The driver pulled up in front of a wholesale plumbing shop in a shabby section of the Bowery. Najib double-checked the number on the soot-covered building and then paid the driver, pausing to replace the lid on an overstuffed garbage can near the curb. There were no lights on in the windows above the shop where Rahmin lived. Perhaps he should give him an extra hour to sleep? A nearby coffee shop advertising homemade biscuits and breakfast served 24 hours a day caught his eye. He saw it as a place to kill some time.

A bell tinkled as he entered the grubby premises of the coffee shop, which reeked of stale tobacco. He slid sideways into a red leather booth with slashes in its seat.

"Sorry, this section is closed," a sallow faced woman with blue shadowed lids said, as she waved him to a table in front of the window. Najib moved to the designated seat secretly amused that this was necessary since he was her only customer. But then everyone had his or her own turf-their own little power game. "So what would you like, gorgeous?" the waitress called to him from behind the counter.

"How about a few kind words?"

"That only comes if you order the full breakfast."

"What do I get with just coffee?"

"Cream and sugar."

"Cream, please." Slowly he unfolded the newspaper he had stuffed in his pocket at the airport. He was happy to see that news of the civilian demonstrations in Afghanistan had made the front page but comments on the editorial page were discouraging. *The New York Times* was predicting genocide for the fiercely independent Afghans, noting at the same time that America could not afford to intervene now that Afghanistan was in the Soviet sphere. Najib grimaced inwardly. He knew he was taking a risk in his decision to engineer Dr. Aziz's escape from Kabul. There was no room for sentiments or loyalty to the past when one signed on as a player in the 'great game.' However, the family of Aziz was an exception to his self-imposed rules; Rahmin's father was under surveillance by the puppet government in Kabul and Najib had assigned himself the unhappy task of informing Rahmin.

The waitress with the frizzy bleached hair arrived at his elbow, coffeepot in hand. "Are your eyes really that green or do you wear contact lenses?"

Najib looked up from his paper and stirred the creamer into his cup. "What do you think?"

"They look real enough. My brother is a fireman and they have this dog at the station—Engine 33--he's a Husky. He's got eyes like yours."

"Your brother?"

"No silly, the dog. They call him, 'Wolf Eyes' because his eyes are transparent. They reach out and kind of pull you in."

"Is that good?"

She smiled. "I think you know that."

Najib flashed back his crooked grin, enjoying their banter. He wondered if Rahmin ever ate here. Probably not. In his letters Rahmin had complained of the hospital food.

"You do know that's *yesterday's* newspaper you've got there," she said.

"Doesn't matter. The news is always the same." He carefully refolded the paper and stuffed it into his jacket pocket. The waitress reminded him of a worn Persian carpet-- pretty in the weave of her but faded now and a bit tattered at the edges. "Tell me something. What do you think about Russian troops marching into Afghanistan on Christmas Eve?"

"Was it Christmas Eve? What a bummer." She hesitated, as though considering his question very seriously. "Well, I guess I feel sorry for the Afghans. They say those people are a fierce lot—nothing but a bunch of dumb camel drivers. You know, like kind of barbaric. Just the same, I hope they get those Russian bastards. Skin them alive."

It made his stomach churn just thinking about it. He had been suckled at his mother's breast to be a warrior but he hated violence and the fact he had been saddled with the family tradition. The death of his two older brothers in a fiery car crash in Herat years ago had sealed his fate. There was no escape: his father's foolish policies had disgraced the family name and he was stuck with having to redeem it. Or so his mother had pleaded.

"What does your brother at the firehouse have to say?"

"About Afghanistan?" She shrugged. "I doubt if he even knows where it is. Say what is this? 'Twenty Questions?' ... What do *you* think?"

Najib held out his cup. "That I'm ready for a re-fill."

"You're a cagey one, aren't you."

"Yes." He was thinking about the Russian foot soldiers that she wanted to skin alive. Poor bastards. There was some truth in what she was saying. The Resistance took no prisoners. As a result the Soviet military personnel he knew on a first name basis in Kabul were an unhappy and drunken lot and without a clue as to why they were in his country.

"How did you get that scar on your face?"

"Playing at soldier."

"Is that what you do for a living?"

"No, I'm an undertaker."

"Yeah. Sure." She retreated smiling to behind the counter.

From his seat in front of the window, Najib watched a homeless man sorting through the garbage can in front of Rahmin's flat. It was not a happy sight. He was loath to pass judgement on the West but it bothered him to see the homeless. Despite the poverty, there were no beggars in the streets of Kabul. An Afghan took care of his own. It was easy to understand why Rahmin's letters had sounded so depressed. Now that the Soviets were in Kabul his dreams for a new clinic there had been shattered. For years Rahmin had nursed a kind of shame for Afghan medicine. Their hospitals had no diagnostic labs—two or three patients in the same bed. And Rahmin's fierce pride could not deal with the humiliation that the American Embassy had found it necessary to build their own hospital because Afghan facilities were so bad. He was now working in one of the finest medical facilities in the world and yet his wounded pride salved itself by finding fault. There was no sense in trying to show Rahmin the error in his thinking. His passions ruled.

Najib checked his watch thinking it was time to roust his over-worked friend out of bed. He dug into his pocket for his billfold, wondering what the waitress would think if she knew that she had been chatting up a spy. He loved to profile people and he had concluded she would probably get a good laugh out of it. "What do I owe you?"

"It's on the house."

"I can't let you do that, Agnes."

"Agnes? Why did you call me Agnes? My name is Mary Ellen."

"You see, it works every time."

"Like, I said, you're a sly one."

He wanted to admit he was. It bothered him that he could lie so easily and so well. He had sailed through the puppet's interrogation in Kabul, having been expertly coached by Langley. He was to confess that the CIA had tried to recruit him and the puppets, as predicted, considered this a plus. From Kabul he was to funnel information to the Resistance—just enough to put him in a position to stir up trouble among Mujahideen leaders who were organizing in Peshawar. Bickering among the Afghan tribes and the fueling of ethnic hatreds were to be subtly encouraged. He was also to pretend to go along with the CIA in their plans to lobby Congress for stinger missiles and weapons that the Congress was fearful could fall into the hands of terrorists. Leaders of the Resistance would be brought to Washington to whip up sympathy and public interest, thus giving Najib access to knowledge of their whereabouts inside. At times the thought of his own duplicity wounded him.

Mary Ellen picked up the money he had placed on the table and stuffed it in the pocket of her uniform. "Are you one of them?"

He looked at her puzzled.

"I mean I was just wondering if maybe you come from that part of the world." He was surprised to see her blush. "With all your questions about Afghanistan I thought. . . Look, I didn't mean to call your people dumb. . .or savages."

"Oh, that. Forget it." But he couldn't resist adding. "I think you should know that we do sleep with our camels."

She chuckled. "In your case, that's one lucky camel."

He stood up and gestured to the empty café. "Hope your business picks up."

"Come back at midnight. It's elbow to elbow. A lot of night shift workers in this neighborhood. Have a nice evening, Mr. Undertaker," she called.

"You too, Mary Ellen."

He crossed the street to the homeless man who was now curled up in the fetal position and snoring on Rahmin's doorstep. Gingerly, Najib stepped over him to push the buzzer. The door opened after repeated rings. "Sorry, I'm on the top floor, "Rahmin panted, gesturing towards the man at their feet. "Western civilization, Najib. Isn't it wonderful?"

Najib embraced the overly thin Rahmin. He was shocked at his appearance. Sad eyes, almost haunted; unshaven and a face ashen with fatigue. "Little brother, you look like shit."

"I feel like it."

Najib held his breath as he followed Rahmin up the gritty concrete steps that reeked of urine. "This stench makes me homesick for the open sewers of Kabul."

"Home smells better."

"That's not the way I remember it. . .So what do you do with yourself when you are not playing doctor?"

"On my off days I drive an unlicensed cab in Brooklyn. We take people into the city for half the fare."

"Sounds grim."

"Only when they mistake you for an Iranian. I had this passenger lecture me about our 'evil intent' the entire ride into Manhattan and after all this, he leaves me an enormous tip. Figure that one out."

"Only in America. I love it."

"Uhuh." Rahmin pushed open the door of his apartment. "Allah must have sent you. My father has sent me a letter insisting I stay in the States."

"That's good advice."

'Why do you always side with him?"

"Because he's always right."

The inside of Rahmin's flat looked wretchedly worn but neat; not exactly the sloppy housekeeping one might expect in a bachelor pad shared by two overworked interns. Furniture was almost nonexistent: two fold-up cots, a dilapidated desk with a lamp and a straight back chair. No stove, only a hot plate; a rusty can of bug spray sat on the kitchen sink. Najib stared at a solitary cockroach circling the drain.

Rahmin jerked open the fire escape window and retrieved a carton of orange juice. "Want some?"

"Any vodka to go with it?"

"You know I can't allow it."

Najib shook his head in mock dismay. "'Allow' is such an unfriendly word. His eyes went to a framed watercolor that he had painted in the garden of Rahmin's house years ago. It hung next to a wildlife calendar. "I'm flattered. You brought this all the way from Kabul?" He took it down to study it. "I forgot I did this."

Rahmin nodded solemnly. "It triggers memories, doesn't it?"

"The best." He was thinking of Dr. Aziz reading aloud his poetry to bright and sassy little Annisa. Najib adored Annisa and had sketched her many times in charcoal. It was a shame he hadn't saved his drawings. He remembered Margahalia once tearing one up, accusing him of an unhealthy interest in his best friend's sister.

"For God's sake, Margahalia, Annisa is only 11 or 12 years old."

"Soon she will be ripe and ready to be plucked."

His hand had itched to hit her but instead he had made a joke of it. "Thank you for pointing out to me the sweetest fruit on the tree." He got a hard slap across his face in return. Life with Margahalia was like living on the edge of a volcano.

"Those were golden afternoons," Rahmin said.

"For you? I'm surprised. You always seemed impatient-- eager to escape those poetry sessions in the garden to race your horse. Funny how life turns. I wanted to be an artist and you were hell bent to be a *buzkashi* player like your Uncle Abdul."

"He was incredible, wasn't he? I'll never forget the day we saw him ride before the King at Jeshin"

"Frankly, Abdul terrified me."

"You scare easy."

Najib wondered if it was true. He hated combat and did not share Rahmin's intense feelings of revenge against the invaders. What did this say about him? "I tell you what does scare me. Your father and Annisa still in Kabul. We've got to get them out, Rahmin."

"Where would they go? Certainly not here. I'm going back inside to fight. You should hear some of the nonsense in my father's letter." Rahmin went to his desk and tossed an envelope at Najib. "Here read this. I am not to throw away a fine medical education for a hopeless cause. Hopeless! What kind of talk is that? We drove the British out with hand- made rifles. We can do it again."

"Old friend, it's all about timing. Right now the Resistance is scattered and throwing coke bottles at Russian tanks. We don't stand a chance. Forget our ancestors and their hand-made rifles. We need air missiles—sophisticated shoulder-fired heat seekers. Russian hind helicopters will destroy us without them—particularly in the south." He held up the envelope. "This was postmarked from Peshawar?"

"Look at this." Rahmin pointed to the name on the return address. "Matthew Hardcastle. Remember that British reporter with *Reuters* who used to stay at our house?"

"Sure. He wrote a series about Western hippies invading Kabul for our hashish-- had this silver flask in his hip pocket he was always whipping out."

"He's written some articles from inside Afghanistan recently."

Najib frowned. "What has Hardcastle to do with your father?"

"I'm not sure. But since regular mail is no longer getting in and out of Kabul I thought maybe my father had him hand carry it to Pakistan."

Najib bit down on his lip. "This is not good news. It could only tighten their case against your father."

Rahmin's eyes narrowed. "Whose case?"

"The KHAD has your father under surveillance," Najib said softly.

"A professor? He's of no interest to them."

"Wrong. Young men start revolutions and resistance is nurtured in universities."

"Najib, he's a poet!"

"Who was also good friends with President Amin. Amin was a dangerous man to know at the university. The official party line is that our late president was an operative for the CIA."

"Something you would know about, now isn't it."

Najib was tempted to confide in Rahmin but retreated into silence.

"Well, where *did* you get your information?" Rahmin challenged.

"Your father's good friend, Fritz Werner."

Rahmin scoffed. "What would the old Nazi know about anything."

"He has his pulse on Kabul. You forget he exports more rugs to Germany than anyone—and that includes the shops in Kandahar. The man is an expert at greasing palms. He is probably the most valuable man the Resistance has inside with his collection of some very important I.O.U's."

"God help the Resistance if Fritz is all they can come up with." Rahmin stood up, stretched and yawned. "I'm getting hungry."

"Good. We can live it up tonight. Maybe I can soften you a bit and talk you into staying in New York."

"I knew it! My father sent you!"

"No. I haven't seen your father since the invasion. He doesn't even know I'm here." Najib hesitated. "But I can deliver a message to him."

"You? You're going back to Kabul?"

"I'm an officer in the Afghan army."

Rahmin grimaced. "That ought to make you proud. An army which has overthrown our elected officials and sold our people out."

"Including men like my father." Najib chastised himself for revealing his bitterness

"No, men like *mine* - my father is an ostrich with his head in the sand. I don't have to tell you—naïve men are the most dangerous kind."

Najib was not sure he agreed. "At least Dr. Aziz doesn't speak in declarative sentences."

For the first time that morning Rahmin actually laughed. "You know, my father once said a curious thing. That 'no two young men were more alike than us and yet so different in so many ways.'"

"Then he doesn't know me, now does he? Flaunting our traditions. Lusting for women." Najib returned the watercolor to its hook. "After dinner tonight how about some good jazz and going on the piss?"

"Then you intend to get drunk. Allah, what am I to do with you?"

"For starters you can get out of those grubby clothes. And for God's sake, shave. America's daughters have been warned about the dastardly charms of Afghan men. We have a reputation to uphold."

Rahmin wrinkled his forehead. "I hate to think of you on judgement day." He crossed to the kitchen sink, and jerked on the water tap. Najib watched him, wondering when would be the right time to tell Rahmin about his father's pending arrest. One had to handle Rahmin with care; his ardent nature was too easily bruised. Najib was even worried about his reservation for them tonight at *Windows on the World*, an elegant and expensive restaurant atop the World Trade Center. Would Rahmin consider this an affront to his frugality?

"The West is a cesspool, Najib. Every bit as evil as the Russians," Rahmin announced dramatically as he stared at the cockroach struggling in the water before it swirled to its death in the drain.

High above the city, atop one of the Twin Towers, New York's famous landmark, they dined in an elegant restaurant frequented mostly by tourists. It was after rush hour and the traffic on the streets below had thinned. Looking down upon the city Najib wondered if any one inside those tiny moving dots of light had any idea what was happening to a civilization thousands of years older than their own. It would be almost dawn now in Kabul. People waking up to yet another day of brutal occupation.

Rahmin seemed to be enjoying his meal but complained about the opulence of their setting and the very existence of the tower itself.

"Western Society must feel superior to the rest of the world from looking down on it from such great heights."

Najib smiled and shook his head over Rahmin's constant harangue about American materialism. "Ever tried satin sheets?"

"I bet you have. Does Margahalia know about your British girlfriend?"

Najib smiled. Rahmin loved to lecture him for his errant ways and the sins of the flesh but it never stopped him from wanting to know the details of Najib's amorous adventures.

"I've been in and out of Kabul most of our marriage and it would never occur to my dear wife that a man could look at anyone else but her. She's incredibly vain." He did not add that she was jealous of Annisa. It would have sent Rahmin into orbit.

"Doesn't it bother you that Margahalia cuts her hair so short?"

"Not particularly. She would have a nervous breakdown if she felt she didn't have the latest Paris fashion."

Rahmin wagged his finger. "Someday the men of Kabul will regret this. Letting their women ape the Western world."

"Not to worry. The Russians will soon have them in combat boots and riding tractors."

Rahmin grimaced. "As usual you take none of this seriously."

"But I do. Don't look so glum. We still have a future. It's girls like Annisa who are the future of Afghanistan."

"Suppose that's true. How can I possibly support Annisa over here? The puppets cut off my scholarship fund. I'm barely surviving."

"Fritz Werner can help out financially."

"An ex-Nazi rug dealer? Not on your life."

"Fritz is not a Nazi, his father was. And so were half the Germans in Kabul after the war."

"I want nothing to do with him."

"And Annisa?"

"She is better off in Kabul. Look at this culture. All she ever talked about at home was rock and roll. She even wanted to wear a mini-skirt!"

"Shocking."

"Go ahead and have your joke. It's a wonder the Mullahs don't take to the city streets in Kabul."

"I rue the day they do. We can't go backward, Rahmin."

"Don't be so sure."

Najib was annoyed. "Since when did you become a poster boy for Ayatollah Khomeini? Or would you have Annisa wear the veil? How the hell would you like to spend the rest of your life with a sheet over your head?"

"Don't twist my words. I hate the *chadri*. You can't get enough Vitamin D covered from head to toe. But why must educated Afghan girls go to extremes? It's easy for you to talk with no sisters to protect. Annisa is a worry. Too headstrong. She flaunts our traditions and my father allows it."

Najib was bored with the argument. It was all too familiar. "Don't be so hard on her. Frankly, I admire your little sister's verve—her natural defiance."

"God help the man she marries."

"Why? She's going to be a great beauty."

"Your wife is a great beauty and look how you feel about her."

Najib flinched inwardly but did not rise to the bait. Instead he drained his wineglass and a waiter instantly refilled it. "Margahalia envies the lifestyle of our exiled King. She would sell her soul to join his group in Rome. And of course she is ecstatic that her sleazy cousin is now top dog in Kabul."

Rahmin banged his fist hard on the table. Silverware jumped and red wine spilled from Najib's crystal glass, staining the snowy white linen. Heads turned at nearby tables. "That traitorous bastard Karmal. Lying son of a camel."

"Right. Fortunately for me, the oaf likes me."

"I'd like to roast his balls on a spit for what he's done to Afghanistan."

"Keep your voice down," Najib said, uncomfortable with the amused glances from fellow diners. At the same time, he applauded Rahmin for not giving a damn what they thought.

Rahmin mocked him. "Sorry. I keep forgetting you have no passion for our country."

His old friend's thrust was unexpected and left Najib suddenly weary; aware of his own melancholy, a resignation as to what was to come. It was a feeling he had carried with him ever since he was a boy—a feeling that he had better seize life by the throat because it might be over before it really began. "I've got an idea. After we finish our coffee let's head down to Times Square."

"And give up looking down our nose at the rest of the world from up here? I thought you liked sitting with all the money boys. You know what this building represents, don't you?"

Najib frowned. "Do you? You can't have it both ways. All this disdain for people we are pleading to come to our aid." Najib left the waiter a healthy tip, hoping to make amends for acting like 'barbarians.' And he hated himself for doing it.

Times Square turned out to be seedier than he had remembered it. The bright lights and vitality were still there but the area surrounding the theater district was dismal and wore a hangdog expression. They entered a topless bar where colored lights spun crazily from a crystal ball above their heads. Loud music throbbed and pounded as naked hips undulated under breasts glistening with sweat. Raucous laughter exploded at the table next to them; the ritual stuffing of dollar bills into a woman's G-string.

Rahmin scowled. "You want Annisa to end up like this?"

"Don't talk nonsense."

"Najib, I *do* worry about her staying in Kabul. I know with our mixed blood it will be hard to find Annisa a husband."

"These are modern times." But it was an empty reassurance on Najib's part. The Shah's demise in Iran had slowed down progress against the old ways all over Islam. As modern as the Shah had been, even he had been forced to divorce his first wife when she couldn't give him a son. "At least your father had courage enough to defy tradition and marry for love."

"Ah, what's the use. We are a doomed society. We tried to emulate the West and it was too great a leap. Neither you or I can make a difference anymore."

"Forget that!" Najib decided to hit him head on with the real reason he had come to New York. "Frankly, you could better serve the Resistance by staying in the States and I'm not talking about your medical skills. We desperately need people to sell our cause. Organizing teams of volunteer doctors in the States. Raising funds."

"Me? A fundraiser? That's an insult. I can ride and shoot better than any man you know. I'd go crazy not being a part of it."

"What a waste. They are plenty of men to ride shotgun, Rahmin." He hated that this was their image to the world. Afghans were so much more than this. Hospitality to a stranger; the poetry of a shepherd boy's flute.

"Don't try to patronize me by pretending you don't love the adventure of being part of it. You always. . ."

The shrill sound of sirens invaded their conversation and several squad cars with flashing red lights pulled up in front of the bar. "What's going on?" Najib asked the bartender.

He gestured with his thumb. "Next door. There's an illegal sweatshop of Chinese aliens. Ever so often they haul them off in the paddy wagon. It's kind of pitiful to watch. They come out handcuffed with this bewildered look on their faces. Most of them can't speak a word of English."

"So we Afghans aren't the only ones whose dreams are in tatters," Rahmin muttered to Najib as he settled their bill.

The bartender overheard him and reached out to shake Rahmin's hand. "I hear you guys are the greatest fighters in the world. More power to you. I hope you kick some Russian ass. We ought to nuke them 'til they glow."

Outside a cold wind was whipping up, but Najib insisted that they walk for awhile. "Fresh air clears my head."

"Not possible. Your brain is too addled with wine."

Najib laughed. "And what scrambled yours? On your knees to Mecca too many times?"

The stunned look on Rahmin's face made Najib sorry the instant he said it. And a sullen silence descended between them, threatening to ruin what was left of the night. It pained Najib that it might be the last time they were ever together. "Sorry I dragged you to that bar. I was hoping to loosen you up."

"You couldn't do that when we were kids. What makes you think you could do it now?"

"Oh, I seem to remember the night we mooned the Swiss ambassador's son for calling us descendants of Ben-I-Israel."

Rahmin brightened. "We really nailed the little toad didn't we. To think he had the gall to suggest that if Nassar had commanded Swiss troops, Egypt could have won the Six Day War."

"Ah, yes. Islam's glory days."

Rahmin grimaced. "Why do you always do this? You know how I hate it when you lampoon Islam's humiliation in the Sinai."

"The fun is in watching you get all riled up. When are you going to give up on serious?"

"It's not normal, you know. The way you make a joke of everything. There must be something in this life that doesn't amuse you."

"There is. My father's misplaced trust in the Russians."

"Where is he now?"

"Jalalabad. Red-faced and keeping a low profile. Mother has made it out to Tehran."

"Then why go back? For years you have wanted to escape Margahalia."

"Ironic isn't it that now I have my chance I can't take it..."

"Can't?"

"Forget I said that."

Rahmin did not stop at the curb light but marched out into incoming traffic. A brake screeched and horns honked as Najib chased after him. He grabbed Rahmin by the arm. "What the hell?"

"You are lower than whale shit. Did you know that? I'm not to know what you are doing with your life but you think you can come here and tell me how to run mine. You want me to accept that infidel Fritz Werner's money for my family. Never!"

Najib was no longer able to silence his exasperation. "That's pretty damn selfish. All you're purist talk about wanting to do well. Boasting you could make a pile of money in the States as a doctor, but you would never be one of those money grubbing foreigners who forsakes his own people. What about forsaking your family so you can ride ambush in the mountains?" He released Rahmin's arm. "Go ahead. Play hero. Impale yourself on your faith. And leave us to plant a martyr's white flag on your grave. What was that crap you said earlier? That 'a Christian lives his life to keep from dying and that a Moslem dies in order to live in paradise.' Is that what you are after?"

"What are you after?" Rahmin said evenly.

"This may shock you, but I don't want to die. Nor am I eager for Annisa to. If she stays in Kabul and your father is arrested she'll do more than wither here under what you consider a morally lax society. She won't survive. Would you prefer that?" Najib made no effort to check the harshness in his voice.

"How can you be so certain my father is going to be arrested?" Rahmin challenged.

"Because his name is on a list. And that's not from Fritz Werner. I saw it myself."

"Oh, I see." Rahmin walked over to the curbside and picked up an empty Coke can from the gutter, hurling it with considerable violence at a street light. Then he started to laugh. Deep from the belly.

"What's so damn funny?"

"You. Thinking I wouldn't know you were working both sides. I assumed it from the minute you called me from Washington. Good old garden variety Afghans like myself do not just fly in and out of Kabul. And to think I'm the one who is supposed to be too serious. . . . Get a grip on yourself, Najib."

Najib was silent for a moment and then a pleased, rather amused smile appeared on his handsome face. "Well done, my friend. Well done." Najib was always honest in his dealings with himself. "I owe you an apology."

Rahmin looked at him skeptically. "Why?"

"For not trusting you. . .They say that if there is something that annoys you in others it's because you don't want to deal with that in yourself."

"Where did you get that rubbish? In some Western self-help book? Whatever happened to 'Inshallah, God Willing' in accepting one's lot . . . Look, you don't have to go back, Najib."

"What and have you miss the opportunity to wave me off to war?"

"I hate you for that."

"Yes, you've made that clear." Najib detected a hint of tears in Rahmin's eyes and once again reached out, resting his hand on his shoulder. "So what is it?" he said, trying to curb his own emotions.

"I was thinking about my father."

"About what the puppets could do to him?"

"No, it was about what they could do to *you* for trying to help him. My father is an old man. You must love him one hell of a lot to risk getting involved in his escape."

Najib searched for an answer and was fearful to face it. That he had always loved the family of Asiz more than his own.

"I envy you that love. . . and yes, I envy you being a part of the fight." Rahmin kicked his toe against a street sign. "How will I know when my father and Annisa are coming?"

23

"Then you are going to stay."

"Was there ever any doubt?"

"Yes. Very real doubt. I know you, Rahmin. I know how it eats at you to stay out of the fight. The truth is I envy you." He did not want to think of his return trip to Kabul, which was going to be extremely distasteful. He was going to have to woo his foolish wife and spend more time with her insipid friends in Barbak's inner circle. Perhaps he also envied the depth of Rahmin's faith—Rahmin truly believed they could drive the Russians out. And Najib wondered what would happen to Afghanistan if by some miracle they did.

CHAPTER 3

Panna stood at the foot of the wooden stairs, leaning on the hand-carved railing to relieve the pain in her legs. She stared at her swollen ankles and a solitary tear rolled down her cheeks. Once she had been young and able to chase the wind.

"Annisa?" she called, slowly pulling herself up the staircase, pausing to catch her breath as she went. Panna rapped lightly on Annisa's door but there was no response. With apprehension, Panna entered the room and scowled at the untouched milk and pieces of *nan*, the flat bread she had baked fresh that morning. Once again, Annisa had only picked at her breakfast tray. When was this foolishness going to stop?

Panna confronted the silent child. "I think your father has spoiled you. You wallow; you glory in your grief. Other Afghan girls are not afraid of the Russians. I see your friend Umariah walk past the gate. She has returned to school."

Harsh words but words which provoked a glint of anger in Annisa's sad eyes; Panna felt heartened to see it. She would continue to goad her. "You disgrace your father's house with your fears. How dreadful you were too frightened to pay your respects to young Kassim."

"I'm not afraid," Annisa muttered, clenching her fists.

"Then why do you refuse to go to school?"

"There is no longer any reason to go."

"Now, more than ever." Panna scowled to under-score her disdain. It was difficult for her to be hard on Annisa despite her vow never to give her heart to anyone again. She chose to live life as an observer; to side-step the quicksand of attachment. But Annisa's vulnerability had roped her in. Early on she had rejoiced in Annisa's bold and open defiance and understood the mask Annisa wore to protect an overly sensitive nature. The girl had an aura about her and Panna was convinced that Annisa was a very old soul who had entered this life with a difficult task. Panna searched Annisa's face, looking for a glimmer of her life force. But her aura was dulled now and deadness lingered. It sickened Panna to see it.

"You are a coward, I say. Afraid to go to school. You bring shame on this house." She picked up the tray and left the room. Better to leave the girl alone to ponder the sting of Panna's unfair judgments. Annisa was not a fearful child, but accusing her might work. At least Annisa had spoken. It was a good sign. And no one knew this better than Panna. She too had suffered the agony of silence, a silence inflicted by the sight of unspeakable violence during the early days of India's partition. The memory of the day her own eyes went dead never left her; a day she had gone mute in that blood-soaked train station of Lahore. In the beginning, she had muttered fragments of sentences, calling out names of her mutilated children, unable to move her hands and feet. She had been certain she would not survive. As the night advanced and she cowered in dark alleyways, she had been terrified of the very whispers of her own breath. It was not until days later that an incredible rage came out. A scream of anguish like that of a wild animal tore from the back of her throat. Only then had she been able to touch her grief.

"*Abhaya mudra.* Do not fear," Panna muttered. The time would come when Annisa would scream.

Panna returned the tray to the kitchen, grumbling. She liked to complain; it relieved the drudgery. Twisting the dial on the radio, she picked up some rousing march music, only to have it interrupted by the strident voice of the new Afghan President Karmal. As usual, he was raving against the freedoms lost by the Afghan people under President Amin:

"This bloodthirsty spy of U.S. imperialism. . ."

Panna switched off the station in disgust. "Barbak Karmal, I spit in your soup."

For a moment she thought she heard footsteps behind her and spun around, half-expecting the ghost of Sultan, the murdered gardener to appear. Too unnerved by his death, she had not greeted his relatives when they came to take his body for burial in his village of Paghman. Had his spirit lingered to shame her?

Panna shook her head at her own foolishness. She was getting feeble in the mind. Professor Aziz had resumed his teaching and only the grief- stricken girl, dreaming of the young boy Kassim, remained in the house. "The boy's death has shattered her," Panna confided to the kitchen cat which rubbed against her legs, demanding to be fed. Panna had guessed the truth of Annisa's grief. Panna knew of such things. Love for the first time. An aura of happiness whenever Annisa had looked at the boy. Panna had noticed and said nothing. Annisa would soon be 13. Young girls must dream.

"*Mahadeva*, Great God Shiva," she muttered, chastising herself for even dwelling on the sadness of Annisa. Life was endurance. "Do not let suffering agitate you," she admonished the cat as she filled its bowl. Now that the Russian devils ruled, the suffering would begin in earnest.

A searing pain shot up Panna's leg from her swollen ankles. "Fluid retention. Congestive heart . . ." Sinister words pronounced by the white-coated doctor. Well, she could live without salt but she would not waste one rupee on medicine. Her life had been longer than most and now that the Russians were here she no longer cared. They were methodically setting out to erase a people and its culture. Afghan children were already being shipped to Moscow to jumble their thoughts. Panna shuddered. She was certain that the invaders would occupy this fine house with its hand-carved ceilings and marble terrazzo floors within the year. At first they would stay hidden inside their tanks and behind the high walls of the Soviet Embassy in Karte-Se, but later they would boldly walk the bazaars. She was certain that within the year daggers would be stuck in their backs. The Afghans would have their revenge. She leaned against the table cursing the dark days that lay ahead. Brother against brother. The old ways confronting the new.

Panna reached over and stroked the cat. She was not by nature fond of animals, but this rag-tag creature had captivated her. An unwanted stray, it had arrived at the gate undernourished and frightened by its very shadow. "Just like me," she muttered.

She was almost glad she was ailing and ashamed for thinking it. She must try to hang on for Annisa's sake. But hang on for what? Kabul was overcrowded with refugees. Too many cars and trucks. Soon the beautiful clear air from the mountains would be choked with smoke, and people escaping from the fierce fighting in the countryside would huddle together inside a pocket of sickness and death. She had lived it during partition. Starvation. Rats and rubble. Nothing but shattered dreams.

Lamenting her fate, Panna unrolled Annisa's black school uniform and took out the ironing board. The material for Annisa's dress was the finest available in the bazaar. Such extravagance! On a teacher's salary, Dr. Aziz could ill afford the extras. The fine house he had inherited from his father belied the few coins in his pockets. The professor was not a rich man, but despite this, nothing for Annisa was ever spared. How could the girl ever hope to marry? No other man would pamper her so. Nor would he tolerate her quick temper and autocratic ways.

Panna slammed the iron on its trivet. "Dr. Aziz expects too much from me!" she told the cat. Ever since the secret police had taken that fool *baccha* away she had been forced to clean the house in addition to the cooking and the care of the girl. Amir, the *baccha*, had made a thorough nuisance of himself from the first day he was hired, bragging about the things he that he had learned from the Americans when he worked at their hospital in Karte Se. Amir had even insisted Panna boil the water for washing the dishes, going on and on in his own self-importance about amoebas and the liver. Well, the simpleton had paid his price for having worked for the American diplomats. Taraki's men had taken him to the Ministry of Interior and Amir, who was a lowly Hazara, had never been seen or heard from again. Dr. Aziz refused to hire anyone to replace him. He was certain his loyal servant was coming back. Panna never ceased to wonder how the professor could be so deaf and dumb to the goings on around him. But then, what could you expect from a poet? Her employer lived in a world of books.

The bell on the front gate rang and Panna flinched. In these times it could only mean trouble. She slipped on her coat and shuffled down the garden walk to open it. Now that Sultan was dead she had to tend the garden and answer the gate, too.

Panna recognized Captain Najib Duranni instantly. Such a dashing figure in his military uniform-- he was always her favorite among Rahmin's friends-- a welcome tonic for the overly serious and melancholy Rahmin.

"Come in. Come in. Dr. Aziz will be disappointed. He has gone to Istalif today."

"Yes, I know. I've just been to his office. I'm here to see Annisa." The captain brushed raindrops from his overcoat as he started up the walk ahead of Panna. "I can't stay long and it's important I talk with her."

Panna was taken back by his sense of urgency--it was not his usual manner. Alarmed, she hurried after him. "I'm sorry, but Annisa has locked herself in her room. She refuses to come out. I even have trouble getting her to eat."

"Why?"

Panna hesitated in answering him, not knowing exactly how to explain it. "She grieves. A young boy she fancied was killed on the night of the demonstrations."

"Fancied?" Najib frowned. "Is that possible?"

Panna smiled inwardly. It was not her place as a servant to correct others but Najib seemed to have turned his eyes away from the budding beauty of Annisa. "She is no different than any other young girl. They romanticize; they daydream. They imagine things bigger than they are."

"She is much too young for that."

They had reached the front door and Panna was pleased Najib had waited to open it for her. Najib was always courteous, even to a servant.

"I want to hear more about this boy. Did he encourage it?"

"Captain Duranni, we are speaking of the dead."

"That makes no difference to me."

His reaction and her thought of those internal mirrors that dog one's life amused Panna. Najib Duranni had always had an eye for the ladies.

"Please, tell Annisa I'm here. She won't refuse me."

Panna prayed he was right as she willed her tired legs up the stairs. Her first rap on Annisa's door was answered with a hiss. "Go away."

"Captain Duranni is here. He wants to see you."

"You lie. Najib will never come back to Kabul. He is with the Resistance. I'm sure. "

"He is standing at the foot of the stairs this very moment."

"This is only a trick to get me to leave my room."

"Annisa," Najib shouted from below. "Come down here."

The door to her room edged open and as soon as Annisa saw him she let out a squeal, racing down the stairs; crying out, "Najib, Najib!" She flung herself into his arms. "You're home, you're home."

Panna marveled at the sudden change--the sullen and listless girl was hopping up and down.

"Have you seen Rahmin? Father sent a letter with Mr. Hardcastle. We haven't heard a word."

Najib held her at arms length in front of him. "Whoa! Slow down, little one. I'm speechless. In one short year you've grown up on me!"

Annisa clapped her hands. "Did you bring me a present?"

"Annisa!" Panna scolded.

"I did." He rummaged in his raincoat pocket and pulled out a small box. "Sorry, I didn't have time to have it wrapped at the airport."

"Oh, it's wonderful." Annisa held up a tiny heart-shaped necklace. "Fasten it for me, please," she said, lifting her long dark braids from the back of her neck.

Panna frowned. "You spoil her."

Najib winked at Panna in return. "Well, she has to give it back if she doesn't go to school. Right Panna?"

29

Panna nodded. "What do you think of that, my stubborn girl?"

For a moment, Annisa's face clouded over. "I can't go to school. I am mourning Kassim."

Panna and the captain exchanged a look that needed no explanation.

"Najib, father is in Istalif."

"I'm here to see *you*."

Annisa's face flushed with pleasure and Panna witnessed yet another transformation. The exuberant child had become the grown-up lady of the house. "Panna, bring us some tea," she ordered.

"I can't stay that long." Najib removed an envelope from inside his jacket. "I want you to give this to your father. Don't lose it. There are very important papers inside."

"From Rahmin?"

"Yes, and you must promise me not to repeat anything I tell you. I saw Rahmin in New York. He is fine and he misses you. Wants you to come."

"To New York?" She clasped her hands with unbridled pleasure and then abruptly unfolded them. "Will you be there?"

Panna frowned. "You mustn't ask the Captain questions he can't answer. These are treacherous times."

"I can't go to America," Annisa said. "I'm going to stay here to join the Resistance."

Najib reached out and affectionately patted her head. "I believe you, Annisa-jan, but in your brother's absence I am your sworn protector. Do you understand?"

Annisa nodded solemnly.

"You must go to Rahmin."

"Does my father know about this?"

"Yes. In the meantime, you must promise me you'll go back to school."

"Why should I if I am going to America?"

"Because no one must suspect this is your plan. Things must look normal."

"Normal!" She spat out her words. "That's a bogus word. How can things be normal when those pigs are in our land."

"Annisa, it's all a game. We have to learn to pretend."

His words seemed to sober her because she retreated to a bench in the hallway and sat there turning the envelope over and over in her hands. "Najib, do you think I am a coward?" she asked, her eyes on Panna.

"A coward? That's a question you have to answer for yourself."

"Panna says I am. She says I'm afraid to go to school."

"She also says you refuse your food. I don't think that's being a coward. I just think it's silly. I like my ladies with meat on their bones."

Annisa giggled. "I shall make myself fat, just for you."

Again Panna scolded her. "Don't be rude, Annisa. Captain Duranni means he wants you to be healthy."

"How do you know what he thinks!"

Panna rolled her eyes at Najib and he nodded his head, acknowledging her dilemma. He turned to Annisa. "I can't stay, Little-One." He leaned down and kissed Annisa's forehead. "Listen to Panna. She is one of the wise ones."

It pleased Panna to hear this. "I suggest you leave from the servant's quarters. No one watches the back street and there are no servants to report you were here. Amir, the *baccha* was taken away by the secret police and Sultan, the gardener, was killed in the demonstrations."

"You are managing this big house by yourself? Panna, it's too much for you."

Panna smiled, grateful that someone had acknowledged her overwhelming task.

"As for you, young lady," Najib wagged his finger at Annisa. "Not one word about our conversation to anyone."

"They would have to torture me."

He nodded. "Yes, I believe it." He headed down the hallway towards the back of the house but then stopped and retraced his steps to Annisa who was still seated on the bench. "Annisa-jan, you must never forget you are my special girl. You are not to be afraid. I am your sworn protector."

She did not look up and lingered in the hallway long after he was gone. "Do you suppose I am the reason Najib has come back to Kabul?" she asked Panna.

"You? What a foolish thought. The man has his family here."

"Father says Najib's parents have fled to Tehran. And his wife is a viper. Everyone knows that he hates her."

"How many times have I told you never to repeat gossip."

"I think Najib fancies me."

"*Mahadeva*, Great God Shiva. You refuse to eat because Kassim is dead and now you imagine things that aren't true about Najib. He is your protector--- a brother. Nothing more, nothing less."

"But Najib thinks I'm special. He brings me presents when he travels. Rahmin never does."

"So? Najib once brought me a silk scarf from London town. Does that mean he desires old Panna? Don't take Najib's little attentions or his teasing as anything more than they are."

Annisa went on, as though she didn't care whether Panna believed her or not. "I know he wishes he could have married someone like me instead of his wife."

"Merciful heavens. You talk like those romance magazines you hide under your covers."

Annisa's face flushed. "How would you know they are romance? You can't even read."

Panna sucked in her breath. "Even so. . . You heard Najib. 'I am wise,' you rude girl. You should apologize to me."

"I didn't mean to hurt you."

"Yes, you did. I warn you. Your father would not like to hear your foolish school girl talk about Najib."

"Father? How could he possibly understand? He's such a robot."

"Wicked, wicked child. It is disrespectful to speak of your father like this. I never knew you were such a shallow girl. And where is your grief? How easily you forget you were mourning young Kassim."

The color drained from Annisa's face... "Panna, don't say such a thing."

"Then don't think it."

"Are you sorry Najib came to see me today?"

"Certainly not. Najib is a blessing on this house. For the first time I see you smile. I hear you laugh."

Annisa looked almost fearful to hear it. "Panna, am I really a shallow girl?"

"I don't know what to think."

"Najib is my hero. That doesn't mean I don't love Kassim. Tomorrow I will visit his grave. There is a shop on Jade-i-miwan, which sells flowers to rich foreigners, even in winter. I have been foolish to hide behind my door. Yes, tomorrow I will return to school. Show them I am not afraid."

Sudden warmth and the sweet flow of relief swept through Panna's tortured limbs. "Oh, Annisa, it is good you say this."

"Do you still think I'm afraid? Well, I'm not, you know. My faith is my weapon."

"Be grateful for that. Life gives meaning when one accepts the wisdom of their ancestors."

"Then it's wrong of me to go to America?"

"I think the secret to life is to tend your own garden. Your own earth."

"But you left your home, your people?"

"It was come or be killed."

"But why Kabul when you are not a Moslem?"

"Any faith is safe here. Besides, my country is gone. The India of my childhood is now Pakistan."

"If father decides to take me to America, will you go with us?"

"Your father will never go. Your mother's grave is here." Panna also knew escape was no longer possible. Professor Aziz had waited too long. Russian helicopters patrolled the borders and they were mining the paths that refugees had to cross. She had no idea what was in that letter Najib had brought but it could only spell trouble by getting Annisa's hopes up.

"Now that Najib is my sworn protector. . . maybe I *should* stay in Afghanistan.

Panna was exasperated... "Your duty is to obey your father. Whatever he decides. Forget Najib. Forget Kassim."

"Forget!" Without warning, Annisa began to wail. "I hate you! I hate this stupid war," she shouted, as she fled back up the stairs. "Why did they have to kill Kassim? Why? Why?" The bedroom door banged behind her.

Panna debated if she should follow. Her heart begged for a rest but it also ached for Annisa. It made her cross that she must pull herself up the stairs again. Outside Annisa's bedroom door she waited, listening to the screams of protest. Holding her breath, Panna turned the handle. Annisa had thrown herself on the bed and was beating her fists on the pillow. Panna was much relieved to see it. The tears had come at last.

After the hysterics had subsided and Annisa's sobbing was little more than tiny gasps for breath, she slowly lifted her head. "Panna, I can't go to America. I won't go."

"I don't think that is your decision to make."

"No one can make me go if I don't want to."

"Fickle child. You promised Najib you would."

"No, I didn't. I only promised to give my father that envelope and I didn't promise when."

"Shame on you. Causing trouble for everyone in these troubled times. One minute you want to go and the next minute you want to stay here."

"My father has not said one word to me about this. He doesn't want me to go, I'm sure."

"I warn you, Annisa, life is not kind to people who think they know what others think or should think."

"I don't care. I want to stay here. Every day I will go to Kassim's grave and I will pray he can have a white flag--like the holy Mujahideen. Oh, Kassim. . ." The sobbing began again and Annisa writhed on the bed.

Panna, who was never comfortable in showing affection, walked over and sat by her. "There. There." She reached out and gently stroked Annisa's hair. "I am sorry the world has shattered your dreams. But you are young. There will be. . ."

Annisa stiffened under her touch. "I will never be young again."

Panna said nothing because she knew the girl spoke the truth. She drew back from Annisa. "If you are no longer young, it does not mean you can never love. Love is your nature. Let it be your *sadhana*, your highest attainment."

"No, I am finished with love. Kassim is dead and Najib is only a brother to me . . .I will never marry."

It was difficult for Panna not to smile at this solemn declaration.

"My mother died giving birth and my father has told me many times that he promised her I would never have to wear the *chadri* or a veil. He would give me a fine education. I shall devote my life to my studies and be a doctor like Rahmin. Only I will be a doctor in Afghanistan. I am finished with love."

Panna turned her eyes away and sighed. She doubted if bliss was ever to be found in books. Lord Shiva had manifested himself into this world out of love. Existence meant nothing without it. Of this one thing she was sure.

CHAPTER 4

A fine rain covered the mountains, spreading a gray veil over the garden. Achromatic shadows and the sweet aroma of *gosh-e-feel* sizzling in the kitchen filled the room. It was late afternoon. Two men sat across from each other, empty tea glasses in their hands.

"I shall miss all this. It is tangible. Solid." There was wariness in the deep-set eyes of Dr. Sulaiman Aziz. "It was my wish to die here--to be buried next to my wife."

"You may get your wish, if you do not leave soon." His companion, Fritz Werner, a short intense man, spoke with a slight German accent.

Aziz made a mental note of his friend's features, hoping to memorize them. "Sorry, I am old and stale and slow moving." His smile camouflaged his inner turmoil. "I do not belong in New York. Better Denver. My associate Nur Rabini tells me the mountains there match ours."

He leaned forward and poured himself a fresh glass of hot black tea; sugar filled almost a third of the glass. "Nur Rabini considers himself safe from any purge. He is friends with Karmal's new mistress Anahita."

"Everyone is friends with Karmal these days. It means nothing. Sulaiman, you have no choice. You must leave."

"Indeed." All afternoon Aziz had exercised self-control. The dismay of impending separation. His land! The smile on his face faded when he spoke again. "There was a time when Barbak emptied the prisons and declared an amnesty." His voice trailed off and he bowed his head. "See how desperate I am to avoid the truth."

"No more than the rest of us."

The steady ticking of the clock filled the room and seemed more tangible than all the discourse of the afternoon. Time was running out while their inane conversation had focused on the weather, the shortage of food and fuel, the frequent power failures in the city when the Mujahideen blew up the transformers. Most of it had been a monologue with Professor Aziz ruminating over how the puppets could have come to power, as though if he could put it into words, a kind of exorcism would take place.

Aziz removed his handkerchief from his pocket and wiped his glasses. His face had aged dramatically since the invasion. A

man in his mid-60's, he looked to be much older. "Taraki. . . his atrocities. To think that he was also a poet. I never paid much attention to his politics. I remember. . ."
Werner stood up abruptly and began to pace. "Enough. We need to discuss details of your escape. Captain Duranni has contacted me twice to warn. . ."
"Najib Duranni?" Aziz's face lit up. "He is involved?" Werner looked stunned. "Did you not get the envelope?"
"What envelope?"
"Dear God. Important papers were left for you. Najib gave them to Annisa."
The light in the hallway clicked on behind them. "It is dim in here. How can you see?" It was Panna with a plate of crispy, sweet dessert. Professor Aziz motioned for her to leave it on the table.
"*Gosh-e-feel!* My favorite," Fritz said.
Panna did not acknowledge the compliment. It had always been clear to Dr. Aziz that she was not fond of the German. "Dr. Aziz, the man has eyes the color of steel. With such a father! Not to be disrespectful, but how can you befriend such a man? He deals more in drugs than Afghan carpets!" Once Panna had even come to Aziz and told him, "I think your German friend gathers information."
"Panna?" Dr. Aziz hesitated, wondering if he should ask her if she knew of any envelope from Najib but decided against it. It might alarm Fritz to know he confided in her. "Where is Annisa? Is she home from school yet?"
"Yes, she is in the garden. She plants the peach tree."
"A tree?" Fritz asked. "At this time of year?"
"It is in honor of the dead boy Kassim."
As soon as Panna had left the room Fritz asked, "Can we trust her?"
"Panna wonders the same thing about you."
"There must be no talk of your leaving in front of her. The Khad woos the Sikhs and Hindus in Kabul with huge sums of money and the promise of privileged jobs."
"Panna has little or nothing to do with the Indian community. She keeps to herself." He would not tell Fritz because it would only upset him, but Panna would have to know of the planned escape and soon. Telling Annisa would be difficult and he would need help. He hardly knew his daughter anymore. She was so high strung and disrespectful these days.

"Are you sure she does not inform?"

"Absolutely. Panna has suffered much in this life."

"Yes, a sad story there."

"There is one for each of us, is there not? Your father. Panna. Now my Annisa. What will her story be before this horror is played out?"

"Hopefully, America will befriend her with the same kindness you gave my family."

Aziz drained his glass, wiping his lips on the back of his hand. Hendrick Werner, Fritz's father, had been an excellent teacher and they certainly had needed men in the sciences, but he never cared for the old Nazi. Quarrelsome and demanding. When the West had asked for his extradition, Aziz had been one of those at the university who fought to save his position. A guest in Afghanistan was a guest. Always under your protection whether you approved of him or not.

"I have made arrangements through the diplomatic pouch to notify Rahmin you are coming. A friend in Frankfurt is going to New York. He will deliver the details to your son personally. You can trust no one these days. Do not use the phone; it is tapped. Send no letters. No written message and whatever you do, Sulaiman, do not leave this house for the next three days."

"But my students. . ." Dr. Aziz looked to the hall. 'Yes, Panna what is it?"

"Is Mr. Werner staying for dinner?"

"No. I thought we discussed that."

Panna shrugged her shoulders and shuffled out of the room.

"She worries me, Aziz. The Russians are very clever. Like dogs, they sniff out family trouble and use it as bait."

"Panna has no family. She is loyal. My main concern is what is to become of her when I leave."

"I will find employment for her."

"How much this relieves me! Having to abandon her. . . You are right about the Communists. They look for the disgruntled; they recruit the boy with pimples on his face. President Amin was always the blacksheep. Barbak Karmal is another. Kicked out of the house when his father remarried. He drinks too much. He beats his wife, they say."

"I did not mean to get you started on the Saur Revolution again."

Aziz raised his glass of tea in a mock toast. "To our new and glorious leader, Karmal, the wife-beater."

"Hopefully, he'll meet the same fate as Taraki and Amin."
The poet smiled. "All these years in Kabul, Fritz-- you will make an Afghan yet. The Hindus have a saying: 'Oh Gods! From the venom of the cobra, the teeth of the tiger, and the vengeance of the Afghan--deliver us.'"
"Deliver us from your avoidance of the business at hand," Fritz grumbled. He walked to the window and stared out at the garden. "Sulaiman, there is something I haven't told you."
Aziz did not hear him, lost in his own thoughts, as his eyes scanned the familiar objects in the room. The prayer rug his wife had embroidered; the framed picture of her on his writing desk. Her long hair had been done up in braids for the photograph. How sweet the memories of unbraiding it for her at night, watching it fall in waves to below her waist.

Be slow the comb,
my heart is nestled there.
Your memory comes at midnight,
my arms cradle my head and the pillow is wet.

The British journalist, Matthew Hardcastle, had taken that photo of her in their garden and mailed it with a note acknowledging that he knew Aziz's faith disapproved of taking one's picture but that 'when one is confronted with such beauty it would be a sin not to capture it.' Dr. Aziz had been grateful and it tore at his heart when Fritz told him he could not take it with him. None of his possessions. It was brutal. Yet Fritz's father had said over and over that the Jews who escaped Europe were the ones who were not weighted down by their trinkets.

Werner turned from the window. "It is starting to rain. Annisa should come in the house."

"Poor child. She will not be here to see her tree blossom." Sulaiman's eyes returned to the picture of his wife. He wanted to ask her forgiveness. If only he had fled with Annisa after Daoud had been overthrown. Werner had urged him to do so at the time. Annisa's face had been yellow from jaundice. They could have flown to India, allegedly for medical treatment, and then on to the States to be with Rahmin. Now a terrible ordeal awaited them. A long trek on foot through the mountains. Had he violated the code of *namus* by leaving his daughter so defenseless? He could not bear to think about it. "Fritz, why was it necessary for them to invade?"

Werner turned from the window with an exasperated look. "Sulaiman, you have spent the afternoon asking why."

"I personally think it is territorial expansion. If Afghanistan is the Rhineland, will Pakistan and Iran be Austria and Sudetenland?"

"Aziz, be done with it! You are leaving. It is settled."

Asiz asked himself if it would ever be settled for his country. The ghosts of Darius, Genghis Khan and the British Raj owned the night. Along the old silk route, Roman influence mingled with Buddhism and Afghans sang of the fair Roxanne and the Great Alexander who constructed Alexandria-of-the-Aryans near modern Herat. But like every other conqueror, Alexander failed to realize that the tribal kingdoms of Afghanistan would fight to protect their own form of mountain independence, which eventually forced Alexander to retreat to Babylon. Would the Soviets meet the same fate?

Behind him the front door opened and Fritz turned to the hallway. Annisa entered, the spade held against her shoulder like a rifle.

"More like her mother every day."

Aziz nodded. "Yes. It hurts me to look upon her."

Annisa paused to brush the smudges of dirt from her black cotton stockings. Her cape dripped rivulets of rain upon the tile floor. "Uncle Fritz, I did not see you come in." Annisa seldom called him Uncle to his face. But she considered him as such. It was Fritz who had convinced her father she should have riding lessons. When she was eight he had taken her to the German Club to ride her own chestnut stallion. The stables at the German Club were empty now, the horses seized in a raid by the Mujahideen. It pleased Annisa to think of a freedom fighter attacking Russian convoys astride the beautiful stallion she had loved.

"I hear you are back at school." Fritz spoke to her in German.

She answered in English. "Yes. My life will be my studies. I want to be like Rahmin."

Fritz saw his opportunity. "And live in America."

"No, that is finished. I have dedicated myself to the Resistance. I could never leave Afghanistan now."

"I see." Fritz Werner gave a side-ways glance to her father. "I always thought you wanted to go to New York?"

"Not any more. Only cowards leave our country. I will stay and avenge Kassim."

Werner cleared his throat. "Annisa, Najib Duranni left an important envelope with you for your father."

Her eyes blazed. "How did you know this?"

"Where is it? Why did you not give the envelope to him?"

"Because I opened it," she said defiantly. "There were papers inside for America."

Professor Aziz was incredulous. "Annisa-jan. You opened something that was for me!"

"Yes, and I'd do it again. My name is on those papers too."

"I am shocked. Where did you put them?"

"I don't remember."

"Annisa!"

The anger in her father's voice rattled her resolve. "I am not a stupid girl. I did not destroy them. I promised Najib I would give them to you but I promised myself only if you asked for them."

"This is unforgivable."

Annisa looked crushed. "Please, no. . . I don't want to leave for America without you. I would be miserable by myself with Rahmin. Please don't make me go alone."

"Alone? Never. Who put such a foolish idea in your head?"

"Panna says you will never leave mother's grave and that is true." Her voice was suddenly pleading. "Please, I want to stay and fight. Najib is here. He will protect us."

Fritz Werner was alarmed "Annisa! Najib is in a very sensitive position. Only because he is so fond of you and your father does he take the risk. You must make no attempt to contact him at anytime. You would only put his life in danger."

Annisa stared at him wide-eyed.

"And do you know if you stay here they can send you to Moscow for your studies."

"Yes, my friend Umariah is going next term. She wants to. Umariah has swallowed their filth."

There was no mistaking the hatred in her eyes against the invaders and this was yet another cause for Fritz Werner's concern. Annisa would have to disguise her contempt for the new government until she was safely out of the country. Informers were everywhere, particularly in the middle school. "The problem is your father tells me you are progressing rapidly in your Russian."

"Yes. Soon I will be able to converse with our stupid liberators."

"Do you not know they can send you to Russia for further study without your father's permission."

"Never. I would die by my own hand first."

Dr. Aziz was alarmed. "Annisa. Never have I heard such talk. The Koran forbids one to take their own life."

Fritz Werner raised his hand to wave the matter aside. "She is only distraught. We all are these days."

Annisa stood in the doorway. "I am not distraught. Why are you trying to scare my father into leaving Afghanistan? You should leave us alone!"

"Annisa!"

But she had disappeared up the stairs.

Dr. Aziz was beside himself. "What has gotten into her? She has never acted like this. She loves you."

"She is not herself."

"Frankly, I am worried. Did you see how pale she is? She never plays her tapes of Western music she used to enjoy so much; her friends who would come to the compound after school have been conspicuously absent. Each day Annisa returns home alone."

"It is sad to see her like this," Fritz said, flinching at the sound of a door being slammed at the top of the stairs. "What has happened to childhood in Afghanistan? All the laughter is gone." He turned to Aziz. "When did you last talk with her about going to Rahmin?"

Aziz felt defensive. "We've never really discussed it. I always thought she would be eager to go to America. But after she returned to school--she's become so strident, militant. You heard her. I am fearful she will consider me less a man because I do not stay to fight."

"For God's sakes, Aziz!"

"Don't look so worried. Of course, I'll go. But I wish I could stay to bear witness. It is the blood of the poor and uneducated that will soak the land--the very people the Russians say they came to free. There will never be another time like this. The old ways, when a man's word was his honor, will finally be put to rest. Here. In Afghanistan."

"Sulaiman, we've been over this."

"Perhaps I could stay and organize the intellectuals? What is left of them."

"Damn it. You haven't heard a word I've said. Wake up, Aziz. You can do nothing from prison."

"Here they are. You're stupid old papers."

Startled, both men turned to see Annisa standing in the doorway, an envelope in her hand. She threw it on the floor at their feet.

Wearily, Dr. Aziz bent over to retrieve it. "Go to your room," he said, without looking up.

"But Father."

"Go to your room!" A vein on his forehead bulged and blood pounded in his ears. "Leave us," he suddenly shouted.

Annisa stood before him trembling. "You don't understand," she murmured.

"That is true. I understand nothing about you."

Annisa put her hand to her mouth as though to stifle a sob and fled the room. Fritz Werner began to pace. "This is no time to quarrel with Annisa. You need to face the truth and I am inept in getting you to see the danger you are in." He looked at his watch. "It will take 50,000 Afghanis for the guide to take you to the border and you do not pay the full amount until you cross." He reached for his money clip.

"Fritz, that is a great deal of money."

"Agreed. But the Mujahideen need money for ammunition."

"Yes, of course. Escorting cowards like myself safely out of the fighting." His tone was sardonic. "I will hate living in a country which is not interested in hearing our story."

"That is too simple an answer. The world is peppered with outrages now. The outrage taking place here is very far away from America." The German pressed a large wad of bills into Aziz's hand.

"Do you know the Russians boast they need salvage only one million of us to run the country? You tell me the world hears this and looks the other way."

"Sulaiman, put the money and the envelope in your pocket before you lose them."

Startled, Aziz looked down at his head. "What is the money for?"

"A down payment for the guide. . .Sulaiman, have you been listening?"

"I can't accept it."

"You must. I lied to you. You are not going to prison. You are to be executed on Friday morning."

"The Holy Day. . . without a trial? Dear God," the poet whispered, staring at the money in his hand. "To hear you say it."

"Captain Duranni confirms it."

"I confess I barely have the 50,000 Afghanis for the guide. I must sell the house and the furniture. There is the matter of

Annisa's education."

"There is not enough time. It would arouse suspicions. I will advance you the money."

"But what if you are unable to dispose of my property? How can I repay you? An Afghan poet in New York."

"Your hospitality over the years is my payment."

Aziz continued to stare at the money. "I can't take this. I will go to a refugee camp in Pakistan and wait my turn like everyone else."

"Would you have Annisa raised in one of those camps? Take the money for her sake. She is the daughter I will never have. Let me help pay for her future."

Slowly Sulaiman folded the bills and stuck them in his pocket. He reached for Fritz's hand. "I honor the risks you take for us." His eyes were moist.

Fritz Werner gently removed his hand. "No matter what excuse they give you, Karmal's men are expert in devising ruses. They want prominent men like you to go peacefully, without a fuss. It is a pattern oppressors use the world over. A man opens the door to an old friend and just disappears. There are over 200 names on their list for Friday. Fake an illness should they come to you before you are to leave for Peshawar. They will figure they can return the next day or the next."

"And Annisa? Should she go to school?" Aziz clicked the spoon in his empty glass.

"Yes. If she stays home, it would only arouse suspicion. Say nothing of your plans to her until the night before you leave. The less she knows the better. She is too overwrought--a danger to herself. I leave for Delhi tomorrow but a chit for the money bazaar in Peshawar will be delivered to your home tonight. It is for Annisa's education. And on the morning you are to leave, a boy from the village of Tezeen will come to your gate before it is light. His name is Zia. Together you will take a taxi to a safe house." Werner stood up abruptly. "I must go. Remember you are not to leave this house on any excuse."

Aziz followed him to the archway, embraced him, kissing him on both cheeks. "I am amazed. All these arrangements."

"We have Captain Duranni to thank."

"Yes. Najib a fine boy. Ardent. Integrity. He is well named." He was reluctant to let go of his friend's hand. "Then it really is good-by?"

"Yes."

"I shall miss you. You have my respect; more than any man I know."

"You do me a great honor." Werner turned abruptly, and without looking back, marched out the door.

Aziz watched him down the walk. "The son pays for the sins of the father," he whispered. "I weep that you should ever think you were born with a fundamental flaw. Good-bye, old friend, I shall pray for the burdens of your soul. May Allah be with you."

The poet looked up at the sky. The drizzle had ceased. The gray clouds would no doubt lift before morning. The last of March. Soon the jonquils would appear. How sad he would not see his beloved garden when they reached full bloom. How his wife had loved the garden, had loved to watch him fuss with his roses with young Rahmin playing at her feet.

You were sitting by when I planted these flowers.
Now they have blossomed and you feed grave worms.
God, it is spring and the flowers bloom;
What autumn frost has stricken my heart?

He looked over to the peach tree Annisa had just planted. It was thin and scrawny, and she had placed it too close to the garden wall. He did not have the heart to tell her that trees should be planted in the fall.

Did I do right, my *barai shoma mahbub,* my special love? Was it wrong to raise little Annisa without the veil? She has no dowry. No skills as a wife. *Insha'llah.* If God wills. Once again his eyes embraced the outlines of his beloved mountains, towering in the distance above his garden walls. The Pushto proverb he had learned as a child echoed over and over:

They put the nightingale in a golden cage,
but still it sang, Home. My home. My home!

CHAPTER 5

That night Annisa was awakened by the sound of her own screams. Fragments of a nightmare. Her quarrel with her father. Kassim's grave. A Russian soldier with his truck parked at the bottom of the hill. Her senses hovering in that place where reality and dreaming interface as she tried to sort it out:

My name is Annisa. I am in my own room. My father's house. It is the 26th of April. My heart is racing. I see a ghost or is that a nightgown hanging on a hook? Heavenly relief. Safe. Safe in my father's house.

The Russian soldier who had triggered her dream was real enough; he had harassed her on her way to school. Only he had not been in a truck but leaning out of the open hatch of a tank, smoking a cigarette.

"Krasee'vee!" he had called to her. "Let me spill my juice in your silky long hair."

She had walked past him, head up, eyes straight ahead.

"You hear me? Afghan bitch. How many men have you had? *Sko'lka?* I save my cock for you."

She had understood enough of their hateful language to know the meaning of his words and bolted up the street, pursued by raucous laughter from the tank. The horror of the soldier's obscenities had obsessed her all day. In the afternoon, when she had visited Kassim's grave, she could not stay in the burial ground, as she was too unsettled to offer her usual prayers.

"Hayya 'illa's-sala." Annisa sat up in bed to the reassuring sound of the mullah calling the faithful to prayer from the minaret.

Grateful it was dawn, she took her prayer rug to the balcony, faced Mecca and said her four prayers, but her mind was elsewhere. The soldier's ugly words were crowding out her prayers. Ashamed she could not concentrate on God, she went back inside.

A pair of scissors inside her sewing basket caught her eye. Scissors! Yes. In one rash moment Annisa determined she would use them; cut off her shame. Her hands were shaking as she began to hack furiously at the thick braid that hung below her waist. The scissors were old and dull and she cursed her clumsiness. When she had cut one side she started to cry but did not stop, until with one final ruthless snip the braid fell to the floor.

"There, you Russian pig. No more insults about my hair." She kicked the braid across the room and threw herself on her bed, crying, sobbing until her body went limp and she sank once more into sleep.

When she awoke, a bright sun was streaming in her window and Panna was rapping furiously on her bedroom door.

"Annisa? Why do you not come for your breakfast? Your father wishes to speak to you. It is important."

"In a minute," Annisa mumbled. What could she say to her father? Would he forgive her? Sluggishly, she dressed herself, but when she caught sight of her head in the mirror she gasped; the impact of her deed hit full force. "Oh, no," she wailed. The girl in the mirror looked pitiful; her hair in jagged edges above her ears. "What have I done to myself!" Annisa shook her head violently from side to side but nothing moved. The image in the mirror did not lie. Her hair was gone.

Panna knocked again. "Are you coming?"

"Tell my father I am sick. I cannot go to school today."

Panna jiggled the handle on the door, but it was locked. "Annisa, must you not start this nonsense again!"

No answer.

"Ungrateful pup. You are beyond help." Panna fussed all the way down the stairs.

Annisa waited until she heard the door close on her father's study. Strange that he should still be home. He always left early for the university. He must not see her like this. Her short hair would only add to his anger from last night. Hurriedly, she tied a white scarf around her head, grabbed her schoolbooks, and inched her door open. She could hear the radio blaring in the servant quarters. Panna would be in the back of the house. Annisa raced down the front stairs and past her father's closed door.

Outside the compound she broke into a run, sprinting across the street to a path that wound through Liberation Park. Three blocks ahead on the corner was a beauty salon. She would stop there after school to inquire how much they would charge to curl her hair.

"Wait up. Wait for me," a young schoolmate called from behind. It was little Mira who was two grades below. "Annisa, why do you run from me on this glorious day!"

"We are late," Annisa answered. However, Mira's words opened her eyes to the day, and truly it was beautiful. Clear and fragrant with the faint smells of spring.

"Slow down, please. There is plenty of time." Mira thrust her arm under Annisa's nose. "My new watch. Even a second hand."

Small for her age, Mira appeared to be eight or nine when actually she was eleven. When she talked, her piquant little face and a hint of a lisp gave her an elf-like quality. "Tell me your secret, Annisa. Where do you go each day after school?"

"It has nothing to do with you."

"Why are you always so angry?"

"Because I am. Now stop asking silly questions or I won't walk with you."

"Is it because we can no longer study the Koran and have to memorize the propaganda of the Russians?"

Annisa was shocked. The girls at school were careful not to talk about such things, having been warned repeatedly by their parents of the danger in doing so. Annisa had to admire Mira's courage. "Yes. That is why I am angry. I wish to study the Koran."

"Me too."

"Then there is no need to talk about it anymore."

They had left the park and were approaching the corner where the only gasoline station in Shar-i-Nau was located. From a distance, they could see a young Afghan boy in tattered clothes, a soiled turban on his head. He was talking to a Russian soldier who was guarding a large black sedan parked at the pump.

"Look." Mira pointed to the soldier who had handed the boy something, which the boy quickly stuffed inside his baggy pants. "My father says they trade bullets for hashish."

"Yes. The stupid pigs. Only an idiot Russian would trade you bullets to shoot him with."

"My father says that many of their soldiers desert to the Mujahideen and that they take drugs because they are ashamed to be here."

Annisa was glad Mira had joined her. And she was relieved that she had not noticed her hair. Perhaps if she did not remove her scarf, no one would guess the horror she had done to herself.

"My brother is going to Herat to join the freedom fighters."

"Mira! You must not talk of this. There are others at school who would tell the Khad."

"I know. Umariah is one. Did you know her father is an official in the PDPA? She doesn't scare me. The older girls are planning a demonstration under her very nose."

"You know of this?"

"Yes. A friend told me. Have you not heard the news? Yesterday four students were shot dead at the Omar-e-Shaheed Lycee and one at the Habibiyya High School. It is time we join in the defiance and. . ."

The rumble of a truck behind them drowned out her words.

"Hey, girls," Russian voices shouted.

"Don't look around," Annisa ordered Mira. But of course Mira did.

The truck drew alongside them and the driver honked its horn. "Show us your tits."

"They have none," another soldier guffawed. "Only their little girl cunts."

Mira could not understand Russian. She looked over at Annisa and asked, "What do they want?"

Before Annisa could answer, a magazine sailed through the air and fell at Mira's feet. She bent over to pick it up amidst clapping and hooting from the truck.

"Here, give that to me, "Annisa ordered, tugging on Mira's arm and pulling her along the street. "Hurry, Mira. We must run. Run!"

It was not until they reached the gates of Zargoona and were safely inside the school grounds that Annisa saw what she held in her hand. She was horrified. Pictures of naked women. She looked around, hoping to drop the magazine unnoticed but one of the Afghan guards at the gate was watching her.

"What is it?" Mira asked. "More of their propaganda? Let me see."

"Never mind." Annisa hid the magazine inside her notebook. "Those soldiers are filth, Mira. Tomorrow you must wait for me. I will come to your house and walk you to school. You should not walk alone. The streets are not safe from these infidels."

An old man carrying a birdcage crossed from the caretaker's quarters and set the cage down in the archway of the school. Then he reached for the wooden mallet he had tucked inside the top of his pants and began to bang on a gong; a summon to morning classes. Groups of girls who were milling around the playground fell into long lines as they waited to march up the steps.

"That's the one who told me about the demonstration," Mira whispered to Annisa. "Her name is Siddiqa."

Annisa knew her. Siddiqa was good in sports.

"Liar!" Siddiqa's face was flushed with anger. Something Umariah was saying as they waited in line? Annisa and Mira moved closer to hear what the fuss was about.

"The Americans threaten to withdraw from the Olympic games because they are afraid to compete. The Soviets always beat them."

"How can you be so stupid?" Siddiqa sputtered. "They will boycott the games in Moscow as a protest against the occupation of Afghanistan."

"You are the stupid girl if you think the Americans care about us."

Annisa could not contain herself. Yanking the offensive magazine from inside her notebook she shoved it into the hands of the startled Umariah. "Here. Take a look. Is this what you go to Moscow to study!"

Umariah looked at the magazine and gasped. "Have you no shame! Where did you get such a thing?"

"One of your great liberators threw it at Mira on our way to school. See how godless they are. They defile women. How can you believe in what they say? They do not believe in God."

"God? There is no God," Umariah snapped. "Show him to me. Is he there, up on that cloud above you?"

Siddiqa was livid. "How dare you talk this way in front of the younger girls."

"I speak the truth. Our people are in rags. The Dark Ages. The Soviets will make everything equal. . . .Not God."

"God does not steal our natural gas, our emeralds."

"Puppet. Puppet. Daughter of a Puppet," Mira began to chant. Umariah shoved Mira backwards just as the second gong rang for class. Annisa leaped forward to defend her.

"Puppet. Puppet. Daughter of a Puppet," Mira sang out again.

In the scuffle that followed, Annisa's scarf was torn from her head. The girls, who had formed a circle around the combatants, let out a collective gasp at the sight of Annisa's butchered hair.

"Look at you," Umariah ridiculed. "Your father has done this to show your disgrace with the soldiers. Now we know why you have such a magazine. A girl like you invites such things."

Annisa stood there white-faced, her fists clenched.

"Do you wish the soldiers to ravage you?" Umariah jeered.

49

Seima, a delicate girl with large somber eyes, began to weep. "Please don't say these things. Every morning I pretend I don't hear them. They shout foul words at me."

"I hate you, Umariah," little Mira screamed. "You are evil. There is a God. There is!"

"Stupid. Stupid. Umariah is stupid." It was a singsong cry and chanted in unison. "*Ahmaq* Umariah."

One of the Afghan guards by the gate crossed the compound to investigate the rumpus. Pushing his way into the circle he found Annisa standing in the middle. "What is this?" he laughed. "A plucked chicken has come to school?"

A desperate quiet followed. Annisa stared at him. Slowly she leaned down and picked up her scarf. "Here, you wear it. Put this on your head. You work for the puppets. Wear my scarf. You need it more than I do. You are like a girl."

His face crimson, the soldier pointed his rifle at her.

"Go ahead. Shoot me. I am not afraid to die for Islam."

Alarmed, Mira rushed up behind the soldier and began to flail him with her fists. "Death to Barbak. Death to the puppets."

Annisa shook her fist in the air. "Death. Death. Death."

At this, the soldier raised his rifle and fired warning shots above her head. It was the sound of the shots that signaled the school compound to erupt. Those few girls who had already filed into their classrooms began to pour out of the building screaming: "*Murda Baad* Karmal. Death to Karmal."

Forming a wedge, a group of girls crowded together and began to push toward the gate. Again, warning shots were fired.

Passersby on the street stopped in amazement to see schoolgirls climbing over the high walls and dropping into the streets, shouting, "Death to the Communists."

Inside the gate another group continued to taunt the guards. "Wear a scarf. Wear a scarf. Weaklings! Women!"

Angered at the insults to his manhood, an Afghan corporal, who looked to be no more than 16 himself, swung around and fired directly into the crowd. Two girls fell backwards. One of them was Mira. A circle of blood seeped through her white blouse.

It was the sight of Mira's blood that did it. Those girls who had been too intimidated by the guards to take part in a protest began to scream, swarming in terror towards the gates. With a roar they pushed against the great doors which yielded in the crush and broke from their hinges. Stampeding through the archway they swarmed into the street, shouting, their numbers growing as others deserted their hapless teachers, who no longer had any control over them. Traffic came to a halt. No taxis, no men on horseback, no Hazarahs pushing their flatbed trucks could get through the sea of black and white school uniforms.

"Go back inside," an old mullah astride a donkey pleaded. "Daughters of Islam. This is not for you."

But Annisa and others swept past him and marched instead towards a tank of Soviet soldiers stalled at the end of the street. The soldiers stared at the advancing girls in disbelief. "Death to *Shuravi.*"

Two Afghan men on the sidewalk began to cheer this bravado and ran to join the demonstration, but others shouted them back. "Stay out. They are only schoolgirls. The puppets will not dare to hurt them."

"A mast for our flag." Khalila, a tall girl in the sixth form rushed over and asked an old man for his cane. She pulled off her dark green jacket and hoisted it on the cane high above her head. "They have robbed us of our flag. Green is the color of Islam." Eyes bright with excitement, she ran towards the front of the line. "Long live Afghanistan. Death to the invaders."

The sight of this set grown men to weeping. The hated puppets had taken away the traditional red, green and black flag of Afghanistan and replaced it with a red one. Now the innocence of childhood defied those in authority. Like a general leading her troops into battle, Kahliha waved her banner and directed them towards the street that housed the foreign officials.

"Out. Out. Out. Out with the Russians!" Startled diplomats watching from the safety of their second story windows could not believe their eyes. School girls marching and shaking their fists.

A woman in a blue chadri, carrying a small child in her arms, rushed into the street and held the child high over her head. "Long live the Mujahideen," she shouted and then rapidly disappeared again into the crowd of onlookers, a small ghostlike figure who had defied centuries of tradition by drawing attention to herself.

The marchers were passing the girls' school of Malali and when they drew abreast of the large iron gates, the gates swung open and the girls of Malali stampeded to join the girls of Zagoona. The people on the street went wild with cheering and saluted the makeshift flag carried on an old man's cane. Liberation! A fever swept through the crowded city streets. "On to the palace," the onlookers shouted as the girls grew in numbers and boldness. "Long live Islam."

A Soviet tank stationed at the intersection of the mosque began to roll down the center of the street, heading directly toward the middle of the march. "Long live the Mujahideen," Khalila screamed. The tank aimed its guns at the flag bearer and without warning began spraying bullets.

More than 10 girls fell in that first wave, and 10 more in the terrible moments that followed, among them Khalila--clutching her flag, blood pouring from her nostrils. The top of her body was almost severed from her hips.

Annisa stumbled towards Khalila and picked up the cane. Bullets screamed past her as she hoisted the makeshift flag again. "Assassins. Swine!"

"Stop. In the name of Allah, stop," a man in a business suit pleaded. He rushed into the street towards the dying children and attempted to move Khalila's body to safety. The Russian gunner cut him down before he could move her. And when the people on the sidewalks surged forward in protest, the tank swung its guns and pumped bullets into the crowds that lined the street. The bullets tore holes in the thick mud walks that fronted the Ministry of Education.

Amidst the screams of the wounded and cries from the helpless onlookers, the girls regrouped. There was no stopping them now. It was better to die. Better to be gunned down in the streets than to live under the Communist pigs.

"*Hkuda Bzanet,* we damn you," they yelled. A line of girls charged over those who had fallen, running directly towards the tank. To the crowd's amazement, it ceased firing.

Annisa, who had dived behind a vegetable stall when the second round of bullets hit, worked her way back through the mob to where the American Information Center and its library stood. "Give us guns, America. Give us guns," she shouted, waving the cane.

"Guns. Guns. Give us guns." Fists were raised once again in unison.

Their numbers had begun to dwindle but still they pushed onward, passing sidewalks jammed with people who stared in disbelief as rows of Russian tanks now mysteriously held their fire.

When the procession entered Zarghuna Maidan, an old mullah ran in front of them. "Please go back. This fight is not for our women."

But another man pushed him out of the way. "We should praise Allah for their inspiration. I bow to such valor." The people began to applaud. Up and down the full length of Zarghuna Maidan, the valiant army of schoolgirls paraded. They would not stop until they reached the palace. But the Russians had prepared for their coming. The palace was ringed by tanks and surrounded by hundreds of soldiers. There was no way to get through.

Annisa remained at the front, arm and arm with Siddiqa--both of them hoarse from shouting; their school uniforms stained with perspiration. When they reached the palace gates, the defiant schoolgirls demanded to see the governor.

Afghan guards outside the palace wall stared impassively ahead but did not raise their guns.

Annisa suddenly broke ranks and ran up to one of the guards, a handsome boy with fine white teeth. "Coward. I have only a pen. You have a gun."

"Don't make me use it on you," he answered.

"Go home," another guard pleaded. "Our job is to protect you."

"The Mujahideen are our protectors. Surrender your guns to them," Annisa shouted.

Suddenly the palace gates burst open and Russian soldiers swarmed out, swinging clubs. Passing motorists leaped from their cars, attempting to pull the girls to safety. But a handful of girls were captured and the people cried in anguish to see them dragged inside and the great palace gates close behind them.

"*Nazah't.*" A Russian sergeant barked, backing them against a stone wall. He turned to an Afghan guard and shouted, "Tell them not to move or we will shoot them down."

Looking distraught, the Afghan soldier moved to obey.

"How can you do this to us?" Annisa asked. "We are your sisters. They have cut us down in the streets. See their blood on my sleeves." At this, the Afghan guard began to weep, and threw down his gun.

A shout came from the building. A tall Afghan official stood at the top of the palace steps waving his arms and screaming. "Idiots!" He turned towards the hapless girls and said in a placating tone. "The Russians are here to help us."

"Death to the Russians," Siddiqa shouted back.

"Stop. I command you." Racing down the steps in his shirt sleeves, his tie askew, the official waved a pistol in his hand. "Shame on you. You are nothing but children."

"Shame on you!" Annisa challenged. "You work for the puppets."

"How dare you," he gasped. He reached for Annisa and held the barrel of his pistol to her temple. "This one gun is good enough for all of you."

"Make us martyrs," Annisa taunted.

"We are like Malay's daughter," Siddiqa said. "We will be as famous as she."

Another Afghan official had emerged from the palace and motioned the man away. He was older and portly and wearing a two piece suit. As he came down the steps Annisa recognized him as the governor. He held out his arms towards Annisa in a fatherly gesture. There was a smile on his face.

"My child. Return to your school."

"With a gun at my head?"

He motioned for the man to release her. "The Russians are here to help us. To give you opportunities you never dreamed of."

Siddiqa stepped toward him. "Opportunities to inform on our parents? At school they ask me if my father keeps a picture of Karmal on his wall. Does my mother give food to the Mujahideen? If I want to go to summer camp, I must join the party. You give me opportunities. You take my soul."

The governor walked over to Siddiqa who was trembling after her little speech. "There. There. You are young. We have ordered food for you. You must be tired and hungry. You have shouted since early this morning."

"No food from the Russians," Annisa snapped.

His eyes narrowed. "Who is your leader?" he asked.

"Mohammed is our leader."

The coldness in his eyes did not match the warmth of his smile. Annisa could see his cheek twitch.

"You are young and misguided."

"We are daughters of Islam."

"Then stop this nonsense. True daughters of Islam do not make a spectacle of themselves. You disgrace your families."

"What are you going to do with us?" Annisa asked boldly.

"Send you home to face the wrath of your parents."

"We have come to tell you we will not live under the Russians," one of the younger girls piped up.

"Such impudence. Would you rather I give you to the Russian soldiers to enjoy? Now what do you think of that!"

It occurred to Annisa there might be things more horrible than death. She was prepared to die but she could not face the disgrace of being spoiled by the soldiers. The way some of them stood there leering at her was terrifying. She attempted a brave face.

"You may go home after you have written a note, promising never to do this again," the governor cajoled. His soft mannerisms had returned. He was acting fatherly again.

"Never. We will not write it."

"Then I shall write it myself and you shall sign it." He turned and marched back up the steps and into the palace.

"I am afraid," Siddiqa whispered to Annisa. "We must not bring disgrace to our families."

Trying to calm themselves the girls huddled together against the wall. A flock of finches flew into the compound and fluttered above their heads. Time passed. Staring at the dark gray stones, Annisa grew increasingly anxious. Finally, when she thought she could certainly faint from exhaustion, the governor returned with his paper. "There will be no more of this. Sign."

Annisa was the first to step forward. She thought of putting down a false name but decided against it. She had defied them, face to face. She wanted them to know who she was. "I am Annisa Aziz, daughter of the poet, Sulaiman Aziz," she said with pride.

"Ah, yes. Poor child. Your father was friends with the traitor Amin and your mother was a Tajick.

Annisa stiffened. "My cousin Abdul is the famous *chapandaz* from Mazar-i-Sharif."

"Yes, I know of him. There is a price on his head."

Annisa was thrilled to hear it. It could mean nothing other than her cousin was part of the Mujahideen.

When the last girl had signed the paper, the gates opened and they were escorted into the street where anxious parents waited.

Siddiqa's father was among them and he whisked his daughter and Annisa into his car. He was weak with anger and relief. "I am proud of your defiance," he uttered. "But in the name of Allah never do this thing again!"

Not another word was said on the drive back across town, a drive that held painful memories. Both girls looked away when they passed the street where Khalila had fallen.

"How many died?" Siddiqa asked her father when they pulled up in front of Annisa's house.

"No one knows. But a woman came to your mother asking for you. Little Mira is going to live."

Annisa felt limp. Her friend Siddiqa collapsed in tears. Annisa would not cry.

"Great God Shiva. You are alive!" Panna said when she saw Annisa enter the compound. In the next breath she scolded. "You wicked child. To worry us so. And look at you. There is blood on your uniform."

"Where is my father?"

"He has gone to the house of Nur Rabini to get help in looking for you. Your poor father is beside himself. He is sick with fear."

"My father is not afraid. He will understand. Besides, they let us go. We simply had to sign a stupid promise paper. Panna, you should have been there. We told them what they were."

"Reckless girl. . . What have they done to you? Your hair. Your beautiful hair."

Mortified, Annisa reached up and touched her head. She had forgotten her shame.

And then this bold, brave, blood-splattered daughter of Islam ran towards Panna and collapsed in her arms like the child she still was. Panna's arms around her felt eternal. Soon her father would be home and she would ask his forgiveness for quarreling with him last night. She would honor his wishes. It wouldn't be so bad to go to America now that she had vented her rage. She had made a fist in the face of the puppets. Her father would respect her for that. In her father's love she was always safe. All would be well.

CHAPTER 6

The dilapidated station wagon Professor Nur Rabini had purchased from an American AID officer in '65 pulled over to the curb on Shara Ra Road. Although it was after midnight, every light in the massive office building was aglow. Two Afghan soldiers opened the door and waved Dr. Aziz out. Aziz did not even look back as Rabini sped away.

Standing in front of the lighted building, it took a moment for Aziz to realize that his friend of 22 years at Kabul University had just delivered him to the Ministry of the Interior! There was not an Afghan in Kabul who did not know what went on inside its marble-fronted walls. Nur Rabini had betrayed him.

Aziz was immediately filled with self-loathing; he had destroyed his chances for escape. Fritz Werner had warned him not to leave the compound for any reason. But when Nur Rabini arrived with news about a riot at the girl's school, he had panicked. Annisa had not returned home. He must go look for her.

"Sulaiman, you have been ill! Let *me* do this," Nur Rabini volunteered.

Aziz now realized this has been his first mistake. He was so grateful for Rabini's help that he confided in his fellow teacher the reason he had faked an illness. Of course, Nur Rabini had been sympathetic and argued that under these circumstances it would be best if Dr. Aziz waited at Nur's house instead of Shar-i-Nau. Annisa might be in trouble with the authorities and if so, it was best that Nur try to find out where she was before Dr. Aziz showed his face. What if the KHAD came to the home of Dr. Aziz to question him?

Grateful that his friend would take such risks for him, Aziz went with him and anxiously waited out the afternoon in Nur Rabini's modest living quarters. It was hours before Rabini returned but when he did, he brought good news. Annisa had not been injured and was being held at the Palace. Friends on the inside assured him she would be released to her father's care that night.

Aziz stared at the sinister building that loomed in front of him, debating if he should try to flee. He turned to cross the street, but his foot was not off the curb before one of the soldiers reached for his arm and ordered him up the steps. Dr. Aziz did not protest and the words of Hendrik Werner filled his head--the old Nazi

57

describing how people had allowed themselves to be shuffled off to gas ovens. Docile. Without a whimper. He had repeated this story with contempt. Aziz had never understood how this could happen. But here *he* was, meekly following his captors when he knew what lay ahead. He made no effort to shout for help or to try to run from them.

Was this what came of a life that only observed, a life that let the world act upon it instead of seizing the moment? His moment had passed, back there when he questioned Nur Rabini's wrong turn at the traffic circle in front of the Red Tower. Now, as he walked up the steps, a distant rocket, fired by the Mujahideen towards a Soviet military post, lit up the sky. It made a perfect arc. A rainbow of red, yellow and pink. It was a rainbow that held no promise.

They entered the lobby filled with men milling about. Some of them Aziz knew by name, but there was no time to greet anyone. He was whisked into a side office, told to sit down, and then the door was locked behind him.

This was not the palace and this was no meeting to sign officially for Annisa's release. The whole thing had been a fabrication. How very clever of them. Nur Rabini's story to lure him out of his house in the first place had been ingenious.

Papers littered the floor of the room. There were office chairs, a single desk, a water cooler, and one filing cabinet, its drawers ajar. A black and white poster of Leonid Brezhnev was tacked on a second door leading to an inner room. The body of Afghanistan was not even cold and already the widow had taken a new master. Aziz sat down.

On the desk in the corner of the room were two dinner plates with bits of fat congealed on them. An old calendar on the far wall showed December 24, 1979. Perhaps after the invasion, time had stopped in here.

Angry voices shouting in Russian suddenly erupted from behind the second door. Aziz was not very adept in the language. He could pick up only fragments.

"Sasha and her big tits . . ."

"You're drunk, Corporal."

"Pigshit. . . if you tell Vladimar."

"Court-martial you for this."

A crash followed and sounds of a scuffle. "You piece of shit. You bastard," a man shouted.

The door flew open. A KGB colonel ordered: "Captain Duranni, call security."

Aziz was startled to hear the familiar name. He looked at the vacant desk. For a moment, hope surged. Was this Najib's office? Had Nur Rabini been telling the truth after all? Had Aziz been brought here for safekeeping or had there been a change in plans concerning the guide?

Behind the sour-faced colonel standing in the open doorway, Aziz could see a burly Russian pulling himself up from the floor. He staggered towards the colonel whose back was turned towards him. "You cock sucker. You rob me of my commission. You send me to this hellhole. Still you threaten me with my brother."

The colonel turned just as the man tackled him. Both men pitched through the door and rolled over and over together at Dr. Aziz's feet. Although the colonel was not as big or strong, he managed to pin the corporal against the water cooler and bang his head against it. Intimidated by the violence, Aziz stood up and stepped back into a corner behind the door. Just then the victim managed to free himself and butted the officer against the far wall. A powerfully built man with legs like tree trunks, the Russian corporal hurled himself at his adversary. "Steal Sasha! I will kill you before you tell my brother."

On his feet again, a solid right to the jaw caught the colonel. He pitched backwards, hitting his head against an open drawer of the filing cabinet as he fell. He did not move. The corporal turned and stared at Aziz, a dazed look in his eyes. Then he stumbled over to the door and locked it from the inside. "I hope he's dead," he told Aziz as he began to knock piles of folders from the desk top, shouting in Dari, "The butcher! The fiend!"

"Open up in here!" There was a loud banging on the outside followed by hurried footsteps in the hall.

Aziz stared at the drunken bull of a man weaving before him. His appearance was riveting. He had a tanned and youthful face with brilliant blue eyes and a thick head of hair that was prematurely white.

A key turned in the lock and the door swung open. "Yuri, for God's sake, what the hell is going on."

Two Afghan officers entered the room. At first glimpse, Aziz thought he was seeing things--the man giving orders was Najib! "Get an ambulance," he barked as he bent over the unconscious colonel, opening his eyelids, taking his pulse. He did not see Aziz who was half hidden behind the door.

As soon as the other officer left, Captain Duranni grabbed the drunken Russian by the collar. "You've had it, Yuri. They will ship you back to Moscow."

"Is he dead?"

"No. I'd get out of here. Fast."

"Hah. And go where?"

"If you can make it as far as the river, follow it to Damazan Park. Sher-Shar Mina Avenue leads to the village of Paghman and Resistance forces. Use my name."

The white-haired corporal grunted an answer, picked up one of the straight chairs and hurled it against the window. Flying splinters of glass sprayed the floor as he crawled through the jagged opening.

Dr. Aziz could hardly get his breath, choking on Najib's name. "Najib. Najib."

Captain Duranni spun around, his eyes opened wide in recognition and disbelief. "Professor Aziz!"

Nothing more could be said. Two soldiers entered with a stretcher and loaded the unconscious Russian colonel onto it. Captain Duranni gave Aziz a look of desperation and reached for the phone. "Get me Colonel Saddozai. . .Well, where the hell is he? This is an emergency." He hung up the phone and hurried out the door.

Aziz's limbs quivered from the tension. Should he try to leave? He forced himself to move to the open doorway. At the far end of the hallway were two Russian guards eating a sandwich with their machine guns resting on a table in front of them. Did he have the nerve to stroll nonchalantly past them as though he had permission to go? Or was Najib coming back? Aziz was paralyzed with indecision and this shamed him. Sick with fear, he returned to his chair and sat down to await his fate. His mind was in a fog. Nothing seemed clear anymore and at the same time everything was all too clear. They had known how to snare him. Pride. Playing to his stupid vanity, his fellow teacher, Nur Rabini had set the trap with words that were now hauntingly transparent. "Sulaiman, your views must be highly respected in the West because Mr. Hardcastle, the British correspondent, is anxious to see you."

"How do you know this?" Dr. Aziz remembered being a bit puzzled because Matthew Hardcastle had made the dangerous trip inside Afghanistan only a few months ago.

"He is hiding out in Parwan Minda and yesterday he sent someone to the university to look for you. Fortunately, that someone came to me," Nur boasted. "Disastrous otherwise. Our young freedom fighters are brave and bold but not always prudent whom they talk to. 'Why does this Matthew Hardcastle want the professor?' I asked. He told me. I could hardly believe my ears. That my old and prudent friend, Dr. Aziz was considered a great asset to the Resistance."

"Why would he say such a thing about me?"

"Everyone knows you refuse to distribute party literature at school."

"I am not the only one."

"Yes, but it is you he wants to see." Rabini had given him a sly smile. "And now you and Annisa are planning to leave Kabul-- you must admit, it all seems to fit. Don't get me wrong. I am happy for you. My only wish is that when you reach the West you will not forget me."

The door opened once again. Najib was back, a senior officer with him. The officer, a major, looked familiar to Aziz. He carried a black box.

"What happened to the Russian corporal?" The officer questioned Najib.

Najib pointed to the smashed window. "He must have gone out through there. Corporal Vitrovich has a drinking problem. This is not the first time he has quarreled with the Colonel. Some kind of a vendetta, I suspect."

"We have received word that a rebel attempt to blow up the gasoline storage tanks near the Monopoly Bureau tonight has been aborted."

"A good piece of intelligence work on your part. You are to be congratulated, Sir..."

"As are you." The major nodded towards Aziz. "Stay with him until I am ready for the interrogation." Then he left the room and the black box went with him.

Captain Duranni crossed to the desk and picked up the phone. His eyes never left the face of Aziz as he did so. "Tell Khushal we have had a man delivered to our office whose name is not on the list. Yes, a mistake. . . No, Colonel Saddozai is not available. . .Then damn, it, I'll hold."

Aziz heart sank. He was not supposed to be here. He was not safe. There was such a pained look in young Najib's eyes that Dr. Aziz wanted to reassure him. Fritz Werner had warned him. It was not Najib's fault he was here. What a blessing it was to see this young man he loved like a son.

Najib put his hand on the receiver as he waited. "Who delivered you here?" he asked Aziz.

"Nur Rabini. A friend and colleague at the university."

"The slime."

"I am very worried about the safety of my journalist friend, Matthew Hardcastle. He is inside Afghanistan and Nur Rabini knows where he is staying."

Najib shook his head. "Hardcastle is in Cairo pursuing a lead that Egyptian money is backing the resistance. His contacts in Peshawar keep me informed."

"But Nur Rabini said. . ."

"Hello?" Najib took his hand off the phone's mouthpiece. "Yes, I'm still on the line. . . Well, tell him to call me back immediately. This is an emergency. A very delicate matter and a mistake that could have terrible repercussions. . . Yes? Of course." He slammed down the receiver.

"Najib, please don't put yourself in jeopardy for me. I. . ."

"Do you have the papers? The visas?"

"At home. In my desk drawer. Fritz Werner told me you saw Rahmin in New York."

"Yes. Right before I returned to Kabul. He had your letter. Rahmin takes your advice."

"The first time ever. . . How is my son?"

"I think he's disappointed not to be here, but he's resigned. Rahmin has thrown himself into recruiting volunteer doctors for the resistance. He will make you proud."

The phone rang and both men jumped. "No, Colonel Orkunium is not here. Give me your number and we'll get back to you."

Aziz watched Najib record the number on the back of an envelope. Dear Najib. A loyal friend to Rahmin who was brooding and awkward in contrast to Najib's sunny nature. A born leader, yet not brash. A quiet fire smoldered in Najib's dark eyes but the fire was under control. Like a fine diamond, he gave off light. Too bad the boy had such a miserable wife.

Najib looked up at him. "About Annisa. She is safe at home now."

"Allah be praised."

"She is a wonderfully brave girl. Have you heard what she did? Our Annisa stood up to them. A real heroine."

Tears welled in Dr. Aziz's eyes. "Her mother's child." His

hands were shaking as he walked to the desk and opened his billfold. Inside was the chit for the money bazaar. A huge amount. Werner had sent it over with more papers before he left for Delhi. Aziz handed it to Najib. "Just in case. For Annisa. Her education. She does not know we are leaving tomorrow."

Najib looked perplexed but said nothing because the door to the inner room opened behind him. The major re-entered the room carrying a folder.

"Sit down," Captain Duranni said firmly to Aziz, deftly palming the chit. "You are not permitted a phone call."

The major approached Aziz. "Dr. Sulaiman Aziz? You are a professor at Kabul University?"

"Yes."

"Come inside."

From the open doorway Dr. Aziz could see that the black box was now sitting on the floor and was open with wires running from it. His heart sank. Najib's efforts were too late. Dr. Aziz had heard stories of what the black box could do.

"Shut the door behind you."

The officer settled himself behind the desk and began to read a paper he had taken from his brief case.

"Why am I here?"

"I ask the questions, Professor. I have certain information here."

"What information?"

"Never mind. We are only after the truth."

He leaned over and fiddled with the wires in the box. "Take off your shoes."

Without protest Dr. Aziz removed them.

"Your socks."

"My socks," Aziz repeated like a parrot. He was embarrassed. He had a hole in the toe of his right sock and marveled that he should be concerned about such a thing at this moment. He pointed to the black box. "What is this?" he asked the officer, knowing full well what it was.

"A hand generator." He walked over to Aziz and tied his wrists behind his back. "Please sit down," he said in a monotone, slipping a rope around his waist and attaching it to the back of the chair. Then he leaned over and clipped two wires from the box to the toes of his victim. "What was your real relationship with President Amin?"

Aziz looked up into the clear gray eyes of the man. He was only a youth. Much too young to be a major. "I remember you. You were an engineering student at Kabul University. Your father and I journeyed to Jiddah together."

Clearing his throat, the officer began to pump the handle on the box. Dr. Aziz was thinking how fascinated the Great Emperor Babur would have been with this instrument of modern torture. Then the first pain hit, a severe one, which tore up the front of his legs and cramped his belly.

"More?"

"Please, I have done nothing against the government. Tell me what you want from me."

Again the handle went up and down and the pain shot up into the arms of Aziz.

"Hafizullah Amin was a collaborator of yours," the officer accused.

"Only an acquaintance." Aziz was struggling for breath. "I knew him in the teacher's training institute."

"He chose your son for studies at Columbia University. Yes or no?"

"I have no knowledge of this. My only recollection is Amin had a Master's in Education from Columbia University in New York."

"You son stays in America."

The pain felt like a steel band encircling his forehead, pressing in. "I have not heard from my son in many months."

"That does not answer my question. He has not returned to Afghanistan."

"Correct. But I have done nothing against the government."

Dr. Aziz flinched when he saw him reach for the handle again.

"You shall have to try harder, Professor. President Amin was recruited by the CIA during his student days in the U.S. He was an American spy assigned to destroy the true Marxist leadership in the PDPA."

"I have never heard such a thing. Amin was a Communist. Always. From the very beginning. . ."

"How do you know this? Did you discuss politics with him?"

The next jolt moved faster than the others, up Aziz's legs and hitting his chest. His lungs were burning and he cried out in pain. The room started to spin. The Major pumping the hand generator was a blur. *"Naz-em, my naz-em,"* Sulaiman Aziz cried out, as the hot white knife of electricity ripped through his brain.

Later, when he regained consciousness, he was mortified to see that he had wet himself. He could feel his tongue move against the roof of his mouth, but no sound came out.

"So you have a special girl?"

Aziz nodded, his eyes brimming with tears. "My daughter." He prayed to Allah that he had not revealed his plan to flee with her.

"We know you worked with Amin. In return he gave your son a visa to study in America. We also know you feed information against the People's Party of Afghanistan to a British reporter." He looked down at a paper in front of him. "Matthew Hardcastle. Do you deny it?"

Aziz tried to shake his head, but his neck wobbled crazily from side to side.

"I see we need another treatment."

Aziz attempted to protest but the searing pain that hit him catapulted him into darkness once again.

Two hours later he awoke in a room filled with many men. An old mullah was bending over him, squeezing the juice of an orange into his parched mouth. The mullah wiped Aziz's lips with the hem of his shirt and stroked his forehead.

Grateful that he had been saved from perdition, Aziz eyed him. There had been a point, while he was spiraling downward into the darkness, when he lost all faith in Allah. This single act of human kindness brought him back from spiritual ruin.

The mullah seemed to sense this transformation. He held Aziz's face between his thin hands as the tears flowed unchecked.

Aziz was stunned to see his right hand puffed up beyond its normal size. The wall clock above his head read 4:10. But was it afternoon or night?

With great difficulty he pulled his torso up to see if there was a window in the room. There was. There was darkness outside. It must be just before dawn. The taxi was to pick him and Annisa up and deliver them to a Mujahideen station in Kah'homi. -- after the first rays of light.

A man lay on the floor directly across from him. Aziz's stomach turned over at the sound of the man retching into a tin bucket. "This is no longer my country. Afghans did this to me. Puppets, not Russians!" the man sobbed, choking on his vomit.

Two soldiers entered the room and yanked Aziz to his feet. His rubbery legs gave way under him. Cursing his weight, they dragged him by the armpits down a narrow corridor. Posters of Barbak Karmal shaking hands with the Soviet premier framed the passageway.

This new room was different. Family photographs were on the desk and there was a vase of white blossoms.

He was only a lieutenant, but the man behind the desk was older than the one before. He stood up smiling when Dr. Aziz was placed in the chair before him.

"I have brought you a cup of tea," he said, offering it to Aziz. But Aziz was unable to hold it. There was no strength in his grip. Obligingly, the soldier came around the desk and held the steaming liquid to Aziz's lips. "I must apologize for our mistake, but we thought your name was on the list. We want to release you. Now."

"Yes?" He choked, gasping for air.

"Here, sign this paper and you may go."

Aziz tried to focus on the paper but the lines would not hold still for his eyes. Najib had worked a miracle.

"It is your release. I am glad you are not guilty, Professor Aziz. I have long admired your work. My very favorite is your poem about the white dove on the dome of the Caliph Ali's tomb in Mazar:

The shrunken moon sinks before the horizon as a man lifts his head to the. . ."

"Stop." Aziz gasped. To hear his own words. Here! Words he composed at the purest moment of his life. It was more painful than the black box.

"I apologize again. My recitation was presumptuous. Here is your release. I am honored to have met you."

Aziz tried to steady his hand. He could manage only a semblance of his name.

His captor looked at the scribbling and smiled. "That will have to do. You are free to go now."

"I fear I cannot walk."

"Then I will have someone drive you home." The officer stuck his head out the door and motioned for help. Two soldiers appeared and half-carried, half-dragged the prisoner outside the building.

Aziz welcomed the fresh sweet air of dawn. He opened his mouth and sucked it in. Praise Allah. He had survived. He could still escape with his child.

He was taken to an open jeep and deposited in the seat next to a sleepy-eyed driver.

It was difficult for Aziz to sit up. His mind was in a maze through which he tried to grope his way. It was too late for them to leave Kabul this morning; he was too weak for the trip. But as soon as he was well enough, they would go. Besides, the danger was past. He had beaten the legendary black box.

The jeep pulled out into a street devoid of traffic. The inhabitants of Kabul were just finishing their prayers. Past the shuttered stalls of the bazaars they sped through the center of town. But instead of turning right towards Shar-i-Nau, they made a left turn towards Old Clock Tower.

Aziz was absorbed with the pain in his burned out limbs and grateful to be alive. It was not until he heard the planes taking off from Kabul airport that he realized they were going the opposite direction from his house.

"You should have turned back there. My home is behind us." It pleased him that his voice was gradually coming back, that he could make himself understood once again.

The driver did not take his eyes from the road, leaning hard on the horn as a stray donkey wandered out in front of the jeep.

The road they traveled paralleled the Kabul River and the Jeshin grounds. Further along was the new prison of Pol-e-Charkhi, a mammoth structure built by Daoud. So this was where they were taking him? But the jeep did not stop, traveling a few blocks beyond and making a sharp turn onto a narrow dirt road.

The early morning light was wonderfully pure and the landscape hushed except for the bells of a camel in the field beyond. Patches of wild lavender grew along the roadside. The pale purple flowers gave a sweet flavor to the new day as the jeep bumped along the rutted road. Ahead of them a shepherd boy with his flock blocked their way and the driver swore at him. The jeep was forced to halt as the sheep bleated in defiance, surrounding it, taking their time moving on.

"This part of our land must never change," Aziz said to himself. His eyes followed the shepherd boy across to the canopy of early blossoms of white on an almond tree.

He wished for his pipe and tobacco. He fumbled for them in his pockets but everything had been removed, including his wallet. He would have no *baksheesh* to bribe the guards; to get news to Annisa from prison. At least Najib had the money chit Fritz Werner had sent.

The driver started his vehicle again and they proceeded down the winding path to a steep valley below. He parked the jeep and yanked Aziz from his seat. Ahead stood a large number of men in front of an enormous pit, a big yellow bulldozer behind them.

"I was released," Aziz said pitifully. "You have made a mistake."

"You signed a confession of guilt," the guard answered and shoved Aziz into the crowd.

Aziz sunk to his knees, unable to stand by himself. From his position he looked up into the gaunt-faced men. No one spoke to him; no one even recognized that he was there. Were their minds gone? Were they drugged? Like robots, they moved on command when the guards began to herd them towards the edge of the pit.

Aziz had to crawl to keep from being stepped on, and when he reached the edge he looked across into the square-jawed faces of two Russian soldiers holding machine guns.

The Afghan lieutenant had said he liked the poem about the white dove and the Blue Mosque. The ultimate betrayal. At least Allah would let him die outside in a field of lavender rather than to rot in the stench of some windowless cell. And it was Russian guns and Russian bullets and Russian hands on the triggers.

In the distance, he could see a tiny dot of red, the new Afghan flag atop the fort on the hill. Nur Rabini had told him the dead child Khalila had carried the flag of Islam and they had gunned her down. With all his heart he prayed that she be remembered in legend and song. If only there had been time he would have written a poem to her. And little Annisa. He had raised his voice to her. His last words had been harsh. His insides shook with remorse. If only he had listened to Fritz in the very beginning and sent Annisa on ahead. On Judgment Day the Prophet would ask him how he had treated the females in his family and he would have to face up to the fact he had not been strict enough. No veil, no arranged marriage. In these terrible times had it been right to humor his sweet *naz-em?* He bent his head in prayer. His beloved daughter was in the hands now of Najib.

Without any warning, the machine guns opened up and above his head men pitched forward into the pit. Another round was fired and then another and then all was silent until the large bulldozer started its motor.

In anguish Aziz called to the Russian gunners across the pit. "Shoot me. For God's sake. You missed."

The roar of the bulldozer moving the mounds of fallen bodies was deafening, and he called out again. "Shoot. Be merciful. In the name of Allah, shoot."

Then his body flew forward, landing inside a pit of blood soaked flesh and earth.

Aziz lay there face down, tasting the blood on his lips from the man beneath him. It was a miracle that he was still alive and a curse that he would go on breathing for some time in the debris. The man whose blood was in his mouth uttered one wrenching gasp. Then the struggle ceased and the body beneath Aziz trembled ever so slightly. Aziz was thinking of a bird that he had once held in his hand when it fell from its nest: the beating heart, the flutter of life, then stillness.

With a final push for his life, he struggled to pull himself upwards. A hand to the right of him in his silent tomb reached out and grabbed his, holding it firmly as the second wave of earth crashed down over their heads. Their clasped hands remained uncovered. A single moment of triumph.

Aziz prayed for deliverance, choking for air. He could hear the sound of the clear water on the rocks of the Daru River where his father had walked with him as a boy. He could feel the soft lips of his wife on his cheek as she lay entwined in his arms under a blanket of stars. In a great surge of love, he squeezed the hand in his, mistaking it for the hand of his young son Rahmin on their way to the mosque. He was leaving this miserable life now to be delivered into the hands of Allah. Peach blossoms swirled before his eyes, spiraling him towards Paradise into a glory of spring.

When the last mound of dirt had been shoved into the pit, the soldiers climbed back into their jeeps and drove away. The sun rose and a flock of white doves flew down the valley. They perched on the yellow bulldozer, which had been left behind for another day. The air was so still that not a blade of grass stirred.

Late that night a small shepherd boy returned to his family, telling them of what he had seen. He sat in his tent and he thought of the ritual of making nan, which his mother had prepared for his meal, and he thought of that remarkable sight on the hillside- a flock of white doves covering a yellow bulldozer.

Turning to his father, he told him of the two hands clasped together above the mound of earth. For a moment he had imagined they moved. Frantically, he had torn at the dirt around them but to no avail; the ground sunk in on itself and no cry came to him. The white doves flew away. For a long time after, he had stood guard at that very spot and had prayed for the souls of the dead. That was all a small boy could do.

CHAPTER 7

Captain Najib Duranni was visibly shaken. On the list of executions outside Pol-e-Charkhi prison was the name of Sulaiman Aziz! Blood flushed the jagged scar on his cheekbone. He pushed back his chair. It was mid-morning and the office was still in shambles. There was no time now to straighten the folders the Russian corporal had scattered during the fight and it would take others to repair the broken window. Praise Allah, Colonel Orkunium's concussion would keep him away from the office for several days at least. The sly dog would be asking questions about the disappearance of Corporal Yuri Vitrovich and a phone call made on behalf of Dr. Sulaiman Aziz, a phone call that failed.

Najib and Margahalia had quarreled again this morning, as she was on her way to the hospital with flowers for Colonel Orkunium. It was a sinister game they played. She knew how much he hated the man. Her actions shamed Najib--cultivating the KGB in exchange for creature comforts. Food was scarce in Kabul but not in Najib's household. Their pantry included gift tins of caviar.

There was no time to dwell on her treachery. Najib was committing *koh-koshi,* an act of suicide, but the chit for Annisa, the money voucher, had to be delivered and in person. He would have to risk going himself to the home of Aziz.

To the guard at the desk, he announced he would be working all afternoon at KHAD headquarters in Karte-Se. The man grunted and leaned over to wipe a smudge from his boots, an unusual gesture for the Soviet military. Dress code was lax in Kabul, far from the mode Duranni himself had learned from his years at Sandhurst.

The sun shone hot for early spring. He would walk. The house of Aziz was not that far and taxi drivers kept records. It would give him a chance to collect his thoughts. The guide had been scheduled to pick up Dr. Aziz and Annisa this morning. Only with luck had he been able to send a message to Kart-i-Denau and instruct them to come instead tonight. But was it wise for Annisa to go to the border alone with a male guide? Rahmin would be livid with such an arrangement. By everything that was holy, Najib knew he should escort her out himself. But it was out of the question. There were too many loose ends in Kabul and too many lives jeopardized if he were to leave his post before key people could be alerted.

Najib crossed the intersection in front of the military hospital. A green Coca-Cola truck turned the corner and lumbered past; citizens of Kabul would stone anything painted red. A university student staggered and dropped his books in the middle of heavy traffic. Yuri Vitrovich, the Russian corporal, was not the only drunk in Kabul. Najib wondered what Babur, the great Mongol Emperor, would think of his beloved gardens with the young men of Kabul getting very drunk among the flower beds.

How much longer could he stomach it? A man could take only so much. He had returned to Kabul, unaware that his father had been caught in Herat on his way to join his mother in Tehran. Three days later his father had hanged himself in his prison cell, an hour before Najib could get there. This left dear Margahalia and her cesspool of relatives. When the time came for Najib to defect, she could refuse to join him. Let her. Now that his father was gone his sense of duty was up in the air. His father's sudden death left him angry and burdened with guilt. There had been no closure--no peace for his ambivalence. He suffered from insomnia. If he didn't get some sleep soon he would crack.

Aziz's house loomed ahead of him. It was imposing, a two-story structure with one of the finest gardens in Kabul--the professor's pride and joy. It was sickening to think what might happen to it now that Aziz was gone and his children would be out of the country. He rang the bell on the front gate wishing he could roll back the clock to a time when he had visited this house bringing hope.

Old Panna seemed relieved to see him as she ushered him into the garden where Annisa sat, her face tear-streaked; her nervous hands folding and unfolding in her lap.

Najib's stomach did an involuntary flip-flop. Had she guessed the purpose of his visit?

"My father did not sleep in his bed last night. My father is dead, isn't he? I dreamed it."

Najib's eyes held hers and then he looked away, fearful he might lose his composure. The effort to hold in his anguish had drained him.

"I know he is dead," she repeated.

Najib's silence was her answer.

"I knew it." She leapt to her feet as though to take flight.

"Annisa." He reached for her and gathered her into his arms. A tiny moan escaped her.

"Your father was a great man, Annisa. It is a dark stain on our country."

"Tell me it's not true," she sobbed.

"Annisa, I can't."

She pulled away from him and sank back down on the bench, her fists clenched. "No, no, no." She made small whimpering sounds and closed her eyes.

Najib felt helpless, not knowing how to comfort her. If only he were going with her. It was too much to ask of a young girl. He studied her dear face, those thick closed lashes. Little Annisa. So innocent and with such great promise. The artist in him could not resist exploring the angle of sunlight hitting her face at this moment. It would make a stunning portrait. She had the same delicate bone structure as Claire. Only Claire was blonde and Annisa was dark with those incredible green eyes, translucent and framed with thick lashes. 'Her eyes are like yours,' Rahmin had said. "Wolf eyes" the waitress in New York had called them.

Najib found he was holding his breath as he watched her; praying she would speak. Her eyes were open now and filled with a gut-wrenching sorrow. "Did they take him. . .did they kill my father because I took part in the girls' demonstration?"

"Don't think such a thing."

Her voice broke. "I gave them my name."

"Your father was proud you were part of the defiance. He told me so last night."

"You saw him!"

Najib nodded, desperate again to keep his emotions in check.

"As my protector, swear you will kill the men who did this to my father."

"I swear."

He waited beside her, uncertain of what he could say. It seemed insensitive for him to launch into the details of her escape. But he had to. Aziz had told him Annisa knew nothing of their plans.

"Can you take me to my father's body? I need to arrange the funeral."

He was shocked by her request. It seemed too adult at a time like this. "Annisa, that's impossible. I do not know where he is," he lied.

"Then why have you come?"

"I have the chit you are to take to the money bazaar in Peshawar." He had decided to pretend she already knew of the plan. "The money you take to America."

Agitated, Annisa rose to her feet. "Not now. Not ever."

"It was your father's wish."

She looked at him askance and her eyes darted over to Panna who was watching them from the patio. "Panna says Nur Rabini came to our house and that my father left with him. He too was my father's friend. And now my father is dead."

"Are you saying you don't trust me? Annisa, don't let my uniform fool you. I too fight the puppets."

Her face brightened "Then you are going with me!"

"No, I stay here."

"Why are you not in the mountains? A Mujahideen." Annisa made a fist. "I will stay and fight."

He knew he must act like he was taking her seriously. "How will you do this?"

"I am skilled on horseback."

"Yes, that's true." The audacity of what she proposed buoyed him and on one level he wanted to cheer her on... Instead, he said, "Annisa-jan. You must go to Rahmin. You are all he has left."

"Does he know our father is dead?"

"It was only yesterday."

"What if Rahmin decides to come back to Afghanistan? I know my brother. He would want me to stay here and help avenge our father."

"That is my task." Najib motioned for Panna to join them. He was getting nowhere with Annisa. "You are to leave tonight. It is arranged."

Panna wagged her finger at Annisa. "Pay attention. Captain Duranni has come to help you."

"I must bury my father first. . . next to my mother."

"How can you when you don't know where he is? Now, go to your room. Finish your tears."

Annisa glared at her. "I do not cry. I will never cry again."

"Good. Because your suffering must wait. When the guide comes, you must be ready to leave."

"Leave Afghanistan? No, I will go to Doshi. I can live with my uncles, My mother would like this."

"Rahmin waits for you in New York."

"He does not know our father is dead."

Najib interjected. "I will make sure they tell him in person. He will not get such dreadful news by letter. I promise you that."

"There is no need to make such a promise. Dead is dead." Najib felt chilled by the coldness in Annisa's voice.

"I wish to go to my Uncle Abdul."

Panna went on the attack. "You selfish, wicked girl. Your uncles have mouths of their own to feed."

"Abdul will provide. He is famous. He played before the King."

"The King is gone," Najib said softly. And soon there will be no more games on horseback. No *buzkashi* -- only bombed-out villages. More important, there are no schools left in the villages to the north. Your education was your father's dream."

"But my father..."

"I think Annisa is much too soft for village life," Panna interrupted, giving Najib a sly nod as she said it "She is nothing but a cry-baby."

Annisa dug her toe into the ground. "I saw your look at Najib. If my mother's family can't take me, I can live with Uncle Fritz in Kabul. He says I am like a daughter. So there."

Panna had finally had enough. She reached out and grabbed Annisa by the shoulders, shaking her violently. "Fritz Werner is a foreigner, a *ferrangi* and unmarried. Do you wish to dishonor your father's name?"

"I don't care."

"Annisa!" Panna struck her hard across the face.

The tears that only moments ago Annisa had announced she would never shed again suddenly welled in her eyes.

Panna was livid at Annisa's disrespect, her anger fueled by her own grief over the death of Dr. Aziz. "Go to your room. Get hold of yourself. Save your tears until you are safely through the mountains."

Najib, who had been a bit taken-back by Panna's savage attack, saw the effect the old nursemaid's words had on Annisa as he watched her cross the terrace, her head held erect, and her stride determined. "I'll show you. I am not soft," she shouted.

"Will you travel with her?" he asked Panna.

"Of course. Do you take me for such a fool that I would let a young girl travel alone, without a chaperon?"

"She will need to wear the veil, if she is not to draw attention on the trek to the border."

"I have already purchased a *chadri*. Only getting her to wear it will be our greatest struggle. As you see, our Annisa has a mind of her own. Why in the world are we arguing with a 12-year-old-girl? Why do we give her such power?"

There was a flicker of a smile on Najib's lips. "Because she is Annisa."

"With Annisa the anger always comes first. It covers up her hurt."

"Annisa will need her anger. An arduous trip awaits her." Najib paused, appraising the obvious infirmities of the old nursemaid. "And you."

He reached into his pocket and pulled out the money chit. "Fritz Werner gave this to Dr. Aziz. It is worth a large sum of money. It can be cashed in the money bazaar when you reach Peshawar."

"This is a fortune."

"To pay for her education. In the envelope I gave Annisa there are forged papers—they will permit her to wait in Peshawar without going to the refugee camps. They are in the desk of Dr. Aziz along with airline tickets. Also an entry visa to the States. When you reach Peshawar, the Reeds will take you in."

"Who are the Reeds?"

"American missionaries. The guide knows where they live. Annisa will be staying with them while her papers are processed. I repeat, under no circumstances is she to go to a refugee camp. They are a snake pit of greed and abuse. The Paks pocket much of the relief money the outside world is sending. . . Also, you would be unable to stay with her there."

"Don't concern yourself with me. I'll get Annisa safely delivered. Does Rahmin know when she is coming?"

"Werner will take care of that. Don't worry about the guide. I will make sure he is paid in Peshawar."

"I wonder what Rahmin will think of Annisa traveling to the States alone."

Najib felt defensive. "It can't be helped. She leaves tonight. My decision. My responsibility."

There was a pounding on the front gate and Najib's hand automatically went to his pistol belt.

"It is only the water seller. He comes each day at this time."

"Don't let him in. . . One more thing. Annisa must take only the clothes on her back. Warm ones. It will be cold in the mountains at night. Hide the money chit on her person, in case you are separated."

"I will hide it in her shoes."

"No, the first place they look."

"Annisa has a belt with a hollow buckle."

"That is better."

"You will be paid for your services when you return to Kabul and Fritz Werner is making arrangements to find you a new position."

"I will not come back."

"It will be impossible for you to go to America with Annisa."

"Again, you take me for a large fool. There will be things for me to do in Peshawar."

Najib knew this was not true but said nothing. "You are a generous woman, Panna. Annisa is fortunate to have you."

"She is my life."

The door onto the patio opened and Annisa hurried outside carrying a small box.

"What is she doing?"

"She buries her treasures. Inside the box are memories."

"Perhaps I could keep them for her."

"You?"

Najib knew it was not wise to confide in the old woman but today he had thrown caution to the wind. "It might reassure her. There is a chance I will soon be seeing Rahmin in America myself."

Panna smiled. "That is glad news. But do not tell the child. It would only add to her fantasy."

"Fantasy?"

Panna did not elaborate. The less said about Annisa's schoolgirl crush on Najib the better. "She must get used to emptiness, to leaving it all behind."

Najib sighed. "That is the hardest task. For all of us."

"You care for others, Captain Duranni. I honor your courage in coming here. Dr. Aziz smiles from his grave."

"I wish I could believe that." For a moment his voice wavered. "I was unable to save him."

"Dr. Aziz loved people for their motives, never the results."

Najib let what Panna had said sink in, then nodded and thanked her with his eyes.

"I'll go inside now. To search his desk. The papers. Annisa hid them once before, you know."

Annisa was in the garden on her knees, her hands pulling at the earth as she prepared a hiding place for her box.

Najib wondered what she could possibly have in it as he crossed to the stone bench and sat down to watch. He unbuttoned his collar. So many happy days were spent in this garden. He would see the long fingers of Dr. Aziz carving a wooden slingshot. Rahmin nearby, taking turns with a kite

"There. I have finished," Annisa called, brushing the dirt from her knees.

"You will have to wear the veil on the way out."

"But why? Women in the village seldom wear the *chadri* because it interferes with their work."

"The war is turning our customs upside down."

"My father thinks the *chadri* is a joke. It's supposed to keep women from being coveted by other men but it is also used for clandestine assignations."

"Assignations? Clandestine? Little-One, I didn't know you were so worldly."

"I won't wear it."

"You will. At least when your guide thinks it's prudent. Girls in the countryside do not have your short hair."

Her hand flew up to her head and her face went crimson. "I did this myself. The Russian soldiers threatened filthy things."

"I will kill any man who harms you," Najib said softly.

Her face was wistful. "You would do that for me?"

"I am pledged to be your protector."

"Then join the Mujahideen and kill Russians in my name. If only I could ride and fight with them."

Najib looked at her with affection, remembering how Rahmin had always worried about what he called Annisa's need to be heroic. 'My father is foolish to let her ride that horse. She takes terrible chances,' Rahmin had complained. 'No one could be as perfect as she wishes to be. She thinks she is above the feelings of everyday life!'

"Tell me, Annisa, if you could make one wish for your future what would it be?"

"If I told you—- you would only laugh at me."

"Have I ever done that?"

"I wish I could be like 'Sleeping Beauty'—that a handsome prince on a white horse would come and take me away and I would never have to worry about the war again."

"Does his horse have to be white?"

"Yes. I have another wish too." She sat down beside him on the bench. "I want to be like Sheila who distributed *Shabnama*," she said solemnly.

"You know of this?" Najib was surprised that Annisa would have heard about the young woman student caught passing out night letters for the Mujahideen.

"Kassim told me. Kassim and I passed out night letters too."

Najib was stunned. "You did this!"

"Yes, and I would do it again. Kassim is dead. Everyone I love is dead."

"I share your grief." Najib sighed. "My father has hanged himself."

"Rahmin said you always hated him."

"That makes it even worse. Your father loved you very much. You must always carry that with you." He leaned forward to comfort her but she would have none of it.

"Sheila was very brave, wasn't she? Kassim told me she slit her throat with a nail she had sharpened in prison and wrote, 'Liberty' in her own blood. On the walls of her cell. . .Like Sheila, I will die for it."

The intensity of her feeling worried him although his growing sense of outrage responded to hers. The death of Professor Aziz had brought him to a different level. He could not share his feelings about this atrocious act with Margahalia; his wife had not the depth to comprehend. 'In the long run we will be better off under the Russians,' Margahalia had assured him. 'Why are you so restless when you enjoy such authority? Most men would envy you. What is it you want out of life?' Margahalia remained oblivious to the suffering around them and Rahmin's words in New York about killing Russians with his bare hands had begun to haunt Najib. He would lie in his bed at night thinking of ways to destroy Colonel Orkunium, each way more sadistic than the first. Ironically, the unhappy Russian, Yuri Vitrovich, had almost done it for him. Najib smiled at the thought of Yuri. Knowing Yuri, he was willing to bet the Russian had made it to Paghman and Resistance forces.

Annisa had turned to look at him in a moment so poignant and intense that he deliberately looked away. The anguish on her face unnerved him. How could a mere girl make such an impact on him? Was Annisa Aziz the essence of Afghanistan: all its boldness, its suffering and vulnerability written on that young face? He was sending her on a dangerous trip that many did not survive. "Don't talk of dying, Annisa. It upsets me."

"Will I ever get to come back here?"

"I promise," he lied. He could not share his fears that there might not be anything to come back to. He wanted to reassure her. "Little One, you will like America. They are people with spirit."

"Don't call me 'Little One.'"

"Sorry. I forget. Americans are friendly. They have great freedom. It's so ingrained they are unaware of it." Najib pointed to the garden. "See how beautiful it is. There is beauty left in this world despite the war. You are young. Happiness is ahead for you. I promise."

"You make many promises."

He smiled. "Some you think I don't always keep?"

"But you will always be my protector?"

"Always."

"If I go to America I must be a doctor like Rahmin; I must come back and help our people!"

"If that's what you want." Under all that defiance she felt so fragile to him. Without thinking he leaned to her and kissed her lightly on the forehead.

Annisa jumped back from him. "You have lived in the West too long. You must never do that again. You are married --much too old for me."

Najib was amazed and amused at the same time. "Please accept my deepest apologies," he said formally. He wondered if he should be concerned that young Annisa had taken it as a romantic gesture? She was still a child in his eyes but maybe Panna was right--young girls dream. "Annisa, when you see Rahmin, tell him I saw your father right before the end. Old friends are important when you are far away."

Like a baby bird, which had fallen from its nest, Annisa began to tremble and she shook so hard that he put his hands on her shoulders to steady her. She did not bury her face but held his eyes instead. Unblinking, the silent tears rolled unchecked down her cheeks, soaking her bodice, dripping from her nose. He had never witnessed such anguish and it tore at him. He did not trust himself to speak.

"It's easy to be brave but it's very hard not to cry, Najib."

"I know. I know."

"Do you want me to tell you what I put in my box?"

"Only if you want to."

"If you had a box of memories what would you hide inside?"

"My treasures are intangible. I cannot even put them into words." Once again, Annisa had touched a forbidden place in him. His return to Afghanistan had little to do with wanting to serve his people; it was rather more what Professor Aziz's poems were all about. Najib loved the majestic solitude inside the shadows of their mountain kingdom: sunlight shimmering through silver birch trees, fields of wildflowers and a solitary hawk above the deep canyons. Nights in Afghanistan were like no other. There were desert skies over Kandahar with their road map of stars, or the timeless journey through ancient villages lit only by candlelight. On these nights, he could hear the footsteps of his ancestors.

A loud pounding on the gate interrupted his thoughts. Before he could stop her, Annisa had hurried across the courtyard to open it. Fortunately, it was Zia, the guide. Gangly and russet faced, he stood in the passageway grinning at them, like an awkward schoolboy come for tea.

"You are hours too early," Najib said, relief in his voice.

"It is necessary. There has been another mix-up. They sent word not to come until tonight. It is impossible. I have no headlights. I do not choose to drive the Kabul Gorge at night. And the delay, it causes great personal concern for my family. The family of my brother's bride will visit my father's house tonight. If we do not leave now I shall be late for the first night of the wedding ceremony, the *nikah-namah*. I must be there for my brother. "

"I have no problems with daylight. The journey can be started now."

"Yes, but is there anyone to ride? They tell me the professor was killed--one of the masses bulldozed into the pit this morning."

Annisa's face went white.

"The girl!" Najib said angrily. "You speak of her father."

Zia, who did not look much older than Annisa, stared down at his feet. "How was I to know? I am an ox."

"An old woman goes with her."

"That was not part of the deal."

"We are paying for two."

"Then pray she is not feeble. Much of the way beyond Jalalabad is on foot. We climb among the clouds. Only a strong heart can survive."

"Love gives the old woman great endurance."

"Pretty words, but up in the mountains one needs more."

"Don't think you have to worry about me," Annisa said with bravado. She had put on a haughty face. "You think I cry because I'm afraid. Well, I'm not. My tears are for my father's soul. Without a proper burial. Robbed for the call on Judgment Day!" Then she looked to Najib, her hand on the heart necklace around her neck. "I will make you proud, Najib."

"Yes, I believe that, Annisa-jan." Their eyes held and for a brief moment shut out the rest of the world.

CHAPTER 8

The door was missing on Annisa's side of the ancient and battered sedan, which carried them through the Kabul Gorge with the guide. Terrified, Annisa gripped the rusted frame. It was a sheer drop of several thousand feet to the river that snaked through the canyon below.

The driver, Zia Khan, was disgruntled. Against his wishes he had agreed to take the old woman and she had given him the devil ever since. He had not volunteered for this trip. Usually, his brother Ishaq made the run from Kabul to Jalalabad. It was Zia's task to take the refugees on foot through the Khyber Pass and beyond. But orders from the *malik* were that Zia was to go all the way with them; in fact, he was not to let them out of his sight until the girl was safely settled in Peshawar. Such a fuss. One would think this orphan a daughter of the exiled King. She certainly acted like royalty, refusing the onion he gave her when she complained of being hungry. "I can't eat an onion all by itself."

"Some people eat only onions. . .for days." He turned his head and glared at his companion, faceless under the gold silk *chadri*.

"Keep your eyes on the road."

"I drive this car, little princess. Not you."

"God help us."

The old woman in the back seat was clutching her belly. He suspected she was carsick. She had breath like rotting melons. He had insisted the girl ride in the front. Better to have foul breath down the neck than vomit in the lap.

Zia switched on the transistor radio that hung from a cord looped behind the rear view mirror. His prize! He had taken it from the body of a dead Russian, along with his boots and his bronze-buckled belt with the Red Star. The rest of Zia's outfit was Afghan--black turban, black pajamas and a black velveteen vest with gold braid embroidered on the front. Two crossed bandoleers holding two tiers of bullets covered his chest. On the seat beside him was a Czech-made top loading light machine gun. He had painted his name on the handle in black.

"You like music?" he asked Annisa.

"Yes."

He grinned. "Does this ride give you fear?"

"Yes."

"When we are through the gorge we are through the worst. The Khyber Pass will be nothing."

The radio played one of Zia's favorites and he snapped his fingers in time to the music.

"Keep your hands on the wheel."

Zia felt rebuffed. "You will never pass for a village girl, *chadri* or no *chadri*. No man has tamed you."

"I am not a horse!"

"A mule maybe? Braying at every turn in the road."

"What else can I do? My life in the hands of a lunatic!"

"Not to worry. I never make an accident. You are safe." What he didn't tell her was that he had made the trip only once before and that the brakes were bad. He would offer prayers when they started the steep descent on the other side.

"Safe? I will never be safe again," she mumbled, swallowing her words inside her veil. But Zia heard her and felt a pang of guilt. Despite her bad manners she had just lost her father. The bulldozer. If only he hadn't blurted it out

He reached into his pocket. "Chewing gum?" he asked. "It helps the thirst."

Annisa shook her head.

The old woman in the back seat was snoring.

"How do you stand it?"

"What?"

"The noise she makes."

"Someday you will be old."

"I think not. I have survived many bullets intended for me. My luck is bound to run out."

"I hope it holds until we get to Peshawar."

He smiled. "And after that?" Zia shoved the gear stick into first as they started down the almost vertical slope of the mountain. Around a curve he could see the crumpled hulk of the Afghan lorry which had gone over the side the month before. Tattered strips of cloth, remnants from the hapless passengers, fluttered in the wind. Skeletal remains hung from the windows. No one could reach the wreck. The lorry had landed on its side half way down the razor-edged rocks, caught on a boulder, and so remained--a grim marker, a testament to the hazards of driving the refugee run.

"Slow down," Annisa screeched.

Zia, too busy wrestling the hairpin curves, didn't answer. He would risk land mines on foot any day. Driving this piece of junk! But his brother was getting married and deserved a precious few days.

For an instant, the right wheels went off the road. Annisa screamed as Zia spun the car back. The old woman woke up. "Child, what happens?"

"Nothing. Go back to sleep."

They sailed down out of the pass at a terrifying pace onto an empty ribbon of highway. Allah was with them. The way ahead was clear.

"Do you enjoy scaring people?" Annisa asked when the truck was once again under control.

"Only you," he teased.

A gentle laugh from behind her veil. It was a musical sound and it pleased him. The girl had spirit. Her grief would not defeat her. He wished he could see her face again. He had only caught a glimpse of her in the garden but he remembered those green eyes. How old was she? The silhouette of her body was young but it evoked his blood. His body ached for the mystery of sex. The girl Annisa wore a *chadri* of silk--not very practical for the trip but wonderful when she moved. What was funny and very out of place were the Nike jogging shoes that stuck out from under her robe.

"I like your shoes," he said.

"Yes. They will be good for the walking. My brother sent them from America."

"Is that who you go to?"

"Yes. He studies medicine. In New York City."

"*Hub bakht*. Some people have luck."

Fields of bright green clover covered both sides of the road; the change in temperature from the mountains was dramatic. In the flat land of the valley the air was hot and still. They had left early spring behind and had driven into summer.

Three small children playing atop a burned-out Russian tank waved to them as they passed. One of them, a boy in white pajamas and sandals with a red tulip behind his ear, gave Zia a salute. "Long live the Mujahideen," he called.

Zia honked his horn and shouted back. "Long live Islam."

He was feeling good. They had survived the pass. The rest of the trip into Jalalabad would be smooth. He had plenty of *baksheesh* to bribe any army vehicles that stopped him and the Russian helicopters that patrolled the area had been surprisingly quiet the past week. The only movement in the noon time sky had been a stiff-winged hawk circling downward into the gorge.

"Oh, look, a pond." Annisa pointed to a pool of stagnant green water.

"It is only a bomb crater filled with rain water."

Again the girl complained of hunger and again Zia offered an onion.

"It would make me sick."

"It is good you go to America. Here you would have to make do with much less. My mother says we will all be eating grass before this is over."

"I can't help it. I'm hungry. I haven't been able to eat a thing since yesterday morning."

"Soon there will be food aplenty. My family has been saving for months for tonight."

On the road ahead an Afghan army truck waved them over to the side. Once again, Zia patted the money in his belt. Prices were skyrocketing--even bribes. Each night he dreamed of a motorcycle in Peshawar. The money he had been saving for it was dwindling.

The Afghan corporal who had waved him over asked no questions, nor did he bother to stick his head into the sedan.

"We go to a wedding in Jalalabad."

The soldier nodded, stuck out his hand for the money, and motioned Zia back onto the road. In his rear view mirror Zia could see the soldier standing on the roadside counting the bills.

Zia had been given a large advance for the trip, the rest to be paid in Peshawar. The girl must get through, or there would be trouble with very important people in the Resistance inside Kabul.

"I wish there really was a wedding," Annisa said wistfully. Then she chided herself. Her father was dead. She was being shallow again.

"But there is. Tonight is the second day. We will spend the day of ceremonies, the *takht-i-khinah* in my village before leaving the next morning for the village of Gerd. You will be an honored guest."

'You mean we will delay our journey." Her voice was agitated.

"Unless you can find some other fool to take you the rest of the way."

"I don't think I should go to the ceremony."

"Have you ever been to a village wedding?"

"No."

"You think us quaint?"

"Oh, no. The traditions...the groom coming for his bride on a white horse--he will do that, won't he?"

"No bride in our village marries any other way."

"How wonderful. So romantic...But I must mourn my father."

"How can you? A daughter should wear white for a year and put lamps on the grave on the fourteenth and fortieth day. And serve *pilau* in remembrance on Thursday evenings at the home of the deceased. Your father has no grave. You have no home. How can you keep up your obligations to the dead?"

"I could put a dagger in your heart for saying that."

"You would kill me for speaking the truth? I know how to solve your problem...so you can go to the wedding."

"How?"

"Do you have any money on you?"

"Yes, but Panna says I am not to tell anyone."

"Panna is right. There are evil people everywhere. But you can take some of your money and pay the mullah who performs the wedding ceremony. For the right amount he will pray for the soul of your father for a year. That should do it."

"But it is only a receipt for the money bazaar. To be cashed in Peshawar."

"Not to worry. I'll pay for you."

"You? Where would you get that kind of money?"

"I save for a motorcycle."

"I could pay you back when we get to Peshawar. Zia, you give me wings. This frees my soul."

The sudden eagerness in her voice gladdened him. If he were a rich man he would just give her the money. At times when he took people over, it was hard to quell the envy in his heart. After a terrible bombing. After the children had been killed. But this girl! So full of life. He had no resentment. He was glad she would escape and live.

"Have you ever been wounded, Zia?"

"Twice," he lied, wanting to impress her. It had only been once. Nothing to talk about--a bone chip in his elbow, a little stiff when he bent it, that was all.

"And have you killed many Russians?"

"Many." This time he was telling the truth.

He could not keep his mind off the *chadri,* and his visions of what was under it. He felt evil for thinking it but he had so little knowledge of the female. Five brothers in his family; not one sister.

He was the youngest. His brother Ishaq would be the first to take a wife; she would move into their house the night of the wedding. The only woman he had ever touched was his mother but thoughts of the soft skin of a woman drove him wild. It would be years before he could marry. A bride cost many more *Afghanis* than a motorbike. It saddened him to think he might go to Allah before ever tasting a woman.

"Your brother? Is it love?" Annisa asked. "Did he pay for his bride?"

"Yes."

"I don't believe in a dowry. No man will pay *mahri-mu'ajjal* for me."

"In America he won't have to. That is difficult for me to accept. I believe in *Pushtunwali*. The code of the Pathan, the *Namue*, the honor of a woman, is stronger than the Koran. Before the Russians came, a woman in our country never had to fear rape. We protect our women. The ancient laws of our tribes are best."

"You are not a woman or you would not say this. In America, women come and go as they please."

"Bah! America! Not so old, I think. In their families everyone divorces. Their women are out of control. I have heard it many times."

"You live in village. How much do you know about the modern world. . . the outside?"

"No need to insult me. I believe in the laws of Islam but I am an Afghan. I love my freedom. This is not Iran. No spiritual dictator for me!"

"Or for women!"

They heard a hissing sound as the right rear tire collapsed and wobbled on its rim. The scowl on Zia's face dared Annisa to say anything and he would explode. "Get back in the truck. I'll attend to this." He kicked the wheel in anger and frustration. He carried no spare. He was surprised it had not happened before. All the tires had little or no tread.

"How many more miles to go?" Annisa asked. "We are in the middle of nowhere." She climbed down off her perch and walked around to where Zia stood shaking his fists in the air. "Anger is for children," she said.

"We have no spare."

"But that's stupid. What will we do?"

"Wait. Wait for someone to come along."

"So we can ride with them?"

"Leave my brother's car here? Are you crazy in the head? *Dewana?* I am to stay with it at all times...and you."

"No need to shout at me. I did not break your stupid tire."

Zia peered in the window at Panna who had not awakened even though the vehicle was stopped. "A flat tire is bad enough. Just look at her. If the old woman wasn't snoring you would think she was dead."

"You are not very nice. How can you joke about such a thing?"

"I see people die every day. Sometimes very young. If I do not laugh about these things, I go mad."

"And my father?" Sudden tears spilled from her eyes and she turned her head away from Zia so that he could not see them through the embroidered window of her veil.

"Forgive me. I forget how fresh it is. I told you I'm an oaf."

Annisa pointed to a clump of fruit trees 500 yards down a gentle slope from the road. A small stream wound along. "At least we can wait in the shade."

"Yes, wake up the old woman. I will stay up here until someone comes. You see, it is not so bad being a girl. You do not have to sit in the hot sun. You can cool your feet in the stream."

Gently, Annisa shook Panna. The old lady woke up choking on her own phlegm. She lumbered out of the sedan, coughed deeply and spit on the side of the road.

Zia was disgusted. Men were supposed to spit, not women.

"I am suffocating to death. Would it be safe for me to take off this *chadri?* Under the trees?" Annisa asked the startled Zia. "I never wear these silly things in Kabul and I am not the least bit afraid to show my face. To anyone."

"Do as you like, but put it on if I wave my arms to you from the road. Or get behind a tree."

"Oh, thank you," Annisa spontaneously grasped his hand. A charge shot through Zia. She must have felt it because she withdrew her hand hurriedly and ran down the slope. "Don't forget to signal."

Zia nodded, still savoring the touch. He stomped over to the other side of the sedan and sat on the narrow running board. Surreptitiously, he lifted the hand that still tingled to his cheek. What kind of girl was this Allah had entrusted to him? Zia could neither read nor write but he was not stupid. Annisa was excitement and danger, an entrapment. She was also very angry and he suspected it was to hide the pain of her loss.

An hour passed. A black redstart about the size of a sparrow flew to a small juniper near the roadside. Zia stretched his legs and yawned. Not one vehicle. He could not take his mind off Annisa and disciplined himself not to look her way. But then why should he worry so much about her honor? She would soon be with the Americans and their ways. He had only pretended to Annisa that he liked America. In truth, he no longer cared for them. All their money and nothing came of it. The equipment they promised was always wrong or the ammunition did not match. Empty promises. Sitting in the hot sun gnawing on his onions, he hoped her new life would not disappoint the girl.

In the distance arose the hopeful sound of an approaching car. In it were Gul Hekmatyar's men from the party of Hizb-i-Islami--the most powerful, the richest and, some who envied them said, the most corrupt. They drove a very fine vehicle indeed. Over 20 Mujahideen were packed into the bed so tightly no one could sit. Bright colored beads dangled in front of the windshield. The driver, a fierce-looking man with three fingers missing from his left hand, agreed to leave word for Zia at the teahouse up the road to send someone back with a spare tire.

His assignment taken care of, Zia half ran and half rolled down the slope to where Annisa and Panna waited. Annisa had climbed to the top of an apricot tree. She stood shaking fruit to the ground. Her green eyes took him again but her boyish haircut that had been hidden under the chadri puzzled him. Had it been this way the day before? No, he remembered now; she wore a scarf on her head in her father's garden. Again he looked at her and was disappointed; she was much younger than he had guessed and her hair made her look like a boy.

"Look," Annisa shouted and jumped from the lowest branch onto the ground, landing on her hands and knees. "We have plenty of apricots to eat."

"They are too hard; too green," Panna muttered.

"See what I have," Zia said, triumphantly, holding up a cloth with biscuits in it. "Our Mujahideen friends gave them to us."

Annisa clapped her hands. "God bless them"

The old woman had removed her veil too and Zia was amazed to see she was an Indian. How could this be the girl's family? "I am Annisa's *ayah*," Panna answered, returning his stare. "Here. I have something to offer too." From her pocket she drew a small bag of hard (lavender colored) candies that she had squirreled away for the trip.

"They bring a tire for us from the tea house. We should arrive at my father's house before dark." Zia felt important. "Not to worry. I also told them to bring one headlight."

Panna smiled at the earnest young man. "One?" Then she asked, "Why do you dress all in black?"

"When the Prophet journeyed to *Jihad*, he carried a black flag. War is not a good thing. This is my protest."

"I like the sound of you," Panna replied.

"Hurry, you two, I am starving," Annisa called from the crystal stream where she had gone to get water in the copper jug Zia had brought from the truck. She had removed her shoes and was hopping barefooted from stone to stone.

"Careful or you will fall," Panna warned. "I thought you said you were hungry."

"I am. It is very shallow here. Panna, it is amazing how clear the water is."

To Zia she looked like a wood nymph come down to earth to bless the harvest. Young, beautiful, innocent. For a minute he forgot the color black and the terrible war. "It is good to see her enjoying herself," he told Panna.

The apricots were indeed hard and green and the bread was stale; the rock candy so old it stuck together. But never had there been a sweeter meal. The sun set and the distant mountains colored plum and the water of the stream shimmered golden. The three sat together and laughed a bit and talked. Those who stayed and those who go, Zia thought. Then they heard the sounds of a truck. Help had arrived and the moment was gone.

CHAPTER 9

The Russian corporal, Yuri Vitrovich, had made it without incident to the Resistance forces in Paghman, but they did not greet him with any enthusiasm. The novelty of a Russian soldier defecting was over for the Mujahideen; lengthy interrogations cost valuable time and this deserter appeared to be a drunk. They would have to wait for him to sober up before they could question him and if his reasons for joining them were suspect, he would be shot on the spot.

At first Yuri's interrogators doubted his story. "You say you are valuable to us because you were an ordnance officer in Moscow. If you trained in explosives why are you now a lowly corporal and with the KGB? How is this possible and why did they send you to Kabul?"

"Afghanistan is where you go when you are out of favor."

"But the man you claim is responsible for your disgrace was sent here too?"

"He is ambitious and can make a name for himself in the war."

"It makes no sense. An officer has you demoted and than asks for you to be assigned to him?"

"To keep an eye on me."

"You are that important?"

"No, we shared the same mistress. . . Have you heard of Colonel Orkunium?"

"We call him the butcher."

"I tried to kill him. That's why I fled Kabul."

"Then your coming here has nothing to do with wanting to help the Resistance."

"Correct."

"You are not a Moslem. You do not fight for Islam. How do we know you haven't been trained to infiltrate us?"

"You don't. But I have the names of some that have."

"Name them."

"First you promise I can join forces with you."

Half of his interrogators were impressed with his toughness and the forthrightness of his answers. The others doubted every word he said. So much of the Russian's story about Colonel Orkunium didn't ring true. It was hard to believe that the corporal had been railroaded out of what he described as a promising career by a man whose mistress he had violated. How could the colonel control him like this? What Yuri stubbornly refused to tell them was that the mistress was also his brother's wife in Moscow and that Orkunium had threatened to reveal this.

If it hadn't been for the unexpected arrival of Omar El-Ham, a Mujahideen fighter from the northern city of Mazar-i-Sharif, the resistance in Paghman would not have taken the risk of keeping Yuri alive. But Omar El-Ham, who had come to Paghman in search of help to blow up the bridge at Amu Daryu, viewed Yuri Vitorovich as a valuable man. Loss of this bridge could interrupt the flow of Russian supplies. Yuri Vitrovich claimed to have knowledge of explosives. Omar could use him.

And because Omar was not a man to judge others solely by their words, he believed Yuri's story. It was in the eyes. The anger when Yuri mentioned Colonel Orkunium was real. Against the advice of the local Mujahideen commander, Omar insisted on taking responsibility for the corporal. "Release him to me. I have more than enough men and dynamite to do the job. What we need is expertise in setting it off. If the Russian is lying about his skills we will know soon enough."

The debate continued late into the night and it was almost dawn before Omar was granted custody of the surly Russian who kept shouting that he wanted some vodka.

"There is no vodka where we are going and if I ever catch you raising a glass to your lips I will cut off your hand. Is that clear?"

Yuri grunted.

"Just so we understand each other. . . This mistress? Was she worth it?"

"What do you think? When you look at me what do you see?"

"I see you have a young face but hair that is white. Did she turn your hair white?"

Yuri smiled at the thought. "No, I am anemic."

"What does that mean?"

"My blood is a little sick. Not to worry. I have lived with it all my life. I am strong like an ox."

"Ah, like me." Omar thumped his chest. "I am not as young as you but I have the strength of ten men."

"You are also modest."

"You make fun of me?"

"I make fun of life. Nothing of this miserable existence has any meaning."

"Is that why you let a woman destroy you?"

Yuri stared at the man who was to be his keeper. He liked what he saw. Omar El-Ham was ugly but in a bold and reassuring way. Short and stocky, with unusually long arms, Omar's walk was ape-like. His skin color looked like photos that Yuri had seen of American Indians and his large liquid brown eyes were emphasized by the baldness of his pate. "Destroy is the wrong word. It's more like women control me. I can't get her out of my thoughts."

"Is that so? I think I envy you. It has never happened to me with my wife."

Yuri shrugged. "Count your blessings. Must we dwell on this? The more we talk about that woman, the more I crave the vodka."

"Vodka makes you stupid."

"It also numbs the memories--the pain."

"I leave you with your sad thoughts. I must check on the staples for the trip. You should rest, it is not an easy journey."

Yuri nodded and leaned his head against the wall of the cave where they had brought him after the interrogation. He closed his eyes. He was weary with all the talk of Sasha but she was still there. A treacherous tease; earthy and base. Her brassy blonde hair was always dark at the roots and her make-up was overdone. But it was the way she moved her voluptuous body that drove him insane. The wiggle of her hips--the way she thrust her breasts in his face when she leaned her head back and blew smoke rings from her cigarette. He could see her now:

The tiny flat. Frost sculptures the windowpane. The wind rises. The kitchen is cramped. The smell of the black pekoe leaves fills his nose. He sits on a wooden bench next to his brother. Across from him is Sasha and next to her, Mother. Sasha's knees touch his under the table. She gives him a look. Vladimar has the night duty at Botkinsky. Mother is going somewhere else. To visit a friend? He is not sure.

"Mother, I think you should stay in tonight," Vladimar says as he carries his plate to the sink. Vladimar puts his hands on the back of their mother's shoulders. He leans down and kisses her neck. "Plako. Snow. Snow. Snow. And they say more is to come." He leaves the room.

Sasha does not take her eyes off Yuri. Under the table she kicks off her heels and slides her silk stocking foot up under the cuff of his trousers, rubbing his calf with her toes.

Terrified and thrilled, he asks his mother for more of her *kabasoo*, her thick, nurturing stew.

Vladimar returns to the kitchen wearing his great coat. He gives Sasha a peck on the cheek. "Be sure to thank Colonel Orkunium for the wine," he says. "He is so generous."

His wife sips her tea, as Vladimar pushes out through the front door of the flat.

Vladimar does not know about Orkunium and Sasha, either. Fear gnaws at Yuri--fear his mother will go out, and fear she will decide to stay home.

They are in bed. Flowers dance on the bedroom walls. Sasha is on top. Sasha is always on top. She likes him to suckle her breasts as she moves up and down on him. "Orkunium says you make a good agent."

"I do not like what I do. I prefer my old job."

A smirk on her mouth. "Ungrateful pup. The KGB is the place to be. The seat of power."

"Why did you tell him about us?"

"It excites him." She laughs and pulls away from him, sitting back on her heels.

"How much do you tell?"

"All."

"You bitch. Your inner being is devious. Convoluted."

"And yours? You screw your brother's wife."

She leans down and begins to lick his penis.

He hates himself for his gratefulness. Sasha is a sorcerer in what she reveals about himself. The back of his head now is pounding like a freight train. Soon there will be no going back.

She lifts her head and again moves on top of him. "Is it certain they are sending Orkunium to Afghanistan?"

"Yes. He asked for it."

"He is ambitious for a promotion, unlike some people I know." His hands grip the sheets as she begins to ride him. "Orkunium tells me he does not want you in Moscow. Why should you have all the fun?"

Wet and slick inside, her powerful muscles jerk him upward. "Chew my nipples," she demands. "Bite them. Hard. Harder. Ah," she moans. "More." Beads of sweat form on his forehead. Her face contorts as she milks him. She cries out as he squirts up into her. "Yuri. Don't stop. Don't stop," she screams.

Her big white breasts fill his hands! His torment.

"Give me more."

"Sasha, I am spent." It is the third time. "Don't go," he pleads, watching her move off the bed and across the bare floor. She slips her sweater over her head. It is tight and pulls across her beautiful breasts. He reaches out. "Give me a rest. I'll be ready again. Soon. I promise."

She pulls away. "No. You are finished for the night." She lifts the phone. Orkunium's black limousine will be waiting at the corner.

Yuri wishes he had the courage to kill them both. "Please Sasha. Don't go...Sasha."

"Here take this. Warm your insides before we start our trek to the north." Omar El-Ham is standing above Yuri holding a cup of hot tea.

Yuri does not know how to respond to this unexpected kindness from a Mujahideen. No one has fed him for 24 hours. What sort of man is this Omar? And why is this man who claims he is only a farmer by day treated with such deference by the leaders of the Mujahideen in Paghman? Is it because they say his brother is a great player in the Afghan *buzkashi* games? Yuri has heard rumors that the games still go on in the northern provinces. In the conversations between Omar and the rebel leaders they seemed more interested in hearing about the games and his brother's feats than Omar's daring scheme to blow up the bridge. Yuri thinks they are shortsighted. Fools. One of the greatest fears of the Russians is sabotage to the bridges. The bridge at Amu Darya is essential, a lifeline. Perhaps Colonel Orkunium was right in his estimation of the Afghans. Fierce fighters but each wrapped in his own personal glory. "Thanks for the tea."

"I have news for you. Your tormentor is not dead. Colonel Orkunium is in the hospital instead."

"The bastard. I wish I had cut his tongue out."

"His tongue is a danger to you?"

"It could destroy my family." Yuri threw what was left of the tea in his cup on the ground. He could not bring himself to admit he had betrayed his own brother. "Why do you stare? Is it my gold tooth?"

"Yes. It betrays you. People will know you are a Russian."

"Shall I pull it out?"

Omar's laugh was deep and from the belly.

"Do you still want to ride with a man like me?"

"I would ride with a pig if I thought he knew about explosives. But I should warn you. My brother, Abdul, will not welcome you. He is fierce and unforgiving. He fights with everyone."

"He sounds like me."

"I doubt if you hate Afghans as much as he does Russians."

"And you don't?"

Omar shrugged. "Abdul will try to make your life miserable."

"So much the better."

"You want to be punished for your sins?"

"No, I am just uncomfortable with people who pretend to like me."

Omar laughed again. "You are a very strange man."

"If you say."

"In Moscow... Tell me about the life."

"It is dull. We live crowded. Most of all, we keep our mouth shut."

"But you are a proud people?"

"Our pride has turned to envy. We know we don't have what the West has."

"So? Neither do we." Omar pointed his index finger at him. "I hear the West is not so good. Drugs. Bandits."

Yuri smirked. "Just like Afghanistan. Hashish. Bandits in the Khyber Pass."

"At least our women are safe on the streets."

"But are they in their own home? You and me. We can't really have a discussion about women. They are little more than property to you Afghans."

There was sadness in Omar's eyes when he answered. "Then you know nothing about us. We treasure our wives and daughters. Do they do this in America?"

"How should I know? I've never been there. All I know is that to the Americans we Russians are a joke. It's pitiful. We were so proud of Sputnik--to be the first in space. So we put all our treasures in a building to show them off. Our space capsules. Pictures of our astronauts."

"That is proud, not pitiful."

"But it is. In summer, the air inside the museum stinks. In Moscow it costs too much money to bathe frequently. And in winter we have to wear our overcoats inside our great building because we do not have enough money to heat it. It is a disgrace."

"I think you worry about the wrong things."

"My mother says this too. One night, for her birthday, I purchased tickets for a special show. The tickets cost me almost a month's salary and that's because the good seats are saved for the tourists. Moscow has the greatest folk dancers in the world and I was determined we were going to have seats in a box near the stage. Up close the dancer's costumes were dirty and the women had hair on their legs. My English is good. American tourists in the box next to ours were laughing about it. I was mortified."

"So that is why your people invade my country. So the Americans won't laugh at you anymore?"

"That's as good a story as any other. It's hard to swallow your pride when you are a big people with a big history. Nothing is small in Moscow. Our boulevards. Our drinking. Our heroes. Tolstoy. . ."

"Ah, yes. The great Russian general."

Yuri looked amused. "Tolstoy was big in books."

"Again, you ridicule me. The Americans laugh at Russians and Russians laugh at the Afghans."

"Okay, I was being stupid. Why should you know who Tolstoy is? I had never heard of your brother Abdul until today. Yet, they say he is a big hero in Afghanistan, yes?"

Omar's eyes glistened with pride. "The greatest of the greatest."

"How would *you* like to do something great? Kidnap the colonel from his hospital room and hold him for ransom--exchange him for some of your political prisoners in Kabul. The Soviet officials do not want to loose Orkunium. They would make a deal."

"Is such a thing possible?"

"I think so. Orkunium treats his staff like dogs. His bodyguard, Sergi hates his guts. I know him. He is eager for American dollars. One can double their worth on the black-market when rotated home."

"I'm not sure the commanders here will trust any of your suggestions."

"Perhaps not. But I tell you, Orkunium knows a lot about their sources of information in Kabul."

"You refused to name names."

"I was saving them as a bargaining chip for my life."

"Give me a name to give them."

"Captain Najib Duranni."

"The man you claim sent you to us?"

"Yes. Orkunium suspects Captain Duranni passes information. He has ordered him followed. Never underestimate Orkunium. He is clever like a fox. He waits his victims out. The colonel will feed him false information until he can reel him in with some even bigger fish."

"I do not know this Captain Duranni but I will report this before we leave for Doshi."

"Shall I come with you?"

"No, it is better coming out of my mouth than yours. I will tell them I tricked the information out of you."

"Well, didn't you? I am not a stupid man. I know you only pretend to be my friend."

"Friend? This you have to earn. But I am willing to take a chance you could be. If not, I dare not take you with me to blow up the bridge."

"I want to fight."

"I can see that. And like Abdul, anyone will do."

Yuri's voice was guarded. "Then you do understand me."

Omar nodded. "I warn you again. It is not easy in the mountains. The north is not the soft life you had in Kabul. If you are wounded in a raid, you bleed to death. It is rare we can get someone to a doctor."

"Death holds no fear for me. I come from a city of zombies. Moscow is the walking dead."

Omar laughed. "You play with words. I like that. It is very Afghan."

CHAPTER 10

The vastness of the flat land soothed Annisa. Ahead she could see the village of Tezeen, an island of flickering kerosene lights set amid fields of wheat and sugar cane. The air was soft and still: it was hard to believe that *Jihad*, the holy war, stalked the countryside.

Tawab, a blind boy from Zia's village, had heard the motor of Ishaq's old car long before the others. He waited in the middle of the dirt lane that led to the bridegroom's house, waving his arms in the approaching headlight he could not see. "Zia," he shouted, "your family waits. You are late for the night of henna."

"Come Tawab, I have a surprise for you," Zia called, banging on the side of the car.

Annisa shuddered when she stared down into the boy's disfigured face. A mass of ugly red scars covered two empty sockets where there should have been eyes. His face was blank as a death mask. Only his voice was vibrant.

Zia reached into his knapsack and pressed a tiny egg-shaped music box into the blind boy's hands. "Feel this? Turn the key until it is tight. Hold it to your ear."

When Tawab heard the tinkling sounds, he bobbed his head up and down in excitement. "It sounds like the wind, the water, like the shepherd boy's flute."

Zia rubbed his knuckles affectionately on top of the boy's head. "The people of Tezeen gave me money to buy this. To honor you."

In the broad beams of moonlight, Annisa could see clearly the square houses of the village that formed a pattern in the palm trees. There were no whitewashed walls as in Shar-i-Nau. The walls here were neither high nor painted. The town was the color of mud baked in the sun. There was no smell of diesel fumes, nor the invasive sound of Army trucks rumbling by. Instead, Annisa smelled a slight odor of decay: animal excretions and rotting vegetables and orange blossoms. And now faint laughter came from inside the house of Zia.

Panna sat up and stretched her arms. She complained of a sharp pain in her legs when she stepped down from the battered vehicle.

"Come with me," Tawab said. "So you can rest."

It touched Annisa to see the blind boy grope for the old woman's hand, take it in his, and lead her in the direction of the laughter.

"How does he know where he is going?"

"Tawab hears every blade of grass. Allah leads him."

"Did the war do this?"

"He was delivering a message to Commander Sadaqat in the Mujahideen headquarters of Tor Ghar. The Russians caught him; he refused to talk. They poked out his eyes and left him to die by the roadside." Zia flicked his cigarette into the dirt. "He is as great a hero to our village as any man."

"His face makes me want to cry. . . And that wonderful gift."

"Diplomats with UNESCO in Kabul were selling their belongings. I told them the music box was for a blind boy. No need to bargain. 'Half price' they said."

"My son!" From the doorway of the house a woman waved to them. "At last. We were worried when you did not come last night. Hurry. We are already late for the procession."

A heavyset woman with a small mole on the side of her nose, Zia's mother was earthy and pleasant-voiced. She welcomed Annisa into fat arms. "Poor little bird. You are too thin, No one feeds you in the city? Come eat with us. We feast on this glorious night." She turned to her son. "Your brother is anxious. You should see Ishaq in his new clothes. A proud peacock. Such a sight."

Annisa followed the mother into the house. It was without furniture, but a fine Turkoman carpet covered the floor, and beautifully embroidered pillows lined the walls.

Zia's father sounded cross. "Without you your mother is too solemn. You missed the visit of the bride's family. Why have you come so late?"

"A flat tire."

"A day's delay for that?"

Zia motioned towards Annisa. "Her father was executed. I had to wait in Kabul."

Annisa turned away from their sympathetic stares.

"May Allah watch over you!" Zia's mother exclaimed. She motioned Zia over to the men and pushed Annisa inside the women's room, where the female relatives of the family already waited.

Annisa removed her chadri, and the women lowered their eyes from the sight of her short hair. All except Zia's mother. "What's this? Poor child. A trimmed tree is no place for songbirds. Never mind. I give you my best shawl to drape over your head."

The mother's hospitality overwhelmed Annisa; her *mailmasti,* considered a sacred duty among Afghans, knew no bounds. "Tonight we forget death. Tonight we celebrate life." She pinched Annisa's cheek. "Such a fine face should not be without jewels."

Annisa's hand automatically went to her heart necklace from Najib.

"Earrings. Wear my earrings."

"But I couldn't. My father never allowed. . ." Annisa stopped and took in a deep breath. She wanted so much to say the right thing. To fit in. Thoughts of her father would trigger tears and she did not want to burden others with her sorrow on such a night. "You do me an honor. Show me how to put them on."

"Such a tragedy!"

Annisa stiffened. She would surely collapse and scream and tear her hair if they spoke of her father again. She had held her grief in on the long ride with Zia. But now, cradled in the warmth of a circle of women, she was no longer sure she could pretend to be brave.

Zia's mother repeated herself. "I tell you this is a tragedy. There are no holes in this child's ears for earrings. Such a pity."

The female cousins and aunts of Zia shook their heads in disbelief.

Panna sat down in a corner of the room. "I wish to be a part of tonight but my legs are swollen. I stay here and rest. There will be enough walking on the road to Peshawar."

None of the women argued the point. The faded eyes in the pale face hinted a longer journey in the days ahead.

"You are a Hindu?" Zia's mother asked Panna. "How can this be?"

Annisa answered for her. "Panna worked for *ferrangi* in Kabul. My father believed one must experience the culture of others: I would learn from Panna."

"And what have you learned?. . . Oh, never mind. Who am I to judge? I suspect it is for the best. You go to live in a country not your own. America is very far. I weep for you. Better you stay here and marry one of my fine young sons."

Annisa was aware of the sudden rush of blood to her cheeks. "None of them would have me. I am much too impudent. You have only to ask Zia."

In the courtyard the giant drums, *dol tablas,* had begun their rhythmic pounding and the sound of a bow drawn across a stringed *ghichak* pierced the air. Annisa was thrilled by the sound and suddenly very happy to be here. To be a part of something she had only heard in stories from her father.

The march to the bride's house was about to begin. Zia's mother grabbed a tambourine, as did two of his aunts, and led Annisa outside where the groom and his brothers were waiting. Zia looked very different with his beard clipped and wearing a sky blue shirt. But it was the sight of Ishaq, the groom-to-be, which captured Annisa's imagination. To think of such a man for her own wedding day! Eyes of a dreamer; a poet's eyes. Like her father's. All day Annisa had tried not to think of him, but it was impossible. A knot tightened her throat.

The father of Ishaq and Zia led the procession as it wound its way through the village. There was dancing and singing, the pounding drums and a happy rattle of tambourines; a sensuous moon lighting their way.

From their doorways the people clapped and shouted to Ishaq: "A lighted heart. . .immortal torch. . .capture a lover. . ."

Ahead, Annisa could see Zia dancing with his brothers. If the Americans wanted to know what it was to be born an Afghan, she would tell them about this. Freedom to twist and twirl to the drums, to march and sing and clap hands. Centuries old rituals. She was a modern city girl, but she could feel them in her blood.

When they reached the bride's house, the thunder of the drums frightened some chickens under a flat bed truck. They scattered clucking across the path of the handsome groom. Annisa clapped her hands, her eyes always on Ishaq. "The face of great strength," she thought.

One by one the procession filed into a candlelit room. Ghulam, an uncle of the bride, tapped on an inner door where the bride waited with the women of her family. Zia's mother, carrying the clothes the bride would wear for her wedding day, was ushered inside along with Annisa and the female relatives. The mood behind the closed door was very different from the men's laughter and hearty congratulations outside. The bride's mother had been crying and her sisters stood there sad-eyed.

Annisa saw none of this, so taken was she at the sight of the bride. Her soft voice, the gentleness in her soft brown eyes, the bright purple shawl draping her long black hair.

She took Annisa's hand with a radiant smile.

"Welcome. My name is Sabra. You do me a great honor to share my precious night."

Sabra's rough hands surprised Annisa. Her skin felt like shoe leather, hard and browned from years in the sugar cane fields.

"Ah, you have the sweet, soft hands of the city. What shall we do if the Russians stop Zia on the way to the border and ask to look under your chadri?"

Annisa stepped back in horror. "Surely, this will not happen."

"It does. Sometimes. They suspect it is a man hiding under the veil. You are tall. I fear this for you."

"Insha'llah," Zia's mother chimed in. "Tomorrow we will take salt and wet her hands many times and dry them in the sun until they are cracked and raw."

Little Habiba, Sabra's youngest sister, giggled "Yes, and put black kohl under her eyes and smudge her face with dirt."

"She must go bare legged and wear scuffed shoes. Those will never do." Zia's aunt pointed to Annisa's American jogging shoes. The women laughed heartily.

Annisa felt hurt and was unable to hide it.

Sabra reached for her hand and squeezed it. "We only wish to protect you and we are sad you will leave us so soon."

"She should live in my house," Zia's mother repeated. Again the women laughed. They knew the mother was suggesting a bride for her sons. "It is difficult for a man to marry during Jihad and the war will only get worse. Better my sons take wives while they can."

Sabra's mother opened the box of red henna she held in her hand. "Annisa seems a high-spirited girl. She would handle the younger one, for sure. Now, come let us go to the groom. I suspect we have made him nervous enough."

Annisa did not follow the others but stayed behind the closed door with Sabra. "I feel stupid. I know nothing about the henna. I have no mother. No sisters to teach me our traditions."

"Then I think you should not go to America. I hear it is a very wicked place. The women are unfaithful to their husbands." Sabra lifted her skirts and began to spin around. "I am such a sinful girl. I am supposed to act sad tonight but I cannot help myself. My heart bursts with pride and happiness to be chosen by Ishaq. I cannot pretend. I can't wait to be in his arms. When I was little I used to tell my mother I would perish without him."

"Did your father arrange the marriage?"

Sabra smiled. "My father thinks so. My mother is a very clever woman. She manages these things. During the engagement she even lifted my veil and let Ishaq peek. I shall miss her. She is dear to me."

Annisa thought of the mother she had never known.

When the women returned with the box of henna, Zia's mother reached for Sabra's palm and drew a large red circle in the center. Then she turned to Annisa. "And you?" She reached out and marked Annisa's palm in the same manner.

"But I am not the bride," Annisa gasped.

"You are the honored guest. You leave your people, your land. Dear child, for you tonight we pretend. Now tell me. Which one of my handsome sons do you like?"

Habiba tugged on Annisa's skirt. "I know. I know! An American will pluck Annisa. An American." The little girl sang as she skipped around Annisa.

"Yes. His name will be Peace Corps," an aunt giggled.

Annisa shook her head. "I shall never marry. I have no skills."

"You have been to school. In America they like girls clever with books."

Sabra's mother was studying Annisa, a sad look in her eyes. "What will you do with your life there?"

"I will study to be a doctor. Then I shall return to our people and care for the wounded Mujahideen."

"But how can an honorable woman touch the body of a man?" Sabra's mother scolded.

"In Kabul, it is different. We have many women doctors and..." Annisa stopped, afraid she had offended.

"It will never be so in the village. A woman must not touch a man who is not of her blood."

Out of respect, Annisa did not answer.

Sabra was smiling at her. "Tonight is my last night as a maiden. Sleep in my house. Share my thoughts, little sister."

"Oh, could I!"

The two girls threw their arms around each other. The women in the room nodded in approval.

105

The night was sweet and outside the drums grew louder as the men danced the Afghan dance, the *attan* in the courtyard under a full moon.

It was to be a big wedding. Ishaq's father had brought ten kilos of grain and three sheep had been slaughtered. Sabra's mother had fussed all morning, preparing the *maleeda,* a sweet dessert. Annisa busied herself washing her clothes so that she would smell sweet. In Kabul, Panna had always done this for her. She did not wring the clothes tight enough and little Habiba teased her. "They will not dry in time for the ceremony." With servants in the house Annisa had never learned to cook or clean. She watched the women, contentedly chattering together at their chores and was eager to help. She was pleased when they asked her to gather the orange blossoms that were to be sprinkled over the head of Sabra when she left her father's house. Habiba and Tawab, the blind boy, went with her.

The morning was fresh and pleasant, the scent of the blossoms intoxicating. Annisa found herself much more relaxed as she walked with Tawab through the orange groves, bending the limbs near the ground so that the blind boy could help in the plucking.

"This Hindu lady, what is she like?"

"Bad tempered but wise. I love her dearly."

"If you wish, I can take her to Dorbaba. The village is not far from here and it is where the great Indian saint is buried."

"That is kind of you, Tawab, but there is no time. Tomorrow morning we leave early for the border."

"Yes. They tell me you desert our people to go live with the *ferrangi.*"

His words stung and she did not answer. Tawab groped for her hand. "It is all right. My father says some of our people must go get guns so we can fight." Then he tilted his head backwards and held his face up to the sky. "Planes are coming. Find us a place to hide."

Annisa shouted to Habiba to take cover. She pulled the boy with her under a large tree.

"We are small fish but sometimes they shoot at us only in sport."

Annisa could hear nothing and wondered if the boy had been mistaken, but when she raised her head she saw a plume of white streaking across the sky.

"There are two of them?" Tawab asked. "I think they fly at a very high space. They will do us no harm."

Annisa prayed Tawab was right. She was not afraid to die because then she could join her father. But not today. Please. Allah, not today. Let her see the glorious wedding first.

The jets were directly overhead now but they did not lower their altitude and disappeared into the haze.

"They will not be back," Tawab said. "I can tell from the sound. They head for Baghram. We can finish now." He turned his small blank face towards her and held up the music box that he was re-winding. "Would you like to listen?"

Annisa was seized with a desire to reach down and kiss the boy on each cheek. That dear scarred face; the dirt covered hands, holding the precious egg. "Your music box is magic," she said.

"The Hindu lady gave me sweet candies to suck on. She says you fly on a plane across the ocean. I wish I could fly. I used to watch the planes when I tended my goats on the hillside. One day I will go up in the air--high like a bird." He raised his arms over his head. "Allah is up there."

When they arrived at the village, arms laden with blossoms, Annisa saw a woman enter Sabra's house carrying a small red suitcase. It was the makeup woman who had come from the next village to prepare Sabra's face for her wedding.

Annisa gave the blossoms to Sabra's mother and hurried into the room to watch. The many pots of powder. The rouge. Black kohl. Tiny bits of glitter glued onto Sabra's cheeks. The ripe pink lip color applied to Sabra's full mouth.

"You are prettier than any girl in Kabul."

Sabra laughed. "It is only because I am a bride. When a girl is in love it shines through her eyes." Sabra threw up her arms and like the night before, she began to twirl around the room.

"God turn me into a rose; I want to fall petal by petal into his arms."

The make-up woman laughed. "A bride is supposed to be demure." She left the room and once again Annisa was alone with Sabra.

"Little sister. Better you stay here and marry one of Ishaq's brothers. I have seen how your face flushes when they talk of Zia. Zia is good-humored. He laughs easily. He will make a good husband."

Annisa said nothing, ashamed of her thoughts. Yes, Zia was all this but he was only a farmer. Uneducated. Without the refinement of Kassim. Or the eyes of a poet like his older brother, Ishaq.

"The necklace you wear? Is it the heart of another?"

Annisa hesitated, then told Sabra about Najib who was like a brother "I wish I could have someone like him for a husband."

"Then I desire this for you but I'm not sure how you'll find a good husband in America."

The bedroom door pushed open and an elderly woman walked over to Sabra and whispered in her ear. Sabra shook her head. "Annisa does not have to leave the room. We have no secrets from each other."

"This is something I should not discuss in front of a young maiden."

"My friend leaves tomorrow for America. She may never return to our land. She has no women in her family. She has the right to know of these things."

The woman sighed and brought out a white piece of cloth. "When we go to the home of the groom tonight I will place this under your pillow. As soon as you feel the pain of the wedding night, you are to take this cloth and wipe your blood onto it. This is very important. It is proof to Ishaq's family that you are virgin. You must not forget to do this."

"I know. My mother has spoken of this."

"What happens if she forgets?" Annisa asked, fascinated yet fearful.

"Tomorrow I will carry the cloth on a white satin pillow and show it to Ishaq's parents. If there is no blood on it Sabra's head will be shaved, as well as mine, our faces blackened, and Sabra sent home on a donkey in disgrace. Or worse, she will be kept in the house as a servant for the rest of her life, but never to share Ishaq's bed or bear his children."

Annisa shuddered visibly. "How could Ishaq allow such a thing?"

"I told you the girl was too young to hear this."

"Tell me, where does this blood come from?"

Sabra looked shocked. "Forgive me. Does this mean you are not a woman yet?"

"What do you mean?"

"A woman must bleed to have children. Do you bleed?"

Annisa was aghast. "No, never. Will I not have children?"

"Soon. It will happen to you soon. And when it does you are not to be afraid. You must learn to expect it by the time of the moon."

"I don't understand if this only happens the night you are married."

"No, that is a different blood. . .I see I confuse you. It is all so complicated but I shall try to explain."

Sabra's mother and sisters entered the room carrying the wedding dress. The bride's moment had come. Her mother kissed Sabra on both cheeks. "My joy. My light. May Allah give you many fine sons."

Annisa stood there aching for her own mother. Who would kiss her on the cheeks if she did marry? Who would call her their light, their joy?

Drummers entered the courtyard. The women rushed to the doorway and peeked through the beads. The *doliar*, a sedan chair was covered in a fine red cloth and carried on the shoulders of the groom's family, led by Ishaq, all in white: a white turban, white shirt and pants. He was riding a white horse decorated in red, yellow and green *zundi* with a purple saddlecloth.

"Stand back, daughter. They will see you."

"Please, just one small look."

"Sabra, come here. It is time we put on your veils."

Annisa remained at the doorway, her heart pounding. The moon was perfectly round and lighted a path for the handsome groom as he dismounted and walked towards the front door with his family and the mullah. Annisa felt dishonorable for thinking it, but wouldn't it be wonderful if she too could be Ishaq's bride. If a man could afford it he was allowed more than one wife and this was sometimes practiced in the countryside. She knew what Panna would say. That she was senseless for always wanting someone who belonged to another.

Inside her bedroom, the women had formed a circle around Sabra and sang:

"*Wro za laila. Wro za laila.* Walk slowly darling. Ishaq's heart is at your feet; walk slowly or you will hurt him."

Zia's mother and his aunts had come with Ishaq and now entered the bedroom. A hush fell over the women. "Your Ishaq asks the mullah for your hand in marriage. Put your ear to the door, Sabra, you can hear."

Just then the door opened and Sabra had to jump back. Her father entered. "Ah, little Sabra, what mischief you make. The groom will be dazzled when he lifts your veil. The mullah waits outside to bring his message."

Part of the ritual was to refuse the groom several times. Not until the third time the mullah had knocked on the door to ask for her hand, did Sabra accept and when the mullah returned to the anxious groom, cheers of jubilation could be heard. Sabra and Ishaq were now man and wife; the dancing and the feasting could begin.

Sabra's mother handed the bride a large green sash to tie around her waist. Only Ishaq could untie it. Midnight had come and gone when the bride finally stepped out of her room. A hush settled over the wedding party as the women escorted Sabra to the *dolair* singing:

"Cry dear sister. Crying is not a shame.
This is your father's home and there are many shoulders to cry on.
There you have no one, they are all strangers."

At this, young Sabra began to weep as the wedding party covered her head in orange blossoms. Ishaq's brothers raised her sedan chair to their shoulders.

The moon hung full and low to the ground as the red *dolair* swayed ever so gently. Tawab had begged to help carry it, promising not to stumble or fall. By putting his hand on the hem of Zia's shirt, he tagged along at the back.

Annisa suddenly lost all of her feelings of joy. Like Sabra's mother and sisters, she had been struck with a sense of loss. All this was hers yet she had never known it and tomorrow she was leaving it behind. In America she would never ride in a *dolair,* even if she were to love a man with a poet's eyes.

When they reached the doorway of Ishaq's house, the groom dismounted his horse. A small lamb, which he must hold up in honor to his bride, was brought to him. The *dolair* was lowered to the ground and Ishaq slaughtered the lamb at Sabra's feet.

Annisa gasped when she heard the lamb's cries and saw the blood-soaked ground over which they must now step before entering the house. She remembered the blood of Kassim in the drainage ditch and talk of a bloodstained cloth on a pillow.

In the ceremony that followed, the members of Ishaq's family took turns removing Sabra's veils. Each time a layer was removed, a ring was given to her. The final thin veil, however, remained for Ishaq to remove in the privacy of their bedroom. Ishaq would lift the veil and untie the green sash.

Annisa fought against her tears. Isolated behind the high walls of her home in Kabul, her inheritance had been only pictures in a storybook. She recalled her father's voice as he read aloud to her of the ancient wonders of Afghanistan: Bamiyan, with its giant Buddhas carved into the cliffs of Bamiyan Valley; the rounded hills of Herat, dotted with pistachio trees in spring and the legends that lived in the ruined city of Balkh--the mother of cities, home of the ancient silk route where the poet laureate Firdausi had walked. "My father, you have taught me our history but I know nothing of love," she whispered to herself. "I am alone."

      Suddenly she felt a small hand reach out for hers. It was little Habiba who had come to sit by her side.

CHAPTER 11

Matthew Hardcastle of Reuters News Service sat alone in Harvey's, the restaurant of Presidents, in Washington, D.C. Irritated, he drummed his fingers on the linen tablecloth. He prided himself on never being late for an appointment and he could not abide tardiness in others. Where was this Dr. Harris? In Hardcastle's opinion, doctors had a natural arrogance, genetically programmed to think their time was more valuable than yours. He was also annoyed with Rahmin Aziz for asking if his friend, Dr. Harris, could join them for lunch and then canceling out at the eleventh hour. What Rahmin didn't know was that the purpose of the meeting was a ruse. Rahmin had to be informed of his father's death and since Matthew Hardcastle had a trip that was scheduled to Washington, he had drawn the short straw. He was researching an article about efforts being made in the States to help the Afghan cause--interviewing people at the Heritage Foundation who were trying to convince the U.S. Congress to provide stinger missiles. Rahmin's plans to recruit American physicians to volunteer their help in Afghanistan might dovetail nicely. Or so he had told Rahmin. Personally, he was against it.

"Mr. Hardcastle?.. I'm Ethan Harris."

Matthew had not seen the young man enter the side door of the restaurant. He pushed back his chair and stood up to shake his hand.

"Sorry I'm late. Couldn't find a parking spot. Hope you haven't been waiting long."

"I was on time," Matthew said bluntly.

The young doctor was handsome, clear-eyed, and wearing blue jeans with his sport coat. He nodded at Hardcastle as he stood by his table, but said nothing, as though waiting for a further reprimand.

"Sit down. Sit down...Your friend, Rahmin. He's left me in a pickle."

"I'm sorry to hear that."

"Nothing to do with you.. .Rahmin tells me he has recruited you to go to Afghanistan."

"Yes, as soon as I finish my residency."

"When will that be?"

"Next year."

112

"So there is plenty of time for you to learn about Afghanistan and even more for me to try and talk you out of it."

The young man before him relaxed and grinned. "Not a chance . . . I can't wait to go."

"Who sold you? Kipling, or was it James Michener and 'Caravans'? Hot love under a nomad's tent?"

"All of the above."

"Well, it is an interesting part of the world; a nation of poets. To an Afghan, poetry is a spoken, not written art. How many places can one meet an illiterate shepherd boy who can recite you verse after verse from Omar Khayyam?"

Ethan Harris cleared his throat. "Rahmin says you have been inside since the invasion."

"Twice. It's not an easy thing to do."

"That's why I'm here."

Hardcastle frowned. "I'm not in the escort business. I hope Rahmin made that clear."

"Not exactly."

The veteran and somewhat jaded newsman studied the earnest young man seated across from him, deciding that there wasn't a snowball's chance in hell that Ethan Harris was going to get beyond Peshawar, a jumping off place for men and supplies in the Resistance. If young Dr. Harris did make it inside Afghanistan, he wouldn't last long. He was too squeaky clean and definitely not red brick university. And he suspected that he might be a bit too eager to please. Hardcastle wondered if the doctor frequented a tanning salon. Patches of snow still remained on the sidewalks of Washington D.C. and Ethan Harris was the shade of Palm Beach.

"Been on vacation?"

"No, I go to a tanning salon."

Matthew mentally chalked up a plus for his young luncheon companion. At least he had no pretenses, a refreshing quality in the yuppified air of Washington. "I admire your intent but the American embassy in Pakistan will try to stop you from going inside."

"But French doctors. . ."

"Irrelevant. Your State department is right on this one. America doesn't need another hostage situation like they had in Tehran. If you want to help the Afghan cause, why not settle for the refugee camps in Peshawar? Plenty of sick Afghans are streaming over the border."

113

Ethan Harris grimaced. "You want me to pretend my motives for going inside are purely altruistic? I'm training to be a surgeon. I want to treat gunshot wounds."

"Then stay here and work in your ghettos. I understand they shoot people every day."

"I'll level with you. Afghanistan is also a chance to practice my skills under adverse conditions and not get sued."

Hardcastle gave him an approving look. "I take it all back. Without the altruistic bullshit, you just might make it inside."

"So what's the attraction for *you* in Afghanistan?" Ethan asked.

"It's a great story. Little David with his slingshot. First time I went to Kabul was in '67. I was ostensibly working on a feature story regarding the status of the Communist Party in Third World countries. But the real reason I tacked Afghanistan onto my list was personal. The place reeks with intrigue. It's very name. Afghanistan was originally called 'Ariana.' In fact, some experts claim the Aryan race originated there. Up in the Nuristan region, you can see Afghans with fair skin, blonde-hair and blue eyes. They call it 'blondism.'"

"That's hard to believe."

"Not when you consider Alexander the Great tromped through--along with some other lights--Darius, Genghis Khan. Even in Khan's descendants, the Moghols, you can find people with pale skin. That's why the romantics call Afghanistan 'the crossroads for conquerors.'"

"I've read the English call it 'the great game.'"

"Poor bastards have always been a pawn. When we split the Pushtun tribes in the South and established the Durand line, the Russians systematically divided the Tajick and Uzbeck tribes in the North. . . End of history lesson." Hardcastle signaled the waiter for another drink but the man turned his back on him. "The service here is frightful," he announced in an exaggerated English accent.

Ethan Harris buried his head behind his menu. He made it a point never to reprimand a waiter, empathizing with their difficult task. "I have a personal reason for going too," he said, reaching for his billfold and removing a snapshot to show Hardcastle. "The one on the right is my brother. He won the Henley regatta in the two-man scull and has qualified for the Olympics. But the President is threatening to boycott the games in Moscow. It's heart-breaking. Four years from now my brother will be too old to compete. Do you think that's fair?"

"Fair is an outdated word. I'm convinced your President Carter will do it. The man's an idealist, sees this protest as a moral obligation."

"Whatever. I felt I had to do something."

"I don't get the connection. You would risk getting your head blown off just because your brother didn't get to row? It's got to be more than that. Running away from or running to something. What am I dealing with? An incurable romantic?"

Harris laughed. "Have you been talking to my girlfriend?"

The dour-faced waiter suddenly reappeared and delivered Matthew Hardcastle his drink. His lower lip curled as he took their orders of spaghetti with meat sauce and a house salad on the side.

"I also want you to bring me a beer with my meal," Hardcastle added.

The waiter rattled off a long list of beers to choose from in a voice that rang with irritation.

"Would you run through that again?"

Ethan Harris cringed as he waited for Hardcastle to make his selection.

"Imagine that," Hardcastle said after the waiter finally had their order. "The natives seem unfriendly."

Feeling a bit sheepish for showing the photograph, Ethan Harris returned it to his wallet, sensing that Matthew Hardcastle did not empathize with his brother's disappointment. "I guess my brother's loss is not so tragic when you compare it to what has happened to the Afghans."

Hardcastle shrugged. "I'm trained to ferret out the facts--not get attached to them."

"But Rahmin says you are sympathetic to the Afghan cause."

"As a people, yes. But once you start taking it one on one--a personal level--you're no good in what you have to do." He was thinking of the unpleasant assignment he was facing with Rahmin. "Stay detached if you plan to function over there."

"Has Kabul changed much since the 60's?"

"Definitely. Western hippies came in search of enlightenment and stayed for the hashish--exploited the cultural generosity of the Afghans. A stranger can come to an Afghan's door and he will take you into his house, share his food and then give you his own bed for the night-- regardless of how poor he is."

"Was the King still on the throne?"

"Yes, in fact, I interviewed the gentleman. Not a bad sort. But he was up against a semi-feudal society. He was making some inroads but he failed to recognize the need for a crackdown on government corruption. Kabul was full of well-educated Afghans and many of them were high-minded for the future. Granted, there were some rumblings about Western influence on their culture-- but they were also very excited over a posh Intercontinental Hotel going up in Kabul. An affluent tourist trade was anticipated."

"What happened to the King?"

"Ousted by his cousin Daoud, a leftist. They called him, 'Crazy Sirdar' and he was the beginning of the end."

The scowling waiter appeared with their pasta, looking very put-upon when Hardcastle reminded him he had asked him to bring a beer with his meal. "And who said the Afghans were 'Third World,'" he quipped.

Ethan Harris pretended not to hear.

"Right. . . now who else have you talked to about sneaking into Afghanistan?"

"Only Rahmin."

"Well, it's essential you know the lay of the land. Stay out of the politics--here and there-- the situation is more complicated than you might suspect. America walks a high tightrope with no net in that area. If Iran gets too strong, they will have to bolster that bastard in Iraq. If they equip the Afghans with stinger missiles they will have to worry about those lethal toys falling into the hands of terrorists. There are terrorist training units in Libya that could use those stingers to blow commercial aircraft out of the sky. And you also have to worry about the Paks. One of the best-financed lobbies in your nation's capitol. They intend to get rich off this conflict. The West props them up because India's courtship of Moscow scares the be-Jesus out of them. Meanwhile, all that hashish flowing out of the Afghanistan corridor is really owned by wealthy Paks who are using the poor Afghans as a front to take the heat from the West. Am I boring you?"

"No, I think you are trying to scare me off. . .Is it true what *The Washington Post* reports? About the Russians carpet bombing the countryside in Afghanistan with mines shaped like miniature toy trucks and dolls."

"Yes, and for your information--Reuters had it first. The object of this diabolical endeavor by the Soviets is to produce a nation of crippled children. But in case you didn't know, the Afghans can be just as brutal. There are rumors of captured Russian soldiers being butchered and strung up in the bazaars like a side of beef."

"That has to be Soviet propaganda."

"I'd take a pass on that one until you've been there. The Afghans are a vengeful lot. Did Rahmin ever tell you about the Afghan game of *buzkashi?*"

"No."

"It's their national sport and it's a license to kill. Men on horseback fight over the carcass of a beheaded goat, which in the modern day game of polo would be considered the ball. There are no holds barred. Whips. Chains. It's not unusual for a horse or its rider to be beaten to death during a match."

"That sounds barbaric!"

"It is, but it's exciting to watch. I've never seen anything like it. Rahmin has an uncle named Abdul El-Ham. He's a great *chapandaz* --that's what they call their *buzkashi* players. And in Afghanistan, a *chapandaz* is like a pro-football star over here. Adulation wherever they go. . .What you have got to understand, is that you are going into a different culture. Talk to me after you witness your first public hanging or a man's hand cut off for stealing. It's great for law and order but goes against our grain. I once interviewed a young Peace Corps doctor in Kandahar who fell apart when they brought a woman to him with her ear cut off--the Afghan penalty for adultery."

"That's sick."

Matthew Hardcastle raised his empty wineglass in a mock salute. "Still want to go to that part of the world? Still want to go inside and risk getting shot? I repeat, Afghan refugees in Pakistan and Iran are in need of medical attention. Half the deaths in those camps are from dysentery."

"Granted. But are 'incurable romantics' really into shit?"

Hardcastle looked pleased. "Got to you, did I?"

"Not to change the subject but do you think the Afghans can win this thing? Some of the pundits are saying this could be Russia's Vietnam."

"With the Afghans anything is possible, but the Russians are pouring in more and more troops. And, unfortunately, the Afghans are starting to flee the battleground. It will become a war on two fronts--fighting to drive the Soviets out, and fighting to keep their own people within. In the meantime, everyone seems to be overlooking some real diplomatic efforts underway in the U.N. Of course, nobody pays much attention. There are vested interests who would like to put a stop to any negotiations."

"That's disillusioning."

"So is point shaving in a ball game." Hardcastle reached for the salt shaker and vigorously shook it over his remaining pasta; a little act of defiance on his part against his arteries. It was hard not to envy all this youthful vigor seated across the table from him. "I hope Rahmin told you that you must be in good physical shape to go inside. Rugged terrain to cover and most of it on foot."

"He made that clear."

"And did he also make it clear that you stay away from their women? Afghanistan is definitely a place where you keep your zipper up."

"Are their women treated like those under Khomeini?"

"A different sect of Islam altogether. Afghan females are in the professions, a significant part of the work force in Kabul. However, the Iranians are funneling agents into Afghanistan to bolster the stricter fundamentalists in the south. That faction is getting stronger by the day. . . Blast it, where is that man with my beer?"

Ethan Harris put down his fork. "It's really a shame Rahmin couldn't finish his internship. Did you know he's driving a cab at night full time? During the day he's out beating the drums for the cause."

"Rahmin concerns me. He doesn't always know when to keep his mouth shut. There are some pretty unsavory characters out there whose toes he could step on."

"Such as?"

"Well, we have the little matter of an international drug cartel which would benefit if the Paks regain parts of Pushtunistan."

Ethan Harris laughed. "Now *that* sounds like bullshit."

"Have it your way." Matthew signaled the waiter over to their table. "I ordered beer with my pasta. Where is it?"

The waiter frowned and left without an apology for the omission.

"Can you get booze in Afghanistan?"

"Don't even try. Western diplomats manage to crate it into Peshawar. But once you cross the border you are in for a dry spell. The Afghans take a dim view of the grape, which is really ironic. They grow some of the greatest tasting grapes in the world. A few years before the war, an Italian firm was interested in setting up a winery. It would have brought in much-needed foreign exchange but the Afghans were having none of it. . . . And one more thing. If you attempt to set up an operation inside you'll have to have private backing to pay for your supply of medicines and the money to transport by mule any equipment you may need."

"Rahmin has told me this."

"Did he tell you it's not a cheap trip? The Mujahideen want their money up front and charge a fortune. Which gets us back to the Red-eye stingers the Afghans want so desperately and which so far your government does not see fit to supply. Money talks and the Afghans know it. They are looking for every means to get some cold cash."

"Is that how you manage to get inside?"

Matthew Hardcastle scowled. "I never discuss my contacts or my sources. Just be aware there is big drug money with muscle in that region. I would even go so far as to say that I think that the drug cartels are the major reason America will eventually cave in to the demands of the Resistance for those stinger missiles. With enough dollars you can purchase anything in this world. If not from the Americans, you can be sure they will eventually get their hands on them."

Ethan Harris looked genuinely puzzled.

"My message is simple. If you make it inside you may see a lot of things you don't like, I guarantee"

"Can you be more specific?"

Hardcastle leaned across the table. "The Afghans are a heroic lot and their cause is admirable, but there is one thing you should know. They are like everyone else in this world. They will bend the twig to fit the wind. Don't be disillusioned if you run across some Afghan heroes who are also smuggling out drugs that end up on your city streets. It's all about survival. It takes money to run a war. People you will grow to trust--men your life depends on once you get inside--they may not want you asking questions. Your friend Rahmin has been knee deep in anguish over the unsavory side to his cause. He's a rigid character and because he is not a man to give an inch, I predict he'll get a lot of people mad at him." He paused and grinned. "Have I managed to unsettle you."

Ethan Harris smiled. "No, but nice try."

"I warn you, keep your eyes open and don't stick your nose in places that smell bad. You're too tall for a smart fit in the coffin. As you said, getting inside is a challenge. Afghanistan is a place for a man to test his mettle. And who knows? Maybe we can get Richard Chamberlain to play you when the movie comes out."

Dr. Harris signaled the waiter for the check. "This is on me. . . . Anything you want me to tell Rahmin when he gets back from Peshawar?"

Hardcastle did a double take. "Peshawar? Is this a joke?"

"No, he left last night. I thought you knew that."

"All I had was a cryptic message on my answering machine. He couldn't make it and you could. He would ring me tonight. I've got some unhappy news for him and it has to be delivered in person."

"Is it about his father?"

"You mean he knows? Why in God's name didn't you tell me? You let me sit here pontificating on the politics of Afghanistan and meanwhile, Rahmin is on his way to Peshawar! How did he learn about his father?"

"A friend at the University of Oregon called to tell him. Evidently word was gotten out to him that his father was executed on the same day as Rahmin's. Rahmin was in a panic. Worried about his little sister that is on her way out. What with their father dead he thought he should be there when she arrives."

"I hope to hell they don't miss each other in Peshawar. That's easy to do. Everything is so chaotic there. Does he know where she will be staying?"

"He didn't say."

"Well, I know. She is to wait at the Reeds, American missionaries. There are no plans for her to go to the refugee camps. That is where he would look for her first. If he doesn't call me tonight then I'm really in a bind. I'm due to fly out of here for London in the morning. What a monumental balls-up."

"Anything I can do?"

"Yes, if and when you *should* hear from Rahmin, tell him where Annisa is staying. I repeat. The Reeds. American missionaries. Want to write that down?"

"No, I can remember it."

"Also tell him I'm sorry about his father. He was a very unique man." Hardcastle pushed back his chair, offering his hand. "I've got 20 minutes to make it across town for an interview. Good luck on getting 'inside."

Ethan Harris thanked him and suggested they keep in touch. Hardcastle agreed without meaning it. Rahmin's rash action and the possible screw-up with his sister had left a sour taste in his mouth. In hindsight he should have told Rahmin about his father's death on the phone while making arrangements to meet with him. But hang it, the whole purpose of his involvement was for Rahmin to hear it in person. Why had he let himself get sucked into this? None of these little errands were ever easy. He'd be damned if he'd get involved again.

At the exit door of the restaurant, he turned and waved goodbye at his waiter. "Enjoyed the beer you didn't bring me," he called.

The waiter scowled as he crossed to clear their table. He resented being singled-out like that. They had tied up his space for an hour and a half and had left him a meager tip. An obvious bunch of cheapskate, long-winded do-gooders. The snatches of their luncheon conversation he had picked up in passing were stupid. He had no use for the British. They always undertipped and tried to act as though they still had an empire. And who the hell cared about Afghanistan? A half-baked country of half-stoned goat herders who wanted to drag the U.S. into war with Russia. When would Americans ever learn to tend to what was going on in their own backyard?

CHAPTER 12

Zia was in a surly mood, up dancing half the night and now the two women were quarreling as they walked behind him.

"How you go on!" Panna scolded Annisa. "You think if you lived in Tezeen that each day would be a wedding feast? Sabra works the sugar cane. When she gives birth, there will be no doctor. It is a hard life and it will get harder. The Russians will burn their fields. You would not last. You are too soft."

"You twist my words. I did not say I wanted to stay--only that my heart was in Afghanistan."

"And what will life in America be without a heart?"

They were in the flatlands beyond Sultanpur, heading for Dorbaba, a village hidden in mountains covered with pine. In Dorbaba, there was a secret spring and the tomb of the Hindu saint that Tawab, the blind boy, had mentioned.

But first they must stop for lunch at a teahouse. Flies covered the food on the plates Zia brought out to them. Annisa turned up her nose. "After last night I am not hungry."

"Eat." Zia ordered. "All of it. I have only the food in my handkerchief to carry us. It may be a long time before our next meal. I don't forget how you whined for food all the way through the pass."

Chastised, Annisa bit down into the round flat bread that was gritty and coarse compared to the delicacies of the wedding.

"We will rest over there before starting the climb." Zia pointed to a small building about fifty yards from the teahouse. Halfway there he halted, listening to the sound of bombs. Smoke rose in the still air and then a jet climbed high in the sky, trailing a stream behind it. The jets circled and dived again.

"What are they bombing?" Annisa asked.

"The nomad tents we passed earlier."

"But why a Kucchi camp? It was only camels and sheep."

"If they can cripple our livestock, they starve us."

The noise closed in. "Take cover. They are headed our way."

In her haste, Panna tripped on her chadri and pitched forward in the middle of the road. Annisa ran to pick her up but Zia motioned her back. "Lie flat on the ground" He leaned down, threw the old woman over his shoulders like a sack of grain, and scurried back to Annisa as a bomb exploded just behind the tea house.

"They have seen us. For God's sake, Annisa, keep down."

The impact of the next bomb shook the ground beneath them. Instinctively, Zia threw his arm around Annisa and pinned the trembling girl to the ground as the fires belched forth around them. Two more bombs exploded less than seventy-five yards away with ear-splitting force, throwing a giant boulder into the air. The jets circled and dived again. A few minutes later another bomb fell further up the valley. Annisa remained with her mouth in the dirt, the strong arm of Zia around her. Eventually, silence returned. A small brown marmot scurried across the path in front of them as Panna struggled to her feet, wobbling unsteady.

"Sit down," Zia commanded. "They may be back."

"I need to relieve myself."

Zia jumped to his feet and brushed the dirt from his tunic. "I will wait straight ahead. Hurry. In times like this we must learn to discipline our bodies."

Annisa put her hand to her mouth to smother a giggle as Panna squatted beside her.

When they re-joined Zia, he scowled at Annisa but said nothing.

"Why are you are so cross today? On the ride from Kabul I thought we were friends."

Zia did not answer. He had been forced to lie to Annisa about that miserable mullah refusing to pray because Zia didn't have enough money. For her sake, Zia had pretended it would be done-- only to double his sin by saying it was his gift when she asked how much she would owe. To add to his woes, his father had warned him to keep his distance from her. "You must be on your guard. You say she is only 12 but she has city ways and the yearnings of a woman."

Zia could never recall a time when he had disagreed with his father. After all, his father was a Haji. He had made the sacred pilgrimage to Mecca as a young man and the village paid homage to his wisdom. But all this did not erase Zia's longing to see Annisa's face once again. A phantom in the *chadri* she had redonned for the trip, she seemed so out of reach. When she laughed he could not see her lips, her eyes hidden behind a slit of embroidery.

"Zia, why don't you speak to me?"

"I am tired. Only two hours sleep. And the old woman is a burden. We lose time because she moves so slow."

"Panna is in pain."

"You think I don't know this," he snapped. He could see the blisters on Annisa's heels from the ill-fitting shoes Sabra's mother had insisted she wear. No doubt she was hurting too, but thankfully she had not complained. Panna had called her soft. Zia smiled to himself. He thought not.

"How much further to Dorbaba?"

"We should reach the village gates before the sun sets. We will rest for a few hours before pushing on in the dark."

"The dark! I can barely see to walk in this stupid *chadri* when the sun shines."

"It is safer by night. The Russians are afraid to come out."

"Then I won't have to wear the veil?"

"We'll see." He dared not admit to himself that his blood was warmed by the thought. "Today's bombing shows they have stepped up the fighting in our province. The next few days may be a nightmare."

Zia's estimation of how long it would take to reach Dorbaba was off by more than three hours. It was well after sunset when they stumbled into the village and Zia was stiff with fatigue. He could only imagine how the old woman must feel.

But Allah smiled on them. A dinner of tasty chicken, eggplant and yogurt was waiting, with glasses of hot tea to wash it down. That night they bedded down on the rooftop of the local malik and slept under a blanket of stars. The heavens seemed close enough to touch. "The stars embrace each other," Zia thought and rolled over, pleased with himself and with the sound of Annisa's gentle breathing beside him. She slept without the veil and it was difficult for him to close his eyes, too intoxicated with the innocence and the beauty of her face.

In the morning, they awoke to the song of a woodlark. Zia stood up, stretched and peered over the side of the roof. Below were long lines of Mujahideen bowed towards Mecca. Each man had placed his weapon on the ground in front of him. At the end of their prayers, the men turned and shook hands and kissed one another. It inspired him. They could beat the Russians. With men like this, how could they fail?

But at breakfast there was tragic news. An informer in Tirah, one of the villages that lay ahead, had led the Russian troops to a cave where twenty Mujahideen made their quarters and the Russians had sealed off the entrance with dynamite, entombing the men inside the mountain

"Have they caught the informer?"

"His carcass hangs upside down in the market place for the people to spit on," Zia sighed. In the few precious days since they had left Kabul, he had forgotten about death. The open countryside had felt safe and peaceful, compared to the over-crowding--the feeling of entrapment with the Russians in the city. Here, at least one was free to move around.

"I am glad they did this to the informer," Annisa said. "Let it be an example to others."

Zia nodded gravely. "Good. You think like us. Maybe the city has not spoiled you after all. The Mujahideen have warned me the Russians are mining the hills around Tirah. We will have to go another way. I know every step through Tirah but the new route is unknown to me. This will slow us considerably."

Why was he secretly pleased? Yesterday he had wanted to be rid of them. But at breakfast Annisa had given him soft smiles before she put on her veil. The delay meant more time to be with her. It was obvious her senses were heightened. He had seen it before. Danger did that. "You shall miss us, fair Annisa, so try to remember the taste and the smell of each day you have left in Afghanistan."

Panna looked at him and belched.

By late afternoon they had reached Girwada and again there were sounds of gunfire in the hills beyond. Zia determined they should rest until after evening prayers, when it would be safer to move on.

Happily, the old woman's face was not so gray, revived by the long rest at the wedding. She offered up the last of her lavender candies and Zia looked over at Annisa and they exchanged smiles. The three of them seemed to have exhausted their talk, each alone with their thoughts. Zia knew he would never forget Annisa. If he survived the war and if he could ever save enough for a dowry, the girl he took for a bride would have to live with the shadow of Annisa. It would be a comfort to think Annisa might remember him too-- on moonlight nights in America; it would fill his emptiness pretending that she did.

"I am grateful for the moonlight," Panna said as they started once again up into the hills. "You hold the light of your lantern too low."

Zia lifted his lantern high over his head but he only walked a few steps before he shouted for them to stop. The moving light had revealed a large black snake stretched full length across the path. "Not to worry. It's not poisonous."

Annisa shook with fear. "How evil it looks. A terrible omen."

"Nonsense," Panna said. "The snake is sacred. It is the serpent that sleeps at the base of the spine--the *Chiti*, the *Kundalini power*, the creative force of the universe. Release the *chiti* and a man can move mountains."

"I hate the thing," Annisa insisted as Zia pounded the snake's head with a large stone.

Panna was clearly upset. "Why did you not get a stick and nudge it away?"

Zia reached down for the tail, twirling the dead snake in the air and flinging it as far as he could. "Annisa is right. They are evil things. There is no reason not to kill it."

"It will bring us bad luck."

Annisa was annoyed. There were times when Panna's superstitions got on her nerves. America was a nation of Christians. Would their faith be as foolish?

The three of them continued on in silence, each absorbed in their own thoughts and the meaning of a serpent across their path.

The climb had steepened and several times Zia had to reach out and help the old woman. The rocks under their feet crunched. In the distance they could hear a Kucchi dog barking. Kucchi dogs were fierce and trained to attack.

Zia patted his gun.

He saw that the old woman was shivering. The higher up they climbed, the colder the air became. "I can think of nothing else but the warm rug on my bed in Kabul," Annisa said.

When they halted by a barren outcropping of rock, halfway up the mountain, Zia took out his compass and held it up to the lantern. "Good. The right direction. We can rest."

Panna sank to her haunches and Zia was alarmed to hear how heavy was her breathing.

"Are you all right?" Annisa asked.

"Foolish question. The air is so thin up here." Panna kicked a stone with her foot and it echoed as it rolled down the mountainside.

"It is her heart. I can tell. Her lips turn purple the higher we climb."

With his arms folded across his chest and his head lifted to the wind, Zia listened to the sounds of the night in the wild briars and fir trees. If there were not war on the land, this spot would be a very romantic place. He looked over at Annisa and thought of the

Pushtu poem, a landri: "Hold me in your arms while we stand; God knows what will happen at the interval by the time we sit."

"Zia? May I ask you something? Have you money for a bride?"

He felt embarrassed. Had she read his thoughts? "I save money to buy a motorcycle."

Annisa threw back her head and laughed. "Then you should come to America. My brother tells me they have many motorcycles."

His voice was suddenly gruff. "I have no desire to leave my country. I am loyal."

"Then you think I'm not?"

"No, it is best you go. My mother is sad for you but in the same breath she says girls like you are the hope of Afghanistan. We may be simple and uneducated but we are not stupid. We know we have many things to learn. You must not fail us. I have seen many men die of their wounds. I am glad you will study medicine. I know you will come back."

"Oh, Zia. Do you really believe that?"

He closed his eyes and prayed for forgiveness for pretending to know. He did not expect what happened next. A warm sensation shot through his body; his limbs were on fire. He felt like he was bathed in a white light of utter bliss. "It is written," he said "You may leave many times but you will always return."

Annisa swallowed hard. He sounded so certain. She had been thinking of Zia's refusal to tell her how much he had paid the mullah. After they reached Peshawar she would ask the price of a motorcycle. She wanted to help. "Have I offended you today? You seem so far away from me."

"You imagine things. I must scout our path ahead," he said gruffly. "If they planted mines around Tirah it is only logical they may have mined this way too. Wait here."

"Careful. . . .please."

"Not to worry. Our only danger is the mines and whenever I suspect the ground ahead, I toss a stone in front of me."

"Don't go too far."

Zia was pleased with her concern. "Do you worry for my safety or are you afraid of the wolf packs in the mountains?"

"Don't frighten me."

"Forgive me. I sometimes make little jokes when I too am not sure."

"Did you hear something ahead?"

"No. It is just a feeling."

"You said I was coming back to Afghanistan."

"Yes, of that I am clear."

"I believe you. Take care." She reached out and touched his shoulder and it quickened his heart. He left her with a feeling of happiness; his lantern bobbing ahead until the light disappeared in the scrub.

"Panna, it is good you rest. Zia was right. Your lips are purple."

"What nonsense. You cannot see my lips. Besides, my lips are no concern. It is your foolishness we should worry about. A girl who is supposed to be so smart, supposed to be educated--you know nothing of the ways of men. Have you no idea what your flirtation does to poor Zia?"

"Flirtation! You mean when Zia took my hand to help me up the mountainside. How else was I supposed to get up?"

"You know what I am talking about. Your smile excites him. You have no idea what to do with the feelings of the heart. You are still a little girl. All this romantic nonsense about village life. Zia's world is not real for you."

"I am an educated girl. I would never consider a farmer."

"Then you are cruel. You give the boy expectations. All that nonsense about you coming back to Afghanistan."

"He said that, not me. And I pray he is right."

Annisa leaned over and picked up a small stone, tossing it violently into the dark. "You only think you know how I feel about Zia!" She did not want to admit that she did not know either. She had dreamed last night that Zia was staring at her and that when she opened her eyes he had gathered her into his strong arms, smothering her with kisses. It was only a dream but she had not wanted it to end.

"I know that you care for Zia."

Zia announced his return in a loud voice. "The path ahead is safe. Follow me." He was light-headed with joy. He had heard the old woman accuse Annisa of caring for him. When the snows came and the wolves howled in the mountains he would warm himself before the fire and think of Annisa's green eyes.

"Don't walk so fast," Panna complained. "What has gotten into you?"

"Sorry."

"How many times must I tell you. Hold the lantern higher. Moonlight is not enough for these old eyes."

Zia's arm went up with the lantern at the same time his foot hit the mine. The explosion tossed the lantern high into the air. It landed upside down, its light gone out.

"Zia!" Annisa screamed, pushing past Panna. "Zia. Zia."

But there was no answer. Running forward, she stumbled and fell several times before the moonlight revealed his mangled body a few yards ahead. "Merciful God," Annisa mumbled as she choked on the bile, which had risen, in her throat. She sank to her knees and stretched her arms out in front of her. Supplicating herself before Allah on the desolate path, she moaned. "No. No. No."

Panna's voice was moving towards her in the darkness. "What has happened? Did he throw the stone?"

"A land mine. He stepped on a land mine!"

"Is he alive?"

"No," Annisa started to scream.

"Stop that. Annisa. Annisa!" The name echoed through the mountains. "Annisa, Annisa. Annisa."

It was one of those moments when wisdom fails. The girl convinced now of her own futility, refused to move as she continued to wail.

"No, no, no," the mountains reverberated.

Crawling on her hands and knees, Panna had finally reached her. "Get his gun. We will need it to defend us from the dogs. And take his money."

Annisa uttered a sob.

"Do as I say. We have only the chit in your belt. A piece of paper good only in Peshawar. Zia carries *afghanis* to bribe the border guards."

"Panna, I beg you. Don't make me touch him."

"You must."

Gritting her teeth, Annisa reached forward. Quickly she withdrew her hand from the wet, slick blood. "You do it. I can't."

Panna inched forward. "His insides are like jelly."

"I tried to tell you." Annisa could barely see her hand in the moonlight. Red circled the center of her palm.

"Annisa, what are you staring at? Have you lost your reason? We must look for the gun."

"No, Panna. There is no sense going on."

"We must. Think of life."

"I want to die."

A dark cloud passed the moon.

129

"If Zia had not been our guide he would still be alive. I did this to him. I destroy my father and now Zia."

"You are not almighty. Only the great God Shiva has the power to decide these things. It was Zia's karma. His choice."

Annisa's voice was shrill. "Zia wanted to live."

"Yes, but perhaps he fulfilled his task."

"Task. You crazy old woman. That is all you ever talk about. The task. The task. The task. This lifetime. I do not believe in your stupid reincarnation."

"You are hysterical."

The cloud passed and Annisa forced herself to look again at Zia in the moonlight. She began to cry bitterly. "I hate this life, Panna. I hate God. How could he do this."

Panna reached out and slapped Annisa as hard as she could. "If you don't stop this, you too will die."

"I don't care." Annisa clawed at the rocky ground with her fingernails and began to beat it with her fists.

"Stop this. You have lost your senses." Panna extended her arms to the wailing girl and gathered her in. She held her, rocking her back and forth, crooning to her. "My poor sweet lamb. Panna does not know how to help you. Grief is not a shirt to wear with age."

Annisa continued to sob.

"We cannot move without a lantern. Let us rest here until morning. But away from the body. I fear the jackals will come."

"No! I stay with Zia."

Panna sighed. "As you wish."

In the distance, the howling of the Kucchi dogs could be heard again and the coldness of the altitude descended upon them. After Annisa had fallen asleep, Panna removed her own *chadri* and wrapped it around the girl. She tried to stay awake but her head was soon nodding, and she lay down next to Annisa and put her arms around her for warmth. Panna slipped into sleep, as the sound from the howling dogs grew fainter.

When the morning rays hit the side of the mountain Annisa awoke. For one brief, sweet moment, memory failed her. She pulled away from Panna and sat up and rubbed her eyes but the sight of Zia's bloodied remains a few yards ahead jolted her senses. Her limbs were stiff from the cold as she leaned over to shake Panna awake.

"Panna, wake up. Panna, I'm sorry I screamed at you. . . . Panna?"

Annisa stood up and backed away in disbelief. Yet another horror had befallen her. Panna's face was ashen, her tongue hanging out of her mouth as though gasping for air.

Slowly Annisa moved back towards her and sank to her knees beside her. "Panna?" With trembling hands, Annisa gently pulled back a strand of thin white hair. Panna's breath was gone. "Forgive me, Panna." Pulling the old woman's head onto her lap she sat there stroking her face until the sun was mid-heaven. Hunger pangs in her stomach broke through her grief. Her limbs cramped from sitting so long. She must collect her senses. She was alone. All she had to protect her was Allah and a scrap of paper in her belt.

First, she must bury the dead. She would gather stones from the hillside and pile them one by one until the remains of Zia's body were covered. The task gave her hope. It was something she could do. But when she returned with an armful of stones cradled inside the folds of her dress, she saw vultures circling in the sky. One hideous creature swooped down over her head with a bit of torn flesh in its mouth. Annisa dropped the stones and vomited into the dirt, praying that Zia would forgive her. She was too weak for the task. She knew she was on the edge now. She returned to Panna's body and began to pile the stones on her. But she had placed only a few when it struck her that Panna believed in cremation. Annisa sat down and wept. She was helpless; she could not even honor the dead. Without any means to make a fire how could she burn her beloved Panna? She too would have to be left to the birds of prey.

The tears had weakened her and Annisa realized from deep within that Panna had been right. Grief kills. She must leave this place, go for help. She must head for the border. Yet the path ahead was probably strewn with more mines. Someone had to inform Zia's family he was dead. Which way should she walk? Panna would want her to go forward and so would Zia. She could not stay here. She knew she had to move. In a daze, she searched for Zia's gun but soon realized he had been carrying it across his chest and, like his torso was now in bits and pieces. The money he carried she could not find. She patted her belt where the chit for the money bazaar in Peshawar was hidden. At least she had that. She must make it through. She returned to Panna's body and with sudden determination removed Panna's thick socks and put them on her own feet. Her ill-fitting shoes were useless. Walking in the woolen stockings relieved the blisters on her heels but the ground was sharp and full of stones and the bottoms of her feet were soon badly bruised.

Once she thought she heard the tinkle of bells on the lead camel of a caravan and shouted. But no answer came and she could see nothing ahead.

Near the end of the second day in the mountains alone, she collapsed under the limbs of a birch tree. In a daze, she watched the leaves shimmer above her head. She prayed to Allah that he would receive her and forgive her for her sins.

But death did not meet her and she awoke the next morning from a dream of her father. In the dream he had handed her a white dove to hold for him but the dove's heart beating within her palms had frightened her and she had opened her hands and let it fly away.

There were terrible cramps in her stomach. Blood trickled down the inside of her legs and soaked her chadri. In terror, she looked at the bloody garment and wondered if she too had been wounded without knowing it. She couldn't remember. An animal perhaps had bitten her in the middle of the night?

Half crazy with fear, she stared at the mysterious blood seeping onto her *chadri*. Then it came to her--the secret of womanhood Sabra had foretold. How could she go to anyone for help now? Men would see her bloodied clothes and turn away in shame.

"Oh, Allah, what have I done to deserve this terrible humiliation?" she cried.

And so it was that young Annisa entered womanhood, lost and alone on a desolate hillside in Afghanistan in the springtime of the war.

CHAPTER 13

For the first few days after she began her trek towards Peshawar Annisa had been certain she would make it. But on the morning of the third day she awoke to the realization she had been wandering in circles. Could she survive? She had managed to quench her thirst in a tiny trickle of water between the stones but how long could a human live without food? She had never paid much attention to nature and the bounties it could offer. What plants were safe to eat and what were not? Panna knew these things. And Panna was gone. But instead of feeling sorry for herself she began to look at her surroundings in a different way. The nudity of the universe was not to be feared, it could be her friend. She had never known what it was like to be truly alone nor had she heard the sounds of nature. They spoke to her. They told her there was a rhythm to all things. By the time the afternoon shadows had began to pool ahead of her path she was convinced that she was the only person left in the world. She was walking through the valley of death or was it the beginning of a new life? She felt pulled by an invisible string.

On the ridge. At sunset. A solitary figure on horseback appeared. His voluminous blouse, a blur of azure blue, was silhouetted against the red and pink of the sky.

As he galloped downwards towards Annisa, she could see that he was barefooted. He wore a *khortom* (a cord with a leather-covered stone on the end of it) and there was a rifle slung over his shoulder. The horn of a gazelle and a knife were tucked in his gun belt.

Annisa's feeling of terror at the approach of the fierce-looking tribesman, his long black turban whipping in the wind, suddenly turned into praise of Allah and the blessing he had bestowed upon her. God had sent a champion to defend her, a *Pay-yi-luch!* The man's uniform was that of the fierce, secret order of chevaliers-- the knights on horseback of Afghanistan.

In Kabul they were known as *kakas*--men from their earliest childhood respected for their piety. To join this sacred order, they had to pass many difficult tests. Her father had regaled her with stories of their secret duels with evil men and of how burning charcoal was placed on their back to test their fortitude. The *kakas* also carried *botah* with them, believing that hashish brought them closer to God and prevented them from committing sins. A *kaka* could never marry or look at the face of a woman; when one approached, he was to close his eyes or take another path.

But this man did not. And he spoke to her as he stared at her blood-soaked *chadri*.

"You are injured?" he asked as he dismounted his horse.

She felt ashamed if he should guess the true nature of her wound. "I am lost. Am I near Peshawar?"

"The other direction." His voice was intimidating. "A city filled with men with evil intent. Where is your home?"

"I have none." It was useless to try and explain. "The guide is dead. His body lies dishonored."

"There are many such bodies to be found in the mountains. . . Why do you ask about Peshawar? It is a wicked place. The Pakistanis are not Afghan; they were afraid to fight the British."

"I go to my brother in New York."

"Bah!" He spat on the ground. "Worse than Peshawar. What kind of a brother is this to leave you unprotected?"

"He studies to be a doctor."

The fierce-looking man held up his hand to silence her. "You must not go. If a lion cub spends too much time with donkeys he will lose his claws and his valor. The Americans will rob you of your nature. You should not wander like an ignorant seeker, from country to country. Countless men of our tradition stand behind you. What will become of your honor with the *ferrangi*?"

"But I have no one. I must go."

"I forbid it."

"Why do you even talk with me? Are you not a *Pay-yi-luch*?"

"The war has changed my intent. I have my own vows now. I must refuse no one in distress--particularly a sister."

His stern manner frightened her, but oddly enough, she also felt relief. She was lost and wandering aimlessly, not knowing where to go and now, someone was deciding for her. If only he would give her a little food and point her in the right direction--she was certain she could make it to the border alone.

He continued to stare at her blood soaked garments. "We must get help for you."

"Yes, in Peshawar."

"Better you die from your wounds than to enter that wicked city."

Annisa's mind was racing. Sabra and Ishaq could help her. She shuddered thinking she would have to give Zia's mother the terrible news of his death if she returned.

"I have friends in the village of Tezeen. I can stay with them."

"Climb up on my horse and I will take you there."

He watched her struggle to mount the horse that had no saddle, but did not offer to help.

"It's too difficult. I can't do this alone."

He removed a cloth from inside his tunic and placed it over his cupped hands. "Step on here but do not dare to touch me."

She was mortified because she knew she would bloody his blanket draped over his horse. What would he do if he knew the true nature of her wound, which was like the green henna leaf: fresh outside but bloody within.

After she had mounted, the *Pay-yi-luch* took the reins of his stallion and led it down the mountainside. It would be a long trip back to Tezeen because he could not share the ride with her--their bodies must not touch. Several times Annisa came close to falling off the horse when she dozed, only to have her head jerk violently when her benefactor shouted, "*Balla. Balla.* Up. Wake up."

Hours passed before they finally reached a highway that was dotted with potholes; the horn from an ancient taxi tooted as it passed them at great speed. "Demons. They go too fast. They could break an axle," he said, choking on the dust from the speeding car. "Deserters from the Afghan army."

"How can you be sure?"

"They carry new AK 47's."

On each side of the road stretched the fertile valley. The terrain began to look familiar to Annisa. It was reassuring. "I am very hungry," she said.

"There are raisins inside my knapsack." He undid the bag and handed it up to her. She scooped up a handful.

"Do you want some?"

"No, they are for you."

Their taste was sweet and juicy and their sugar content revived her spirits. "Am I allowed to ask you where you are from?"

"Wardak."

"Then you go out of your way to take me."

"Allah has willed it."

Not another word was exchanged between them until nightfall came and he motioned for Annisa to dismount. He tied the reins of his horse to a tree near an icy cold stream and left her to wash his face in the water. Then he built a fire with some sticks he had gathered and roasted a hunk of goat's meat from his knapsack. The stringy tough meat smelled of blood and it turned her stomach but she forced herself to eat and washed it down with water from the sweet tasting stream.

"You are an educated girl?"

"Yes."

"That is a stone to carry if you grow up disobedient."

"It was my father's wish I study."

"A woman should marry and have sons." With his barefeet he began to stamp out the hot coals of the fire. "Do not lose faith in yourself. Faith is the warmth in the embers when the fire has gone."

He made a bed for her on a bough of green leaves and motioned for her to lie down. Annisa was too weary to be afraid of him. Without hesitation she curled up at his feet and fell asleep, unaware he stood guard over her, searching the darkness for those with evil intent.

She dreamed she was in Kabul before the King. "You sit on a throne of judgment. Hear me out," she begged. Before the King could answer she awoke with a start and smelled the sweet, sticky odor of burning hashish. But she was too tired to sit up and plunged back into her dream where she now imagined *she* was the King with the face of a street urchin. A *sher-bacha*. One of those barefoot boys who roamed the bazaars and stirred up trouble.

In the morning the *Pay-yi-luch* told her, "In your sleep, you cried out for Zia. Your brother?"

"The guide who was killed."

"You have me to protect you now. Come. Daytime is meant for prayer and work; night is for dreams. Let us pray."

He unrolled his prayer rug and Annisa knelt down directly behind him. It was comforting to repeat the familiar words in the crystal light of early dawn. And when she had finished she thanked Allah for the gift of memory-- grateful she could close her eyes and still see the faces of those who had gone. Her father had been dead no more than a week but already she was fearful she would forget him. His face. His long delicate fingers. The sweetness in his voice reading to her his poems. It was a miracle she was still alive and did she deserve it? She knew now that she was a stranger in her own country. Her privileged and sheltered life in Kabul had shielded her from the harsh realities. Panna had been right; she was a shallow girl. Poor Panna who had catered to her every whim. She prayed she had not died judging her. Panna's faded blue eyes had stared out to her in death. Did they accuse or did they challenge? Without Panna to scold her she had nothing to push against. And all her life she had been pushing. Where should she go? What life should she choose? Had not Panna told her that the secret of life was to tend to one's own earth?

She also felt much stronger than the day before and the closer they came to Tezeen the more confidant she grew. Perhaps Ishaq himself would escort her to Peshawar. Hadn't Zia said that Ishaq usually made the trip? At the sight of the familiar archway above the entrance to the village, she was elated. Soon she would have clean clothes and a warm bed and once again she would see the endearing face of Sabra and be in the presence of the mythical figure Ishaq. As she was thinking this, a small pebble hit her in the shoulder. Startled, Annisa looked up to the top of an abandoned teahouse near the city gates. She saw a girl in a red dress and pigtails. It was Habiba, Sabra's little sister. She waved. "Habiba. It's me. Annisa."

But the little girl threw another stone that missed its mark and then ran to hide. Had she not recognized Annisa? Was she, perhaps, angry to see her returning without Zia?

"You know that child?"

"Yes."

"She acts very strange."

The *Pay-yi- luch* led Annisa on his horse through the gates of the village. She was puzzled to see the bazaars deserted at this time of day. The tinsmith's shop was padlocked, as was the shop where Zia had stopped on the way out to purchase cigarettes for the trip. "Where is everyone?"

"It is curious."

The road under the archway curved to the left and continued up the dirt road that led to Zia's house. The courtyard looked deserted. In the center, a basket of washing sat near the line with the clothes rolled neatly in balls. A large black dog with clipped ears was asleep beside it in the sun.

Nothing moved. Annisa spied a figure seated by the well where she had drawn water to bathe Panna's tired feet. It was an old man with a grizzly beard. He brushed a fly from his face as they approached.

"The people in this house? Where have they gone?"

"Dead," he answered, eyeing Annisa suspiciously. "The enemy came here."

"Dead!"

"Don't shout. It offends me." When he opened his mouth he revealed that he had no teeth.

Annisa leapt from the horse and in her haste tripped on the *chadri,* pitching headfirst in the dirt. Her benefactor did not move to help her up. She limped to the threshold of the house, which had so recently been filled, with the laughter of the wedding party. She peered inside. No one. It was heavy with the silence of a tomb. The smell of *sabsi,* a mixture of spinach and yogurt cooking in mint leaves on the *tandori* filled the room. She crossed to the large black pot and stirred the mixture. The sight of it made her mouth water. Two bowls sat in the middle of the carpet as though waiting for her to serve up, as though the food had been prepared to honor her return. Her eyes went to the bedroom door where Sasha had gone with Ishaq. It was ajar. Holding her breath and treading softly, Annisa crossed the room and entered. Then she screamed. Zia's mother lay on her back; her eyes like Panna's -- open to death. In one hand she clutched a handful of yellow flowers, in the other an earthen vase. The treasures of Sabra's hope chest were strewn around the room... The Russians had not only killed, they had looted. The fine jeweled pendant given to Sabra on her wedding night was missing from her slim neck, which hung limp over the side of the bed... 'This pendant has been in our family for generations,' Zia's mother had said on the night of *henna...* 'In America, does the family give the bride jewels? I think not if they do not honor their women.' Folded neatly on a satin pillow next to Sabra was the green silk veil she had worn on her wedding night and on top of this the *Zardi,* a veil that had covered her, multi-colored with golden threads.

Annisa sank to her knees beside the lifeless bodies on the bed and gently kissed Sabra's cheek. There were no marks on her body. How had she died?

One item the Russian pigs had missed. On the floor was a red and purple cape on which Sabra had embroidered flowers: a *degere desmal,* a special bib for Ishaq to wear around his neck when he shaved. It was all so senseless. Nothing was sacred. Honoring one's traditions was no guarantee of anything. Annisa backed away from the bed. It was then she spied her Nike jogging shoes on Sabra's feet... She looked down at her own feet and Panna's socks, which were torn and of little protection. Without hesitation she began to untie the laces of the shoes on Sabra.

The tall *Pay-yi-luch* had entered the room. "What is this? You steal from the dead!"

Annisa face grew hot with indignation. "I do not steal. These are mine and I need them."

He stood there watching her put on the shoes. "Hurry," he snapped. "The old man says he expects the Russians will return and soon. They are convinced these people know the hiding place of Commander Sadaqat."

"But everyone in the village is dead."

"Only this house. The others have fled into the hills to tell the men who were on a raid last night not to return."

It was a tiny ray of hope for her. Was Ishaq still alive? "I'll take my chances. I'll wait here."

His eyes blazed. "Come outside. Our talk disturbs the dead."

Annisa followed him into the brilliant sunlight. It was hot but her hands felt like ice.

"I will not leave you without protection."

"Are you certain no one is here?"

"Only the old man and just look at him."

She stared into the old man's milky eyes—-the eyes of glaucoma and she thought of Tawab. "Do you know where the blind boy is?" The *Pay-vi-luch* answered for him. "He told me the trouble started when a blind boy came out of this very house and fired a rifle. Without any sense of direction. It angered the interrogators."

"Tawab!"

"The boy is safe. By a miracle he escaped and has gone to join the men in the caves."

"I must go to him. I must tell Ishaq his brother Zia is dead."

"I forbid it. The caves are no place for a woman."

The black dog awoke, walked over to Annisa and began to sniff the blood between her legs. "Get away from me," she yelled and she began to run in the direction of the city gates. The disgrace. The humiliation. "I forbid you to go," the *Pay-vi-luch* shouted. She had to escape this man. He had rescued her only to become her jailer. She must get to Peshawar.

Once again he ordered her to stop. "Where do you run to?"

Annisa had no answer. She only wanted to flee.

He was by her side now. "The old man knows where we can go for help with your wounds."

139

"No. It is nothing. More blood shows than the wound deserves."
"But you are ill."
"I don't care. I can go no farther. Let the pigs take me. Let them take our country."
"How dare you speak this."
"I just want to go to my brother," she wailed.
"You are a stubborn girl."
"I am sick of the dying. There is no one left for me. No reason to live."
"Allah weeps to hear this."
"I wish to die."
"Then you are *dewana* like the girl. Look at her pawing at the earth--sticking clumps of dirt in her mouth."
"Maybe she is hungry."
"No, she is crazy in the head. Like a wild animal. She runs in circles."
"It must be fright from what she saw."

Habiba was pulling on her hair now, rocking from side to side.

"It's so sad. I can't take any more. I wish to die," Annisa repeated.

"Order yourself a coffin then and kneel before me. I have slain many before you. You are no good to anyone like this."

Annisa sucked in her breath. "You mean to kill me?"
"That is what you are asking."
"I just want peace. A place that is safe."
"There is no such place. Peace is only in the grave."
"In America. . ."

He leaned over and picked up a handful of dirt and held it under her nose. Slowly he let it sift through his fingers. "In each pinch of earth there are whole worlds. You refuse to see what is in them. You want to run away. You mock the memory of your people."

Annisa made her hand into a fist. "That is not true. My memory of Afghanistan is death. It was my father's wish I go to America."

"Hah. You wish to die. Miserable girl."

"Hail storms come from your part of the mountains. Others run away. I curse you. I run to meet the storm."

He stared at her. "Those are not your words."
"My father's. His poems."

"And do you know their meaning?"

Annisa lowered her head. "I do."

"That is better. . .A great evil has happened here. But you must choose to live. That will be your revenge."

"It is impossible to drive the invaders out without rockets. You said so yourself." She was fighting the sensation that she was going to faint.

"I saw a boy in Wardak who believed so much he grabbed the cannon of one of their tanks with his bare hands and burned the flesh off."

"Let me stay here. In this village," she begged.

"And leave you in the hands of the Russians when they return? Never. Have you no blood relatives left in Afghanistan?"

"Only my mother's people. . .I have uncles in the North. Outside Mazar-i-Sharif. In Doshi. They are Tajick. My father married into another tribe."

"No difference. We are all Afghans. Better you go to Doshi. The Tajiks are great fighters. There is much fighting in the north against the Russians."

"But my brother waits for me in America."

"That is between you and your relatives. I will deliver you to your people but my allegiance to the sacred vow of *namus* does not allow me to take you to a brother who lives among the infidels."

"The child. Habiba? Can I bring her with us? She has no one."

"If you wish. But I warn you, her mind seems empty."

Annisa nodded, aware of a strange sensation in the back of her head.

"You belong with our people."

Again Annisa nodded but the words to answer him would not come. There was a ringing in her ears, whispers that Ishaq was still alive--that she must try and trick the *Pay-yi-luch* into letting her stay in Tezeen. Then the orange blossoms on the ground came up to meet her and she pitched forward, a frail figure in a golden *chadri* soaked with blood. She need not worry. The fierce *Pay-yi-luch* would protect her. He would see her delivered safely to her own people in Doshi. It was his will and thus he believed the will of God.

141

CHAPTER 14

Najib Duranni would have liked not to face his wife until he had time to compose his thoughts. Her irate phone call had sent his heart racing. "I've told you never to call me at work. We'll discuss your crazy suspicions when I get home."

But within the hour Margahalia appeared in his office, brandishing the letter from Claire. Caught off guard, Najib went on the attack. "You have no business coming here."

"Say what you like. I have proof of your treachery." She threw a plain brown packet on his desk and Najib could feel his innards twist.

"Want to know where I got it?" The look of triumph in her eyes sickened him. "Lelah gave it to me. She caught a boy handing it off to that stupid husband of hers."

Inwardly, Najib cringed. The boy, who carried messages to his contact in the cloth bazaar, had made a fatal mistake--passing the packet off in front of the contact's wife. The wife, Lelah worked as a beautician and was a part of Margahalia's inner circle of gossips. Unfortunately, the drop of personal mail hand-carried in from Peshawar occasionally included instructions from the Resistance. It was always a risk. What if there was more than just a letter from Claire?

"You sneak, how do you think you're going to get out of this!" Margahalia snarled. A string of accusations followed and Najib stood up hastily and closed the outer door.

"Lower your voice, you are creating a scene."

"I'll create more than that, you piece of camel dung. You are going to pay for this."

"First, you have to tell me what I have allegedly done."

She pointed to the packet. "Go ahead. Open it. I want to watch the look on your face as you do."

Najib was so relieved to see the packet held only an empty envelope with Claire's name on it that he regained some of his composure. Claire knew nothing of the details of his work--only who to contact when she wanted to get a message to him. "There's nothing in here."

She unfolded the letter she held and smoothed it out on his desk. "Read it. Read this filth."

"I can't make it out. The handwriting is terrible," he bluffed.

"Want me to tell you what it says?"

"That won't be necessary." He willed his features to remain composed as he scanned the pages. Fortunately, Claire made no reference to the rendezvous in Cairo he had proposed. Evidently, she had not received his message yet. Rather, it was a love letter which was highly unusual for Claire. The very guarded Claire, was not one to reveal her passions verbally, let alone, put them down on paper. She had refined the chosen isolation of the English to an art form. A successful career girl at the BBC, Claire was often a clever mimic of the sentimental. She abhorred the image of the rose covered cottage and the platitudes that went with it. In fact, so much of their time together he had wondered if it all meant as much to her. In the confiscated letter, Claire dwelled on some of the more intimate details of their relationship, and in particular a night they had spent together on a secluded beach in the Canary Islands. No wonder Margahalia was livid.

Najib looked up and glared at his wife. "This is gibberish you bring me. I don't know this person."

"Liar."

"I told you to keep your voice down."

"Why? I want the whole world to know."

"You also want me to get a promotion."

"Hah, so that you will travel even more than you do-- sneaking in and out of the country to British whores who service you in Pakistan."

"That's a lie." This time his indignation was real. "I have never had a whore in my life."

"Oh yes, you have."

The conviction in her voice alarmed him. He could feel his lower jaw begin to twitch. "This letter makes no mention of whores. The lady sounds much too personal."

Margahalia smiled. "There was *another* letter in this packet of filth."

"Let me see it."

Her eyes narrowed in triumph. "Not on your life. This one names time and places. "

The back of Najib's shirt felt wet from his sweat and he was fearful it would soak through his jacket and reveal his fear. The only option he had was to out bluff her.

143

"Then don't show it to me. A packet of lies is of no concern to me."

"It is to me. You will bring no bastard children into our house!"

"Have you lost your senses? What bastard children?"

"I'm not leaving here until you tell me the truth."

"How can I tell you anything if I don't know what you are talking about?"

"Your friend in Peshawar, a Mr. Reed does. The Reverend writes it is urgent you contact him. What should he do? The girl Annisa is 'long overdue.'"

Najib could feel his jaw twitching and struggled to contain it. Margahalia's misinterpretation of the message—that Annisa was pregnant-- would have been humorous if it did not have a more sinister indication. The message meant that Annisa had not yet made it to Peshawar. This was a real cause for concern. She had left with Zia almost three weeks ago and he had thought by now she would be on a plane to Rahmin.

"What do you have to say for yourself?"

"That you have been duped. I gather intelligence for our government in Peshawar. Part of my job is to stir up trouble between the tribal leaders. I have to be away from home. You know that."

"I also know you have other women and now I have my proof."

"I swear on all that is holy I have never been to a whore."

"Then just why was this packet to be delivered to you? I warn you, I intend to get to the bottom of this. And Lelah is very curious indeed as to why her husband is receiving messages to be hand delivered to Captain Duranni."

The possibility of his contact being interrogated devastated him. "Look, if it will put your fears to rest, I'll ask to be transferred out of intelligence or at least not to travel outside Afghanistan. I don't like being away from you anymore than you do."

"You expect me to believe this."

"You have to, it's true. . .Perhaps you can help? You are a friend of Orkunium. The Colonel likes you. I'm sure he would try to do you a favor if possible."

"Najib Duranni, I know you. You are hiding something. You are being much too slick about this. It is one thing to go to whores, but to arrange to have them send messages to you from Peshawar? Something else is going on."

Najib thumped the pages of the letter he held in his hand. "Please note, *this* letter is addressed to 'Dearest,' not 'Dearest Najib.' It could be meant for anyone."

"So the boy who brought the packet just happened to make up your name? You really think I'm that naive?"

"Margahalia, did you even stop to think that this might be a way to frame me?"

"Who would want to do that?"

"There are people jealous of our position. Some of them work in this very building. Because of our connections, we enjoy special privileges and you know it. Or, it could even be some low-life who works for the Resistance. I have a reputation with the Mujahideen as someone to fear. What better way for them to destroy me than to discredit me with my beautiful wife?" He could see a glimmer of doubt in her eyes now and he breathed a little easier. "Margahalia, as God is my witnesses, I have nothing to do with whores."

"And the pregnant one in Peshawar. Annisa?"

He could feel his guts cramp at the mention of her name. "The only Annisa I know is the young daughter of our late friend, Dr. Aziz."

"That brat. Good riddance. You had your eye on her. I was glad to hear she has disappeared from Kabul."

"I'm sorry to hear that. Her father's death was a terrible tragedy. The man practically raised me."

"Spare me your pitiful sentimentality. Dr. Aziz was such a bore. His poetry sounded like an old woman and he looked a mess. Scuffed up shoes; soup stains on his tie."

Najib wanted to pummel her but instead he spent the good part of the next hour in cajoling; playing to her vanity. How could he possibly be interested in other women when he was married to such a beauty? Everyone said so. Najib knew on some level that Margahalia wasn't buying his act and that she would do further checking, but at least he had bought some time. He had to keep his wits about him. Annisa had not made it to Peshawar. Where was she? Rahmin would be frantic with worry. On top of his wife's suspicions he had another cause for alarm. From his hospital bed, Colonel Orkunium had asked for an inquiry into the disappearance of Corporal Yuri Vitrovich. Najib knew he was suspect and that his home phone was being bugged. He would have to move fast. His sources outside of Kabul must be warned immediately that one of their drop off points in Kabul had been compromised. Discovery of the packet was a costly mistake. His biggest worry was that preparations were underway for him to see Gregory Meirnardus again. The newly appointed Egyptian ambassador to Pakistan was taking a terrible risk in these clandestine meetings. The truth was that Gregory Meirnardus was circumventing his own government in an effort to negotiate some order out of the chaos between rival Mujahideen factions. There were long term plans for Najib to work closely with a member of his staff--once Najib had made the break and defected from the puppet government in Kabul.

After Margahalia left his office, Najib remained slumped in his chair, staring into space. He was exhausted and totally drained of his self-respect. The flattery, which his greedy wife so easily devoured, had made him sick of himself. He had to get out of here. Away from his own deceit and the rapacious people who made up his life. He distrusted his mood, aware that his disgust might overrule what was prudent.

If only he could have kept Claire's letter so that he could memorize every word. It had been almost three months since he had heard from her and anything from Claire always turned him inside out. This letter was such a breakthrough from her guarded self that it was almost hard to believe she wrote it. But she had. There were too many intimate details from that night on the beach. Thinking of it left him weak with desire.

He closed his eyes and saw Claire racing toward the ocean, pulling her cotton dress over her head as she ran. He did not follow her but enjoyed her wantonness as she splashed naked through the water. He burned with lust--so much so that for a moment he thought he had imagined her.

"It's much colder now," she called. The moon caught her beautiful body as she turned to him, arms outstretched. She was alive, triumphant, bountiful and free, far beyond the mystery of the veil.

Najib met her in the water and carried her to their blanket on the sand and took her.

Afterwards they talked for the first time about a future.

"You're married, aren't you?" she had asked him.

"Does it matter?"

"Only if you decide to come back to England for good."

He had wanted to believe that he would.

"Najib, does it bother you, this business of being split in two like a wishbone. Another place, another life."

"Never before tonight."

Beyond their blanket in the moonlight, the waves lapped the sands. The surf was gentle. She traced her name on his chest. "Talk about your country."

"Crystal steams, high up in the mountains, pools of moonlight etch the ridges. . . ." He reached down and kissed her full, welcoming mouth. His hands on her white buttocks pressed her tightly to him as he entered her. She met him, a perfect tension; a living pendulum set in motion. They did not rush the act. Confident, feeding each other's rhythms, they peaked. He read the pleasure in her open eyes. He had known many women in his life but never anyone like this. It was her independence that held him. She was quick to challenge but even quicker to surrender. She also had a remarkable wit that was subtle and never cruel. Everything about her enthralled him. The day after they had first met in London, he had followed a woman for several blocks who was wearing Claire's perfume. Claire had been amused when he repeated the incident. "You believe in things other than words don't you? No wonder they warn young maidens to beware of Afghan men."

"Is that a compliment?"

"I'm not sure. Englishmen are rather good with words and that can be a bloody bore at times. But that is nothing compared to the tragic tales about Afghans-- the pitfalls of your legendary dark good looks and instant charm and then stories of being whisked off to Kabul where one meets the first wife, the children and his mother who all live happily under the same roof in a mud house with no plumbing. Forget the photographs of the palace he's represented as pictures of his home."

"Unfortunately, I don't have any pictures with me."

She smiled. "You I don't worry about. You are such a dandy I doubt very much if you would settle for a mud house."

After their first meeting he had pursued her for months despite her lack of encouragement. It was Claire who called the shots. The night of his graduation from Sandhurst she had left a message for him to call. She had a week off and was going to the islands.

It would be years later before he would discover that Claire was not as casual about him as she wanted him to believe. But she was simply too proud, or too sensible to give it credence. In return, he had never really confessed how serious he was about her.

"Captain Duranni?"

Najib looked up, startled to see one of the guards standing in front of his desk. The man was out of breath.

"Sir, come quickly. You are wanted upstairs. The Commander."

"What's the rush?"

"A terrible thing has happened."

Najib had an acid taste in his mouth, imagining the worst. He had been exposed. Perhaps there were other papers in that packet Margahalia hadn't mentioned. The woman was diabolical.

He entered the office of the Afghan in charge of the KHAD, the dreaded Afghan secret police. Najib's face remained stoic but his kneecaps were shaking under his uniform pants.

"You sent for me, sir?"

"Yes It's about Colonel Orkunium."

Najib rushed to say something. "His recovery has been much slower than expected. I assure you that we are handling. . ."

"The Colonel has been kidnapped, snatched by the Resistance forces from his hospital bed. They demand the release of political prisoners for his exchange."

Weak with relief, it was easy for Najib to feign concern. "This is a terrible blow to the KHAD," he said.

"It could be disaster if they force certain information out of him."

"My thoughts exactly."

"Then we must see this doesn't happen. I understand his driver was taken with him. Safiq, you know this man?"

"Yes."

"You are to be our contact with the Mujahideen. Ask to speak with Safiq before the Colonel."

Najib was startled at this turn of events. It was common knowledge that Safiq was disgruntled and that he flirted with the Resistance.

"What are we willing to trade for Orkunium?"

"You are simply to stall them."

"For how long?"

"Long enough." He threw up his hands. "It won't be easy. They are an impatient lot."

Najib immediately got the drift. Orkunium had outlived his usefulness to the Afghan secret police. Was this a hint of yet another coup? He had heard rumblings about a change in command.

"Moscow must be convinced of how great an effort we made. The rest is up to you."

"It will be as you wish." It was hard for Najib to suppress his glee. Allah had just sent him his one-way ticket out of Kabul.

"Will that be all, sir?"

"Not quite. Why did you intercede on behalf of Dr. Aziz."

Najib stiffened his fingers. His exuberance had been premature. "Dr. Aziz was an old family friend and . . ."

"I know that."

"He was of no threat to the government."

"That was not your decision to make."

"Yes, sir. I was wrong."

"And then there is that little matter of your wife. She is a loose cannon. Hurling false accusations about your womanizing to anyone who will listen."

In a split second Najib decided to admit a truth in order to cover up a bigger lie. "My wife has good reason."

"I see." The director pushed back his chair and walked around the front of his desk, positioning himself only inches from Najib's face. "You are either very clever or very foolish." He tapped his finger on Najib's chest. "I think foolish. This is what happens when we send our brightest young men to be trained in the West."

"My wife accuses me of things that happened years ago. When I was at Sandhurst, sir."

"Well, I want all her complaints stopped and now. We are grooming you for big things in the government. If you can't control your wife you are of no use to us. If we are to legitimatize ourselves with the rest of the world there must be no hint of scandal in our leaders."

"Consider it done."

"I'm going to trust you, Duranni."

"Thank you, sir."

"Your father made a big mistake in attempting to leave the country. We had big things planned for him had he stayed. But then he always was too rigid for his own good. You agree?"

"Indeed." Inwardly, Najib burned. The very thing he had spent a lifetime accusing his father of he could not tolerate from the lips of others.

"The people's government will bring a bright future to Afghanistan. I believe that."

"So do I, sir."

After he was dismissed Najib hurriedly left the building. He was exhilarated-- almost giddy. He was about to become a free man. His original plan was still in place. A large number of handpicked men waited for his signal to empty the jails before making their move over to the Resistance. The pretext that he was going to Paghman for negotiations concerning Colonel Orkunium was the perfect foil. As for Orkunium? Najib was certain the Resistance in a very short time would dispatch him--Orkunium would refuse to cooperate. The man was tough. He would not bend. Too bad Yuri Vitrovich wouldn't be there when he met his demise. Najib would have loved to see the look on the Russian's face.

It wasn't until Najib had walked several blocks that the reality of his situation set in. This time he was leaving Kabul for good--perhaps never to return. He would shed his smart uniform and the only way of life he had ever known for the challenge of the mountains and the equally harrowing existence of intrigue among diplomats. His military career was finished--his future uncertain. How could he hope to support a girl like Claire? Her job at the BBC paid more now than he could ever earn. In his mind he was already rehearsing sentences he could never say. It was hard to admit that he had no hope for himself but could not accept hopelessness in others. And what had become of sweet Annisa-jan? Where was she? He must find her and deliver her safely out of Afghanistan. As soon as he was finished in Paghman he would head for Kakark and try to re-trace the route she took. He was pledged to be her protector. This he would honor above all else.

1983

CHAPTER 15

A cloud of dust rolled across the playing field, which stretched as far as the eye could see. The team from Mazar-i-Sharif had arrived. Waiting for them in a jagged line were the *buzkashi* players of Baghlan Province, fierce-looking men in wolf skin caps astride horses which measured over 17 hands tall. It was the 16th of August. *Jeshin Isteqlal.* A hot day. A day the color of dust. To the crowds milling around waiting for the clandestine celebration of *Jeshin* to begin, it seemed a poor replica of yesteryears. Gone were the high silk flags whipping in the wind, the gleaming brass trumpets and the drum rolls. No fireworks. No grandstands of Afghan dignitaries for the horsemen to parade before. No cash for the winning *chapandaz* when he tossed the beheaded calf or goat into the Circle of Justice. Only a few food vendors weaving in and out of the crowd of bearded men and Tajik women in long red dresses, their picnic lunches tied up in scarves. The puppet government in Kabul had announced that the Afghan people were no longer to celebrate their annual Independence Festival. Next year, in the spring, they would commemorate the anniversary of the Communist Saur Revolution instead.

"How many players have they brought?" asked Abdul El-Ham, the famous *chapandaz* from the village of Doshi.

His older brother, Omar, son of their father's first wife, shielded his eyes to the sun. "Fifty--sixty, perhaps more." He threw down the lime sack he had just emptied drawing the Circle of Justice in the middle of the field, and brushed his big, callused hands on his pantaloons. "Daldal champs to do battle."

Abdul pulled in the reins of his mount Daldal, who pawed frantically at the parched earth. "He smells the sweat of our opponents."

Omar reached up and patted his brother's horse. It was as handsome and arrogant as its rider was. Five years in the training and three years more in the game--nothing was ever spared for Daldal. This morning he had breakfasted on melons and barley mixed with raw eggs and butter. The horse ate better than the family of Omar El-Ham. "How is your leg, my brother? This is the first time you play with a Russian bullet in your knee."

"I can ride with one stiff leg better than men with two that bend."

Omar smothered a smile.

"Have Zinjarani's men delivered the dynamite?"

"Yes. We start our long journey to the Amu Darya tomorrow." Omar's plain yet expressive face broke into a satisfied grin. "Oh, to hear those Russian pigs squeal when we blow up the bridge." It was their second attempt. They had failed the first time.

Suddenly Abdul turned in his saddle and shouted at a little girl who had come up behind his horse. "Idiot child. Stay back."

Omar bent over and scooped the girl with the vacant stare into his arms. "Habiba, jan. Abdul's horse is trained to kick and bite." He called to a woman standing nearby who was haggling with a soft drinks vendor. "Annisa, come get little Habiba."

Her eyes bright with excitement, Annisa ran towards Omar. "Sorry. I was so busy looking around she got away."

"I told you not to bring Habiba," Abdul growled. "The game will go all day. Your hands will be full with the half-wit."

Annisa tossed her head back and glared at her uncle Abdul, sitting high above her on his magnificent horse.

"Don't give me your evil eye. If ever I hear you have ridden my horse again, I will have you whipped. No one rides Daldal but me. Do you understand!"

Omar, the family peacemaker, signaled Annisa it would be wise not to answer as he handed her Habiba. "After the game I will buy you both some sweets."

"You reward her for riding my horse?" Abdul was furious. "It disturbs my rhythm with Daldal."

Fatima, Omar's pregnant wife, who had followed after Annisa, arrived out of breath, her face crimson from the heat. "Annisa not only thinks she can ride. Twice I have seen her down by the river shooting your pistol, my husband."

Omar looked incredulous. "Is that true!"

"Ask her if you do not believe me."

Annisa avoided his eyes.

"Annisa. Is this true? You waste valuable ammunition needed by the Mujahideen?" Omar, who never wore a turban or a hat, reached up and wiped tiny beads of sweat from his baldhead. "I asked you a question."

"Yes. . .I practice to kill Russians."

"Russians!" Abdul made a rude gesture. "It won't be Russians you kill. Your cooking will finish us all. What did they teach you in that miserable school in Kabul?"

Annisa's contempt for Abdul showed in her eyes. "They taught me it is better to have a bad rider on a good horse than a good rider on a bad horse. No wonder you always win. It is Daldal, not you."

"It is good your face is not plain, Annisa. With a tongue like yours it would be impossible to get a good bride price for you."

"Bride price. Never. I will choose the man I marry."

But Abdul did not hear her retort, having galloped towards the center of the field to meet with the captain of the opposing team.

Omar's voice was gentle. "Annisa-jan, take Habiba and go sit by the concession stand. The child has no sense. She could get hurt."

As she turned to go, Omar called after her. "Don't be upset. I honor your desire to help. But you must never play with my gun again. We will think of other ways you can be a part of the resistance."

Fatima glared at her husband as he watched Annisa wend her way with Habiba back through the crowd towards a cluster of trees more than 200 yards from the edge of the playing field. "You have eyes for the girl."

"She is only a child."

"Then you are blind. She is 16 now and should be married. I tell you she is no help to me. A real nuisance in the village with her talks about a school. Yet you encourage her."

"Annisa is skilled. The world spins very fast, my wife. Our children must learn to read and write. Look at me. I get a box of dynamite and detonators to blow up the bridge and I cannot read the instructions. It was Annisa who helped me. The girl is smart."

"Unlike you--believing that the Russian dog Yuri knew all about explosives. He lied to you."

"I would have lied too if it meant not being shot. Yuri did what he had to do in order to stay alive."

"And yet he goes with you on this second attempt."

"Certainly. Yuri is the bravest man among us. A warrior. He would die for me."

"Not before he eats your share of the food. He is a glutton. And I don't like the time he spends with Annisa."

"Hah, if you had your way Annisa would never leave the house."

Fatima, a woman who would be considered pretty if it were not for her heavy brows and a large mole on her chin, gave him a dark look. "I forbid you to take Annisa on the raid this time. She is trouble. With her hot blood the sooner we marry her off the better. She will destroy this family yet."

"Enough," Omar said wearily.

"No, it is not enough. When I talked to her of Abdul for a husband, she had the nerve to tell me it was not right for relatives to marry. This from a mother and father from different tribes. Only in Kabul could such a thing happen."

"Woman. Enough of this!" Omar stomped off towards the Circle of Justice, which was now ringed by players on horseback from both teams. He was hounded by his guilt. No one but Yuri knew that the letters Annisa wrote to her brother were never passed on. Instead, Omar would burn them late at night in the *tandori*, praying that she would never discover his treachery. He could not bear to lose her and he justified this by telling himself she would not fare well in America. Annisa was an Afghan girl. She belonged here. And yet, the dejection, the disappointment in her eyes when she never received an answer, had begun to gnaw at his innards. It was not all his fault. Hadn't the tall *Pay-vi-luch* who had delivered Annisa to Doshi advised him to hide the truth? 'Do not tell the others but I plan to leave word in Kakark that I found her body in the mountains along with her guide. She said his name was Zia. This should stop any further mischief to send her to America. The girl belongs to us. She is educated and she is bold. She can teach your sons.'

At the far end of the field Omar looked to the mud house shaped like a beehive. Through the hole in its dome roof, smoke curled from the cooking pots. It had been decided that this house would serve as the turning point for the riders. If a player managed to grab the goat carcass and lift it to his saddle, he had to carry it to the house and circle it before returning to the center of the field. If the carcass should slide outside the Circle of Justice, no goal would be scored. It was uneven terrain. Many riders and horses would fall before the day was won.

When Omar stepped through the lines of horsemen into the circle, he drew back in revulsion. Lying inside the ring of players was the body of a decapitated Russian soldier, fresh blood oozing from his severed neck.

The slant-eyed captain from Mazar grinned. "No farmer could spare us a goat, so we saved this Russian pig for the ball."

"*You* are the swine." Omar shook his fist under the man's nose.

"Don't heat your blood. This Russian gets better than he deserves. The wife of a Mujahideen refused to reveal his hiding place to this vile creature so he made her watch her baby roasted alive on a spit."

"Our invaders are bestial. Do you want to be like them?" Omar pointed to the headless corpse. "This sickens me."

"You are not in the game. You have no say."

Abdul gave his older brother a disdainful look. "Our ancestors played with human corpses."

"Then curse our ancestors. I want no part of this." Pushing his way out of the circle, Omar hurried to the edge of the crowd and stood beside the old mullah, Makhmoor. The holy man would officially start the game.

"Are they ready?"

Omar nodded. "But you will not like what you see."

With great flurry, Makhmoor raised the ancient rifle that his great grandfather had used against the British and fired. The sudden noise flushed out a covey of quail as men and horses too exploded in a frenzy inside the circle. Holding the whips between their teeth the riders charged each other in a fierce battle to be the first to pick up the headless soldier.

Triumphant shouts went up from the spectators when they saw that the men from Baghlan had seized the "ball" first. Abdul El-Ham rode ahead of the pack of over a hundred horsemen who thundered after him as he raced for the dome-shaped house. "*Raftan.* Go. Go. Go."

Soon the riders were out of sight, enveloped in a cloud of dust. The spectators that ringed the field surged forward onto the playing ground in an effort to see better. Then the dust lifted and the crowd roared, "Pick it up." The corpse was on the ground.

Annisa, who had once again defied Omar's orders to watch from a safe distance, fought her way to the front of the crowd, holding tight to little Habiba's hand. "*Raftan. Raftan,*" she shouted as she saw Abdul retrieve the carcass and disappear behind the house.

"Annisa!" Omar thundered. "You disobeyed me."

"Oh, please. In a minute. It's so exciting."

"It is a gruesome sight. Go and sit with Fatima. She spreads a lunch for us."

"But you promised I could see Abdul play. Fatima says there may never be another game. . .Oh, no," she gasped and pointed to the field. "Omar. A man. It is not a goat he carries. It is the body of a man!"

A roar from the crowd drowned Omar's answer out. A horseman from Mazar had cut through the riders protecting Abdul's race for the Circle of Justice and wrested the corpse from his arms. Once again the mutilated body fell to the ground and riders folded in and out of the circular mass, arms dangling to the ground, each man trying to snatch the fallen prize. Two men from opposite teams grabbed the body at the same time. Clinging to their mounts by their stirrups, they pulled on it to gain control. An arm ripped from the torso. Annisa stared in horror and fascination. She could not look away. Reinforcements from Abdul's team whizzed by the struggling pair. Knocking his opponent to the ground, Abdul emerged from the melee with the "ball" slung across his saddle.

"Omar shouted. "Shift. Your bad leg. Pull Daldal to the right."

Abdul was heading again towards the distant beehive house and the crowd roared its approval. But before Abdul could round the goal, three horsemen from Mazar headed him off. Daldal veered to the left and the riders chased him back across the field they had just crossed straight towards the crowd where Annisa stood with Habiba and Omar. Spectators parted in a frantic wave to avoid the stampeding horses. Legs and arms flailed the air in a mad scramble to escape. Vendor's trays of sweets and drinks went flying and little Habiba broke away from Annisa and ran directly into the path of the oncoming horsemen. Omar chased after her and snatched Habiba out of their way. He held her high over his head as the horsemen thundered by.

Her mouth full of dust and shaking, Annisa ran towards them.

"Take her back to Fatima." Omar handed her the frightened child who was screaming in terror.

Fatima stood watching, hands on her hips, as Annisa came up to her. "I saw what happened. Omar warned you."

"It's so terrible."

"You insisted on coming."

"Up close. They play with the body of a Russian soldier."

"So? Are you not the girl who wants to kill Russians."

"But Fatima, it is savage. It makes me ashamed to be an Afghan."

Fatima spat at her feet.

Her eyes defiant, Annisa ground her heel in the spit. "Abdul is a mad-man to play such game. My father always said. . ."

"I am sick of your father and sick of you. For months you pester us to see *buzkashi* and now you complain. Your wonderful life in Kabul is all you ever talk about. We are your family now. You come to us for shelter and bring another hungry mouth with you. Mad! I'll show you something mad." She pointed to Habiba whose crying had ceased and who was happily smearing her face with *burini*, a mixture of eggplant and sour cream which Fatima had set out for their lunch. "That is mad."

Annisa grabbed the bowl from Habiba's hands. "The war has done this to her."

"Yes, and it wasn't Afghans. Just look at her. There is no end to it." Habiba had taken the lid off a dish of *torshi* and was squishing her fingers in the bowl. "The child is an animal."

Annisa was not to be denied the last word. "So are the men playing this game. I should have gone to Peshawar and on to Rahmin."

Fatima was busy wiping Habiba's fingers clean with a rag. "More threats again? You think of no one but yourself. Months go by and still no word from your glorious brother. Rahmin does not care for you."

"Omar says my messages must not be reaching him."

"Omar will say anything. He wants you here." Fatima bit down on her lip. She had said too much and without thinking. She knew for a fact that Omar took the letters from Annisa and only pretended to pass them on. She had overheard the Russian defector Yuri accuse her husband of this very thing. Yuri, who lived in a cave by day and rode with the Mujahideen at night, was against Omar letting Annisa help with their plans. The Russian saw Annisa as frivolous but worse yet as a source of tension between the men. The girl knew none of this.

"Do you?"

"Do I what?"

"Care if I stay, Fatima."

"Why should I? You spend all day chasing after this idiot girl. What does she mean to you? She is not even your blood."

"Habiba has no one." Annisa's face suddenly crumpled. "I know I upset you, Fatima, but I don't mean to. I know how much you love Habiba."

"Love? Hah. I am sick of that child."

"I see the extra food you give her when no one is looking. It is often your share."

Fatima looked embarrassed. "So? A child has to be fed."

"*Zafar*," the crowd cheered behind them. "*Zafar!*" Both women turned in time to see Abdul holding his whip high above his head. "We have scored," Fatima said. "There will be great rejoicing in the house of El-Ham tonight."

"How can two brothers be so different. Abdul is so full of himself. I would die before I would marry such a man."

"You are crazy like the child. There is not a girl in Doshi who would not be the bride of a famous *chapandaz*."

"He's much too old for me. And coarse and stupid. Abdul has the manners of a peasant."

"So you think you are better than us?"

Annisa's face flushed.

"And this man on a white horse, this Ishaq you daydream about. Did he not work the fields?"

"I don't want to talk about him and I'm sorry I ever told you about that beautiful night of the wedding. It was perfect love."

"Well, you had better get this Ishaq out of your head or there will never be room for anyone real."

"If Abdul is 'real' than I want no part of it."

"How can you be so unfair? Abdul is devout. Unlike my Omar, Abdul prays each day and he knows by heart many verses of the Koran. Your uncle is a prophet! Do you know that before father Ismael died, Abdul foretold the Russian invasion and that troops would cross a bridge from Termez."

"Then Abdul was wrong. I should know. I was in Kabul when it happened. All day, all night you could hear the planes ferrying in the troops. They came by air."

"Yes, haughty girl. But now they come by bridge, and tomorrow the men of the family of El-Ham start on their long journey to the border to blow it up." Fatima patted her pregnant belly. "They will be gone many days and my husband will not be here when I birth. A woman gives life but it is how a man meets death the world honors. I think the men enjoy this war too much. Especially my Omar."

"Omar hates fighting. He is gentle and kind."

"A lot you know. A woman never experiences a man until she lies down with him. I know this will disappoint you but Omar has promised me he will not take a second wife." Fatima's eyes

159

gleamed with triumph as she studied Annisa's face. "Despite your gushing over his every word, Omar has no lust for you."

"Your thoughts are disgusting."

"Go ahead, turn up your nose at me. You will not have my husband."

The riders were almost parallel now to where the two women were arguing. Fatima grabbed Annisa by the arm. "See. Again, Abdul has the prize."

But as soon as she spoke, a circle of horses surrounded Abdul. Slashing whips and the weight of the torso slung across his saddle threw Abdul sideways. When he regained control, horse and rider were one. "Look how he moves. It is beautiful. No man in the province can ride like Abdul."

"*Raftan.* Go. Go. Go." The crowd roared.

Without warning a horse from the Mazar-i-Sharif team came from the sidelines where its rider had remounted after a fall. Rider and horse charged head on into Daldal, knocking both horses to the ground. Abdul fell in the maelstrom of flailing hoofs.

Omar shouted for his brother, racing out from the other side of the field.

The game did not stop for the fallen. Another player had the carcass on his horse and was heading off in the direction of the goal. A great wail went up from the crowd. No one could catch him.

At the other end of the field the riderless Daldal stood guard over his unconscious master while Omar, on his knees, struggled to lift his brother to carry him to safety. He struggled towards a clump of trees, waving aside those who would help. He laid Abdul on the coverlet Fatima had spread for the food.

"He is finished," Fatima gasped.

"Tear off the bottom of your skirt. I need it to stop the blood."

Abdul opened his eyes and groaned. "Send the women away."

Fatima grabbed Annisa by the arm. "This is your fault. You ruined Daldal's timing by riding him secretly at night. It is you who have caused this."

Annisa jerked away from her in horror. "No, no."

"*Bash.* Leave the girl alone," Omar barked. "Go for the Mullah, Makhmoor. And Annisa, bring Daldal over here."

The two women ran to do his bidding.

"Have they gone?" Abdul whispered.

"Yes, my brother."

Omar undid his brother's belt and stared in disbelief. The horses' hooves had mangled Abdul's manhood. Quickly he covered Abdul's pelvis with the coverlet.

Abdul's eyes burned with agony. "No one must know of this."

"On my honor. Only I will nurse you."

"Daldal?"

"Not a scratch." Omar was watching his brother beat his fists on the ground as he fought against the pain.

"Take my gun, older brother. Put it to my head before the women return."

"I am not brave enough to do such a thing."

"Then I shall live as half a man." Abdul gave an agonizing moan and his eyes closed. The great *chapandaz* was unconscious again.

Omar raised his fists over his head and shouted at God. "Damn you. You play tricks! Is this how you reward those who believe? I make a bargain, Allah. I bend to your will if he survives."

"*Adalat. Adalat. Adalat.*" The chanting grew louder as another horseman from Abdul's team galloped in the direction of the crowd. The crowd roared as he tossed the remains of the Russian's body into the Circle of Justice. The rider's arm shot high in the air, waving his whip. Once again, the men from Baghlan Province had scored.

161

CHAPTER 16

The ambush of the Russian convoy was to take place an hour before dawn. For the trucks coming out of the Salang Tunnel, renamed "the maw of hell" because it belched out a deadly flow of tanks and troops, there would be no place to go except straight ahead into the roadblock. Next to the entrance, the embankment dropped off sharply into deep, snow-filled canyons below, where tiny points of light sparkled in the winter air. The Mujahideen, positioned on the jagged ridge directly above, sent up flares to warn the guerrillas preparing the barricade that the enemy had emerged from the mouth of the tunnel too soon.

"No! We are surprised. Not now!" Yuri Vitrovich, the Russian defector and second in command for the raid, shouted the orders from his vantagepoint high in the frozen mountain. His companion, Omar El-Ham, the leader of the ambush, pushed his horse down the icy incline, ignoring the warning. He lobbed an incendiary grenade under the lead truck as he rode. The attack was on.

A flash from the explosion lighted up the slick, black band of highway that snaked out of the mouth of the tunnel. Soldiers from the burning truck scrambled to the ground, their clothes on fire— becoming human torches of burning flesh. They were not Soviet troops, but Afghan army regulars. The Russians had played an old trick: putting Afghan soldiers at the front of the convoy. In case of trouble, Afghans would slaughter Afghans. The middle trucks, loaded with heavy equipment and back-up Soviet guards, would stand a better chance of getting through. It was a familiar ploy.

The Soviet machine gun, a deadly DShk mounted on the flat bed of a truck, opened fire on the hapless men in the middle of the road. The Mujahideen, caught in front of their own barrier, foolishly did not head for cover behind the spur of rocks above the road. Instead, they stayed to fight, charging the convoy head-on. The big Russian gun cut down a dozen Mujahideen in less than a minute.

The slaughter on the highway was illuminated now in a kaleidoscope of color. Golden arches of light and flaming tracer bullets crisscrossed the heavy sky. From ill-chosen pockets in the hillside, the rocket grenades fell short of the target.

Yuri was disgusted. The whole action was a terrible waste. Anti-tank missiles were precious and hard to procure. They should have held their fire when they saw the rout below. Instead, the Afghans exhausted what little ammunition they possessed.

Cursing the rashness of Omar's action, Yuri picked his way down the cuts in the glacial ridge, two grenades in his pouch. His initial throw had missed the mark, wounding only the mountainside, which rose barren and desolate from the road. But the second throw destroyed the cab of the second truck, blocking the entrance of the tunnel.

Suddenly, the machine gun slicing through the freedom fighters was still. One shot from the mountainside had picked off the Russian gunner, who stretched upwards, hands held high in bootless supplication. From his position in an outcropping of rock directly above, Omar watched the man fall.

No Mujahideen remained on the road to take advantage of the silent gun. Those who had not been wounded had fled down the ravine in search of safety. Nothing on the roadway moved.

A group of Russian soldiers, trapped inside the tunnel by the burning vehicle, surged out of the mouth now, and formed a human wedge to push the remnants of the makeshift barrier over the edge of the ravine. Not stopping to retrieve the body of their dead gunner, they clambered back into the trucks, which lumbered past piles of mud and stone that had formed the barricade. The wheels thumped over the bodies of the fallen Mujahideen lying in their path on the way to Kabul.

"We are finished here," Yuri shouted to Omar below.

Omar did not answer. He urged his horse down towards his dead brothers. He would have to shoot anyone who moved. There was no time to take the wounded down the mountain before the second wave of trucks would come through. A bullet was salvation from the packs of wolves that could attack a helpless man before the sun rose. He must leave no wounded. It was his rule.

Reaching the mouth of the tunnel, he moved slowly among the bodies, searching for life. His light found the Russian gunner curled over his gun. Had he seen a finger move? Merciful even to his enemies, Omar fired a bullet into the Russian's brain. He could never forget how his brother Abdul had begged for this and had cursed Omar ever since for letting him live. Abdul no longer joined in the raids. He remained at home in the village with the women and children, a bitter man who said few words to his family. Instead, he talked to Allah from his prayer rug.

Behind him now, Omar heard a moan, and spinning around on his horse, he saw a young boy from his village, sprawled on a mound of snow, his eyes open in terror, the mask of death set on his mouth. The boy had begged to come along. It was to be his first skirmish. There was no blood on the white snow where he lay, only a clump of wild habel containing the promise of purple berries in the spring.

Omar dismounted, leaned down and listened for the sound of breath. None came, so he closed the boy's eyes with his thumb and whispered, "Sleep well little warrior." Allah was merciful. The boy did not know their mission had failed.

In anguish, Omar stood up, aware that the blood of the ambush was on his own hands. He had been too sure, too headstrong. Yuri had warned him repeatedly not to attack with fewer than 20 men, to set up the barricade of dirt and rocks a good two hours before schedule. Yuri had not trusted their informant in Mazar. Yuri trusted no one and, as usual, Yuri had been right.

Wearily, Omar climbed upon the flat bed of the truck to inspect the machine gun. Rounds of ammunition hung from it. A pity there was no way to bring the machine gun down the mountain. He pushed the Russian's body aside. At least they could carry away some of the ammo. But as he reached over to unload, the floodlights of a Russian helicopter appeared over the crest of the ridge beyond the tunnel. That dreaded whirling sound so often filled his nightmares. How he hated those awkward machines which carried death to his people.

From the slope directly above, Yuri shouted. "Take cover."

Frightened by the sudden noise of the helicopter, Yuri's horse lost its footing and began to slip sideways towards the roadway below. Grabbing a branch from a tree, Yuri halted his slide just short of a boulder.

But Omar did not move. He stood boldly on the bed of the truck. He would wait until the helicopter came down to get a better look, and then he would open fire. He knew it was senseless, a futile gesture, but he could not help himself. He aimed toward the sound, blinded now by the floodlight, and fired in rage. The Russian pilot hovering above him toyed with his impotence. Omar wasted round after round; the chopper did not return his fire but circled the smoking ruins. Then it dropped out of sight over the mountain, surveying the bodies lying on the slope that led to the valley below, swept up again then above the ridge. Omar felt like a gnat on its backside. He thrilled, however, when the copter made its second pass; it returned his fire. He had become a worthy adversary. He had pulled the enemy into his own foolishness. Instinct told him to fall forward over the gun--play dead and hope to entice the pilot downward for a better look at his prey.

"Omar," Yuri shouted in anguish, as he saw his friend slumped over the big gun. "Omar!"

The ruse worked. The pilot lowered his machine towards the prostrate figure. "Omar," Yuri shouted, only this time in surprise. With lightning speed, Omar righted the machine gun, and blasted the underbelly of the helicopter, aiming for the Red Star which covered the oil pan now directly overhead. A hit! Israfil, the angel of Islam who would sound the trumpet at Resurrection, was with Omar El-Ham this night.

The helicopter tilted like a wounded bird, its engine suddenly silent, and then slid out of control, spinning crazily, then plummeting out of sight over the side of the mountain.

"You are a crazy man," Yuri shouted with relief. Omar was alive and standing triumphant on the flatbed truck.

Omar raised his fist in the air. "What do you think of that, my friend!"

Yuri answered Omar with the Mujahideen salute as he watched Omar climb down from the truck.

Within moments, the two men had walked the edge of the road and peered over the mountainside. There was no sign of fire or smoke from the wreck below. It was still too dark to discern a crash site.

"Was it real?"

"I am sure."

"If the equipment in the helicopter survives the crash, it will be the answer to our prayers. Let us ride to the bottom and search."

Yuri nodded, pointing back to the mouth of the tunnel. "The second convoy comes. Be off."

It was then that they noticed Omar's horse had been slain. The stallion was lying on its side, its belly torn with bullets. "My *sakhra*, my *rafiq*," Omar wailed.

"Here," Yuri barked, reaching out his hand and pulling his friend up behind him on his mount. "Omar there is no time for this. We must ride."

But riding double down the steep slope into the valley far below proved slow and treacherous. Pockets of moonlight beneath the tree line now made it easier to see, but there was always the danger of deep ravines camouflaged by snow.

165

"Perhaps it did not crash," Yuri said, discouraged when there was still no sign of a wreck.

At that instant Omar nudged him from behind. "Look! Down there."

"Where?"

"No, to your left. There! Yuri, what a prize! The West will pay dearly to get a close look at this new Russian equipment."

"Damn, what a sight!" Yuri whipped his horse and galloped recklessly in the direction of the downed craft.

It was an awesome sight indeed. The helicopter lay upside down; its giant propeller imbedded in deep snow. The pilot could not have survived, but some of the avionics gear might be salvaged. There had been no fire. Omar was jubilant. "Allah has sent us a gift. This could help finance our plan for a 'Red-Eye.' "

"You dreamer." Yuri knew his friend was a wild man with grandiose schemes, yet he loved him for it. Life with Mohammed Omar was yeasty compared to life under the State. "So you think if you can get your hands on the American Red-Eye you can win the war single handed?"

"No," Omar chuckled. "I would need your help a little."

"You know that the Americans will never let an Afghan have that missile."

"Our contact in Peshawar swears he can deliver it to us through the Saudis."

"Rubbish. The man talks big. Besides, it is out of our reach. Do you have any idea how much such a missile costs?"

"What are you telling me? That our money from the helicopter parts is only a drop of piss in the ocean?"

"Not even a drop."

Omar shrugged his shoulders. "God willing. I trade up."

"Better we take the money we get from Western intelligence for the parts and buy some dynamite. I vote we go for the bridge over the Amu Darya again."

A scowl clouded Omar's face.

Yuri knew Omar did not like to be reminded of his failures. Had it not been for faulty detonators they would have succeeded in blowing the bridge sky high during the Soviet dedication ceremonies. Of course, he, the Russian defector had gotten the blame. It had been his first raid with the Mujahideen and some of them suspected he had deliberately sabotaged their efforts. Omar knew better but for Yuri's own protection, he had pretended that

Yuri was merely stupid. Their second attempt to destroy the bridge had been aborted when Abdul was injured in *buzkashi.*

"Fermez is too far away," Omar grumbled.

"You did not think so last May."

"Last May we had a truck."

"Which you traded for a shoulder launcher from Abdul Haz's men."

"So, I'll throw that in too when we bargain for the Red Eye."

"Rave on, you fool," Yuri said affectionately. The makeshift army of Omar and his friends never ceased to amaze him. Afghans swapped parts from village to village until someone could get enough together to launch an attack. He had been with them almost four years now and their fighting prowess was awesome; the Afghans would be invincible if properly armed. So despite the misery and the hardship, Yuri savored his life among them, the Mujahideen were brave beyond anything he had ever known. "I hear there are plans in Mazar to cross the border into Tajikistan."

"Only to distribute religious pamphlets to Soviet Tajicks. It is a stupid idea."

Yuri nodded. "A waste of time. So why not invade the Al Zulfiqar and kidnap Bhutto's sons? They train only six miles outside of Kabul to overthrow President Zia of Pakistan. Offer their heads to Zia for more weapons from Peshawar. Annisa has suggested this many times."

Omar threw up his hands. "Now who is the fool! Bhutto's sons train to overthrow President Zia in the heart of Soviet fortification. I think I made a big mistake, Yuri Vitrovich, when I did not let the Resistance shoot you in Paghman. You will get me killed yet."

"I bet your foolhardy actions will beat me to it." Yuri dug his heels into his horse. "At least listen to what Annisa has to say. She has a good head on her shoulders."

"Why do *you* listen to Annisa? Or do your attentions to her grow each day along with the size of her breasts?"

"Can I help it if our girl-child has grown into a sensuous woman? Every man in our village lusts for her—all, of course, except Abdul."

"My brother loves horses more than women," Omar said, pretending to be amused. But there was an edge to his voice and Yuri was sorry he had mentioned Abdul. It was not difficult to guess the secret that festered between the two brothers. Omar had refused to let anyone attend to Abdul's wounds after his accident and the once proud and haughty Abdul had become a sullen shadow of his former self. Well, it was none of his business. He certainly hated the questions about Sasha and his own blood brother Vladimar in Moscow--the brother he had betrayed. "The snow is too deep to risk going ahead," Yuri said. "Let us look for a cave."

"No, we must get help to bring the helicopter parts out and soon."

"We will freeze to death first."

"No, I see the lights of Khinjan ahead."

"The snow has frozen your senses. It is only a mirage."

"Trust me."

"I trust no one, you know that."

Omar gave a belly laugh. "And my friends say I am crazy to trust you. 'Omar El-Ham is now a brother to our enemy. True, the man has courage but he is a Russian. Omar El-Ham trusts too much.'"

Yuri worked his fingers trying to pump blood into them. "The one not to trust is Annisa. She still wants to get to her brother and the day she finds out you have fooled her-- it will be hell."

"Why must you harp on that?"

"Because Fatima is right. Annisa will be trouble if she isn't married soon."

"I don't believe Annisa would like America. She can not bear to leave Habiba and how could she take the senseless girl with her? I save her heartache by not forcing her to make such a choice."

"Or is it that *you* would miss her too much?"

Omar was indignant. "Only because she is a symbol. It is girls like Annisa who are the heart of Afghanistan."

"And your wife?"

"Fatima is not our future. She is our past."

An uncomfortable silence settled between them but Yuri could not let it go. "Go ahead, lie to yourself. You and I know the truth of it. Annisa heats up your loins. You never take your eyes off her."

"I am a fool, but not that much of one."

"You are in danger if you believe that." Yuri hesitated again, but only for a moment. "I have never told this to anyone. But for your own good I tell you now. I was obsessed with my brother's wife and I betrayed him, only to discover that the bitch had taken Orkunium for a lover, too."

Omar was incredulous. "Orkunium's mistress was your brother's wife! Why did you not say this before?"

"For the same reason you can't admit why you can't let go of Annisa. You and I both know she doesn't belong here. The girl is educated. My God, she speaks three languages. She does not belong in this miserable and primitive life."

"Primitive? Don't say things to me I can never forgive my friend."

Once again, Yuri regretted his words. He had not meant to wound Omar.

"Tell me something, Yuri. Did your brother ever find out?"

"No. That was part of Orkunium's hold--to keep me in line out of fear he would tell."

"This Sasha must be a she-devil to twist you like this."

"I would have killed to have her. It can happen to *any* man."

"Not Omar El-Ham. There is not a woman alive who could make me want her that much. Annisa was a child when she came to us. She is still a girl in *my* eyes."

"You are sure of that, are you? I'm warning you. I sense she is hot blooded. You must either send her to Peshawar or find her a husband and soon."

Omar shrugged. "Then I give her to you!"

"Me! So you want me to wake up with a knife in my back? Annisa wants to kill Russians --to ride and fight like a man instead of doing women's work."

"What about your Russian women? They serve in your Army. Should we offer up Annisa for training?"

"Joke if you want to."

"Yuri, why the fuss? Has this Moscow Sasha with the big tits soured you on all women?"

"No, but she has taught me that a woman can turn brother against brother."

Omar's smile was tight. "As you said, Abdul has no desire for her."

"But I do and so do you."

"Bah!"

"You deny you only pretend to send Annisa's letters to her brother?"

"I deny nothing. But it is too late for her to go to America."

"No one need know you destroyed her messages."

169

"My sin is far greater. I have played God... When I heard her brother had come to Peshawar to search for her I let it be known she was dead. The *Pay-vi-luch* had already volunteered he would tell them this in Karkak. My story would be confirmed."

"What compelled you to do this? Do you take her for a second wife?"

Omar was indignant. "Of course not!"

"What is it then?"

"She makes me feel alive. It's like breathing fresh air. I never knew my life was so dull until she came to our village."

"That's lust. Pure and simple."

Omar hesitated. "No, it is much more powerful. Annisa is something I can believe in—-perhaps, the only thing."

"Does Allah know about this?"

"Ha, very funny."

"Do you think her brother believed she was dead?"

"Yes. A man came looking for her in Tezeen where she had left with the guide. His name is Duranni. Captain Duranni. A big important man. He sits at the right hand of our leaders in exile. Duranni knows her brother. I'm told he delivered the sad news to Rahmin."

"My God, I know this Captain Duranni."

Omar smiled. "Yes, you gave us his name in Peshawar."

"You are dead meat. Duranni will pulverize you if he ever finds out."

"He has no idea the report of her death came from me. There is only one man who could tell him the truth. And that man is determined that Annisa not go to the West."

"Yes, that religious nut who brought her to Doshi. Omar, that man was too weird to be believed . . .. And what happens if Annisa ever leaves and heads for Peshawar on her own?"

"She won't. Annisa is at heart an Afghan girl." Omar gave him a sly smile. "She wants to kill Russians, remember?"

"Annisa's brother? Is he still in Peshawar? Won't he kill you if he ever finds out?"

"They say Rahmin has returned to America."

"Then you can rest easy."

"No, I can't. For what I have done I will never see paradise."

"Paradise!" Yuri roared. "Forget paradise. It doesn't exist except between a woman's legs. And than you pay hell for it."

Omar was not listening, too excited to see the lights of Khinjin. "See. I told you. It was not a mirage. We are almost there."

"Curious, isn't it?" Yuri said. "You are older than me but your eyes are much better."

"That's true, but your vision of the future beats mine. Poor Annisa-jan."

The wind on their faces was so bitter as they rode into town that their breath came hard. The snow was frozen stiff on the end of their turbans, which were wrapped across their mouths. Yuri pointed to the sun, which was beginning to edge itself over the snow-capped peak. "Old friend, we will have those helicopter parts."

"Yes," Omar answered, the enthusiasm having disappeared from his voice. He spoke as though emerging from a fog. "I've been a foolish man." Despite the thrill of the downed helicopter, he could not stop thinking about what Yuri had said about Annisa and he was filled with remorse. His actions had been treacherous to those who would give him their trust. Yuri had spoken yet another truth and Omar's head ached with it. Annisa was a danger to them all. A danger if she left and told her story and a danger if she stayed. The girl had juice.

CHAPTER 17

Annisa stared at the frail child wading in the icy stream and realized that each day Habiba lived was a victory over nature. By all rights, Habiba should have died on their long trek north. Scars from the ugly lesions which covered her body remained, but she had ceased to spit up blood. Annisa was attuned to the thin rasp in her breathing at night, and like the mother of a newborn would awaken instantly at the slightest change in the pattern.

"*Nazeem*, my special girl," Annisa called out. It was sweet relief to find her but worrisome that she was without a sweater and wet up to her knees in the freezing water. "Thank God. You are safe."

Habiba did not look up at the sound of Annisa's voice.

"Why must you always run away?" Annisa scolded as she snatched her from the stream. "You are lucky I found you. I've searched all day. And just look at you. Fatima will be cross. Your hair. What have you been doing, rolling in brambles?"

Combing Habiba's hair was a ritual between them. Each morning Annisa would braid it with ribbons. During Habiba's illness, great clumps had come out in Annisa's hand, and Fatima had predicted the little girl would be dead before the first leaves fell.

Annisa refused to accept this verdict, and kept Habiba alive through the long winter and into the next with little more than the strength of her own will. One morning when Annisa herself was sick and unable to get up from her cot, Habiba had come to her and held up the ribbons, jabbering the names of Sabra and Tawab and Ishaq--names which Annisa often repeated to her like a mantra--hoping for a glimmer of recognition from the past which never came. "She understands more than we think," Annisa had announced triumphantly to Fatima, but Fatima only shook her head and muttered, "You waste time."

Annisa reached down and wiped Habiba's runny nose with the hem of her skirt. The pink in Habiba's cheeks had slowly reappeared and she was healthy enough, despite the fact she had not grown an inch since the day Annisa found her in Tezeen, throwing stones. Habiba's small body had been arrested in that horror of time but her mind had traveled backwards. Sometimes Habiba would make baby sounds and coo at Annisa. More often than not her eyes were vacant. No one would get near her except Annisa and, strangely enough, Yuri, the Russian defector. Annisa did not understand it. Yuri was gruff-voiced and said very little to anyone. He seemed annoyed with the world. She had once overheard him tell Omar, "Nothing pleases me."

Omar had collapsed in a belly laugh. "That's why I trust you. Never have I known a man who enjoys his own suffering as much as you."

"What have you got in your hand?" Annisa asked Habiba, catching a glimmer of gold between her fingers. "Where did you get this?" Annisa pried a gold watch from the child's hand. When she held it up for a closer look in the waning light, a cold shiver gripped her. On the back was engraved Russian lettering. Certainly the watch was not Yuri's. His was black with a leather strap. This one was too fine.

Habiba began to cry and stretched out her arms to retrieve her find.

"Where did you get this?" Annisa repeated.

Habiba only screamed and stomped the ground.

"Shush. Here. Take it. It's a long walk back home."

She took Habiba's hand and gently led her up the rocky incline to the road towards Qalagai. Habiba broke away from her and sat down in front of a mud wall of the deserted village, her arms folded across her chest.

"Okay, we'll sit here but for only for a minute." Annisa had learned that the easiest way to handle Habiba was to give in instantly and as soon as you did the little girl was content and would follow you. Habiba loved to imitate. If Annisa smoothed her blouse, Habiba patted the wrinkles in hers. If Annisa leaned her head against the wall, Habiba did likewise. And when Annisa put her hand to her forehead to survey the bombed out houses, Habiba repeated the gesture.

"You little mimic." Annisa stuck her tongue out and Habiba did so too and then burst into giggles. Annisa loved to see her happy and playful like this. A smile from Habiba was so rare.

Despite the grimness of their surroundings, they might have stayed longer but soon it would be dark. Annisa hated the thought of going home and she was ashamed of herself for thinking it. Unlike many Afghan girls, she had a roof over her head. Her relatives were good to her. Fatima was nicer than before. It was Omar who had changed. Annisa had thought of him as her friend, her champion in her struggles but lately he rarely spoke to her and refused to look at her when she entered the room. His tongue was sharp with her when he did speak. Abdul had noticed it too and shocked Annisa by telling her not to judge Omar. "He has too much on his shoulders now that I am worthless to anyone. It's not his way to be unkind." But what really hurt was Omar's sudden announcement that she must write another letter to Rahmin and soon--it was either that or he would personally escort her to Peshawar and the refugee camps. What had she done to offend? She had wanted to please Omar more than anyone. But there were times when he acted as though he hated her.

"Time to go," she told Habiba. Dutifully, Habiba stood up and took her hand. Annisa was feeling apprehensive. They were several miles from the nearest inhabited village. And this place appeared sinister. After repeated bombings, only one building remained. There was a massive wooden door and wooden shutters over the windows, but the roof was missing, and birds with red tail feathers perched on top of a charred beam in the lengthening shadows. They were hideous with predatory eyes. Twice they swooped low over Annisa's head, flapping their great wings in the ebbing light, their ugly talons a few feet above. In front of their perch was the twisted shell of a red bus, tilting crazily on its front axle. The steering wheel had been stripped away and the seats inside removed. A tattered white scarf tied to the window on the driver's side hung limp, as if in surrender.

"I don't like this place," she told Habiba, lifting her into her arms. But Habiba squirmed and wiggled out, laughing as she ran towards the old bus. "Come back here," Annisa shouted, tired of humoring her charge.

Afghanistan was filled with many such villages, inhabited only by a stray dog or two and ghosts of a life before the Russians came. She had heard that the people in the village of Nawar had been herded into an irrigation ditch where the Russians poured oil into the water and then set it on fire. Every Afghan for miles knew the gruesome details. Nawar had been a major supply stop for the Jihad trail. So the Russians had made it an example. Those few villagers from Nawar who had survived the burning had moved up into the mountains. During the first year after the disaster, they would come down at night to farm their land. But the Russians came back and burned the fields. All that remained was a straw stuffed scarecrow in a black jacket and a turban standing guard over the now barren fields.

"What is to become of us?" Annisa muttered to Habiba. She motioned for her to return but the little girl shook her head and ran around behind the bus.

Annisa was angry now. Frustrated. "Soon it grows dark. I'm tired of these silly games." At times like these, Annisa was tempted to lie down in the freezing cold and just go to sleep. Unlike Omar, who was filled with passionate hope they could still drive the Russians out, Annisa was no longer certain. No matter how many Russians they killed, more kept coming. The new troops were better fighters than the ones before them.

Perhaps Omar kept his faith because he occasionally smelled victory after a successful raid. For Annisa, life was a procession of dull little defeats. Omar could act out his dreams; she was constantly chastised for hers. Fatima announced to everyone that Annisa was hopeless in the kitchen. And she continued to needle her about having a Pushtu father. "Mixed blood makes you lazy; bad-tempered."

Annisa had fought back. "Then why do you want to marry me to Abdul?"

Poor Abdul would get up and leave the room whenever Fatima started in on it. It was painful to Annisa. Their village ways got on her nerves. Had he guessed she felt this way? Well, she couldn't help it. They knew so little of the world she had been raised in. But this did not mean that she thought she was better than Abdul. At least he made an attempt to learn. He listened regularly to the BBC, and the Voice of America too when it was not jammed. In some ways he reminded her of her brother Rahmin--overly serious and taut in manner and speech. They were both tall and thin--like pillars on a porch--and their features were sharp in contrast to Omar's broad face and stocky build.

Abdul also had a disposition like her brother's. He was easy to anger and quick to forgive. Both men enjoyed their solitude.

Omar was just the opposite. He was always in the middle of things and it was usually an argument with Fatima. "It is better for my husband that Annisa goes to America where she won't cause problems without the veil."

The veil was a never-ending quarrel between them. "Forget the old ways, woman."

"Do you want me to go without my veil? To travel around the countryside talking to strange men."

"You are different. You belong to me."

Fatima would turn her anger over Omar's indecision regarding Annisa's future onto Annisa herself.

"If you do not go to America, you must marry Abdul!" Fatima had screamed that very morning for no reason at all. "We have no books here. Better you go to the infidels. You act like one of them."

At this, Abdul had thrown the tea from his cup on the ground. "Leave the girl alone. She is welcome to stay in this house as long as she wants. She is our blood. I'll hear no more about two more mouths to feed."

"And what do you do around here to help feed them?"

It was yet another one of Fatima's awful little truths. Abdul, who walked stiff legged from the bullet lodged in his kneecap, did little more than tend the horses. And bury the dead. The *buzkashi* accident had subdued him; his pride was gone. Unlike Omar, who never bothered to pray, Abdul was exceptionally devout and spent a great deal of his day studying the Koran. He knew whole sections by heart. He had told Annisa that the Russians' attempt to ban the Koran or re-write it for the Afghans would never work because too many people knew it word for word. He was also very observant and startled Annisa by telling her he knew she had money hidden in her belt. "You should be more careful."

At first, Annisa had hotly denied it, angered he had discovered her hiding place and ashamed she had not offered it to help pay for her care. Once it was gone, America would be gone as well. "It is only a chit; good only in the money bazaars of Peshawar."

"Tell no one in the family you have this," Abdul warned. "You have no father or husband to care for you. These are harsh times and they will get harsher." And he had spun on his good leg and hobbled out of the room before she could answer.

Annisa had taken this as Abdul's way of letting her know he lacked interest in her as a wife. She often imagined what it would be like to have the strong arms of a man around her. But she never thought of Abdul. He was old like Omar. And an uncle. Relatives should never marry. Her dreams were of the dead. Kassim and Zia but more often it was Ishaq, the storybook hero who had belonged to Sabra. She also wondered what it would feel like to carry life and to give birth. She envied Fatima's swollen stomach and was fascinated when the women nursed their children. To have a sweet small mouth suckling on your breast--what would that be like? The young men of the village had no time for marriage--too busy fighting the

Jihad. She would not settle for being second wife to an older man. The thought of old flesh repelled her. There was a man in the village they called Niaz. He was a grandfather and he had asked for her. He had offered Omar a good price. She refused. Her first time with a man would be sweet and wonderful like Sabra's. Better the sweetness and intensity of few days with a doomed warrior than the sour smell of an old man night after night. She told all this to no one --no one except little Habiba, her friend and confidant, who understood nothing of what she said.

"I have no fate," Annisa murmured and brushed aside a tear of self-pity. She must guard against these feelings of despair or Panna's prediction that she would not last in village life would come true. Annisa stared at her hands. She had taken great pride in their blisters the day after her first harvest. To think Zia's mother had worried she could not pass for a village girl. Her hands had become as tough as Fatima's. There were times she did not even recognize them as her own when she held them up before her eyes.

"Nail polish!" She laughed out loud thinking of how she had coveted the bright red nails of the film stars in her movie magazines in Kabul.

Habiba, who had returned to her side, looked up and laughed too.

"At last. Let's go." Annisa lifted Habiba up to the wall and then backed up for her to climb on, piggyback. For a moment Annisa imagined she saw something move in the shadow of the old bus and scolded herself for her fear. She was not only losing hope but her nerve as well. Then she heard a soft moan, and in terror she spun around and snatched Habiba from the wall and ran out into the road. She could hear the sound of an approaching jeep. It was dusk but the driver did not have his headlights on. Hopefully, he had not seen them. Clutching Habiba, she scrambled across the road and halfway down the rocky incline towards the small stream. But there was not enough time to reach it before the jeep passed so she flung herself down behind a large boulder and put her hand over Habiba's mouth.

The jeep did not pass them as she had anticipated but screeched to a halt on the road above their heads. Annisa waited. Had they been seen? No one came or called out.

"He's over there," a gruff voice shouted in Russian. "Behind the bus. I tell you he was alive when we left him."

There was the sound of boots crunching on the road. Then silence.

"Holy shit! God damn this stinking place. Look at him. They have cut off Sergi's testicles. These people are devils-- the scum of the earth."

"The poor son of a bitch," another voice growled. "He was almost out of this shit-house. Sergi was due to rotate home to Leningrad in two weeks."

"How many villagers were you taking in?"

"We had five but the last man was too old for the army and we let him go."

"Afghan butchers. I hate to take his body back to the base. The sight of this demoralizes the troops. At least they will send the casket home sealed. They always do."

Annisa could hear the thump of the body as they tossed it on the hood of the jeep. The motor started up.

Suddenly, little Habiba broke lose and scrambled out of Annisa's arms. She darted up the steep embankment.

The driver of the jeep slammed on his brakes and leapt out, grabbing the little girl who had run out into their path, jabbering at them. He reached down and lifted her high in the air above his head. "Filthy little beggar. Where did you come from?"

Habiba squirmed in his arms and the gold watch fell out of her hand and onto the frozen ground at his feet. Annisa, who was watching from her hiding place, felt a cramp in her innards as the soldier bent over and picked up the watch. "The little Afghan bitch. She has Sergi's watch."

"How do you know this?"

"See. His initials are on the back of it. Filthy little Afghan turd." He struck Habiba across the mouth with the back of his hand

"Put her down," Annisa screamed, revealing her hiding place. She charged up the side of the slope and rushed the startled soldier. "Don't touch her!" She pounded him with her fists. "Don't you dare strike her again," she shouted in Russian. Strong arms grabbed her from behind and pinned her wrists together.

"We have captured a wild cat."

"Put the child down. *Pleasebo.*"

"Ah, she says please so nicely. And in Russian, too. I wonder what she really pleads for."

Habiba reached up and scratched the face of the man who held her, clawing at his eye. In haste, he dropped her to the ground. "Shit. Look what she did." He reached for his pocket-handkerchief but stopped when he saw Habiba running away from him down the road. His hand grabbed his pistol from his holster instead.

"Don't" Annisa screamed as he took aim and with great deliberation pointed the barrel of the gun at the escaping child and pulled the trigger. The impact of the bullet spun Habiba around, her eyes wide open. She staggered towards Annisa, her arms outstretched, before pitching forward onto the road.

A roar of anguish tore at Annisa's throat. She fought to jerk away from her captor. Her lips quivered as she watched the man with the gun walk over to Habiba and roll her over with his boot. "She's dead," he said looking back at Annisa. "A crazy child. You could see it in the eyes. She is better off."

"Pigs. Filthy pigs," Annisa lunged forward but another soldier grabbed her by the back of her long hair and dragged her over to the front of the jeep where the dead Russian lay sprawled face down across the hood. "Pigs, huh? Is this what pigs do?"

Annisa fought to turn her head away from the naked bare bottom staring her in the face but the soldier held her head rigid, pushing it downward. "Turn him over. Rub her face where his genitals were."

"What's the sense of it. Let's show her ours instead."

"Bastards!" she screamed.

"I saw her first."

The other man shrugged. "We can share her. Take your time."

The soldier holding Annisa pulled her across the yard and through the doorway of the roofless house where he shoved her against the side of a wall, pushing his pelvis against her. Instinctively, she let her body go limp, slumping to a dead weight in his arms. When he leaned over to pull her up she jerked up with her head, butting him under the jaw and knocking him sideways. But as she turned to run, her foot caught in a rut and she pitched forward losing her sandal as she fell. Scrambling to her feet, she raced towards the jeep. She could hear the laughter of the other soldier who stood by a tree, smoking a cigarette.

The man she had thwarted tackled her from behind, knocking her head into the right front wheel of the jeep. Blackness engulfed her.

He must have dragged her face down across the yard because when she came to, she was lying on the ground, the smell of human excrement near her head. "Your Mujahideen friends leave their droppings," the soldier grunted. With a violent jerk he rolled her over on her back and pinned her arms to the ground above her head. She could see the outline of the other soldier now. Loud music blared from the transistor radio he had pulled from his pocket.

"She's a hot one all right. Want me to hold her down for you?"

"Nyet."

Her tormentor lifted her head and then banged it repeatedly against the frozen ground. The dim light and the music began to fade for Annisa, replaced by a loud ringing in her ears, and then the sound of cloth ripping as the soldier yanked her skirt above her waist. Warm blood began to ooze down the back of her neck from her head. Merciful Allah. She would die.

He was on his knees now. Over her. Unzipping his trousers. "Shut up, bitch, or I'll slit your throat."

Despite his threat she let out a shriek of pain when his penis rammed into her, stabbing her insides, and tearing her membrane.

"Tight little pussy, you cunt."

Annisa was fighting hard not to lose consciousness.

"You love it," he panted. "Say it. You love it."

She didn't answer and he leaned down and bit her furiously on the neck. Again she screamed in pain, but it was more from the incessant pounding inside her. There was a putrid smell to him. Worse than garbage. Like the decomposing corpses she had helped pull out of the rubble following the bombings. Edges of black curled like shriveled mushrooms around her head. She prayed to die, to escape the shame.

Suddenly, he was off her and panting. He yanked her up to her knees in front of him, holding her head. "Now you are going to suck my cock."

Vomit rose in her throat as he pulled her head against him. The ground undulated.

"I come in your mouth, Afghan bitch. Swallow it. Swallow every drop."

She tried to turn her head.

"Open your mouth."

She uttered a scream low in her throat.

He reached down and pulled her face up sharply, clutching her by the hair. He yanked so hard she could feel bits of hair coming out in his hand. It reminded her of Habiba. She screamed between her teeth.

"Open your mouth or I'll slit your throat."

The world was spinning again, only slower this time. She could see her brother's face before her; Rahmin's eyes burning with shame.

"Damn you, open your mouth." He slapped her repeatedly across the face.

Slowly, she released her clenched teeth and her jaws slacked open. He jammed the hot flesh into her mouth. Almost instantly a ball of sweet-tasting snot sprayed the back of her throat and she started to gag, but he would not let go of her.

One last flash of rage drove her to bite down hard upon him as she shoved upward with her fists into the base of his testicles.

He reeled backwards, cursing and screaming as Annisa staggered to her feet. She was confused and dizzy and without direction. Further back in the dark shadows the other soldier stood watching, his hands on his hips, puffing his cigarette.

The man who had raped her lay cursing in the rubble. She knew that once he recovered he would kill her. "Bitch, bitch," he hollered, his voice filled with a savage rage.

"My turn," the other man said in a monotone and ground out his cigarette.

It was dark now. She could not see the other man's face but the strong smell of tobacco clung to his thick lips which were wet with saliva. He was not as brutal as the soldier before him but that made it worse. Defeated, Annisa had no strength to fight back but lay semi-conscious as he unbuttoned her blouse and slipped his hand on her breast. The gentleness of his hands and the softness of his lips as he began to nibble on her breasts shriveled her insides and filled her with self-loathing. She prayed she might shed her skin like a snake.

"You have beautiful eyes. So green."

Quickly she closed them and slipped into darkness, and the second time he entered her she had no knowledge of what happened next.

When she came to, she was alone in the deserted village. Dim light from a half moon filtered through the shadows. Annisa stared, mute with disbelief, the hot tears salting her cheeks. With great effort she pulled herself to her hands and knees and crawled out towards the road. The jeep was gone. So was Habiba's body. What had they done with it! Annisa lay still for a moment, half-frozen, remembering another night when the moon was full and there was a green ribbon tied around Sabra's waist. Her hand flew to her waist and relief flooded over her when she realized they had not taken her belt. The chit for money was safe. But her sense of shame was overwhelming. Panna was right. She was not strong enough. With trembling hands she ran her fingers over her exposed breasts, remembering how her body had been defiled. The stream! She would cleanse herself in the stream. She pulled herself to her feet and, trance-like, made her way down the steep slope and entered the water below. The water came only to her knees. Slowly, she removed her torn garments in a sliver of moonlight and tossed them onto stones beside the riverbed. Then she sat down on her haunches in the freezing water and attempted to wash herself. Throwing her head back, she floated face up in the shallow water, staring at the crescent moon. She was no longer a maiden. She could never marry. Her husband would blacken her face and make her work as a servant in his house. Despite the freezing water, Annisa had no sense of cold. She was aware only of a white anger in her soul. "No one must know," she whispered to the moon. "I will kill anyone who finds out." Then she stood up and walked out of the water. Her clothing would cover most of the bruises on her body except the ugly one on her neck where the Russian had bitten her. She could never go back to Doshi; there would be no way to escape the prying eyes of Fatima. Suddenly her hand flew to her throat. It was gone! Her heart necklace. Najib's gift ripped from her neck in the violence. Allah was having his say. Her loss of innocence had stripped her of her right to wear it.

"There is no God," she muttered as she staggered down the road. She would walk to Peshawar or die. She now understood why Omar looked bitter when Abdul was down on his prayer rug. She could no longer believe. If Allah allowed such evil, then he was hateful and if he could not stop it then he was powerless and there was no faith in the world. "There is no safe place. Only the grave," the fierce *Pay-yi-luch*, who had brought her to her uncles, had warned.

In the wasteland behind Annisa, a few miles down the road the yellow eyes of a jackal glowed in the dark. The remains of a child's body tossed from a speeding jeep lay before him. It was Christmas Eve, the fourth anniversary of the invasion. There was the smell of fresh snow in the air.

CHAPTER 18

Night had slipped into morning before Omar reached the rim of the valley, where he paused only long enough to give his horse a rest. Not once during the long cold night had he closed his eyes. They burned too bright. He was feverish with worry. For weeks now he had searched in every direction for Annisa and little Habiba. No one had seen them. Disappeared. Swallowed up by the earth. Yuri, who waited for him in Charikar, had no luck either. It was Yuri who counseled they should give up the search. The helicopter parts had to be delivered to Peshawar.

Poor Fatima. When Annisa was with them she had done nothing but quarrel with her. Now that she was missing, Fatima was beside herself with grief. "If only I had not told her we would send her to the Saint's Shrine at Jalalabad."

"'We will have you trussed up and left overnight at the shrine so that the holy men can pray over you,'" Abdul mimicked cruelly. "If I were the girl I would have run away, too."

This was Fatima's hope--that Annisa had run off to Peshawar.

"She would not leave without goodbye," Omar had said bitterly. "She is a sensible girl. She has no means of support in Peshawar."

Abdul thought differently. "Her biggest problem will be the half-wit Habiba."

Fatima wept when he said it.

The ceremony at the birth of Omar's second son a few days later had seemed joyless. Guns had been fired, drums pounded, and Fatima had removed the cloth stopper on the large ceramic storage vessel in order to distribute some of their grain to the poor. But without Annisa and little Habiba, the celebration seemed empty.

On the road ahead Omar saw a small boy carrying a load of sticks piled high on his back. The boy raised his arm in a salute to the proud Mujahideen fighter on the great *buzkashi* horse. "Death to the Russians. Death to Babrak. Long live Massoud," the boy shouted.

Omar returned his salute and felt suddenly refreshed from his long ride. At least the news from Kabul was good. The Resistance had penetrated tight security around Kabul airport and damaged two aircraft belonging to the Afghan civilian airline. It was also reported that a large Soviet-built grain elevator had been set afire.

Omar looked below him to the valley. It lay peaceful in the morning sun: a valley of apricot orchards and bombed-out, mud houses; a valley surrounded by monolithic stone mountains standing sentinel to the outside world. Gone were the dreaded Soviet SU 25 ground-attack aircraft which could dive so steeply and turn so sharply. Omar respected the weaponry of the enemy. Its troops might be alcohol-ridden and demoralized but they had the equipment with which to fight. This morning, however, the skies over the valley were empty; it was too early for the smoke from the village charcoal vendors. Neither a solitary falcon nor a Soviet gunship claimed the sky.

Omar reached down and patted his horse. "'Daldal is yours, my brother, the fastest in the valley,'" Abdul had said.

"I can't take him."

"Don't be foolish. Go to Peshawar. Bring back a missile. Attend to our cause. I shall stay home and pray for your journey and your soul. And I will also pray that he has granted a miracle and that you find Annisa in Peshawar."

Omar urged Daldal down the steep and winding mountain path. Would his brother ever forgive him for letting him live? Abdul, now a shell. The bullet was still lodged in the knee. But it wasn't the bullet which had zapped Abdul's zest for life. Abdul was able to urinate but would never again have an erection. Only Omar knew this truth.

And perhaps Yuri? Abdul's angry refusal when Yuri told him he knew where he could get his knee operated on had puzzled the Russian, especially since the bullet in his knee was all the stiff-legged Abdul had ever talked about when he played *buzksashi*.

"I think Abdul nurses a wound far greater than his knee," Yuri had confided to Omar. "There are operations available for *many* wounds."

"Keep your opinions to yourself," Omar had snapped.

So Yuri had never mentioned it again.

A gentle breeze cooled Omar's cheeks as he rode. The day showed promise. Yuri was to meet him at Charikar where he had gone for help in transporting the captured helicopter parts. Yuri was good at logistics. He had worked in Moscow's command headquarters, Yuri had valuable skills.

Yuri waited under a clump of mulberry trees. He was too sturdily built to look like an Afghan, even from a distance. He had enormous thighs, powerful shoulders and arms, a square body, a thick neck. His white hair looked out of place with his unwrinkled face, as did the Afghan tunic he insisted on wearing. His pale skin and deep-set gray eyes made his face stand out in a camp of olive-skinned Mujahideen. His facial expression suggested a contradiction. The mouth could broaden into a disarming grin while the eyes remained impassive; dead in the center. The Mujahideen did not like him despite his bold and daring actions. He was much too surly and too serious to suit them. The war was all the Russian ever talked about. Around him one felt guilty for pausing to drink a cup of tea. The man had no sense of humor. He forged ahead in life rather than letting life come to him.

"You are miserably late," Yuri grumbled to Omar.

"I made one last trip to Banu looking for Annisa. Abdul still thinks Annisa went to Peshawar."

"Yes. You might as well know. He told me she had money to buy a plane ticket to America."

"How can that be?"

"Ask Abdul. He did not say."

"If she reaches Peshawar they will stick her in a refugee camp. I do not wish this."

"Only last week Annisa told me you threatened to send her."

'Yes, but you know I could never do it."

"That was the problem all along."

"I have a deeper one now. Even if Rahmin never discovers I was the source of the news about her death --well, he will surely tell her there were ways to get word to him. Annisa will lose all respect for me and curse my memory. She had such trust."

"Dah, don't be so hard on yourself. How important is respect if the girl arrives safe?"

"Respect is the one thing I live for."

"Then you are talking to the wrong man. Sasha took care of mine." Yuri shoved a handful of sugared almonds into Omar's hand. "I bet Annisa at least makes it to Pakistan."

"How much do you gamble?"

"You decide."

"Your watch for my pearl-handled dagger."

"Done. It is my hope I lose."

"And the helicopter parts?"

"Abdul Haz's men will bring a truck for us from the mouth of the valley through hostile tribes. They tell me the Soviets have bought off some of the leaders in Konar Province."

"On again, off again. We'll have no difficulty getting through. Did they want to know the contents of the truck?"

"I told them mostly armor. Avionics gear from a M 124 'Hind' helicopter gunship you shot down." Yuri gave a crooked grin. "They were impressed--so if it's respect you are after. . ."

A mullah with a long white beard approached them. It was hard not to laugh. He used one half of his broken spectacles as a monocle. "Defector," he screamed and spit on Yuri's feet.

Omar was incensed. "I trust him as a brother. He has saved the lives of many of our people."

"Perhaps to throw them away for bigger stakes. They are trained to infiltrate."

"Yuri is the best man in my command."

"I laugh at your command."

"If you are thinking of my failure at the bridge over Amu Darya, then you mock me." Omar's hand was on his dagger.

"Your reputation is known even to the Soviets, even in Termez. Others ridicule your attempts. Like the over-zealous men of Herb-i-Zalif, your people planted land-mines upside down."

Omar clenched his fist. "On the bridge, we put nothing upside down. I tell you they sent faulty detonators. As for the stupid Herbs, they could not tell the belly of a mine from the backside of a yak."

"And this man?" The mullah raised a long bony finger and poked Yuri in the chest. "This man is the enemy. His words count for nothing. How dare he ask our village for a truck." Again he poked Yuri. "A curse on you. May you die at the hands of a woman." He shuffled off muttering to himself.

Yuri looked over at Omar and grinned. "He has met Sasha?"

Omar threw back his head and roared. "Is it possible? For the first time in months, I see you make a joke. Good. Life goes on. Now, let us go before the old donkey starts throwing stones."

In the early hours of the next evening, they reached the last Mujahideen way station on the Jihad trail taking them through the Khyber Pass. Kerosene lamps had been fired in the hidden valley below. Resistance fighters were sprawled on blankets and mats, drinking tea and Coca-Cola, listening to cassettes of religious chants and popular Mujahideen songs. It was hard to believe there was war.

The plains of Jalalabad, now far below, had once been fertile ground for American AID agricultural experiments. Such efforts were now in ruins. Like Kandahar to the South, the Soviets wanted to cripple the Resistance food supply and, like Genghis Khan before them, they had burned, looted and destroyed. Even now, red and yellow tracer bullets could be seen lighting up the twilight. An hour after leaving the base camp, Yuri and Omar would thread their way through two separate war zones. The road wound through desolate rock and swept upwards past the graves of fallen British soldiers buried on the rocky slopes. Plain stone markers spoke of men, drum rolls, bugles, and flying banners--ghosts of another war which the Afghans had fought successfully, with tactics they were still trying to use, tactics that were no match for the dreaded Soviet helicopters. "The mullahs will lose this for us yet if they keep insisting we surround the enemy and charge. These are different times. Our enemy fights us from the sky."

"And from within," Yuri answered, urging his horse up the rocky grade which still held ragged patches of snow.

"So many times I have wondered why your people invaded us? What was there to gain?"

"If I told you, you wouldn't believe me."

"Let me be the judge of that."

"We feared the emergence of Islam. Our military was disturbed by the instability along our southern rim. We wanted to forestall any potential Muslim unrest in Central Asia--particularly those within the Soviet Union."

"That will never happen. Moslems have no real quarrel with the rest of the world."

"Saying it won't make it true. Ten years from now you may be singing a different tune. There is always a struggle for power and what better place than here? This is fertile ground for conflict and fundamentalists from all corners of Islam can carry the seed to Afghanistan."

"Bah! I hear you came because you wanted to be closer to the south and a warm water port."

"Oh, that's brilliant. We invade a land-locked country in search for a port when we have no need for one! In East Africa we have naval facilities and also on the southern end of the Arabian Peninsula. Our Asiatic fleet operates in the Indian Ocean. All this talk about warm weather ports is ancient history. I tell you we invaded out of fear of Islam and that is why we are stupid. Trying to avoid the hornet we have stirred up his nest."

They were in the shadow of a Soviet post now. Although spring was near, ice was still in the shallows, in the furrows of soil that lay between the rocks. On the other side of the valley below, they could just make out the outline of Mujahideen figures on horseback, galloping at a determined speed. "Heading for an ambush on the road to Jalalabad," Omar said. "I wish we were going with them."

"I know. It will be a good fight. But we must hold to the plan. Are we going to try and blow up the bridge again?"

"No more talk about that blasted bridge. The memory haunts me. In truth, I have eyes now for the munitions dump outside Mazar. That should shatter their sleep. Let them know we are still here."

Behind them they could see the flat plains where Soviet helicopters ferried troops towards the fighting in Khost. Fortunately, they flew too high to concern themselves with ground operations. At one point, Omar decided it was unnecessary to hide behind boulders as the copters hovered overhead.

"Agreed. They have their hands full in Paghman," Yuri said. "Abdul Haq may be with the Younis Khalis faction but he is bold. He terrifies Kabul and brings war to the doorstep of Babrak."

"Abdul Haq would be a fool to strike the air base at Baghram. Too heavily fortified."

"Perhaps Abdul Haq might try to capture Bhutto's sons."

"I am sick of hearing about Bhutto's sons."

Daldal, more sure footed than Yuri's horse, was in the lead now as they climbed single file a narrow path that appeared to go straight up the mountain side.

Two Afghan army deserters, both of them barefoot and heading for the refugee camp outside Terri Mangal, were directly in front of them. They stopped to warn Omar that they had heard Soviet tanks guarded the pass ahead.

Omar gave each man a piece of *nan* from the rag he kept tied to his bedroll.

"You are too generous," Yuri grumbled, well after they had passed them.

"They have not eaten for days."

"If you keep this up that will be you."

When they reached the pass they found no tanks, but only bloated dead horses covered with maggots and sprawled across the road. They rode around the rotting carcasses, their own horses skittish and hard to control.

It was a moonless night, the ascent hazardous and slow. The mountains were quiet, except for an occasional boom of a rocket grenade or the thump of a mortar in the distance. Yuri was having trouble with his horse and kept falling further behind.

Impatiently, Omar called to him. "You will be a handful of dust if you don't keep up with me. The night is black with mischief." He waited on the path until Yuri's horse closed the gap. "I'm thinking if Annisa reaches Peshawar she may change her mind about going to America. She loves this land more than she realizes."

"Annisa has lost her spirit. I have seen this coming."

"You are wrong. A girl like that is like a prized *qawk-i-jangi*, a fighting partridge. It is our loss that she flies away. . . Help me Yuri. I do not wish to forget her. Help me to keep her memory alive. Talk to me of Annisa."

"That is the worst thing I could do."

"She leaves such a space. I miss her youth, her appetite for life."

"And her beauty. Hang your worries. I am convinced that we have not seen the last of Annisa."

A kucchi dog could be heard barking in the distance. From behind a clump of trees, a shepherd boy appeared carrying a lantern. "You must detour," he cried. "The Soviets install a new station. Straight ahead. On this path. Up there."

In the shadows of his lantern it was difficult to see the ragged boy. Omar guessed him no more than 10. It made him proud to think the whole nation had rallied against the invaders. Had his first son lived, he would be approaching this age. Praise Allah for giving him a new son this week.

They turned their horses up the jagged side of the mountain to follow the shepherd boy. "How far is it?" Yuri asked.

"Not far."

Twice Yuri's horse lost its footing and the loose rocks underneath rattled down the hillside, sending echoes through the steep canyon below. Yuri swore at his clumsy horse, cursing the night. At one point he was fearful he might have to abandon his animal. The terrain was indeed treacherous. In the dark the ground was almost invisible. Thank God, the shepherd boy guided them.

"Keep your eyes on the light. There is a great drop to the right," Omar called to Yuri.

So they continued for another ten minutes.

As they neared the top, the boy signaled with his light.

Omar, who was close behind, called out again. "Yes, what is it? Are we in the clear?"

He never heard the answer.

A shot rang out and the bullet hit his chest with such force that it knocked him from his horse and he tumbled backwards. An ambush. The shepherd boy, the little traitor--Omar's only thought as he slipped into a blackness more awesome than the night.

CHAPTER 19

Captain Najib Duranni was bone weary. He stared at the sign above the darkened gates of Rokeh: SPIES WILL BE HANGED.

To think, a few years ago, Massoud had fewer than 30 followers and 17 rifles. Now, at age 27, he commanded 5,000 fighters and his influence spread far beyond the Panjsher Valley. Still, his rivals, the leaders of the Herb-i-Islami, complained bitterly about him. "Massoud is for Massoud; he declares himself King of Panjsher," they jeered.

Najib was worn out with the idiocy of it all. Massoud was the one leader who could unite the Resistance and inspire a valley of rag-tag men against an empire. The jealous fools spent more time squabbling with their fellow tribesmen than fighting the Russians. They had no strategies, no concrete plans. He did not relish his task and each time he left the war zone he was tempted not to come back. He was free of Margahalia and could make that final step towards Claire, but it was a step he could never quite bring himself to start.

The narrow path he followed towards the city gates of Rokeh danced in patterns of dark and shadow. Clouds moved over the moon, now light, now gone. Across the distance, he remembered the play of moonlight on the water and on Claire's face.

"Allah is with you," the guard at the edge of the garden compound said, after he recognized the partisan who had just ridden through the gates.

"And with you," Najib answered, as he moved to tether his horse for the night.

A shadow emerged from one of the side tents and hurried towards him, the glow from a lantern weaving them into a circle of light. It was the old warrior Ghulam, a deputy to Commander Massoud, who had come to greet Najib with great ceremony. Najib felt proud. Approval from Ghulam would have pleased his father. Ghulam was a legendary fighter who had served King Nadir Khan in the struggle against Habibullah.

Words from the ancient Afghan song his mother had sung filled Najib.

"Better come home stained with blood
Than safe and sound as a coward."

His mother had sung of men like Ghulam.

"Captain Duranni, you do me honor."

Najib stared at Ghulam's wizened face, his bold clear eyes. Could this man be over 70? His shoulders were not slumped or even rounded with age. There was no softness in his middle and he moved across the compound towards his tent like a caliph, motioning Najib to follow. "You are weary. Come inside."

"I have ridden two nights. . . Massoud. I must see him."

"He left when the light passed."

"When will he return?"

Ghulam shrugged his shoulders. "It is uncertain. A big price on his head. He sleeps in a different place each night."

"But I must talk with him."

"First, sit down. Eat. Rest."

"Is it possible I could get a message to him?"

"Only after you have had your tea. You are like a goat in heat, pawing the ground of my tent."

Najib smiled despite his fatigue.

"I hear you spend much time with the Americans."

"There is a lot of talk about Massoud among them."

"Yes, and all of it twisted. The last foreign news devil you sent us gave us. . . how do you say it? 'Bad press.'"

Najib was amused at Ghulam's use of the Western phrase. "The correspondent from Los Angeles? I had nothing to do with his coming here. The man is an American. My contact is Matthew Hardcastle of Reuters News Service. He is well informed. Even before the war. He knows us."

"Bah. I have heard about this Hardcastle. No Englishman knows us. And those who think they do are the most dangerous. This American devil is no stranger to Afghanistan either. He claims he lived in Jalalabad as a boy when his father was with the American government. Says his father taught us how to plant wheat. Hah! And now he writes that Massoud is a Communist. Such a word as this for the hero of the Panjsher Valley! Did the idiot think we would not hear about it?"

"That's why it's crucial Massoud comes with me to Peshawar. Matthew Hardcastle will be there. I tell you he is a good reporter. Fair. Also French television wishes to interview Massoud."

Ghulam ignored him. "To think that infidel American stayed in my tent, my honored guest, dined on my best mutton. . .Ah, forgive me, you have not eaten. I am sorry your long journey ends with only an old man full of bile." He walked over and put both hands on Najib's shoulders, looking him in the eye. "You did a bold thing when you deserted and brought fresh blood to the Resistance. They tell me you are the glue which holds our shattered tribes together in Peshawar."

Najib could not resist. "Are you saying I have *good* press?"

The old man guffawed. "Your impudence pleases me. I trust that in a man. My aides tell me only what they want me to hear. If you weren't so valuable to us with the West I would insist you stay here. Fight with me."

"I think I would rather chase women."

"You like to hurt an old man, do you? Make him grieve his youth?"

"You? I doubt if age has curbed your appetite.

'A hawk when he grows old,
Becomes more subtle in the chase.
His stoop becomes more bold:
Surrender then to me, for though
I seem no longer young,
The fervor of my love will taste
Like honey on your tongue.'"

"Ah, you recite my favorite poet. Khushal is a tonic for my soul."

"Even though this particular translation was written by an Englishman?"

Ghulam poked at the fire. "The English can only envy us. Habibullah with his four wives and thirty-five concubines. And you, my son?"

"I can't count that high."

Ghulam chuckled. "You are a clever dog. Have you heard the tale of how the Resistance stole a Volvo that was being shipped to a Russian general in Kabul? And how they carried it in pieces across the mountains and reassembled it for Massoud to drive?" He nudged Najib with his elbow. "What kind of man could manage such a thing?"

Najib shrugged. "I just thought the war needed a little levity."

"Good, that's good. You give us laughs. . . Now tell me of your family."

"That story is not so funny."

Men's voices could be heard in the compound. Najib looked up hopefully.

193

"Sorry, my friend, it is not Massoud. Only the guards exchanging for the night. . . Now tell me what goes on in Kabul."

"The latest gossip is who killed General Wodud? The Parchamis? Or the Soviets for colluding with us? No one trusts anyone."

"You avoid my question. Your family. Your wife?"

Najib looked at him evenly. "Margahalia has remarried; they say her new husband works for the Parcham."

"Yi! And her brother with the Khalq? That household will explode." Ghulam grinned. "Life goes on, does it not? We must find you a new bride so you will stay with me and fight. A man should not be without the comforts of a woman."

Najib smiled, thinking of Claire. "You know my weakness."

"I think I do. And it is not what you pretend it is. 'Even the severed branch grows again.'"

Najib shook his head, admiring Massoud's choice in a deputy. Ghulam was clever. He easily read a man.

"Come, you share my *pilao*."

"I have eaten, but I have a great thirst."

Ghulam nodded and went to the *tandori*. He took the steaming teakettle and filled a cracked cup, stirring the sugar with his thumb. "Drink this," he said, gesturing for Najib to sit.
Consumed with weariness, Najib crossed to the carpet that was spread near a hole in the ground, full of burning coals. He dropped on his haunches; grateful for the warmth, the welcome. "What is this I hear about Khomeini's men coming here?"

"It is true. They offered us help if we would quarrel with America. Of course, the foreign devil wrote this too."

"Blast it! How many times must we turn the Iranians down!"

"Don't heat your blood. You and I know the truth." Ghulam leaned forward and punched Najib on the arm. "That miserable son of a camel who sat before this very fire. Full of questions. He asked me. 'Why does Massoud study Mao Tse-tung?' Sly devil."

"Only his military tactics."

"Of course. What else!" Ghulam spat out his tea. "He heard only what he wished to hear. He called Massoud the future Castro. Is it any wonder that Massoud thumbs his nose at newsmen?"

"But we *need* for them to stay focused on Massoud."

"Ah, who cares? It is all a dance." Ghulam squatted on the ground beside his visitor. "A waste of time to talk to infidels. You know what they say. 'Massoud is a Tajik and a Tajik has never ruled Afghanistan.'"

"I don't care if he is a Hazara. Massoud holds the Russians at bay. He has established civil law. . ."

"But on this the newsman was right. Massoud can never rule. Old ways die hard."

When Najib did not answer, Ghulam reached over and nudged him. "Forgive an old man's distress. These are hard times. With the death of Sadat, our supplies from Egypt have dwindled to almost nothing."

"Another reason I want Massoud to come to Peshawar. The Egyptian diplomat, Gregory Meirnardus, arrives in three weeks for talks with the Paks. I want him to meet privately with Massoud."

"Three weeks? That can be a lifetime in the mountains."

"We have to make plans."

"I thought you were here to put Massoud on French television?"

"That too. He is a great hero to the French and soon the world."

"The French have been in this tent many times. Let other commanders talk. Massoud prefers to fight."

"His image could raise millions"

Ghulam scoffed. "Image! It is a word invented by fools. We must not let the West dominate our thinking. Wait here for Massoud. Hear these same words from *his* mouth."

"No, tomorrow I must leave. The Soviets use poison gas in Negarhar Province. I go to find proof for the Egyptian, Meirnardus, to show the UN."

"Proof? They still do not believe us!"

"They want discarded gas masks. Empty canisters. The world demands proof."

"The world is full of donkeys."

"Yes, but if Massoud pleads our case on television. . ."

"An Afghan doesn't plead. We can talk again of this in the morning. Sleep. You need sleep."

"Ghulam, words are important. Like weapons. The story of Islam's struggle is simply not that well known to the West. We must convince them that we fight the Communist menace for them."

"Good. That's good," Ghulam said, rocking back on his haunches. "You make good speeches, huh? Perhaps you should have been here with Massoud when he met with the infidel from America."

The old man had guessed his thoughts. "The Americans have promised us shoulder-fired surface-to-air missiles, S-A7's."

"Don't believe it. All the help we have seen from them are these miserable pieces of paper." Ghulam pointed to Massoud's plastic coated set of U.S. military maps of Afghanistan. "Promises! Bah!" He threw the remainder of his tea upon the ground. "The West blows *Siah Bad.*"

"But we need their equipment if we are to have any chance of winning this thing."

"The Pakistanis have seduced the Americans." Ghulam reached over and stirred the coals. "And it's the Paks who bog us down."

An old story. Najib's father had believed the same thing: all the evils of the world came through the Paks' door. Najib lowered his eyes, pretending to listen. A horse whinnied outside the tent. Across the compound a shepherd's flute sounded thin and clear under the low sky, far beyond the mountains.

He thought of Claire:

"Why did you have to be born on a mountain top five thousand miles away?" she had asked.

It was a question without an answer.

"Najib, I am not a fearful person but sometimes when I am with you I am afraid."

"That I won't come back?"

"I don't know what it is. A fear I can't put into words."

Claire was a woman who was impudent to fate. She laughed in its face. And yet? He too had a sense of doom when they were together and strangely enough, he was more worried for her.

The tea Ghulam had placed in his hand smelled of sweet oranges. Najib could feel his eyes beginning to droop. He studied the coals smoldering in the *tandori*.

Soon he would see Claire again, this time without a wife. He knew he would have to tell her but he had his misgivings in doing so. His marriage for too many years had been his excuse to himself. It had saved him from making the final break from his land.

The tea spilled from the cup. Najib's head jerked. "Forgive my bad company, Ghulam. I *am* tired." He reached for the piece of warm *nan* Ghulam had placed on a greasy plate before him. "I see I have hunger. . ."

"A good sign, always."

Ghulam's voice filled Najib's loneliness. "The Paks fear the Russians. We score a great victory. Their borders are bombed. Arms from the Saudis end up in the hands of the Paks." Ghulam pounded his chest. "Weapons sent from Peking intended for us -- the Paks steal."

"In Pakistan, General Zia had promised. . ."

"Don't talk to me of Zia. He could fall any minute. Jatoi says that if he were in power he would send our refugees back. Force them out if they refuse. Who wants to listen to Zia? His prisons are full. Terrorist bombs in Islamabad--Lahore."

Ghulam rose and stomped to the front of the tent. Pulling open the flap, he pointed to the West. "There. In that direction. Tell me the truth. What comes of your efforts in Peshawar to unite us?"

Najib sighed. "The Jamit can agree on nothing. They shout: 'Bring back King Zahir. No, let Pazhwak establish a government in exile."

Ghulam hit his forehead. "My head aches with it."

"As does mine."

The tent flap opened and from the shadows a young woman entered carrying a plate of sweets. "Khalila sends this to you and your guest," she murmured, not looking up.

"*Tashekor.*"

The girl hesitated.

"I have thanked you. *Tashekor. Tashekor.* How many times must I say it? Now be off." Ghulam waved her to go.

Najib was suddenly very wide-awake. He leapt to his feet. "Annisa?" he thundered.

She raised her eyes to him.

"You know this strange girl?"

Tears welled in Najib's eyes. "To know you are alive." He stared in wonderment as Annisa stood meekly before him. Her hair was long now, below her waist, her breasts, full and pointed. The same light shone in her green eyes. "Annisa. It's Najib. Najib Duranni."

She nodded; her eyes fixed now on the carpet.

"How did you come here? I went out of my mind when they told me you were dead."

"Dead?" she said softly.

"And no word from you all this time." He was pacing up and down.

Ghulam walked over to Annisa and put his hand under her chin, tilting her face upward towards the kerosene lantern that hung from the top of his tent. "So you have a name? You come to us pretending to know nothing. Deaf. Dumb."

"When you found me, I did not know my name," she whispered. "My senses returned. Then I was afraid you would send me back."

"Back where?"

"To my uncles in Doshi."

"Doshi!" Najib exploded. "My God. Four long years with those people. A girl like you!"

"They took me in. They were good to me."

Ghulam snorted. "So good that you ran away? They beat you." He turned to Najib. "My wife says bruises covered the girl's body."

Annisa pulled back into the shadows of the tent; a worried look on her face.

"Annisa, is this true?"

"No, . . please, don't talk of this."

"Did I not tell you she was strange?"

Najib defended her. "She is loyal to her family. But I know these people. They are coarse and crude. The child has been through a terrible ordeal."

"She is not a child. She is a woman. We found her wandering outside the gates, the look of a mad dog in her eyes."

"I was going to Peshawar . . .Panna died." Her eyes pleaded with Najib. "Please, it is true."

"My sweet Annisa. Can this really be you?" Najib held out his arms to her and she ran to him sobbing.

"I tried. Panna said I was not made for village life. But I made myself useful. I did. I did. I still have the chit. I can pay for my plane ticket."

"There. There. It's okay, Annis-jan... It's going to be okay." He looked over at Ghulam. "To think I almost didn't come tonight. Everyone said Massoud would refuse."

"Allah gives reason to your journey." Ghulam's eyes narrowed. "Is she family?"

"Sister to my dearest friend. I made arrangements for her to join him in America. She never made it out to Peshawar."

"The girl tells us nothing. She comes here. She eats our food. A big appetite, I tell you."

Annisa looked up at Najib as though Ghulam was not with them in the tent. "The guide. He stepped on a mine. Panna's heart gave way."

"You were left alone in the mountains!"

Her body shook with her sobbing. "I could not bury them. Little Habiba. A *jinn*, an evil spirit will inhabit her remains and enslave us all."

"Stop, Annisa. You make yourself sick with tears. You are educated. There are no evil spirits."

Ghulam smiled to hear this but said nothing.

"Please do not send me back to Doshi. Ishmael. Omar's first born. The dysentery. I ground leaves of the halarrhena plant. Omar praised me. But still Ishmael died. In his mother's arms." Her words and her tears came in starts. "Fatima gives birth again any moment. I pray she has rich milk." Annisa lifted her head. "Oh, Najib. She wants to send me to that awful shrine."

"Give her some *botah*, some hashish to calm her nerves," Ghulam said.

Najib shook his head, still holding the hysterical girl in his arms. "Annisa I am here now. Your protector. Nothing will ever happen to you again. I'll take you with me. I promise you will not go alone to Peshawar."

"You promise," she sobbed; her head still buried against his chest.

"I will not let you out of my sight until you are safe with Rahmin."

Ghulam cleared his throat. "It is good you have come, son. Too many men in the camp had eyes for her. You are without a woman. She is unsettled in the mind but as fair as the girls from Astanah in the Panjsher. More lovely than Alexander's Roxanne."

A smile formed on Najib's lips as his fingers gently twisted a strand of Annisa's lustrous hair. Ghulam's gnarled hand shot up and made a sign of victory. "Allah, you sly dog. I think you make wise mischief tonight."

CHAPTER 20

"The boy cares too much," his father said. "Better he be like young Abdul who has patience with the seasons--Abdul is content to let things mature."

"Omar is a thunderbolt," his mother argued. "Such energy I have never seen."

"And he spends it recklessly. Omar has no discipline. You do wrong to encourage him in his passions. When he becomes a man, they may cause him pain."

"My son is an eagle. He will soar."

"Your son does not study the Holy book. You may live to see him fall to the ground. It will not be a pretty sight. He flies too high."

The people in their village simply said that Omar was a woman's first born--blessed by his father's faith, and cursed by his mother's expectations.

In a network of secret caves, approximately eight miles from the last Soviet command post in the Khyber Pass, a team of French doctors ran a small hospital for the Resistance. It was to this hospital that Yuri brought his friend Omar El-Ham.

Two doctors, one of them a woman, performed the surgery on Omar's chest wound, laying him on a crude, wooden table and operating by the light of a kerosene lantern. They were without anesthetic but it was not necessary. Omar was unconscious when Yuri brought him in. He had lost much blood and they had no serum to give him. It had seemed senseless to operate. But Yuri had insisted.

"Why not?" the woman doctor had said. "If the Russian can carry the man on his back ten miles through the mountains, then we can operate on a man with no pulse."

Through four long days and nights of fever, Yuri never left Omar's side and he watched with admiration as the woman doctor worked to save his friend. The morning Omar awoke and began to stare at her ample breasts, Yuri was elated. Omar-El-Ham had strength to look at a woman; Omar El-Ham would survive.

During Yuri's vigil he built endless imaginary scenarios around the ambush in the mountains. The boy who volunteered to show them a detour? Who had put him up to it and why?

As soon as Omar could speak, he asked the woman doctor who stood by his bedroll on the dirt floor of the cave, "Why do you help us? Why do you leave your people?"

"In France I pay high taxes." Her smile was droll.

"We owe this woman your life," Yuri said.

"No, it is to your friend you owe thanks. He has the legs of a mountain goat."

"How soon can I go to Peshawar?"

"Is he a madman?" the doctor asked Yuri.

"No, he is driven."

Omar did not hear them, having slipped once again into a gray-lined cloud. So tired. The journey so long. Annisa. The Red-Eye. Daldal. In the cloud he saw his brother Abdul hand him the reigns of his horse.

"But Daldal is your life, my brother."

"He will carry you into the heavens. Like the prophet Mohammed, you will ride across the sky."

Daldal was hurtling upwards now, galloping, kicking up stardust with his hooves. Stars scattered and fell. "I have trouble in believing," Omar shouted to Abdul far below.

"Your disbelief drives you to do things that I, who know I am mortal, cannot. Our people need a man who lives in this world and triumphs over it. I will stay home and hold the land and pray for your journey and your soul."

The horse had begun to spiral downwards, and Omar could see the blackness coming up to meet him. "Daldal," he called.

Yuri was holding his hand when Omar opened his eyes

"My brother's horse? Did they take him?"

"Yes. Daldal is gone. And my horse was shot out from under me."

The woman doctor came up behind Yuri. "Leave him. He needs his rest." She put her hand on Omar's forehead. "The fever is back. Who is this Daldal he calls out for in his sleep?"

"A horse. Named after the horse Mohammed rode into heaven."

"No," Omar muttered. "Daldal was the horse of Husain." Omar opened his eyes and watched the woman doctor cross to the opening in the rock and step into a bright shaft of sunlight. He wondered if the irregular granite cliffs that protected the cave gave way to the central range of the Safed Koh. "Where are we? Who is this woman?"

"You forget, a woman doctor from France. She works for no pay."

"Then Allah has sent me an angel." His eyes closed again.

Yuri left his friend and the dank smelling cave. A dozen chickens scattered at his feet. It was a glorious day, filled with the promise of white pear blossoms. He had only two cigarettes left. It might be weeks before Omar would be well enough to travel to Peshawar.

He watched the woman doctor. The small of her back was stained with sweat. She passed him, carrying a chipped enamel pan and a jug. Water splashed from it, spilling down on her blouse. Her breasts breathed like Sasha's and he shuddered, thinking of his brother's wife. Last night he had dreamed of the French doctor and her tits. Now he held them in his eyes. She sat down on a rock just outside the entrance to the cave. Lines of fatigue etched her otherwise youthful face. It had been almost four years since he had been inside a woman. Anne-Marie. The doctor's name was Anne-Marie.

For a moment he was tempted to chat with her but he checked himself. Never again. It was a vow.

The aroma of the soup simmering on the open fire stirred his hunger. He got up and served himself a bowl.

Another night passed into morning before Omar was totally lucid or wanted to eat. "You have eyes for the woman doctor," he accused Yuri who was spoon-feeding him his breakfast.

"Me? Speak for yourself!"

"Why deny your hunger? The *ferrangi* woman wants it. I can see it in her eyes."

"The fever has left you soft in the head."

"Answer this for me. Are the French good people?"

"No better than anyone else."

"But the doctor leaves her home to help us. She is like you."

"Only in that she has lost her idealism."

"How would you know of this?"

"She spent half of last night complaining about how the Afghans had stolen the 30 sacks of medical supplies her group had brought in with them from Peshawar. The medicines she herself had collected in Paris. She also carried medicines that were collected by an American doctor who waits in Peshawar."

Omar was indignant. "It is stupid to steal from people who help us."

"The woman doctor has many worries. A member of their group was arrested for espionage in Kabul and sentenced to eight years in prison. There is typhoid in the valley beyond. Her other friend narrowly escaped capture."

"So why is she here? A cave is no place for a woman-- even a *ferrangi*. Massoud has good hospitals. Why does she not go to him?"

"Soviet leaflets were dropped accusing Massoud of keeping 'French whores.' She showed me one. They tried several times to capture her friends. They would make them confess to having sex with the Mujahideen and discredit the Resistance."

"An injustice!"

The doctor stuck her head in the entrance. "I told you to let him rest, Yuri. He talks too much."

"I survived the gun, did I not?"

"So you did." She threw up her hands and left.

"With Anne-Marie's help."

"Ah, she has a name. Anne-Marie."

Yuri was annoyed. "Yes, you survived. As Abdul says, you are not mortal. "

Omar's eyes clouded over at the mention of his brother. "Did they take Daldal?"

"You forget. We talked of this before. Daldal is gone."

Omar closed his eyes and muttered. "It is sad when a small boy can be bought for a few coins. The little traitor with his lantern."

"To me it is nothing new. In my country, children are raised to spy on their own flesh." Yuri stood up. "It is our way."

"Don't go Yuri. Stay and talk with me."

"You heard the doctor."

"Bah." Omar opened his eyes "The ambush may have been a blessing. Allah may have a reason for the delay."

"I am not a fatalist. To me life is only the luck of the draw."

"We pull life to us like a magnet. You do not believe that?"

"If I did I could never forgive myself for drawing Colonel Orkunium my direction."

"And do you forgive yourself for being born a Russian?"

"You expect me to deny my own soul? We are a proud people."

"What do you miss most about your home?"

"You always ask me this. Why?"

203

"Because I like your answers. You Russians have big appetites. You eat big--you make love to big women. You have a big square in Moscow. But I ask myself what good is your 'bigness' without a choice?"

"You mean because our life belongs to the State? You forget, the mullahs own yours."

"Strange, isn't it. That here you are in Afghanistan with me, Omar El-Ham. I'll tell you a secret. I believe there are people who cross our lives many times, sometimes they never touch, but all a part of a plan?"

"Whose plan? Allah's? Christ's? The great god Buddha? I prefer to think a god created the world and then abandoned the mess he made."

"But you do believe in miracles?"

"I do now. When Anne-Marie first looked at you she told me I had a dead man in my arms."

"I am greedy. I wish for yet another miracle. . . Do you believe I will ever see Annisa again?"

"Certainly. I still have my eyes on your pearl-handed dagger. I plan to win our bet."

"If you could wish for a miracle what would you wish?"

"Vodka--just one glass."

"Rather than Annisa?"

"Absolutely." Yuri walked to the opening of the cave. "It is better we talk of fighting or drinking than of women. The doctor says you need rest. I am going out now, to sit in the sun and worship it as the ancient Egyptians did."

"Rascal. May it fry your eyes. Here I lie in this damp, dark cave while you feast your eyes on the woman doctor."

Yuri chuckled and stretched. "Yes, my garden is full of flowers." And he left the cave.

Much to his surprise, Anne-Marie crossed the clearing to join him.

Il fait tres beau. A beautiful day."

"Uhuh."

"Yuri, I'm curious. What do the Russian people *really* think about this war?"

"It is dangerous for us to think because our heart isn't in it."

"But do you discuss the war?"

"Yes. But we get very little real information. When they send us here we are told we are here to keep the Afghans from stirring up trouble with our Moslem minorities."

"You believe this?"

"Yes. Islam has been a sleeping giant in this century; it is awake now and flexing its muscles."

"I know very little about their religion. But I find the Afghans fascinating. They are so extreme. They can be very gentle and the next minute unbelievably fierce. I don't think they have bought into our latest Western fad--to be 'cool.' Laid-back. Afghan men seem so . . .so emotional."

"They are circumcised by their seventh year."

She laughed. "What has that to do with anything."

"You wouldn't say that if you had your jewel stick butchered by an itinerant barber. And than your family celebrated your agony with a big feast."

"You are impossible. Did you know that?"

He shrugged.

"How many wives can an Afghan legally have?"

"Four and all the concubines he can support."

"Your friend, Omar?"

"One and she is enough to make his life miserable enough."

"In Russia women are treated pretty much as equals aren't they? Or is that just propaganda?"

He stared at her. "I'm not the one to ask about women. I haven't had much success with them."

"That's begging the question. I'm curious about how Russian men feel about their women. The Russian women I've seen are pretty healthy looking."

"Healthy?"

"You know, stout. A bit matronly. Not exactly the helpless type."

Yuri scowled at her. "You are French. I don't see you as helpless."

She smiled. "*Touche*. You aren't into stereotypes."

"Yes I am. Women are a plague. I don't give a fig about them in any culture." He said it with such a vengeance that she immediately suspected that the opposite was true.

"I think that's my cue to leave you alone," she said softly, re-entering the cave.

Yuri found himself a large boulder on which to sun. The Afghans disliked nudity of any kind but today he didn't care what

205

they thought. He had just embarrassed himself with his surliness. He didn't really want to be left alone. Slowly, he removed his tunic and bared his chest to the hot rays of noon. The heat from the boulder underneath him softened him. He closed his eyes. Life was madness, an illogical whirl of strange doings--a puzzle he did not care to figure out. Rather he ached for release. Escape. A woman, yes. Sasha. He could never get her out of his head. The sun felt good on his face. Yet thoughts of Sasha were always in a setting of snow.

"Yuri!" He could hear Omar's shouts from inside the cave. He leapt to his feet and raced back. Omar was sitting up, his back resting against the granite wall.

He looked contrite. "I tried to stand up. It is difficult."

"Damn it! You will rip out everything they stitched together."

"Then you must leave for Peshawar. Without me."

"No."

"Yes. The parts will be delivered and who will be there to receive them? There are nests of thieves in Peshawar. We will lose our prize."

Yuri dared not tell him that he suspected they already had. The boy who volunteered to show them a detour? Who had put him up to it? "Forget the helicopter parts."

"No, as you said, we must stick to the plan." Omar winced suddenly with pain.

Yuri reached down and grabbed Omar's hand. His eyes were on a small brown lizard crawling up the wall behind Omar's head. "You have lost a great deal of blood. If I go will you promise to do as the doctor tells?"

"Take orders from a woman?"

"A woman gave you life."

"And a woman will be the end of me. So it is prophesied."

"Horse droppings. The fever confuses you. The old mullah said that to me, not you."

Omar laughed again but doing so gave him pain.

Yuri looked at him and was fearful.

Omar seemed to read his eyes. "I will join you in Peshawar," he said firmly. "We will bring back a missile. A Red-Eye."

"And then? "

"We can make our plans after we get it. Who knows what the future will hold."

"Yes, Omar. Who knows." Pretending to be nonchalant Yuri stretched his arms over his head and yawned. "Who knows." Meanwhile, above the cave in the vanishing light, a giant eagle soaring towards the western rim of the canyon suddenly dived into its shadow.

CHAPTER 21

Anne-Marie stood dangerously close to the edge of the cliff watching the caravanesi as it snaked up the mountainside. She lifted her field glasses and focused on a body draped over the lead donkey.

"Poison gas," Yuri said. "That is the word they sent ahead."

"I'm glad you didn't leave yesterday as planned."

"That was only to pacify Omar. I won't leave him."

She leaned over and stared into the jagged canyons far below. "Are you ever tempted? To throw yourself in the air and hurtle down and down."

"Because I am a defector, a man without hope?"

She looked surprised at his outburst. "I think about it a lot. I thought everyone did."

"But why?"

"It would be over in a minute. At least one would be in control. To decide where and when to meet death. Not like those poor bastards struggling up the mountainside." She moved back a few feet from the edge. "Too little sleep and too much to do are unraveling my nerves. I shall end up like Dr. Phillipe--broken and babbling and having to be sent home to Bordeaux."

Yuri stared at her, wrestling with his desires. He wanted to reassure her --to comfort this woman. But he also wanted to keep her at arms length. He wanted her. His mind was on nothing else.

"If only those well-meaning souls who donate free medical supplies could know what it does to your morale to open a box containing treatments for hemorrhoids! " She raised her field glasses again. "In Peshawar I received a letter from my family. They think I exaggerate. My father enclosed a clipping, which said an American scientist had discredited our claims of yellow rain. Claimed the vial the Mujahideen sent him was yellow from bee shit!"

"The whole war is bee shit," Yuri growled.

She sighed. "I agree." She was suddenly all business. "Please go inside and help move the patients to the back. We will need more space."

He nodded, grateful to give her distance.

"And Yuri, I warn you. People who have been gassed--it's a grim sight. Sometimes their skin comes off in your hands."

He left her, still brooding about the conversation he had overheard the night before concerning him. 'The Russian is cold and aloof; his only reason for existence is Omar; now there is a man!' It was one of the nurses talking to Anne-Marie. The sound of their laughter had disturbed him. 'I think the Russian has the hots for you.'

'Well, if he does he can keep it in his pants. I haven't time for sex.'

'A real Neanderthal. I bet he's a gorilla in bed.'

Anne-Marie had countered. 'Don't be so harsh. I suspect he is tender. There is a sadness in the Russian. An old wound.'

It angered Yuri to hear it. He'd be damned if he would tolerate a woman's pity. He had half a mind to confront Anne-Marie and tell her so. Instead, he busied himself moving boxes of medicine further into the depths of the cave to make room for new victims. It all seemed so senseless. He hated the smell of the cave. Mold and dank and medicinal. Omar was sound asleep with the innocent look of a child.

Well, to hell with innocence. To hell with women in particular. The more he thought about it the more he was convinced that Anne-Marie had misled the nurse. It was true, he did have an old wound but he sensed or at least wanted to believe that Anne Marie was drawn to him too-- a tension so powerful between them she would not understand it herself.

When Yuri returned to the sunlight he saw that Anne-Marie had walked down to meet the lead donkey. The tall Afghan leading the caravanesi raised his arm and saluted her. She signaled back.

"*Salaam Aleikum.*"

"*Shoma shotar hasted?*" Anne-Marie answered.

Yuri grinned. She meant to say, "*shoma chetaur hasted?*" Instead of "How are you?" she had asked the Afghan, "Are you a camel?"

"Do you speak English?" the man shouted.

"Better than Farsi or Pushto."

The Afghan had reached her. They were shaking hands. He turned his face upwards in the direction of the cave. He had the bearing of a malick, tall and proud. Experience had put lines in his face but his bottle green eyes were young, Afghans to Yuri often appeared older than they really were. No adolescence for them. They grew from childhood into adulthood with no steps in between. A handsome devil, he was clean-shaven, unusual for a Mujahid. A noticeable scar ran across his right cheekbone. My God, it couldn't be but it was. Suddenly, Yuri was racing downwards to greet him. "Captain Duranni!"

Najib stared at Yuri unblinking and then grinned. "Allah plays games." He stepped forward and hugged the Russian. "I knew it! I knew you would make it through."

"Thanks to you."

"I have great news. Our mutual tormentor is dead. The Resistance captured Orkunium shortly after you disappeared and held in a cave outside of Paghman. Eventually they shot him when they couldn't work a trade."

"Who do you think suggested the kidnapping!"

Najib shook his head. "I should have known. You were always too independent to be Russian. And you dress as an Afghan. No wonder I did not recognize you."

"How many people have you brought?" Anne-Marie asked. "We have only ten bedrolls left. But the cave is deep. There is space for more."

"Good. Anything will do. Most of them complain of dizziness. Vomiting. Those who died in Tor Khama were bleeding from the eyes, the nose, and the mouth. When we tried to move their bodies, their flesh disintegrated."

"Nerve gas. They've used it before."

"There is also terrible itching and trouble breathing."

She turned to Yuri. "Bring those who cannot walk inside the cave. I will see them first."

"So you know this Russian?" she asked Najib as they headed back together to the plateau above. "He seems very dedicated to the Resistance. Pretends he doesn't give a damn. But he has a heart bigger than most."

"Yuri was always drunk when I knew him."

"I can imagine. . . Sad isn't it. He can never go home again and he will never be accepted here. It must be miserable to contemplate."

"Yuri has a talent for living from day to day."

"I guessed as much. This war makes strange bedfellows doesn't it?"

"Indeed." Najib smiled. "I particularly like the French speaking ones."

She smiled. The Afghan was a flirt. Incredibly good-looking, he could easily turn a girl's head.

He smiled back. "I thank you for what you do for our people. We owe a great deal to the French."

"*Nous le faisons avec plaisir.*"
"If nothing else, you bear witness for us to the world."
She threw up her hands. "How much good does that do? Twice I have written reports to the World Health Organization on the victims I examined after attacks near Jalalabad. Their skin was blackened and bloated and there were signs of severe internal hemorrhaging. All of the symptoms of gassing."

"I have something to show you," Najib said, reaching into a sack he had tied to his waist. He opened it and pulled out a gas mask. "We took it off a dead Russian. We also have four canisters that we retrieved and have brought with us. I left them at the way station below." He held up the gas mask triumphantly. "Now let them try to deny it."

"Don't hold your breath. A Dutch journalist actually filmed Russian helicopters dropping canisters, producing a yellow cloud and a few hours later photographed victims with blackened. . .*Mon Dieu!*" she suddenly shouted, pointing to the sky above. A lone Russian jet was approaching. "The vultures. We've moved twice this month. Word gets around we are here, and some nasty informer leads them to us."

"Take cover," Najib shouted, running back towards the column below. He plunged into the line beside Yuri who was carrying a small boy on his back.

A woman further back in the line called out. "Yuri! Over here." Startled, Yuri looked over his shoulder, dumbfounded to see Annisa waving at them. He had no time to respond to this apparition. The jet came straight for the long line of caravanesi spread out in a single trail that snaked all the way down the mountain. It moved very fast and made no sound. Then came a terrifying howl when it dived, and a bomb exploded near the center of the narrow trail, hurtling donkeys and the nerve gas survivors down the side of the mountain. A deep crater had been cut into the middle of the path.

"Annisa. Run for the cave," Najib shouted.

Yuri had given the child he carried on his back to Anne-Marie and ran back with Najib toward the lead donkeys, frantically pulling people to the ground. "The other side. They are trapped."

"Down, get down!" Anne-Marie screamed from the mouth of the cave. "Helicopters!" The shadows of two war birds loomed large as they approached the mountain sideways. Hovering over those men and animals unable to pass around the crater the bomb had made, they systematically flew the line, spraying bullets. Like a

211

row of dominos, the injured toppled, rolling down the path on the edge of the mountain, some into the canyon below.

Smoke was rising now from the deep canyon floor. "God damn those bastards," Najib cursed. "They have bombed our way station. The canisters."

Anne-Marie stood up still holding the child in her arms. "Take the survivors inside the cave. They will return. Once they have found us they always come back."

That night heavy rains came and lightning bolts thundered from mountaintop to mountain top as the small band worked feverishly to pull the few survivors up to safety, and to try and bury those dead still remaining on the trail. It was a night filled with frantic movement, quick tempers, and the moans of the wounded.

Shortly before dawn, the rain stopped. Annisa rose to go outside the cave and start a fire for breakfast. Already the stench of death was in the air from the remains of dead animals too heavy to move from the path.

The only other person up was Najib. He stood outside the cave, his back to her, his woolen cloak pulled tightly around his shoulders.

Shivering from the dampness, Annisa joined him. It was a desolate sight. Najib stood in mud up to his ankles and the murky water trickled down and around the bloated carcass of a goat near his feet.

"Would you like some tea?"

He turned around. "Ah, it is you." His face was drawn and there were dark circles under his eyes.

"Did you not sleep?" she asked.

"No." He seemed distracted--listless.

She walked over to the fire he had already started and put the copper kettle on. "We need warmth. I am sorry about the canisters. At least you have the gas mask to give to the Egyptian diplomat."

"Yes, a gas mask," he sighed. "We had the evidence in our hands. How could I be so stupid to leave the canisters at the way station."

"It's not your fault. It was the logical thing to do. The canisters were too heavy to drag up here—you said so yourself. . ."

He held up his hand to stop her. "You are sweet to be concerned my 'Little One.'"

"Please, no more 'Little One.' You promised."

He laughed. "*Tu hasti drost.*" His eyes boldly caressed her for a moment and she basked in his open admiration. "You were amazing help yesterday," he said. "The French doctor says you have a gift with the sick."

"I hope that is true. I am very worried about Omar."

"The sight of you makes him well. The joy on his face when he first saw you!"

"He thought I was dead."

"A fear I shared for years with Rahmin."

"But I did try . . .Omar sent message after message to Rahmin... There never was an answer."

Najib's eyes narrowed. "I see." He felt suspicious of Omar's alleged attempts but there was no sense in confronting him. He did not want to be the final nail for his coffin.

"But you don't see. I can tell by the look on your face. I desperately wanted to reach Peshawar. I still have the chit and the money for my tickets."

"Yes, you told me. I'm going to get you to Rahmin and soon. Without the canisters for proof there is no longer any urgency to my mission. Our testimony falls on deaf ears."

"Does Rahmin know you have found me?"

"Ghulam promised to get a cable sent to him from Peshawar. Knowing Rahmin I am certain he will be waiting in Peshawar to greet you by the time we arrive. But I confess I was afraid you might not want to go. I have vivid memories of a tearful girl in Kabul who wanted to stay and fight."

"She still does."

"Then you are torn?"

"Yes, I am miserable with it. I care for Omar. . .even Yuri. The Russian and I have become good friends. He serves as a buffer for me with my tormentors. I never thought a Russian could be human. . ." Her voice trailed off. Visions of her very real Russian tormentors had surfaced. She shuddered. "The past few days with you have been my happiest."

Najib wanted to avoid the subject. He did not want to dwell on how happy he had been with her too. "The doctor says Omar will not make it."

"The French lady is wrong. Omar wills it."

Najib warmed his hands over the fire, which sputtered and hissed from the damp twigs. "He loves you very much, Annisa. It is easy to understand."

She blushed. "He has been good to me."

"I think you hurt him. Not telling him you were leaving Doshi. Why did you run away?"

Annisa looked down at her feet.

"It's still not clear to me how you came to Ghulam's tent? You were reckless to travel alone. You should never. . ." The look of sudden terror on her face made him stop mid-sentence. "Annisa?"

"No more questions. Not ever!"

He was puzzled by the abrupt change in her. In the few days since they had begun their travels, she had been so docile, not at all the fiery Annisa he remembered. This little outburst secretly pleased him. It was good to see her spirit was back.

"I can take care of myself. I can ride and I can shoot."

"That is not a woman's role."

She sounded anguished. "And what is that? I wanted to teach the children but there were no books. Fatima made fun of me in the kitchen and was angry I would not marry Abdul. The only thing I was good for was to take care of Habiba. Little Habiba. It's my fault she is dead," she sobbed.

"Annisa-jan. Forgive me. I made you cry. I mean well but I say all the wrong things. What do you want?"

"I want to be with you."

Najib smiled. "You'd soon change your mind. I can be miserable company."

"No, I'd be happy with you."

"Ah, sweet Annisa. That may not be so wise. I have memories of a tearful little girl in her father's garden, yet here is a young woman before me." He gently brushed her check with his fingertips. "The bud has blossomed."

She did not look up--her face burned to his touch. He pulled away from her suddenly aware of the magnitude of what she had been saying. Her look of adulation made him cautious.

"Najib, the beautiful heart necklace you gave me." Her tears began again. "I promised to wear it forever. It is. . .it is lost."

"Not to worry, I'll get you another."

"No! I don't deserve it."

"You deserve the moon."

"I don't want the moon. I want to be with you."

"Annisa, that's not possible."

"What happens after you deliver the gas mask to Peshawar, where do you go?"

"Germany. France. To talk about the Resistance."

"What can you tell them?"

"That the Russians spend big money to divide us. Politicians squabble in Peshawar, but the men do the fighting--here--inside--more and more we are working as one. We can't survive with tribe against tribe."

Anne-Marie emerged from the mouth of the cave. "What a miserable morning." She yawned and stretched her arms high above her head and Najib's eyes went immediately to her voluptuous body. The look did not go unnoticed by Annisa, who backed away from the two of them.

"I eavesdrop, no?" the woman doctor said. She held out a tin cup and Najib poured her some tea. "Tribe against tribe! They said the same in Algiers. The world thought they were too divided. But fighting against the French unified them. Doesn't anyone ever mention the common Russian enemy?" The two of them launched into a conversation about the intricacies of world politics.

Feeling inadequate and shaken by what she had told Najib, Annisa left them and returned to the cave.

Yuri, who was awake, watched her enter and was amused at the instant response she evoked. The male doctor could not take his eyes off her and a wounded Mujahid, who had shown no interest in his surroundings, appeared suddenly alert.

Annisa was totally unaware of the spell she cast as she stood silhouetted at the mouth of the cave, her wet dress clinging to her firm young body. The sky showed a miserable gray and it was even darker in the cave. Annisa took a candle from a ledge, lit it. Holding it close, she approached Omar--the flickering light illuminating her green eyes, even her dark damp hair.

"Jesus, she grows more luscious each day," Yuri muttered under his breath. He could afford the luxury of such thoughts. She was leaving the country. Annisa leaned over the sleeping Omar, her thick black braid touching her waist.

"Is he any better?" she whispered to Yuri.

Omar opened one eye. "I am dead but you have brought me life."

"Oh, you."

"Do I still have a fever. Is it really Annisa-jan?"

"Yes. It is me. I'm sorry, Omar, for all the worry I caused you. Did this terrible thing happen because you were looking for me?"

"You are not that powerful, Annisa-jan. The bullet was mine. I had them save it. Now, I give it to you." He raised up on his elbow. "Yuri, where is my bullet?"

215

Yuri lifted an earthen bowl in which the bullet rolled back and forth and passed it to Annisa. "Here!" It was hard for Yuri to comprehend their superstitions. Omar truly believed the legend that bullets that have wounded but not killed are positive charms and have great protective powers.

"You must carry this when you go to Rahmin. Have you discussed this with Captain Duranni?" There was a worried look on Omar's face. Yuri saw it and interrupted them. "Everything is fine, Omar. There is nothing to worry about. You . . .she will be safe."

Annisa opened and closed her fingers over the bullet several times. "I can feel the power. It is warm in my hands. . .I am happy to hear Fatima bore you another son."

"He is strong with the lungs of a giant. His cries keep the whole village awake."

Anne-Marie appeared carrying a cup of goat's milk. "Drink for your strength."

Omar shook his head.

The doctor put her hand on the back of his neck. "His fever is up again." She looked at Annisa and gently shook her head. Omar did not see or hear her, having slipped once again into a gray-lined cloud where two brothers stood at a mountain stream in the shadows of the Hindu Kush. The water was crystal clear and cold from the melting snows.

"Why is it, Abdul, you have always been like a father to me? Why was I born first?"

"Because you were more eager to join the world."

The jets did not return the next day as expected; nevertheless, the hospital would have to be moved It was certain they would be back. An old barn used for drying raisins had been found in a valley on the other side of the mountain. It would have to do. Those who were too sick to make the trip would simply be left behind in the cave. It was accepted; it was part of the culture, the heritage. When their nomad ancestors had herded livestock to greener pastures, those who could not travel were left to die in the wasteland. It was for the common good.

Omar was adamant with the woman doctor. He would not go with her to the raisin barn. He insisted he was well enough to sit on Najib's horse. He would leave for the border with the others, infection or no infection.

Anne-Marie did not try to stop him. If he stayed with her, he would die on her hands. She was fearful that peritonitis was setting in. Ugly red streaks branched out from his incision.

The next morning, they were a scraggly crew who started down the mountainside as the first rays of sun splintered the dawn. Najib was in the lead, along with Gul Bas, a quarrelsome old man who had brought the French doctors two camels to help move their supplies. Yuri and Annisa brought up the rear behind Omar, who was strapped to Najib's horse and in obvious pain. Their plan was to spend the night in Terri-Mangal before heading to the Jamit's last base near the border, the city of Parachinar.

Anne-Marie was the only one to wave them goodbye. The other doctors had left late the night before and those patients who remained in the cave were too weak to stand. Arrangements had been made for food and water to be brought to them, but under considerable risk. The only hope was that the Russians were after the medical team and once word leaked out they had deserted the cave, those patients who stayed behind would be free to live or die in peace--according to Allah's will.

The mud had dried and the air was fresh and clear. The stragglers labored with great difficulty over a makeshift bridge that covered the crevice the bomb had created. The structure could hardly be called a bridge. It was three logs tied together barely the width of the horses' hooves. Yuri was apprehensive as Omar crossed over ahead of him. On the valley floor beneath them he could see clusters of yellow jonquils in bloom. It was the 21st of Wray, the beginning of the New Year.

Yuri was pleased to be on the move again. He had felt imprisoned in the darkness of the cave. If he was going to die by bombs let it be in a meadow green with the promise of life, rather than entombed forever under mountains of rock.

Yuri looked over his shoulder and waved to Anne-Marie, a tiny speck now, and then he turned to smile at Annisa. He had changed his mind about Annisa. Someday she would come back to Afghanistan and take over the good work of women like Anne-Marie. Annisa had learned many things during the two days she had been in the cave, just by watching the French doctors at work. She could stop the flow of blood by applying a tourniquet and Yuri had watched her help set a bone. Anne-Marie said she would make a good doctor and had given Annisa a tiny silver locket. 'I pass this on. *Je comprend* more than you think Annisa. Take this with you as a promise that you'll return.'

Anne-Marie had not read the guilt on Annisa's face over the jealous feelings she harbored. Yuri had watched the three of them together: Najib, Annisa and Anne-Marie. It was easy to see that

Annisa was smitten with Najib and that she felt intimidated by the confident sexuality of the French woman. Unsure of herself on how to act, the outspoken and bold Annisa he had known in Doshi, was showing a timid side. It amused Yuri. If the girl only knew what fire she kindled. He preferred her defiant and challenging; it was not her nature to be coy and withdrawn with men. Or was it something else? The change in her was dramatic--as though Annisa had discovered fear. Yuri hated fear. It made people stupid.

"Anne-Marie, I can't take your locket," Annisa had protested. "Najib gave me a beautiful heart necklace and I lost it."

'Then all the more reason you should have this. Now be gone before I do something very unprofessional and cry.'

But of course Yuri knew that Anne-Marie did not cry. She was not a crying woman. No doubt she had watched them go with a sense of relief. They were alike. He and the French woman. Both of them believing it did not pay to get too close. Perhaps that is why she had slept with him on their final night. Not one word had passed between them when they met by the stream to carry back the goatskins of water. No need for words. It was something they had to do-- something powerful and primitive and life giving. Nothing like Sasha. He was grateful Anne-Marie had understood. He had said no words to her this morning and the wave at the last minute had been a compromise. Life went on. He felt renewed.

CHAPTER 22

Terri-Mangal was small with narrow streets. There was much coming and going. It was a city heavy with rich-smelling tobacco smoke and the sour smell of sweat on rough men who brandished rifles. There was not a woman to be seen among them.

"Do not speak to anyone," Najib whispered to Annisa as they stopped in front of a large wooden gate set in a high wall. "Your Pushtu sounds bookish. We are surrounded by those who earn their living by informing."

Annisa waited with Yuri and Omar. Many eyes were on her chadri which Najib had insisted she wear until they reached the refugee camp. Yuri stood behind her, shielding her from the street. Men on the second story rooftop of the building Najib had entered stared down at her. When she moved, she felt a sharp pain in her abdomen and her forehead burned. If only she could sit down.

She looked at Omar, who had dismounted his horse and leaned heavily against the thick, mud wall. His face remained impassive, but she could see he was in pain. Her discomfort would pass; it would be weak to complain.

Najib returned with a man called, "Toothless One." He reeked of garlic and the ring of dirt around his neck looked so permanent it could pass for a tattoo. Toothless One had disturbing news. They could not stay in the town.

"Go down by the stables. There is a *kishmishkhana* there, a hideout."

Najib was annoyed. "Why must we leave our horses? My friend is injured."

Without a word, Yuri walked over to Omar and hoisted him up on his back.

"I can walk," Omar protested.
"Not while I'm around."

They made their way past several houses along the edge of a muddy stream that flowed near the town. A large gathering of men loaded carts pulled by donkeys. Next came a stretch of flat land where many horses were tethered against a fence of rocks.

"Why couldn't we have brought our horses here?"
"Those are my orders. I do what I am told."

A man from the Hazzara tribe passed them. He carried two, large tin trays filled with bullets, balanced on each end of a pole across his back.

"The town is filled with rumors," Najib told Yuri. "You among them."

"Me?"

"They heard Omar call out your name. There is news that a captured Soviet chemical specialist named Yuri Pavarnitsyn is being escorted to Peshawar to testify."

"About what?"

"About his dirty job. He examines villages after chemical attacks to determine if they are safe for Soviet troops."

"I hope you set them straight."

"Yes, but I am not sure they believed me. I do not like leaving the horses behind. We will have to stand guard tonight. There are people in this town who would quickly deliver you back into Russian hands. If you are the Yuri they think you are, you would bring a big price."

Annisa followed close behind, listening and watching. She studied a group of men milling around a string of donkeys at the far end of the compound. There was no kindness in their faces.

"Smugglers," Najib told Yuri. "The price of hashish grows larger every day. Two thousand Kalnifov bullets for one kilo."

"I bet the DEA screams about that."

"You know about the Americans?"

Yuri smiled. "It's no secret. They have a tough time. It's hard to run a clandestine operation and not look the other way."

"Well, there is nothing we can do. The smugglers help to keep the borders open so that we can move men and supplies. They are a necessary evil if we are to continue the war."

Annisa was disillusioned to hear it. The shame of it would make it easier to leave Afghanistan.

Toothless One exchanged greetings with a man outside the stable. The man pointed to a house in the field beyond. "They can sleep on the roof."

It was getting dark. It was difficult to see the rungs of the flimsy ladder leaning against the outside wall. Najib's strong arms pulled Annisa upwards. Yuri came next with Omar slung over his back like a sack of flour. He bulldogged his way through men who had already found a spot on the roof and stretched Omar on a place near the edge. "I will go for his sleeping mat. We left it on the horse. Save me the space next to him, in case I have to make a hasty exit in the middle of the night. I will stand guard first."

"I'll be glad when we are out of here," Annisa said.

"Shsssh. Do not speak."

Annisa settled down between Najib and Omar. Her teeth were clenched. Her insides felt full of poison. Anne-Marie had talked of a village where the Russians had poisoned the well. It was not like her to be sick. Yet no one else had complained. She prayed it was not the amoebae or worms. Old Panna had been sick with them for years.

The night air in the desert grew cold rapidly.

"Does your wife mind sleeping without a blanket?" Toothless One asked Najib.

"No, she is fine. She is not feeling well but she has my arms to warm her."

Najib's words sent the blood to her head. He had not denied her as his wife. No doubt he considered it safer to pretend. But how did he guess she was ill? "Did Anne-Marie tell you of my complaints? She promised. . ."

"I told you not to talk." His voice was harsh.

Annisa turned her back to him. Crossing paths with Najib had been wonderment. Without Najib she would still be back in Guliman's tent denying to herself she was even alive. Najib was delivering her to Rahmin but instead of the great joy she had anticipated, she was filled with an incredible sadness. She could not bring herself to believe she was worth all this effort and for the first time in her life she felt uneasy around Najib. He was kind and patient with her as always but something had changed between them. Gone was his easy banter—the joy she used to feel when he teased. He was overly polite to her, almost formal and on their long ride with the caravan to retrieve the gas canisters he had only talked of mundane things. She sensed he wanted her to keep her distance and that his attention to her was only out of a sense of duty. Had he guessed the Russians had sullied her or did he find her boring after her four long years with people who could neither read or write? It hurt her feelings when he avoided her but she was too proud to ask him why. She noted that Omar had pulled himself up and was sitting near the ledge, his rifle resting across his lap. It was too dark to read his face but she knew his eyes were watchful, waiting for Yuri to return.

Below in the courtyard angry Pushtu voices sounded. "A curse on you! The box is empty."

"An honest mistake."

"No, you have cheated me." A shot rang out. "An honest lesson for you, thief."

Annisa closed her eyes. There would be little sleep for any of them. Terri-Mangal was a different world. The unity of the mountains was missing. On the faces of men, she saw only greed.

"Damn them. As I suspected. The horses are gone!" Yuri had come up behind them.

Toothless One sat up. "They have been taken to a safe place."

Omar growled at him. "My dagger will make sure you speak the truth." A soft moan of pain escaped his lips. He handed Yuri the rifle and lay back down.

Yuri lifted Omar's head and placed the bedroll under him. "You forget. It is my dagger now. I won the bet."

"Has Captain Duranni asked any more questions about Annisa?" Omar whispered. "About the report on her death?"

"No," Yuri lied. "He suspects nothing." In fact, Najib had questioned him at length and when Yuri had asked him to drop it because it would only upset Omar--Najib had agreed, saying he would figure out a way to pacify Rahmin.

Omar raised up on his elbow. "Do you think Annisa will ever suspect me?"

"Keep your voice down. She might hear you. The answer is no. Never." Yuri truly believed this. Annisa was too trusting of others. "No more talk. The night has eyes and ears of its own."

Soon Omar was asleep and snoring.

The sound of his snoring reassured Annisa. It reminded her of Doshi-- all of them crowded together for warmth around the coals of the *tandori*. She never thought she would miss it but tonight she did. She prayed she too would soon meet sleep. But Terri-Mangal came alive at night with movements of supplies and men. Now the sounds turned from heated arguments and insults to laughter and music. A Jews harp played. Annisa sat up and peered over the edge of the roof. A bonfire had been lit. Longhaired men danced around it.

"Homosexuals!" Yuri grumbled. "They disgust me."

Najib was restless, flopping about like a fish, unable to settle himself comfortably.

"Shall I give you more space?" Annisa murmured.

"How many times do I have to tell you. Be still."

Why was he so bad-tempered? What had she done to anger him? She would try to entice sleep by telling herself a story. Her father's favorite. Lila and Majun. A legend of selfless love where the lovers sacrificed themselves, Majun's arms embracing Lila's gravestone. It was not long before Annisa had slipped into dreamland where she saw Ishaq approaching on a white horse. The moon was full.

Sleep did not come for Najib. Stretched out next to Annisa, every part of his being was tense. He did not worry so much about the horses; if necessary he had money to buy them a ride in a truck to Parachinar. He worried about what he had not told the others. Toothless One had confided that the helicopter parts, delivered the day before they arrived, were now gone. Stolen. "Pirates," the old man had said. "Six men from Paktia. They mean to purchase a tank. 25,000 U.S. dollars." Apparently, they learned of the contents of the truck and left with it for Peshawar to see what Western intelligence would give them.

It infuriated Najib. Not only had Omar risked all to get what he called his "prize" --the theft further exemplified how egos got in the way of fighting the war. The men from Paktia felt perfectly justified in doing what they had done. It was crazy. Men wanting a tank, when they had no central fuel supply, and when a Russian helicopter could take it out of action in a minute. He feared their belief in the magic of technology would be their undoing. One tank would not win the war. Stealing from one another would lose it. He dared not tell Omar the parts were gone. That blasted missile he dreamed of had kept Omar alive. It was pitiful. Men like Omar were unsophisticated and child-like in their thinking. They were brave beyond all others but also a roadblock to unity. Too many Afghans were like Omar, wanting to win the war all by themselves.

In her sleep, Annisa rolled over and threw her arm over Najib's back. He stiffened. He knew she was drawn to him and it was the last thing he wanted. In her innocence, Annisa did not know her eyes revealed a yearning. He could feel her young breasts against his body, awakening memories of the female he tried to forget. Strange, he had not thought of Claire for days, not since he had held Annisa's face between his hands in Ghulam's tent, her eyes bright with excitement because he would deliver her to Peshawar. Perhaps he should not have promised to buy her a new red dress to wear in America. Had she misread his good intentions? Her eyes always seemed to follow him. Last night, he dreamed she had come to him and told him of her desires in her father's garden. Thoughts like this would have to stop. Why had he said a red dress? Was it because Claire looked so desirable in red chiffon the night they had met? As beautiful and tempting as she was, Annisa could not compare to the smoldering Claire, so calm and poised in every social situation and a tigress in bed. Diplomats and journalists ate out of her hand. She was always the lady, elegant and sophisticated. He had once told himself these things did not matter, but they did. At the end of the day, this made him more like Margahalia then he ever cared to admit.

He could feel Annisa's even soft breathing on his neck. It was disconcerting; sent shivers. He treasured her innocence, his role as her protector and her sweet surrender to his care. But the magnitude of her beauty was tempting, giving him thoughts which took away his sleep. Claire. He must think of Claire. She had agreed to meet him in Peshawar. The Ditchfields. But he was not counting on it. Twice, she had reneged.

"Better you come to London, my handsome warrior. The war is all you talk about. You need escape. I will give you safe harbor."

Najib smiled in the dark. Her harbor! Light blonde hair curling atop her mound. He preferred Margahalia clean, waxing away all the hair from her body. But Margahalia in his bed was wooden. What would young Annisa be like? Her soft arm still rested on him. What a delight it would be to awaken the passion which waited between her thighs.

"Najib." Najib's hand tightened on his gun as a hand touched his shoulder. "I must talk to you," Yuri whispered. "No, not here," Najib answered.

The two men slipped from the rooftop and crossed the compound to where men were loading burlap sacks of bullets onto donkeys. The dancers with their long hair were gone.

"If you are worried about the horses. . ."

"Our helicopter parts were delivered. I went to check with our contact. He claims they are gone."

Najib sighed "He speaks the truth, Yuri. Men from Paktia."

In the light of the dying bonfire, Yuri's face contorted in anger. "This will kill Omar, surer than any bullet."

"I have contacts in Peshawar. I meet with a powerful Egyptian diplomat from Islamabad. Perhaps he can free up some.. ."

Yuri spit in the ground. "You know the price of a Red-Eye."

"Yes. What Omar wants is impossible. I was hoping he would settle for less."

"All night I have thought of this. I have a plan. The money you mentioned the Russians would pay to snatch their chemical advisor back?"

"A big sum, I'm sure. His testimony to the UN would be very damaging."

"Then turn me in here. Say I am Yuri Pavarnitsyn and collect the money for Omar."

"God, Yuri. Have you lost your reason? When they discovered they had the wrong man to deliver to the Soviets you would have a knife in your heart."

"That is my concern. Old Toothless One has already agreed to help me escape them once you have the money safely in your hand and are out of Terri-Mangal."

"Whoa! You go too fast. You have talked to him?"

"Yes, he thinks you will split half with him if he delivers me safely to the refugee camp."

"I would not trust that man an inch."

"You will have to. I have already struck a deal. He had gone to tell them he knows of my whereabouts. In the morning you are to escort unsuspecting me to the tea house to make the exchange."

"Yuri, you are throwing your life away."

"I take care of my life better than you suspect."

The darkness passed without incident. The morning air was dusty and warm.

"Get a move on, Annisa." Yuri stood over her. "Najib prepares to go."

She sat up and rubbed her eyes. "Where is Omar?"

"We have moved him to a house closer to town."

"Why?"

"He is not well enough to continue the trip. His head is like hot coals. We have found an old woman to drain the pus from his wound."

"That is unsanitary. He should go to the hospital in Peshawar."

"Annisa, believe me. Omar is too sick to continue the trip."

"I will not leave without him."

"You did once before."

Her temper flared. "You know nothing about why I left--why I did not come back to Doshi."

Yuri stared at her. "I am nobody's fool. Your story about Habiba being shot and you falling into a ravine, about bruising yourself--I guess more than you think."

"I hate you."

"That is nothing new."

"I'm going to stay with Omar."

"No, damn it!" She had never seen Yuri so angry. "Stupid woman! Don't stir a ruckus. Don't upset Omar. God knows how long we will be stuck in this god-forsaken place. We will catch up with you later. Najib says you will be many weeks in Peshawar before they process your papers."

Annisa was thunderstruck. "You mean you are not coming either? What about the helicopter parts? The truck?"

"I stay with Omar."

"Can I say goodbye to him?"

"Fatima is right. You are too dramatic. You will be seeing him again. Soon."

Reluctantly, Annisa climbed down the ladder behind him. "I need food in my stomach. My insides hurt. . .Yuri, wait. Where are you going in such a hurry?"

"I am to meet Najib at the tea house. You are to wait for him under the city gates."

"Alone?"

"What worm has sucked at your courage? For heavens' sake, Annisa, stop this schoolgirl talk. Wait for Najib. He will care for you as a sister. You have nothing to fear from him. He has no interest in you as a woman. He has a wife in Kabul. I met her once."

"I will make no trouble. I want to go with you to the teahouse."

"Forget it. You are more trouble than you are worth."

As they approached the teahouse, they could see Najib outside shouting at Toothless One. "You son of a camel. You made the whole thing up."

"Wait here," Yuri ordered Annisa and hurried towards the two men. Annisa paid no attention and followed. Najib turned to Yuri with a look of exasperation. "He claims the captured Russian chemical advisor passed through early this morning. Now he must leave with us for Peshawar or they will have his head for trying to pass you off."

"What has happened?" Annisa demanded.

The men ignored her. Najib, enlightened as he was, did not include her in his plans as Omar always did. This was, after all, the business of men!

Yuri threw up his hands. "So take the old fraud."

"And you?"

"It was worth a try. At least now I am safe to stay with Omar. There is no longer a price on my head."

"Az Khud-i-ma." It was a meaningful phrase. Afghan to Afghan. *Az Khud-i-ma* meant that Yuri was one of their own. It showed a deep affection. A bond.

Yuri appeared overwhelmed when Najib embraced him. His answer was unintelligible and he made movements with his hands as though to ward off something.

"He considers you a blood brother," Annisa said, staring at Yuri, amazed to see him so rattled.

"So why do you gawk?" Yuri scowled.

"You. . .take good care of Omar."

Yuri brushed his eyes with the back of his arm. "And you do as Najib tells you. He is your *kaka* , your protector, now. . .May your life be long."

Old Toothless One nodded and shuffled away to wait by the gate. From the distance he saw the Russian step forward and awkwardly embrace the girl. Heathens. All of them! The wife of an Afghan was allowing a *ferrangi* to hold her. He wanted no part of this blasphemy!

CHAPTER 23

A few miles outside Peshawar the refugee camps were dotted with white canvas tents, unlike the black, goat-hair tents of the nomads. Issued by the Pakistan government, they were new, without patches or tears. New arrivals received 50 rupees per month, which was generous, compared to what Afghan refugees in Iran received.

But Annisa did not like what she saw in the camp and did not want to stay. Najib promised her it would not be long before they went into Peshawar.

"I will be gone only a few days. First thing when I get there I will go to Dean's Hotel and ask for Rahmin. He should arrive in Peshawar any day now. And when I return it will be with the new red dress!"

"Why can't I go with you?"

"You have a fever. Your face is pale. Better you rest. I have many meetings in Peshawar and it is best I check with my friends, the Reeds, before I bring you to their house." Then he grinned. "Your arrival is about four years late."

Annisa made a face at him. "These missionaries? Are they good people?"

"Yes, well-intentioned despite their jumbled thoughts. They are here to convert us to Christ."

"Will they try to convert me?"

He laughed. "I doubt it. Five minutes with you and they'll know you are not easily swayed."

Annisa was trying not to pout but to have come this far and be so close and still having to wait! "Are you sure I can't come?"

"You forget I meet with Ambassador Meirnardus"

"He must be very important and he is coming all the way from Islamabad just to meet with you!"

Najib could not hide his exuberance. "Miernardus is a powerful ally for the Resistance. His work behind the scenes may be the bridge for our push for stinger missiles. That could change the course of the war. Things are looking up, Princess."

"No wonder you are so happy!"

He nodded, feeling a bit sheepish. There was another reason why his blood was up. It would not have been that difficult to bring Annisa to the Reeds unannounced. But Claire was flying in tomorrow and he selfishly wanted some time alone with her. "When

I return you will be feeling more fit. I promise you, dear Annisa. You will be seeing Rahmin and soon."

He prayed what he said was true. In Terri-Mangal he had sent a message ahead to Dean's Hotel for Rahmin to leave word for him at the refugee camp. But when they arrived at the camp there had been no message waiting for him.. It was frustrating. Had Rahmin received the cable Guliman had promised to send ahead?

"I hope Rahmin is waiting in Peshawar to surprise me."

"I hope so too."

Najib cautioned her not to call attention to herself while he was gone. "In a few weeks you will be on your way to a new life. The injustice you see here will be like a very bad dream."

"But how can I forget the misery?" She had only been in the camp a few days and was appalled at the conditions. All those people who had made the torturous trip through the mountains with hopes for a better life only to settle for an existence as demoralizing as the one the communists had to offer in Afghanistan. Children in the camp were losing their Afghan pride of independence and self-sufficiency. Many were undisciplined and so many were sick-- aches, coughs, fevers, digestive troubles. Better to fend for oneself in the countryside than to sit here with a hand out, expecting to be fed. Also the Pakistanis were resentful. They did not like sharing their water or their jobs. It was true that they were proud of their Afghan cousins who were fighting godless communism --it meant victory for Islam. But they did not like their children wearing Afghan-style baggy trousers, long shirts and vests. The Pushtu spoken in and around Peshawar had many Afghan phrases in it now. 'Don't go into Peshawar,' other refugees warned her. "You will be unhappy there. We are not really welcome. They are jealous of us because we are smarter and work harder. Peshawar does not welcome an Afghan girl."

Najib told her that everything she heard was exaggerated by both sides. "The Paks say that half of our people earn their living by smuggling heroin and that we plan to rise up and overthrow them. That is why they are afraid of our guns. They make us a scapegoat for their domestic tensions."

Annisa sighed. "I want to be of help but perhaps it is good I do not stay. It is my nature to speak out. They would send me right back to Doshi."

"I wouldn't let them! We never want to lose you again."

She felt weak with happiness to hear such words.

"Annisa-jan. Don't ever change. You are going to love America. It will feed your high spirit. Now run along, Soon it will be dark and you don't want to miss the evening story in the fortuneteller's tent."

"Go with God, Najib."

Haji Baz, one of the maliks, passed by her as she wended her way through the maze of tents. Annisa glared at his back. She despised the man. Najib had told her he was corrupt and kept for himself some of the wheat flour that foreign sources donated. There was no doubt that the women and the sick received unfair distribution in the camp. The maliks should not be in charge of handing out the food, but Najib had warned her repeatedly to say nothing; it made sense in terms of tribal traditions, and any attempt to undermine malik authority would only cause problems. Najib was more patient than she. After all, people in the refugee camps outside Peshawar were lucky; Baluchistan was receiving little in the way of relief items. She wanted to challenge them but she did not want to bring trouble for Najib. Her heart was glowing with the thought of him as she slipped into the circle surrounding the fortuneteller, Mabaie.

"Yusuf, son of Ya'kub, was the youngest son, but the most beloved. He went with his brothers on a trading caravan from Caana, somewhere in Arabistan to Egypt. The brothers dumped Yusuf in a well, killed a sheep, wrapped up the sheep in a cloak, then took the bloodied cloak to Ibrahim. A caravan came along, looked in the well, dragged out Yusuf, and sold him as a slave in Egypt.

The handsome young slave became the favorite of the Pharaoh's wife, Zulaika. Tongues among jealous females began to wag, so Zulaika held a banquet for her lady friends. She served apples with knives. Then Zulaika asked Yusuf to come in with some grapes. All the lady guests began to swoon and accidentally cut their wrists while looking at the beautiful Yusuf. Zulaika then said, 'See, you are just as guilty of secret lust as I am.'"

The audience was spellbound and asked for more as the sun slipped over the horizon and the lighted candles inside the tent flickered and danced in shadows on the eager faces surrounding Mabaie. Annisa was not so much enthralled by the stories, as she was by the feeling of comradeship inside the circle. She felt her roots, her inheritance. These were her people.

After Mabaie, the gypsy story teller from the Jat Guji tribe, had finished with her tales and dismissed the audience she motioned to Annisa to stay. "I have something to tell you."

A look of concern crossed Annisa's face. "You give fortunes. You see bad things for me?"

"No, I only want to tell you it is not wrong to love a man. This Najib who brought you to the refugee camp is not your husband?"

Annisa was alarmed. "How would you know such a thing?"

"I make it my business to watch all new arrivals and you in particular. Women with your beauty can create trouble . . ."

"Oh, no. I'm not like that. Please, say nothing of this. We travel as man and wife in name only. For safety."

Mabaie rubbed her fingers over the stubble of hairs on her chin. "Once my skin was smooth, unlined, like yours. Your secret is safe with me. I tell no one in this miserable place."

"How did you guess he was not my husband?"

Mabaie laughed hard and passed wind as she did. "He looks at you like a man who has not tasted you."

"You mean he desires me!"

"Do not deceive me. You lust for him too." Mabaie stood up to collect the coins left in her dish. "He is rare among men. He will not pluck the fruit. He wants your happiness above his own."

"He helps me go to America."

"I guessed it. You are privileged. Not poor like the rest of us."

"I go to America to study. To be a doctor."

"Unhappy girl. You should marry instead. All the curses of this earth are bearable in the warmth of a man's loins. I have been a widow many years and my body still aches for my dead husband."

Annisa looked up amazed. It was hard to believe that the old woman had these thoughts.

"I think you are a girl who knows the answers in books but she has much to learn about life. The greatest thing a woman can do is give birth to a son. Nothing else matters for us. Nothing. When you are old like me you will look back and remember my words. Ghosts, my child, visit your eyes. Only the love of a man can drive them away. Tell me, do you still bleed?"

"Yes, it is with me now."

"Then what is this pain in your gut?"

"I have no pain."

"You do not fool me. You clutch at your belly. Your face is flushed. A red rash down there, I bet. She pointed to Annisa's private parts. I think you have the sickness of men. It can eat up your brain. Make you crazy."

Annisa stared at her horrified. "I am a girl. How could I possibly . . ."

"Men give it to you when they stick their baby maker inside you."

Annisa gasped and hurriedly left the tent, not wanting to hear another word. Did the Russian soldiers give her this? Would it really eat up her brain? She prayed Mabaie would keep her secret! And all this talk about Najib had upset her. She could not admit to herself that she idolized him and that she would stay in Afghanistan if he asked. She would even be a second wife. But she was too proud to let him know this and she did not believe Mabaie had any real insight into the thoughts of Najib. Najib was in love with his work for the Resistance. She had watched him come alive when he talked to the maliks in the refugee camp. They looked up to him. He was a man of great honor with many things to do

She turned in the direction of the tent she and Najib shared with a Turkoman family. It was unusual for the Turkomans to be among Pushtuns but Najib had requested to be with them. He was intent on communicating with ethnic minorities whenever he had the chance. "You should understand the need for this more than most.. A Tajik mother and a Pushtun father. The only hope for Afghanistan is for the tribes to live together in peace."

"It was not easy. Najib. Even in Kabul."

"Annisa. Annisa!" Zarghuna, the eldest daughter of the Turkoman family came running toward her. "Did you hear a wonderful story again tonight?"

"Yes. After I have eaten I will tell it to you and the others." Annisa felt sorry for Zarghuna, who worked with her sisters weaving carpets sun-up to sundown. Zarghuna had no time to go to the tent of Mabaie and listen to stories.

Annisa entered the tent and crossed to the fire where the evening meal simmered inside an iron pot. She settled herself on the carpet beside Zarghuna's mother. The woman wore a red conical hat with coins sewn on it. The metal shone in the firelight. "I shall leave here soon," Annisa said. "You have been so kind to me. When I get to America I shall tell them that Turkomans make the finest carpets in Afghanistan."

The mother handed Annisa a piece of bread to dip in the stew. Annisa knew the mother did not approve of them staying in her tent. But her husband was a great admirer of Najib and she had no say in the matter. She raised her hand up and touched Annisa's locket. "Not Afghan," was all she said.

"No. A French lady doctor gave it to me."

"The tall American doctor came looking for you."

"Oh?"

"His name is Dr. Harris," Zarghuna added with some importance.

Annisa had seen the tall, blonde American in camp. "I wonder what he wants?"

"He has heard you speak good English." Zarghuna held out her hand. "Look, he gave me five afghanis to send you to his tent. Hurry. I will give you half when you get back."

"Me? Take *baksheesh*!" She saw the hurt on Zarghuna's face and was immediately remorseful. Five afghanis were a fortune to these people and Zarghuna had offered to share. "I'm sorry, I didn't mean it that way. I'm not angry with you. Only with the American for thinking he has to pay us to do anything."

Zarghuna attempted to smile but it was obvious she was fighting back tears. "Please, forgive me," Annisa said. "You have done nothing wrong." She looked over at Zarghuna's mother who glared at her. Oh, God, when would she ever learn to curb her tongue!

All the way to the American doctor's tent Annisa tried to calm herself. And why did she feel such anger for the American doctor? She had seen him from a distance and judged him to have a kind face. She had only been in the camp a few days and already she was becoming like the rest of the refugees--hating the outside world.

The tent where the American doctor was staying was the tent of a *rishi-i-saif*, a white beard, an elder in the Village Council. He had permitted the American to be with him and had promised Najib when he returned he would introduce him to the American doctor who came to the camp for two weeks in the spring and again in the fall.

"You wanted to see me?" Annisa asked.

The young doctor stuck out his hand and shook hers. She felt awkward with his gesture but did not want to correct him.

"Thank you for coming. I have been told you are good with the sick?"

She liked the strength in his hands, the eagerness in his eyes. He seemed boyish. "I know very little about medicine. Only a few days up in the caves with some French doctors. The patients were gassed."

233

"Then it's really true? I've heard so many rumors about poison gas."

She was indignant. "Of course it's true. Their skin fell off in our hands."

"We need to get photographs of that. Proof."

"Captain Duranni thinks the same thing. I am sorry. He has gone to Peshawar. You should talk with him when he returns tomorrow night."

"Captain Duranni?"

"He is the one you want to talk to, isn't it? Najib has brought out a captured gas mask as proof."

"Actually, at this moment I need the help of a woman. An Afghan brought his wife to the tent earlier today and asked me to prescribe some medicine for her. Unlike you, the woman had on that blasted veil. I could not see her face but it certainly was not hard to tell she was in the early stages of labor. She was very upset. Jabbering at me in Farsi. I knew only a few words of Pushtu. Today is your Holy Day. Not a Pak doctor in the whole damn camp. The husband refused to let me examine her. When I made him understand I knew she was pregnant, he denied it. I didn't know whether to laugh or cry."

"Afghan men do not talk about these things."

"That's obvious! It's been bugging me all day. I thought why not send for you and let you ask the woman certain questions for me. We might be able to help her. Is that allowed? For you to help me?"

"Why not? Show me where they live."

Ethan Harris walked with Annisa to the edge of the clearing. "The tent nearest the road. There. Where the green shirt on the pole is whipping in the wind."

"Yes. I know of these people. The woman has just given birth. The baby was born dead."

"Jesus. What are you telling me?"

"The child came less than an hour ago. I know. I was in the tent of Mabaie the storyteller when her husband came for help. Mabaie has many herbal remedies."

"Witchcraft, you mean. Damn it. Under my very nose."

"I'm sorry." She felt her face flush as she said it.

"What can I do with people who don't want my help?"

"We do want help. It is just that a *ferrangi* is not allowed to touch an Afghan woman."

"So why did he come to me in the first place?"

"I suspect the wife knew something was wrong and begged him. We are not stupid. We know your medicine is better."

Dr. Harris picked up a stick and hurled it across the open field. "Maybe it's just as well I didn't make it 'inside.' I'm having trouble with your rules. And ours. In the three years I have volunteered my help, the American government has refused to let me go into Afghanistan."

She was overwhelmed "Three years you have been coming here? That is a very great gift." She felt embarrassed that this nice American doctor would have such a low opinion of Afghans. "It is rude to ask you but why do you come?"

"Pig-headedness, I suppose. I don't like being told there is something I can't do."

"Ah, yes. This I understand. But your interest in Afghanistan?"

"I have a good friend in the States who is an Afghan. We interned together at a hospital in New York. He is a very good salesman for your cause."

"My brother does this. He recruits . . ."

"Wait a minute." Incredulous, he looked at her. "You don't mean Rahmin? Rahmin Aziz!"

"Then you know him!"

"It never dawned on me you could be *that* Annisa! When they told Rahmin you had died trying to escape to Peshawar he came back a different man. Quit his internship to devote all his time for the Resistance."

Annisa was horrified. "My brother did not finish his studies?"

"No. He drives a taxi at night and in the daylight hours he is on the phone, badgering, cajoling, and raising funds for volunteers. But you should know that he never gave up hope you might still be alive. He even asked me if I could be of help when I came over. I went to several people he gave me to contact in Peshawar. He said new refugees arrive every day. I checked for your name in all the camps but there was no one by the name of Annisa Aziz."

She blushed. "I'm only here for a few days and Najib put down my name as Annisa Duranni."

"Ah, I see. Then you're married."

"No."

"Sounds a bit tricky."

235

"It makes it easier to travel together. Not so many questions."

Dr. Harris looked pleased. "Are you still coming to the States?"

"As soon as my papers are ready."

"Rahmin must be over the moon."

"Pardon?"

He grinned. "Never mind. Does he know you've been found?"

"Najib has cabled him. I am hoping he is on his way to Peshawar."

"Fantastic. Wonderful. With all the misery I see here day after day I'm happy to learn of a happy ending." Dr. Harris reached into his billfold and pulled out a card. "I hope it's not against your rules to take my address. I'm a good man to show you around if you should get down to Washington, D.C. I'm at George Washington University hospital. I try to make it over here on my holidays. I managed a month this time." He handed her his card. "Go ahead, take it. I'm only here for a few more days myself."

Annisa smiled. "I leave the camp tomorrow to stay with American missionaries in the city."

"This is probably breaking another one of your rules but did anyone ever tell you how pretty you are?"

She could feel the blood rise to her cheeks. "No."

"Well, what's wrong with the men in Afghanistan?"

She didn't know how to respond. "Are all American men like you?"

"You mean brash?" He stood there, half-blocking her exit from the tent, as though he didn't want to see her go. He had a generous smile and nice even teeth. His features were perfect. Too perfect. There was no flaw to make his face memorable.

"You really aren't married?"

"No, Najib has a wife in Kabul."

"Then all is not lost. You have made the trip over here worth the taking." He followed her out of the tent. "I should apologize for dumping on you."

"Dumping?"

"American slang for putting your own problems on others."

"I am guilty of this." She was thinking of Zarghana. "When one is troubled it is hard not to do. Thank you, Dr. Harris, for coming to Afghanistan. Thank you for caring."

Annisa awoke the next morning with a terrible burning sensation in her pelvis. She did not want her breakfast and hurried to the tent of Maebaie to ask her if she had some herbs for 'this sickness of men.'

Mabaie rummaged through some bottles she kept in a basket by her bed and handed her one. "The root of the Great Burdock tree . . . And Annisa, it would not to be wise to tell anyone you have this sickness."

"I won't. Never. And thank you." Once again, she was so grateful that her secret was safe.

On the way back to her tent she saw two boys kite fighting in the distant field. The strings of their kites were covered with a paste made of flour and broken glass; the object was to cut the other boy's kite down. For some reason it disturbed her. Why did little boys always want to fight? Her father had never been like that. 'Oh, well. There is too much wind today,' she told herself. The wind would rip their kites to shreds before the contest was over. Maybe a great wind would sweep through Afghanistan—a wind of peace. Or Allah might bring a terrible earthquake. There must be some way Allah could show his displeasure at all the killing.

Dusk was hovering over the camp when Najib returned from Peshawar. Weighed down by tangled emotions, he walked doggedly against the wind that whistled across the clearing, whipping the tents. A spring storm. Mostly dust. Only sprinkles of rain.

It was hard for him to grasp that Claire had arrived. They had agreed to meet on the fourth but she had surprised him, arriving a day ahead of time. She had been waiting at Dean's Hotel when he arrived. Last night in their room, he had confessed he was no longer married. She made no comment, flashing only an enigmatic smile. Nothing between them had changed. In bed he could not get his fill of her.

But today his happiness had been shattered beyond repair. He carried heart-breaking news; news of Rahmin that he was not yet ready to share with Annisa. He had to get his thoughts organized first as to what his next step should be.

Annisa ran to greet him. "You look so sad. Did you miss the important Egyptian? Was there a message from Rahmin?"

"Not yet." He tried to mask his feelings—to act cheerful. "I have a surprise. We are invited to a party."

"Me? To a party? Where, Najib? A party?"

"I see there is no need for the purple medicine that you asked me to buy for your stomach ache in the bazaar. You look much better."

"Oh, I still want it." Between the stomach remedy from the bazaar and Mabaie's Great Burdock plant she had faith she would soon be well. She threw her arms around his neck. "Najib, tell me about this party...Wait, what is that behind your back?"

He held out a brown paper package tied with string. "It is red as I promised."

Annisa's eyes shone with pleasure as she opened it. "So beautiful. So expensive!"

"From a Western boutique in the Khyber Inter-Continental Hotel. Do you think it will fit?"

"I am certain. I shall be a grand lady." She twirled around, holding the dress. "Will there be many people at this party?"

"It is a dinner, Annisa. Good friends. The Ditchfields. He is British and I think she is Danish. Mr. Ditchfield has been a lawyer in Pakistan for many years. He is old and bald and ugly. But she is blonde and not so old. And he is very rich."

Annisa laughed. "I understand. . . I too have news. I met the American doctor in camp. You were right. He does know Rahmin."

Najib's face went white at the mention of his friend. "What did he say about Rahmin?"

"I was shocked. He says Rahmin has quit his studies. That he is driving a taxi? He says that Rahmin has always refused to believe I was dead. Asked Dr. Harris to look for me. Isn't that amazing? That I should meet him here in the camp? Allah is guiding me. First you and now Dr. Harris. I am so grateful. My heart so full."

"Yes, wonderful." Najib felt a surge of relief that Dr. Harris had evidently left for Pakistan before the tragic news of Rahmin.

She held the dress up to her again. "Thank you, thank you. I have never had anything so special. I can't wait for the party."

"Someone who wants very much to meet you will be there."

Her eyes lit up. "Can it be? Rahmin is coming to surprise me?"

Again, the blood drained from Najib's face. He shook his head.

She paused, a worried look on her face. "Did Ghulam send the cable to Rahmin?"

"We had better go inside the tent. The storm blows heavy sand."

"No, please, Najib. I like it out here. It is exciting. I like it when the wind howls."

"Your new dress will be covered with dust."

Quickly she stuffed it back inside the wrapping paper. "See, it is protected."

He could not bring himself to tell her. On the ride back from Peshawar, he had debated this decision over and over. If she knew the truth about Rahmin, she would go back to Omar and Terri-Mangal--back to the deprivation and the nothingness of village life. He had made the decision to get her into Peshawar, and settled with his missionary friend before he broke the news. In a few days he would leave for Hamburg with Claire. Paris was off, now that he could not deliver Massoud to television. Hopefully, he would be back in Peshawar within a week. The Reeds knew of the terrible tragedy—that she now had no one to go to and were offering to contact people in their church to act as sponsors-- they had promised to look after Annisa until his return from Frankfurt. Both Mrs. Reed and Claire had warned against giving her bad news about Rahmin and then leaving suddenly. How would he manage it? Annisa should at least have the joy of her new red dress and the party. He would wait until the morning after.

He still couldn't believe it himself. Rahmin murdered. For a few pocket dollars driving his cab. Jack Westerman, the CIA station chief, had offered to see what he could do for Annisa. The consular officer knew of religious organizations in Nebraska who were sponsoring Afghan refugees. But Najib refused. He must get her a private sponsor so that Annisa would not be stuck in a refugee camp for two years.

Annisa was suddenly subdued. "Something is wrong, Najib?"

"Nothing. Come inside now. The sky is black with evil-looking clouds."

She reached out and put his hand in hers. "I want to help Rahmin."

Najib was wary. "What are you saying?"

"I have many thoughts about the money Fritz Werner gave me for my education. Rahmin should have it for *his* school."

Najib sucked in his breath, searching for the right words. "Being a doctor. You talk of nothing else. Ever since Anne-Marie."

"I have dreamed of it much longer than that. But if there is only money for one, it should be Rahmin. He is the man. I may be going to America but I am still an Afghan girl."

"Annisa, no. . ."

"You want to hear something funny? The American doctor was so happy to hear we were not married. I think he likes me. He said I was pretty."

Najib frowned. "What else did he say?"

"That he lives in Washington, D.C. You know, where all the important people live. I guess I shouldn't have told him you already have a wife."

"Annisa, I'm not married anymore. I thought you knew that."

She looked at him, her eyes incredulous. "But Yuri said in Terri-Mangal. . ."

"Before we found Omar in the cave I hadn't seen Yuri in years. He would have no way of knowing."

"What has happened? Was your wife killed in the bombings?"

"No, we are divorced. She has married someone else."

"How sad for you."

"Hardly."

"Then maybe I shouldn't go to the States. Maybe I should stay here in the refugee camps?"

His heart froze. The very thing he feared she would do once she learned of Rahmin. "This is no place for you."

"But you have no one to take care of you."

"Annisa. . ." The words wouldn't come. What could she be thinking?

"Oh, look." She reached for his hand again. "Isn't it wonderful the way the clouds are swirling over the mountain tops. They are dark and powerful but they do not frighten me"

"That is good. I don't like it when you are afraid. And you mustn't concern yourself about me. I will see you often enough. I am in and out of America more often than I am here."

Her face lit up. "Then you will come see us in New York! I am so pleased. A new dress. A party. Soon to see Rahmin. Thank you, Najib."

Najib could no longer keep the tears from his eyes and he hurriedly wiped them away.

"Najib. What evil thing have I said?"

"Ah, sweet Annisa-jan. There is no one in the world like you."

Annisa babbled on, unaware of the depth of his sadness. "What shall I do about my rough hands? I suppose the rich wife of Mr. Ditchfield will have red polish on her nails. Shall I wear my hair in braids or brush it down my back? Najib, you aren't listening to me."

"No, I am not." Suddenly he grabbed her, and embraced her. Before he understood his own response he had kissed her hard on the mouth. When he pulled away, he said huskily. "It does not matter how you look, Annisa-jan... Forgive me for this."

"Forgive you? Oh, Najib. You make me so happy." Her arms encircled him again, her mouth lifted towards his. He knew he was sinking into quicksand but there was no going back. The sweet taste of her skin as he nibbled her neck. His hand on her breast.

"Dear God, Annisa," he moaned as he pressed her to him.

"I will love you forever," she whispered.

Her words sent a shock wave through him. And once again, he pulled away. "Go inside Annisa," he said, "before I say things I do not mean."

Dazzled by his kiss, she wanted to stretch her arms and twirl in happiness but his words had diminished her. She waited for some kind of sign but he had turned his head from her and stared at the swirling sand. "Are you angry with me again, Najib?"

"Of course not. I am angry with myself."

"I guess I am too bold, Najib. I know nothing about these things."

"Annisa-jan. It's not you. Forgive me, please."

"Thank you for my lovely dress," she said softly and went inside, aware he would not follow her. Something was hurting Najib. She sensed it in the way he looked at her, as though it made him sad to be around her. If only she knew why she made him unhappy. Was it wrong to love Najib?

CHAPTER 24

Brass kerosene coach lanterns flickered under the crescent moon as the open horse-drawn carriage clomped rhythmically on the brick streets. The heady smell of night jasmine mingled with the light perfume of the woman seated next to Captain Najib Duranni. "You smell delicious," Najib said, reaching over and taking Annisa's hand. "Annisa-jan! Your hands are like ice. Here, let me feel your head. Naughty child, the fever is back. Why didn't you tell me?"

"Please, Najib. Do not treat me like a child."

"You are right." He kissed her forehead. "You look a woman tonight."

She wanted to answer, 'And yesterday? When you kissed me?' Instead she murmured, "Thank you," knowing he would not want to talk about it. She was thrilled at the way he had looked at her when he picked her up at the Reeds. All afternoon, Mrs. Margaret Reed of the Evangelical and Reform Church had played with Annisa in the cosmetic box. It was like painting a doll. Out had come the curling iron, because after earnest debate the hair was not braided but piled high on the head. Next, Mrs. Reed added dangling jade earrings, earrings which had belonged to her mother but she never wore herself--a bit too much for a minister's wife. All these years they had waited inside a velvet box in her dresser to be taken out and worn on such a night. And, of course, Annisa insisted upon red nail polish.

"I can hardly wait for my surprise," she said to Najib.

"A friend of mine. All the way from England," he replied.

The *gaadi*, their two-wheeled buggy with its sleepy-eyed driver, turned into the street which led to the old city, a street that edged the Khyber Bazaar. The night air was steamy. The little shops lining the road teamed with life. From a side street came the sound of hammers tapping in the tin bazaar. Ahead lay rows and rows of gun shops. Leather bandoleers strung on clotheslines draped the narrow lanes. The smell of jasmine now blended into that of rotting vegetables and sweat. The old city belonged to men, men in turbans and beards, men brandishing rifles.

An officious policeman directed traffic. The *gaadi* stopped in front of the gold seller's bazaar. Across the street one could see inside the delicate mosque of Mahbat Khan, empty except for a custodian filling the oil lamps hanging from the ceiling.

"You want a woman?" The high shrill voice of a street urchin called in perfect English to a passerby. "I am very discreet."

The man shook his head and walked briskly on. The grinning boy followed him. They were now abreast of the *gaadi*. "You want to go to the other side? See the war? My friend can take you. We have a camel."

The man laughed good-naturedly. "How do I know you wouldn't steal my watch and leave me in the wasteland?"

"You wear a cheap watch, mister." The *gaadi* moved forward. "You like hashish? Very pure."

Slowly, they pulled away from the old city, the wild frontier town, and passed into the new--ghastly and modern, crowded and polluted. The noise of braying donkeys mixed with the roars of motorcycles.

"All these motorcycles make me sad. They remind me of my guide. All Zia ever wanted was to own one," Annisa said.

Najib squeezed her hand in the darkness. "Don't be sad tonight, remember what we promised. No talk about the dead or dying."

"Sorry. I forget. It's never far from my thoughts."

"Or mine." Najib hastily turned his head away from her. God how he dreaded tomorrow and giving her the news about Rahmin. He would rather face a thousand deaths.

Down a wide boulevard lined with palms, the *gaadi* horse trotted, clomping its hooves on the cobblestones. The houses were fewer now and farther apart. High in the distance, the creamy bricks of the Great Bl Hisar Fort dominated the city, another nostalgic relic of the British Raj, from when they had controlled the Indian subcontinent.

"I am nervous, Najib."

"Don't be. Everyone will love you. The Egyptian diplomat, Meirnardus, was very impressed when I told him you were the daughter of the poet Sulaiman Aziz."

"You discussed me with him!"

"Certainly."

Annisa smiled in the dark.

Then they heard the sound of bagpipes. In a beautiful garden lit only by kerosene torches, handsome young Pakistani soldiers in white dress uniforms danced on the green lawn to a band of bagpipers, while turbaned waiters circled the dancers and moved in and out among the tables.

"It is like a dream," Annisa gasped as they passed the Pakistani Officers' Club.

Further along was the British Club, surrounded by well-kept hedges. The roses were in bloom.

Najib leaned forward to the driver. "*Dast e rast.* On the right."

They turned into a long, narrow drive. A great house, fronted by terraced steps and a large verandah, lay ahead. The figure of the moon in its last quarter had climbed higher and its slim light silhouetted the rows of turrets on the roof. Dance music and laughter wafted through the open windows. They were entering, returning to a world where one still had permission to aspire to romance and elegance and the pleasure of leisure. A uniformed Pakistani in chartreuse green and gold tassels and wearing a purple turban helped them from the carriage. Another opened the front door of the mansion for them.

"Dear Najib. At last." The woman advancing towards them was a middle-aged brass-colored blonde. She walked deliberately, swinging her hips. The gold-lame of her dress was cut low to reveal an ample cleavage. "Gordon, darling, come help me introduce our guests. I'm frightful with names."

"Good evening, Mrs. Ditchfield."

Annisa edged closer to Najib but a diminutive woman now took his arm, elegant in long black silk with a slit up the side. This woman's hair was also blonde, but natural looking, short, cut blunt, her makeup understated. "So this is our Annisa. I've heard so much about you. I'm Claire." Her voice was musical and light. The hand she offered was soft, without polish on the nails.

Annisa murmured, "Thank you," trying to hide her bewilderment. She watched her squeeze Najib's hand, wondering who she was.

"Najib darling, she is even more lovely than you described. What a treat! And I'm so happy to see the dress fits," Claire said.

Annisa was suddenly propelled away from Najib by her host, the portly Mr. Ditchfield. Her foot slipped for a moment on the high polished marble floors but she regained her balance. They passed clusters of faces. Animated. Laughing. The women looked elegant but none with skin as smooth as the milk-white Claire. Annisa looked back at her. The English woman was also watching her. Mr. Ditchfield paused before three men deep in conversation, sipping cocktails under a massive fern.

"Agreed. Always the danger, however, once our side escalates, Russia will have the excuse to go in and wipe them out utterly." The square-jawed American placed his empty glass in the dirt of the potted plant and deftly snatched another glass from a passing waiter carrying a silver tray. Unobtrusively, the waiter retrieved the discarded glass. Annisa smiled at him. His face remained impassive. Was she invisible? She was beginning to feel so as she and Mr. Ditchfield stood waiting for a break in the conversation. "There is no convincing them. The Afghans are a tenacious lot." With a fresh glass of whiskey, the American gestured towards Najib, who was now standing with his back to them. "Men like Captain Duranni there. I'd be willing to bet he talks the right people into supplying the Afghans with stinger missiles whether it is prudent or not. And you can quote me."

Annisa eyed the teal-colored satin draperies, which framed the windows. They were embroidered with peacocks in gold thread. Never in Kabul had she seen such opulence.

Mr. Ditchfield interjected himself into the conversation. "Ambassador Meirandus. The young lady you have been waiting for. Annisa. Daughter of Sulaiman Aziz."

The tall Egyptian diplomat gave Annisa a welcoming smile and clasped her hand between both of his. "What an honor to meet you. So many pleasant hours your father gave me. I have every one of his books in my library."

Annisa wished he would release her hand. Her palms were rough despite Mrs. Reed's creams and lotion. And what could she say to this great man--a man Najib admired so much.

The American diplomat next to him nodded at Annisa and eyed her appreciatively, but there was no break in his conversation with the small-boned Pakistani official at his side. "Don't you get your belly full of complaints! Hell, we've spent $300 million on relief alone--50 percent of the international food contribution is ours!"

The slight Pakistani official coughed. He looked frail next to the chunky American. "Tell me, Mr. Westerman. Off the record. Is it true that article in *Time* about CIA activity in Pakistan was a plant? Minimize the obvious to take the heat off?"

The American had a very expressive face. He rolled his eyes. "Jamal! You forget. I'm the lowly economics officer. Not much above stamping passports. Talk to the big boys in Islamabad."

Ambassador Meirnardus smiled as he saw the American put his arm around the Pak civil servant and lead him away towards the table of hors d'oeuvres. The Egyptian turned to Annisa. "Politics. Always politics. And with such a lovely young lady beside us."

Annisa gave him a faint smile, glancing anxiously over her shoulder for Najib. He had disappeared to the verandah. His familiar laugh could be heard through the open French doors. She felt deserted and vulnerable.

"You prefer to talk politics?"

"Oh, no. . .I mean, whatever you like." Annisa was embarrassed. She had been so confident earlier. Mrs. Reed had said everyone would want to talk to her. Yet she could think of nothing to say. Why had Najib told that woman about her dress?

"Captain Duranni tells me you are going to the States, that you study to be a doctor. I applaud your endeavors."

"Thank you." It was hard to concentrate on anything but her feet. The shoes Mrs. Reed had insisted she wear were not high, but Annisa felt tilted, like she was standing on a mountaintop. "Do you have a family, Dr. Meirnardus?"

He beamed. "Yes. A son Alexander and a daughter Neamet. They live in Cairo. I'm afraid Neamet is a bit less serious than we would like her to be. She dreams of being a movie star."

"How old is your daughter?"

"Ten, wishing she was 20."

Annisa smiled at him with her eyes. She liked this man. He was easy to talk to. "All little girls wish to be in the movies."

"One that plans to be a doctor?"

"Oh, yes. You should have seen my bedroom walls in Kabul. Covered with photos. My favorite was the Indian film star Parveen Babi."

"So when did you decide it would be medicine instead?"

"When the Russians invaded. War grows you up pretty fast."

He nodded. "Najib was telling me . . ."

They had not seen her coming. Mrs. Ditchfield swooped down upon them from out of nowhere. She had a young Pakistani officer in tow. "Annisa, you have an admirer!"

The young man whom she introduced as Kahil bowed as Mrs. Ditchfield expertly maneuvered Ambassador Meirnardus away. "We mustn't monopolize this charming man. I promise to return him, dear."

How strange. It seemed like a dance to Annisa. People whisked in and out. Snatches of conversation that no one listened to. There was no time to reply.

"Our hostess is not as rude as she seems," Kahil said. "It is their custom. A party is not a success unless one circulates...Makes small-talk."

"Small talk? What is that?... Oh!" Annisa was stabbed by a sudden sharp pain in her abdomen and clutched at her side.

The young officer moved towards her. "Would you like to sit down? Your face is very flushed."

Annisa put her hand to her head. "It's so hot in here."

"Let's go outside. There is music on the verandah"

"Oh, yes. I would love the fresh air." Her fever was always higher at night but at the moment she actually felt dizzy.

Outside was not much cooler than the drawing room. There was no breeze in the walled garden.

"How long will you be in Peshawar?" Kahil asked.

"Until my papers are ready for America. I am going to join my brother."

"Where does he live?"

"In New York."

"I see."

A long pause followed.

Annisa saw that Najib and the woman Claire had left the terrace and were standing below on the lawn. Holding her breath, Annisa watched as Najib leaned over and plucked a red camellia from a bush. He brushed the flower with his lips and handed it to the woman. Annisa was starting to perspire. Fire filled her insides. If only she could lie down.

"So many stars tonight," Kahil said, trying to make conversation. Self-consciously, he leaned against a stone pillar and looked up at the sky.

"Yes." Annisa answered, unable to concentrate on the heavens. She heard Najib say, "No reason to pout, kitten."

"Listen to you." Claire's voice was well modulated but it carried to them across the garden. "No wonder this war fascinates you. With a companion like that. Sleeping out under the stars. Blood and sand. Think of what you and Annisa have shared!"

"Claire, she is only a child."

"Have you looked lately? Surprise. Surprise."

Annisa watched Najib lean down and take the woman in his arms. His lips were on her mouth, her neck. "I think it may be

247

cooler inside," Annisa said, trying to hide her distress. Her companion followed her back into the party only to lose her as she hurried towards Ambassador Meirnardus, who was now chatting with two women in silken saris.

Before she could reach him a brass gong sounded, and the doors to the dining room swung open, revealing four large circular tables. Annisa stood spellbound at the sight. Silver baskets of fresh flowers on pale lavender linen. Hovering behind ivory in-laid chairs stood uniformed Pakistani waiters. Tall turbans. White gloves. A hand-cut crystal chandelier hung from the pink silk that canopied the ceiling.

A murmur of appreciation rippled through the room from the guests.

"Move over, Cecil B. DeMille," the American, Jack Westerman quipped.

"Precious girl. Did I spell your name right?" Mrs. Ditchfield asked Annisa as she ushered her to a table, which included place cards for Najib, Claire, Jack Westerman, and a newsman from London, who introduced himself to Annisa as Matthew Hardcastle.

"Remember me?" he whispered as he pulled out her chair.

"For my father? You took a letter to Rahmin?"

On her right was Mr. Jamal Hashim, the Pakistani official whom Mrs. Ditchfield introduced as having made a killing off the war.

Annisa was curious about the British journalist who said he knew her. He must have read her thoughts because he answered for her. "You were a very little girl the last time I saw you in Kabul."

"Yes." She smiled demurely, wondering if this Matthew Hardcastle was the surprise guest Najib had promised.

"There you are. . .Where have you two lovebirds been?" Mrs. Ditchfield asked as Najib and Claire arrived late to the table. "As if we didn't know." She raised her wineglass. "Here's to romance. I'm making a rule: no talk of war at this table."

"Then I am going to have to move my chair," the newsman joked.

"What? And miss sitting by the fair Annisa?"

Annisa looked up from the rows of knives and forks in front of her. Claire had said it. "The fair Annisa." Was she making fun of her? Annisa busied herself by counting the silverware at her plate. Four forks. Three spoons and three knives. In her father's house, they never ate from the bowl with their fingers as Omar's family did. There had always been one knife, one fork, one spoon. But what did one do with all this? Her eyes went to Najib for help. He was smiling at her with such a proud look on his face. Their eyes held and for the first time since she had entered the party, Annisa felt reassured. He looked so handsome in his white suit! It thrilled her to look at him and that he had looked back.

"Don't pay any attention to Jack," Mrs. Ditchfield told the British journalist. "It's his official duty to complain about trips inside. Frankly, if I could do what you do, Matthew, I'd be in Kabul in a minute."

The wine in the cut glass goblets shimmered golden in the candlelight. Annisa was tempted to taste it. She noticed that Claire only played with the stem of her glass but Najib drank his. Annisa followed his lead.

The American, Jack Westerman, exaggerated a groan in response to Mrs. Ditchfield. "Don't encourage him. Matt knows he can find out all he needs to know right here. He is too ready to be a Yahoo as it is."

"So we are back to T.E. Lawrence are we?" Claire lifted her glass. Although she was small, she sat high and straight in her chair. "Pray God that men will not, for the love of glamour of the exotic, prostrate themselves, or their talents, to serve those of another race.'"

"Clever girl," Mrs. Ditchfield said as she rang the ceramic bell on the table to signal the soup course.

Jack Westerman tossed down the whiskey he had brought with him from the drawing room. "Lawrence left out money. The town is crawling with mercenaries ready to prostrate themselves for the dollar...the name of the game."

"An old cliché, but I happen to agree with you," Matthew Hardcastle answered.

"You are very quiet, Mr. Hashim. What are your thoughts?" Claire asked the Pakistani official. Annisa watched to see which spoon Claire picked up for the soup.

Mr. Hashim cleared his throat, looking pleased with Claire. "Well, of course it is strictly against the policy of my government. The more people involved, the greater the risk to us from the Soviets. Whenever you cross the border, Mr. Hardcastle, as you have already discovered--you are not always with Afghan people who are for the Resistance."

"Hear that, Matt?" Jack Westerman slapped the journalist on the shoulder.

Mr. Hashim was trying hard to convince him of his folly. "Believe me, Mr. Hardcastle, my country has had long experience with refugees, beginning with its inception in l947."

"I'm afraid Matt likes to see more than refugee camps."

"Precisely. I understand. But the point is, who is to guarantee his coming will not be broadcast ahead?" Jamal Hashim had his forum and was not to be denied. "We have been very good to the Afghans. The whole world says we are more than generous."

Jack Westerman leaned back in his chair and stifled a yawn.

"Furthermore, Pakistan subsidizes the cost of transporting relief goods from the port of Karachi into the hinterland. Such an undertaking places severe strains on our roads, our rail infrastructure. Refugees have deforested many areas for firewood. It is a misery."

"I couldn't agree with you more." Mrs. Ditchfield rang the little ceramic bell again. "But it has also produced millions in additional foreign aid for Pakistan."

Jamal Hashim ignored her and the exquisite cut crystal ashtray beside his plate. He ground out his cigarette on his unfinished salad. Mrs. Ditchfield looked pained to see it.

"We take great risks in letting all these arms into our country. They could fall into the wrong hands," the Pakistani announced to no one in particular.

A white-gloved hand now filled the second wine glass in front of Annisa. The amber color disappeared The new liquid sparkled burgundy, the same color of her dress The memory of Claire's words hurt her. She hated the dress now. The English girl was pleased that it fit. She must have gone with Najib to buy it!

A tiny puff pastry filled with mushrooms and steaming bits of beef was placed before her. The rich aroma filled her nostrils and made her want to cry, thinking of the food her friends in the refugee camp would be eating tonight.

Jamal Hashim leaned across Annisa to speak to the journalist again. "Is it true, Mr. Hardcastle, that the CIA planted an article in *Time* magazine about their alleged help to the Resistance? Training camps? The. . ."

Jack Westerman interrupted. "You never give up, do you, Jamal? I've got a *better* story. British intelligence has done it again. Would you believe one of their agents was in Paktia province for l2 years. Get this. Posing as a mullah! Came retirement time in the rose garden in Bolton Percy, and this Yorkshire gent gets to feeling guilty. Thinks maybe he should send word back, 'fess up.' All the Afghans he had married, the babies he had blessed."

Annisa looked shocked. "Is that a true story?"

"From the horse's mouth. No wonder the Brits knew the Russians were coming into Afghanistan long before the rest of us."

"Here, here." Claire raised her glass once again "Here's to Her Majesty's secret service. And how marvelous, Jack. A mullah? Imagine calling the faithful to prayer with a Yorkshire accent. I love it."

Annisa reached for the red colored wine. Why was everyone laughing? How could they think this absurdity funny?

"Najib, dear. Tell them about that ridiculous little man in Kabul," Claire prodded.

Najib looked uncomfortable.

"You know, the one the Afghan secret police thought was CIA. They found an American social security card on the poor man."

Jack Westerman chuckled. "Maybe that's what we oughta do with Social Security. It's going belly up any way."

Annisa's glass was empty and as soon as she set it down the waiter behind her chair refilled it. At least the pain in her stomach was beginning to ease.

Claire leaned forward. The candlelight picked up the lights from the small heart necklace she wore around her neck--her only jewelry. "I'd like to hear what Annisa has to say about all this. After all, she has been inside ever since the war began!"

Alarm registered in Annisa's eyes.

"She doesn't like to talk about the hardships," Najib said.

"Darling, let Annisa speak for herself."

But Annisa remained speechless, her eyes transfixed on the heart necklace. It was exactly like the one Najib had given her!

Mrs. Ditchfield jumped in immediately to save her. "Shame on us. Remember, we are not to talk about the fighting. Give me 20 lashes for violating my own rule." She signaled for the lemon ice to clear the palate. "Annisa doesn't have to talk about this ugly war, especially when she wears the loveliest dress in the room."

Annisa bristled inside at her obvious patronizing.

"Red suits her, don't you think? We had such fun picking it out." Claire gave Annisa a very sweet smile.

They were talking about her as though she was not there. Invisible again. She would make an effort to make them see her. Annisa reached for her wineglass. Was Najib's frown intended for

251

her? She raised the red liquid to her lips and took a sip, slowly setting her glass down, her eyes on Najib. "I think the troops in the mountains owe much to..."

A sudden exclamation from Claire thwarted Annisa's attempt to enter the conversation. "But how lovely. This looks divine."

Annisa looked down at the Cornish hen glazed with apricots the white-gloved hand had placed before her. So much food! A miniature whole chicken and for just one person! Impossible. And the wine had changed color again.

Claire had her hand on the journalist's arm. "I know we aren't supposed to talk about 'it' but Matthew I do think your articles about the war are terrific. Your competition is in a scramble to match you. How do you do it when you sneak inside? Do you wear brown contact lenses to disguise those very penetrating blue eyes?"

Mrs. Ditchfield giggled. "A mustache, I bet. It's a regular masquerade party these days in Peshawar. Everyone in disguise. Next time you go inside, Matthew, I vote for Kandahar. I'm bored silly with Massoud and the north getting all the press."

"I thought you ladies all have the hots for Commander Massoud." Jack Westerman was beginning to slur his words

"Oh, we do He's dark and dashing and mysterious. But he's hardly a matinee idol like our dear Najib." Mrs. Ditchfield raised her glass to Najib. "To hear people talk, you'd think Massoud was the only hero of the Resistance. He has a whole mountain range to hide in. Those poor devils around Kandahar have to fight on open flat lands. Besides, Massoud prefers the French."

Annisa looked to Najib, waiting to hear him defend Commander Massoud. But not one word. Najib acted as though he hadn't heard.

Matthew Hardcastle was playing with his napkin ring, spinning it from one side of his plate to the other and then back again. "I'm afraid I'm all talk, Mrs. Ditchfield. Kandahar is out this time. I leave for Delhi in the morning."

"Or so you would have us believe." Claire tilted her head back and smiled at the ceiling. "I don't think Matthew trusts us."

Annisa could not bring herself to eat her dinner. The gold-edged plate swirled before her. She could see the battered wooden bowl. Eager hands. Fatima hoarding a carrot she had found buried inside the rice. Now the sound of glasses clinking. Annisa raised her hand to yet another toast. This time from Jamal. Hashim, the Pakistani.

Najib shook his head at her but she drank her wine anyway. She hated to see Claire was now whispering in his ear.

"No fair. No secrets," Mrs. Ditchfield giggled again.

Claire threw back her graceful white neck and blew cigarette smoke towards the chandelier. Annisa watched it curl toward the pink silk canopy. In the smoke she saw faces. Frightened. Starving. The blind boy, Tawab.

"If you really want to go to Kandahar, Matthew, I suggest you talk to Captain Duranni. He can direct you to the right people." Claire turned to Najib. "Can't you, dear?"

Najib appeared hesitant. Jack Westerman gave him a nod, a subtlety Annisa did not miss What was going on? What did Najib have to do with this unpleasant man?

Najib cleared his throat. "Yunus Kahli's men. Take a taxi to the compound of Syd Ahmed Gailim. He is not anti-West. He speaks good English. He'll know how to put you in touch with Khali."

The American consular officer threw down his napkin with great flourish. "You ladies who do not like to talk about war are going to get our friend here killed. Kandahar is exceptionally dangerous business."

Annisa was confused. Why did this man say one thing and then look over at Najib and wink.

"Don't be so hard on us." Mrs. Ditchfield was exaggerating a pout. "We are only teasing. You heard Matthew. He has to leave for Delhi tomorrow."

Jack Westerman sighed "I've got someone I wish he'd take with him. I've been hounded the past month with some skinny idealist from D.C., a regular Brahmin. His umpteenth visit to Peshawar. He pops up wanting to go inside and play doctor. All we need is another hostage crisis. 'Why the hell don't you go to the International Red Cross Hospital?' I asked him. 'Plenty of work there. Or go home and collect medicines and ship them over.' What the hell is the motive for risking his neck?"

"His brother didn't get to row in the Moscow Olympics after the Soviets invaded Afghanistan," Matthew Hardcastle said, leaning over to light Mrs. Ditchfield's cigarette.

"You know this guy?"

"Yes, he was recruited by Annisa's brother, Rahmin. A few years back I had lunch with him in D.C. and tried to talk him out of it. He's a persistent chap."

Annisa's eyes lit up at the mention of her brother's name but before she could say anything Najib hurriedly raised his glass and proposed another toast. "Here's to youth and idealism."

"Here. Here."

Annisa thought it a silly thing to say but she was busy watching Claire who was using her fingers to tear away the leg of the small capon. Not her knife and fork? Surely the English girl knew you were supposed to use a knife and fork or was she imitating Afghans? Once again, Annisa was thoroughly confused.

Jack Westerman answered his own question. "He didn't say it but I know what the young doctor is all about. The Olympics? Not on your life. He wants to be a footnote in a history book. A glory boy. This town is crawling with would-be heroes. A lot of people just looking for a cheap high. The Afghans have got better things to do with their time than to escort the lot. You won't believe it but we were actually contacted by some fool travel agent that wanted to run a tour bus to points where his clients could, quote, 'see some of the shooting.' Christ!"

Annisa reached for her wineglass and drained it. "The American doctor? Was his name Dr. Harris?"

"Yes. You know him?"

Annisa looked over at Najib who had a worried look in his eye. "I met him in the refugee camp. He is very sincere. He wants to help our people. He already has sent supplies inside. With the French. He is *not* a footnote." She made no effort to hide the contempt in her voice.

"I applaud his efforts. And if he gets his ass shot off, I'll have to escort the coffin home, " Jack Westerman said, motioning for the waiter to give his whiskey glass a re-fill.

Annisa was shocked by the man's language. Did men in America talk this way in front of women?

Westerman wagged his finger at her. "Your doctor friend is sophomoric. Peace Corps mentality. Believe me, that is live ammo they are using inside."

"Yes, Mr. Westerman, I know," Annisa said softly.

"There's no talking to Dr. Harris. He sees everything in black and white. There are no shades in between."

Annisa put down her fork. The faces around the table were beginning to blur. Their eyes glowed yellow, like those of wolves circling their prey.

"Gentlemen, are there really any shades in-between in this struggle?" Claire asked of no one in particular as she raised her hand to her throat, fingering her necklace. Annisa stared at it again. Inadvertently, she let out a sob.

"Annisa-jan, what is it?"

"Nothing. It's nothing," she answered as she clutched at the arms of her chair so tightly that her knuckles were white. Her world was collapsing about her. Claire had the very same necklace. She was sure now.

"Dear, do you feel faint?" Mrs. Ditchfield asked.

"No!" All the holding in of her feelings towards these dreadful people was about to explode. "I'm upset with Mr. Westerman. He mimics Dr. Harris and Dr. Harris is a very good person."

Najib signaled her with a look, which spelled caution. "Annisa- jan, Mr. Westerman is helping us. He processes your papers for America."

The American smiled benevolently at Annisa. "Right as you go."

But Annisa was not about to let it be. "Dr. Harris is my brother's friend. He told me that Rahmin. . ."

"Ah, then you know. I'm truly sorry about your brother. A shocking waste, that was." Jack Westerman drained his glass in an absent toast. "Najib here is on my tail to get you a new sponsor. Tell you what, I'm working on it. I may decide to take you to the States myself."

"A new sponsor?"

"Jack!" Najib was on the edge of his chair. "Annisa doesn't. . ."

"If your brother was still alive, he'd qualify. As it is. . ."

"Still alive?" Annisa's eyes went wide with terror. "If my brother were still alive?"

"Najib asked us to double check the morgue report in Queens. Just to be certain."

The room was once again beginning to spin. Claire looked to Mrs. Ditchfield. "I advised Najib against telling her right away. There's always the possibility of a mistake in cases like this." She reached for Annisa's hand across the table.

All the yellow eyes had narrowed to slits. Annisa stood up suddenly, knocking her chair over backwards and dropping her wineglass to the floor. It shattered. Her hands went to her throat. A pitiable moan escaped her. Everyone froze for a moment; talk at the other tables in the room subsided. Then she turned and rushed toward the French doors and was gone.

Najib chased after her and caught her at the bottom of the terrace steps leading to the drive.

"Let go of me," she cried. "Don't touch me." Annisa was raging. "Rahmin, oh my brother." The tears she had fought back in front of the others flowed freely now.

"Annisa." Najib's voice was desperate. "I didn't know until yesterday when I went to the embassy. Rahmin was killed less than two weeks ago."

"Get away from me. I hate you. I hate your stupid friends. You let me sit there when they all knew. You humiliate me." She began to flail him with her fists.

He grabbed her hands and held them together. "Stop it. Stop this. Are you crying because of your pride or for your brother?"

"You fake. Go back to those silly people. That pompous American."

"You misunderstand. Jack plays the buffoon. But it is only a mask. He secretly works day and night to help us."

"Liar." She jerked away but he grabbed her by the arm. "Annisa, for God's sake calm down."

Her fingers pried at the hand holding tightly to her arm. The dinner party had assembled now at the top of the stairs. As they watched from the terrace, Annisa broke free again and ran towards the street. It took Najib only a moment to catch her. "Annisa, you are acting like a child. Jack is only trying to help you."

"Help? He lies. Rahmin is young. He is alive."

"Rahmin was shot and killed."

"America is not at war."

Najib held her shoulders and forced her to face him. "It was a robbery. Rahmin was driving a taxi . . . ."

"My brother is a doctor," she screamed. "You make stories."

"Your brother is dead. Rahmin is dead."

"No! No! I will not hear it." She pushed him away. "The man who tells you this is evil. I will never go to America."

"You must. It was Rahmin's wish."

"Who cares? You say he is dead. My poor brother. You lied to me. Let me go."

"Annisa, my God. It burns my hands to touch you. You're skin is on fire. You are sick. We must take you to the hospital. Now. Tonight."

She pulled away from him, kicked off the hateful shoes, and raced towards the gate.

"Annisa, don't be foolish. Come back. You cannot go out on the streets alone. It is not safe."

Indeed, night had closed over the city. Low clouds above the bazaars gave back a faint light, but the street in front of the Ditchfield's looked dark and almost deserted. A thin flute sounded far away in the shadows. Annisa beckoned to a passing cab and the driver stopped at the curb. The driver leaned over and opened the door.

Najib had reached her and barred her way. "No, I will not allow this." He pulled her back away from the waiting cab. "This was all my fault. I was crazy to let you drink all that wine. You need care."

She turned to him accusingly. "I saw you in the garden. You and that woman. You kissed her. Go back to her. Go back to your British whore."

Najib was livid. "How dare you call her that."

"Get out of my life," she screamed. "I never want to see you again."

The cab driver's grinning face framed the window. "Here, come. Both of you. Quarrel tomorrow."

Najib was pleading. "You have to believe me. I was going to tell you about Rahmin. But I wanted you to have this night."

"This night?" She waved her arms wildly. "Selfish pigs stuffing themselves while we starve. Making fun of our efforts to fight."

"Annisa, don't do this. I beg you." He knew he did not have the right to say it. To tell her how he really felt.

"I hate you, Najib Duranni."

"No, you don't. You love me. . . And God help us both, I love you."

"Liar. I'm glad I lost your necklace. It has no meaning for me now."

"Annisa, did you hear what I said? I love you."

"You are cruel to tell me this." She reached for the jade earrings of Mrs. Reed and pulled them from her ears. "Make sure you take these back," she said, flinging them at him. "They don't belong to me. None of this does!" She pushed him back and slammed the taxi door in his face.

Those standing on the terrace watched as Najib bent over to pick up Mrs. Reed's jewelry. He paused, but only for a moment before he ran after the red taillights of the taxi disappearing behind the tall brick fence. None of the guests on the terrace understood the extent of the small melodrama that was being played out before them. None except Claire.

Jack Westerman was the first to speak. "Christ! What a fuckin' mess."

Mr. Gordon Ditchfield was wheezing. "I will never understand why my wife dotes on these Afghans. Uncivilized lot if you ask me. Totally unpredictable."

Jack Westerman stopped to light his cigar and then pronounced, "The poor dumb bastards. They haven't got a snowball's chance in hell of winning this war."

Ambassador Meirnardus, standing in the shadows at the top of the steps, a brandy glass in his hand, shook his head sadly. "Even so, they will keep on with it. And we must do what we can."

Matthew Hardcastle, who had started down the steps from the terrace, returned. He was sick at heart. He had been out of the country and had not heard of Rahmin's death. Rahmin Aziz had raised healthy sums of money for the Resistance. His latest project had been to find sponsors who would fly some of the freedom fighters with limbs missing to the States. Fit them with the latest prosthesis. And Rahmin had been smart enough to parade them around. Elicit sympathy with the American public. It would be a terrible blow for Resistance efforts in the States. It rattled him to think he had spent the night at the dinner party thinking how thrilled Rahmin was going to be now that his sister had been found! It was like those asinine bumper stickers Americans loved to plaster on their cars: "Life's A Bitch and Then You Die."

"We've had enough excitement for one night. Everyone inside," Mrs. Ditchfield ordered. "Our chocolate soufflé will fall."

Jack Westerman pretended to clutch his stomach. "Lead me to the Romans and their vomit pits," he whispered to Claire.

"Pull yourself together, dear boy. We mustn't disappoint our hostess."

"Right. I've done enough damage for tonight." He took Claire by the arm to usher her inside. "Coming, Mr. Ambassador?"

"In a minute." Meirnardus stood alone, staring into the now empty garden. Behind him, the French doors were ajar to the wine and laughter and Mrs. Ditchfield's party. The young girl Annisa had affected him deeply. He had witnessed her reaction to the banality of the evening and shared it. Captain Duranni had told him of her ordeal in Afghanistan. To think that the daughter of

Sulaiman Aziz would be exposed to such hardship. He went inside, thinking he would call his wife tonight. Hear her voice. Tell her how much he loved her and his family. He couldn't wait to be home in Cairo-- with his sweet daughter, Neamet and his bright and precious little boy, Alexander. He was grateful to God that his children would never be exposed to the ravages of war.

CHAPTER 25

The last members of the audience for the evening reading trickled out of Mabaie's tent. She had dismissed them earlier than usual, feeling out of sorts from the tongue-lashing that the American doctor had delivered before he left. Who did he think he was? God? Ridiculing her attempts to cure Annisa. Going on and on about his precious penicillin. He had even tried to frighten her—-insisting that the sickness not only could eat up your brain but it might leave scars on Annisa's tubes and if so, Annisa would never be able to have a child. He berated her over and over for not bringing Annisa to him earlier.

She walked to the *tandorri* and poked at the fire. Smoldering bits of wood, angry at being disturbed, burst into flames. Sparks flew. Sparks that hissed and snapped and matched her mood. The nerve of him. What did Dr. Harris know about sickness or death or what to say to the dying? He waltzed into the camp a few weeks each year and then returned to his soft life in the West. She was left with the day in and day out despair in the camps. Who was he to make fun of her herbs or her get-well charms? She had learned a long time ago that a little faith in magic could work wonders in the sick. If they thought they could get well, then more often than not they did. Well, the joke was on him. Annisa was cured now and everyone in camp thought it was the skill of Mabaie, the fortune teller that had snatched the ranting and delirious girl from the jaws of death. No one knew that after dark the American doctor had visited the tent of Mabaie, armed with his bag of tricks. She thought his great concern for the girl was suspicious. To get that upset over a single patient when there was so much sickness around them? This Dr. Harris had to be enamoured with the girl like every other man in the camp. And now she had left the camp for God knows where? Annisa might be cured in the flesh but it was her confusion about what to do with her life that worried Mabaie. The girl was a danger to herself.

"May I come in?" A young girl had pulled back the flap of Mabaie's tent.

"Sorry, the stories are over for the night."

"I'm not here for the stories."

"You aren't? Then what do you want? Speak up. What is your name?"

"Zarghana,"

"Well, what do you want Zarghana? I am tired and ready for my sleep."

Zarghana held out her hand and showed Mabaie a few coins. "A man gave them to me if I would bring you to him."

"Put the money back in your pocket. This place is full of thieves. You must never let them know you have money."

"Please come to the gate and see him."

Mabaie groaned. "What does he want? Why me?"

"He is looking for Annisa. I told him you knew where she was."

"Not Captain Duranni again!"

"No it is not Captain Duranni. I know him. He lived in our tent."

"Well, it had better not be or I will have your head. Annisa did not want to see anyone and each time he came here I lied to him and said she was not in the camp."

"This I know but Annisa is gone now and the man is not Captain Duranni and please come so I can keep the money."

"As a favor to you," Mabaie grumbled. She was not going to admit that she felt more than a little curious. Could this be the man who had caused Annisa's sickness? Annisa had refused to say who gave it to her.

Mabaie slipped into her shoes and threw a woolen scarf over her head to guard against the night chill. "Show me where he is." She grunted.

"He is dancing around the fire outside the guard's house."

"Dancing?"

"He says he is a Russian bear. And he is singing too. I think he is a little mad. His hair is white and he has a gold tooth."

"A gold tooth? Then he must be a Russian and mad indeed if he comes here! They will have the gold out of his mouth by morning."

When they reached the gate the fire was out and the guards had retreated inside their tent. Zarghana looked around. "I don't understand. He was just here. . .Oh, there he is. Leaning against the truck."

Mabaie walked over to a giant hulk of a man who looked to be asleep standing up. "I am Mabaie, the fortune teller," she shouted in his ear. "What do you want?"

He opened his eyes with a sheepish grin. "I want it all!" He pulled out an empty bottle from beneath his cloak and waved it in the air. "Want some? It's Stolichnaya. Mother's milk."

"You're drunk,"

"Nooooo. I never, ever, ever. Allah knows best." He waved his arms and began to sing.

"His balls were big and roundo
They hung upon the groundo
The constipated, masturbating, son of a bitch Colombo."

"You want to shock me? Well, you can't. I've heard worse than that."

"Yes, your royal highness. My czarina, mother of all Russia." He made a sweeping bow and in the process almost pitched over.

Mabaie turned to Zarghana who was watching from inside the shadows. "Go back to your tent. You should not hear such vile talk."

"Vile? Vile? Did someone say vile?" he was weaving about, unsteady on his feet

"Yes, vile. You should be ashamed."

He grinned. "I'll tell you a secret. A very big secret. It's not me talking, it's the vodka," he hissed.

She leaned over and picked up the empty bottle he had dropped on the ground.

"Where did you get this?"

"In the bazaar. A man with money can get anything he wants in the bazaar."

"And you have money?"

"Not any more. I spent it all on the Red Eye but there will never be any Red Eye. They stole Omar's parts. Stole Omar's parts!"

If he had no money she was no longer interested in talking to him. "Why don't you go back to where you came from."

"Can't. Moscow is a very, very, very long ways away. Got to find Annisa." He wagged his finger under her nose. "Naughty. Naughty. You know where she is."

"No, I don't." And this time she didn't have to lie.

"Got to find Annisa. Najib came looking for her. Terri-Mangal. You see, Annisa is lost. She is always getting lost."

"And this time she wants no one to find her," Mabaie muttered.

For a brief moment she thought her words had sobered him. He looked at her puzzled, rocking back on his heels. Then he shook his head and began to sing off-key.

"A simple Afridi boy am I
Far from the hills of home."

Mabaie shook her head. "More like simple minded. Go home before they cut out your gizzard. You have some nerve showing up here."

"You don't like my singing? How about a poem. All Afghans are poets. I am an Afghan. I fight for them. Do you know that? Did you know that?" He began to weave again and she reached up to steady him. "I am an Afghan," he repeated. "A true friend is a saddled horse. How's that for an Afghan proverb?"

"Life is not a bed of roses." She countered. "Abur Rahman said that."

He hiccuped. "Who is Abur Rahman?"

"If you do not know Abur Rahmin than you are not Afghan. Abur was a famous Afghan King. You would have liked him. He was sent to prison for drinking wine and smoking Indian hemp."

"Give me a kiss," he said, "just a little one."

"What!" Mabaie stepped back. "The girl is right, you are mad. I'm an old woman."

He grinned. "And ugly."

She laughed, "And ugly."

"Very, very, very ugly." He pitched forward on his face.

"What am I to do with you. If I leave you out here like this you'll be dead before morning." She lifted his arms and half-pushed and half dragged him towards the wooden barrel where they stored the rainwater. "Stand up," she ordered. Slowly he pulled himself to his knees. "Up I say." She had him by the back of the collar and jerked him to his feet. "Now walk."

"Walk?"

"Walk." She shoved him ahead, and whenever he started to falter she would kick his bottom. It was like leading an unruly donkey.

"Humpty Dumpty sat on a wall.
Humpty Dumpty had a great fall.
And all the kings horse crapped on him."

"Be quiet. You'll wake up the whole camp." They had reached the barrel of rainwater and she shoved his head in, holding it under as long as she considered it safe. He came up sputtering. "Unhand me, woman."

"Not yet," and she pushed him under again.

Several people had come out of their tents to watch the ruckus but she waved them back inside. She would drag him to her tent until he sobered up enough to defend himself in the night. She had no fear of what the mullahs thought of her taking a man to her tent. She was Mabaie the fortune teller. A woman who could raise evil spirits and put a curse on you. They let her alone. She was to be feared.

The Russian followed her into her tent; water dripping down his face and wetting his tunic. He was smiling. Docile.

"Sit down," she ordered. "Over there. You need some food in your belly to settle the poison you have poured in your mouth."

"Poison? You are going to poison me?"

"I could, you know. Without blinking an eye." She ladled a bowl of soup with bits of chicken and rice for him. "Do you not poison school children? We do not forget the 12th of June when hundreds of students were taken to hospitals in Kabul. It is said the poison was released into the air from a small 'cartridge.'"

"No, it was the drinking water and to this day no one knows who is responsible."

"Ah, I see the mention of 'poison' sobers you."

"Don't want to be sober," he muttered.

She said nothing as she watched him eat the *nan* she had put before him. He ate his soup slowly and without slurping -- despite a vulgar and foul mouth, the man had good manners. "So what is your name?"

"Yuri. Yuri Vitrovich."

"And you are a defector?"

"Not exactly by choice."

"At least you are honest. I am glad you got drunk."

He gave her a bewildered look.

"This war robs us of our laughter. Why dwell on the sadness. We were born crying. Let us learn to laugh."

"There is nothing funny about war," he burped "I am soooooo sleepy. Can I lie down?"

"No, but you may stay here until you are sober enough to defend yourself."

"Where did you come from, old woman?"

"The desert in winter and the mountains in summer."

"Ah, you are a *Koochi*, one that moves. I see you don't cover your face."

"Never... You are not to ask me any more questions. In my tribe older people rule."

He sighed. "Yes, particularly women." Before she could stop him he stretched out on the carpet and began to snore.

She watched him with his mouth agape. In sleep he looked innocent and vulnerable... She thought of her sons killed in the war and wished she could cradle his sleeping head in her lap. Several times he snorted and called out the name Sasha before settling back into sleep. Poor fool. She wondered what his story was.

An hour or more must have passed before she dozed off only to be rudely awakened by the Russian. "Who are you?" he demanded. "I want to know. Did you try to poison me?"

Mabaie sat up and rubbed her eyes. "I wish I had not dunked your head in the water. You were more pleasant full of Vodka. You are the one who answers questions, remember. Tell me again, why do you look for Annisa?"

"Najib says she is lost. And that she is ill."

"You told me that. Why would *you* risk your life looking for her?"

"Omar was too sick to come."

"Omar? How many men are in love with this girl?"

Yuri laughed. "You are not only old but you are wise."

She smiled. "And ugly. Even when I was young. That is why I learned to live by my wits." She gestured to the fine carpets on the ground and the embroidered pillows on her *charpoy*. "I tell people their fortunes and it pays for all this." She jingled the many bracelets on her arms as though to emphasize her wealth.

"What is my fortune?"

"Certain death if you don't leave here soon. You are a fool of a Russian to come into Peshawar alone."

"How do you tell fortunes?"

"I read palms. Or ask what sign was in the heavens when you were born."

"Most Afghans don't know their birth date."

"Doesn't matter. I'm good at faces. My knowledge doesn't come from books. I was just born with the 'knowing.'"

Yuri stuck out his palm. "I don't believe in any of this but what do you see?"

"That there is no money in it."

Yuri chuckled. "And so you deny a poor Russian down on his luck. Why did you help me? Why did you try to sober me up?"

"I have many sins but killing is not one of them. I would have blood on my hands to send you away in such a state." She took his palm. "I see I was right to do so. Your palm says you will die at the hands of a woman and I don't want it to be me."

"Not that again." He took his palm back. "I've been told that before."

"See. I am very good."

"Can you tell the fortune of someone you haven't met?"

"Sometimes. If I have a picture of them. A lock of hair. Or something that belonged to them. Who do you want to know about, Annisa?"

"No, I was thinking of Omar."

"The Omar who looks for Annisa?"

"I do have something of his on me." Yuri removed the pearl handled dagger from its sheath. "Here take a look."

"I need to hold it in my hands." She closed her eyes and waited for something to come. "The blade is hot. This is a man of great ambition. He dreams big dreams."

"They have robbed him of them. The bastards stole the helicopter parts."

"Tell him he will get his dream," she said, making it up as she went. She liked to give people hope.

"And what about Najib? What do you see for him?"

"You ask a lot for a man who can't pay. Besides, this Captain Duranni is a man of many contradictions. Too difficult to predict. He could be a twin to Annisa. They both are beautiful and with emerald eyes from another world."

Yuri chuckled. "I bet you are going to say they are really brother and sister? How could that be?"

Mabaie shrugged. "It would make a good story. I could have them switched at birth?"

"Not easy to do when Afghan babies are born at home."

"Ah, but the mothers could switch them without the fathers ever knowing. How many fathers pay that much attention to a new born?"

"Why would a mother want to do that?"

"Out of boredom? Out of wanting to have the last word against the male. To sit and laugh behind his back at his ignorance."

Yuri chuckled. "Far-fetched but fascinating. You do weave a good tale. The trouble is you have one big flaw in it. Najib is many years older than Annisa. They could not possibly be switched."

"Ah, yes, but the brother Annisa was going to in America? Did she not tell me they were like brothers."

"You are making up all of this?"

"Of course, I am... But isn't it fun to play with. I have the gift. I can keep people coming back for days on a single story—twisting and turning it as I go. Making them hunger for the end."

Yuri stood up and searched his pockets, looking for some money to give her.

"No, this is for free," she said. "Save it for another bottle of Vodka."

"I should tell you that when Najib came to Terri Mangal looking for Annisa, he said he suspected that she had returned to the refugee camp. That you lied. You honestly don't know where Annisa has gone? "

"No, but you shouldn't worry. The girl says she has a chit for the money bazaar. She is going to put her money in a bank so she will be free to choose her own destiny."

"And did she say what that was? You ought to be able to read her future." His tone was accusing. "You have something of hers." He pointed to the necklace around Mabaie's neck. "A French doctor gave that to Annisa, she would never give it away."

"You think I stole it?"

"I never trust anyone."

"And what if I did? My sins are little ones. I save lives...Yours."

Yuri grimaced. "You're a hard one to figure out. I think you know more about Annisa than you are telling me."

Again Mabaie shrugged. "Did I not tell you she is like Captain Durani? Full of contradictions. But I'll tell you one thing I do know. Despite what she says now, I think Najib is her life. Annisa will always toss everything over for him."

267

1986

CHAPTER 26

The sound of the rooster came first, followed within minutes by the cluck, cluck, clucking of the hens.

Alexander Meirnardus pulled the blanket up under his chin and grinned to himself in the darkness. Only three more days, and they would be on the plane to America where his father was going to be a very important man.

"How many Coptics have ever held such a post?" his grandmother had bragged. "Christians in Egypt should be very proud of my son."

Larks chorused outside his window now, the only sound in Cairo in early morning. In another hour or so, the loudspeaker atop the minaret of the corner mosque would begin to wail, calling the faithful.

Alexander rolled over and stuffed his face in the pillow, gleeful that he was a Christian and didn't have to rise from his warm bed at 4 a.m. to face Mecca like Ali, their snaggle-toothed gardener, who would soon be down on his knees outside the kitchen door.

But try as he might, Alexander could not get back to sleep. He would miss his school and Ali, of course. But America! So many toys. At Christmas, the family would drive to Florida and Disneyworld, a promise from his father. Father seemed eager to leave Cairo. He said things had not been the same ever since his good friend Sadat was assassinated.

"God was looking after you, Gregory Meirnardus," Alexander's mother had said on that terrible day. "Why else would you have been home with the gall bladder?"

His mother always worried about his father's health. But then his mother was a chronic worrier. She worried about moving to New York, too. "All that crime! Violence on the streets! Cairo may be dense and loud but her people are not lawless. To walk the streets of New York --even when the sun is shining--is not safe."

Father did not agree.

"I tell you, Captain Duranni sat in this very room last night and told me of his good friend Rahmin, gunned down in a New York taxi. The son of your hero, the poet Aziz!"

"That was late at night. A robbery."

"A bullet is a bullet, my husband."

"Woman-- don't speak of things you know nothing about."

"I know what Najib Duranni tells me. Poor man. Three years he searches for the sister."

His father had sighed. "I can't help thinking about that lost girl Annisa. A tragic family, the family of Aziz. She was an exquisite young woman. Ever since her disappearance, Najib Duranni seems to have put his life on hold."

"On hold? What does that mean?"

"Oh, nothing really. It's none of my business."

"I know. It's that English woman, isn't it? My husband, that's exactly what could happen to our Neamet. The idea of saying one doesn't believe in marriage. A career instead! I shudder every time that woman, Claire comes here."

Alexander liked to sit on the marble steps in his nightshirt and listen to them at night. But not when they quarreled. Last night had been particularly noisy.

His mother's voice was angry. "Mark my words, Captain Duranni will get you into trouble yet. Gregory, you take risks in your work with the Afghans. It has been seven long years now and still they fight. How much longer will you go on? When we left Islamabad, you promised no more trips to Peshawar."

Alexander admired Captain Duranni. A great freedom fighter from the land of high mountains, Afghanistan. He had told everyone at school how Captain Duranni had been wounded his last time inside. His arm was in a cast.

The Captain had laughed to hear this. "Alexander, I fell from my horse and broke my arm. I'm afraid you make me out to be something I am not."

After he was gone, his father said he liked the Captain even more for admitting he fell off his horse. "My son, I too thought he must have been shot in a raid. I trust a man who doesn't have to make himself out a hero."

"You trust too much and for all the wrong reasons. Just because Sadat sent them guns is no reason for you to stay involved in this mess," his wife nagged. "Sadat has been dead a long time now. Afghanistan is none of your concern. How can Egypt's new ambassador to the United Nations stay involved in such a thing? Do you see how foolish you would look, my husband, if the authorities should find out? You are a Christian representing a Moslem nation."

"Yes, and I am worried sick over the growing strength of Moslem fundamentalists. There will be no peace for anyone."

"Tch, tch, tch, I do not know who will kill you first. The PLO for your friendship with the Jews, or the Russians for helping the Afghans."

"You had no business eavesdropping on my conversation with Duranni," his father shouted.

At that, Alexander had hurriedly fled back up the staircase to his bed. His father hated people who were "sneaks." He must never know Alexander sat on the steps each night.

"Your poor sad-eyed father has so many enemies in the government, He does not need trouble in his own home." These were his grandmother's words. Grandmother also quarreled with Mother. For different reasons.

The toilet flushed down the hall. Alexander could hear the soft footsteps of Neamet, his dark-eyed, older sister, whom everyone said had inherited his father's melancholy ways. Unhappy Neamet hated moving to America, especially after what Grandmother had done to her because she was going.

The sound of water running through the pipes from the toilet into the adjacent wall made Alexander want to go to the bathroom too, but he was too warm and cozy to get out of his bed and risk the cold marble floor. He would lie there until he could stand it no longer.

Poor Neamet. She was crying. He raised up on one elbow and strained to hear the muffled sobs from her room. But the house grew quiet again. His hands behind his head, Alexander stared into the empty dawn and wondered when Neamet's terrible pain would end. Neamet, whose very name meant "growing things," had been cut down, "butchered" by Grandmother. His mother's very words. "Had not the family agreed Neamet would not be circumcised?" she had screamed.

The family was modern and enlightened and proud of it. But Grandmother had tricked his docile sister by secretly taking her to a doctor for a female examination. The horrible job was done before Mother knew. Mother had wept when she heard it, but Grandmother had insisted. "The old ways are best. The girl will be living in America. To cut out the seat of pleasure is our duty."

Grandmother knew all about American women and their ways. She never missed an episode of *Dallas* on the television Father had purchased for the family. "You see what comes of Western women who still have a clitoris!" Grandmother said.

Alexander did not know what the word "clitoris" meant, but he did know it belonged to that dark and mysterious world between

Neamet's legs. He also knew his Mother had refused to speak to Father for days afterwards, and when she did, she blurted out that there was "no hope for the world. What good are your dreams to make life better for Egypt when your own mother clings to barbaric customs?"

"What is done is done," his father had sighed. "You will make yourself sick if you don't forget."

"Forget? Is that what Neamet is supposed to do? Our daughter is so destroyed she will turn on us. Would you have her grow up to be like Captain Duranni's plaything? I don't care if this Claire works for the BBC. She is empty-headed."

Alexander remembered the beautiful lady with the golden hair. She always smelled like flower blossoms.

"The way that woman talks with men, my husband. As though she knows as much as they do. Disgraceful. Her hair color comes out of a bottle and she exposes her breasts to the sun. Out on our terrace I tell you. She is brazen."

"We have more important things to discuss than the Captain's mistress."

Alexander had asked Ali what "mistress" meant and Ali had told him he was too young to know.

"Ali, why did the British lady get so mad at Najib when I brought him the picture?"

"What picture?"

"On the cover of the yellow-edged magazine in my father's study--a girl with a red shawl draped over her head. She has green green eyes--kind of spooky and haunted looking."

"Trouble maker. Why did you bring this picture to Najib?"

"Because mother said the girl was from Afghanistan."

"And you wanted to look important in the eyes of the Captain."

Alexander did not like being found out. "I didn't know it was going to cause a fight, honest."

"Who was fighting?"

"The Captain and the mistress."

Ali's look was sly. "Did the Captain say the girl in the magazine was pretty?"

"No, he said she looked just like Annisa. Then father said, 'How can this be? This was published in July of last year. The girl in this picture is much younger than the Annisa I met three years ago.'"

"Then what happened?"

Najib said he thought it was an old photograph. That they should contact the *National Geographic.*
"What's that?"
"I don't know. Anyway, the Captain said he would follow any lead to find her. This made Claire very angry."
"Claire?"
"The mistress. She says, 'This is not the Annisa I met in Peshawar all powdered and perfumed' or something like that. Then she takes the magazine and throws it at Najib."
Ali chuckled. "Then what?"
"The captain picks it up and tells her she never knew Annisa when she wandered the countryside-- half-starved and a wildness in her eyes. Then the mistress stomps her feet and says, 'The wildness is still there. No amount of make-up could hide that.' The captain gets really mad then."
"I bet. . .but who is Annisa."
"Annisa is the one he loves."
"Who told you that?"
"No, that's what *she* said. The mistress. She said the Captain was 'obsessed.'"
"Mercy. What did your father do?"
"He left the room."
"I told you. Your father is a very smart man."
The voice of the muezzin from the minaret loudspeaker had begun to call and Alexander snuggled further under his covers. Ali would be unfolding his prayer rug. The voice was only a recording now but in the olden days a real muezzin had climbed to the top of the lofty tower and stepped out on the slender balcony for prayers. His mother, who was scornful of Muslims, had told Alexander that only blind Mullahs had been allowed to ascend the tower. Muslim men had not wanted another man peering into the back yards of their women.
"Your mother feeds you nonsense," Ali said. "One of the trials of working for Coptics."
The rumbling of a donkey cart came to a stop outside the iron gate of the compound. Its metal wheels, salvaged from tanks after the great battle of El Alamein, announced the arrival of Saneya, their fat, sweet-smelling maid with the large round breasts and plump hands that patted the bread loaves before she put them in the oven. How he loved the smell of Saneya and the warmth inside her great arms as she hugged him. Sometimes when he couldn't sleep, he stuck his hands between his legs and thought of Saneya. What

puzzled him was how Saneya could be so fat and her little girl, Taha, who rode up front on the garbage wagon with her father, so skinny. Poor Taha, her legs were always covered with flies.

"Christians!" Ali always spat on the ground when he said it. "Coptics, only fit to feed the pigs."

His mother fired Ali on the spot whenever she heard him say such things about Coptics. Each time, Ali would wail and wring his hands and throw himself on the ground crying. "But what about my two wives and seven children in Luxor? What will become of them?"

Of course, Father always let Ali stay, insisting he was old and sick and had been with them too long to be sent away.

"You have a soft underbelly," Mother had hissed. "How can you tolerate a man who tells your own children they are infidels?"

"It would not be Christian to fire him."

"Your Christ is too humble. The Christ I know overturned the tables of the moneychangers."

The arguments had been pointless, because now that the family was moving to America, Ali would no longer have a job, and what with yet another new bride, it was sad, very sad. Hebra, the young wife who did not look much older than Alexander's own sister, had been sent home three times for being jealous. The last time, Ali had torn up the marriage papers from the Sheik. She had returned docile, promising never again to make accusations against Ali and other women. So Ali had accepted her back into his one room attached to the garage where their quarrels could start all over again. From the balcony off his room, Alexander could hear their bickering.

"Everybody in this household fights," Neamet had said sadly.

And it was true. Ali accused Saneya of poisoning his bride's mind against him and Grandmother told Father that indeed "Saneya is a mischief maker."

Mother believed Ali made up stories against Saneya because she had refused his "advances." "I'm sick of their squabbling. They remind me of children. It will be a blessing to go to America, if only to be rid of their fights."

But she also knew it would be difficult in New York with only a cleaning lady that came once a week.

Father insisted there was no reason for the squabbles. It was simple. Give Saneya full reign of the house and tell Ali not to enter. "Everything outside--the garden, the car--are his."

"Oh, and what do I do when Ali does the shopping and Saneya tells me he is cheating us? Buying fruit from a stand that belongs to the people of his wife."

"*Maelesh*, so be it!" his father had said, throwing up his hands.

And his mother had smiled in spite of herself. "And you, Alexander. What will you do without your Saneya? There will be no one to spoil you."

Alexander hated his mother when she said this. It made his ears turn red, remembering those times with his hands between his legs. "What will happen to Ali after we are gone?" Alexander had wanted to know.

"Perhaps he can go back to the sugar boats," Grandmother suggested.

"He is too old for that life now; his back is no longer strong."

"Better he go back to Luxor--before the plague comes," Mother had answered. "We shall die of garbage on the streets. It is not certain Egypt was the beginning of civilization, but there is no doubt it will be the end. Cairo is not what it used to be."

On this, Grandmother and Mother agreed. Mother was forever wanting to return to her girlhood home of Aswan and the beautiful gardens. "How can one smell the roses in our garden? They are covered with dust."

She blamed the high dam for all their problems just as Grandmother blamed the floods that came before that. "I don't care what anyone says, life was good when the British were here," Grandmother always insisted. She loved to talk about her youth and the British and how festive Cairo had been when they had returned during the Great War. "Shepherd's Hotel was splendid--red-tabbed British colonels at the bar, back from the fighting in Libya."

"Your grandmother romanticizes war," Mother had told him.

"And you?" Father asked.

His mother sighed, "Look at Ali, the miserable fool. Calling his son's death in '67 part of a great victory. For how many days did we hold back the Jews? A victory! I have to laugh."

"That's enough," Father scolded.

"All of our problems now, Gregory Meirnardus--they stem from one thing--Sadat made friends with the Jews."

"She speaks the truth. You are tarred with his brush, my son."

Father was pained to hear Grandmother say it. But then he always felt pain when there was talk of the Jews. Ali had told Alexander he didn't know any Jews in Cairo, but if he met one he "would spit in his face." Ali, whose sons had died in a glorious victory.

Alexander knew a Jew. At the International School there was a girl Jew, who smiled at him each day on his walk home with Neamet.

"New York is full of them. Another reason you should think twice about taking us to live in America," Mother had told Father.

"Our savior was a Jew!" Father's voice had been angrier than usual. "There will be no more talk in this house against the Jews or the mistake Sadat made in going to Palestine."

"How can you hate the Russians and not the Jews?"

His father had stormed out of the house and did not return for two days.

Grandmother had told mother not to worry. "He simply fights with you to cover up his nervousness over the move to New York."

Alexander rolled over in his bed and raised his arms above his head, making a fist into the room. Soft streaks of light had begun to filter through the shuttered windows. Outside the garden walls below, the taxi drivers would soon begin quarreling too, as the noisy, crowded city began another day. "When I grow up I will never fight with my wife," Alexander said out loud. "And I will live in Cairo and see a blonde lady who smells sweet and runs her fingers through my hair like she does the Captain's. She won't get mad because I will never show her pictures of my love." He turned his head towards the night stand and reached for Alexander the Great, one of the 12 silver warriors in miniature his father had given him. Napoleon, Julius Caesar, Alexander--"All of whom," Father had said, "once stood at the foot of the great pyramids of Giza."

Alexander rolled the soldier over and over in his palm. Some day he would be a great warrior like Alexander, his namesake, or better still like Captain Duranni. The captain was coming for dinner again tonight and mother was fussing about it even though the British lady had returned to London. Father said she had to go on business and mother said she thought there had been a tiff--a rift between them.

It was full dawn now. A woman's laughter could be heard in the driveway. Strange, it did not sound like the voice of Saneya or even Hebra, Ali's young bride. Maybe the tiff was over? Maybe Claire had come back? Alexander swung his feet out onto the gritty floor. No matter how often Saneya wiped the floors down with a damp rag, there was always that fine layer of dust under bare feet. Forgetting his bladder was full, he pushed open the shutters and walked out onto the balcony which gave him a fine view of the driveway and the street beyond the iron gate, now open for the day.

Ali was washing the car down with a bucket of dirty water and wiping a window with a greasy rag--as though he was trying to make up in these last few days for all the times he had neglected his duties and fallen asleep in the shade of a mango tree.

Alexander was curious about the girl--young woman, to be more exact. What was she doing there, leaning up against the car and laughing with Ali in the early morning? She looked like pictures of the Queen Nefertiti in history books at school. Did she not know about Ali's jealous young wife? If Hebra should come out of the house now and see them together, there would be yet another fight. Alexander knelt down on the balcony and tucked his flannel nightshirt under his feet, half hoping that indeed Hebra would come out and make a fuss.

The early morning light was not strong enough now for him to get a good look at the woman's face. She did not wear the traditional gown, the long flowing *galabaya* like Ali's wife always wore, but rather high heels, blue jeans, and a green shirt with white daisies embroidered on the sleeves. Alexander loved the color green. Saneya had said it was the color of healing.

No wonder Ali's voice was getting louder; he was showing off. Just watching the girl move around Ali, Alexander knew for certain there would be trouble when Hebra came out. The girl was slim and cat-like with pointy breasts like Neamet, and she had wonderful sweeping hands. They were making too much laughter not to be heard. Alexander smiled; knowing that Grandmother would call the girl "a temptress." It had taken Ali to explain what a "temptress" was.

Alexander turned to pee in the honeysuckle vine that ran up the side of the house. His heart stopped. The girl had heard the sound on the leaves and was watching him. It was too late. He was caught. Then she smiled. Putting her finger to her lips, she signaled their secret.

And he knew she wouldn't tell.

"Alexander. Alexander?" It was his mother calling. Alexander hurriedly left his spot on the balcony and his view of the little scene in the driveway.

"Yes, Mother, I'm up. Yes, I am awake. Yes, I am out of bed. Yes, I am getting ready," he called.

He had dressed in his bright blue pants, black tie, and the white shirt and jacket of his school uniform. Then he went out on the balcony and took one last look at the beautiful girl.

The car door was open. She had snatched the lucky blue sandal that hung from the rear view mirror over the driver's seat. She was teasing Ali, refusing to give it back.

"Alexander? Your breakfast is getting cold."

Knowing he would miss the big fuss with Hebra in the driveway, he reluctantly went down the stairs.

"Good morning, son."

"Good morning, my father. Ali just gave the lucky blue sandal away to a girl."

"The what?"

"Hush, Alexander. Hurry and eat. Your father is late."

"You know, the one that hangs in the car for good luck."

His father smiled at him. "I do not care about the blue sandal. Ali hung it there. It is not Christian to be superstitious."

"Ali is flirting again." Alexander felt important to say it.

"Oh?" His father smiled.

"Mother, where is Neamet?"

"She is not going to school today."

"Then why do I have to go?"

"I thought you were looking forward to your farewell party?"

A wave of guilt swept over him. His friends had been unkind about his father.

"Father?"

"Yes?"

"Why do my friends say the UN is a joke?"

"Because they are jealous of your father's important new position," his mother interrupted. "Here, you haven't touched your egg."

Alexander's eyes were steady on his father's. "Do you think it is a joke, my father?"

His father set his coffee cup firmly on its saucer. "The UN is a place where nations meet to make the world a safer place. That task is not a joke, my son."

The boy nodded his head, his round eyes serious. "That is what I told them. But they laughed. They said the UN has voted many times to say the Russians should get out of Afghanistan. But nothing happens. It is all talk."

His father threw his napkin on the table and stood up abruptly. "Hurry, Alexander, I cannot be late," his voice was gruff. Alexander reached for his tea and gulped it down. The hot brew seared his tongue, which he knew would be sore for the rest of the day. Then he took the stairs two at a time. He scooped the miniature soldiers up from his bedside table and tossed them into the ivory inlaid box they had come in. Alexander loved the blue lapis lazuli clasp--the stone of the high priests. "A stone that comes from Afghanistan," Captain Duranni had said when Alexander showed him the box. His father had given him permission to take his soldiers to school on his last day.

The girl was gone when Alexander came out into the driveway. Ali was there talking to his father in front of the car. "Can I steer this morning? Sorry to be late, my father."

His father shook his head as he unfolded his arms and reached for the brief case he had left lying on the hood of the car. "Another time. We are much too late."

"Oh, please, just for a minute. I am a careful steerer."

His father reached over and affectionately roughed up Alexander's hair. "Why is it I can say 'No' to a cabinet minister but I can never say 'No' to you?"

"You spoil the boy," his mother said from behind the kitchen screen door where she stood watching. But there was a smile in her eyes.

"How can one spoil innocence?"

Alexander knew he had won and raced to the driver's side of the car, jerking open the door and sliding his box of soldiers over onto the seat. "Ali, look at me," Alexander shouted gleefully, "I shall drive us all the way to New York. What do you think?"

"*Maelesh,* so be it. "Ali showed his snaggle tooth grin.

"New York. We are coming." Alexander twisted the steering wheel and leaned on the horn.

His mother waved back.

When the explosion hit, all the windows on the kitchen side of the house were shattered. Ali, his face covered with blood, was

279

running in circles in the driveway, his right eye pierced by a piece of flying glass. At his feet, Alexander's father lay moaning, both legs blown off from the blast. Black smoke filled the driveway. The animal screams of Ali's young bride could be heard all the way to the mosque.

The mother of Alexander stood silent, unable to move, frozen in time behind the screen door. "My baby, my baby," she whispered, addressing what was left of her only son inside the smoking car, her sainted boy with the soulful eyes. She lifted a prayer toward heaven and caught sight of one of her husband's legs caught on top of the drainpipe of the garage roof.

"Oh, merciful Jesus," she sobbed, and then fainted onto the cold tile floor, safe inside the kitchen door.

CHAPTER 27

In late afternoon, the hot and sand-laden southerly wind of *Khamsin* raised the temperature in Cairo to over 100 degrees. Choking the air of the city, it covered everything with a fine gray film.

On his way to meet with Gregory Meirnardus and his two wealthy Saudi friends, Najib Duranni felt concern. His freshly pressed suit might not look presentable by the time he reached Ataba Square. The porous material of his arm sling absorbed the fine sand. It had been foolish not to take a taxi.

Near the Babylon Fort in Old Cairo, he stopped for cigarettes at a newsstand. He was feeling down on himself for letting his fight with Claire trigger an old habit. Suddenly, dry-mouthed, he dropped the packet and reached for a paper:

NEWLY-APPOINTED U.N. AMBASSADOR WOUNDED,
SON KILLED IN TERRORIST BOMBING

When he wandered from the stand without paying, the proprietor shouted after him. Too dazed to be concerned, Najib handed him some *piasters*. Two separate terrorist organizations were taking "credit" for the deed.

"Barbarians!" Najib shouted, startling passerbys. Moslem terrorists had destroyed his only hope, Meirnardus, who believed the Mujahideen should be included in the U.N. negotiations between the Paks and the Soviets. Meirnardus, who had faith in the young commanders inside Afghanistan, wanted to by-pass the money-grubbing politicians in Peshawar.

Without a sense of direction, Najib stumbled through the crowd of faces. Eager voices around him assaulted his senses as they called to one another in their daily commerce. So many people in Cairo. "Why, you God-forsaken bastards, why?" A few heads turned to stare at this crazy man shouting obscenities.

He rounded a corner and the hot wind caught his tie and whipped it across his face. In anger, he reached up and yanked it from his collar. This useless tie purchased especially for this all-important day. Useless. All was useless. Just when they were making headway. Only last month, he had accompanied Commander Gailani to testify before the U.S. Congress, and before that the conferences in Strasbourg and Florence had been a success. The world was beginning to pay attention.

A wooden cart, its side piled high with mounds of garlic, waited at an intersection. Its ancient driver nodded to Najib. For the old man with his garlic to sell, today was like any other day. Najib pushed past him and out into the traffic. Running now, running down the street of Al Azhar, he headed without intent into the City of the Dead. Ahead were mounds of gray trash, which bled into a horizon of sand and desert, enveloped in diesel gases from nearby streets. The exhaust hovered over the neglected gravestones like a pall. He sank dejected to the ground, possessed by the evil genie *Ilfrid*, the genie of despair. Beside him, a crumbling marker stood amidst scattered orange peels, broken bits of crockery, and fresh donkey dung. The City of the Dead was where he belonged. He was without a wife or family or a place that was his own, a man caught between two different cultures, different centuries. For six years now, he had been shuttling back and forth between those bountiful banquets served to him in Europe and the States and starvation at home. Little or no rain the past three years had brought a terrible drought to the fields of Afghanistan that the Soviets had not already torched.

"Did you ever see such eyelashes on a man?"

This had been the idiotic response from a group of socialite women to whom Commander Gailani had just delivered an impassioned speech for funds. Gailani had come out of Afghanistan at considerable risk. The Soviets had a $40,000 price tag on his head. It was tiresome--having to parade Mujahideen and crippled Afghan children like a sideshow at a circus. What a ridiculous war! Field commanders sneaking out of the country, leaving the battlefields in order to plead for bullets.

In a sudden panic, Najib reached into the inside pocket of his jacket and groped for the letter. Ambassador Meirnardus had shown ultimate faith by choosing him as his courier. The letter was still there. The attempt on Meirnardus's life might change things but he had counseled how important it was that Fritz Werner receive the letter, to be hand-delivered. Najib pulled it out of his jacket wondering if he should open it. If the seal were broken, their informant inside Barbak's council might think the packet had been tampered with. This was not the time to decide. He would have to leave Cairo tonight for Afghanistan instead of waiting until the weekend. Whoever had done this terrible deed had kept a close watch on Meirnardus's house. And this meant other parties might be aware of his own whereabouts. He had been to the home of Meirnardus many times in the past few weeks—several times with

Claire. This was worrisome if they connected her with him. Too many revenge seekers were out there operating in the name of the prophet, often at cross-purposes. He should know. He was one of them. He had compromised his own work for the Resistance by doing the very thing he always counseled others against: letting his desire for restitution stand in the way of his judgment. He had killed a man to even the score for Rahmin Aziz. It was true that Rahmin had been shot in his taxi but it was not a hold-up as the papers reported. Rahmin in his zeal to help raise funds had inadvertently stumbled upon a splinter group of Muslim zealots in New York negotiating a very lucrative drug deal. Rahmin had been incensed when he learned what they were up to and because he was never known to keep his mouth shut, it was silenced for him. Najib's suspicions about the shooting had started with a throw-away line at a party in London by the journalist Matthew Hardcastle, 'I'd like to think it was a robbery instead of a rumor that Rahmin was involved inadvertently in a money laundering scheme,' Hardcastle's words had set Najib off to uncover the truth. He was not able to prove or disprove the rumor but in his investigation he came up with the name of Rahmin's alleged killer. There had been no going back. He could not honor his vow to Annisa for her father's death but he could avenge her brother. As a result his own name was now on the list of a group of terrorists operating out of Libya. It never stopped once you started it. An eye for an eye.

The best thing he could do would be to leapfrog his way to Islamabad, stopping in Athens where he would switch to a Greek passport. He looked down at the sling. It would make him an easy man to spot in airports. He would break the cast.

The taxi driver had the radio on a music station.

"More word on Meirnardus?" Najib asked.

"He lingers. But with both legs shot off, what kind of life? They are saying The Party of God did it. Fucking Shiites. They give Islam a bad name."

Najib nodded. Damn the Ayatollah. Damn his secret deal with the Soviets. Khomeini had agreed to put a lid on his arms shipments to the Afghans if the Soviets would temper their assistance to Iraq. Meirnardus had told him all this. Now, Meirnardus might be dying.

The cab driver raised his hand in a gesture of despair. "Always there is trouble from the foreigners. The Americans give us mini-skirts. And the Russians would take away our prayer rugs."

"So what's the answer? Do we keep the modern world out?"

The cab driver shook his head. "Let wiser heads than mine figure out the answers. I just ask questions."

The taxi stopped in front of an art studio that specialized in Egyptian papyrus prints for the tourists. Najib had taken a room on the top floor. He was halfway up the landing when his landlady called from above. "I don't want trouble. Two policemen were here looking for you! And the day before a man with a salt and pepper beard. He had one funny eye. Kind of crossed."

"What did *he* want?"

"Not much. Asked me if a man with his arm in a sling lived here."

Najib handed her a month's rent in advance. "If he comes back, I have left for Alexandria to visit my sister."

"You have no sister. A man doesn't look at his sister the way you did at that blonde lady you brought here."

"Suit yourself. I have done nothing wrong."

"That is what they all say. So self-righteous in their own cause. The world is self-seeking, I tell you, and it grows more so every day in the name of religion." But she did not hand back his money and was busily counting it as she headed down the stairs.

He entered his room. It had been turned upside down. Thank God, he had his papers and his plane tickets on him. His picture of Claire had been removed from the frame. But her goodbye note was still on his dresser top. He reached for it and crumpled it in his fist. Her jealous outburst over Annisa in front of Ambassador Meirnardus and his family had caught him off balance. He had never made any secret of his on-going search for Annisa. Why had the cool and collected Claire revealed this side of herself in front of others? In a peculiar way her jealousy pleased him. It made her much more real. But she had not allowed him to confess this pleasure in the privacy of their room. Instead, she had wordlessly packed her suitcase "I've had it with you," she shouted, as she flounced out the door. "Go piss up a rope." Najib smiled at the memory of her word choice. So out of character for the lady-like Claire… He knew he couldn't give her an honest answer about Annisa because he didn't know for sure himself. How much of his going back to search for Annisa had been because he was her *kafka*, her sworn protector, and how much was fueled by a desire just to be with her? That night in Peshawar, there had been no clear cut answers and there might never be any. Once again, Annisa had been

284

swallowed up into the catacombs of war. Claire was right. Despite the passion in their relationship, Annisa remained unresolved. Like every other woman, Najib suspected Claire wanted marriage even though she professed many times she did not. Claire was everything he wanted. But he couldn't ask her now. He had no future. It would be irresponsible before this war was over.

"You have got to decide someday where you are going to grow old," Claire had said the first night she arrived in Cairo. "Will we bury you in London or Afghanistan? Right now you are only half a man in each place."

"Half a man for you?"

"That's not what I'm saying."

"Claire, forcing me to choose is not the answer."

"I'm not talking countries."

Slowly, he uncrumpled Claire's note and smoothed it out on his dresser top. *'Okay, you win. You've got to find Annisa and sort this out if we are ever going to have a chance. It is dangerous for me to love you because how can I ever get over it if I lose?'*

Damn. He felt the same way about her. But Claire's leaving Cairo was for the best. God, what might have happened if she had been here when these thugs arrived? It was selfish of him to keep seeing her. Despondent, he took one last look around the room and closed the door. He chastised himself for even thinking of Claire at a time like this. They had tried to kill Meirnardus and he had to find out who they were.

What was it Mrs. Meirnardus had said at the dinner table earlier that week? "Gregory, your friend Cordovez will get nowhere with his U.N. negotiations in December. As long as the Soviets are in Afghanistan, America has an excuse to interfere in Central America. I suspect the CIA is not that pleased with you working with the Mujahideen, my husband."

The vein in Meirnardus's forehead had stuck out he was so incensed.

"You forget the years here under Nassar and the Soviets."

"There is no difference between East and West--both are enemies of the Egyptians. Besides, New York is full of Jews. I don't care if Jews do read from the Book."

Meirnardus had motioned for his wife to leave the table. He was enlightened but not enough to be abused in front of a guest by his wife. The conversation had ended there but the gist had stayed with Najib. Surely, the CIA had nothing to do with this attempt on Meirnardus's life? It also bothered him that he had let

Claire badger him about Annisa in front of others. Maybe, he too, was not so enlightened as he thought.

A few blocks from the studio Najib found what he was looking for: a building was being torn down to make way for a high-rise. Workmen with sledgehammers were breaking up pieces of the stone. He approached a young Egyptian in a tee shirt which had a picture of the British rock-star, Sting, imprinted on the front.

"I need to break this," Najib said, holding up his cast.

The man put down his sledgehammer, leaning on it as he wiped the sweat from his face with the back of his arm. *"Izzay?"*

"I'll give you 50 piastas to break this open for me."

"Put your money away. I can't do this!"

"100 piastas."

"Crazy man. Go to a hospital. It is a terrible risk."

"That is for me to decide. 150."

The worker motioned to a window ledge. *"Dra!* Put your arm up there. But don't blame me if I pulverize it."

With two swift blows the cast cracked open. At first there was no pain, only a numbness. But by the time Najib boarded the plane late that evening, he was questioning the wisdom of what he had done. They could not recognize him as easily at the airport without the cast, but the pain in his arm was more than he had anticipated. He also knew cabin pressure would cause the blood to expand and push against the fracture. Oh well, he should be grateful for being delivered out of Egypt on time. God willing, he would deliver the message from Meirnardus.

The passenger who boarded TWA flight #390 in Athens gave Najib a second glance as he headed down the aisle.

Dr. Ethan Harris buckled his seat belt. Where had he seen that face? The Afghan looked familiar. They were taxiing down the runway when he remembered. Of course. Captain Duranni. Najib. The man in the refugee camp with the girl Annisa. How many years had it been? Two? No, three. He wondered where Annisa was now. Memories of her tear-stained face his last night in the refugee camp still disturbed his sleep.

The doctor craned his neck around. Yes, that was Duranni all right. Najib was thinner now and his hair was short, a military cut. But there was no mistaking the scar on the side of his face. It was hard to believe he could have so misjudged the man. Miserable creep. Giving the girl a case of the clap and then cutting out on her.

If the old woman Mabaie had not called Ethan to her tent, Annisa might have died from the infection.

"I gave the girl the root from the Great Burdock plant but the sickness stays," the gypsy-like woman had told him.

"How long has she been like this?"

"Two days."

"With this fever? Damn you!"

Annisa lay before them semi-conscious.

"The girl has great shame. I tell her I think it is a sickness that comes from men. She makes me swear to tell no one."

He had not given Annisa a pelvic examination. He was not going to risk it in this culture. If the girl died who knows what the old woman would tell about the *ferrangi* who had touched her. He had no slides to take a culture, but the symptoms of gonorrhea were all there. He had done the only thing he could think of. He had given Annisa a large enough injection of penicillin to cure a cow.

"You miserable hag. Why didn't you come to me before?" He was fearful Annisa would be left with endometriosis--pelvic scarring of her tubes. "She may never be able to have children now!"

The sight of Annisa's silver locket around the old woman's neck had made him livid. The thief. Stealing from a girl who was delirious.

"Doctor, tell no one she is here. The man who passed as her husband is looking for her. I think *he* is the pig who gave the girl this sickness. I told him I had not seen her. He does not deserve to know where she is."

Ethan had never known the outcome for Annisa. His plane for the States had left the next morning and when he called Rahmin in New York, the number had been disconnected. It wasn't until a few months later that he learned from Matthew Hardcastle that Rahmin was dead, killed a few days after Ethan had arrived in Peshawar. And yes, Matthew Hardcastle knew the sister had resurfaced. He had met her at a dinner party. Ethan decided not to tell the journalist that he had seen Annisa in the refugee camp a few days after that party. He also didn't tell him that despite the fact he had seen Annisa only twice, she had made an impression on him. Memories of her remarkable stoic demeanor and beauty lingered.

Ethan sighed and picked up a discarded newspaper on the seat beside him. It was in Arabic but he recognized the picture of the Egyptian, Meirnardus. The papers at Heathrow had been full of it. Last thing he heard was that the U.N. diplomat was not expected to live.

A red-headed stewardess who looked a bit like his girlfriend Jan, trundled the drink cart down the aisle. Hell, it was ll o'clock in the morning. Too early for rotgut. His head ached with tension. This time he was going inside. This time it was for sure.

The man in the window seat pointed to the newspaper in Ethan's hand. "A shame about the Egyptian diplomat."

"Criminal. They ought to string up whoever did it by their thumbs."

"Do they say who?"

"They think it was the Iranians. But there's also speculation it might have been the Arafat faction of the P.L.O."

"I doubt that. Meirnardus was no friend to the Syrians. His connections with King Hussein were believed to be the best"

"You seem very knowledgeable about this part of the world."

"I try to be. But you need a scorecard to keep up. Every time I think I know who is on what side, the players change. Are you staying long in Islamabad?"

"No, I'm going on to Peshawar." Ethan hesitated. He was talking too much as usual. The doctor with the International Medical Corps in Los Angeles that was sponsoring him this time had told him to keep quiet about his intent. He was to let only one other person Stateside know he was going in. All he had was a Peshawar phone number for a contact, not even a name.

The red-headed stewardess was back again with a plastic tray of food wrapped in aluminum foil. Her hair was the color of Jan's--lovely Jan, who had called him "sophomoric" for wanting to go back. "All your education, your years of training--risking it for what? So you can brag about how macho you were?" She had even protested his stopover in Athens.

"It was cheaper than flying direct."

"I'm terrified of that airport."

"I'm a fatalist. When your number is up, it's up."

"Interesting, from a doctor. A real comfort to your patients... I know, why don't you get a phony passport. Carry an extra one; Canadian perhaps? In case of a hijacking you won't be the first to go."

"Jesus, girl. They would cut off my balls if they found out."

His seatmate coughed. Then cleared his throat. "You will find Peshawar very hot this time of year. Crowded. Full of refugees."

"Tell me, what do the Greeks think about the situation in Afghanistan?"

"We don't pay too much attention. Too busy agitating against NATO and the Americans, I'm afraid."

"We seem to grow more unpopular each year."

His seatmate smiled. "It goes with power. When I was a boy we hated the British, and my father's father was furious with the Turks. You pay a price when you're--what is it your American footballers say? 'Number One.'"

"So you have been to the States?"

"Many times. Most enjoyable."

Captain Duranni was standing in front of Dr. Ethan Harris while they waited to clear customs. It was too tempting. Ethan had to speak to him, if nothing else then to find out what had happened to Annisa.

"Najib?"

The man gave him a blank stare.

"Captain Duranni? I met you in..."

"I am sorry. I do not know you. My name is Nicholas Venizelos."

Ethan was confused. He found himself replaying in his head the man who had been in the camp. It was mind-boggling. It had to be him. He looked down at Najib's discolored fingers on his left hand. His hand was swollen to twice a normal size.

Ethan waited until Najib had cleared customs before he decided to try again. He dashed towards Najib who was heading for the exit door. "I only wanted to talk to you about Annisa."

The scar on Najib's face turned a brilliant red. He grabbed Ethan by the elbow and herded him over to the side. "Perhaps I can be of help? I speak good English."

They were out of ear shot of the other passengers; standing in the front of the entrance to the toilets. "What do you know of Annisa?"

"I was asking you."

Najib's face fell. "You are the American doctor, aren't you? I'm surprised you are back."

"I'm just stubborn enough to try it again."

"How long did you stay in the refugee camp?"

"I left a few days after you did."

"I was wondering if you saw Annisa. . .if she came back to the camp after the two of us left together."

Ethan hesitated, but only for a minute. "Yes. Annisa returned. She was sick."

"Then the old woman lied to me."

"So she told me."

Ethan noted that Najib kept looking anxiously towards a man standing near the vending machines. The man had a full salt and pepper beard and was a bit cross-eyed.

"Your hand? Want me to take a look at it, Captain Duranni?"

"I broke my arm. They took the cast off too soon."

"That's bad business. It may have to be re-set."

The bearded man stood up and crossed to the automatic doors that led to the street. He went out.

Captain Duranni looked relieved.

"I really think you should get that arm looked at."

"When I get to Peshawar."

"Why not let me see to it now?" Ethan held up his carry-on case. "I have the fixings for a temporary splint in here. You need to take the weight off of it. Put that arm in a sling."

"No. . . But there is something you can do for me." Najib reached for an envelope inside his suit jacket and pulled it out. "This has to be delivered. A man named Fritz Werner. It's important to the Resistance."

"But I can't even speak the language."

"I'm not asking you to deliver it. That's my job."

"So what are you asking?"

"How are you getting into Peshawar?"

"Air India. Tomorrow morning."

"What time?"

"10 o'clock."

"I'll be on that flight with you. But in the event I don't show up at the airport, I want you to call this number." He removed a pen from his shirt pocket and wrote the number on the envelope.

"How long do I wait before I make the call?"

"About ten minutes before boarding is announced."

"Then what?"

"Arrangements will be made for the letter to be picked up from you "

"Does the number have a name?"

"No, we don't operate that way. You just give your name and number and tell them Najib Duranni has a birthday present for Fritz Werner."

"Fritz Werner?"

"Don't write it down. Remember it. Fritz Werner."

"Let me get this straight. I'm to hold this letter until you show up here tomorrow morning."

"Please. It's crucial to the Resistance."

"Where are you going?"

"It would only jeopardize you to know."

"Why not take it with you?"

"Because there is always a chance I might not be back. This letter has got to get through."

"Shit. I'm a doctor. Not James Bond."

Najib smiled. "You have enough fortitude to go inside and operate under fire. You risk kidnapping or torture; the last man I would worry about." He checked his watch. "One other favor. I won't be going inside this time but I do have feelers out for Annisa at every way station on the Jihad Trail. In the event you should have any news of her."

"I struck out last time." Ethan wanted to add. 'And so did you.' But he didn't. Captain Duranni evidently had a full plate. He was tempted to tell this Afghan swashbuckler that he had very possibly given Annisa a venereal disease and that the consequences might have been tragic.

"I have left messages for Annisa for three years, but nothing." Duranni looked genuinely concerned.

"Maybe she gets them but doesn't want to contact you?"

Najib sighed. "Very possibly. But just in case." He pulled a cocktail napkin from his pocket and scribbled a name and address on it.

"Claire Lipscomb? The BBC?" Ethan was curious. "Does she know about the letter?"

"No, this is a place where I hang my hat when I'm in London. I have no permanent address. I'm a floater. But I keep in touch with the lady. If you get word of Annisa, tell Claire. . .No, just give her *your* name and how I can get in touch with you. Whatever you do, don't mention Annisa."

Ethan was beginning to get the picture and felt more resentful by the moment for being included in Najib's plans to contact Annisa. If she was still alive, she was probably better off without the guy.

"Sorry to be rude. But I've got to hurry." Without so much as a goodbye or a handshake, Najib Duranni walked away from Ethan and crossed to the exit doors.

Ethan watched him go. From the back he looked like what he was. Military, straight backed. His long stride was more of a march than a walk. Ethan picked up his duffel bag to get back in the customs line. What the hell? Duranni had left his carry-on case on the floor. Shit, he was not to be saddled with this, too. All those stories of people giving you things at airports. What if the guy didn't show up? He was not about to carry someone else's briefcase on board. Ethan dropped his own bag and ran past the custom's officers towards the exit to wave Najib back inside.

Najib was at the corner now, and about to turn out of sight. Damn his ass. Saddling him with this briefcase.

The roar of the motorcycle, which whipped from behind an airport storage building, was deafening. It traveled fast. Horrified, Ethan watched it plow directly into the back of Najib Duranni, tossing him in the air. He landed face first in the middle of the street. The motorcyclist did not stop but roared away full throttle.

Ethan broke into a run and pushed his way through the crowd gathering around the victim. "Let me through. I'm a doctor. Let me through." Someone had rolled Najib over on his back. "Don't move him," Ethan ordered, bending over him. "Get an ambulance," he shouted as he opened Najib's shirt collar. Ethan took off his own suit jacket and covered Najib for warmth. Najib opened his eyes.

"An ambulance is on the way."

"The letter," Najib whispered.

"We'll have you to a hospital in a minute."

"No, don't come with me. The Sprinzar Hotel. Fritz Werner. Fritz. . ."

"I hear you. Fritz Werner. The Sprinzar Hotel."

A small trickle of blood had started to ooze out of the corner of Najib's mouth. Internal hemorrhaging.

"I'll go with you to the hospital first. Never sure about the medical treatment over. .. ."

"Please no. . .This was no accident."

"Don't talk."

"For Meirnardus. Deliver it, I beg you." His eyes closed and he lost consciousness. But Ethan could still get a pulse.

When the stretcher-bearers arrived, Ethan was pleased to see they had modern equipment and were well trained in moving the injured. Too late, he realized he had thrown his suit jacket over Najib, whom they were now carrying through the crowd to the waiting ambulance. "Wait," he shouted. His passport and air tickets were inside his jacket. "Wait." He chased after them and yanked his coat off the injured man just before the ambulance driver slammed the door shut on the stretcher. "Sorry, I need this," Ethan said to the sea of curious faces surrounding him. Then he remembered the envelope in his hand and hastily tucked it inside his pocket, sprinting down the street for the taxi stand. "The Sprinzar Hotel," he told the driver.

"The Sprinzar Hotel?"

"Yes. Sprinzar."

"No such place."

"Oh, Christ, maybe I'm not pronouncing it right. SPRIN--ZAR HOTEL. You take me fast. Fast."

The driver looked indignant. "No need to shout at me. I speak English. I tell you there is no such hotel in Islamabad or Rawalpindi and we are halfway in between. Now, where do you want to go?"

"I don't know."

"What do you mean you don't know."

"I'm confused."

"I see that. Do you look for a place to stay?"

"No, I mean yes. I leave for Peshawar early tomorrow morning."

"Well, why didn't you say so. In Peshawar. There is a Sprinzar Hotel."

"Shit. I forgot the duffel bag."

"Sir?"

"My fucking suitcase. I left it in the airport."

"You have it in your hand."

"That's not mine. It's his."

"You confuse me."

"Never mind. You just wait outside while I go back through customs and get it..."

The cab driver threw up his hands. "You did not go through customs!"

"No. I had to . . ."

"I do not want you in my taxi." The driver leaned over to open the door. "I don't want trouble."

293

Ethan was shouting again. "No, god-damn it. You will take me back to the airport. Now!" He was surprised with his own tenacity.

The custom's area was closed when they got there and much to Ethan's amazement his duffel bag was sitting out on the curb.

Well, he sure wasn't going to go around asking questions about how it got there. He had enough craziness to deal with as it was. Christ, he wasn't even inside Afghanistan and all his carefully laid plans not to call attention to himself had gone by the boards. He had been screaming like a banshee ever since Captain Duranni had been struck down.

The taxi driver delivered Ethan to Flashman's, an old-fashioned but clean establishment in Islamabad that charged only a few rupees a night. At the desk Ethan tried calling hospitals in Islamabad to check on the condition of one Najib Duranni, struck by a motorcycle near the airport. No one by that name had been admitted and he could not remember the other name Najib had used at the airport.

"What is this shit?" he said to the desk clerk. "How many people are hit by a motorcycle every day in this town?"

"Maybe they took him to Rawalpindi? Or maybe your friend was dead on arrival?"

"God damn it, no. I don't want to hear that. . . Sorry. How far are we from Peshawar?"

"100 miles."

"Can I rent a car?"

"First thing in the morning. Shops closed today. Holy Day... ."

"I suppose the plane would be faster."

"Here, can you find this number for me?"

"Very expensive phone call, sir. London."

"Try it anyway." Ethan was hoping against hope that this Claire Lipscomb might know of some of the aliases Najib used.

He was flabbergasted when they got through immediately and a satin voiced woman was on the phone. She sounded concerned with Ethan's request. Was Najib in trouble?

"I'm not sure." He was not about to tell her how serious it might be. "He is using a Greek name which I can't remember. It would be helpful if you were familiar with it."

"Who is this again?"

"I'm an American doctor. Ethan Harris. A friend of Najib's."

"How do I know this?"

"You don't."

"I'm not sure I should be talking to you. Najib is taking extra precautions these days. Is he all right?"

"I'm not sure. Look, if you honestly don't know a Greek name he might be using I need to hang up. This phone is costing me a fortune."

"I honestly don't know... Please, tell him to get in touch with me as soon as you see him."

"Will do." He hung up. Poor woman, she had sounded very upset. And little wonder. But what else could he do?

He noticed that his breath was coming in gasps and he had better slow down. All the tension. He was starting to hyperventilate. There was only one other phone call he could make. The telephone number without a name. "Deliver it," Najib had pleaded... Trouble was, he had forgotten to mention the Sprinzar was in Peshawar.

"Here, try this," Ethan told the desk clerk who was watching him, a wary look in his eye. He handed him the number.

"Ah, this is a good number."

Ethan raised an eyebrow. "You recognize this number?"

"No, but this one is good. Not expensive. Not another country. Peshawar is also in Pakistan."

Ethan drummed his fingers on the desktop as he waited with the desk clerk. "No answer, huh?"

"No, they answer."

"Well, what did they say."

"That the number is out of order, sir."

"Shit!"

"Will that be all?"

"No, can you get some soda water delivered to my room."

"Consider it done."

Ethan thought it prudent to leave him a very large tip.

Inside his room, Ethan pulled off his boots and opened the bottle of Jack Daniels he had in his duffel bag. One good thing about playing hopscotch with customs. He had run the risk of their confiscating his liquor stash.

Gingerly he removed the brown packet with a red seal of wax on it, and put it on the bed. He stared at it as though it had a life of its own. Perhaps it did. What were the odds with being on the same plane with Duranni after all these years? Not so big if you thought about it. Afghanistan had five million people but it was an elite handful that flew in and out of Islamabad trying to form a government in exile. But to be handed an envelope for the Resistance! Jan, who believed there were no coincidences, would call it providential.

For a minute, he was tempted to open the damn thing. How did he know for sure what he carried was what Duranni said it was? Meirnardus had been bombed and now Najib had been run down. He, Ethan Harris had been a personal witness to an attempt on Najib Duranni's life. What the hell was he carrying in his pocket for this man? Stupid to take chances. But then wasn't that why he had come back to Afghanistan-- to prove something? Only God knew what. Jan had laughed at him when he tried to tell her. "For Christ's sake, Ethan you are over 30. It's grow-up time."

Her words had stung because they had an edge of truth. In fact, he wasn't ready to join the so-called "adult" world at home. It was boring. For the past three years he had stared at the baby poo green walls and florescent lights in the hallways of the hospital and each morning he had asked himself. "Is this all there is? Routine tonsillectomies and old men with hernias? And then settling down with Jan and raising a raft of kids? What comes in between?" Also, he had never failed in anything he had ever tried to do in his life. It was like climbing that proverbial mountain just because it was there. First time around he hadn't made it into Afghanistan. Well, this time he was going to prove to himself that he could.

Exhausted, he put his head on the pillow, loving the smell of soap and fresh air on the sheets. How extraordinary. It was a smell from his childhood and it pleased him. To hell with clothes dryers and bits of wax paper you threw inside for an artificial smell of lilacs or some other synthetically contrived scent. This part of the world smelled like life.

He poured himself yet another glass of whiskey. On the other hand, a good stiff drink was not part of the scenery over here. He raised his glass and toasted himself. "Okay Commander Bond. Admit it. The old adrenaline is pumping." He sure the hell was curious about the message he had promised Najib to deliver. Who was Fritz Werner? His head swirled with possibilities.

Perhaps he should open Najib's briefcase? Maybe his new identity was inside? He leaned over to the nightstand and picked up the case. Najib Duranni traveled light. Inside he found a razor, a toothbrush and some worry beads. There was also a small bottle of pain pills, and, of all things, a copy of the magazine, *The Economist*. There was no address book or secret messages. Only a hand-written note that said he should go look for Annisa and that he was a dangerous man to love.

The phone rang by his bedside and he jumped at the sound. It was only the desk clerk confirming his wake up call for the morning.

Ethan stared at the ceiling. He was too revved up for sleep. Was Jan right? Was he out of his league? He decided he wasn't dumb enough to think he could make a difference over here but he wanted to be a part of it. Something very big was dying in Afghanistan, where mountain tribesmen were taking on a superpower. Maybe it had to do with what Annisa had told him in the refugee camp. "This is not life. Only a passing of time." She had pointed to the distant mountains. "Behind those mountains, every moment counts."

Ethan Harris wanted every moment.

CHAPTER 28

The desk clerk at the Sprinzar Hotel looked impatient.
"Checked out."
"Did he leave a forwarding address?"
"I am sorry. I can not give out that information."
Ethan Harris reached into his wallet and laid an American 20 dollar bill on the counter.
"Kabul," the clerk answered without looking up as he pocketed the bill.
"Any particular address?"
"Mr. Werner has a rug business there. That is the extent of my knowledge." He turned his back on Ethan and returned to his cubbyhole. Ethan could see him nonchalantly sorting the mail. Meanwhile, the message from Meirnardus was still in his keeping.

Outside, the day was miserably hot. He was tempted to go to Dean's Hotel and sit in the garden with a lemonade. It was familiar. But the doctor in Los Angeles had told him to stay away from Dean's and any other place where foreign tourists gathered. He would be wise to attract as little attention as possible. Pretty funny when you thought about how visible he had made himself in Islamabad.

It was easy to see that the tenor of Peshawar had changed. It was more crowded than he remembered and there was more tension between the Paks and the Afghans. The Paks were tired of their guests; the government had kicked the headquarters of the various Resistance organizations out of town. Now most of them lined the roads to the refugee camps. And the camps had deteriorated drastically; the Paks were refusing to register new arrivals. Refugees camped along the roadside and there were constant fights over water and jobs.

There was no sense in going to the American consulate for advice. Officials remained uptight about Americans going inside. A journalist from San Francisco had been shot in ambush a few weeks before.

Ethan did try to call Matthew Hardcastle in London to see if he might have any advice or people he could put him in contact with to deliver the message. But the journalist was in Lisbon and not expected back for two weeks. Did he want to leave a message? He did not.

His only hope was that his Mujahideen escort that he was to take inside to the clinic would have some idea of how to get a letter to Kabul. But he had to be careful-- to make sure he knew whom he was dealing with first.

Much to his surprise, the number he was to contact for his guide was picked up on first ring. A man who identified himself as Rahmatullah told Ethan to wait where he was--the Fasial Restaurant.

Ethan was not expecting the short, tobacco-chewing character in knee-high boots and a long cloak who showed up.

"You look too young to be a doc." Rahmatullah shouldered Ethan's duffel bag and then transferred it to his head. "We go to the Khyber Bazaar. We buy you turban. Afghan outfit. The whole gig."

Ethan grinned. "Gig?"

"You got it, man. You make silly looking Afghan. But we try." He patted the duffel bag and then pointed to Najib's briefcase. "All this has got to go. We carry our belongings in pieces of burlap."

"You're the boss. . .My medical supplies?"

"You bet. Arrived last week. On the way in by mule. Be there before you, the rate you walk."

"Have you ever heard of a man named Fritz Werner?"

"Nope."

"How about Najib Duranni?"

"Captain Duranni? You keep dangerous company."

"I thought the captain was highly regarded in the Resistance."

"He is. But some nasties have been around asking about him. Drugs."

Ethan stopped in his tracks. "You mean Najib Duranni is involved in the drug traffic out of Afghanistan?"

"Nope. I mean people who *are* have been looking for him."

"Would it be possible for you to take me to Kabul?"

"What's this? They have sent me a crazy man."

"Agreed. But I've got to deliver a message to a man in Kabul. It's important for the Resistance."

"Bah, it's always the same. Every message is the most important."

"I think this one is."

"Doc, many people walk many miles to see you. Long lines waiting. Forget this message. You came here for the sick."

"I can't. Captain Duranni may have been killed in trying to deliver it."

"Ah, me. The wind blows bad. I'll see what I can do."

"He told me it has to be hand-delivered. We can't just give it to anybody."

"You need to tell *me* that!. . . I'll think on it but Allah makes miracles, not me."

Before the night was over, Ethan decided it would be up to Allah if they survived the trip inside. Their lives were in the hands of a seven-year-old boy who Rahmatullah dangled by his feet outside the window of the truck. The boy held a lantern. It was his job to coach the driver, "Bashir" -- to tell him whenever the wheels of the ancient vehicle got too near the edge of the road. There were no shoulders--only a straight drop into eternity.

In the morning Ethan surveyed the open stretch of desert they were to cross by foot. They would be totally vulnerable: easy to spot by Soviet aircraft. Bashir, his soft-spoken bodyguard, who weighed around 300 pounds, told him "not to worry." This was not too comforting because it had become apparent that "not to worry" was the extent of Bashir's English.

"Ten more miles in the truck before we reach the border," Rahmatullah said. "Not so flat beyond Parachniar." He pounded him on the back. "Okay, Doc?"

Rahmatullah, his madcap interpreter, who had learned English by cooking for Texans visiting the Wakhan Corridor to hunt Marco Polo sheep before the war, pointed to the hands on Ethan's watch and to the sky. "Russkies don't fly this time. Same time each day. You savvy, Doc?"

Ethan laughed despite his trepidation. With Rahmatullah's constant "What's up, Doc?" he had begun to feel he was the centerpiece of a Bugs Bunny cartoon.

Outside Parachniar, a border patrol shone a light in Ethan's face and ordered him out of the back seat. Before he could move, a gun was shoved in his stomach. Nervously, Ethan watched a big hairy arm shoot out from the window with a fist full of money. Bashir growled and the Pak guard allowed them to pass. But as he turned to go, Ethan's turban, which had been unwinding like a snake from the top of his head, now trailed to the car floor.

"Shit fire and save matches!" Rahmatullah said, rewinding the turban for the hapless American.

"Where did you hear that expression?"

"Texans. My kind of Americans."

Bedded down for the night at a safe house in Terri-Mangal, Ethan needed to urinate. Outside, behind the house, Rahmatullah came up behind him in the dark and slammed his hand down on Ethan's shoulder, forcing him towards the ground.

"Afghans don't pee standing up," Rahmatullah gasped. "Only *ferrangi*. . .Here. Like this." He squatted on the ground to demonstrate. "That's good, Doc. Now you know how to piss like an Afghan."

Ethan was thinking he should write in his diary that Jan had insisted he bring along. Jan was not going to believe any of this. "I give you three or four days, Ethan, and then you'll be bitching like crazy," was Jan's prediction. "You've only been to the refugee camps. I know you, you like your creature comforts. You're not going to take too well to eating out of the communal bowl."

He wanted to prove her wrong but his stomach was in constant revolt from the assault of stringy goat meat swimming in grease. Poor people were offering up their best meals along the way and he felt ungrateful if he didn't finish his plate.

On the second day inside, his temper and his stamina were stretched. Despite his six months of training at home--jogging five miles a day and a rigid program of pushups--he was not in good enough shape to keep up with his guides. His feet were a mass of blisters and he had a constant charley horse in his right thigh. It was humbling. He was half the age of his companions.

"Sorry, Doc. Next village, we get you a mule. We sing a song for you. Cheer you up." It was cartoon time again. Rahmatullah had a voice like Kermit the Frog and Bashir sang off key:

"When you're wounded and left on Afganistan's plains,
And the women come out to cut up what remains,
Jest roll to your rifle and blow out your brains
An' go to your Gawd like a soldier."

"Go, go, go like a soldier." Ethan chimed in. "That's a poem by Rudyard Kipling, He was British, you know."

"Must be. A British newsman taught it to me. 'Beer, beer, beer for the soldier.'"

It was obvious that one of the reasons Rahmatullah was in such good humor all of the time was that he was stoned. A generous soul, he offered Ethan his pipe, but Ethan declined. He should be grateful for small favors-- Bashir did not indulge. Bashir kept guard at night, sleeping sitting up with his rifle on his knee. His big liquid brown eyes and a drooping mustache gave him the benign appearance of a Pancho Villa.

"Bashir looks like bandit? No?"

"Big time."

"Before the war, Bashir wrestle on Afghan national team. Very strong. Pick up Russian soldier and snap him in two."

Bashir gave Ethan a gentle grin.

It was strangely reassuring.

Finally, they arrived at the first clinic. It was located under the trees outside a whitewashed mosque. And as Rahmatullah had predicted, many people were waiting patiently for him as he rode into town on his mule. Cheers and adulation greeted him. Little girls brought him flowers.

Ethan wrote in his diary that night: "A bit like Christ on a donkey. Shades of Palm Sunday."

An epidemic of measles had racked the village. Many children had died. It made him furious with the Russians. Why the hell weren't they brought to task for this? Measles and diphtheria had been all but eradicated in Afghanistan before the invasion. But the big killer of children was dysentery. The men had bleeding ulcers, brought on by the tensions of trying to fight a war without adequate weapons and feed a family on ruined land. He saw a lot of stress-related complaints ranging from migraines and insomnia to neuroses and schizophrenia among both active Mujahideen and the civilian population. A number of mad children roamed the countryside.

All of this he recorded in his diary, adding "I am receiving more from these people than I give. I feel needed. Useful. But I'm also losing sleep over the message for Fritz Werner. Rahmatullah seems to be dragging his feet."

The next day was to be a day of rest. Rahmatullah had ordered it. Ethan was stretched on the ground in the sun outside their makeshift clinic at the end of a gorge. Hidden from the world in the long canyon, the Mujahideen had constructed a ramshackle clinic for him against a granite wall. The back was the mountain and the sides were made of rock piled upon rock. Overhead was a clay roof and across the front were two large Afghan carpets hung over a pole. When he wanted air and light, he had only to raise one of the carpets.

His doorway commanded a view of the narrow gorge, which twisted below him within giant walls of granite looming 800 feet straight up. A tiny river flowed through the center. Anyone entering the gorge could be seen immediately. Because of the wind currents, Rahmatullah assured him they were fairly safe from aerial attack. Men from the village guarded the passes and checked those entering.

News of the American doctor's skills had traveled ahead of him and he was deluged with patients. At this rate, he would soon be out of medicine. Bashir had sent word to the guards at the pass that the doctor was finished for the day, but still the people came, a large group of them camping out on the canyon floor waiting their turns. Some of the little girls had organized a game of hopscotch and it tore at Ethan's heart to see one little tyke attempting to play on one leg with her makeshift crutches. The boys were off by themselves shooting stones at crows with slingshots. The chatter and happy faces below revealed nothing of their ordeals.

"Good news, Doc. More supplies come today. You stay longer?"

"How could I part from you?" Ethan hugged Rahmatullah, a spontaneous gesture. He surprised himself. He never hugged men. He and his father always shook hands. He came from that kind of family.

"We friends now, Doc. We fight. Air clear?"

"No. Only when we get that message delivered to Kabul."

"Doc, the word is out. Wait."

"I was told it was urgent."

That night a man delivered a sack of walnuts to Ethan, who had treated his son the day before. The family lived 12 miles away. The father had made a round trip of 24 miles on foot to say, "Thank you."

"You study long time? Fix sick people."

"Long time, Rahmatullah."

"No wife."

"Nope."

"Women best part of man's education."

"I won't quarrel with that."

"You good man, Doc. America very far away. You help us. So we give walnuts. Understand."

"In spades."

Early the next morning, Rahmatullah sat on a rock in the sun, cleaning his gun. A man in a Russian fatigue jacket approached.

"Mohammed Omar. At last you come. Here is your man, Doc. For a message."

303

Omar held out his hand to Ethan and Ethan winced from his grip. The Afghan had arms like pile drivers. His face was also arresting, and he was bald except for a fringe at the back of his neck. His features were not Mongoloid like Bashir, the Hazara. Fascinating. With his russet toned skin he could pass for an Apache warrior.

"You stare at his face. He is handsome, you think?" Rahmatullah chuckled and poked Omar in the ribs.

"I hear you are a good doctor," Omar said.

"Best in Afghanistan," Rahmatullah interjected. "You have sickness?"

"No, but I need help for Yuri, my Russian friend..."

"Where is he?"

"I didn't bring him until I was sure the American would treat a Russian."

"A man is a man to the doc. Is it true Omar El-Ham you blew up the munitions dump outside Mazar?"

"You have heard this?" Omar asked, looking pleased with himself.

"Tales of your daring are legend, my friend. I also hear your chest is made of leather. That you cheated death."

Omar raised up his tunic and showed Rahmatullah the scars. "Would you believe a woman did this? A *ferrangi*."

"The Russians have women soldiers in Afghanistan?"

"I mean a woman saved me. She made these stitches when others gave me to the dead."

"That does not surprise me. Women are good with a needle." Rahmatullah laughed uproariously at his own little joke. "Heard any funny stories lately about the Mullah Nasruddin?"

"No stories."

Ethan sat down. His back was killing him. Seeing patients 14 hours a day while seated cross-legged put his back in spasms at times.

"Doc needs a chair," Rahmatullah said.

"I will bring him one."

"You speak good English," Ethan noted.

"No, my English is bad. It only sounds good when you listen to Rahmatullah's."

Ethan laughed.

"It gets better. My niece has taught me. She speaks better English than you do. Yes, it is the truth. English like the real English. She is the one who urged me to come for the message. She says it must be important because she knows you. Or at least she thinks she does. And she says she knew a Doctor Harris in the refugee camp."

Ethan got a strange sensation in the back of his head. It couldn't be. "What is her name?"

"Annisa."

Ethan could not hide his excitement. "Annisa, of course I know her. Is she aware that everyone in this world is looking for her? This is wonderful, wonderful news." The look on Omar's face indicated it was not so wonderful.

"Who looks for her?"

"Captain Duranni."

"She would not like to hear this."

Ethan did not know exactly what he was supposed to say to that "Well, I am certainly pleased. Relieved. The last time I saw her she was very sick."

"Strong as an ox. She rides like the wind. . . And the message?" All of a sudden Omar was all business.

"It has to be delivered to a rug dealer in Kabul. His name is Fritz Werner. As soon as possible. It comes from an important diplomat who was with the UN."

"I would have to read it first."

"Fair enough." Ethan was so relieved to be rid of it he didn't care if it was opened. It had been a week now. Whatever it said might be too late as it was. He handed Omar the envelope and watched him break the seal.

"I cannot read this."

"What are you telling me?"

"It is not in Farsi."

"Here let me see that. . .Damn. This looks like German."

"I will bring Annisa with me when I bring Yuri, the Russian. She knows many languages. She can tell me what it says and if it is worth the trip to Kabul . . . .I wouldn't bother her with this Captain Duranni."

Ethan decided to change the subject. "What is the Russian's complaint?"

"It is the malaria. Fever. Chills. The bed shakes."

"I have medicine to help him."

Rahmatullah stood up. "I fix special meal for us. Kebabs. I go to the guards at the pass. They will send in meat."

"Hold on." Ethan said. His stomach had been much happier on a diet of rice and vegetables.

"Not tough goat. But lamb. A celebration. The message will be in Kabul soon enough."

Omar walked over to Ethan and put his hands on his shoulders. "I am glad Rahmatullah leaves us. I have an important question to ask you."

Ethan was really leery now. He was sorry he had mentioned Najib. He certainly didn't want to get mixed up in any family feuds.

"It's about my health."

A long pause followed but Omar didn't speak.

"Is it the malaria? Do you have chills? A fever?"

"No, it's a very personal thing."

"A doctor never reveals what his patients tell him."

"I have your word?"

"My honor."

"It is my pleasure in bed. I fear the worst. I can only take my wife two times a night now."

"Two times a night. . . but"

"Then it goes all limp--like a sick fish."

Ethan had heard tales of Afghan libido in the refugee camp. If they were to be believed, they went off the chart. "Your wife? Does she complain?" he said, trying to keep a straight face.

"Oh, no. She welcomes it. I disturb her sleep."

"How old are you, Omar?"

"I have no idea. Forty? Fifty years? Maybe more, maybe less."

"In my opinion a man who does it twice a night at your age is a stallion."

"Then he is not an Afghan."

"Maybe Afghans tell tall tales like all the rest of us."

Omar studied his face. "You try to make me feel good with lies? That is your medicine?"

"No, I speak the truth as I know it. But who am I to say? You fight a nuclear power with slingshots and rocks. For all I know an Afghan can hump all night."

"Hump?"

"Mount a woman."

"Oh, good. I like that. 'Hump.'"

Ethan, who was a great believer in the power of the mind, decided it would be prudent to practice placebo medicine. He took out a bottle of Vitamin B-12 he had brought for his personal use and doled out 30 pills. "Here, this should help. One every other night before sleep." He was mentally calculating the number of days he had left in Afghanistan. Two months at the most. Hopefully, he'd be out of the country before Omar found out. And who was to say-- the power of suggestion might "cure" the patient. Ethan figured he was as bad as the old storyteller Mabaie and all her hocus pocus. "It's a slow process. It may take a week or two to see a difference after you have finished with the pills."

Rahmatullah returned carrying long sticks on which to roast the kebabs. "Red sky tonight. No rain. Many people come tomorrow."

Ethan turned to Omar. "When will you deliver the message?"

"If Annisa decides it is old news, then tomorrow I go to Kandahar instead. To shoot a plane out of the sky."

Rahmatullah leaned forward, a gleam in his eye. "What plane, Mohammed Omar?"

"A plane with Russian officials. Besud Zalmair will be on board."

"The great Mujahideen commander!"

"The great traitor, you mean. He hides out in Kandahar. The plane leaves on the 4th."

Listening to the conversation, Ethan was suddenly impressed. Perhaps his remark about slingshots against a super power was out of date. Commander Balisar was a very big fish.

"Kandahar is too far to reach by the 4th."

"You joke. I have over a week."

"With what do you shoot this plane down?"

Omar beamed. "A SAM-7! The launcher and six rockets cost me four thousand U.S. dollars three years ago. I have three rockets left."

"Four thousand U.S. dollars," Rahmatullah gasped. "You traffic in drugs?"

"Do I look that stupid! It was Allah. For many years I save and scrimp. And then they steal my Hind helicopter parts. It is our Annisa who saves us. She gives me big sums of money she brought back from Peshawar."

Ethan frowned to hear this. Was this what had happened to her plans for America? She had been so eager to go to medical school. Why didn't she? His feelings of good will towards Omar were beginning to fade. No wonder she had not gone on to the States if she had given her money away. And where had she been all these years and what would she be like when she arrived tomorrow?

He was just now trying to fill in the blanks. Surely, Annisa hadn't been all this time with this man? He realized he was flattered that she had remembered him. Even his name. With a sudden start, he thought of Najib. Warnings or no warnings from Omar he was going to have to tell Annisa he had seen Najib. How would she take the news? The girl had obviously been in love with him.

Rahmatullah was shaking his head. "The great Zalmair would not betray us. Many people believe in him."

"He plays both sides," Omar snapped.

"Whose word is this?"

"Yuri, the Russian. He learns Zalmair leaves secretly for Tashkent from Kandahar on the 4th."

"It's the malaria. Your Russian sees things that aren't there. . . And why all the trouble to shoot the plane. Why not a knife in the back?"

"How would I know where Zalmair stays in Kandahar? And if I did, how do I get through his bodyguards?" Omar's face was turning red that anyone would dare question the wisdom of his plan. "Zalmair will be on that plane and my heat seeker will sniff him out. Blow him to hell."

Rahmatullah was reveling in Omar's indignation. "But why you? Why not send word to Kandahar. It is very far away. I bet you have never been there."

"So?"

"So. You will wander the countryside. Not get there in time."

"You would have me tell men I do not even know that the great Zalmair betrays? Who would believe it? I have no proof. Only Yuri's word from his friend in the GRU."

"Never trust a Russian."

"Only this one. What kind of man are you that you would deny me my prize?"

"A jealous one. I go with you, Omar? I know Kandahar." Ethan shook his head. "No way, Rahmatullah I need you here as my interpreter."

"Omar needs me more. He has only a sick Russian. This is big stuff, Doc. Big. Did you not listen?"

Ethan was beginning to understand what the newsman Matthew Hardcastle had counseled years ago--that the biggest problem for the Afghans was that every man had his own plan on how to win the war. Getting them to agree on a major strategy was impossible. The war was being fought without any real coordination. There seemed to be no central command.. But still they hung on. Men like Omar were a double-edged sword. Fighters beyond belief but with little or no discipline. "Omar, is this a civilian or military plane?" Ethan asked.

"The Antanov 27 flies Reconnaissance and passengers. Both."

"Won't shooting down a civilian airliner cause some flap?"

"Flap? What is flap? Zalmair betrays us or why would he go secretly to Tashkent!"

Rahmatullah rose to Omar's defense. "Zalmair big man, Doc. Omar does great thing."

"A footnote to history, huh?"

Omar frowned. "Flap? Footnote?"

For the first time Ethan reached over and took a puff of Rahmatullah's pipe. "An American diplomat in Peshawar once accused me of this. They put an asterisk which is a little wigglely star by something important in the history books and your name is there at the bottom of the page."

Rahmatullah grinned. "You mean I will be famous? I like this footnote. Big things happen and the wigglely star tells people it was Omar's idea?"

"Kind of. A small bit of recognition."

Omar smiled broadly. "I shall blow this traitor to Afghanistan out of the sky. Then I will be a footnote, no? I can't wait to tell Annisa. I bet she knows all about footnotes. She knew who you were. That woman is always right. The most valuable fighter in my command."

Ethan choked to hear it. Fighter? Annisa? He had better leave that one alone.

CHAPTER 29

    Rahmatullah and Bashir left before dawn to pick up more medical supplies donated from funds raised by school children in Sweden.
    Ethan was happy to be left alone. The heavy sweet smell of hashish from Rahmatullah's pipe lingered where he slept, along with the smells of Bashir's indigestion. Last night had been a particularly musical time for Bashir's innards, which were accompanied by the rattle and whistles of his heavy snores.
    Ethan stretched and pulled back the rug at the entrance. An amber colored sky. He yawned and stretched again, his arms over his head. His "protectors" wouldn't be back for awhile and the guards would not let the patients enter the pass until their return. It was like a mini-vacation for him.
    A figure entered the gorge and even from this distance he could see it was a woman. She was without the veil and her walk was determined. It had to be Annisa. He raised his arm and waved but she did not wave back. Her long dark hair swung freely down her back and when she drew closer he could see the luscious pink of her ruddy complexion. She had a radiance; a glow of good health. He was gratified to see it. That last night in Peshawar, Annisa had been a shadow of herself, white and wan and fragile.
    The woman coming up the path towards him was a different woman than he expected. There was not a hint of young girl's shyness in her. Even the dress she wore suggested boldness. It was the dress of the nomad women; vibrant and multi-colored with tiny round mirrors stitched on the bodice. Her eyes were as he remembered--a sea grass green.
    He wanted to run down the path to greet her but thought better of it. The guards at the mouth at the pass would realize she was alone with the *ferrangi* and any suggestion of intimacy on his part might be misinterpreted. Perhaps that was why she hadn't returned his greeting. He felt a bit apprehensive that his heart should quicken at the sight of her. Even the crunch of her footsteps on the loose rocks of the canyon made his pulse quicken. He felt like a schoolboy, fearful he would be tongue-tied in her presence.
    "Good morning, Dr. Harris. I was happy to hear you came back to Afghanistan."
    "You look fit. I think the mountain air agrees with you."

Neither one of them looked at each other. "I hardly know you," he said, attempting to break the awkward silence. It's been three years."

"Omar tells me you have a letter in German I should read."

"Yes." He felt rebuffed. And pulled back the carpet over the entrance and ushered her inside. "Where is Omar? I thought he was coming with you?"

"He will be here later. He has gone with his brother Abdul as far as Jamu. Abdul is on his way to Peshawar. He has a bullet in his knee and his leg is stiff where it was trampled by horses. It mended wrong. He is hoping to make the list for an operation."

"Well, if he doesn't make the list, whatever that is, I may be able to help. I know a group of doctors out of Salt Lake City who are performing reconstructive surgery on wounded Mujahideen. They fly them to the States if they think it's warranted. If Abdul is still in Peshawar when I return I could take a look at him."

"It would mean a lot to him. He's very morose. For many years he was a great athlete--a famous *buzkashi* player. After his accident he isn't fit enough to ride; stays home with the women and children while his older brother stages ambushes on the enemy. He is bitter and bad-tempered but I understand how he feels."

"You? You are much too young to be bitter and bad-tempered," Ethan teased.

"I know what it feels like to be a cripple, Dr. Harris," she said evenly.

He was taken back by the vehemence in her tone. "Are you? A cripple?"

"You know I am. You told the fortune-teller Mabaie I could never have children."

"What? I did not use the word 'never.' I said there was a possibility. Annisa, have you been to a doctor about this?"

"No, and there is no reason to go now. It is too late . . .We waste time. I have come to translate the message for you."

Ethan was hurt that she sounded so cryptic--so business-like. There was not a hint of the friendship he thought they had shared.

He walked to a crevice in the granite wall where he kept his passport and other important papers and pulled out the envelope. She scowled when he handed it to her. "This is unfortunate; the seal is broken."

"We decided to open it. Omar did not want to risk the trip into Kabul if the message was no longer of any use."

311

"A message without a seal is always suspect. Omar should stick to what he knows."

Ethan was put out. "Give me a break. How do you think we knew it was in German if we hadn't opened it?"

Annisa's cheeks burned, trapped by her own high-handedness. When she spoke she still did not look him in the eye. "This is in German all right. But it is gibberish. Some kind of code."

"I was afraid of that."

"Who were you to deliver this to?"

"A man named Fritz Werner."

Her voice was agitated. "Fritz Werner is very high up in the Resistance. A message to him would probably be of the utmost importance."

Ethan felt defensive again. "I did what I could. It was one hell of an impossible situation. In the past week I have not met an Afghan who could read or write--let alone read German. Rahmatullah was calling the shots and, frankly, he wasn't that interested in helping me out."

Annisa fingered the envelope. "I have no way of knowing if this is important or not. This will have to be taken to Kabul as soon as possible."

"Does that present a problem?"

"A big one. Abdul has already left for Peshawar. And Omar plans to take Yuri with him to Kandahar as soon as he is well enough to sit a horse."

"Omar says the Russian has malaria?"

"Yes. Omar brings Yuri to the clinic this afternoon. Hopefully, on a litter. He's too weak to walk."

"Has he had these attacks before?"

"Not that he tells us. Yuri is the packhorse of the Resistance. He keeps to himself. He does not complain. But Yuri is a very sick man. Too sick to travel for Omar's foolish scheme for Kandahar."

"You say foolish?"

"I misspoke. Omar dreams big dreams. There is nothing wrong with that."

Ethan was beginning to see a pattern—she would contradict him no matter what he said... "It did sound a little far-fetched when he talked about it."

"You are not Afghan. You wouldn't understand."

Something about her suggested a strange authority over his emotions and suddenly he was mad. "Why are you acting so snotty?"

"Because you judge me. I know what you're thinking. That I should have gone to America as I planned or that I should have stayed in the refugee camps and helped with the sick."

"You are putting a lot of words in my mouth."

"I dare you to tell me different," she snapped.

"You are so very angry and I'm not sure why."

"Then I will tell you. You remind me of my shame."

"Shame?"

"My sickness in the camp."

Ethan was annoyed. "That's a bum rap. I admit I'm disappointed you didn't come to the States, but I never. . ."

"How could I go? My brother was dead."

"There were others who offered to help you. Me included. And yes, you could have stayed at the camp. You'd make a damn fine nurse."

"I want to be a doctor."

"Then be a doctor. The International Red Cross is training para-medics in Peshawar now. It would be a start. And if you ever want to come to the States we can get you into a nursing school. You're very bright Annisa. You should have no trouble in getting your G.E.D. I can send you books to study for it and..." He stopped mid-sentence. "You aren't interested in all this are you."

"No."

"I give up. Omar tells me you are a 'fighter'? What's that supposed to mean?"

"Omar talks too much."

"And you don't talk at all."

"Understand this. I couldn't stay at the camp. Mabaie knew I had the sickness of men. And Mabaie has a loose mouth. I had nowhere to go but to my uncles."

The way she said it was a revelation to Ethan. Underneath the bold new facade she was still that hurt little girl. "You are very wrong. I don't judge you for the sickness."

"I don't want to talk about this anymore."

"Then let's talk about you coming to the States. It is never too late. If you should change your mind . . ."

"What's so special about America? If it's so great, why are you here?"

313

Ethan cringed. It sounded too much like Jan. "Forgive me for remembering how happy you were in the camp, helping with the sick." He knew he was being sarcastic but it annoyed him that she should challenge everything he said. "It's none of my business if you want to live the life of a nomad. Maybe you know something I don't know."

Her face suddenly relaxed. "Dr. Harris, I know you only want to help. But it's too late . . . I was weak and frightened when I left the refugee camp. I made some foolish decisions."

"How foolish?"

"I had nowhere to go but my family. So I came to them on their terms."

"To be a fighter? I can't believe they demanded that of you."

"No, joining in raids against the Russians was my idea. So don't blame them!"

"You actually go on raids! I've never heard of a woman in Afghanistan who . . ."

Annisa smiled. "Never underestimate an Afghan woman." She turned and crossed to the fire where the coals were still hot from Rahmatullah's early morning breakfast. "Shall I fix us some tea?"

"Tea? I guess. I suppose so." Damn her. She was treating him like she was granting him an interview. What had gotten into her?

"How did *you* come by this message for the Resistance?"

Ethan had known this question would be coming and did not look forward to having to tell her about Najib.

"I was in Islamabad and an old friend of yours gave it to me to deliver for him ."

"An old friend?"

"Yes, Captain Duranni."

She dropped the teacup to the ground but it did not break. Together they watched it roll across the cave. The look on her face said it all. She was still smitten with the Captain.

"You have seen Najib?" Her voice was small, almost child-like.

"Yes, in Islamabad."

"I was told he was living in England."

So Annisa knew about the girl friend, Claire. Ethan hedged. "I think he goes in and out. Najib told me he has looked for you many times. That he's left messages for you on the Jihad trail."

"I know nothing of this but I'm not surprised I wasn't told. My husband is very jealous. He has forbidden me ever to see Najib."

Ethan felt like he had been sucker punched. "Your husband?"

A look of resignation in her eyes. "I am married to Abdul."

"The man with a bullet in his knee?"

"Yes. It was something I had to do. Omar's wife, Fatima, refused to let me come back to the family without a husband so I agreed to it on certain terms: I would never ever wear the veil. And I was to be free to come and go as I pleased."

"And your husband went along with it?"

"It is a marriage of convenience. And because of it, Omar sees me as some kind of saint."

"This is all a bit hard to follow."

"Omar knows that because of his injury, Abdul can never perform as a man."

"I thought it was his leg?"

"*Buzkashi* horses are trained to stamp and kick their opponent. He was trampled in many places."

"That's grim. But *knowing* this, why would you marry him?"

"Because of my shame. This way no one but you and Mabaie will ever know. The family still thinks of me as a virgin."

"Jesus Christ!"

She stepped back from him, surprised at his outburst. "You sound angry. Why?"

"That you would agree to a loveless marriage on the strength of what that old fortune-teller might say. This culture is just a little crazy. You throw your life away over what other people might think?"

"In my crazy culture, as you call it, if on a woman's wedding night it is discovered that she is not a virgin, her face is blackened and she becomes a servant in the household of her husband."

"So you marry a man who can never fulfill you. I would think that would be worse than being a servant girl."

She glared at him.

"I know you had the money to come to the States. Omar told me you gave him a large sum to buy this rocket launcher."

315

"I have more than enough left," she said evenly. "And I am not the fool that you think I am. It is in a bank in Peshawar. I can withdraw it at any time."

"And your husband? Does he know of these funds?"

"Yes, he does. When I offered to give the rest to him for an operation on his leg, he refused. He said that money was mine from my father and was for my security. He feels badly that he never had any money to offer for my dowry. Don't talk to me of things you know nothing about."

"Annisa, you just said you made a mistake. I could have helped. I still could."

"I don't need your help," she said stiffly.

"Well, if not me, I'm sure Captain Duranni would try to find something for you. He knows many people."

"Najib is the last one I would ever ask for help."

"Don't be too hard on him. I'm sure he didn't know he gave you a venereal disease"

"Najib! How can you say such a thing? Najib never touched me."

Ethan was taken back. "Then who did?"

"I was raped by Russian soldiers. Are you satisfied to hear this--now that you are the *only* person in this world to know this shame."

"Jesus Christ. You mean to tell me the only man you have ever had sex with in your life was a Russian soldier who raped you?"

"Two. There were two of them."

"Goddamn. Goddamn it."

"Why must you shout? It is my shame, not yours."

Ethan glared at her. "I am sick to death of hearing about shame. Forget that word. You are a very desirable young woman. My god, the rest of your life! Married to a cripple. Wandering around the countryside. Risking getting killed. No education. It is a crime, Annisa. A God damn crime."

She was visibly shaken but when she spoke, her voice was calm. "This is none of your concern, Dr. Harris. My life is not as empty as you think."

For one quick moment his mind went to Omar and the vitamin pills to help his libido. Surely, this couldn't be. Omar was old enough to be her father.

"There is only one man I have ever desired and that is not to be."

"Najib Duranni?"

316

"Yes."

He slumped down on his haunches, his back against the wall. "I need to tell you something."

She threw back her head, a defiant look. "He has married the English girl? I expected that."

"Annisa. . . he was badly hurt in an accident. Islamabad."

"Najib hurt?" Her voice ratcheted up. "How badly?"

"I don't know. I suspect there was internal bleeding. But I didn't go with him to the hospital."

"You were with him?"

"It was urgent. He insisted I deliver the message for him to the Resistance."

"So urgent that you waited a week?"

"Don't tar me with that brush! I did my best. It's a complicated story. I even volunteered to go into Kabul. But Rahmatullah would not hear of it. Pushed my 'care' buttons. All the people who were waiting for my help. All the lives that had been risked to ferry my supplies in. And now that fickle bastard wants to go to Kandahar and shoot off rockets with Omar. Rahmatullah has suddenly lost his great passion for the sick."

She paused, a thoughtful look on her face. "Maybe that is not such a stupid idea after all. For Omar to go to Kandahar. He will need help holding the shoulder launcher and Yuri is not that fit. This Rahmatullah can go with him."

"Hell, no. I need an interpreter here. Bashir knows only a few words."

"Yuri speaks the language and his English is good. He could stay here and recuperate with you."

"And you? Where will you be?"

"I'll deliver the message to Fritz Werner in Kabul."

"By yourself? Rahmatullah tells me Kabul is dangerous as hell."

"I know the city. And I know Fritz. I'm the logical one."

"That may be. But I can't imagine a woman traveling that far alone."

"I have done this for years. Who is to stop me? Abdul is on his way to Peshawar and possibly the States and Fatima is in the north awaiting the birth of her fourth child."

A wave of panic swept over Ethan. "You mean to leave now? Before the others arrive?"

"Why not?"

"They will skin me alive for letting you go, that's why. Annisa, what you are telling me doesn't exactly jive. You marry a man you don't love in order to please the customs of your people and at the same time you are free to traipse around the countryside by yourself? I haven't seen many Afghan women doing that and that includes the Koochi tribes. And even if you did go by yourself, I'm not so sure it's worth the risk. The message may be old news. You said so yourself. Or it may be a message that shouldn't be delivered. I'm told Najib may be acquainted with some pretty unsavory people"

"That is an insult to Najib."

"Then I apologize."

"You should."

Silence.

"Annisa, you wouldn't be going to Islamabad instead? To try to find Najib?"

"You are a large fool. I told you, Najib and I are finished. He may have left messages for me because he feels responsible since I have no father, no brother. Najib is my sworn protector but he loves this English woman. Tell me he still does not see her. I dare you."

Ethan did not answer, thinking about that phone call to Claire. There was obviously still a connection...

"I knew it. Najib is in love with a *ferrangi* and I have a husband, Abdul! There is nothing more to be said." She stomped out of the clinic.

He decided not to follow her. Instead he watched as she ran down the trail. But there was to be no escape for Annisa because two Mujahideen carrying what looked like a front seat from an old car suddenly blocked her way.

"Dr. Harris. I promised you a seat!" Omar shouted.

"Omar, he delivers," Rahmatullah called from behind him. Bashir was carrying a man on his back. It had to be the Russian.

It amused Ethan that Annisa had not made her exit in time. Annisa was always running away--disappearing--but there was only one way out of the canyon. She was trapped into coming back.

She returned with the others and gave Ethan a look so threatening if he should say anything that he burst out laughing.

"Ah, you like my seat," Omar said. "The driver's seat for you. Here try."

Ethan sat down on it and the back collapsed, sending him sprawling. This broke the tension. The two men who had carried the seat up the steep incline began to laugh. Annisa reluctantly joined in. "You can coax an Afghan into Hell, but you cannot drive him into Heaven," she said.

Omar hooted. "You heard her, Dr. Harris. That is an Afghan!"

And, of course, Annisa had been exaggerating about her freedom to move about because in the end it was decided that Rahmatullah would go with Omar to Kandahar, Yuri would take the message to Kabul as soon as he was fit and Annisa would stay with Ethan as his interpreter. It would not do for Annisa to travel to Kabul alone. Of course, Abdul would go ballistic if she were left alone with the *ferrangi* but that was easily solved. Bashir would stay in the clinic with them. Bashir was a formidable chaperon.

Noontime came and Annisa had prepared a meal. "Yuri is asleep. His shaking has stopped."

Ethan shook his head. "I'm afraid it will be days before he is ready to make the trip."

"Then I must go in his place."

"I thought that was settled."

"The message has to be delivered. You promised Najib."

The patient opened his eyes. "I can make it," Yuri growled.

"I am the doctor. I decide."

Yuri was not well enough to travel the next day or the next. When he was not sleeping he watched Annisa and Ethan work side by side in the clinic.

Ethan was impressed with her talents. Annisa was a quick study. He had only to tell her something once. "You are a natural-- with good instincts. It is a sin you don't go to Peshawar to train as a paramedic."

"I belong inside."

"Living in a cave, under a tent? What about all those things you have been telling me about your father? About the beauty in stretching the mind? What will happen to your mind traipsing around the country with a bunch of goat herders."

"Don't ever speak like that again!"

"Well, damn it, Annisa. Stop making your terrible deprivation a religion. . .all this talk about your country. It's finished. You certainly know it. I do."

"Such a weak stomach. You are here only a few weeks and already you talk of quitting."

"Say what you want about me. The Russians will wait you out. Maybe not this year or the next. They will engulf you and swallow you like they did Tashkent, Baluchistan. Your

319

grandchildren will serve in the Soviet Army and recite the teachings of Lenin."

"I will not have grandchildren, remember."

"Come outside. I have something to say to you."

"You've said enough. That is all you ever do. Talk, talk, talk."

"I think you should go to Kabul with Yuri."

"Ah, I see. You are ready to throw in the towel. Head back to Peshawar with Bashir. Use Annisa as an excuse."

"I told you before what you think of me doesn't matter."

"I think that is a lie."

"Probably." He leaned over and picked up a small stone, hurling it into the canyon. "I worried too about the message. You can't go to Kabul alone and it wouldn't be wise for Yuri to go in without you. I've watched you with him the past few days. You make a good team."

"You would have to close the clinic. Give up what you came to do."

"Bashir indicates we may have to move the clinic soon. Evidently the Russians know we are in here now."

"So you are speaking Farsi now with Bashir?"

"Enough damn it, Annisa, I'd like to think what I've done here isn't a total waste. I'm sorry you have so little respect for me."

"Oh, but I do. The trouble is you do not respect me. . . I will not be pitied. Don't try to help me because you feel sorry for me."

"Is that what you think?"

"I think you want to rescue poor Annisa from the wilds of Afghanistan when it is really yourself you want to save. You are dissatisfied with your own country or you wouldn't come here to mine. Surely there are sick people in America. If we are such a lost cause, why are you here?"

"I'm a sucker for lost causes."

"I think you are a quitter. . . And what did you mean telling Omar you can look into the eyes of a man and you can see if he is not afraid to die. How can you know this? You are not God!"

"A doctor sees death many times over. There is a look on those who are afraid and those who have hopes of salvation."

"You think you are the only one who has seen death? You are so full of yourself." She lifted the rug and went inside.

In the morning, he handed her his diary.

"What is this?"

"Here, you fill in the empty pages. I can see where it was vain on my part to bring it. Some kind of nonsense about saving my thoughts of this experience."

"I am not a poet. I do not record my thoughts like my father."

"Use it to take down notes on what you learn from me during the day. You'll have your own little medical textbook when I am gone."

"You ridicule me."

"No. I save that for myself."

That evening when the last patient had gone she questioned him about his medicine and began to jot down his answers. "This special kind of malaria which kills the brain?"

"Don't worry. Yuri doesn't have it."

"But I need to know the symptoms."

The first week with Annisa passed into the second and still Yuri was too weak... Secretly, Ethan was relieved. His days were full, working side by side in the clinic with Annisa. At night, after the evening meal, they took long walks into the canyon together.

Yuri would scowl at them but Bashir showed no interest when they disappeared.

"Can we go over my notes on insulin tonight?" Annisa asked.

"Forget it. I feel like going for a walk." He was hoping she would follow and she did.

It was the last night of August. The sky was brilliant with stars.

"I never see the sky like this at home."

"Are skies so different in America?"

"Annisa, I dreamed about you last night."

"Omar should be in Kandahar now. The plane leaves on the 4th."

"Don't change the subject."

"Yuri says you like to be alone with me. That it is written all over your face."

"Yuri is right."

"He does not want to go to Kabul and leave me alone with you."

Ethan laughed. "He really thinks I'd lay a hand on you in front of Bashir?"

321

She looked very solemn as she said it. "That is not his concern. He says you are much more dangerous than that. That you play with my mind. You make me discontent."

"Do I?"

She shook her head. "No, I knew I had made a mistake before you came. But I'm not so sure I want to go to America. I do know I want to study medicine. Do you think you could help me? I mean do you know people at this International Medical Corps."

"I have friends who do."

"Yuri thinks he is well enough to go to Kabul tomorrow."

"He is. And I repeat. You should go with him. I don't think you would ever forgive yourself if you don't. Yuri can take you to the outskirts of the capital but it would be a suicide mission for him to take the message into the city. He sticks out like a sore thumb."

"You have been eavesdropping on our conversations."

"No, I figured that one out all by myself."

He tilted his head back and stared at the stars. "You know, it's funny. Despite the fact he watches me like a hawk, I like the Russian. He lives a greater tragedy than all of us. Choices can be painful but that guy doesn't have any. He's in a no win situation. There is no place where he could fit in now. . . You love him, don't you."

"As a brother, yes."

"And me?"

"You too are my brader-jan."

"I understand enough Farsi to know I do not wish to be your dear brother. That's Yuri's role."

"What would you be?"

"Rahmatullah tells me the Turkomans are into wife-stealing."

Her laughter surprised him. "I misjudged you. You are very bold!"

"Only with you." He wanted to show her that he was and for a moment, he thought she wished this too.

"Annisa?"

"No, please." She backed away from him. "You know about the Russian soldiers and what they did. You think I am easy because I have been soiled."

Ethan stared at her anguished face. His voice was hoarse when he spoke. "Never say that about yourself again. Never." He turned away from her. "Forgive me. Yuri is right." Without looking back he started up the path.

She followed him. "Don't hate me, please."

"You ask too much. I go crazy with it. You give out signals. There is something between us."

"You imagine this."

"No, that is why we fight so much. . ." He stopped abruptly. "My god, the rest of your life! To deny your feelings. It makes me want to kill."

"But if I lie down with you it will be me who dies. How can I miss what I have not known." She reached out and touched his lips with her fingers. "The very thought makes me afraid."

"Annisa. . ."

"No. This will not happen." And before he could answer she had hurried past him.

From the top of the steep incline Yuri stood watching. When Annisa reached him, he looked straight through her. "Tomorrow we leave for Kabul."

"Yes."

"And the American?"

"He is innocent."

"His innocence angers me. Innocent men are dangerous. He would betray you."

"No Yuri. I have wanted to be betrayed. I betray myself."

CHAPTER 30

The terrain they traveled was unfriendly--jagged ridges and deep ravines. On the first plateau of rock, Omar reined in his horse and, taking the goatskin bag from inside his pack, he shared water with the stallion. Behind him, he could see the crags peaceful and flattened in the lie of the moonlight. Rahmatullah followed, towing the donkey with the shoulder launcher strapped to its back. Omar's stallion shook his mane and trembled, reflecting Omar's own impatience with the distance to be covered while it was still night. Tomorrow they would be in the flat lands, unprotected.

"You are not your jolly self, Rahmatullah. Or did you act the clown with the American doctor on purpose?"

"To settle his nerves. You should have seen him in Peshawar. He was like a frightened chicken: running in circles, clucking about his all-important message for Kabul. He was a worry to both of us. Bashir threatened not to come along."

"But he is a good doctor?"

"Yes, and a good man. But he takes himself too seriously."

"I'm not so sure it was wise to leave him with Annisa."

"*Bawar kardan*! Believe me, Bashir would snap him in two. Unlike the Western hunters I used to take into the Wakhan Corridor, the doctor has respect for women. Nothing will happen."

"It's not the doctor I'm worried about. It's Annisa. The girl is hungry."

There was nothing Rahmatullah could say about that but he did find it curious. Annisa had a husband.

They rode on in silence until Rahmatullah asked, "Your brother? Abdul. Will he really go to America if the American can arrange an operation for him?"

"It is my hope. For years, I have pushed him to have his leg looked to. But Abdul is stubborn. He buries himself in the Koran and his prayers. His judgments are as brittle as his leg."

"The Americans may be a shock to him. They are such a foolish but generous people. Never have I seen such big appetites for life. Everything is a challenge. But there is also a yearning to do good. Even the hunters from Texas. They were so pleased I did not steal their sugar like some of the other guides that they gave me a big tip. Enough money for me to buy sugar for a year! I do not understand their thinking. But I tell you the Americans have money to do anything. They can buy the world."

"I think this is so." Omar pointed to the distant moon. "It is magic to think the Americans walked on the *mahtab*."

"Maybe we should shoot me in the knee," Rahmatullah joked. "I go next time. So many things to see in America."

Their banter continued throughout the night as they rode without stopping.

Morning came and early sunshine glowed on the delicate wisteria that grew on the trellis of the house--a complicated wooden structure sitting alone on the side of a hill.

"I have seen houses like this in Nuristan and Paktya but never this far south."

"See the curtains on the window. I think a *ferrangi* lives here."

Omar had started up the steps when a young boy opened the door and pointed a pistol at him.

"Stop or I will shoot."

Omar threw up his hands, pretending to be alarmed. "Small Inglace--what are you doing here?"

"I live here. And you have come to steal our food."

"We have only thirst and we need water for our horses."

"Wait here. My grandmother decides these things."

The woman appeared, carrying a pitcher of water and a bowl of oranges. "Excuse my grandson, but in these troubled times we have learned to be cautious."

Omar knew it was rude but he could not help asking. "How did you get here? And how can the boy be English when you are Afghan?"

"His father built this house for his bride. She was as fair and delicate as the flowers on that vine. She died of the fever when the boy was only five years."

"And the father?"

"My son is dead. Tarkai's men took him to prison and we never saw him again. But they leave the boy and me alone. You must stay and rest in the shade. A Russian patrol passes this way within the hour. Ahead of you, the land is open. From the large gun I see strapped to your donkey you are up to brave deeds."

The boy ran to examine it.

"Look at your friend, he nods off standing up." The grandmother gestured to Rahmatullah who was indeed almost asleep on his feet. "Stay until the patrol passes. I will serve you pieces of bread in warm milk and sugar, and sheep's fat. It is special. It will give you strength."

She invited them inside and Omar was amazed at the furnishings. There were books and a table and two chairs and china dishes with flowers painted on them.

"My mother brought these all the way from Devon," the boy said. "Not one piece was broken. We guard it with our life." He ran and turned on a radio. "It is battery operated. It is grand, don't you think?"

Omar stared at the rug on the floor. It had the sunbird, the phoenix, woven in it. It was not Afghan.

The grandmother brought forth a jar of sweet, plump raisins.

"You are a Mujahid!" The boy could hardly contain his excitement.

"Yes," Rahmatullah beamed. "We go to Kandahar to blow a plane out of the sky."

"Oh, let me go with you. We can stay in the house of my uncle. From his house you can see the planes take off."

Omar was astounded. "Is this so?" he asked the grandmother.

"Yes, my oldest daughter is married to a man who works at the airport. His health is too poor for the army but he is well enough to load and unload boxes from the planes."

Omar was thunderstruck. "Allah has sent us to you. How else could we get close enough? We do not know any safe house in the area."

"Why do you fight in the South?"

"We are after a particular plane which flies from Kandahar."

"Without mountains to hide in the enemy can follow your every move."

The boy leapt up. "I know. From the rooftop. From the roof of my uncle's house, you can shoot it down."

"No, it is too far," the grandmother corrected him. "And if I let you go with them who would stay here with me?"

"The Army will draft me in a year or two. You have said so many times. Oh please my *madar-kalan* I want to be a Mujahid. In the Afghan army, I would only run away."

"Why not let the boy show us the way?" Omar asked. "No harm will come to him. I will see to it."

326

"It is not up to you. Only Allah can protect him . . . What is this plane you shoot down?"

"It carries a traitor. An Afghan who does dirty work for the Russians."

"But how will you know which plane?"

"Surely there cannot be more than one civilian plane a week for Tashkent. It leaves on the fourth."

"You shoot down unarmed men?"

"Men who would betray us. Yes."

She motioned to Rahmatullah. "Take the boy outside. I must talk alone with your friend."

Turning to Omar, she raised her hand to her breast. "I have a large lump growing here. Inside. I am ill. If the boy goes to live with his uncle--you see his beautiful face, the blue eyes of his mother--he will bring a good income to the uncle who will have him sleeping with men. Believe me, the boy's uncle would tolerate such evil. If I let the boy go with you and if I should be unable to care for him when you return--will you promise to help him? I fear for him with his mixed blood. Would you treat him as your own?"

"He would be a gift--a comfort for my sorrow. Had my first born lived, he would be this age. My brother's wife has studied in Kabul. She can teach him many things."

The grandmother sighed. "He is a greater treasure than these teacups. If only I could rid myself of this illness." Her eyes clouded over.

Omar looked at her. "Allah has brought us together. Each one has a gift to share. We shall know how to care for the boy if you are gone. Tell me his name."

"Akhmed. But his mother called him William."

"Then it is decided. William Akhmed will come with us."

"I must warn you. There is much fighting in Kandahar now. Many helicopters."

"The boy is eager for this. To be with Mujahideen."

The grandmother nodded. "Yes, he wants to join the world of true men." She saw Omar to the door. "The world grows stranger each day. I suppose it must be. But do not forget. I am Pathan. Do not break your word. A Pathan is a very good friend but a terrible enemy."

"I will not forget," Omar said. "May Allah bless you for your hospitality and your wisdom. To prune the tree is to love fully. This is true of all growing things."

She nodded. "*Hodai Pahman.* Go with God."

Mid-afternoon of the fourth day they reached the village of Akhmed's uncle, located to the north of Kandahar Airport, a gleaming white modern structure rising out of the desert. Built by the Americans in the early 60's, it had been the source of much local pride.

The boy's uncle was nervous about their coming. "You will get us all killed. Only two of you. Impossible. The airport is patrolled, fortified. How will you do this thing?"

Akhmed whispered in Omar's ear. "Be careful of him. He pretends to like me but I would rather join the Army than live with him."

Omar squeezed his hand. "It is arranged. You are to come with me when the time comes."

"In the north. The fields are mined." Akhmed's uncle paced the room. "You do not have a plan? No scouts?"

"There was not time."

"Tell him about the traitor," the boy whispered to Omar again.

"Secrets?" the aunt asked. A pleasant-faced woman, she seemed happy to see them, serving them generous portions of eggs and mushrooms and onions. "It comes to me. Our house is too far away. Go south. Ask for the house of Naka, my cousin. He can provide you men. Cover."

"Yes, Naka!" Her husband grasped the idea. "Naka knows. Naka can show you where the mines are planted. Naka knows where their secret new airfield is located--the airport where the Frogfoot aircraft hide."

"I have not heard of this Frogfoot."

"The Sukhoi-25's," the uncle said importantly. "They drop bombs with steel needles inside. I cannot describe the damage they do to people. Western intelligence offers big money for information about them. It is a new secret weapon."

"Steel needles? What next?"

"I hear there is terrible fighting now on the borders. The Russians have poured in many fresh troops. All the Jihad trails to Peshawar are under fire. It is the heaviest fighting of the war."

Omar was alarmed, thinking of Annisa and Dr. Harris. They were to leave with Bashir for Landi-Kotal the end of the week. "When did the heavy fighting begin? How do you know these things?"

"I keep my ears open. People who work at the airport always know first."

"My husband is very knowledgeable," the wife added.

Omar stared at them, wondering if they could be trusted. He did not like the way the flesh drooped over the uncle's eyes and his hands were restless, always moving agitatedly as he talked. Omar hesitated. Should he share the details about Commander Besud Zalmair and his treachery?

Rahmatullah spoke up before he could be warned. "What time does the civilian airliner fly to Tashkent?"

"Exactly at noon on Thursday."

"I think not," his wife whispered to Akhmed.

"You have already missed today's flight."

"No matter. Tomorrow is Friday. Tomorrow is the 4th day of the month. Tomorrow is the day we want to shoot down the plane." Rahmatullah leaned back, patting his full belly.

"There is no plane for Tashkent tomorrow. I tell you it left today. You have come a long way."

"Not to worry. My information is good."

"This plane carries someone special?"

"No," Omar answered, signaling Rahmatullah to hold his tongue.

"A civilian plane? It will tarnish the name of the Resistance."

"Yes, but it will also put the fear of God in them. The very reason we target it."

The uncle shifted his eyes to his wife.

"Spend the night here is better," she said. "Go to Naka's house early morning before first light. We enjoy your company and that of the boy."

"I shall tell Naka to expect us," Akhmed said eagerly. He jumped up and was out the door.

"A fine boy."

The uncle nodded. "It is his grandmother's wish he come live with us."

Rahmatullah looked over at Omar and crossed his eyes.

Omar choked on his tea, trying not to laugh and hoping the uncle had not seen it.

But the wife did.

It was to be a good night. The air was soft, the breeze gentle. The wife served then *Naranj pilau,* a sweet dish of rice with dried orange peels and *chutney-morch*, a special hot chili sauce.

"We eat like kings," Rahmatullah belched, showing his satisfaction.

Afterwards Omar told jokes about the Mullah Nasruddin and Rahmatullah played *joft-o-tag,* odds and evens, with William Akhmed, careful to let the boy win.

"When Jihad is over, we will remember this night above others," the aunt said.

"Memory is difficult," her husband grumbled.

"To remember is the most important thing in life," she answered, smiling with affection at Akhmed. "I look at Akhmed and I see the face of my brother."

"Woman, you need glasses. He has the looks of his mother's people. A real little *ferrangi.*"

Everyone laughed, including Akhmed.

Omar could only marvel; their house functioned so smoothly; their provisions were so plentiful. So much of Kandahar had been destroyed. Perhaps the grandmother was wrong. The wife appeared to love the boy. A pity her husband appeared so full of avarice.

That night, Omar was unable to sleep. He knew his plan was reckless. A very big bite. He would be blowing up the last of the rockets Annisa had bought for him. And what if Yuri had the date wrong and the plane had left yesterday instead of on the fourth? Why would the uncle lie? And why did he, Omar El-Ham, want so much to destroy Commander Zalmair? A foolish question. He knew the answer. One could mourn an enemy who fought with valor. But to the win the hearts of his people and then sell them out--no, this man had to be shot down!

There was something grumbling in Omar's stomach-- it concerned him. In the dark, he reached out and shook Rahmatullah awake. "I feel as if I have been poisoned."

Rahmatullah grunted. "My belly pains me, too. I have the *psych.*" He rolled over and began to snore again.

Omar picked his way across the floor. In the adjoining room he could see the boy lying next to the aunt but the blanket of the uncle was empty. The boy's eyes were open. Omar listened for sounds of movement in the house. It was as quiet as death. Omar signaled to Akhmed to be quiet as he stole out of the room and returned to where his friend slept. Rahmatullah continued to snore. "Wake up, you lazy camel."

William Akhmed had followed him. "Careful. You will wake my aunt. I come with you. Please wake up, Rahmatullah. We have been betrayed."

Rahmatullah sat bolt upright, his hands instantly on the rocket launcher, which slept, by his side.

"My uncle is gone."

"*Maskhara!*" Rahmatullah hissed.

"Don't," Omar said. "You forget. He is only a boy."

"But the mines? In the dark, danger awaits us."

"Naka will show us. Hurry, my uncle may return any minute." William Akhmed led them outside. Dawn was still an hour away. The boy held up his father's pistol that he had hidden inside his knapsack. "My grandmother said, 'Use it like a man.' I go with you."

"No. I promised no harm would come to you."

"You think I will not be harmed when my uncle returns and finds you gone?"

Omar checked the RPG grenade, his only one. It was designed to kill a tank on impact. Silently they strapped on the rockets and the launcher.

Rahmatullah leaned against the wall. "My stomach. It is in my mouth."

"No time for that," Omar snapped. "Follow Akhmed. He leads us to the house of Naka."

"Dare we? Can we go there now?" Rahmatullah asked Akhmed. "Where is your uncle?"

"He would not be with Naka. Naka does not pretend. He truly wants to help. I think my uncle brings the enemy here--to this house-- to take your rocket launcher while you sleep."

"Your aunt? Was our food poisoned?"

"He forced her. But she is clever. She added just a little-- only enough to make you a little sick. She did not expect him to leave in the middle of the night. My uncle is a coward. He must think there is a reward on your head."

Omar raised his fist. "He will fail. Does he think he can ensnare an eagle? Hah!"

They started across the barren land single file. There was little cover--rocks, a few dunes, an occasional juniper bush. For the most part, they crossed in the open, unprotected, inviting attack. But all was quiet. Darkness served them as a shroud.

When they reached the small adobe house of Naka bordering the east-west runway of the airport, it was still dark. Quietly, William Akhmed led them inside. A kettle still simmered on the coals. The smell of tobacco hung in the room. But the house was empty. Puzzled, the three slipped back outside. Nothing stirred.

There were no chickens left in the small outhouses nearby. Omar motioned to Akhmed to tether the mule with the rock launcher strapped to its back behind the one farthest from the house.

When he returned, Rahmatullah grabbed the boy's shoulders and shook him. "Just where is this Naka?"

The boy's voice squeaked with fear. "It is a mystery. He was excited when I told him of our plan. Proud to be a part of such boldness. He promised to help. Why would they be gone? I don't know. It is still night."

"Just as I thought," said Rahmatullah "It is a trap." There was no real concern in his voice, only annoyance. He walked to the side of the house and regurgitated in the sand "Son of a turtle. I hope a bullet finds me today. My body runs at both ends."

The wind was rising in the west.

"When there is too much dust the helicopters do not take off," the boy said.

Omar grunted. "You are smart, a good companion, but I fear I have brought you to very big trouble. See ahead."

The headlights of an official vehicle approached. It rolled to a stop not more than 50 yards in front of the house. The three hung back in the shadows of the chicken house.

A Russian voice shattered the stillness. "*Stroli!*" A soldier leaped from the cab of the truck, attempting to read a piece of paper he held in front of the headlights. The gold threads on his red and yellow epaulettes shone in the light. Omar always aimed for epaulettes; without their officers, Russian soldiers tended to run in the heat of battle.

Rahmatullah had dropped to his knees in the loose dirt and Akhmed crouched behind a small stack of hay.

Carrying a flashlight, the officer in his brown dress top and khaki-colored pants marched smartly towards the house, an AK-94 in his hands. He pounded on the door. Then he raised his black jackboot and kicked the door open. No reason for this. The door was not locked.

"His AK-94," Omar whispered to Akhmed. "Makes wounds that do not heal."

"But the plane . . ."

"Be still. I am not ready to take him yet."

"We will miss the plane."

"It leaves at noon."

"My aunt whispered to me it was daybreak. Soon. It will be very soon."

"On my head and eyes! Climb to my shoulder. Tell how many men in the truck?"

"Only the driver."

"The arrogant fool. This *Shuravi* is cocky. Wait here. On your life, now. Do not stir." On his belly, Omar crawled back to where Rahmatullah lay with the dry heaves, his head in the sand. "Pull your guts together. Go into the house and put a knife in his back. We race the dawn."

A car door slammed. Both men raised their heads. It was the driver. He leaned against the hood looking like any ordinary man; smoking, watching the sky brightens on the distant horizon.

"I will secure the truck. Can you manage to put Nicholai out of his misery and then go back to the grip stick?"

Rahmatullah nodded. "It is medicine for my stomach. The Russian is already dead as you speak."

Omar returned to the boy. "The three tubes hold the rockets. Each weighs 20 pounds. After I attack the driver bring them one at a time to the back of the truck. Make three trips. Understand?"

"Yes, my lord."

Omar grinned to himself. His lord? This was no ordinary boy!

Rahmatullah reached the back stoop and waited, his shoulders flattened against the wall.

Suddenly the door opened. Rahmatullah's hand went up and with one swift blow to the neck, the blade stuck in the throat and the man fell without a sound.

Omar stood up, shouting, "*haraka, haraka.* Let's go." With his Kalashnikov 47, Omar aimed at the startled driver and fired one shot. The driver fell, blood gushing from his mouth. In the distance, they could hear the low whir of a helicopter approaching the field. Rahmatullah raced up behind Omar, hauling the precious rocket launcher they had hidden behind the chicken house. Together they lifted it onto the rear of the truck. Then Omar took the first rocket from the boy and ran back to help him with the other two.

"Good boy. *Hub baccha.* Now get in that house for the chickens. Stay there until I come to you. No words between us."

The first streaks of morning provided a vivid red backdrop as the helicopter came down out of the sky and landed on the runway. A military plane, a small fighter, followed. Omar stumbled towards the truck, holding the third rocket in his hands. "Climb in the front," he barked. The two mujahideen were off, driving without headlights, careening; bumping along in the field Omar knew was mined. They parked about 30 yards from the cyclone fence that guarded the airstrip. Green light floated high above their heads, casting an eerie glow on their faces and defining artificial pools on the wasted landscape at their feet. Beyond the wire barricade, Omar could see the faint outline of the Antanov 26 at the airport terminal. The "Reconnaissance," which doubled as a civilian plane.

"See there, the old stone fence, just as William Akhmed promised. If luck is with us, the plane will lift off almost directly overhead."

Omar looked at the watch Yuri had given him even though Yuri had won the bet. "Let's get ready. I fear it is growing light too fast."

"You are God sure this is the right plane? We will have one chance only."

"The boy trusts his aunt. She swears one Antanov takes off at this hour, only one."

Omar climbed down from the bed of the truck hugging the launcher to his breast, motioning to Rahmatullah to follow him with the rockets. They hung close to the ground and zigzagged towards the stone wall. "Allah sent us the boy, I tell you. This is a perfect launch site."

Rahmatullah returned with the last rocket.

"Check the battery. Is it working properly? Test the signal light. Red is on. Green is ready for target."

"I have checked it twice."

Omar's hands were shaking. "You are surprised, my friend? A Mujahid afraid? Bah. I wash my sour stomach."

They waited each breathing his own prayer. A small brown marmot scooted out from under a nearby rock and raced across the desert floor.

"That's it. Right on time." Omar's stomach knotted as he heard the roar of the twin engine turboprop on the runway.

He pulled himself up to a standing position atop the stone wall. Rahmatullah jerked on his leg. "Over there. A Russian jeep."

The vehicle was racing down the road that paralleled the runway. It had already begun to fire at them. Omar dropped to his knees and pulled the grenade from his belt. "Throw yourself flat," he shouted, as his arm went up, tossing the grenade high into the air directly at the oncoming vehicle. Suddenly, an orange ball of flame flared, followed by an explosion. A perfect hit.

Omar crawled again atop the stones. The plane had turned on the runway and was picking up speed. Rahmatullah handed the launcher up to him and Omar steadied it on his shoulder. Then he fired. The heat seeker began to spin. The green light was on. A miss.

Rahmatullah's hands were lightning fast in reloading the second tube. Once again Omar aimed. Machine gun fire from behind the airport fence opened up spraying the stone wall. The plane was now directly overhead. Tiny fins popped out of the tube. The green light flashed. The missile sang, hovered and then went straight for the tail. The plane tilted crazily and in a burst of flame, plummeted to the ground. For a moment there was silence. Then Omar too seemed to explode. "We did it," he roared in exaltation, unmindful he was still a target. The launcher and the rockets had cost thousands of afghanis--more than he could make in two life times. It was all worth it. "Rahmatullah, you are a *jawan*. A true hero. Allah claps for us in paradise."

But Rahmatullah gave no answer. His hand held yet another tube for the reloading; a Russian bullet had found his brain. Omar's friend was no longer a hero. He was *shaheed*, martyred, killed in Jihad. For only an instant Omar hesitated. There was no time for the dead—not any time even to close Rahmatullah's eyes. He would bid his fallen friend a proper farewell at a better moment. He leapt from the wall and began to crawl the length of the stone. Another burst of shots rang out. The airport runway was bristling with guards. The heat of the burning plane whipped like an inferno across the desert. William Akhmed! Suddenly Omar remembered the boy. If he tried to reach him by the truck he would be marking a path to the hiding place. Better to keep to the ground. Bullets were whistling at the stone wall now above his head. The barrage of firing had intensified. He reached the wire barricade. He was breathing hard as he stood up and sprinted now across the bare fields to Naka's house. A bullet grazed his hand, tearing the skin from his thumb. They had him in their sights. He dropped behind a boulder. Bursts of gunfire seemed to surround him. The house of the chickens was just ahead now. He could see it. Praise Allah, he could reach it.

William Akhmed crouched on the floor, sobbing; his head between his knees as Omar burst through the door and threw himself on top of the boy.

"Your friend. Your friend is dead. I saw it."

"Inna lillahi wa'enna' illaiji raji un. We come from God; to God we return."

Now they could hear the scream of sirens. "Infidels," Omar shouted. "I defy you." Omar went to the window. Orange flames

335

still flashed amid the black smoke rolling above the airstrip in their direction. A sudden burst of machine gun fire came from the roof top of Naka's house, the hayfield behind it, and from behind the boulders beyond. Omar flung open the door. Twenty, perhaps thirty Afghans had appeared out of nowhere and were returning the Russians' fire. William Akhmed was beside himself with joy. "Naka's men are holding them off."

"We are trapped, small friend. There is no way out."

"Follow me. I know the way. Naka's men will give us cover. An irrigation channel, just across the road. But we must travel under water once we are in. Can you swim?"

"If it serves my purpose."

As soon as they were out the door, several Mujahideen leapt from the roof and began to run in all directions.

"Good, this is good," Omar shouted. "They confuse our enemy. Which one of us to chase?"

Under cover of the black smoke swirling over their heads, the pair slid headfirst into the cement-lined ditch. When they had swum about 200 yards, the boy pointed to a distant tower. "We can hide there. It is for pigeons. We collect their droppings for tanning."

Omar looked at the boy's small white face. "Pigeon shit. Bah! It is better we take our chance in the open fields."

"There is only desert beyond. A single road."

"That is good. Only a fool would walk the open road but they will be looking for two of us. You go alone. A small boy can dissolve into the horizon."

"But you promised. Grandmother has a black sore eating her chest. You are a Tajik. Are you all words and no fire?"

Omar patted his wet clothes. Behind them he could still see the black smoke billowing towards heaven. He prayed the traitor, Commander Zalmair had burned alive. "Yi! I, Omar El-Ham, am a footnote!"

The boy held up his fist and gave Omar the Mujahid salute.

Omar reached for his hand and held it tight. "Show me the way, fearless one."

"I can run faster if you let go of my hand."

They raced across the hard-packed sand to a cluster of boulders. "They can only spot us now from the air."

The boy looked at Omar and smiled. There was a chord of triumph between them. "Ahead lies the village of Robeth. There will be plenty of people to hide us."

Omar knew life would never taste so sweet again--a juicy ripe melon cooled in a mountain stream. At last he mattered. No need to fear the future. The new life Fatima carried in her womb would inherit his brave name. If only Yuri had been here to see it! "I am proud of us, William Akhmed. Some day they will sing of us in story and song. Bless Rahmatullah. What more could a man ask for at this moment?"

"To make it out of this alive."

Omar laughed. "Our hero is a practical man." He noted the boy had lost his sandals in the drainage ditch. The sun was scarcely up but already waves of heat shimmered on the sun-baked earth.

"Faster, Omar. Run faster."

"I hear you small one. But I think we should walk at a leisurely pace now so that from the air we look like a farmer and his son. Running will only call attention to ourselves." He could see that the hot sand was burning the boy's feet. "Here, I shall carry you."

"No! I am not a baby. Today, I am a man."

"I see that. But it takes more than courage to be a man. One must have integrity."

"What is this word?"

"Integrity is when a man does not pee in the stream from which his brothers must drink."

The boy's face was troubled. "Many times I have peed in the stream thinking no one would know."

"No one does. Only you. So when you don't pee-- that is the meaning of the word."

They did not have far to go before they came to the road. Nothing was in sight but a straight path to emptiness. When they had walked less than a mile, Omar heard the creak of wooden wheels behind them and the slap of leather on flesh. He spun around, his gun in hand.

It was a farmer sitting on a wagon hitched to a moth-eaten horse.

The boy waved. The wagon would have passed them by but William Akhmed called out. "Stop. You must hide us. My friend just blew the Russians out of the sky."

The wagon rolled to a halt. The old man looked at them with white milk eyes. The dreaded glaucoma!

"Praise Allah. I heard it. I smelled the smoke."

"How can you tell where you are going?" William Akhmed asked.

"My horse leads the way."

Omar and the boy scrambled into the cart, filled with dried camel dung for winter fuel... Again Omar laughed. "We turned down pigeon shit for this? It seems, young friend, we cannot escape the droppings. It is our fate."

CHAPTER 31

Kabul was not as Annisa had remembered it. Could it have changed this much in six years? It was so much larger and the scars of war were everywhere. The once crowded street of Zarghuna Maidan where the tourists had come to buy samovars and fine carpets was mostly boarded up now. Small boys for change hawked Old Russian rubles, pre-1917 Revolution notes, on the streets. The modern government buildings her father had boasted about looked shabby--tiles were missing on the outside, and everywhere there was litter. The modern Hotel Inter-Continental seemed more a part of an ancient past rather than the future.

Soviet armored trucks shuttled back and forth between military installations along city streets that were dying from neglect. Most of the troops Annisa and Yuri saw on the streets were Afghan. The few Soviet soldiers afoot served as an armed escort for Soviet civilians who still did not venture out without protection.

Yuri was not an easy companion on their journey through the city. He was anxious for them to make contact with Fritz Werner and leave as soon as possible. Unhappy with Annisa because she had insisted he accompany her into the residential district, he complained, "I cannot hide behind a *chadri* like you. I am too easily recognizable."

"That is no longer true. The sun has browned your skin and wrinkled your face. Now that you have been ill, you are slim like an Afghan. See what happens when they pass you? They take you for a Pathan. No one looks your way."

"Then I had better be careful. I still look able-bodied. They will snatch me into the Afghan army."

"If Kabul makes you so nervous to come inside, how did you get your information on Zalmair's secret trip to Tashkent?"

"My contact works at the military club. We meet always at the slaughter house on the edge of town."

They had reached the dark green wooden gate that fronted Werner's house.

"Annisa, I'll wait outside for you."

"Now that *would* call attention! And what if Uncle Fritz wants me to stay for awhile? It would be cruel if I refused. He hasn't seen me in years."

"This is not a social call and I am nervous about the German. Werner has always worked both sides."

"He would never do anything to harm me."

"And me?"

"Don't be such a pessimist. It's not like you. It must be the malaria talking."

The house of Fritz Werner stood behind high walls across the street from a new apartment complex. Refugee tents were pitched in the yard fronting the building and on tent lines pieces of lamb had been hung to dry in the sun. Annisa pointed to the apartments. "None of this was here before the invasion."

"I don't like it. From the top windows you have a good vantagepoint of the street. Anyone who goes in and out of Werner's is in full view."

Annisa was surprised her palms were wet when she rang the bell. She had lived with danger for so long she thought she had grown used to it. Perhaps her real fear concerned the questions Uncle Fritz might ask. Why hadn't she gone to America as planned? What was her life like now?

The servant who answered the bell was not Yassim, the man who had served Fritz Werner for years.

"I am here to see Mr. Werner."

He eyed her *chadri* with suspicion. Only peasant women in Kabul wore the veil.

"Do not keep me waiting here in the street like this. My father is a good friend of Mr. Werner. He has traded fine rugs with him for many years. He will consider you rude."

"The German does not live here anymore. Across the river. In Shari-Nau. The house which belonged to the poet, Aziz."

Stunned, Annisa had him repeat the information.

"Yes. Yes. The professor's house." He slammed the gate.

Yuri was unhappy they had to double back. "Are you sure you understood him?"

"I am certain."

It took them longer to reach her father's house than it ordinarily would have. The streets were blocked off near the Palace and two black limousines with Soviet flags on their hoods brought traffic to a halt.

Annisa stared at the official cars. "I wonder if this has anything to do with the traitor Zalmair? Pray Omar reaches Kandahar in time."

"Too late for prayers. Yesterday was the fourth."

It was a sobering thought and neither of them spoke again until they reached the street of Annisa's old home.

"At last. This is it!"

Annisa peered through the grill on the gate. The house was freshly whitewashed and the gardens looked well tended. This pleased her.

"Simply give him the message and leave," Yuri cautioned. "And make sure you explain how the seal came to be broken."

She nodded and felt relief when the old servant Yassim answered the bell. Wouldn't he be astonished to know who was under the veil asking for Mr. Werner, but when she told him it was 'Annisa,' he showed no reaction. "Wait here," he announced.

When he returned, Yassim simply told her, "He will see you."

"Make it quick," Yuri growled from behind.

"Yes, I hear you."

She followed Yassim up the familiar walk. She had forgotten the glorious scents of the garden. Such color, a profusion of spring flowers. She raised her eyes to what had been her bedroom window and she could see coral tinted curtains fluttering in the breeze, the same curtains which Panna had insisted needed washing once a month to survive the dust of Kabul.

Fritz Werner appeared at the doorway and shaded his eyes with his hand. He looked much older: receding hairline, a stomach paunch. He beckoned to her from the patio and Annisa broke into a run.

"I thought Yassim had the name wrong. Is this a visitation from the spirit world? Take off that dreadful *chadri* and let me see my little girl."

Annisa felt self-conscious removing it. Underneath her shroud she wore a bright and multi-colored native dress with mirrors stitched on the bodice. What would Uncle Fritz think?

"A feast for the eyes. If only your father had lived to see you. You are more lovely than either of us anticipated."

She kissed his cheek. "All these years. I have missed you. You gave me special love."

"Did I? Tell me where have you come from? Out of the sky? You have given me a terrible shock."

"I have a friend who waits outside the gate. I can only stay a short time."

"Ask him to come in."

"He refuses."

341

"I will tend to this." Werner was off the patio and down the walk before she could answer. She watched him open the gate and exchange a few words, returning within minutes.

"What are you doing with a Russian?"

"You can tell?"

"Certainly."

"Yuri has been with us so long he seems Afghan."

"His gold tooth gives him away. . . I told him to come back, but to wait until dark."

"Dark? He will be furious."

"Don't concern yourself. He looks like a man who can take care of himself. I have so many questions."

Annisa was too engrossed with the familiar surroundings to answer immediately. Her home was as though she had never left it: her father's favorite chair by the window, his books neatly lined in rows on the fireplace wall, even her mother's picture. "It has been waiting for me to come back." Child-like, she ran from room to room. "Uncle Fritz. It is the same! You have kept it all the same. Even those silly movie star pictures in my bedroom."

"I am a dotty old man. I like to pretend you are both still with me."

He motioned for her to sit with him on the large sofa, the only thing he had added to the room. "Now tell me about your life. I have ordered tea. Rahmin was frantic when you did not arrive in Peshawar. My sources have lost contact with him. Does he know you are safe?"

"Rahmin is dead. Killed by bandits. New York."

"Dear child." He left the sofa and began to pace. "What a miserable world. No place is safe."

In the hall she could hear the familiar ticking of the clock. Panna used to wind it with a large key.

"Where are you living, Annisa? Peshawar?"

She hesitated, feeling angry with herself for not wanting to tell him she was married to Abdul. "I live with my uncles. My mother's people in Doshi . . . We move around a lot."

"At least you are with family."

She handed him the envelope with the broken seal. "I have come with a message for you from the Resistance. It was opened by mistake but by people we can trust." She flushed, remembering another envelope for her father she had deliberately opened in this very room. "I tried to read it but it was in code."

Fritz nodded and reached for his horn-rimmed glasses atop her father's desk. "You see how I have aged! I never needed these to read."

She studied his face as he deciphered the message. He looked wasted; great purple circles under his eyes. Watching him reading in her father's chair made her want to weep, or to crawl up on his lap, and pretend she was a little girl again; pretend he was once again reading her fairy tales in German.

"You have done a great service to bring this, Annisa. I know the risk involved in coming to Kabul." He removed his glasses and wearily wiped his eyes. "I'm afraid it is too late."

Annisa was crestfallen. "Was it so important to the Mujahideen?"

"No way to judge. A secret meeting took place here last week between the Paks and the Soviets. The Paks do not officially recognize the Barbak regime. Until now the Paks have refused to negotiate directly with the Russians but there is pressure being applied. The big surprise is that Ambassador Meirnardus says here that Commander Zalmair would take part in the meeting."

"Zalmair! Then Yuri's information was right. He is a traitor."

"A moot question. His plane was shot down in Kandahar airport yesterday. Commander Zalmair is dead."

Annisa leapt to her feet. "Omar! "Her eyes bright with excitement, she clasped her hands together. "I can't wait to tell Yuri."

"My God, you have information about this?"
"Yes, my uncle Omar. This is *his victory!*"
Fritz looked stunned. "Is he connected with the CIA?"
"Omar?" She laughed heartily. "Hardly. Oh, Uncle Fritz this is wonderful. You don't know the great effort this took."

"The government is stunned that the plane was brought down by a shoulder fired-missile. I need to know; did your uncle know that Zalmair collaborates? The Americans have poured a lot of money Zalmair's way. It puzzles me. I wonder if they knew it all along?"

"But why would the Americans support a suspected collaborator?"

"12 SS-20 missiles at Shindand, west of Kabul, are aimed at a top secret US. naval base in the Indian Ocean--Diego Garcia. If the Russians agree to remove the missiles from Afghanistan, the West might be persuaded to look the other way in Kabul." He removed his pipe from his pocket and played with the tobacco he had stuffed in the bowl. "Only rumors, Annisa. The Soviets could annex the north and let the Paks have the south, including the disputed territories of Pushtunistan."

"Partition! I don't believe this."

He sighed. "A nasty bit of business but many people believe it will come sooner or later."

"Why do you say the message came too late?"

"Meirnardus, the man who sent this, was wounded in a terrorist attack at his home in Egypt."

"Yes," Dr. Harris said. "I think Meirnardus is a good person. I've met him."

"Where?"

"In Peshawar. . .I never realized my father's poems were known outside Afghanistan. Ambassador Meirnardus said he was familiar with them. It makes me sad that I was too young to appreciate my father's work before he was gone."

Werner smiled. "You won't be the first child with regrets. I've never met the ambassador. What is he like?"

"Distinguished. Thoughtful. You get the impression he is really listening to you. . .I'm afraid I made a big fool of myself in front of him."

"You must have had a good reason."

"Afraid not. I acted like a spoiled brat." She grinned at him. "It's all your fault, you know. Father always said you spoiled me."

"It was a very great pleasure. The older one gets the more they regret not having children. You must have some for me to spoil."

She gave him a weak smile and looked away.

"Think of poor Meirnardus. They say his son was killed in the same explosion. His only boy." He looked at Annisa. "Well, enough of that. The loss of the Ambassador certainly leaves a gap in friends of the Resistance. He always pushed hard for our groups to consolidate--for recognition at the U.N. It is ridiculous. The U.N. condemns Barbak's regime yet continues to let it represent us. Hekmatyar has been chosen as spokesman."

She frowned. "Hekmatyar is a fundamentalist. . ."

Werner held up his hand. "If Hekmatyar can get our Resistance groups to present a united front, there is a better chance for recognition." He reached for the letter and held it up. "This says Zalmair was to be in Kabul at the secret meeting, to plot the assassination of Hekmatyar when he goes to launch our campaign for a seat in the General Assembly. The Soviets want it to look like inner squabbling for control--a coup for Soviet propaganda."

"The United Nations? Why would they shoot Hekmatyar in New York when they could assassinate him in Peshawar?"

"World-wide attention. The Soviets are never that simple, Annisa-jan. Reactions to events are planned well before the event takes place." He leaned forward in his chair. "I'm told the attempt on the life of the Pope was well over a year in the planning."

Annisa stood up and crossed to the window. "In my world, we live simply, counting our precious bullets each night, hoping there is enough for an attack the next day. Leaders in exile play with our lives like we are small mice. We do the fighting, Uncle Fritz." She turned to him, a sad look in her eyes. "Village life has dulled my brain. We not only do not discuss these things--we know nothing of the people who decide our future."

He stared at her unblinking. "You fight? You personally? You deliver messages for the Resistance? Your father must be spinning in his grave."

"He has none, remember. Only a pit."

"I'm sorry, Annisa. If there was only some way to comfort you. You are still so young--a whole life ahead of you. You mustn't worry about the message. Even if it had come on time, proof of Zalmair's involvement would have been difficult. He was highly thought of in the Resistance. The Russians made a clever choice."

The silence that followed felt heavy to Annisa.

Finally, he spoke again and his words shocked her. "Sometimes I think a secret deal would be a blessing. If America gives the Mujahideen the 'stinger' missiles they are begging for, the Soviets will only escalate their invasion. More troops keep coming. Each unit is better trained, better equipped than before. Their next attack will be in Paktia. It is their intention to wipe out our supply lines."

"But we must have those missiles. They beat us from the sky."

"But what price victory? Is every last Afghan to die in this struggle?"

She did not answer but crossed to the window and stared outside. The sky was robin's egg blue, the mountains beyond russet and stark. The light was pure and it made her shiver. "Remember my father's poem:

'Death is after us. We will go unfilled.

Other men run away from grief. I rejoice when I am drowned in it.'"

She turned to him, smiling. "I feel so at peace here. The peach tree in the garden. It bears fruit."

"Yes, and your father and I both predicted it would die."

"Remember our picnics in the King's gardens in Paghman? Sweet yogurt. Green grapes. My father reading aloud."

"The gardens are destroyed, Annisa. Scarcely a building is left standing in Paghman."

"I wish none of it had ever happened. That I could wake up in the morning and be a child in my father's house again."

"I wish you could too. I remember that little girl. She loved strawberry ice cream. Would you believe they still serve it each noon at the International Club."

Annisa stared at him solemnly and then she began to laugh. "Is it possible? Ice cream! I'm surprised the club is still open."

"It functions. A bit dilapidated. Shabby. Dust on the roses. No water in the swimming pool. And holes in the table linens."

"But aren't most of the diplomats gone?"

"The sensible ones. But we still have some businessmen left like myself. We are a sad lot these days. Remember the American pilot who helped start Ariana airline? He's worth a small fortune. But the Afghans refuse to let him take it out of the country. So here he sits with his money and nothing to spend it on."

"Strawberry ice cream. . . It seems so bizarre. People in Ghanzi and Wardar are starving."

"That does not mean we should not eat."

"It's not right."

"Sweet Annisa. Allow yourself one day. You are not taking food from the Mujahideen. Some Russian will have it for supper tonight, if not you."

Annisa shook her head.

"What did I always tell you? A man's greatest happiness is when he can take care of you. Remember this when you marry."

She dared not look at him.

Yassim entered the room to remove the tea tray.

"I will not be home for lunch as planned. If anyone needs to reach me. The International Club. Noon."

"Mr. Chatterjee's man has brought a note."

"Christ, that man is persistent. I can leave for Delhi tomorrow. No need to go today."

"He insists he talk to you tonight."

"All right. All right. Chatterjee makes a pest of himself. Tell him to come tonight but to come *after* the dinner hour. Our Indian friend always arrives just in time to eat."

"Uncle Fritz, if you have business. . ."

"Heavens, what is more important in this world than to be with you."

Suddenly she frowned as she stared down at her dress. "They would not serve me ice cream at the International Club in these clothes. Or my *chadri*. Heavens. I wasn't thinking. It would look very suspicious for you to be on the streets with a woman who covers her face."

"There is no need for you to wear the veil."

"What if someone sees me? Recognizes me?"

"The daughter of Dr. Sulaiman Aziz fled Kabul years ago. You were only a child. Now you are a stunning woman. People will only see you as a modern city girl and suspect I have a mistress."

"Uncle Fritz!" She laughed again. "A modern city girl dressed as a Koochi?"

"If need be, we can buy you a new dress. . ."

Yassim had returned and Fritz looked annoyed with the interruption. "Now what?"

"A message delivered to the servants' quarters." He handed Fritz a folded piece of paper.

Fritz opened it and shook his head. "The gods are against us. I'm afraid I have to go out."

She stood up to leave.

"No stay. I will only be gone a short time. Then we can go for the dress. The ice cream. Is there anything you need? Want? We will go to the bank this afternoon. There is money for you."

"Please, no. I did not come here asking for money."

"Annisa, I live in your father's house."

"That would please him."

"I have made money in this dreadful war. I have no one to spend it on. Seeing your hopeful young face adds years to my life. For so long a time I believed you dead. Indulge your old uncle. Let him give to you."

She felt shy in saying it. "All I want is a bath. I was wondering if you would mind if I took one? It's been years since I have bathed in a tub."

"But of course. This is your house. Do as you please. I'll tell Yassim to get some firewood to heat up the boiler. . . And

Annisa-- be careful what you say to him. I am sure they make him report to the Khad."

"But you trust him to bring messages? Just now. . ."

"His son is a student of Islamic theology in Peshawar. A secret organization is forming. I am in contact with them. The Taliban."

"I know nothing of this."

"It is best you don't. They would restrict women to the home. Close the girls' school."

"Those days are far behind us."

"Or maybe the distant future? Annisa, I think you should try to go to America."

"America is too late for me. It is my wish to be here the day we drive the invaders out."

He smiled. "You are a stubborn girl. . .Like your father. You must know our future is bleak with or without the Russians. There are killings in Kabul each day. Mostly the Khalq and Parcham disputes. If left to their own wiles, the secret police would eventually do each other in. And bombings. Yesterday 20 students were hurt in a blast at Kabul Polytechnic Institute. The in fighting has started in earnest. It will rip the Resistance apart. There is already widespread corruption."

"That angers me."

"What would you have people do?"

"Well, we can't all emigrate to the West."

"No, but we need leaders trained in their electronic wizardry. Outside of Afghanistan it is a very different world."

Annisa listened to what he had to say but after Uncle Fritz left for his errand she was too happy to think about it, too enthralled with the pleasure of a bath. She luxuriated in the hot water and washed herself with store-bought soap. It was a shock to rediscover what it was like to enjoy these small but all-important things. She had been pampered as a child and she was only now beginning to realize how much she had taken for granted. Coming here had awakened desires for things that she had told herself she didn't really miss. But she did and desperately. She never wanted to leave this house again. Just to stay in Kabul and eat ice cream and take hot baths. Let others worry about the war.

She was sitting on the patio, wrapped in one of Fritz's old bathrobes and brushing her wet hair when she saw him coming up the front walk. He did not look pleased.

"I'm afraid I have to go out again. An old friend of ours is in town. I haven't seen him in years and he takes a very grave risk in coming to Kabul. My contact tells me he is here only until tonight."

"An old friend of ours?"

"Yes. Captain Duranni."

"Najib? Here?" She dropped the towel from her wet hair. "It's not possible." Her eyes filled with tears. "Please, you must tell me about him."

Fritz was in no hurry to answer, curious as to why she was so distraught. "Nothing to tell," he said. "He gave his code name to my contacts and told me to meet him. We have to be careful on the phones, Annisa. We never use them. It seems he too is inquiring about a message."

"I was so afraid for him," she whispered. "Oh, Uncle Fritz. . ." She paused long enough to regain control. "He was injured in Islamabad. The American doctor said it was not an accident. That is how we got the message that was to be delivered to you."

"I see. Then perhaps Najib is here to make sure it arrived."

"How is he?"

"I haven't seen Najib in years. I'm told it is rare he comes inside these days. And never to Kabul."

Her excitement was mounting. "Where is he now?"

"A safe house for the Jamit."

"May I go with you?"

"Annisa, a safe house is much more risky than the International Club. I'm afraid that. . ." He stopped mid-sentence when he saw her crestfallen face. He was not about to say it might be more dangerous for Najib too.

She was pleading. "I live with danger every day. Oh, please. There are things left unsaid between us."

"Yes, I can see that."

"You can trust me to be careful."

He sighed. "I keep forgetting you are no longer a small child. Of course you should go and I think perhaps, alone."

"You would let me do that! Oh, thank you." She leapt up and kissed him, racing towards the staircase. Halfway there she paused and turned to him. "How well did you know my mother? What was she really like?"

"Very much like you."

"And everyone loved her very much?"

"*Everyone.*" He reached into his pocket and removed a money chit. "Come here. I forgot to give you this. For a new dress."

She looked at the amount. "Uncle Fritz this would buy a thousand dresses."

"Then buy a thousand. I have no one to spend it on."

Annisa hesitated. There was money left for her schooling but not that much . .. If she ever went to America?

"Take it Annisa. Make an old man happy. And never forget that money buys power--freedom to choose."

She blew him a kiss and then hurried up the stairs.

He watched her go; wondering if sending her to Najib was wise. Najib was a seducer of women and Annisa had always been headstrong and reckless, hot-blooded like her mother. He smiled at the memory. So long ago and only one stolen night. But then he was never born to taste life and loved it that others could.

In her old bedroom Annisa ran a comb through her wet hair and threw on her brightly colored dress. God was good. Najib was alive. This was the happiest day of her life. Nothing bad could happen to her. Nothing!

When she came down the stairs her cheeks were flushed and her damp hair fell in ringlets below her waist.

Fritz Werner sighed. "Your hopeful young face adds years to my life. If you take a taxi be careful what you say to the driver. They all work for the KHAD."

"Where is Najib?"

"It is a house next to the Swiss Embassy. Two stories. Blue shutters."

"I remember it. My father tutored a small boy in Latin there. I would go with him."

"Ask for *Sheer*. His code name."

Annisa smiled. "Najib is a lion, is he? And you? Do you have a name too?"

"The fox. I am the fox. What else. Don't forget. Your Russian comes to the gate at dark."

She reached for his hand "You have made me so happy, Uncle Fritz. Peace. Be at peace my protector, my *kaka*. "

CHAPTER 32

Annisa did not take a taxi; she wanted to walk. To clear her thoughts. But she couldn't think. She was too joyful. She wanted to skip and sing and swing her hips in her brightly colored Koochi dress. Today she was just another young woman in Kabul, dressed as a daughter of nomads, pretending she was no longer the village wife of Abdul.

She decided she would not buy a new dress. A beautiful red dress from a Western boutique in Peshawar had crippled her. She was a daughter of Afghanistan and today she was ready to claim it.

No one answered the gate at the house of blue shutters. When she pushed it open, she was shocked to see the once lovely garden in disarray. Trash littered the grounds and several windows in the house were broken. What a pity. She had memories of polished brass door handles and starched lace curtains.

The front door was ajar. She entered the darkened hallway. Yes, she remembered now--up the rickety steps. Dust clouded the pools of sunlight at her feet falling from the window on the landing above. She walked down a long hall and encountered three closed doors. She rapped at the first one. No answer. She knocked again. *"Sheer?"*

"Who is it?"

"A friend of the fox."

The door opened a crack and for a terrifying moment she thought he was going to close it. "Annisa!" He drew her in, locking the door behind her.

The room was small and hot, like an attic. Windows were closed off with wooden shutters. The only light came from a naked bulb, which hung on a cord over the bed, a Western bed with a large oak headboard and spindled posts on each corner. And wallpaper. It was the only house in Kabul she had ever visited where there were paper yellow roses on the wall. "How do you breathe in here? It's so stuffy."

He held her away from him, unsmiling. He did not speak. For a moment they were two creatures slowly turned into stone.

"Najib, greet me." She was trembling with uncertainty; fearful his words would condemn her.

"Three years," he said. "Three wasted years."

Annisa bit down on her lip; the validity of his words were more than she could take. "It's very easy for you to say that. You've had nothing to lose."

"Lose? A thousand times I have rehearsed what I would say to you if ever. . . But now, to hear this. I had nothing to lose!" He dropped her hand and moved away from her. "Why have you come?"

The anger in his voice intimidated her. She could not say what was in her heart. "Your message from the Egyptian. I delivered it to Fritz Werner. I'm afraid it came too late."

"Then I have made this long trip for nothing."

"No, it worked out for the best. . .I am here."

He stared at her but gave no response.

"Najib?"

For a second she thought she saw a hint of tenderness in his eyes. Then his gaze fell away and he looked utterly dejected. "The message. Did Werner tell you what was in it?"

"Yes. There are plans to assassinate Hekmatyar in October. At the U.N. Commander Zalmair was on his way to Tashkent to negotiate with the Paks. The Americans betray us."

Najib was wild eyed. *"Pasmanda!* The American President plans to recognize the Resistance in October as the rightful representative of our people. The message must have been garbled!"

"Uncle Fritz did not say this. But Zalmair is dead. His plane was shot down in Kandahar." Nothing has changed, she thought. His mind is always on the war. I am nothing to him. He doesn't know I exist.

"Shot down! But how. . ."

"I think Omar was responsible." She said listlessly.

"Omar-el-Ham! Your uncle? What kind of stories do you bring me?"

"It is not a story."

"Zalmair a traitor? This is not to be believed."

"Uncle Fritz said the Russians were smart to pick him for that very reason."

"This hideous war."

"But with Zalmair dead. . ."

"Forget the message. It's not important. It's over. All of it. . . We are over."

A flash of anger seized her. "If the message was not important then why did they try to kill you in Islamabad?" Her eyes went to the cane next to his bed.

He caught her furtive glance.

"Only temporary. I am fine."

"And your arm? It hangs crooked."

"It did not mend properly."

"The Americans are flying Mujahideen for special surgery in the States. Dr. Harris says. . . I was with him in the mountains. He is wonderful with the sick." She was racing, tripping over her words; nervous and miserable from the coldness she saw in his eyes. "He told me about the motorcycle that hit you..."

"Is that how you came by the message?"

"Yes." She repeated herself. "Dr. Harris serves a clinic in the mountains. Yuri was sick with malaria. I volunteered to come to Kabul and. . ."

"Annisa, slow down."

"I can't. You make me so nervous."

"Look at me."

"Najib, I can't."

"Don't talk anymore."

She raised her eyes to him.

"You are more a woman dressed like this than in those Western clothes we bought you in Peshawar."

"But I loved that red dress. It was beautiful. It just, it just didn't belong on me."

"And why is that?"

She refused to answer. Her pride wouldn't let her.

His voice was gentle. "Annisa, I came to the refugee camp many times. Mabaie swore you were not there."

Annisa lowered her head. "Dr. Harris has told me of this."

"And did he tell you I left messages for you at every way station?"

"I did not get them."

"You expect me to believe that?"

"Yes, because it's the truth. I am sorry I ran away from you in Peshawar. I was confused." Her eyes brimmed.

"Save your tears, Annisa. I have dreamed of this meeting many times. And now that I see you I have an urge to break everything in this room!"

She recoiled from him. The scar across his cheekbone pulsed red with anger.

"Was I so terrible? You had that woman..."

"How could you choose this wretched life? Jack Westerman could have gotten you to the States. Your father planned for your education. You have thrown the best of you away."

These were Ethan's words! She hated hearing them here. And from Najib.

Stung by his harshness, she stepped back from him. "I chose not to go. I do not fit." She pointed to the faded wallpaper and the picture of the Last Supper on the wall. "Even Mrs. Reed, your missionary friend, knew. She kept calling you a Mohammedan. I told her it was not possible. Mohammed was a prophet, not a son of God. But she kept on saying it. How could I live among Christians who know so little of us?"

"You make excuses."

"I was afraid."

"Of what?"

"That I wouldn't belong." She feared she was no longer able to hold back her feelings. She wanted to scream at him; to confess her real truth --that she could no longer masquerade as a virgin. "A terrible thing happened to me, Najib."

"Yes, tragic. A chance to choose a new life."

"Go ahead. Be sarcastic, I don't care. It is something I can never tell you."

"And I no longer want to hear."

"I hate you for saying that."

"Yes, of course. It is a common failing: the belief that putting it into words will turn it into fact."

"Then I don't hate you?"

"Do you?"

"If there was only some way to make you understand." She was furious with herself for losing her composure. She had come looking for him thinking she was so strong.

"Do you understand why you would choose to throw your life away?"

"Why are *you* still here?" she challenged. "Why don't you just stay in your precious England. What gives you the right to judge me a failure."

"You were full of dreams. To be a doctor..."

"That dream is finished. I have found my place."

"Place! You come here dressed like a nomad, a Koochi girl."

Her lower lip quivered. "You just said you liked me in these clothes. That it was better than the red chiffon." She looked up at him with tears in her eyes. "You destroy me. I shouldn't have come. Your anger hurts too much."

"I want it to hurt."

"Najib, please. You have to forgive me. I was not myself. Sick with the fever. Don't look at me like that. After I left the camp I went to Dean's Hotel but you had checked out with that woman. The two of you had left for Lisbon. I had no chance against her. I can't help it. It's been unbearable. I ache for you."

He braced himself against her tears but it was futile. "Don't cry," he said, his voice gruff. "I say the opposite of what I feel."

"Do you want me to go?"

"God, no!" His hand reached out and touched her cheek. "I love what is beautiful when it appears to me."

"What is beautiful?"

He dropped his hand. "I am not a poet like your father. Do not ask me to put it into words. It is a feeling only."

She backed away from him. "Please, I need to know. I need something." Her grave eyes searched his, questioning.

He looked at her and then at the strangely transformed room. No longer did it seem a prison-- the yellow flowers in the wallpaper led him into a garden. A young girl in a sun-yellow cotton dress was planting a box of treasures under a peach tree. At this moment she was as he remembered her. He reached out to touch her again but she turned away "What treasures did you hide in your garden, Annisa? In the box you buried at your father's house?"

"Strange that you would remember it."

"I remember all my times with you."

She turned to face him again. "There were letters from Rahmin and a lock of my mother's hair inside. A small stone from Kassim's grave."

"And your feelings? Are they buried in that box? Are you still afraid of life."

Her eyes snapped. "Yes I am afraid. I have good reason."

He wanted to hold her but she held herself rigid, unyielding. Tears spilled over again. "What can such people be made of?"

"People?"

"The Russians."

He reached out to comfort her, stroking her cheek again with the back of his hand. "Forgive my harsh words. Why do you think I have wanted you to leave the war so badly? You have suffered enough."

Her body shook with fear. "Don't make me say it."

"Nothing can be this bad."

"But it is."

He kissed the hair on the top of her head. He breathed the woman smell of her and sensed the danger. "Downstairs, in the kitchen there is a kettle. We can make tea."

"No, don't leave me." She grabbed at him. "Sit with me." She pulled him over towards the bed. They sat on the edge. He held her hand.

Between sobs, in words so disjointed he did not always understand, she told him. Little Habiba. . .The soldiers. . .Those dreadful moments. Waves of suffering shook her. She could only speak in whispers. "Two. There were two of them, Najib."

He wanted to speak but the rage he felt rising inside was choking him.

"I knew no decent man would ever want me. You would never want me. Never. And you were the only one for me."

He put his arms around her as she sobbed out unfamiliar names: Ishaq on a white horse; the pendant missing from Sabra's neck and Tawab the blind boy. . .and the vulture. All the vultures circling over Zia. The bombs exploding red.

Some of this he knew but he waited, listening patiently, holding her. Each time he felt the tears had finally subsided, she would begin again. His arms ached. Her hand inadvertently touched his thigh. He felt dazed, wary of her sexual innocence and unsure of how he should be with her. Annisa had witnessed violent death many times but she had never made love--in the truest sense of the word. Would it be healing if he were to take her now? He feared for himself. He would have to check the passion that was rising within, a fire that wanted to consume her, to leave her gasping. He could feel the terror still in her body. It was real, born of yearning, and the violence done her by the soldiers.

"Annisa?. . .Look into my eyes."

She shook her head.

He took her face in his hands.

"I don't want you to see me."

"We are here. Together. Is this possible?"

She pulled away from him and stood up. "No."

"What are you saying 'no' to?"

"I wish I knew." She crossed the room. "What is happening to me, Najib? I'm so upset. Dr. Harris has urged me to go to the International Red Cross in Peshawar. They are training para-medics. And you are angry because I stopped my education. What should I do?"

Disappointment that she had pulled away from their intimacy was coupled with relief that she had done so. Najib stretched out on the bed, relieved to be off of his feet. His broken ribs were taped and were excruciatingly painful; his unhealed arm throbbed. He stared at the ugly water stains on the carved wooden ceiling above the bed. "Annisa, are you serious about Peshawar?"

"I can't be. I must remain with my. . .with my family."

"Why must you talk in riddles."

"And you don't! Dr. Harris told me that in Islamabad they tried to kill you. It was no *accident*. You expect me to leave Afghanistan while you. . . "

"Islamabad was personal. A score to be settled." He could not tell her that Rahmin's death turned out to be an execution ordered by the drug-lords and that he had taken it upon himself to avenge it.

"I don't understand what you mean by personal?"

"Let it be. Don't stir up painful memories."

They stared at each other without speaking and the specter of that street in Islamabad appeared to both of them.

"Come here, Annisa," he said softly. "Come to my bed."

"Promise just to hold me." She lay down beside him and rested her head on his chest. "Najib, I'm not a good person."

He played with her hair. "Terrible. You are very, very bad."

But she refused to let him tease her out of her remorseful feelings. Another jumble of words came tumbling out. If she hadn't taken part in the girls' demonstration, her father might be alive. If she hadn't taken little Habiba to that remote village or if she had only mixed the right herbs together, Omar's oldest son might not have died of the dysentery.

"Annisa, stop this. You are not omnipotent. God decides these things, not you. . . Why must you feel guilty for enjoying life."

"I just do. Today I worried because I enjoyed too much having a hot bath in a tub and because I wanted strawberry ice cream. Does this make me a bad person?"

He smiled at her question. "Have you forgotten your father's poem?

'Life is not about comfort -- it is about discovery.' You have always clamored for the answers. As a little girl you wanted to explore everything and to do whatever Rahmin did. You have never sought comfort and you have never made it easy on yourself."

"I worry because I am beginning to forget Rahmin's face. What he looked like. His hands. He always had such wonderful strong hands. . . Najib, help me. Help me. I'm not strong. I only pretend."

The sound of her filled his heart and he silenced her with his lips. Her mouth quivered as he leaned over her. The grave yearning in her eyes gave him courage. Her lips were sweet on his. They kissed and drew apart. She looked up at him and for the first time since entering the room, she smiled. Suddenly the shabby room burst with life. Words formed on his lips but he could not say them. Childhood voices echoed through open windows, the lullaby of the swing on the terrace.

"Oh, Najib." This time she raised her lips to his.

"I fear for us, Annisa-jan."

"What will happen?" she asked. "What will happen tomorrow?"

He touched her lips with his fingertips. "Don't ask."

"But. . ."

"Hush. Don't talk it."

"How does one know if they love someone?"

"It has to do with trust."

His words caused her body to stiffen. She had told Najib everything. Everything except Abdul.

"What is it, my angel?"

Beneath the window a Russian truck rattled past.

A shadow on Annisa's face. "I am afraid," she whispered.

"I know."

He leaned his head down and gently touched his lips to her neck, aware of the pulse in her thighs beside his own. Slowly, he ran his hand down her arms to her fingertips. She shivered as he unbuttoned her bodice and kissed her breasts with his tongue. Her nipples stiffened. His hands upon her warm stomach now inched downward between her thighs. Another tremor shook her.

"Take off your dress," he whispered. "I wish to look at you."

She slipped away from him and stood by the bed, removing her garments without a word. Her beauty descended upon him and left him weak.

For a moment he was torn. How could he let this happen? For a girl like Annisa it should be only as a wife.

Annisa decided for him. Bending over, she caressed him with her eyes and gently laid her nakedness upon him.

She clung to him, holding tight to stop her shaking. Then in one quick moment he rolled her over and straddled her. She became completely still. Eyes closed. He kissed her eyelids. Her mouth. She slipped her arms around his neck and gently they slipped into another world where they ate hungrily of each other. A moan escaped her lips as she opened to receive Najib between her legs.

Then he lost himself, no longer aware of what he must do for Annisa, surrendering instead to their pleasure. Their bodies moved, feeding their hunger, filling with light, caught in the cradle of the universe, then exploding to where they were lost and drifting.

She quivered and lay moist beneath him. He feared to move, to disturb the rich, steady breathing. Then slowly he pulled away from her and gazed down at her peaceful face. His body felt warm and spent. He lay on his pillow and stared at the faded wallpaper and the picture of the Prophet Hasrat Isa and smiled at the irony of it all. Annisa was right about the missionary woman. He got up and walked to the window peering through the shutters. The sun had gone, and in their cloistered room they had not even known it.

"Najib?"

"I'm here."

"What are your thoughts?"

"I was thinking about a little boy named Alexander. In Egypt. How much his father loved him." He turned and walked back to the bed, staring down at her. "Alexander was the son of Ambassador Meirnardus. They blew him to bits, Annisa. I can't get it out of my mind. Someday we will have a boy and we will name him Alexander."

Memory had returned.

Annisa got up from the bed and with her back to him began buttoning her dress.

"Where are you going? Why the hurry?"

"Yuri. I have to meet him at Fritz Werner's house. Did I tell you Werner now lives in my father's house? It is after dark. Yuri will be angry. I am very late."

"I will go with you."

"No, Najib, you cannot. The truck picks you up here at midnight, remember? It would be difficult for you to hurry. Your cane."

"Annisa, you cannot go out another door without me. Never again. We will go to Peshawar together."

"Najib. I must go alone. I cannot go with you. Not now. . .not ever."

"Repeat those words."

Tears began to flow. "Abdul. I did not lie to you, Najib. Until this day no man has ever touched me but the Russians. But I am married. Omar's brother, Abdul."

"The *chapandaz*?" He leaned against the bedpost. "Don't say this. I saw him at the fair grounds as a boy. I hated that man and everything he stood for. It can't be true."

"Najib, it is."

"You, married to such a man? How can you be his wife and not be his?"

"Abdul was injured in *buzkashi*. He cannot perform as a man."

"And still he married? What kind of selfishness is that?"

"Trust. You told me to trust. Why can't you? I had nowhere else to go. Fatima insisted. You had that woman. I hated her too and I cannot even remember her name."

"Claire."

"You had Claire."

"She is finished, Annisa."

"When?"

"In this very room. . .but this time if you walk out that door you will never see me again."

She stood there looking at him, her hand on the knob, spent from their passion, free of anger, and of the newborn hope. "Najib, do not threaten me. Please."

"We could have a life. A family. Sons." He blocked her leaving; his arm held the door.

"No, no family. The fever was from the Russians. My mysterious fever in the camp. I am worthless to you. You would have no sons."

Bawdy laughter filled the room from the street below. "Glory to thee, O God. And thine is the praise and blessed is thy name." Drunken Russian voices mimicked the familiar words from the Koran.

Najib picked up his cane by the bedside and smashed it against the picture on the wall. Glass shattered and fell in splinters.

"Don't, Najib. Please. Please forgive me."

Forgive? Had he not feared this very moment? That he would someday fully surrender himself to a woman only to be betrayed? "You destroy me, Annisa."

"No, please, no." Her voice was desperate. "I must hurry. It is after dark. Yuri will be alarmed."

"Then go. Meet Yuri. Then come back here. The two of you. There will be room in the truck. We have not finished with what we have to say to each other. For God's sake, Annisa, you no longer belong in this hideous war. It is over. The Russians plan a major assault in Paktia within months. Jawar is their target. Supplies will be cut off. There will be nothing left in the mountains. The Mujahideen will be demoralized. . . I will not let you stay married to that miserable Abdul."

"Najib, I can not give you a son."

"I want *you*."

She touched his lips. "If only I could believe that."

The streetlights were dim. No light shone on the front gate of her house. Annisa could see no lights coming from the second story windows. The house looked dark and deserted. She was at grave risk. There was a curfew on the streets of Kabul and she was out alone.

She stepped forward out of the shadows and rang the front bell three times. No answer. What was she to do? She crossed the street and waited in front of Kassim's old house, watching the gate from the shadows. No one passed. The street was almost empty. A few army vehicles lumbered by. Where was Yuri? Had he come early and found her not there? Or was he himself late? This was not like Yuri. You could always rely on him. Yuri never let you down.

She crossed the street again and rang three more times. No answer. The longer she waited the more apprehensive she became. What had become of him? Where was Uncle Fritz? Where was the servant Yassim? She pushed against the gate and was surprised to find it unlocked. Once inside the darkened compound, she at least felt safe, away from any prying eyes on the street. She made her way to the front door and hesitated. It was ajar. Something was terribly amiss. Yassim would not leave the gate unlocked or the front door open. Should she return to the street and wait for Yuri there?

Instead she entered the familiar darkened house, groping for the light switch. She found it, and a small lamp in the hall turned on. "Uncle Fritz?"

"Turn that off." A voice from inside the kitchen.
"Yuri? Where are you?"
"On the floor. Be careful when you open the door."
She groped her way into the kitchen.
"Where have you been?" he growled.
"With Najib."
"That is good news. He will have to get you out of Kabul."
"What are you doing in here? In the dark."
"I saw Werner return and leave again. The servant went out shortly after that. You must leave Kabul. At once. I can join you later."
"What is going on here?"
"No lights, I told you. Did you hear the news? Bandit rebels downed a civilian plane in Kandahar yesterday."
"Yes. Uncle Fritz told me. Omar got Zalmair."
"The paper makes no mention of that. Just a fuss about Mujahideen shooting down innocent civilians."
"All these years, Yuri. Omar could never have done it without you." She reached for him in the dark and when she touched him, she felt the sickening slickness of warm wet blood. "What is this?" she gasped.
"In the bazaar. 'Russki' someone whispered in my ear, and then I felt the blade in my side."
"How bad is the wound?"
"Bad enough. I am sure I left a trail of blood all the way here."
"Uncle Fritz will help you when he returns."
"I was hiding in the garage when he went out. He left for Delhi."
"Then we must get out of here at once."
"Annisa... I am too weak to stand. I can't make it."
"You will. I can go for Najib. A truck picks him up at midnight. He promised to wait for us."
"Before you go I need your help."
"Yes."
"They must not take me alive. I know too much about the Resistance. Use my gun."
"What!"
"Annisa, you must. I haven't the courage. I tried."
"Try to stand up. You can lean on me. We can make it to Najib. Or I can run back and get him. Don't ask this."

362

"You must do this for me or I am without hope of salvation."

"You? An unbeliever!"

"My grandmother read secretly to us from the Bible. To take one's own life is to. . ."

"Shoot you, Yuri? I cannot. I love you."

"Then shoot me out of love as I did Daldal. I lied to Omar about the horse." His voice broke. "I'm begging you Annisa. Lives could be lost."

"You may bleed to death."

"We cannot risk it."

"I'm going to Najib. He will know what to do."

Yuri reached out in the dark and clutched her arm. "No! If the servant returns there would be three of us trapped."

Annisa was desperate now. "Yuri, I did this to you. You waited for me. . .Najib...Oh, my God."

"My gun."

"No."

"Get it."

"Where?"

"On the floor beside me. My hand shakes when I put it to my head."

"It is not your religion. You are afraid."

"Yes, afraid. You have known this always. Afraid to live. Afraid to die."

The bell on the front gate rang.

"Merciful God."

"Have you got the gun?"

"Yes... It can't be Yassim. He would not ring his own gate."

The bell sounded again, followed by a loud pounding.

"Uncle Fritz was expecting a visitor tonight. A Mr. Chatterjee. What should I do?"

"Don't answer and if he enters flick on the light and fire. Aim for the head. You are a good shot."

They waited. An eerie silence. Finally the pounding had stopped. "Put the gun in my mouth. Death will be instant and in the dark, you will not see."

"Yuri, I am not strong. I want to run. To leave Abdul. To go to Peshawar."

"The American doctor had twisted your head."

"No, I want to be with Najib. I love him."

"Enough to kill him if he begged you?"
"Please, Yuri. Don't do this."
"You are strong enough. Now shoot."
"No."
"Damn you, woman. I survive the malaria. Sasha. Only to argue with you."
"You can lean on me. We can make it."
"Now, Annisa, now."
"No." She rubbed her fingers over the barrel of the gun and put her hand on the trigger. She reached out for Yuri's face in the dark. She could feel the tears upon his cheeks. "Omar will not forgive me. He loves you."
"Omar is not to know. It is a gift to me from you. Just tell him I knew. I knew the eagle knocked Zalmair out of the sky. Now hurry. That fool servant. He must not find me alive."
She leaned over and kissed his forehead, repeating his name "Yuri, my Yuri. You gave me so much."
In the darkness Yuri could see the frost upon the windowpane and hear Sasha moaning his name as he sprayed his life force inside her. The barrel of the gun was in his mouth now. Annisa was merciful and brave. She did not hesitate or question him further. No sooner had Yuri tasted the cold steel than the shot rang out.
And Annisa, with six years of fighting in the countryside, had presence of mind not to drop the gun. It was a good one. They could use every weapon they could get their hands on
She stood up quickly and shoved the instrument of death into the pocket of her dress. Groping for her *chadri* that hung on the hook in the hall, she closed the door on her father's house for the last time and slipped outside into the garden. The street outside the gate was clear. She must make it through the streets to Najib. To reach him was all that mattered.
In the distance, the Resistance guns turned towards Kabul had begun to fire, lighting up the night.

CHAPTER 33

The sky had clouded over and the gray light sharpened the contour of the landscape. Inside the hospital grounds, surrounded by a neglected garden, they laid the litters of the wounded in rows. Annisa moved quietly among them. She was grateful to be in Quetta, Pakistan. She had never worked with such fervor or so well. Caring for the sick was her calling.

Her good friend, Akmatcha, the young pockmarked ambulance driver, approached her. "The base at Jawar has fallen."

"Nonsense. Commander Haqqani denied it by radio from Miramshah. I heard it myself. You lose faith too easily."

"How many wounded?" he asked.

"Too many to count."

Annisa knelt beside a burn victim; a young Mujahideen swathed in bandages. She could only see his eyes. "Have faith," she whispered, praying he would last the day...

The boy weakly raised his hand.

The wounded around Annisa seemed to sense her tranquillity of spirit. It sustained them. There were no moans in the courtyard; they stifled any noise of their pain.

With unsteady steps, Annisa crossed the garden. Two days without sleep. Her ears tingled and the tips of her fingers felt numb. Long lines of wounded. She knew so little. Three months training with the para-medics in Peshawar and then to be catapulted into this! But who could stay the sea of blood that flowed? At first, she had done what she was told-- wrapped the heads, salved the burned flesh, and ripped sheets to fill the bloody holes. From everywhere came the plea for water. Children carried it to parched lips. Trance-like, she moved through this labyrinth of twisted limbs. She could not believe the stories coming out of Kandahar. If only half of them were true. Grandmothers attacking with bows and arrows. Hand to hand fighting with only a shovel to bash across a Russian face. Stones in the fists of children.

Annisa raised her hand and brushed at the gnats swarming around her head. She paused outside a small room adjacent to the main building--cement walls, a dirt floor covered with straw. Fresh bedrolls had been laid out for those patients coming from surgery. A former storehouse, the room had no windows, but if one left the door open at least there would be air. It would have to do--in all the disorder, one improvised.

"Annisa." Akmatcha was standing in the open doorway. "I've been looking for you. You have a visitor in the lobby."

"Me? A visitor?" Had Najib come at last? Her heart was beginning to race. "Who is it?"

"He did not tell me."

Annisa hurried towards the lobby, which was a regular beehive — people buzzing and swarming about—as if movement alone could tamp down their sense of panic. The citizens of Quetta were frightened. The spring assault by the Soviet troops in Afghanistan was more massive than had been expected. Rumors were rife. The major supply base of the Resistance in Paktia was in danger. In Kandahar, 125 miles to the northwest, there was hand-to-hand fighting in the streets.

To add to the tension in Quetta, there had been a spate of cross-border shelling by the Soviets. Six Pakistanis died. What if the Soviets decided to expand the war into Pakistan? Najibullah, the new puppet leader in Kabul, had strong ties with the border tribes. Only yesterday, the Paks had shot down an Afghan plane, which had dropped bombs across their border.

Annisa frantically searched the lobby for a familiar face, hoping against hope it would be Najib. In his message delivered to her at the hospital by a Mujahideen he had made no explanation of why he had left Kabul without her. Only that he was in Islamabad and that he was coming to Peshawar the first night of *Ramadan*. "This time you are not going to run away. There is no going back. We are one, Annisa-jan."

To see those words on paper had left her light-headed with joy. It was delicious and freeing.

And terrible. Because his message proved to be false. All through the holy month of Ramadan she had waited for him; preparing a meal for them to share each night after the white thread could no longer be distinguished from the black. But Najib never came to Peshawar nor did he send word explaining why.

Her ecstatic fervor had turned to hurt and disbelief. Over and over she returned to that night in Kabul--to the house of blue shutters, to that empty room where Najib had said he would wait for her to return with Yuri. Empty. Empty. Empty. He had left Kabul without her! Dazed, she had fled the city by stealing a bicycle, pedaling madly to leave behind the sound of a single gunshot embedded in her conscience. And, like a bird in flight that has forgotten how to stop migrating, she had returned to Jalalabad, where Fatima awaited the return of Omar. Fatima had not shared Annisa's adulation of Omar for shooting down the plane.

'His glory may leave me with four children to raise.'

An ugly quarrel followed when Annisa announced she was leaving for Peshawar to train as a paramedic.

"Ha. I wonder how long that will last. You never stick at anything. You are empty-headed and irresponsible." Fatima wanted to know who was going to provide for the children. Abdul was in America and Omar and Yuri had not come back.

"Yuri is dead."

"And my Omar?"

"I have no news of him."

"You ungrateful girl. You leave me to fend for myself."

Annisa did not answer but Fatima's words cut deep.

"You do not have the courage to take life as it comes. There is always something better for you just over the mountain."

It gnawed at Annisa that it might be true. To ease her self-doubts she left a share of the money she had received from Uncle Fritz in Kabul. It was more than enough to see Fatima through for several years.

When Annisa reached the far end of the hospital lobby her spirits sank. It was Abdul, standing by the window. The very sight of him made her want to flee. Even with his back to her, she could recognize the gloom that always weighed upon him.

"Abdul."

He spun around. It seemed forever, but it really was only a few minutes before he answered. "It has been a chore to get here," he grumbled.

"I thought you were still in America."

He gestured to his right leg. The operation had been successful and with the special shoe he wore, he could now walk like any other man. Did she want to see?

"Abdul, that's wonderful." She motioned to a bench where they could sit. "Fatima? The baby?"

"They are well. She has found a job."

"Fatima? Working?"

"As you know she is clever with a needle. They bring her pictures from magazines. She copies. She sews."

"And you?"

He pulled himself up taller. "In a few months I am to have special training on the 'Stinger' missiles. They are complicated to learn. I am one of the chosen!"

Annisa smiled. "Think how proud Omar will be to hear this."

"Omar knows."

"You have news of him!"

"Yes. Word came he was imprisoned in Kandahar. I went there. I saw him. I visited him in his cell."

"Omar alive!" Annisa's clasped her hands together. "Dear God. So many nights I have prayed for him. Did you tell him Yuri was dead?"

"No, and he never said his name. I think he knows Yuri is gone. There were many questions about you. Your work here at the hospital. He is glad for that."

"And did you tell him about us?"

"I didn't have to. He knows I would never allow a wife of mine to touch other men. That if she did I would perform the divorce ceremony of *bahshesang*."

"When Fatima sent word I couldn't believe it."

"Yes, you could. It is what we both wanted. Work is your master, not a husband."

Abdul reached into his money sack and began to count out bills... "Here, take this back. It was good of you to give this to Fatima but I am her protector now. You must learn not to be so generous. I fear you may end up an old woman begging by the side of the road."

She could see that he believed it. "You must not worry about me. I am learning a profession. I will be able to support myself."

"I pray that is true. At least you have courage to work in this place, with all this death."

Annisa was taken-back. Abdul had never praised her for anything.

"The Koran says, 'oh ye who believe. Give of the good things, which ye have earned' You do this for the sick. I admire you."

"But you were always so against my wanting to be a nurse."

"That was before I repeated *tu-ra tala-mejuman* three times in public. Now that we are divorced, my honor is no longer at stake."

He looked so stiff and uncomfortable as he said it, Annisa actually felt sorry for him. "Abdul, as you said, it was right for both of us."

"But it is not right for you to be alone. Fatima worries."

It was hard for Annisa to grasp this, remembering the many ugly scenes.

"Ah, I almost forgot." Abdul reached into his pocket to show her a page from a newspaper that had been folded and unfolded many times. "The newsman that was a friend of your fathers? Mr. Hardcastle. He has sent this to me." Abdul tapped the paper with his index finger. "My picture. Here. You should have been there, Annisa. The banquets. The applause. The cheers for the Resistance. I gave a speech about my shattered leg and how the Americans had fixed it. A great moment in my life."

She was incredulous. Surely Abdul's ego wasn't so out of proportion that he had come here just to show her a news clipping of himself? Then she remembered the money in her pocket he had returned and felt ashamed for thinking it. "This is a good picture of you. I am glad it was such a great moment." A small printed card fell to the floor from inside the clipping. Annisa bent over and picked it up. "You dropped this."

"It's for you."

She looked at the card with the name, Dr. Saul Rosenbloom printed on it.

"I met this man at a 'Friends of Afghanistan' banquet in New York. You can write to him at this address."

"Write to him? I don't know who he is."

"He was Rahmin's roommate in New York. He has a picture he wants to mail to you. A watercolor of your house in Shari-Nau. After Rahmin was killed this man sorted out his things."

"Abdul, you don't know how much this means to me. To have something that was Rahmin's."

"The man is a Jew."

"And?"

"He is a good Jew. He tells me there were no funds to bury Rahmin so his family paid-- even bought a stone for his grave."

"What a blessing! I was fearful my brother lay somewhere nameless, forgotten like my father."

"Well, let us hope the Jew buried Rahmin with his feet toward Mecca, so that on judgment Day he can sit up facing the Holy City."

"Did you visit the grave?"

369

"No, it's in a place called Poughkeepsie."

Abdul's mood suddenly changed and Annisa could see the storm clouds coming. "The newsman tells me you write to the American, Dr. Harris."

Annisa felt wary. "Yes? Ethan was a great help to me in getting me in the para-medics program here."

"Do you plan to marry him?"

"Who put such an idea in your head? Dr. Harris and I are just friends."

"You need a family. A husband to care for you."

She crossed her arms upon her chest as though to reinforce what she said. "I like what I do here."

He looked skeptical.

"Come with me, Abdul. I wish to show you something." Placing her hand upon the dirt streaked window of the lobby, she asked him to look outside. "See what I see." She gestured to a small Afghan boy who stood by a wheel chair on the hospital verandah. From the side, the boy looked like a stork. His torso rested on top of two long aluminum tubes attached to his hips and on the ends of his thin metal legs were two wooden feet. "These are my children, Abdul. All of them. I can spend a lifetime raising them."

"It is not enough."

"I am content."

"You are many things, Annisa. But never that." He paused, and Abdul, who was always so fierce, looked vulnerable and incredibly shy. "I too am to have a son."

Her eyes widened. "You?"

He smiled at her, a rare thing for Abdul. "The Americans can do almost anything but they are not God. No, it is an orphan boy. He was with Omar when he shot down the plane. His name is Akhmed. William Akhmed. He stays with his grandmother now. She is ill. Omar wants me to pick the boy up in Landi-Kotal. I will raise him as my own. I often think of little Habiba and all the love you gave her."

Annisa reached out and gently touched his arm. "It can change your life."

"But I have made this long journey here for *your* life. Here." He slipped an amulet into her palm. "This is for you."

Annisa stared at the green-colored stone. She felt uneasy.

"I give you this *ta'wiz,* this charm."

"What? Why?"

He told her that when they first left Doshi that he had gone to the shrine at Ashushkham and that he had bought the charm from a caretaker at the tomb. "He put a spell on it to give me control over you. I wish to give it back."

Annisa was shaken. She did not believe in evil charms. But to even think one had existed. This was too much, even from Abdul.

"I wish for you to forgive me."

Annisa heaved a very large sigh. "Abdul. I don't wish to feel blame. I try to be without superstitions, but it is not easy. I am grateful you came, but I need to return to my work now. There are so few of us, so many wounded."

"Your life should be more than this."

She could no longer check her impatience. "Everyone is always telling me what my life should be. My life is fine! It is full."

"Without Captain Duranni?"

Annisa froze.

"He told me you were to leave Kabul with him. You. Yuri. But the truck came early for him and they refused to wait. So he made the driver take him to your father's house. He pounded many times on the gate. The house was dark. The lights were out. No one came."

Annisa squeezed the amulet in her hand. She could hear the pounding now. And Yuri telling her not to answer it. She could feel the dark, kneeling on the kitchen floor. The smell of Yuri's blood. The agonizing wait and then the sound of her own footsteps were chasing her through the city streets, desperate to reach Najib and the house of blue shutters. His empty room.

"I told Captain Duranni he talked foolishness. That when you first reached Jalalabad you told Fatima you never went to Kabul at all. And later you said soldiers on the road outside Paghman killed Yuri. The message for the old German in Kabul could not be delivered."

Annisa's face reddened.

"Captain Duranni said I lied," Abdul sputtered. "I tell you the man was so full of you he hallucinates. He swore he spoke to you in Kabul. He came to the gate of your father's house and thought you had left with Yuri."

Annisa put her hands behind her back to hide the trembling. "When did he tell you this?"

"After I returned from America. They brought me to him. He was to make arrangements for me to meet with other groups to tell my story. All that time I thought he was interested in me only because my name was El-Ham. And questions about you! They never ceased. It's no secret to you. I always despised his very name. Now there is only sorrow. His fancy education. His big important office in Islamabad. It meant nothing."

"You saw him in Islamabad?"

"A great city, Annisa. Gleaming marble and glass buildings. Wide boulevards. Gardens of flowers. Many rich people," Abdul frowned. "I used to tell myself--here he sits behind this great desk of polished rosewood and talks on the phone to important people. And I, Abdul El-Ham, a great *buzkashi* player, must go back inside and fight."

Her answer was barely above a whisper. "Did you discuss me with Najib?"

"You rush my story. A terrible thing. His good friend, Baharunuddin, has told me. Baharunuddin works as his assistant--he's the one who was with me at the banquets in New York."

"Yes, yes." It was hard for Annisa not to be cross with Abdul's self-importance in the retelling.

"I was shocked. Najib confessed he wanted you for a wife. He said that he had spent months trying to track you down and that when he did he sent you a message he was coming to Peshawar to meet you at Ramadan and that I must give you a divorce."

She sucked in her breath. "When did he say this to you?"

"I told you. When they brought me to him after I returned from the States."

"But you had already divorced me!"

"It angered me to hear he wanted you. I told him you were going to America to marry the doctor."

"Abdul!"

He held up his hand. "I have tried to make amends. A promise to Allah. I prayed that if Omar was saved I would make it up to him. It was because of Allah's great gift that I went back to Islamabad after I saw Omar in prison. To confess the truth. But Captain Duranni had gone."

"No more, Abdul. Najib knew where I was. And never in a million years would he believe I was going to marry the doctor. There is no need for your anguish," she said bitterly.

"Why must you always rush my story?"

Her voice rose in anger. "Why come to me with it? You want forgiveness? I forgive. You want me to give thanks to you for Omar? I give thanks. No more, please. You have performed your good deed. No more about Najib Duranni or I will think you are here to torture me."

"He has left Islamabad for good, Annisa."

"Yes. To England, I'm sure." She wanted to shout, 'To a woman that can give him a son' but she did not want to give it credence by saying it outloud "Abdul. I must get back to the wounded."

"The woman is dead."

"Who? What are you talking about?"

"The English lady. Najib had this woman in London. Baharunuddin told me of this."

The room began to spin for Annisa.

"It was a terrible death. A car crash. They say she burned to death."

Annisa had gone the color of chalk; her head was reeling. None of this was true. Abdul couldn't possibly know what he was talking about. It couldn't have been Claire. Claire was from another world-- the lucky one. Claire had everything. She had Najib.

"Where is Najib now?"

"I am told he has gone to Paktia. That he fights like a madman. That he is daring death to come for him. That he no longer cares."

She could not stop shaking. "Yes, of course. His grief for Claire." She knew Najib too well. Memories of Claire would entrap him. From the grave she would rule.

Abdul reached out and tentatively touched her arm. "Annisa, I am not a bad man. I tell you this for you to understand. Najib will never come to Peshawar. You must not wait for him."

"He said this to you?"

"How could he? He was already in Paktia when I returned from seeing Omar. But the captain will never come for you and you must not go to him."

"You know nothing about him and you have no right to tell me what to do. Let go of me, you are hurting my arm." She wanted to pound the ground against the cruelty of fate. Instead she turned her rage onto Abdul. "Don't ever come here again! All this questions about the American. If you can't marry me off to an Afghan, you offer me off to a man you call an 'infidel.'"

"I am only trying to make amends."

"I hope you burn in hell."

"Annisa, all the evils of the world are not on my head."

373

His words just hung there—waiting for Annisa to acknowledge their truth. "Abdul, I'm sorry." She knew she had to get away. Air. She needed air. She gasped for it as she pushed her way through the lobby and entered the garden. Outside the first splatters of rain were beginning to settle the dust. Hurrying towards the burn patient on the stretcher, her heart sank when she saw an empty space.

"The boy died," Akmatcha said simply. "Don't look so distraught."

"I am not distraught."

"What a strange thing to say when there are tears on your cheeks."

"Go inside. See if there. . .see if we can move these men temporarily to the room without windows."

"It is already full."

"Damn. Damn it, Akmatcha. Damn."

He took her by the elbow and led her further into the garden. "The sky grows ever darker. See the flock of demoiselle cranes circling the courtyard. They are unable to break through the fog."

Annisa's hands were doubled into fists as she turned her eyes to the heavens. "Oh, no, it is starting to rain." There was panic in her voice. "Hurry, we must get the wounded inside."

"Calm yourself. There isn't room. These are only splatters. The heavens only tease us. It is like tiny drops of spittle. We will wait it out under the trees."

"No."

"Yes."

He took her by the hand and she followed, barely able to put one foot in front of another. "Akmatcha, there is nothing left of me."

"You have said this before."

"This time I mean it. I want to go to sleep and never wake up."

"Then you are human like the rest of us." He rummaged in his pocket for a piece of candy. "Want some?" It was rock hard. Lavender colored.

At the sight of it, Annisa began to sob with thoughts of Panna.

Akmatcha looked bewildered by Annisa's outburst. "What has happened?"

This sad, proud girl could not even bring herself to say it. For so long she had denied the enormity of her loss from this war. What she had done to Yuri had finally hit her full force. Najib had been the one knocking on the door on that dark night in Kabul--a knock which could have saved Yuri from his bloody fate and delivered her into the arms of her lover. The angel of deliverance was at her father's gate and she had not answered--too crippled by her fear. Fear had dictated her silence in that darkened kitchen. Fear killed life.

"I did a terrible wicked thing," she whispered.

"All of us have. It's the war."

"Do you realize we could have gotten help for Yuri. The men with Najib had a truck. If I had opened that door I could have had a life with Najib. Oh my God, I can't take this anymore. Yuri was my friend. I loved him. And Najib never came to Peshawar. He promised!" She began to wail like a frightened child.

Akmatcha felt helpless as he listened. He knew nothing of a Yuri or a Najib--Annisa always kept things to herself. But he did know that her cries came from a wound so deep that the sounds of it could make grown men weep. He dared not try to console her. Better he back off until this terrible agony was exorcised.

And then, not unlike a summer shower, her sobbing stopped abruptly "I must leave this place," she said. "I'm finished here. I'm finished with everything. I have no tears left in me. Do you hear?"

"Yes."

"Do you believe me?"

"No."

"Fatima was right about me. I am worthless. I no longer care about this war. . .or them." Her hand swept the rows of wounded on their bedrolls. "Listen to what I am saying. I don't care about them. I just want to get out. To get as far away from all of this as possible. Does that shock you?"

"No, I often feel the same way myself."

"So why are we here? Why do we do it? It's all so hopeless. There must be some way to escape."

"None. We can't escape ourselves."

"I've truly lost him. Claire is dead. It wasn't about sons. Najib only wanted her."

Akmatcha was fearful she was on the verge of a breakdown. And little wonder. Annisa drove herself day and night. He sighed. "Right now, you are not in harmony with yourself." He lifted a roll of gauze from an empty cot and tore off a piece. "Here, your nose is running."

"I should be ashamed. To weep in front of the wounded." She wiped her nose. "Why should my agony be so special? I need to accept my fate."

"Fate? There is none. I am a Modernist. The essence of Islam is not predetermined."

She shook her head. "You are wrong."

"No. Islam means 'submission,' but not blind submission to an already determined fate controlled by an impassive source. On the contrary, we submit to a way of life or essence only after careful examination. I think you have not yet found your way of life."

"Oh, shut up. You are full of words."

"True ones. This war goes on, Annisa. Maybe they settle it and maybe they don't. And the squabbling within the Resistance grows louder every day. You have no real power to change this. Your power is that you have endured."

Annisa did not answer him but she was thinking it was more than endurance. Much, much more. Panna believed that love was your sadhana, your highest achievement. "I have failed," Annisa murmured. "I do not know how to love." She looked to the distant mountains, to the empty space where the boy's stretcher had been and back to the mountains covered in a thin, gray veil. "Oh, look, the demoiselle cranes. They have found an opening in the cloud. They are flying away."

Akmatcha rubbed his chin, which had only a stubble of growth. "Annisa, what happened with that man you met in the lobby? I saw you run from him and now you are talking foolish."

"He said terrible things. - -That Najib will never come for me. You think he is right don't you."

"I know nothing of this Najib and if I did, it would not be for me to say."

"Is it wrong for me to go to Najib? Make him face the truth about us?"

He sighed. "I repeat. How should I know? You say this man broke his promise to you. If so, I think you should give the man *his* peace."

She looked down at the green stone Abdul had given her and which she still held in her palm. Then she pitched it with a vengeance into the dirt. "I am sick of the killing. I just want to live."

"Then why chase after this Najib if he doesn't want you?"

"What if I told you I killed a man who loved me. That I put a gun in his mouth and pulled the trigger. He was my friend, my brother. I will never see the gates of Paradise."

"Do you really believe this?"

"I don't know what I believe. I'm so tired. I want to forget this war. I wish I could start life all over. What would you think of me if I told you I want to be selfish? Not to care so much?"

"I would think it was part of your search."

"And would you think less of me if I were to go to America?"

He smiled. "Well, now, that is a different matter."

CHAPTER 34

If it had not been for a truck driver who volunteered to drive her to Talluqaan, Annisa would not have attempted it. Commander Massoud's headquarters was many days to the north.

Annisa was suspicious of the driver's intent when he refused to let her pay him and when he admitted that Talluqaan was 70 kilometers beyond his destination.

"Why do you do this for me?"

"Your father was good to my family."

"My father?"

"Are you not the daughter of Dr. Sulaiman Aziz who lived in Shari-Nau . . . Kabul?"

"How could *you* possibly know this?" She quickly realized how insensitive she was in saying it. Hazzars were rarely educated and had little contact with the professional class. Like beasts of burden, they pulled their heavy flat bed wagons through the busy city streets and were shunned by the Sunni majority. Sunni Muslims despised members of the Shi'ah sect.

"My name is Hussein and my brother was a *baccha* in your household for many years. That is how I know your father."

"Amir? Your brother was Amir!"

"Yes, and when the secret police took him away it was your father who came each month to our home and paid us his salary. Dr. Aziz pretended that Amir was coming back and that the money was only an advance. You are blessed. Your father was a very special man. I am grateful for this opportunity to repay his kindness."

Annisa was incredulous. "I'm amazed you recognized me. I was just a girl when they took Amir away."

"You haven't changed that much. But it is your eyes that convinced me." He hastened to add. "I hope this doesn't offend you, but they are unforgettable. Such an incredible green."

She smiled. "Than I am grateful for their color. Your offer to drive me is a great gift--I'm not sure I had the strength left to make the long trip on foot."

"On foot! All the way to Talluqaan? *Dewana.* That is crazy. Who is this Captain Duranni you seek? A god? Do you pay homage?"

She liked Hussein's sense of humor and was astonished how well spoken he was coming from his very limited background. "Did you go to university?" she asked.

"No. I had to leave school when I was eight. But your father always brought me books whenever he visited our house. I am self-taught. I study history and philosophy and, of course, religion."

"Good for you." Again, Annisa hesitated, hoping she hadn't sounded patronizing again. "I should be ashamed of myself. Here you are so eager to learn and I had an opportunity to study in America and I turned it down." Before she knew it she was confiding the terrible conflict within her to this stranger and she didn't know why. Was it because he had known her father, that she automatically trusted him?

The long trip north with Hussein proved an eye-opener for Annisa in other ways. She thought she knew all sides of the war but Hussein was to introduce her to yet another. He was embittered because the Hazzars had no voice within the resistance groups in Peshawar. "Our efforts have not been appreciated."

"It doesn't make sense. The Hazzars started the resistance in Kabul against the PDPA."

This pleased him. "Then you remember the July riots before the Russians invaded. I was part of it," he said proudly.

"Is that why the secret police took your brother away?"

"Yes, I can say that now."

"It isn't fair your people are not included in the decision making."

"When you have Mongolian features in Afghanistan, life is not fair."

"Then it's time we changed it."

Hussein smiled. The girl was not unlike her father. Without prejudice. "It's not only the Afghan Taxims who refuse to give us a voice in Peshawar, it is also the international leaders. Because we are Sh'iah's they think we have connections to Iran. They know so little about us. We want closer ties to the United States. We do not share the Iranian view of the West."

"But, we are all children of Islam and fighting a holy war."

He laughed. "There is an old saying, 'only foreign invaders can unite the Afghans.' I sometimes think religion is only a mask --it papers over the real reasons for our rebellion."

Annisa was aghast. "You believe such a thing?"

"I do. The Mujahideen use Islamic slogans and talk of the holy *Jihad*, but in the beginning the fighting had to do with local grievances. This was true in Pasawand and Herat and in the Chindawal section of Kabul. The war just took on an Islamic appearance because the Islamic parties controlled access to arms and supplies out of Peshawar. Think of it. In the beginning there were over 100 different resistance groups. It was the Paks who selected which ones would have a say. The Paks want us to be weak."

"If we don't fight for Islam, what do we fight for?"

"Unfortunately, the old ways. Our women."

Annisa stared at him in disbelief.

"I tell you it's true. The PDPA was out to destroy the economic underpinnings of the marriage relationship. No more brideprice by the groom to her family. No more forced marriages of young girls or making widows remarry close relatives. Unheard of! In Paktia, government interference in domestic relations was a far more important issue than land reform by the Communists."

"Marriage is sacred to Islam."

"I don't deny that. But the awful truth is that marriage in Afghanistan is also the exchange and control of women, an economic and political mechanism in the patriarchal kin system."

"You talk like a professor."

Hussein smiled. "I only parrot things your father said. He often stayed and read books to me aloud."

"Yes, he liked to do that."

"Sometimes we would discuss ideas. He strongly believed our tribal societies cannot tolerate interference when it comes to women and marriage."

Annisa sighed. "Each day I discover how little I knew about my father."

She turned her head from him and stared out the window. "Yes," she said softly. "I know this first hand. After my father's death, I was forced to marry my uncle if I were to stay with the family. We shared no love for each other."

"This Captain Duranni you seek?"

She blushed. "He is not my husband. . . Do you judge me for this?"

"No, but how could you be a modern girl if you give up a chance for schooling in America in search for a Mujahideen?"

"It doesn't make sense, does it?"

"Not to me. But then the source of a woman's love remains a mystery."

Annisa pointed to a pair of baby shoes tucked inside a jumble of paper flowers and tiny mirrors, which decorated the dashboard of his truck. "Do you have children?" she asked.

"No, I support the sons of my brother."

"And was his widow forced to marry you?"

"I would not ask it of her. I believe in the equality of women."

"So does the man I search for."

"Why does he not search for you?"

Tears welled in her eyes. "That is why I must see him. I must have an answer before I can be truly free."

Najib did not move when he saw Annisa enter Mujahideen headquarters. From the distance he gave her a scrutiny, a moment, then he raised his hand to acknowledge her.

"Yes, it's me," she whispered when she reached his side. It was painful for her to see his first glimmer of joy upon recognizing her fade rapidly from his face. He looked distressed.

"Why are you here?"

"I think you know why."

"Annisa, you shouldn't have come."

"I had to. My life depends upon an explanation."

"No, I don't want to hear this. Please, just go."

The finality in his voice was chilling.

Her lips quivered. "Do you realize how far I have come?"

Najib did not answer, motioning her to follow him outside instead. "This is no place to talk." His walk was brisk and purposeful and she had to scurry to keep up with him as he hurried through the gates of the Mujahideen compound and entered the winding bazaars. He did not look back once as he led her through a maze of bombed-out buildings to the edge of town.

"Najib, wait," she gasped as she watched him plunge down a steep embankment to a clump of trees and the river's edge. Her initial hurt was turning to anger. "Must you be so cruel?" she shouted.

"You are the cruel one-- coming here," he shouted back.

She half slid, half fell down the embankment and Najib made no move to help her up. "I thought you were at least a gentleman," she huffed as she brushed twigs and leaves from her clothes.

"What were you thinking of? Coming here? To take such a risk."

She mocked him. "Risk? You talk to *me* of risk!"

"An armored column from Kabul is moving up the Logar Valley, and another advancing from Jalalabad towards our bases just west of Parrot's Beak. We face some of the heaviest fighting in the war. You aren't safe here."

"So? Armored vehicles ring Kandahar—over one thousand Mujahideen are trapped. Enemy forces around Khost have moved against bases at Ali Khel and Zhawar—they are only a few kilometers from the Pakistan frontier. Show me a place that is safe and it will not be in Afghanistan. I am safe only when I am with you. In Kabul, I believed that. . ."

"I don't care what you believed in Kabul. I broke my promise to come to Peshawar. That should be your answer."

It was not what she had anticipated and his callous words stung her, lacerating any hope that he still cared.

"Don't force me to be harsh," he pleaded.

"There is something you aren't telling me," she accused. "I couldn't have been so wrong about what was between us."

"For God's sake, leave it alone."

"Najib, I am lost without you."

"I can't help that. Go home, Annisa. . .Please, please go home."

"Home? I have no home. I do not intend to spend the rest of my life in Peshawar."

"And yet you still refuse to go to America."

"You know that!" She stomped her foot in the wet leaves. "If I am nothing to you then why are you so aware of what I do and don't do?"

"Never mind."

"You are an arrogant... "

"Say what you want."

"How dare you dismiss me?"

"How dare you come here?"

"Because I promised in Kabul I'd never run away again. I didn't. I wanted you to know that."

"You've come all this way just to tell me this?"

"Yes. Yuri was wounded. He begged not to be taken alive. After you rapped on the door of my father's house I..." Her voice cracked and she dug her fingernails into her palms to keep from crying. "We didn't know it was you. We thought it was the KHAD."

Najib turned his head from her.

"I'm not leaving until you hear what happened. Najib, I killed him. I shot Yuri in the mouth."

"For God's sake. Must I know this?" He walked away from her to the river's edge.

She followed him. "When I rushed back to your room it was empty. I thought you had left without me."

He turned and faced her. "Then it happened for the best."

"I don't believe it. How can you say this? You told me you loved me. That you and. . .and Claire were over."

His face went white. "Don't ever mention her name to me again."

"Why? Does she rule you from the grave?"

With a sinking feeling she realized she had gone too far. She had never seen him so angry. "Najib, I have to speak of her. It's horrible when you want something too much. You have to know why you are rejected."

"Don't do this, Annisa. Where is your pride?"

"I have none. Don't you see I thought you had chosen her over me? Abdul came to Islamabad and they told him that. . .."

"Damn, you Annisa." He turned his back to her and stood staring out across the water at a small branch, floating on the current.

"I know it is wrong of me to be jealous of a memory."

"I forbid you to say one word more."

It was not the Najib she knew. The man whose tenderness had always sustained her. "I came here because there is no peace for me. You have to tell me in person you don't love me. That it was always *her*."

Najib slowly turned towards her but he avoided her eyes. "Annisa, it no longer matters. It just doesn't matter."

"Then I am a dunce. You said we were one." She began to weep.

Najib stood motionless. "We have no choice. We are finished. You must believe this."

"Never."

"God, what am I to do with you. It's over. It never happened."

"I won't go until you say you don't love me."

"Then you leave me no choice. I will have to take you back to Pakistan myself and put you on a plane for America. You are going to leave this part of the world."

She fought back an urge to scream. "Nothing changes. You have been saying this for five years. In my father's garden. In

383

Terri-Mengal. For my salvation you are always sending me to America. I'm a grown woman now. I refuse to go... Abdul lied to you. I am not in love with the American doctor."

"I never thought that. But Dr. Harris has promised me to look after you if you come to Washington. He is sending you papers to study for something they call the G.E.D. A diploma of sorts to get you into nursing school."

"The two of you have discussed me? How dare you! Am I a sack of grain? To be bartered. To be traded off. Hussein knew what he was talking about. Women in Afghanistan have no rights. We never will."

"Hussein? Who is Hussein?"

The hint of jealousy in his voice heartened her. "Hussein is a Hazara. He gave me a ride to Talluqaan in his truck. I confided in him the purpose of my journey."

"You discussed what is between us with a perfect stranger!"

She shook her head in disbelief. "What has happened to you? I have only to close my eyes to hear Abdul talking."

"I won't have you running around the country with an illiterate Hazara. Enough is enough!"

"You know nothing about this man."

"And you do? How *well* do you know him Annisa?"

"Oh, I see. At last you reveal what you really think of me."

"How could you know how I feel!" His agitation was a hopeful sign to her. He did care. She would not back down.

"I have lived by my wits since the war began. I am a freak and you know it. How many Afghan women have ever disguised themselves as boys and gone on raids with the Mujahideen? Or are you suddenly so overly protective of me because I am a fallen woman--succumbing to your charms in Kabul. Am I so wanton now that I must be protected from myself?"

"You must be protected from others who would harm you. It's not safe to be around me."

"Safe! There you go again. That word is laughable. When have you or I ever really worried about that? You make up stories in order to excuse the truth."

"Which is?"

"That I am still poor little Annisa. You took me because you pitied me. And in doing so you have created a monster--a woman obsessed who will dog your steps for the rest of your days. I was just an act of charity wasn't I!" Her eyes blazed.

With one swift movement he grabbed her by the shoulders and shook her roughly. "How dare you sully what was between us?" "How dare you reject it?"

"That settles it." Wearily, he released his grip on her. "I am taking you back to Peshawar. Tonight!"

"How can you leave your precious war?"

"I have business in Karrachi."

"You love this war, don't you. You love the action, the adventure."

"That's enough!" His voice was cold. "I can't believe you think this of me."

"You want to know what I really think. I think you use this war as an excuse because you're afraid. You're afraid to care that much for anyone."

"Then so be it. I am taking you back."

"And if I refuse to go?"

"You won't."

She hated him for his certainty. For his knowledge of her. That she would endure any insult just to be with him. The trip could take days, depending on the fighting. And she knew that he knew she was praying he would change his mind. That she could talk him into leaving this dirty war. That his desire would get the best of his intent. How else could she erase any memories of Claire? In Kabul he had said Claire was over. She had to believe this. Her self-respect would not allow her to accept anything less.

For the trip Najib confiscated a dilapidated sedan from one of Ghulam's men and their first day of travel was as painful to their backsides as the tension-filled silence was to their peace of mind. To avoid a roadblock, Najib had detoured through an empty riverbed--driving a bumpy and rutted path, which snaked between canyons of rock looming above their heads. Annisa experienced the majestic walls as stone gods-- sentinels, guarding their past. She knew she must hold herself together. This trip was her only chance. Several times she caught Najib glancing surreptitiously at her when he thought she was absorbed with the landscape. But still he said nothing, detaching himself, retreating into his own inner thoughts. She could sense his grim determination not to let her break through the wall he had erected between them. So she endured his silence by pretending he really was taking her out of Afghanistan because he wanted her out of harm's way and that the war really was her competition. Not memories of Claire.

They were still in the canyon when night fell without warning. A starless night, pitching them into a sinister blackness. Najib broke the silence. "I have no headlights. We will have to stop here."

Annisa's pulse raced as he opened the door and removed his bedroll. "You sleep in the back seat," he commanded. "I'll be on the ground outside. Here, take this." He handed her his woolen cape. "The nights are cold in the valley."

"I won't need it. I'm going to be with you."

"So help me God, if you don't stop this I'll strangle you."

"That would be less painful than what you are doing to me now."

The argument continued. "Annisa, can't you see what *you* are doing? You will make it impossible for me to say goodbye."

"Good. So you know my intent."

"Don't do this to me."

"Don't do this to *you!*" Waves of humiliation swept over her. How dare he destroy what had been so meaningful. She leapt from the car, coming at him in the darkness; beating her hands against his chest. "How can you deny life? The war has robbed us. You mock my father's words: Life is not for comfort; Life is for discovery."

"Stop it." He grabbed her hands and she struggled to be free of him.

"How much more do we have to give?" she shouted. "We have earned a little happiness."

"A little happiness can be deadly. I dare not risk it. Do you really believe I could just walk away from you again? You are the only one who has any meaning for me."

"Then why, Najib. Why?"

Slowly he released her hands. She must never know that Claire had been murdered because of him. If the drug-cartel assassins knew about Annisa she would be next for their list. "I want you safe, Annisa and you can never be with me. How can I make you understand?"

"You can't because I don't believe you. We have faced danger many times together and you never acted like this. Why? Why?"

He was clutching at straws. "You'll drive yourself crazy in this life with this constant wanting to know 'why.' Life just *is* Annisa."

"I don't believe it."

He didn't answer, wrestling with the urge to tell her the truth.

Annisa was staring at him. "What are you thinking?"

"That you are so young. Only eighteen…"

"Nineteen!"

"Eighteen. Much too young for me."

"Except when you made love to me in Kabul."

"I'm begging you, Annisa, let it be."

"You said in your letter, 'We are one,' Did you mean it?" He looked away.

"Did you?"

"Yes."

"I knew it!" She threw her arms around his neck, her lips searching his.

"No, Annisa." But retreat was no longer possible. Najib was drowning, spinning out of control in his hunger for her. He smothered her face with kisses as they dropped to the hard earth beneath their feet. The most omnipotent god of them all lay between them. The blackness dissolving into the warm light of desire. Longing. Fulfillment. Her yearning answering his thrust. Then peace. The gentle sleep of angels.

When dawn arrived it was blood red and the wind came up without warning. A storm was brewing. Heavy splatters of raindrops were upon them before they could reach the safety of the car. There was no going forward. Heavy rain pounded the windshield and without wipers they could not even see the hood of the car. Najib sat behind the wheel staring at the downpour.

"Do you hate me for last night?" she asked.

"Yes."

Her voice was calm. "I have promised myself. I will do what you want me to."

He turned and faced her unable to take his eyes off of her face. Her wet cheeks. Her radiance. Lingering flecks of joy in her eyes. How could he bring himself to say it. "Then you know this has to end when we reach Peshawar," he said. "It has to."

Her voice was barely above a whisper. "If you will it. The war has nothing to do with it, does it? It's because I cannot give you sons."

"God, no." He gathered her into his arms. "Annisa-jan, you must not even think it. You are all that is good in this wretched life. But I must keep you safe and you will never be safe if you stay with me."

"I don't want to be safe. I would rather. .."

He touched her lips with his fingertips. "Remember, your promise."

"Yes, and I will keep it."

Their last days of travel together were bittersweet. The scars of war were everywhere. Rusted tanks on the road--deserted villages. They traversed a landscape that was bruised and bleeding, but it could not dampen their passion. They were lost in a timeless bliss--a secret society which only lovers can share.

By the time they reached Peshawar, Annisa was convinced Najib would never leave Afghanistan and that she must. The war was over for her. Najib had willed himself to die and she was not certain why. This part of himself he held back from her and in doing so, he defeated her will to stay. She knew he loved her but she also felt the strength of his resolve. They were not to be together. Perhaps Akmatcha had been right when he had suggested that Najib might be in love with loss.

To compensate her desperate feelings of hopelessness over their impending good-byes, Annisa invented a game for herself. She would pretend that if the fighting ever ended and Najib survived that he would come for her in the West. It was a fragile thought, a tiny sliver of hope but it gave her the courage to call Ethan Harris when she returned to the hospital. She told Ethan she was ready to come to America. She was ready to begin a new life.

CHAPTER 35

Ethan Harris had mixed emotions about Annisa's arrival in the States. It was an overworked saying, but true: be careful what you wish for, it might arrive.

He had offered to help her come to America but hadn't anticipated she would decide to come so soon... Her decision had prompted a flurry of activity on his part. A student visa was needed and admission to the Fairfax nursing school had to be confirmed. Meanwhile she would have to study for a battery of tests.

Once again, he had made promises too easily in his eagerness to share his more than bountiful rewards in life. He knew he was no more worthy than any other man--just lucky to have been born with affluent parents in a country of free men. Ethan firmly believed that one must never go back on an offer, whether it was made impulsively or not. As a result, he often ended up inconveniencing himself.

And then there was the matter of Jan, his 'significant other.' Jan's anger had turned out to be more than an inconvenience. She was furious with the whole idea of Annisa coming. The process of getting Annisa there had not been that easy; it had been done with a terrible sense of urgency. Negotiations for Soviet troop withdrawal were part of the urgency because it was rumored that one of the agreements, which included the U.S., the Soviet Union, and Pakistan, would be for all outside aid to the rebels to stop and that Afghans in the refugee camps would be returned to Afghanistan. This might make it more difficult for Annisa to come to the States under political asylum. Jack Westerman, a name Annisa had given as someone who had offered to help, was no longer on the Afghan desk. He was in Rumania of all places. Ethan called Matthew Hardcastle who suggested that since Annisa had no living relatives in the States to sponsor her entry, had she considered the possibility of marriage? In fact, the newsman was pretty cavalier about the whole thing. People married for green cards all the time. The mere mention of this had put Ethan in a cold sweat in case Annisa thought he had offered that! He was grateful when Annisa balked at Hardcastle's suggestion. She announced she had spent too many years of her life pretending to be a wife in name only in order to please tradition and to satisfy Fatima. She was not about to do the same thing in order to please a government. America represented freedom to be herself for the first time in her life and if she came she was coming as exactly what she was--a free woman.

Another option was for her to come as a student, but she did not have the equivalent of a high school diploma and the only way to apply for college entrance was to take the GED equivalent. She could enter on a tourist's visa and take the test. Ethan mailed some manuals to Peshawar for Annisa to prepare for the examinations. She seemed exceptionally bright and he was confident she would pass. But another minor mutiny took place when he suggested that she apply for nursing school instead of pre-med. Stubborn as always, Annisa wrote to him that she was going to be a doctor like Rahmin or nothing else. Ethan assured her that was possible but it was a long way down the pike. Medical school was tough to get into. Rahmin could have told her that. In the meantime, a nursing degree was a plus. Nurses were in big demand worldwide. She had her certificate with the para-medics in Peshawar and he had connections at Fairfax hospital in suburban Virginia. Once she had her high-school equivalency degree, he would have no problem getting her into a nursing program.

The thing that wasn't clear to him was what had made her change her mind to come. She had always been so adamant that she would never leave her part of the world. Her sudden phone call to him in the middle of the night six months ago had taken him by surprise. And her reasons for wanting to come sounded suspect. Her voice was a little too bright and her enthusiasm a bit too forced.

To add to his confusion, the Annisa who stepped off the plane at Dulles Airport was no longer the haughty and sassy girl he had known in the mountains, nor was she the dedicated, somber and shy young woman he had visited in the makeshift hospital in Peshawar. This new Annisa was smiling and expansive and obviously awed with everything she saw. The first place she wanted to visit was an American supermarket and to placate her they stopped at one on the drive home from the airport.

"It's so incredible," she gushed.

This annoyed him. He caught her looking secretly at the other women as they pushed their baskets of bounty up and down gleaming aisles. Annisa was clearly interested in how they looked and he secretly wished she didn't try to imitate them. He would hate to see Annisa cover her natural beauty with make-up. He wanted to tell her this but dared not.

"There is so much to see," Annisa gasped. "I have heard of this but now that I am here. . ." She seemed particularly fascinated by the machine in the meat department, which automatically was sealing boneless chicken into polyethelene packages.

She smiled at him. "What is this?"

"Polyethelene. It's made from natural gas and oil."

"How wonderful. Can you imagine how just one store-- one of your supermarkets would look in Kabul? Everything here comes wrapped so beautifully."

What could she be thinking? How could she so easily adopt a faith in technology as the key to the best of all possible worlds--a world she had mocked in Afghanistan.

But his biggest surprise had to do with where Annisa agreed to stay. She had enough money for her tuition but housing was going to be tough. He had made the mistake of offering Annisa the room he used for a den in his apartment until other arrangements could be made. He was not prepared when Annisa did not balk over his half-hearted offer.

Jan did. Loudly. In fact, Jan went ballistic. Ethan lived in a two-bedroom high rise in Alexandria, Virginia, and Jan shared an apartment with two flight attendents on Connecticut Avenue in the District. Jan had a wonderful apartment-- high ceilings, close to the subway and overlooking the zoo. But that wasn't the real reason Jan had always refused to move in with him. She did not believe in living together before marriage. She might be old-fashioned but it had more to do with statistics--the numbers showed that couples who did so before marriage had a lesser chance of making it. Of course, none of this made her happy that the Afghan girl would be sharing his space, if only for awhile. After all, men were men.

In contrast, Annisa had done an about face on the customs of her culture. She was perfectly happy to accept his offer. She was coming to America to rid herself of the do's and don'ts of Islam. What went on behind closed doors between her and Ethan was between them. *They* knew they were just friends. If others objected, it was their problem. She was through with the tyranny of Fatima.

But the person who really didn't understand this arrangement was Ethan's father. It was a puzzle to him how Ethan could live under the same roof with a beautiful woman and on the weekends see his girlfriend. "It's not normal for a male and female to be under the same roof and not-- well, you know, son. What if you come home with a few drinks under your belt some night?"

"I have lots of friends who have female roommates-- nothing more. It's done all the time."

"Not in my generation."

"Dad, a lot of guys are wary about a live-in girl friend. Once you agree to that, she thinks she is there to stay."

"And you think this Afghan girl won't? I don't see how Jan puts up with you. Has she met the lady yet?"

"No, but I'm sure they will be friends. Besides this is only a temporary arrangement--until Annisa can get on her feet."

"The whole thing is ludicrous, but then you always were bringing home stray dogs and birds with broken wings as a kid."

"Annisa is not a stray dog. You and mom are going to love her. And she is drop-dead gorgeous!"

"Then if there is nothing going on between you, I worry about you, son."

Ethan had hung up the phone with a grin on his face over that one. It wasn't that he hadn't thought about it when he first made the offer. But her rebuff of him in Afghanistan had been pretty final. Annisa was Annisa. He was comfortable with the arrangement and who was Jan to tell him what he could do. As for Annisa she was focused on pursuing her education and learning about America. She was hell bent to savor the western world and at the same time save humanity in general. She also said a very strange thing. That she wanted to learn how to be sophisticated. How to use the right fork and how to laugh at a man's jokes. Did this have anything to do with the dead women she had considered her nemesis? He thought it worrisome that Annisa seemed fixated on Claire.

Contrary to what Ethan had anticipated or at least hoped for, Jan did not like Annisa. The usually effusive Jan had been cold and distant all through the dinner. Later she phoned him in tears. "I've had it. Either she goes or I split. I'm too old to compete with Miss Universe." He tried to reason with her but in a very deep spot he balked at her issuing an ultimatum and particularly in light of what all his buddies had told him for years. He and Jan had known each other since grade school. If it was taking him this long to make up his mind about a commitment, then perhaps the chemistry just wasn't there.

And then came his discovery of Annisa as she began to discover herself. Her enthusiasm for America, which he suspected she had talked herself into in the beginning, was suddenly very real. She was child-like and hungry to experience it all. It was fun to watch her reactions to new things. The proud and courageous woman he had known in their make-shift clinic at the top of a gorge in Afghanistan would not have spent hours in a bubble-bath whether it was available or not. Nor would she have refused to talk about the past. At times his conversations with Annisa seemed unreal; never anything of substance. Annisa loved old movies on television, Domino's pizza and the Washington Redskins football team. The time he took her to a game she created quite a stir with the fans in their section. She had no grasp of the way the game was played but she threw herself into the spirit full-force... Heads turned to see this exotic creature jumping up and down, waving her arms and yelling at the players in her native Farsi. Farsi was the language she used when she was truly excited.

There was nothing she didn't want to try. He took her to Williamsburg, Virginia for a first-hand American history lesson, but it was the near-by amusement park which got her attention, particularly the roller-coaster ride. She wanted to go again and again. Ethan literally had to drag her out of the fun house. And perhaps that said it all. Annisa was having fun for the very first time. Annisa was having a childhood.

Out of loyalty or perhaps habit, he made an attempt to patch it up with Jan but she remained adamant they not see each other for a while. She told him her strategy was to give him some time and space. And it surprised him how easily he went along with it.

It was to be a long weekend to see the fall foliage--yet another outing Ethan had planned in the education of Annisa about the wonders of her adopted land. Her joy in discovery had become contagious and he reveled in his role as guide, teacher, and the person who could make magic in her life.

Autumn's palette had outdone itself for their trip. Unusually heavy rainfall all summer had assured spectacular colors in the foliage. They traveled the Skyline Drive, skirting nature at her best; blinding sunlight bouncing off gold and crimson leaves with touches of flaming bright orange. Annisa was enthralled.

But the best Ethan had saved for last. He had made reservations in West Virginia at Lost River State Park, a rustic paradise with secluded log cabins up in the mountains, complete with a forest ranger who tipped his hat to you as he passed you on horseback and later brought you firewood.

As soon as they drove up in front of their cabin, Annisa leapt from the car. "It's like the houses in your cowboy movies. Ethan, I never want to leave. I want to live *here* ."

Both of them were heady with the smell of wood smoke after Ethan had stoked the fire. He had brought along champagne and her joy in discovering what the bubbles could do to you was exhilarating. She would run full speed down the hillside and then throw herself in a pile of leaves, rolling over and over. Together, they scooped great handfuls of leaves to toss at each other. At one point, Ethan pretended he was a bear coming out of the woods to get her and she had screeched with delight when he tackled her in the leaves.

For the first time since she had come to the States, Annisa mentioned her past. "Think how glorious it is to run through all this and not have to worry about stepping on a land mine." She pointed to the sky. "No planes to strafe us. I've never been so happy in my life."

It was curious that she never talked about Afghanistan. She showed no interest in the news reports and what was going on there. It didn't seem right that she could erase her past so completely.

That night they feasted on porterhouse steaks he cooked on the grill. With their busy schedules they rarely ate at home together--leaving notes for each other when the larder was empty. It was the first real meal he had ever prepared for her and Ethan had gone all out, phoning his mother for her recipe of mushrooms sautéed in wine and garlic with a touch of cream. He also made a special dressing for the salad and had picked up a chocolate cake from a gourmet deli in D.C. All this he had packed into the trunk of his car as a surprise. Annisa loved surprises.

The cabin was without a dishwasher so they played a family game invented before the machine destroyed togetherness--flipping dishtowels at each other's backsides and tossing newly dried plates to each other to be put away in cupboards.

Without television and the radio, they were left to their own entertainment. Ethan had brought playing cards and soon discovered Annisa loved 'slap jack.' She was so delighted with the game, she refused to go to bed until long after the fire had turned to embers. And when they did retire he kissed her good night on the forehead and they each trundled off to their separate rooms.

Morning came late, clear and cold. The weather had changed. The wind was stripping the trees. But after a hearty breakfast, there was no stopping Annisa. She wanted to go for the hike he had promised.

She talked the entire way. Her cheeks were pink from the nip in the air and when she reached over and grabbed his hand, swinging it as they walked, her fingers were cold to the touch. Many things she had to say he had never heard before. Stories about her and Rahmin. But stories only about her life before the war; she had been a very happy girl. When they reached a stream with a tiny bridge to cross, she wanted to go in the water.

"You're kidding of course. It's like ice."

"I know. But let's do it anyway."

Before he could protest further, she had yanked off her sweater and was undoing the belt in her jeans. "Don't be insane."

"Try and stop me."

What possessed her? Annisa, the girl who dressed in a clothes closet, who refused to wear shorts in the humid summer months of Washington, had stripped to her pants and bra. Stunned to the point of near paralysis, he watched her race towards the narrow stream. Her squeals of rapture must have gotten the attention of all the living creatures in the park. "Don't go too far out," he cautioned from the embankment.

"Why? Come on in."

"Your lips are blue. Enough already."

She laughed and shook her head, diving under the water. "Annisa, come back here." He was suddenly in a panic waiting to see where she would pop the surface. "Annisa? Annisa?"

"Over here." She waved from the opposite shoreline. "Come and get me."

"No."

"Chicken, you can use the bridge."

"Get back here. Now!"

"Okay, Okay. You're no fun at all." She re-entered the stream, keeping her head above the water as she dog-paddled. "You look terrified! Watch this." She stood up, her wet undergarments clinging to her. "It's not even over my head."

He watched her wade waist deep towards him. Shaken, but filled with relief, he turned away.

"I never knew you were such a prude" she said, her flesh covered with goose bumps as she hastily donned her clothes.

"I'm going to race you back to the cabin," he said. "You could catch pneumonia over this little stunt."

She gave him an impish grin and took off ahead of him. He could feel his lungs burning as he chased after her. The girl ran like a gazelle!

She was out of breath and laughing when she reached the front stoop. "You let me win, now didn't you?"

"I wish. Get inside. We've got to get you into a warm bath."

"Don't be so bossy. You used to nag me about being too serious about life. And now you act like you witnessed a death down by the stream."

Ethan was shaken but said nothing as he opened the bathroom door and began to run the hot water.

"Don't be cross. I was only having fun."

"I know. I'm just not used to you being a tease."

The extent of her brashness suddenly dawned on her. "Sorry, I've been acting stupid." She closed the door gently behind her.

But was she sorry? He could hear her singing in the tub.

Afterwards, he had wrapped her in warm blankets and carried her to the sofa before the roaring fire he had built in the fireplace. "What you need is hot coffee."

"I'm sorry I upset you back at the stream."

He brought the steaming cup of coffee to her and insisted she drink it.

"You should have gone in; it was glorious. My body is tingling all over."

"I don't like to swim."

"I thought every red-blooded American boy liked. . ."

"There was an accident, Annisa, a long time ago."

"What happened?"

He stared at her. Her wet hair was wrapped in a towel and he fantasized unwinding it and running his fingers through its dampness. "Never mind. It's best left unsaid."

She was suddenly angry. "But it's okay for me to spill my dirty secrets out to you. You know everything about me. Rape. Venereal disease. The fact that I killed Yuri and he was my friend."

"It was the only thing you could do for him. And don't use the word 'dirty' to me about your secrets."

"Why not?"

"It's stupid and degrading."

"So then tell me. What accident?"

Ethan frowned. "It's hard to talk about."

"No need to tell *me* that. Remember, you are the one who always preaches not to keep things in."

"My baby sister, Melissa. We were on Cape Cod. I was supposed to be watching her. I left her for only a minute. Went inside the house to get some more glue for my model airplane. When I came back, she was gone. Under the waves."

"That's terrible. How old were you?"

"Nine. I was nine. My folks never talked about it. I'm sure they were only trying to protect me. But after her funeral, it was never mentioned. Her photographs on the piano were put away. It was as though she had never existed."

The room went silent except for the hissing of the burning logs.

"When I lost sight of you in that stream--I was suddenly back there. That empty beach. Shouting for Melissa."

"I'm glad you told me this. It makes me understand why it's so important for you to rescue me."

"I think there is more to my feelings about you than that."

She looked away. "I know this... Ethan, I live with ghosts. They come between us and always will. When I said goodbye to Najib in Peshawar I secretly wished he would come for me if the war ever ended."

"You've told me this."

"What I haven't told you is that yesterday I heard that Najib has left Afghanistan and is living in Paris. His ex-wife is there too."

"I very much doubt if he is back with her."

"But don't you see. For so long I used the war as an excuse for why he didn't want me. And today I used you. I tried to make something happen."

He nodded.

"And it wasn't real. It was an act and you knew it. Can you forgive me?"

"I'm almost relieved. I didn't know where you were coming from."

"Ethan, I'm so miserable. Why would he go to Paris?"

"Maybe he wants to live on the left bank and pretend it's the 20's. That watercolor of your father's house is pretty damned good. After all the shit he's been through it might be the only thing he wants to do."

"Najib is more serious than that. He always was so full of plans on how to get the tribes to unite once the Russians were out."

"If he believed that then he's probably hung himself in some attic loft. They say the war is winding down but they are never going to solve that mess. Sorry to be so blunt, my lady, but that's reality."

Her face crumpled and she looked so forlorn it left a lump in his throat. It was not unlike the night he had seen her in Mabaie's tent. "Annisa, what can I do to help?"

"Help me to forget Najib."

"No, I'm not taking that on. Maybe you should see a shrink. This is some kind of sickness with you. The man is out of your life."

It was as though she never heard him. "I knew I could never be as worldly as Claire. But I've tried. I've really tried."

"People love you for you. Not some poor imitation of ... of I don't know what."

"Don't you see? I will always be second best to Najib. Just like America was always second-best to me."

"And is it now?"

Her silence was his answer.

CHAPTER 36

Annisa had never experienced the American holiday of Thanksgiving. Ethan was going to his parents home in Boston. Why didn't she come, too?
The meaning of Thanksgiving delighted her. The ritual of giving thanks. To be grateful to God for his bountiful harvest. America had so much--she hardly knew where to start.
Ethan talked so fondly of his family she was looking forward with particular pleasure to staying with them. "Just don't let them overwhelm you," Ethan warned. "Thanksgiving dinner at our house is a great cast of characters in search of a plot. It's organized mayhem. My nephews and nieces usually hold the adults hostage."
"Hostage? I don't understand."
"You can't really carry on a sane conversation when they are around. It's easier to give up and let them dominate the day."
They arrived by train early Wednesday evening and took a taxi to what looked like a castle to Annisa. "You live here?" she gasped as they entered the circular driveway.
Ethan laughed. "Not too shabby, huh?"
"It overwhelms me."
There was a great shaking of hands in the foyer and a flurry about the luggage. Ethan's mother, a pencil slim lady with silver streaks in her hair rushed them up the stairs. "Sorry, dears, but you haven't much time to change. We are giving a little cocktail party to introduce Annisa."
Ethan groaned. "Mother's little cocktail parties could fill a football stadium."
Annisa was ushered to a room that was all in blue: the carpet, the walls, the curtains and the bedding—-even the porcelain drawer pulls on the dresser.
"Call me if you need me," his mother trilled. "I'm so delighted you are here." The many bracelets on her arm made a jingling sound as she closed the door behind her.
There was no reason for Annisa to suspect that his mother wasn't delighted. And yet?
She opened her suitcase feeling a bit apprehensive. She had only brought one dress-up dress because that was all that she had. Ethan had told her the weekend would be mostly blue jeans and

sweaters. "You know, rough-house stuff with my nephews and the traditional family touch-football game."

She kicked off her shoes and walked barefoot through the plush carpet, wiggling her toes. If she lived in a house like this she would never again wear shoes.

Nobody was downstairs except Ethan's father when she descended the staircase. He held up his drink and gave her a wink. "Now here comes my kind of woman. Beautiful and on time. There is nothing worse than waiting for a woman to get dressed."

Annisa smiled, beginning to feel confident and comfortable in her sea green dress, which Ethan had helped her pick out. She had twisted her long hair into a French knot and the only make-up she wore was a raspberry lipstick.

"Your eyes match your dress. I guarantee the clan is going to love you."

She soon began to think that they did. They arrived in drips and drabs: an assortment of all ages. Ethan's maternal grandmother, his brothers and their families and too many cousins and old family friends to count.

Annisa basked in their warmth, their interest in what she had to say. She was treated like a princess, showered with invitations to show her Boston and paraded around for all their friends to meet. Wasn't she beautiful? And wasn't her story amazing? Escape from the Russians through the Khyber Pass. Her father had been an eminent poet. It was all so romantic -- Ethan meeting her while operating on the rebel forces up in the caves! "She even took part in raids by the freedom fighters," his mother gushed. "Our Annisa is a modern day 'Belle Starr.'"

Ethan and Annisa exchanged amused and knowing looks during his mother's monologues. It was a game they played: the world they had shared and what they revealed to others.

"Who is this Belle Starr?" Annisa whispered

He grinned. "A beautiful bandit in the old West. She rode with a band of outlaws. Maybe we should make a movie about you?"

"I'm kind of a joke, aren't I."

"No, you are the most interesting thing that has happened to this family. You dazzle them."

Annisa wanted to believe it. Ethan's parents couldn't have been nicer. That was the trouble, too nice. Ethan's brother Eric was particularly interested in what she had to say about Afghanistan. He was all for supporting the Afghans and felt he had made his small contribution by losing out on his chance to get an Olympic medal.

"I try not to think much about the war anymore. I don't keep up on what's going on over there," she said.

"Isn't that a little hard to do after being so passionately involved?"

Annisa shook her head. "War soon takes the passion out of you. You learn not to care too much about anyone because you are afraid they will disappear."

Ethan's mother raised her eyebrows. "How sad. I mean, you know, not to care about others."

"Well, I hear that the tide is turning." Ethan's father interjected. "That Moscow is bogged down in a no-win conflict. It may be their Vietnam. Your people may drive them out yet. Wouldn't that be something."

"Yes. But even if we do my country is finished. Evil men are standing in the wings. It's best not to get your hopes up."

His father, a man with rather bland features and unexpressive mannerisms, appeared upset by her answer. "That's hard for me to accept. In this family there is always hope. I've taught my children that there is nothing else but 'winning.'"

"Right, you have, Dad." Ethan had Annisa by the elbow and whisked her away. "Don't give that any attention. His bark is always worse than his bite."

"I'm not upset, Ethan. What he said is true. I am a quitter and it's hard for me to accept it too."

Thanksgiving morning was cold and brisk with a burst of sunshine.

"A glorious day, Annisa," Ethan's father greeted her at the breakfast table. He seemed in high spirits and she was relieved that nothing between them seemed to have changed.

"I'm thankful to be with your wonderful family on your day of thanks," she told him. And she was. Everything seemed so ideal. The smell of turkey roasting in the oven and pumpkins pies lined up on the countertop waiting to be served. His mother flying about the kitchen, chirping merrily because her family was back in the nest. She asked Annisa if she would like to peel the potatoes? She would. And would Eric mind running out for some more cream? The convenience store would still be open.

"I'll go, Mom," Ethan volunteered. "Eric wants to take grandma Gilchrist for a drive in his new Porsche."

"He's such a show-off with that car," Eric's wife joked.

"Is your brother very rich?" Annisa asked Ethan.

"Very. An investment banker. You should see his office at the World Trade center. Over l00 stories up. An incredible view."

Eric's wife, who was washing the cranberries, was evidently not so impressed. "The higher you rise, the harder you fall. Eric would trade the Porsche in a minute for more time with his family."

Annisa was tempted to say, "Then why doesn't he?" But she thought better of it. After all, she was in the presence of a family that believed 'winning' was everything.

As the day progressed something didn't feel right to Annisa. She didn't understand why until late that night she overheard a conversation in the kitchen between Ethan and his father. She had gone down for a mid-night glass of milk. From the bottom rung of the stairs she could hear loud voices in the kitchen.

"Son, your mother--well, we both wonder if you see how impossible this relationship is?"

"But I told you it isn't what you think."

"Hear me out. I'm not talking different countries, different religions. I'm talking scar tissue. Annisa is so young to have witnessed all that violence. Christ, her whole family is dead. She'll never be able to adjust. You heard her the other night. What kind of outlook on life is that?"

"Survivors of the holocaust seem to have managed."

"It's common knowledge they never get over the guilt for having survived. You told me yourself--the girl has violent nightmares."

"Wouldn't you?"

"You say she has big mood swings. Is this something like that post traumatic stress syndrome everyone talks about? Think of the burden you are taking on."

"Dad, you aren't tracking."

"Your mother and I want to know how long this 'playing house' together is going to last? When are you going to jettison her? The longer you wait the harder it's going to be for her. Your mother is afraid that girl already has her hooks in you."

In her darkened corner of the steps, Annisa recoiled.

The easy-going and affable Ethan exploded. "Whatever happened to the father I grew up with?"

"I only want what's best for you."

"Give me a break. I'm 32 years old. Enough already."

"That's my message to you. Enough is enough is enough. How many months has she been living with you? Haven't you ever heard of the word propinquity? You could so easily slide into a marriage with this girl before you knew it was happening."

Ethan's tone was defiant. "Would that be such a tragedy? Annisa is beautiful, intelligent. Full of wonderment and joy. Exciting. And she makes me happy to be around her."

"I see that. But by your own admission she is not very stable."

Annisa sucked in her breath.

"I never said that."

"You said you worry she doesn't seem to want to have anything to do with her own countrymen over here."

"Let's be fair. That was right after she first came. I couldn't understand why she wanted to forget Afghanistan after all those years of involvement. Pretend it never existed? Perhaps it was superstition, fearing if she thought about her past she would lose the present. She's told me over and over that she came here to fit into our culture and that she can't be both places at once."

"My point precisely."

"Well, I've changed my thinking on that. First, she has to get over that feeling that she doesn't quite fit--that she will never fit anywhere again. I pushed her to socialize with some of the Afghan exiles living in the D.C. area but it didn't work. Single girls her age still live with their families. They may not wear the veil but they are definitely under the thumb of their parents, who are terrified they will become too westernized. We found that out the night I took Annisa to a banquet organized by the 'Friends of Afghanistan.'"

"What's that?"

"A mixed bag of local Afghans and Westerners who have lived over there. State Department, UNESCO--some former Peace Corps volunteers. Annisa got snubbed and pretty badly by some of her own people. In fact, a girl by the name of Mira that she had known in Kabul before the war was not allowed to speak to her."

"I thought you said these people were educated and enlightened?"

"All of that. And to be admired. Mira's father is a man of great dignity--a former Afghan diplomat who supports his family by working as a cook in a restaurant in suburban Virginia. Mira's brothers wait table. But not Mira and whenever Mira has to go somewhere she needs a chaperone--one of her brothers takes off work to accompany her."

"What must they think! Annisa living with you. I told you, son. People aren't used to this."

"Yes, people can be incredibly cruel. It took just one rebuff by them to throw Annisa. She left the banquet in tears, convinced that her long years in the mountains make it impossible for her to socialize with her own people over here. Let's face it. It was mainly the elite who had the money to get out. Annisa had bad luck --lost on her way out and was forced to live with relatives she had never seen before--a different class than the one she was raised in."

"The more you talk, the worse it sounds."

"To you perhaps. As I see it, the only real problem for Annisa was the shock that she identified more with the Westerners at that party than her own fellow exiles."

"That girl could use some therapy."

"Yeah, but who couldn't. I'll tell you one thing--she's stronger than I am. I could never have gone through what Annisa has."

"That's my point exactly."

"I give up. You just don't get it, Dad."

"But I do and for you to 'give up' on what I have to say is taking the easy way out. Those people over there are just too different from us. I've heard they will tattoo a women's breast with a tribal property symbol. The same tattoo they would put on their camel or their horse. Is that true?"

Ethan was livid. "What is this? A trick question? Am I familiar with Annisa's breasts?"

"I'm only trying to point out how impossible this whole thing is. I'm ashamed of the way you've acted. . . The way you've treated Jan."

"Leave Jan out of this."

"For years, both of our families expected you children to marry."

"That's the trouble. Everything was always so planned."

Annisa felt her heart drumming in her chest. She had not fully understood the extent of his relationship with Jan. Ethan had assured her that his break-up with his old girlfriend had nothing to do with their friendship. Had she destroyed it for him?

"Dad, you've got to let go of thinking you can save me or anyone else from the rough spots in life."

"All parents try to do that. All we want is what is best for you."

"And happy isn't good enough?"

"I'm talking about the future. Wait until you're my age. The long view. This enthralling creature you are investing so much of your time and energy in will get old and wrinkled like the rest of us. And will she still be such good company? Right now everything is still new to her. What happens when the excitement wears off?"

"Look, Dad, we share a lot. Annisa is working for a nursing degree. She understands what I do."

"Well, frankly I've never wanted to sleep with my fellow lawyers. It's nice to have pillow-talk about something other than your work."

"Damn! You haven't heard a word I've said. Annisa and I are not sleeping together. And more to the point, you have no crystal ball as to whether that is wise or not. There are no guarantees."

"I think Annisa's culture would disagree with you. I have to hand it to those people. There is something to be said for ritual. Continuity. Separate roles for women and men."

"Too separate. It's a double-edged sword. The first time I went over there--a woman died in childbirth in the refugee camp. It didn't have to happen. It was because that damn culture doesn't believe a man should touch her--even if he is a doctor and wants to save her life."

"You still do want to save her. Look at you now. On a rescue mission to save some waif from Afghanistan."

"Fuck it. I can't believe I'm hearing this."

His father let out a very long sigh, which was followed by an eerie silence. "Sorry. It's not like me to talk like this. You know that--it's just that your mother is so upset about the ring . . ."

"Ring?"

"My mother's ring... The one Annisa is wearing. Your grandmother put in her will it was to go to your bride."

"Jan never liked it. Said it was too old-fashioned. So I gave it to Annisa. The poor kid has never had any jewelry of her own--only a locket some French woman doctor gave her and it was stolen right off her neck in one of the camps. I guess I was trying to make it up to her. It's a ring of friendship, Dad. That's all."

"But it was your grandmother's. It was intended for Jan."

"I thought it was mine to do with as I wanted."

On the darkened steps, Annisa sat humiliated and ashamed, twisting the diamond around and around on her finger. She had no business with this. Ethan had never said it was his grandmother's.

Their voices in the kitchen had raised another a notch. "Dad, you have got to let go of the old ways. People live together and don't get married these days. We are headed into the 21st century."

His father sighed again. "Without a rudder, I might add."

Annisa did not want to hear anymore. She tiptoed up the stairs and back to the guestroom with its canopy bed and the crystal perfume bottles tinted blue that lined the dresser. It was a beautiful room, but she now saw it as ugly. She didn't belong here either. Dejected, she laid her head on the satiny pillow and stared into the darkness, unblinking, feeling too numb to cry. Ethan must never know she had overheard the conversation. He always tried so hard to please her. Suddenly, she sat up and threw her legs over the side of the bed as though she had to take action. And now. To leave this house this very minute. Instead, she just sat there, her feet dangling over the side--the bed was so high her feet didn't touch the floor. This was what was wrong with her life in America. Her feet hadn't yet touched the floor. She was still a bird in flight. What could ever hold her? Her life had become a retreat from reality. As soon as they returned to Virginia she would come up with a good excuse for her sudden decision to move out of Ethan's apartment. His father was right. Enough was enough. It was time she left Ethan's safety net. But how? Ethan was her friend, her protector in a culture still so new to her. Ethan knew all her fears. It would be hard to hide from him the pain she had just experienced. The realization that America could never be her home. And if not, where was it? Where could she go?

1989

CHAPTER 37

On February 25, 1989, the last Russian troops pulled out of Afghanistan. Annisa was elated. Of course, it didn't mean the fighting was over. President Najibullah, an Afghan puppet of the Russians, was still in control and it would take a big push by the Mujahideen to overthrow him.

To celebrate this auspicious occasion, a dozen long-stem roses arrived at Annisia's bedsitter in Arlington, Virginia. The enclosed card from Ethan simply read: "David beat Goliath with his sling shot. Let the good times roll!"

She was tempted to give him a call but decided against it. Their parting had been amiable and in retrospect, judicious. Less than a year after she had moved out of Ethan's apartment, he announced his engagement to level headed Jan. Annisa was keeping her distance from that relationship.

Feeling nostalgic for the friendship they had shared, she arranged the roses in a vase and then sat down to admire them. No one had ever sent her roses! She played with his grandmother's ring -- twisting and turning it on her finger. Despite her vehement protests, Ethan had refused to take it back, insisting the ring might prove to be a safety net. "The way you bungie jump through life you never know where you might land. Don't forget, 'Diamonds are a girl's best friend.'" Ethan also found it amusing that she thought his grandmother wouldn't approve of her keeping the ring. "Grandma Harris was a bit of a bungie jumper herself. Always marching for something. Civil rights. Vietnam. You would have loved her. You two are very much alike."

The ring took on a life of its own for Annisa after that. She vowed never to part from it, but if she did, it would have to be for a very important reason.

It seemed ironic that Ethan saw her as a risk taker. If only he knew how subdued she had become when he was not around. She thrived on her work but there was another part of her life where she felt overwhelmed by America. Socially she was as handicapped as those patients who needed new limbs in the hospital's orthopedic ward. Her attempts to be a part of the singles scene were feeble at best. She was included by her fellow students in their birthday celebrations and invited to TGIF (Thank God Its Friday) parties. Friday was her Holy Day and even though she never went to the mosque, not to do so felt uncomfortable. Singles bars filled with cigarette smoke and music that could split your eardrums did not appeal to her. Reluctant to join in the inane conversation of the mating game. she preferred to sit on the side-lines and watch. And she always went home alone. 'Lighten up, Annisa,' others told her more than once... There were times when she had been tempted to call Ethan and confess she was a misfit. But she never did. She knew it made him happy when he thought *she* was happy. So she had continued to pretend. Last Christmas he had given her a T-shirt which read, 'Plays Well With Others.' She never told him that it hurt her feelings—-that it was too close to the bone.

She hated to admit even to herself how much she missed him. Life without Ethan seemed harsher. Drab. He could always make things happen.

At that moment her phone began to ring as if to prove her point. It was Ethan on the line. Did she feel like celebrating now that the Russians had left Afghanistan? He had two tickets to a Washington Bullets basketball game. Jan was out of town. He thought Annisa should have some company on such an auspicious occasion.

"Ethan the roses were beautiful. I've never had roses." She felt embarrassed to admit it.

"What's wrong with the men in this town! So how *is* your love life?"

"It doesn't exist. I actually met a man who told me that by jumping into bed straight away you save time by sorting out who you want to invest in. It almost like pinching melons in the market."

Ethan laughed. "What else from a nation of consumers. You've seen our bumper stickers. 'Shop 'til you drop.'"

"Thank God, you aren't that way —at least, you never were with me."

His answer was slow in coming. "Off the record, there are times when I regret that."

She didn't respond, afraid to go there.

"Hey, are you still on the line?"

"Yes."

"Look, it was rude of me to bring this up. Your love life is none of my business. About the Bullets game. . ."

"I'm a big disappointment, aren't I?"

"Hold on. I didn't say that."

"No, I did. I know I'm a misfit, Ethan."

"In what way?"

409

She didn't want to admit the real truth—she felt a failure as a woman. "I guess it's working so hard towards a goal and now that I'm about to graduate I feel so let down. I foolishly expected life to be different."

"Don't we all...Now about those tickets to the Bullets, can I twist your arm?"

"I wouldn't be good company."

"Not true."

"I love you for thinking of me. It means a lot...I miss you."

"Yeah, me too. Twice as much."

Yet the conversation ended shortly after that.

Annisa chastised herself. Such an ingrate. All the wonderful things Ethan had done for her. She must have sounded ridiculous. What was wrong with her? She should be happy. In three more months she would complete her nursing degree. Her admission to nurse's school had been conditional on her academic performance and she would be graduating with honors. So why was she suddenly feeling depressed? Her supervisor had assured her that she would have no problem finding a good job—in fact, she already had been interviewed for a job with the Montgomery County Maryland Health services in one of the most affluent counties in the States. In many ways it was an ideal job—good pay and reasonable hours. But it was primarily paper work. It wouldn't give her that part of nursing that she enjoyed the most. Her greatest interest in school had been the practical work assisting in a hospital. A hands-on contact with the patients. Recently she had spent some time with the amputees on the orthopedic floor and she was very enthusiastic about what she saw. Western prosthetics were very well made, natural looking and light and there were specialists to fit them properly. If she had one wish in life it would be for maimed Afghan children to have access to the same medical treatment. It was hard not to be awed by all the wonderful equipment and the facilities American hospitals had to offer. With special springs in artificial feet, some amputees could even participate in sports. The hospital she had worked in outside Peshawar was in dire need of some modern prosthetics. How could she go about getting some charitable organizations interested in donating some?

She wrestled with that question all the next week at the hospital... It would take some boldness on her part, but she decided she would approach Dr. John Hammond, the chief of orthopedic surgery. Dr. Hammond was a powerful figure in the hierarchy of the hospital. If only she could enlist his help!

Much to her surprise, this busy and important surgeon agreed to meet with her to discuss her plan.

"Are you on duty, tonight?" he asked.

"Until ten."

"Meet me in the staff lounge after I've made my rounds. I'll buy you a cup of coffee."

"I can't tell you how much I appreciate this, doctor."

"No problem. You make a very good case for your cause."

Annisa was flattered and shared her excitement with Marge Larson, a fellow nurse at her station.

"Not too swift on your part," Marge Larson said.

"Swift?"

"There isn't a nurse on this floor that old lecher hasn't tried to put the make on. He's always trying to cop a feel. Backed me into the corner of the linen closet one night."

Annisa was wide-eyed. "You can't possibly mean Dr. Hammond. He's never acted that way towards me."

"Have you ever been alone with him?"

"Yes...no, not really... He seems so dignified and isn't he married?"

"Oh, yes. And a grandfather."

"Marge, he could be of real help."

"True, but... Look, I don't want to hurt your feelings but you are just a bit naïve when it comes to men."

Annisa did not want to sound defensive but she said it anyway. "I lived for years in the middle of a war. Believe me, I've seen their dark side."

Marge shrugged. "Have it your way but watch your backside with Dr. Hammond. Don't say I didn't warn you."

The staff lounge was located in the basement at the far end of the hall directly across from the cafeteria. Hot food service was closed for the night but one could get sandwiches and beverages from the vending machines. Dr. Hammond was seated at a lounge table with two Styrofoam coffee cups before him. He smiled when Annisa entered.

"Am I late?"

"No, right on time. Do you take cream or sugar?"

"No, and thank you."

She was shy at first, feeling a bit intimidated by what Marge had said and by Hammond's commanding presence. But

411

there was nothing out of line on his part during the conversation. Annisa felt at ease. There was no reason to fear him. He was the perfect gentleman and all business and he seemed genuinely interested in her plans. He was going to see what he could do. He'd make some phone calls. It was hard for Annisa to understand why he had such a terrible reputation with the nurses. Had Marge exaggerated her story?

"Can I give you a lift home?" he asked.

"Thanks anyway. But the ride-on bus delivers me right to the front of my apartment building."

"It's raining outside. I insist."

She hesitated, but only for a moment. Dr. Hammond had been generous with his time so she accepted his offer. They walked in silence to his car--Annisa unaware of the impending nightmare that was about to begin. It didn't start until they were just a few blocks from where she lived. Dr. Hammond pulled over to the curb and switched off the engine and the headlights. "I want you to know how much I admire you, Annisa, for what you are trying to do. Not many girls your age are that passionate in helping their fellow man. Or that far-sighted." He edged a bit closer to her as he said it. "It must be hard adapting to a new culture. Away from your own people. Lonely, I bet."

"Not so much," she answered, inching away. "Everyone has been very kind. They couldn't have made it easier. I'm never lonely." She could hear the apprehension in her voice.

He slipped his arm around her shoulder. "You know, one doesn't have to be lonely. You and I could have a good time together."

"It's late, Dr. Hammond. I'd better get home."

"You disappoint me. I thought we could have a little talk." He patted her shoulder.

"Talk?"

He smiled. "You know what I mean. We're two adults and we both have something to offer each other."

She turned her head away from him. "No, I don't know what you mean."

"Don't be a tease." His hand was on her knee and pushing up her thigh under her skirt.

"Dr. Hammond! No!" She tried to pull his hand away. "Stop it!"

"Come on, pretty lady." His voice was like butter. "Don't play games." He had slipped his fingers under her underpants and

412

began to rub her pubic hair. "I thought all you little Arab girls had to shave."

Choking on his words, she pushed hard against his chest. "Get your hands off of me."

"You know you want it. You've been asking for it all night."

"Let go of me."

After she pushed him away, his voice was suddenly hard. "Don't play virgin-queen with me you little wildcat." He grabbed her by the wrist but she jerked away and slapped him hard across the face. "How dare you! I'll report, you for this." she gasped.

He drew away instantly, his eyes cold with anger. "I don't think so."

"I will. I will."

"How pitiful. Do you really think anyone would believe you?"

"Yes. Every nurse on the floor knows what you are."

His eyes narrowed. "Is that so? I suspect they also know I review their job performance. Do I make myself clear?"

"That's sexual harassment. Blackmail."

"I'm warning you. You stir up trouble for me and you won't get a job within 100 miles of Washington. Do you understand that, little Arab?"

"I'm not an Arab. I'm an Afghan," she said haughtily "And I'm not one bit afraid of you." She leapt from the car and slammed the door. "I'll see you in court," she screamed as she ran down the street and out of sight...

"You did what?" It was well after midnight and Ethan Harris had been asleep for over an hour. He sat up in bed, clutching the phone. "Oh, Jesus, Annisa. I don't want to hear this."

But he did hear it and groaned when she was through. "The problem is, Annisa, he can do exactly what he has threatened. Remember the unwritten rule: doctors are omnipotent-- little tin gods when it comes to nurses."

She started to cry. "All my work. My hopes. My dreams. I've got to turn this man in. My honor is at stake."

"No, it's your future. You don't stand a snowball's chance in hell that they would believe you and not him."

"Other nurses. . ."

"Forget that. Nobody wants to be on the losing side. Believe me, Annisa, he can do you a lot of damage."

"I don't see how."

"He could accuse you of patient neglect. Wrong doses on prescriptions."

"We keep tight records on all that."

"Late for work. Talking on the phone on personal matters. Deliberately disobeying a doctor's orders. Worst of all, you are here on a green card. It's open season on you..."

"It's not fair."

"No, it isn't."

"I hate him. I hate it here!"

"Calm down. In three more weeks you get your diploma. Just lay low. Stay out of his way as much as you can. And for Pete's sake keep your mouth shut with the rest of the nurses. You're walking on thin ice."

"This is not supposed to happen in America. Women are supposed to be equals. First thing tomorrow morning I'm going in to the chief administrator and.. ."

Ethan groaned. "I give up. I'm coming over there now. Just give me time to get my pants on. I'm not going to let you throw away three years of hard work."

When he arrived, Annisa was crying so hard he couldn't get her to stop. "Don't do this. You'll make yourself sick."

"I don't care. I don't care about anything anymore."

"This isn't the end of the world."

"You don't understand. I really thought I had a chance to do something good. Then I wouldn't feel so bad about leaving them behind. The crippled children."

"Annisa, you need to get some rest."

She refused.

What was left of the night was filled with tears and recriminations. If only she had stayed in Afghanistan. The humiliation. It was worse than the Russian soldiers... She had trusted Dr. Hammond.

"You were told not to."

It was almost dawn before Annisa was calm enough to talk sense.

"Don't do anything rash. You can't throw away everything because of one sleazy doctor. I repeat, stay out of his way and he won't sabotage you. And there's nothing wrong with the job offer in Bethesda..."

"It was only an interview and I don't want it even if I get it. I wouldn't be happy there."

"Why not?"

"It sounds too easy."

"You mean you want more of a challenge?"

"It's not that so much. I just want to work and live somewhere where people aren't prejudiced against Muslims. England maybe. I hear they have a shortage of nurses."

"Have you ever been to England?"

"No."

"It's all drizzle and overcast skies.. I guarantee you won't like the Limeys. Too standoffish. They don't let you 'in' as easily as us Yanks. And don't kid yourself into thinking they have no prejudice."

"It doesn't matter."

"Ten minutes ago it did. All that business about Afghans getting a bum rap in the States."

She didn't answer...

"Annisa, listen to me. Forget England. Their national health service is going down the tubes."

"Well, what about the people *here* who don't even have health insurance?"

"You mean this is a political statement on your part?"

"No," she said sullenly. She didn't really have a clear answer. "Winning might be everything in America, but wouldn't it be wonderful if one didn't feel compelled to try."

"You think the English don't like to win? In a pig's eye. Don't let that aloof exterior fool you."

She thought of the elusive Claire and sighed. "You're right. You're always right. You must think I'm hopeless always fantasizing about life somewhere else."

"Are you kidding? All the flak I took about going to Afghanistan. It's the best thing that ever happened to me. I'm a much better person for it... And I met you."

She reached for his hand. "I like what you are."

"I wish I did. In my old age I think I'll have a lot of regrets."

Another silence descended upon them.

"Annisa? Talk to me. It's never good when you suddenly go quiet on me."

"Sorry. I was thinking about how you do things just because you have to do them."

"Fair enough, but you've got to do that too. Promise me one thing; that you'll go to the hospital tomorrow and keep your head down."

415

"You make it sound so easy —to sell your soul to the devil."

"And what was your marriage to Abdul?"

She pulled her hand away "That was cruel."

"But necessary. You're a lady who's been known to change her mind."

And she did.

Annisa Aziz received her diploma in June of 1989 and took a job with the Public Health Service in Montgomery County Maryland, lasting a little more than eight months. She resigned to take a job in London as a pediatric nurse working with babies of indigent mothers.

CHAPTER 38

As Annisa had hoped, life in London town proved to be very different from the years she had spent in America. True, the image of the crippled children in Peshawar burned in her subconscious mind. And with it came the guilt for not doing something about it. But in London she decided to insulate herself—not to get involved in any causes or to entertain any grandiose dreams. She made sure that her social life went no further than the local pub. It was nice that she could go there alone without anyone thinking she was looking for a mate. English pubs were a family thing. She learned to drink ginger beer and enjoy a game of darts. It was a lifestyle that suited her. Contrary to what Ethan had envisaged, she loved being a pediatric nurse. Working with babies-- particularly those born with AIDS-- was a constant source of joy. She felt useful—needed in surroundings that had not defeated her as they had in Peshawar.

A letter from Mira, who had married the son of a former Afghan general, arrived shortly after Annisa moved to her new flat. They had a baby girl and were living in Oregon. It rained a lot in Oregon. Otherwise, everything was fine. What puzzled Annisa was how Mira had gotten her address and why she suddenly wanted to resume their friendship? Annisa never answered back.

Her days in England seemed to blend into each other and at times she thought she was in a time warp—never going forward, never going back.

Then good news came out of Kabul in April of '92. The puppet government had fallen. Blocked at the Kabul airport, President Najibullah had taken refuge in the UN compound. A new coalition government was to be formed.

This time Ethan called long-distance instead of sending flowers.

"Looks like the fighting may be over so don't get any big ideas about going back to Afghanistan."

"Not a chance. I love it here."

"Are you saying you don't miss me?" he teased.

"Well, maybe just a little." She wondered how things were with Jan but she didn't have to ask.

"Jan and I are getting married in August. Big time. Preparations galore. You would think it was a rocket launch. Mother is over the moon with excitement."

"And you?"

He paused. "Excitement is hardly the right word. More like content." He paused. "I do miss you, Annisa-jan."

"Me too."

His phone call made her pensive. A little sad. 'Content' was a very good word. It was certainly what she had settled for. Like Ethan, she had found her niche. Her modest, two room flat was nestled in a row of shabby but solid Victorian houses. It was sparsely furnished but boasted a kitchen window that overlooked a small garden in the back. She had chosen it for the view but also because of her landlady, a silver haired grandmother who reminded Annisa of Panna. Her landlady was a caring soul, and like Panna was protected by a rather firm crust. She came complete with garden shears and friendly cups of tea.

The phone rang again, shortly after Annisa finished talking to Ethan. She answered it, half-hoping it was *him* and that he was calling back to tell her the marriage was off. It was a selfish thought. Instead of Ethan, an unfamiliar male voice was on the line. It was Matthew Hardcastle, her father's old newspaper friend.

"I'm flattered that you've tracked me down."

"Well, I'm trying not to sulk but how long have you been in London?"

"Since '90."

"Shame on you."

"You are such a busy man. Important. I didn't want you to think you were obligated. I am no longer a waif who has to be rescued."

"I've never thought that, but evidently Dr. Harris was right. You are a very complex lady." Matthew went on to say that he had it in the back of his head to write a novel about Afghanistan and to write about the war as seen through the eyes of a woman instead of a man. She would be a great source of material for him.

"You won't use real names, will you?"

"No, and I doubt if it will ever see print. I'm a newsman, not a novelist. We can rarely make the adjustment. It may be nothing more than a good excuse to enjoy your company."

They agreed to meet for dinner at Matthew Hardcastle's favorite Indian restaurant, which was located a few blocks from Earl's Court tube station.

"Do you mind if I bring a tape recorder?" he asked.

"No, but I wonder if that will make me self-conscious." She also wondered how it would feel to see her father's friend after all these years. The last time they had met was in Peshawar. The Ditchfield's dinner party where she had made a total fool of herself.

Her fears about talking to him proved to be ungrounded. The minute she pushed open the door of the modest restaurant with it's pungent smells and sitar music in the background she felt at ease. From a back table Matthew Hardcastle stood up and waved to her. She nodded and wound her way through a nest of tables.

"It's wonderful to see you." He pulled out her chair and helped her remove her rain jacket. "I'm grateful you are going to help me with this."

"Why not? I've nothing better to do. I live alone with my two cats." It surprised her that she so readily admitted this. And she felt concerned it hadn't come out right. "I mean," she paused. "I didn't mean to sound so flip— I know what you are doing is important..."

"You're very sensitive to others feelings, aren't you? I like that. I've already ordered for you. Hope you don't mind. I usually get several different bowls that we can share. I hope you like it on the hot side."

"The hotter the better."

"Ah, a kindred soul."

Matthew Hardcastle's questions about her experiences proved to be non- threatening. He was a sympathetic listener. In fact, the evening was cathartic, a blessing in disguise. Talking about the war that she had tried so hard to forget helped to exorcise some of those demons that plagued her dreamtime. Matthew Hardcastle evidently understood her mixed emotions about her country and her very real doubts about her role as a woman in her own culture--or any culture to be exact.

When she tried to apologize about that hideous evening they had shared at Mrs. Ditchfield's dinner party in Peshawar, he interrupted her.

"You looked like an angel that night and had the rage of a trapped lioness. That insufferable ass, Jack Westerman, couldn't stop talking about you until Meirnardus shut him up. You know what the Egyptian ambassador said about you? He said, 'that young woman has more dignity than anyone in this room.' That was quite a mouthful."

419

Most of the evening Hardcastle spent tape-recording her recollections, rarely interrupting unless he wanted a point cleared up. However, he did like to pontificate on his own views of the fighting in Afghanistan and the role of Islam in general.

"It's senseless--a re-run of the Crusades by the fundamentalists. They need a villain to blame for their poverty and loss of law and order. Islam is overreacting against the modern world because they think the infidels are out to convert them again."

"But they are. It's all so subtle but pervasive. Television, movies, records, computers. Americans have wired the world and they are sending out their messages, not ours."

"And your message is?"

"That's the trouble. We can't seem to agree on one."

Before the evening was over Annisa realized once again what a gap Ethan had left in her life. It was good to be with someone like Matthew who made her feel so much at ease. Someone familiar with her culture. The more they talked the more she realized what she had been denying herself. A friend.

They decided to meet again the following Saturday and all the next week she eagerly looked forward to it.

A pattern soon emerged. They would meet after work on a Saturday night to sum up their week and to have a plate of Indian curry in the same cozy, intimate restaurant. It had good food and was inexpensive. It was also an equal distance from where they each lived. Matthew Hardcastle had became her mentor-- deciphering the politics behind the rhetoric of the Western world- - just as Ethan had tutored her in how that world functioned at play.

Matthew also shared her sense of outrage that Afghanistan was now virtually forgotten by the rest of the world. During Najibullah's-six year-dictatorship, thousands of Afghans had been arrested, tortured and killed. But few people were aware of it. As a newsman, Matthew saw it as a geopolitical issue--Afghanistan had virtually dropped off the Western radar screens once the Soviets were out.

"Why don't they write more about what's going on in Kabul?"

"They do, but it only sees print on a slow news day. No one is interested now that the Russians are out. I'm sorry, Annisa, but there you have it: the fact of the free world's limited attention span."

Later, Matthew would confide his worries about the new coalition government in Kabul. He was fearful it was not going to last. And, he was concerned about an organization called the Taliban.

"Uncle Fritz talked about that."

"He couldn't have. It was only formed a short time ago. The West knows very little about it. Was this Uncle Fritz a soothsayer?"

She shrugged. "He said religious students in Pakistan were the base of it-- they were anti-modern but not anti-West. At least not yet."

"My treat." The owner of the restaurant had arrived with a pitcher of beer for Matthew and a lemonade for Annisa. They were special customers now; he even reserved them their own table. It was located in the back, under the staircase. Close to the kitchen but a little more private. "Let me know when you get the problems of the world solved," the owner said as he walked away.

Annisa smiled. "I think he's been eavesdropping. Now where were we?"

"The Taliban?"

"Oh, yes. Why are you so concerned about them? They sound harmless enough. They want to reunite the country on the basis of Islamic ideology."

"True. But harmless? I wouldn't bet on it. It was Matthew's opinion that there was more to it than ideology. It had something to do with an old treaty. The Taliban started in Pakistan and Pakistan was due to surrender some territory back to Afghanistan soon. He argued that there was an international business cartel that preferred that the land stay in the hands of Pakistan."

"With you, it's always a conspiracy." Annisa said.

"Hear me out. The West is not losing any sleep over the Taliban. They want stability in that area at any price. Mistake. Big mistake." He waved his fork as he said it.

"Now you sound like a true Afghan. A Pak hiding under every bed! Matthew, it will never happen. And I don't think the Americans are that stupid to lend their support to a people who they think would deny human rights."

"Stupid? Not at all. There are potential profits in that area- in the billions. And the American Congress wears two hats when it comes to human rights. I'll bet you that China gets her most favored nation status despite Tienanmen Square. Yet Afghan rug dealers aren't allowed to export to the U.S. without paying a terrible tariff.

All of this because they used to be under the rule of the Communists. Does that make any sense?"

"Sense? Matthew, I gave up expecting that a long time ago."

It was Christmas Eve. There was fog and lots of it. The dampness depressed Annisa--she felt weighed down. On a night like this she missed the crisp, dry air of Kabul. Even in heavy snow there had never been this terrible penetrating chill.

Outside there was singing. Revelers from the corner pub had spilled into the street below, serenading any window with a light in it.

Her landlady, who had dropped off a present for Annisa, scoffed. "Gentleman carolers out on a spree, my foot. More like drunken sots."

"I feel bad I don't have a present for you," Annisa answered as she tore at the tissue on the box.

"I hope they fit."

Annisa held up a pair of mittens. "Did you knit these?"

"I wish." Her landlady held up her hands, crippled with arthritis. "I bought them at a jumble sale."

There was a pounding on the door. "Ho. Ho. Ho. Open up in there." Annisa was surprised. She never had visitors. "I know you are home. I see a light in the window."

Matthew. It was Matthew Hardcastle. She hurried to the door.

He stood on the doorstep holding a large basket of fruit; a bit unsteady on his feet. "I know you don't celebrate Christmas, but I decided you should not spend it alone."

"But I love Christmas. Ethan always made it magical." *The March of the Toy Wooden Soldiers* was drumming in her head. There had been red velvet and crystal chandeliers. The magic of the 'Nutcracker' in the Kennedy Center. She had never seen a ballet and it really was true—"everything was beautiful at the ballet."

"May I come in?"

"Oh, sorry. I don't know where my mind is these days."

The landlady had joined them at the door. "I was just leaving."

"Please don't go. . .This is my good friend, Mr. Hardcastle."

The landlady reached for his hand. "I'm Mrs. Brierly. Mrs. Peter Brierly. I'm just out the door for church services." She turned to Annisa. "Merry Christmas, lovely Annisa. Now be nice to him. He's a very handsome man."

Annisa thanked her again for the present and ushered her out the door.

"What was that all about?" Matthew asked as he crossed to the grate to warm his hands in front of the coals. "The poor woman needs glasses."

"Mrs. Brierly thinks I need a beau."

"One that's 56?"

Annisa's smile was almost wistful. "Mrs. Brierly is of the old school. A woman is not complete without a husband."

"Does she have one?"

"Killed in the war. They had only been married a few months and she was pregnant. She keeps his picture on her mantle and every night she pours two drinks and toasts him."

"I bet she drinks his glass too."

"No, that's the sad part. She pours his drink back in the bottle. It's as though she's saving it for his return."

"Why do women do that?"

"Do what?"

"Sublimate themselves. Throw themselves on the burning pyre."

"Is that what I do? Did? Sorry, I guess I was just feeling sorry for myself because it's Christmas Eve and it's not even my holiday. I'm glad you came. I do feel alone."

It was the first time Matthew Hardcastle had ever been inside her flat. His eyes scanned the meager furnishing and rested on a watercolor that hung on the wall behind the sofa. "That looks familiar. It's a picture of your house in Kabul, isn't it?"

"Yes. I doubt if it looks that way now."

He wondered who had painted it and when she told him it was Najib Duranni he had asked her how she had come by it. Rahmin's old roommate had sent it to her when she lived in Virginia.

"Now there is a story for your novel. Rahmin's friend is Jewish and it was his family who saved my brother from a pauper's burial. They interred him in their family plot in Poughkeepsie, New York. I went there with Ethan to visit his grave. They even bought a tombstone; it has Rahmin's name and the date of his death. And under that is just one word: MUJAHIDEEN. Do you have any idea how much that would mean to Rahmin?"

"Certainly." Matthew reached into his hip pocket and pulled out a flask. "I'm surprised you never told me about this before."

423

"I didn't think it would mean anything to anyone but me. Can I get you a glass?"

"No, thank you. And it does mean something. A lot of us have a thorn in our side over what is happening to your country. The very reason I want to attempt the book. A callous world seems to be more moved by fiction--you have to personalize a war to make it real."

She agreed with him and found it curious that he never mentioned Najib. "A lot of my memories of the war involve Najib. You never ask me about him."

Matthew's answer was guarded, admitting that omitting Najib left giant gaps in her recollections. "I've filled in the spaces with the man you call Ishaq. The romantic bridegroom at the village wedding... He's the quintessential hero for a young girl--the man on the white horse."

"I'm still looking for an Ishaq."

"So you can end your days like Mrs. Brierly? Toasting a man you haven't seen for 50 years. I don't man to pry but it's hard for me to grasp why you left Washington. Ethan seems like a chirpy, cheerful soul."

"I didn't fit. It wasn't so much Ethan as it was me and America."

"Anything in particular?"

"Not that I can put into words. In some ways America was just too easy."

"You mean you like to struggle?"

"No, it's more like wishing for a rich dessert. America was something I craved. And when I got there I stuffed myself until I made myself sick. After that, nothing never looks as good to you again."

"So you came here to our impoverished little island. Easier to digest?"

She was surprised to hear an edge in his voice. "Kind of. At least I don't have to feel guilty here if I don't 'make it' whatever that is. I kind of like the class system-- knowing your place."

"That is pure, unadulterated garbage. I know several million Englishmen with the wrong accent who would loudly disagree with you."

"You asked me a personal question. Now it's my turn. Do you know where Najib is living in Paris?" She was trying to sound casual, but her voice betrayed her nervousness.

"Paris?" He raised the flask to his mouth again and then wiped his lips. "Najib is still in Afghanistan."

"How can that be? Are you sure?"

He bristled, reacting to the pinprick in her voice. "Don't push it, my lady. I promised Najib never to discuss him with you."

"Well, you have done an excellent job of that," she snapped.

"It's good to see you are getting into the Christmas spirit."

But there was no joking her out of it. "I'd like to know where he is."

Matthew sighed. "He's with Massoud--working under Rabbani and Hekmatyar. I suspect working for a divided government is one heck of a high-wire act."

"It irks me that you've kept all this to yourself."

"I didn't want to upset you."

"Upset? I'm happy. It was his living in Paris I couldn't understand."

"Why do you insist on Paris?"

"I heard this from the Afghan community in Washington."

"Well, they've got it wrong. Najib may go there on occasion-- a large community of Afghan exiles are there and some of them are maneuvering to get the ex-King back on the throne. Najib monitors politics from all sides. The man has no life. Often works 24 hours a day. One would think he was possessed. I think he also visits his mother in Paris. Didn't she end up there?"

"He never talked much about his family... His father committed suicide, you know."

"I think Najib is doing a bit of that himself. The last time I saw him in Kabul he was drinking heavily."

Annisa was crushed to hear it.

"I didn't mean to upset you. So let's change the subject."

It was as though she hadn't heard him. "It was Claire. Najib never got over her. That's why he drinks."

Matthew hesitated. "I don't think that's true. But, then again, don't throw yourself on your sword in hopes that it isn't. Forget him. Forgive. At the end of the day good men sometimes have to do things they don't like in order to survive."

She looked offended "Najib never compromises. Never. One of the reasons I stayed away from the Afghan community in Washington was because there were so many cruel rumors of what had happened to people I knew. I was told that Najib had been involved with the drug world in New York. I refused to believe it. Do you?"

"I'm not sure Najib would want me to talk about this."

The color drained from her face. "You've got to. I'll never see Najib again."

"Annisa, don't ask me to break a confidence."

"I have a right to know. I have loved that man since I was a child."

"That's precisely my point."

She was growing more agitated. "They tried to kill him in Islamabad. And when I asked him about it, he said it was 'personal.' Why couldn't he tell me? Was Najib involved in shipping drugs?"

"Yes and no. Najib pretended to become involved because your brother was "

Annisa lifted her hand as though to ward off a blow. "Not Rahmin."

"Hopefully, it was innocent enough. I want to believe that Rahmin had no idea where some of those large sums he was raising for the Resistance were coming from or that some of the money was being funneled to terrorist cells. It's my hunch that when Rahmin found out, he threatened to blow the whistle. That shooting in his taxicab was not a random act of violence. Annisa, your brother was executed."

"I don't believe you."

"Najib did. An off-hand remark by me prompted him to do some poking around on his own. Najib made it his mission to pursue what I had learned and he did so by infiltrating their ranks. It took him almost a year and he had to do it in-between shuttling back and forth as the eyes and ears of Meirnardus. Najib walked a very taunt rope."

"He told you all this?"

"No, only confirmed it. I was working on bits and pieces. What happened in a nutshell is that after Najib found out who was responsible for killing Rahmin he settled the score. I later confronted him. He did not deny it."

Annisa was stunned. The magnitude of what Matthew was saying was only beginning to set in. "Najib killed a man in revenge for my brother!"

"Don't dwell on it, Annisa. Najib would be furious with me if he knew I told *you* of this."

"I'm glad you told me. It explains so much that's puzzled me. I feel so responsible."

"That's ridiculous."

"No, it isn't. When my father was bulldozed into a pit in Kabul it was Najib I asked to avenge his death."

"Annisa, you are reaching. Rahmin and Najib were very tight. Maybe he just did it for himself."

She shook her head. "After all these years you would think I could forget him. I never had a chance. It was always the English girl. After her death he left to join the fighting in Paktia. I am certain he wanted to die."

Matthew Hardcastle stared at her and suddenly felt very sober. Words formed on his lips but never came out. He'd have to watch himself. Najib Duranni had confided much more than the events surrounding Rahmin's death to him. It was for Annisa's own good not to know.

She looked suddenly leery. "What are you thinking?"

"I'm thinking you never cease to amaze me. You are under 30 but you have already lived many lifetimes."

"Not the kind most people would pick."

"None of us have a choice. Life is a crap game."

"I refuse to believe that. In your book will you write about Afghanistan as a 'holy war?'"

"That seems to be the current billing."

"I wonder. I once met an Hazara who said he thought the real reason we threw the Russians out was because the tribes were afraid they would lose control of their women."

Hardcastle chuckled. "Food for thought. But obviously the man didn't know *you* very well."

Annisa leaned over and poked at the coals. "The strange thing, Matthew, is that I think he did."

427

1995

CHAPTER 39

Matthew Hardcastle proved to be right in his fears about the Taliban. Not only did Burhanuddin Rabbani, the Afghan president who replaced Najibullah, have to deal with factional contests; the Pashtun-dominated Taliban emerged as a major challenge to his government, less than two years after he took office.

Annisa abhorred what she heard of their methods and especially their attitude towards women. She felt that it would be the end of Afghanistan if the Taliban ever took Kabul.

Matthew was confident they would but Annisa clung to her faith in the fighting expertise of Commander Massoud. Massoud would defeat them. If only he didn't have to deal with the squabbles within the coalition government. The whole thing was disheartening.

It was Matthew who suggested she treat herself to a brief vacation at a seaside inn on the rocky coast of Cornwall. She was looking peaked-- without doubt overworked. It did not take much to persuade Annisa to go. She *was* exhausted and had been driving herself the past few years. Not once had she had to dip into the money Uncle Fritz had given her on her last trip inside. She lived frugally and got a great deal of satisfaction in knowing that the money she had invested was working for her. She had accumulated quite a large amount. Ethan needn't worry so much about her 'bungie jumping.' She now had her own safety net. "Have a little fun in life," Matthew had urged. "You're young. You owe it to yourself."

Unfortunately, the beachside holiday did not meet her expectations. She felt conspicuous amidst the holiday revelers and particularly when eating alone in the dining room. People on vacation seemed to come in pairs.

In addition to her loneliness, the seaside (which she had expected to adore) depressed her. The ocean seemed so endless and impersonal--without a past or present. It washed away her footprints in the sand. She was homesick for her land-locked country. She missed her high mountains--the great earth gesture of the Hindu Kush. Mountains gave her shelter and a feeling she belonged.

Much to her surprise she discovered it was not so easy to put her thoughts on paper. She had promised Matthew she would keep a diary about her feelings. Could she put into her own words what she thought the experience of war had done to her life?

Days went by before she could put a pen to paper—she felt too shy in revealing her innermost feelings even to herself. But after her first attempt, her shyness proved to be rather illusory. Once she had started she couldn't write fast enough. And as the words flowed she realized it was a diary she could never share with Matthew Hardcastle. Nor with anyone.

St. Austell, Cornwall
Hawthorne Inn
May 27, 1995

My name is Annisa. I am lost. I don't know who I am. Sometimes I think I am wise beyond my years and other times I am ashamed of how little I know. There are few things I am sure of because my world has changed so rapidly and so many times. I have seen too many people die and I have killed. It has hardened me. I wonder if I am capable of love. Panna, who raised me, believed love was the highest attainment. If so, I have failed. I have railed against the tyranny of my culture but I have nothing to put in its place. Behind the veil, the real? I have lost my country and I don't know how to be what I was born to be--a woman. I keep waiting for a certainty in an uncertain world. If only someone had the answers. Show me my task and I will do it with all my heart. At times I believe in God but I don't believe. I pray each day as I was taught to do as a child but often I am reciting words, which sound hollow to me. Many times Allah has saved me from disaster and yet how easily I forget to be grateful. My brother was murdered and so was my father. My mother died giving birth. I would welcome such a fate. They tell me I am a survivor but what does that mean? I plant myself in soil other than mine. I water and tend to my growth. But there is no flower. No bloom. I am not enough of a purist to perpetuate a scar. If only my father had lived to explain his poetry to me. Only now do I begin to grasp its meaning. Najib always knew. No matter how hard I try to surrender to the will of the universe--it was always Najib and always will be Najib. Najib. Najib.

When she had finished writing it she crumpled the page and tossed it into a wastebasket. Was there scar tissue? If so, Ethan's father had been right.

It was raining and dreary and Annisa was home in bed with a cold when she rang Matthew Hardcastle. She wanted to thank him for recommending the inn in Cornwall. The view was wonderful and the people who ran it were lovely.

He was pleased to hear from her but sorry to learn she had failed in her attempt to keep a journal. Also, he couldn't talk long. He was leaving for Afghanistan later that evening.

"I thought news over there is old hat."

"Then you haven't read the papers?"

"I was on vacation, remember."

"All hell has broken out again in Kandahar. Rebel Taliban groups are trying to push the coalition government out of southern Afghanistan."

"But you've said for weeks that was coming. Why the urgency?"

There was a very long pause on the phone. "Annisa, it would only open old wounds."

"I thought we were honest with each other."

"You are. I'm not."

She sat up in bed. "Thanks, thanks a lot. I'm a big girl now. All grown up. I don't need you or anyone else to shelter me from the truth."

He breathed a sigh. "This is against my better judgment. Brace yourself. The worst has happened. Najib Duranni has been accused of corruption by his fellow officers and is under arrest."

"Arrested by the Taliban militia?"

"No. His own people. No doubt it is a trumped up charge. Najib has been fighting their double-dealing every step of the way and knew if certain elements weren't exposed and soon that the Taliban militia would get a real toehold on the country. The trouble is he has not been able to get anyone to listen to him. The American government knows very little about the Taliban faction and in its ignorance is going along with it because the Taliban's backing comes from the Paks and not the Iranians. I am certain Najib believes if the Taliban militia takes over, then Afghanistan is on her way back to the Stone Age."

Annisa's voice was tight. "So you are still in contact with Najib?"

"I never said I wasn't. He's a good news source, Annisa."

"I feel betrayed."

"Not by me. You said you were over him."

"Does he know I'm living in London?"

431

"No. I never told him. He's never asked about you."

"That hurts."

She could hear the exasperation in his voice. "Which explains why I never talk about him."

"What can you do to help him?"

"Not much. I'm at least going to try and see him. Write about it if I can. One man's stand against a coming disaster. It was hell getting travel money out of these tight-fisted bastards at work for this side trip. I am scheduled to be in Seoul next week because the North Koreans are acting up again. Management is buying Kabul as a sidebar. It was a hard sell. As you know, Kabul is hardly a stopover."

"I thought you were a senior man."

"That's the problem. The word 'senior.' War correspondence is a young man's game. There are even some rumblings to move me to New York--put me out to pasture in their financial services department. Dow-Jones must be terrified."

"It makes no sense."

"The bigger an organization gets the more nonsensical it becomes. They forget that Reuters News service started with carrier-pigeons flying messages across the channel."

"Matthew, I have a favor to ask. Can you tell me where they are holding Najib?"

"In Dulmagon prison."

"I want to go with you."

"To do what? Engineer an escape?"

"You sound so detached about this. As though Najib was a potential story and not a man."

"At times you have an acid tongue, my lady."

"I'm upset."

"I knew you would be. Don't be foolish. They wouldn't let you see him if you did."

"If I can't go with you, I'll go on my own."

"That is the last thing Najib would want."

"How do you know what Najib wants? I need to be there. To let him know someone cares."

"Caring for someone is giving them what *they* want, not you."

His words stung and she lashed back. "You've never been in love."

"How would you know? Annisa, don't be stupid. You simply can't go."

A petulant silence followed.

"Scratch a man raised in the West and they are all the same under the surface. Women are to be ordered around."

"Balderdash. It's not like you to parrot outdated ideas. I'm beginning to think the States was indeed a bad influence on you. Grow up Annisa. Don't say words you don't mean to hide your anguish over Najib."

"I'm not hiding. Who are you to point your finger at America? You're smug little island is just as disdainful of woman."

"Fickle girl. What happened to your love for our glorious class system?"

"Go ahead. Twist my words. You always do. You Englishmen cling to the past more than you realize. At least the Americans look forward to a dream world. If only *this* country could pick up a little of the American's faith in themselves."

"I'm surprised you left such a utopia for the likes of us."

"I told you. I didn't fit. And I don't fit here."

He sighed. "Since five minutes ago when you heard Najib Duranni was in prison. You can't go and that's it."

"You can't stop me."

"Of course, I can't. But if you knew the truth you wouldn't do this to Najib."

"What truth?"

"That Najib has stayed away from you for your own protection."

Annisa felt humiliated and even angrier. "I'm sick of hearing this. I haven't seen that man in years. If he thinks I'm still so smitten that I can't function without him then he's crazy. This makes me boiling mad."

She waited but there was silence on the other end of the phone. "Matthew? Don't hang up. I'm sorry."

"Annisa, his name is on a list of people who never let up on revenge. In avenging Rahmin's death, Najib is . . ."

"You said that had nothing to do with me."

"Bollox! It has everything. Christ, Annisa, you must have guessed. Claire's death was no accident. She was killed because of Najib."

"That's preposterous. I made a pilgrimage to the local library. There are news clippings: 'BBC Reporter Dies in Fiery Crash.'"

"Claire Lipscomb was murdered, Annisa. The same people who killed Rahmin."

"Ridiculous! There is no suggestion of that in any . . ."

"Annisa, for God's sake, they cut off her ear and mailed it to Najib in Islamabad."

Annisa put her hand to her mouth to hold back her screams.

"There was a card inside that grisly box --a card with the name of the man Najib killed in New York and on it was a message: 'From your British whore.'"

"Oh, no," she moaned. . . "I can't bear this."

"Neither can Najib. He never wanted them to know he had any connection with you. Can't you see? These people will methodically destroy anyone he loves. They create a living torture as their revenge. You would never be safe. First your brother. Then Claire. He's convinced he has her blood on his hands. Don't give him yours."

"Matthew, I've got to see him."

"And if you get yourself killed trying to see him--what would that prove? Leave it alone. Let him die in peace."

"Die?"

"They plan to hang him in Kabul as early as next week! There, I've said it. Are you satisfied? If you show up in Afghanistan I'll throttle you." He hung up on her and for a long time she stood, holding the dead receiver in her hand.

CHAPTER 40

Annisa left the crowded bus on the outskirts of a small village in southern Afghanistan. There were no lights in the houses and at this hour she could see only inches beyond her face. Silence reigned on every street.

Cautiously, she groped her way down the rutted dirt road until she saw a single candle burning in the window of a small house. She approached the open door and rapped on the door-jam. When no one answered, she entered. She was able to make out the shrouded figure of a man seated on the earthen floor. "The prison? How much farther on this road?"

"Too far to walk."

"Can you take me there?"

"What business do you have at Dulmagon? It is a foul place."

"They tell me my. . .my husband is being held there and I must see him."

The man stood up and took the candle from the sill. He held the flame close to her face. "What kind of woman walks the streets alone at night and without a veil?"

"A wife whose husband is to be hanged."

"But a man stays in Dulmagon until he rots. Even here you can smell the stench."

"They are taking him to Kabul."

"Ah, he must be very important. A public hanging in the square. . . It won't be long before the Taliban controls Kabul and it will be a daily occurrence. They now have Kandahar. When they come, order will be restored. We can live in peace."

"Please, I haven't much time."

The man eyed Annisa with mistrust.

"I have money to pay."

"Wait here." He folded his faded rags about him and moved out the door.

Annisa stood in the flickering light, her hands together in prayer. "Please, Allah, deliver me to Najib in time."

The man did not come back. Apprehensively, she looked around the room with its soot-blackened walls; a cracked teacup on the window ledge by the candle was the only sign it was a home.

"Come." A runny-nosed and barefoot boy stuck his head in the doorway. It was bitter cold outside and it depressed Annisa that the boy had no shoes. How easily she had forgotten how desperate things were in her homeland.

She followed the light of his candle to where the hooded figure stood in the road holding an ancient bicycle. He patted the bars in front of the seat. "Here. You sit here."

"I know how to ride. I will go alone."

"I am not such a large fool that I give you my bicycle. I ride with it."

"I have money."

"You will need every coin if you hope to bribe the guards. The price to go inside the prison is high."

"But will I be able to see him?"

"Why not? Like everyone else, they have their price."

The ride was bumpy and hurt Annisa's backside. Each time they hit a hole in the road, the iron bars beneath her bruised her tailbone. In the darkness, one had to trust Allah that the road ahead was clear. Her companion said nothing; the only sound between them was the creaking of the rusty chain that turned the wheels. Annisa remembered the new bicycle her father had given Rahmin one December morning of Ramadan. It was sleek and black and had come all the way from England. Her brother had learned how to balance it by holding onto the garden walls.

"Let me try," she said.

"You are a girl."

Najib, who sat on the patio steps watching them, had crossed over to her. "I will hold it up for Annisa if she can reach the pedals."

Strange, after all these years, to remember this. She could not have been more than six at the time.

Suddenly, the bicycle stopped, throwing Annisa against the handlebars. "What is it?"

"This is as far as I go."

Dawn was approaching and a faint glimmer of light pierced their path. He pointed to a bend in the road. "The prison is less than half a mile beyond. I want nothing to do with Dulmagon. It is not wise to be seen near there."

A mournful note suddenly sounded above their heads as a flock of black-breasted-cranes, traversed the sky, stretched out in long array. The sound of the graceful birds was full of pain and sorrow, a dolorous melody in the stillness of early morning.

Annisa shuddered at the sound and reached into her pocket to pay the old man.

"No, little sister. Keep what is yours. Too soon you will suffer a great loss."

"But we made a bargain."

"You were a guest in my house. Hospitality is all that is left to an Afghan. . .*zindabad Qaum: Sar-buland bashard, baira-i-Afghan!*"

Annisa smiled to hear the words of their national anthem on his ancient lips. "Thank you, my brother. Go with God."

The Afghan army sergeant in a gravy-stained uniform stretched his long legs on the dust-covered desk. The window behind was plastered with yellowed newspapers. An upper sash was down. From somewhere outside came the sounds of men coughing to spit up their morning phlegm.

"You are just in time for early prayer." There was rancor in his voice.

The guard appeared to be younger up close. His hair was slicked back with a sickly smelling rose-oil, but he evidently considered himself quite handsome. Annisa caught him stealing looks at himself in the cracked mirror that hung on the wall to his right.

"Colonel Duranni is a very large fish. Kabul is pleased with its prize."

Annisa clenched her teeth. He was obviously enjoying his power over her. It was all she could do to keep from screaming at him. Instead, she answered his questions politely, lowering her eyes at the appropriate time.

"I will have to search you for weapons."

"I understand."

"Your husband is a very fortunate man."

"To be hanged?" She bit her tongue. She must not offend the guard in any way.

Her tormentor laughed. "No, to have a woman who looks like you."

Where did this boy come from? What bad seed had spilled to give him life? Not only was he a traitor to men like Massoud, he betrayed his heritage with no respect for womanhood.

"Do you have a gift for me?" he asked.

She reached into her pocket for the money.

"No, put that away. Afghanis are worthless these days. Do you have dollars? Pounds?"

437

Her stomach flipped over. If only she hadn't cashed in her pounds in the money bazaar. "What would you consider a proper gift?" she asked, her blood turning to ice as his eyes lazily traveled over her. He reached for her hand and she thought she would retch.

"You guarantee this is real?" he asked as he fingered Ethan's diamond ring.

"Oh, yes. It's very valuable," she swallowed hard, her insides quivering with relief. "You can detain me here until you have it tested."

"But I believe you. Anyone with such arrogance in her eyes would certainly possess the jewels of a princess."

"Please, may I see him now?"

"After morning prayers are finished."

"Yes, of course."

"I would not bore you, but I would like you to know that I have for several years studied English. I understand what you said to my superior officer."

Annisa's stomach began to churn again. She was unable to remember exactly what she had told the man.

"Don't look so concerned. You were smart enough to save the diamond for me. I am your man." He laughed and patted the large ring of keys that hung from his belt. "You puzzle me. Families bring food, a radio, soap--but it is rare for a wife to ask to go inside."

"Perhaps no one else has diamonds."

Again, he threw back his head and laughed "You can't help yourself, can you? You pretend to be submissive, but you would stick a dagger in a man's heart." He leaned over the desk. "I wouldn't be so cocky, if I were you. You tempt fate by not wearing the veil. In Taliban territory you would be stoned for this."

Annisa was fighting to keep her composure. She turned her face away from the sadistic pleasure she saw in his eyes. "I understand. Please, I am anxious to be with my husband."

"Then go. Take one last look." He stood up abruptly. "Too bad he got greedy. I tell you this. I hear he always fought like a lion and never deserted his men when we fought the Russians. A rare thing for an officer."

"You are speaking of the wrong army," she muttered.

"More insults?"

"I think it is going to rain."

Again he laughed and motioned for her to follow him out the door. "Aren't you the sly one. And yes, it's going to rain. I smell it in the air."

But it was the smell of urine mixed with burning charcoal, which stung her nostrils as the guard unlocked the rusty padlock of the cell.

Najib lay at their feet, asleep in the dirty straw.

"So little time left and he wastes it like this." The guard kicked Najib.

Najib moaned when the boot hit his side and rolled over onto his stomach but not before Annisa caught sight of his bruised face. His right eye was swollen almost shut.

"Remember--30 minutes and no more. You are lucky to have that."

Annisa nodded and felt relieved to see the man disappear down the corridor. Thank God, he had not searched her as he had threatened. She carried no weapons but she would not have been able to endure his touch.

She dropped to her haunches and put her hand on the back of her lover's head. "Najib," she whispered. "Wake up. I am here. It's Annisa."

No sound came from him. There was no movement in his limbs. Dear God, was she too late? Had their torture destroyed his senses? Did he even know her name? "Najib. Please open your eyes to me. Turn over. I'm here. Annisa."

She held her breath as she watched him pull himself to his knees. Blood in parallel lines soaked through the back of his shirt. The result of whips? She put her arms around his waist and struggled to help him to his feet. His back still to her, Najib leaned forward and rested his forehead against the wall.

"Najib?"

"A minute."

The tears she had forbidden herself began to spill from her eyes. "Najib, can you hear me?"

"A minute."

She stood behind him fearful he might not know her as she watched him turn slowly towards her.

"A cup. On the floor. It has water. Can you find it for me?"

"Yes, yes!" Frantically she searched through the straw and when she found it she brought it up to his lips, holding the tin cup as he sucked it dry.

439

"There. My head clears...Move by the window so I can see your face."

Annisa did not take her eyes off him as she inched backwards to the barred window.

"It *is* you," he said huskily. He hung his head.

Some few minutes later he spoke again. "An angel appears." He reached out to her but his hands were shaking so violently he pulled them back again. "To see me like this." Puss oozed out from under his right eye and she reached up and wiped it away with her hands. She could not speak.

"It really is my Annisa?" he mumbled.

She bobbed her head, trying to swallow the hard knot in her throat.

"Annisa-jan, we said our good-byes." His voice broke.

"Please, I had to come. I know the truth about Claire's death. I understand now. I..." The dark look on Najib's face stopped her.

"Don't." He slumped backwards against the wall and closed his eyes.

"Najib?" There was panic in her voice. "Can I get you more water?"

He shook his head. "My ration for the day." Then he opened his eyes and gestured towards the bars that fronted his cell. "How did you find me?"

Annisa leaned down to brush away a lock of his hair, which had fallen across his forehead. She had never seen Najib when he was not clean-shaven. "It doesn't matter."

"Who let you in?"

"These are greedy men. I gave them some jewelry, nothing I will ever need."

He reached out and gently touched her arm. "Always so brave. Strong."

"I'm not strong. I am nothing without you."

He pulled himself up and braced himself against the wall.. A faint smile on his lips. "Then Matthew Hardcastle plays with the truth. He says you are very brave."

She felt a surge of hope. "You have seen Matthew?"

"No, they delivered me his letter. A very practical man. He has arranged that I will have a clean shirt and that my beard will be shaved before they hang me. He knows what a dandy I am."

"Oh, Najib. How can you joke!"

"How can I not?"

"Matthew wants to tell *your* story. Put you in a book."

"Make me eternal, huh? Tell him to write of *real* heroes. Afghanistan has more than her share."

She hesitated then found the courage to ask. "Would you have come back for me if I hadn't gone to America?"

He sighed. "How can I answer that?"

"I should never have left Afghanistan. You are my soul."

"Don't, Annisa-jan... The mind is always the dupe of the heart."

"I prayed America would erase my ache for you. Believe me, I tried. In London I remain an empty shell." She was desperate to remain calm... "It was wrong of me to follow you to Talluqaan. I just didn't *know*, Najib. I didn't know the real reason you wanted to send me away."

"Thank God you did come."

"You mean that!"

"With all my being." He stared at her in wonder. "You have this great gift, Annisa --the courage to love. I was a fool. Nurturing my misguided image of myself. Proving my manhood. Wanting to protect you when I should have given *you* a choice. I should have trusted in 'us' more."

The truth of his words tore at her insides. "Oh, God."

"There, there." He pulled her head to his chest. "No need."

She could feel his heart beating against her cheek.

"Words are never enough," he said simply.

She slipped her arms around his waist and clung to him. Her tears now flowed unchecked.

Najib ran his fingers through her hair. Finally he spoke. "Behind you. Outside our window. A flock of cranes circles the courtyard, unable to break through the fog."

"Yes... earlier on the road. I saw them. I always loved to watch them in Peshawar ... Najib, is there nothing we can do?"

He shook his head.

"Soon they take you to Kabul?"

"Give me your word not to follow."

"But you just said. . ."

"Annisa, it's over. I'm to be hanged."

She could not bring herself to speak.

"Swear to it."

She raised her face to him. "I can't. You are not the only fool. You denied me a choice but I should have fought you for it. I too, was entrapped by what I thought I should be."

441

"And what was that?"

"Noble, self-sacrificing. Honoring *your* choice. My heart told me to follow you."

"I would have sent you back."

"Not when you held me. You could not have let me go."

"You know this about me?"

"I know this... Najib, I want to be with you in Kabul."

"No, save me that indignity. Remember me alive. Please.." His voice caught. "You must return to your new life. Modern Afghanistan is finished. For the love of power, they sell each other out."

"But you always came back."

"I thought I could make a difference. But I'm no longer a warrior. I never was. My angel, it was never the war over you." Gently, he reached down and brushed his lips on her forehead. "My sweet, stubborn girl. How I love you... Your hair. The smell is sweet. Remember when you cut it like a boy?"

"Yes. I also remember you drew me in charcoal in our garden."

"If only I could draw you as you are now." He put his hand under her chin and gently raised her face towards him. "There is something you must know... No, don't look away. You need to hear this. I'm not afraid to die. Honor that. Know that I'm glad it will be in Kabul amidst our corrupt leaders-- men who sell out the people who fought so hard with them to drive the Russians out. I will hang defiantly."

Her eyes did not leave his as she pictured the scene--the noise, the crowded square. The ground began to spin beneath her. She couldn't bear to see the rope. She would escape, rise into the air. Far below, she could see Barbur's tomb. White doves were perched on the dome. She turned her head away. "You always spoke of compromise. Why did you challenge them? It goes against everything you ever believed."

His answer was slow in coming. "The time came when it felt right."

"To die?"

"I do not scorn death, Annisa. Defiance does not distract me from the awful truth. But I have made my peace with Allah."

"No, please, no." Her arms tightened around him. She must never let go. She must cling to his life. His warmth. His breath. She was terrified now. Her eyes were closed. The blackness. The abyss. "Najib, I can't believe in God."

"He is with us now. Allah's miracle has brought you here."

With all her heart she prayed that the whimper which was rising within her would not escape. She prayed to conquer the emptiness she would feel the moment she lost him forever. "Why does Allah give us this moment only to snatch it away?"

"Hold it for me. Take it with you."

"You truly believe this is Allah's will?"

"This moment is his blessing. I never dreamed to see your face again."

She burrowed her face in his chest.

"You must promise not to come back inside. Ever."

"No." She threw her head back. "How can I promise such a thing?"

"Because we must not squander Allah's gift. You must live for both of us now. I will see the seasons change through your eyes."

"I can't promise this. I will avenge your death as you did Rahmin's."

"Annisa. We are finished with vengeance."

"Your vengeance for Rahmin was *my* fault. What have I done to you?"

"You have loved me."

Tears rolled silently down her cheeks; she could not will them to stop.

She wanted to scream, but she couldn't. Her father's words came to her now. "How could tulips bloom where bulbs had not been planted?" Her whole life was an unflagging turmoil, her faith shattered. She wanted only to exist. Hate had fueled her for so long, how could she function without it?

She pulled away from him. She wanted to protest. But the minutes were slipping away. So much was left unsaid. She walked to the window. Lost-- she was lost without him. She looked to the distant mountains covered in a thin, gray veil "Najib. The demoiselle cranes. My father said they simply rest while passing through."

He came up behind her and put his hands on her shoulders. "And that must be you. Promise you will keep your new life."

"Look, they have found an opening in the clouds. They are going to fly away."

"Swear it, Annisa."

"They are beautiful birds, aren't they? See the white plumes behind their eyes."

443

"Annisa, answer me."

"No, I don't want to. They look so beautiful..."

"You are the one who is beautiful." He turned her to him. "In Allah's eyes, we are man and wife."

"To hear you say it."

"You are my one true wife," He leaned down and kissed her gently on the lips. When he drew back from her there was a smile in his eyes. "As my wife, you have to obey."

His face blurred before her. 'I love what is beautiful when it appears to me,' he had said in their room with the faded wallpaper. They had made love. It was all about trust.

"If I promise to obey you how can there ever be hope for the modern Afghanistan that you were willing to die for? Am I to lie to you now and say I am sorry in the afterlife?" She lifted her eyes to his. "I will not obey."

Slowly, he shook his head and smiled. "Allah, at least I tried."

Aware that he had bent to her will she began to sob, choking on her tears.

"Hush my angel, the guards will come for you." He brushed her cheek with his lips and whispered, "I cherish your fire. Don't ever change."

Splatters of rain stirred the dust in the courtyard and the doomed couple turned to the window in time to see the last of the cranes disappear over the hills. The rain came heavy now, drenching the land. It would bring a good harvest for the people.

Najib squeezed her hand. "The earth has a great thirst, Annisa-jan. A great, great thirst."

CHAPTER 41

The departure lounge in the airport of Peshawar was almost empty in the early morning hours. A few travelers dozed in their chairs while others watched the half-hearted movement of a barefooted man in pantaloons washing the flyspecked windows. It seemed a futile task. The rag he dipped in his tin bucket of dirty water smudged the windows even more, leaving a thin gray film of grease.

Annisa shook her head at the futility of it all. There was no longer much sense in pushing against life; it had defeated her. She found it hard to believe in a world that would no longer include Najib. And yet, a strange calm had settled over her after they had said their good-byes. 'Annisa-jan, so far-seeking but self-doubting. I love the battle that rages within.' The depth of their 'knowing' of each other had reaffirmed her faith and when the waves of sorrow swept over her she met them with an inner peace. She would honor Najib's request that she not go to Kabul to witness his death.

"Annisa! Annisa Aziz!" Startled to hear her name shouted, Annisa turned to see Mrs. Reed, the American missionary, walking swiftly towards her. She was carrying a tin of sweets and a bouquet of flowers. Annisa stood to greet her.

"God works in mysterious ways." Mrs. Reed gasped, red-faced and out of breath. "To think I would run into you *here*. A Mr. Hardcastle has been calling and calling. Says it's urgent he reaches you. I told him I haven't seen you in years and to try your friend, Akmatcha, at the hospital but he rang back that Akmatcha is no longer there. Mr. Hardcastle said he wasn't certain you were even in Peshawar but that you had talked about going into Afghanistan and that he knew it would take a miracle to find you. And here you are. A miracle. Miracles happen to me all the time." All of this said in one breath!

"Did he say what was so urgent?"

"It's not clear, but he seemed very upset. I tried calling everyone I could think of that might know you but no one has heard from you in years. Shame on you, dear girl. You shouldn't just float in and out of people's lives. And to think I wasn't even going to the airport this morning but, then again, we have a new family coming to post and I thought it best I meet them." She held up the flowers. "Give them a little welcome, you know. Mr. Reed is in Lahore on business. You won't believe how much our mission has grown. Only, these Taliban people are making our life difficult. The Catholics are suffering the same harassment."

Annisa could feel her newfound inner calm quietly slipping away. She repeated her question. "Mrs. Reed, did Mr. Hardcastle say what this was all about?"

"Something about your brother."

"My brother! He's been dead for years."

"Well, according to Mr. Hardcastle, there has been a resurrection."

Annisa sank back into her chair, in an effort to keep the room from spinning beneath her feet. "My brother's alive?"

"Precious girl, are you okay?"

"No. I'm frightened." Her hands were shaking. "I don't know what to do with this news."

It was mid-afternoon before Annisa could get a plane out of Peshawar with connecting flights in Lahore for Paris and terminating in Lausanne. Former Ambassador Gregory Meirnardus was in a nursing home in Switzerland. His wife had died the year before of hepatitis and his daughter, Neamet, was married to an investment banker with Credit Suisse. Matthew Hardcastle had interviewed Ambassador Meirnardus for his book and it was through the Egyptian diplomat that Matthew had learned Rahmin Aziz was alive and living under an assumed name in Afghanistan.

Annisa's phone conversation with Matthew Hardcastle revealed even more startling news...

"Meirnardus says that your brother is with the Taliban and has connections with Osama Bin Laden in the Sudan."

"The wealthy Saudi who fought with the Mujahideen?"

"None other. It's rumored that he plans to reactivate those terrorist camps in Afghanistan he established in the 80's. Bin Laden is courting the Taliban and throwing his money around. He's a clever bastard. His secret organization has tentacles in many countries and a lot of his henchmen use assumed names. Trust me, Annisa, this Bin-Laden is one bad actor. If they kick him out of Khartoum he'll come back to Afghanistan to do his dirty work."

"This has to be a mistake. If Rahmin were alive he would have tried to contact me. My brother is dead. He's buried in New York. I went there."

"Somebody else must be in that grave."

"How could that be possible? Don't the authorities check on these things? There are death certificates. The American hospital I worked in was very strict about recording the cause and the exact time of death."

Matthew agreed. "All I know is that Meirnardus is very sure of his source."

"Well, I'm just as sure of my brother. Rahmin may be intolerant of other religions but he wouldn't hook up with anyone like this terrorist. This Bin-Laden."

"You'd be surprised. Bin-Laden is very charismatic. Adept at turning young idealists into fanatics against the West."

"Is it true that Bin-Laden was trained by the American CIA?"

"Yes, and he's learned his trade well. Frankly, I think he wants to kick the royal family out of Saudi Arabia and has drummed up a hatred of America as an excuse. He's pissed because American troops didn't leave Arab soil after 'Desert Storm.'" Matthew then went on at great length to spell out the flaws in the character of Osama Bin-Laden.

"Meirnardus is wrong about my brother."

"You've met the Ambassador. You know he is not a man who would pass on false information. He keeps close tabs on the Taliban and the al Qaeda."

"From his wheel-chair?"

"Absolutely. Seeking revenge against the al-Qaeda has given him a purpose.. It's become the focus of his life. One of Bin-Laden's right hand men was behind the assassination of his good friend Sadat. And the ambassador thinks they also killed his son, Alexander."

"Najib spoke of the boy. He said if he ever had a son he would name him Alexander." Thoughts of Najib made her stomach began to churn.

"Annisa, you must go to Switzerland. Ask Meirnardus if he knows who can put you in touch with Rahmin. It will have to come from you personally."

"Why should I? All these years and Rahmin has never tried to reach me."

"Because Rahmin may be in a position to help Najib. You've told me over and over they were like brothers."

To even think that someone could save Najib was a cruel joke to Annisa. "Rahmin can't help him. The Mujahideen have control of Najib. You were right. They are taking him to Kabul to hang him."

"Not anymore. The Taliban seized Dulmagon yesterday morning. Or should I say 'bought.' Bribery accounts for most of their turn-arounds."

"My God. I was just there. I saw Najib."

"I suspected as much. How did you do it? I was only able to get a note inside."

She could feel the blood pounding in her ears. "Never mind. Does Ambassador Meirnardus know all this? That Najib is now under the control of the Taliban?"

"I have no idea. When I saw him in Switzerland we talked a great deal about you. And he volunteered that he was certain Rahmin was alive and was surprised you had no knowledge of this."

"What do you think has happened to Najib?"

"He could have been killed. He could have escaped. Or the Taliban may have him. If so, Rahmin might be our only hope."

'Hope.' That gut wrenching word. She had promised herself never to nurture it again.

The winding drive to the private rest home outside Lausanne was lined with evergreen trees. Annisa rolled down the window of her rental car and filled her lungs with the sweet smelling air. From the dust and dirt of Pakistan she had landed into a land of verdant green. It was a crystal clear day and one could see across Lake Geneva the faint outline of the mountains of France. She was thinking that Switzerland must be God's refuge from a violent and untidy world. Unlike Kabul's brown and jagged outcroppings, absent of trees (some Afghans claimed earlier vegetation had been destroyed by years of grazing sheep), the landscape outside Lausanne was a journey into paradise.

She had phoned ahead to let them know she was coming. Visitors were allowed from 2 to 5 in the afternoon but she had convinced the staff to let her visit this morning. If the ambassador really could put her in touch with Rahmin there was not a moment to waste.

The woman at the reception desk was cheerful and welcoming. "Ambassador Meirnardus is very pleased to hear of your visit."

A stiffly starched nurse directed Annisa to a large white stone veranda overlooking the lake. "He tires easily," she whispered as they approached. Gregory Meirnardus was dozing in his wheelchair with a blanket over his knees. A sheaf of papers lay in his lap.

"Don't wake him," Annsia said. "I'll just wait here." She pulled a lawn chair up beside him.

"Let us know if you want some tea or anything."

"Thank you, I will."

Annisa was distressed by his appearance. She had remembered Gregory Meirnardus as square-jawed and imposing; the man before her was hollow-faced, a shadow of his former dignified self. Frail and shriveled looking in an over-sized bathrobe, his thick dark hair had turned the color of Yuri's—- a snowy white. At the thought of Yuri she felt her throat constrict. There was never an end to the forgetting or trying to forgive.

She leaned back in her chair, content to soak up the sun. The morning was so peaceful--not a ripple on the lake. It looked inviting. The serenity of the setting felt almost unreal—a picture post-card or a film set. As though any moment someone would shout, 'cut' and real life would return.

Demons of doubt were invading her head and she was ashamed of her thoughts. A part of her did not ever want to see her brother again. She ached to return to London and resume her predictable and sheltered routine. Unknown and unknowing. There was no strength left in her to do battle. She was resigned to Najib's death and had released him. She might go mad like little Habiba if she had to do it again.

"Ah, Annisa." The sudden movement by Meirnardus in his wheelchair sent the papers on his lap cascading to the stone floor beneath her chair. "How lovely to see you. Forgive an old man who sleeps."

Annisa leaned over and picked up the papers. She handed them to him. "I didn't want to wake you. You looked so content."

"Only in my dreams. In my waking hours I chase the monsters. Did you have a pleasant trip?"

"Very. The drive here from the airport is spectacular."

"You drove your own car?"

She grinned. "Yes, that is one of many things Americans taught me."

"Mr. Hardcastle tells me you are living in London now?"

"Yes. Alone with my two cats."

He shook his head. "A pity. Life is not so much a matter of luck but of choosing and learning how to feel."

"Yes," she answered, wondering if he meant she had made the wrong choice. "I came as soon as I heard you had news of my brother."

"You must have mixed feelings about Rahmin."
She nodded, grateful that he could so readily understand. Meirnardus must have picked up on her urgency to get down to business because he immediately launched into the details of Rahmin. "He is thought to be connected with Bin Laden's group."
"Yes, Matthew Hardcastle has told me. But Najib always said my brother wanted to return to Afghanistan. Isn't Bin Laden in Khartoum?"
"When Saudi Arabia began pressuring Pakistan to get rid of the Mujahideen near the Afghan border, Bin Laden paid for 480 Afghan veterans to come work with him. Your brother was one. I have reason to believe he was part of an unsuccessful assassination attempt on the life of Egyptian president, Hosni Mubarak, in Addis Ababa."
"Rahmin an assassin! Where is my brother now?"
"Outside Jalalabad. He is using the assumed name of Nur Rabinni."
"That's the name of my father's friend who betrayed him to the Russians!"
"Then perhaps his choice of a new identity has a double meaning. Your brother appears to have rejected the teachings of your father by choosing to join such an oppressive force." Meirnardus held up the papers on his lap. "These are from the United Nations -- they estimate there are 500,000 disabled orphans in Afghanistan and over a million widows. Do you realize that in Taliban-seized territory widows are being buried alive in mass graves? And the al-Qaeda, which is behind much of this, has a stranglehold on the Taliban. Mark my word, they will twist the Koran to fit their own ambitions. They are anything but freedom fighters. More like soldiers of fortune. Paid cutthroats. But, oh so cunning politically. They have a 'catchall' philosophy. The U.S. and Pakistan are pleased that the Taliban is attempting to curb poppy growing and heroin refinement. Their so-called anti-drug programs have received tacit backing from Washington and pushing for a pristine Islamic society has found favor with the Saudis. Saudi Arabia is not only helping to bankroll the *madrassas* of the Deobandi denomination but they are funding the Taliban as well. They have suckered in everyone because the Kandahar-based Taliban are using drug production to fund their activities. And their puritanical teachings that seek to cleanse the country are violating human rights. Sorry. I get so agitated when I talk about this. But think of it. Burying women alive!"

"Afghans in the puppet government did the same thing to my father."

"Each side has dirty hands."

"Granted, but Annisa, when you think al-Qaeda, think Nazis. Your people have got to stop the Taliban from taking Kabul or your country is doomed. The al-Qaeda will control the Taliban. More terrorist camps are being set up as I speak."

"It may not be possible to stop them. Our people are starved and exhausted. Our farms are gone. Our land littered with mines."

"Does this mean you are giving up?"

Annisa was taken back. It sobered her to hear someone voice it. To put her thoughts into words. "I confess that I am tempted," she answered. "I'm living a peaceful life now. It suits me."

"There is no peace except in the grave."

Annisa had not come to debate the war or defend herself. She did not know how to proceed. It felt uncomfortable that he was studying her so intently.

"I see it like this," he said. "I don't believe in delaying inevitable confrontations. You are too young to play the ostrich game."

She leaned forward in her chair. "I need to see my brother. Is that possible?"

"I honestly don't know. I can put you into contact with people who can take you to him. Whether he will see you or not is another matter. I hear he is hardened and fanatical."

She wanted to hear the details but at the same time she did not. It was painful to learn of her brother's new life. Of how he encouraged nine-year-olds to blow themselves up in suicidal missions. The Taliban and the al-Qaeda glorified the life of a warrior. Students recruited from religious schools in Pakistan were encouraged to hate women.

"Is it any wonder I left my country and never want to go back." She looked to the lushness of the foliage on the mountains and breathed in the quiescence of the day. "Switzerland is a magical place," she said. "You must love it here."

"Enjoy is a better word. My heart is with my roots. I am here only to humor my daughter. If I had legs to carry me I would run back to Egypt, to help fight the zealots."

His answer shocked her. "Have you not earned your peace and quiet?"

"A true heart never earns anything. It gives."

Although Annisa knew he was talking about himself she sensed that underneath the message was meant for her too.

"You must think me a coward-- forsaking my people."

He answered that he thought no such thing and she believed him because she needed to. Too often she only pretended to be happy. Regardless of the serenity and the safety of this mountain paradise in the neutrality of Switzerland, she understood why Gregory Meirnardus would miss the turmoil of Cairo where the human drama played out on a much bigger screen.

"All my life I've been searching for a cause, my task. I never seem to find it," she confided. And then it all came tumbling out. A purifying moment. A blood-letting. All the different hats she had tried on. From an over-indulged schoolgirl who had tried to adapt to the harsh reality of village life. She had loved and she had lost and was childless. And she had lived the life of a man, riding with the Mujahideen and learning how to kill. America had been good to her but she was unable to accept its bounty --too guilt ridden over the plight of her land. So London had been the logical end of her search. It seemed like a good compromise. She was resigned to her rather uneventful life and found meaning in caring for her patients. The English with their inner reserve respected and tolerated her. "In England I never feel judged."

"Do you think I am judging you?"

"No, only throwing out a challenge."

There was humor in his eyes. "It's difficult for me to picture you as an old lady alone with her pot of tea and a ginger cat."

"Two. I have two cats."

He sighed. "Fair Annisa. You are still so young."

"I'm old enough to know that I can't really make a difference."

"How very sad. You make it sound like your life is finished long before it is over."

She wondered if she should allow herself the tears that threatened to spill. Strange, but she was thinking of Mrs. Brierly and her nightly ritual of toasting her lost soldier husband, dead for 50 years. Would she end up that way too? And hadn't this same Mrs. Brierly told her how different London had felt to her during the blitz? That despite the fear and the hardship, people had seemed to come alive in their common cause. A bonding had taken place.

"You are right about me. It *is* sad."

They talked then of Najib, sharing mutual stories, marveling at his zest for living and his attempts to mask it. "I think he always had to hide that he cares too much," Meirnardus noted. "I never understood why he didn't seek power when it was his for the asking. The man is far-seeking."

"He said that about me. 'Far seeking but self-doubting.'"

Meirnardus gave her a knowing smile and re-adjusted the blanket over his knees. "Then you match. Do you mind wheeling me inside? It feels a bit chilly."

"*Ghamgin, mota'ase.* I've stayed too long. I've over-tired you."

He reached for her hand. "Annisa. You must stop apologizing for being alive."

His words injured her. How did he know she had always felt this way --that she had no real right to be here. Her birth had killed her mother. Aware she was indeed about to cry, she wheeled him into the reception room and asked him if he was ready for someone to return him to his room.

"Not yet." He reached into the pocket of his bathrobe and handed her a crumpled piece of paper. "Don't lose this. It's your contact for Rahmin. He is not to know where you got this."

"Then you think I should go?"

"I can't see you doing anything else."

She sighed. "Neither can I. Thank you for 'giving' to me today. Who knows, maybe you can help me find my task." She leaned over and kissed him.

"'Someday you will meet a young man with a halo of life around his head. Go with him... The zombies may feel obscurely honored by your presence.'"

"What's that from?"

"The poet, Robert Graves. I wonder if your father read him."

"It would be nice to know, wouldn't it."

"Reflect on your father's poetry, Annisa. The answer to your task may be in his words."

"And what path do *you* think I should follow?"

"That is not for me to say. Remember the life of Meena. Meena," he repeated it twice. Then he released her hand and nodded to the nurse to wheel him away. He never looked back and there was also a lesson in that.

There was fog on the road on the drive back into Lausanne, and Annisa was so deep in thought she almost drove into the centerline several times.

Meirnardus had given her advice in a subtle, yet powerful way. Meena was an Afghan woman who had been assassinated in Quota, Pakistan, by Afghan agents of the KGB in connivance with the fundamentalist band of Gulbuddin Hekmatyar. Meena was a founder of RAWA, an organization of Afghan woman involved in widespread activities promoting women's rights. Annisa had known many RAWA women who left Afghanistan to work among refugee women in Pakistan. They had established schools with hostels for boys and girls, and they also taught nursing and literacy courses for women. Now that the Soviets had left Afghanistan they were openly demonstrating against the fundamentalists in an effort to expose their treason and heinous crimes. Any woman who joined RAWA had a cause. RAWA volunteers knew what their task was and the price was sometimes death.

Overwhelmed by the thought, Annisa pulled over to the side of the road and wept.

CHAPTER 42

Annisa felt unpardonably elated. The closer the time came to her meeting with Rahmin the more excited she felt. True, he had refused to let her come to him but at least he would travel to see her. His terms were that they meet in a non-public place in Peshawar and that she be alone.

Mrs. Reed was more than happy to volunteer her house. Annisa was to stay with her and the Reverend. 'What are friends for? It pains me to think you have been waiting for an answer in Nasi Bagh. Everyone knows that is one of the most crowded camps near Peshawar.'

Her visit with the Reeds was a journey back in time. She slept in a four poster bed with a beautiful hand-made quilt that had been made by the ladies of the congregation. It was the same room where Mrs. Reed had taught her how to rouge her cheeks and curl her hair and had helped her button a beautiful red dress. That night at the Ditchfield's was centuries ago and yet vivid as yesterday. Under a blood red moon she had thrown Mrs. Reed's beautiful jade earrings in the dust at Najib's feet.

"I was such a hateful girl. I pray that Najib returned them to you."

"The very next morning. I have never seen a man so distressed. He was frantic to find you. You know what the Reverend and I think? We think he was looking for himself. We think he saw what he always wanted to be in you."

Annisa threw her arms around Mrs. Reed and clung to her—-never wanting to let go. She loved her plumpness and the smell of her lilac talcum powder. She was wearing a blue cotton apron and there was flour smudges on her nose. "I never had a mother. I mean . . .I never knew her. She was good like you."

"And you?" Mrs. Reed stepped back and looked into Annisa's face. "Are you good?"

"I don't know what good is anymore," Annisa answered wistfully.

"Well, I do. You are one of God's children and you are just fine to me. Now, I'd better get going. Your brother is coming soon and it would be a disaster for him to find me here. Try not to judge him, dear. The Bible preaches forgiveness. Forgiveness is the one true path to happiness."

After she was gone, Annisa settled herself on the sofa, trying to calm her fears. Could she forgive? Her brother had left her alone to grieve his death. A legacy of empty years. A struggle was going on in her heart between a desire to admonish Rahmin for his neglect and the consciousness that she must endure anything if he could be of help to Najib.

Her neck was stiff from watching the pendulum clock as she waited for Rahmin. The minutes dragged by. Every sound on the street outside made her run to the window, afraid she would miss the moment. But after almost an hour of waiting her senses began to dull. She looked around the room that was cluttered with knickknacks. Freshly starched lace curtains at the windows made a strong statement against the dust and dirt of Peshawar. Stacks of books and garden magazines overflowed on side tables gleaming with polished wax. It was a ritual of sorts for Mrs. Reed to polish the furniture, cheerfully humming church hymns as she went about her household tasks. Mrs. Reed did not believe in servants even though they were inexpensive—she enjoyed working with her hands. A painting of a blue eyed, longhaired Jesus rested on the mantelpiece. Annisa thought his eyes followed her every move. On each side of Jesus were family photographs of Mrs. Reed's grandchildren who lived in Kansas, a state in the American midwest. What did they think about their grandparents living halfway around the world? What mysterious force was it that led a person to forsake their own people to spread their faith with others? And to go to a place where their religion wasn't wanted? She marveled at the strength of that faith. Mrs. Reed was not unlike Rahmin who had been so certain of his true beliefs. Rahmin had never professed any doubts. He just knew.

Annisa thought she heard the distinct click of the front gate and ran to the window hoping she would see Rahmin coming up the walk. But the garden was empty and she returned to the sofa, aware of the sweat that had formed on her palms. Surely he was coming. He wouldn't be so cruel as not to show up. She had rehearsed what she was going to say to him over and over, but all her words flew out of her head when she finally heard his footsteps outside the door. It was after 5 o'clock and she had almost given up.

She opened the door and at the sight of him her worried face unconsciously expressed not gladness but surprise. Could this hard-faced man in rimless glasses and a long black beard be Rahmin? He hardly resembled the clean-shaven brother in a Western business suit she had waved off to America as a girl.

"Annisa," he said gruffly, stepping inside and closing the door behind him.

She felt as nervous as a schoolgirl. Should she step forward to embrace him? His arms looked too rigid to touch.

"I'm so happy..." she couldn't finish her sentence, overwhelmed by her feelings. She had an urge to run from the room. Instead she gestured to the pot of green tea and bowl of walnuts Mrs. Reed had left on the table for them. "The tea is cold. I'll heat it up."

"No. No tea. I did not come here for tea." His eyes didn't leave her face and she wondered if he felt as awkward as she did. He settled himself in an easy chair and motioned for her to sit across from him.

Meekly, she obeyed him and quickly withered under his steady gaze. Flustered, she looked away. He had always made her feel so inadequate. Nothing had changed.

"Seeing you is like seeing a ghost," he mumbled. "You now wear our mother's face."

"That's wonderful to hear. I know how much you loved that face."

His voice was cold. "What is it you want from me?"

She could hear the pleading in her voice. "You're my brother, Rahmin."

"Rahmin Aziz is dead. You only imagine me."

"I see. Are those the rules?"

"Those are the rules." He reached into his robe and pulled out a pearl handled dagger and began to clean his nails. "I can't see the purpose of this meeting."

"The purpose!" Annisa was reeling from the hurt. "All these years I mourned you. I missed you." Tears welled in her eyes.

"Don't cry. It never worked on me. Why didn't you stay in America? It was always your goal."

"Then you knew where I was? This is perfidy. You were my sworn protector. How dare you deny you have a sister?"

"How dare I?' He smiled "Ah, the real Annisa shows herself. I knew this meek and docile creature before me was only pretending."

She could not stop the blood rushing to her cheeks. "Yes, I'm good at that. I'm to pretend you are dead. That you don't exist."

"I have not come here to quarrel with you."

"Why did you come, Rahmin?"

For one brief moment she thought she had reached him. His face softened and he took his eyes from her, a pensive look on

457

his face. She waited for an answer but nothing came. She saw that he was staring at the painting of Jesus above the mantle. "I might have known you would arrange to meet me in such a place. The home of infidels. I repeat, what is it you want? I am a busy man and it was a great inconvenience for me to come here."

"An inconvenience to see your sister for the first time in 15 years?"

"Sixteen. And I don't like what I see. Look at you. Red polish on your nails. You look the whore. Is it any wonder that Abdul divorced you."

Annisa gasped. "That was years ago. All this time you have known of me?"

"Certainly. I felt great relief when I heard you were married to Abdul."

She could not hide her sarcasm. "Of course, the great *chapandaz*."

"Don't belittle him. Abdul was a true follower."

"You speak of him as if he was dead."

"He is. Poisoned by one of Haji Latif's men. Believe me, the Lion of Kandahar will meet the same fate."

Annisa knew she should feel something to hear the news of Abdul's death but there was nothing left. Instead her thoughts were on Fatima and the children. What had become of Omar's wife? "Poor Fatima. Abdul had been caring for them."

"Don't concern yourself. Fatima is in Tora Bora. In the home of my second wife."

Annisa was genuinely surprised to hear that he was married. She had always thought that he would never seek a bride. Rahmin had always been so contemptuous of worldly things; it was hard to imagine him as interested in the flesh "And the children?"

"Safe in my house--all except Akhmed."

"Akhmed?"

"Did you not know Akhmed? The boy who fought with Omar and was sent to live with Abdul. He was like an adopted son."

"Oh, that boy. I never met him."

"And why should you? You have no interest in children. Only yourself... After taking you in during the war, you desert the family of El-Ham. Ran away. Ran away to the West."

"Those are Fatima's words. I went to America many years after."

"Doesn't matter. You have always worshiped the non-believers."

"Oh stop it, Rahmin. You are talking to your sister, not some..."

"A sister who fills me with shame."

Furious about his condemnation, Annisa wanted to wound him—to strike back. "You say I look like our mother?" She held up her hands. "Did she polish her nails? Did she rouge her cheeks?"

"Leave our mother out of this!"

"No, I won't. She has always been between us. That perfect woman. Do you forget she was a lowly Tajik? And your creepy friends in the Taliban? Do they know you are part Tajik too? How does that go down with their scorn for women and minorities?"

Rahmin leapt to his feet and for a moment she thought he was going to strike her. Instead, he walked towards the door. "I came here out of a sense of duty. I see I am free to go now."

"No, please wait," she pleaded. "I'm sorry. I really am. I sometimes say things I don't mean."

"I pity you, Annisa. That is the only feeling I have left for you."

She thought of Dr. Hammond's haughty use of the word 'pity' and she shivered. "Forget me and my failures. You still care for Najib. You always did."

His jaw muscles tightened and he turned and walked back; towering over her. "Why talk to me of Najib?"

Annisa was desperate, realizing she had gone about it all wrong. She should have mentioned Najib in the very beginning before they slipped into their old antagonistic patterns. "You've got to help him."

"I see. So that is why you are suddenly anxious to rediscover your brother."

"That's not true. I only heard you were alive a few days ago."

"Najib told you this?"

"No, no." She was searching for the right words. She could not mention Meirnardus who wanted his contacts kept secret. "Najib was going to be hanged but your forces captured Dulmagon just in time. I beg you. I know that you are very high up in the Taliban. If Najib is in your hands you have the power to release him. You have always hated me but you loved him like a brother."

"I still do."

Again, tears welled in her eyes. "Then you will help?"

"Save your dramatics for others. Najib is not in our custody. I have no idea where he is."

459

"I don't believe that. Najib was too formidable an enemy of the Taliban for you not to know he was in Dulmagon."

"You call me a liar?"

She tried to stop herself but could not. "Yes. You align yourself with evil men."

"I see. You ask to meet me in order to insult me. You left Afghanistan. You know nothing of what has been happening since the Russians left. Rape, murder, and looting. And not by the communists. By Mujahideen commanders of warring tribes. By *your* friends. The Taliban controls many provinces now. We are the stalwarts of Islam and we conform to the *Sunnah of Rasulullah*."

"No, you are hypocrites. You ban television sets, smash them and hang them from trees and at the same time you allow the sale and transit of truckloads of them in order to collect the taxes. You allow grave-worship and the *mujaawars* to collect money from the ignorant visitors. You absent yourselves from *Mamat Salat* and laze around smoking hookah."

"Where do you hear such garbage?"

"From many different visitors to Afghanistan."

"Now I know you are a fool. You use gossip, the tool of the devil, to malign our good intentions. Annisa, you have never been anything but a thorn in my side. If it were not for the memory of our mother I would have you put in chains."

"Chains! Your only sister in chains because she disagrees with you! My God, what has happened? Are you the same brother who used to braid my hair? Who carved a wooden doll for me? You built me a treehouse in the garden. Was I really so terrible?"

His look was menacing. "Be finished with this."

"Put me in chains!" She was hysterical now and flailing her arms. "Have you no feelings for anyone, Rahmin?" Lost in her sobs she did not notice Rahmin quietly leave the room and enter the kitchen. He returned with a glass of water and stuck it under her nose. "Here, drink this. Calm yourself."

The intimacy of this small gesture of human kindness gave her a small ray of hope. "Please, Rahmin. You've got to understand. Najib is all I have ever lived for."

"You put Najib above Allah?"

The blood drained from her face leaving her white with anger. "You imposter. You twist my words. You pretend to be the true standard-bearer of Islam. I spit on your Taliban propaganda. You ignore the needs of the *fuqara* -- the poor and the destitute. There is no shortage of food in Taliban quarters. Twice daily, mutton is served to all. You drive flashy late-model vehicles. And your call for the strict observance of *Jamaat Salaat* is a joke. You abandoned your roadblocks for prayer after only a few months. Hypocrites that's what you are. All of you, hypocrites."

"Enough, Annisa."

"Oh, no. There is more. Lots, more."

He crossed his arms across his chest and rocked back and forth on his heels. "Your tirade reveals who you really are. You came to me only because you want something."

Annisa could feel her body contract, shrinking in defeat. There was a grain of truth in what he said.

"You don't belong in Afghanistan," he said.

"I belong as much as you."

"No, you have never been strong in our faith."

"Wrong. I am the true believer. Your teachings of the Koran are twisted. You consider yourself so pure and yet you align yourself with a man who had many whores in Lebanon. A drunkard. A spoiled rich son of the Saudis. His own people have disowned him. Kicked him out. So he creates mischief in the Sudan. It is rumored he plans to come back to Afghanistan. I have as much right to be in Afghanistan as your precious Bin Laden. I hope he rots in the sands of the Sudan. That the vultures pick out his eyes."

"You ignorant stupid girl. Bin Laden has no connection with the Taliban. If he comes to Afghanistan it will be to Jalalabad, which is controlled by Haji Abdul Qadir, a good friend of Massoud. Bin Laden is a saint. He renounces his millions to give to the poor. He wants nothing for himself."

"You are the one who is stupid if you believe that. I think he is driven to call attention to himself. Mercy, if I were one of 52 children I guess I would do something different from the others too."

"Yes, that is something *you* would do. Don't speak of matters you know nothing about. The Taliban is good, Annisa. Your friends in Kabul are nothing more than bandits. We must restore order to the land."

"And lose our freedom in doing so?"

"Are you free if you can't feel safe?"

"I would rather be free."

"Bah. You don't know what you want. You never did. Frivolous. Always chasing rainbows. You know nothing of what life is about. What have you ever done for your people except run away? Your life is a joke."

"You know nothing of what my life has been," she said softly. "Or else you would not speak to me so."

"I know you are wrapped up in yourself. You play house in England but where are your goals? I see you have created yet another fantasy..."

"And I see that you are drunk with power. That the zealots of the Taliban have seduced you."

"Think again before you criticize us. We have great plans. Someday the captains of industry will take note of us. Islam has been invisible too long. Akhmed, Abdul's adopted son, will be a name the world will remember. He is a young man now and he trains to be a martyr."

"You would send Akhmed to Bin Laden to train as a terrorist? When is all this killing going to stop?"

"Never. We are a nation of warriors."

"Well, at last the truth is out. You like to fight. You live to fight. You take young boys and make an adventure of it. Children serve as your runners. Nine-year-olds blow themselves up in the bazaars in order to wound others in your name. And all for the glory of what? You have no heart. You are my blood brother and yet you have always denied me."

Enraged, Rahmin reached for his dagger he had placed on the table near his chair. Annisa went cold with fear.

"I'll show you what I think of sharing your blood," he thundered.

Horrified, Annisa watched him walk slowly towards her. Like a high executioner he reached for her finger and pricked it with his knife. Then he sliced the tip of his thumb, smearing their blood together onto the palm of his left hand. She felt she was going to faint as he raised his bloodied palm above her head. "Death to the unbelievers." Annisa was holding her breath as she watched him cross to the mantle and press his bloody palm print onto the face of Jesus.

"You are mad," she said, her voice barely above a whisper. "Jesus is one of our Prophets."

"And in his name they have slaughtered us."

She was truly afraid of him now. Not for herself but for what he wanted to do to others. People like the well-meaning Mrs. Reed.

"Rahmin. Please. Please stop this," she whimpered. "Where has the kindness of our gentle father gone? What have they done to you?"

He did not answer, methodically wiping the blood from his blade and returning the knife to inside his garment.

Annisa could not take her eyes off the bloodied handprint on the painting and her body began to shake. "I can't believe that I actually thought you would help Najib. Dear God, you can't even help yourself." She knew in this moment there was nothing left she could do for Najib. "I hope you go to your grave thinking of Najib and how he loved you. He would have done anything for you. He went to New York several times, searching for news about you. He even killed a man to avenge your alleged death. And he has paid a terrible price for it."

Rahmin did not respond.

"Who lies in that grave that bears your name?"

"Some homeless man, they tell me."

"You are vile. Evil"

"I have no time for this."

"You deliberately killed a man so that you could change your identity. That is monostrous."

"I killed no one. The cell made the arrangements."

Annisa exploded. "Arrangements! How cold-blooded can you get? Our father is spinning in his grave to hear this."

"You forget. Our father has no grave and yet you cry for the infidels."

"I cry because you are so full of hate. Najib is not an infidel yet you refuse to help him. You violate every ancient code of honor. You will not help your friend."

"I curse you! They emptied the jails before we entered Koimar. There was hand to hand fighting in the streets."

"That's not true. I hear the Taliban bought their way in as they always do."

"You think you know everything."

"No. You do. You have the power, Rahmin, and you abuse it. I'm begging you. Please help Najib."

"There is no help for Najib. He could be anywhere. He could be lying dead in a ditch or back inside Kabul. I don't know where he is!"

"And if you did? Would you have tried to save him?"

"Allah has spared me that terrible decision and you are not about to force me to make it now."

From the anguish on his face she suddenly believed him. She had forgotten that Rahmin had never been able to lie convincingly. No wonder he flew into a rage when she called him a liar. It was part of their childhood. Najib could tell you an outrageous story as a joke and be believed. But when Rahmin tried the same thing his jaw would begin to twitch and he couldn't look you in the eye. Rahmin was telling the truth. He truly did not know Najib's fate. She was more upset now than before. Najib might still be alive. And perhaps no one would ever know.

Amazed to see that Rahmin had brushed a tear from his eye she reached out and awkwardly put her hand on his arm. But he recoiled from her touch. There was incredible pain in his eyes as he backed away from her. "Go back to London, Annisa. You no longer belong here and I do not say that to be unkind."

Her voice was softer now. "Yes. I know this. And you must know I will always love you. They have twisted your mind, but you mean well, my brother-jan." She knew that in his own warped way of thinking, Rahmin had always thought he had her best interests at heart.

A look of relief swept across his face. "*Khoda Hafez*. Then my journey was worth it. God be your protector."

"*Az amadon e shom, khush hastam*. From your coming, I am happy." But she was not sure that she meant it when she looked at the bloodied handprint on Mrs. Reed's picture of Christ. Forgiveness. It was all about forgiveness, Mrs. Reed had said.

CHAPTER 43

Strangely enough, Annisa's decision to return to her 'roots' was not questioned by Matthew Hardcastle. In London she moved like a whirlwind to settle her affairs: sold her belongings and found a home for her cats. Who was he to dampen such zeal? In fact, he aided and abetted her journey to Kabul. He was going back inside to do a feature story on landmines. The UN Mine Action service report had suggested that Afghanistan had perhaps the greatest level of mine concentration in the world. Half of mine accidents were children under eighteen and half of those injured died before reaching a medical facility. Land mines were becoming a hot news item.

It was decided he would take Annisa with him as far as Kabul before heading on to Herat. He had an interview scheduled with Taliban leaders who were eager to show the world how their black-turbaned troops were winning over the population by clearing roads of mines.

His stated purpose made their ride through Taliban controlled territory easier than expected. The few times their Land Rover was stopped they did not even bother to check Annisa's forged papers. She was traveling as a member of the press with a Lebanese passport.

Matthew had not tried to talk her out of going back to Afghanistan but he certainly acted the mother hen on their ride inside that country. Was she certain she had enough money and was it accessible? The answer was 'yes' and yes it was true that the average Afghan lived on less than fifty dollars a month. Her childhood friend Siddiqa had assured Annisa there would be no trouble finding work with the hospital—so many trained doctors and nurses had fled Afghanistan there was an absolute dearth of them now. Siddiqa had a local staff job with a European relief agency and Annisa would be sharing her flat in Kabul. Together they could survive for years.

"And if the Taliban takes over Kabul?" Matthew asked. "What then?"

"It won't happen." Annisa pointed out that few in Kabul believed that an ill-trained force of mostly young and idealistic men could seize the well-defended capital.

"Do you think you'll ever come back to London?"

"No, I'm finished with chasing rainbows. Rahmin was right about me."

"And the rest of us? Were we so wrong?"

"No more than I was."

They talked about his novel on Afghanistan and if he would ever finish it. Matthew did not have a timetable. "Afghanistan is a work in progress."

"If you do finish it, could you do me a favor? Could you make my Uncle Omar an asterisk?" She told him about Omar's wish to be remembered and Matthew promised that Omar would be included and probably in a bigger role than a footnote.

"Of all the stories you have told me, Omar intrigues me the most. Now you take care, I want a happy ending for my book. Modern readers only want happy endings."

"Then end it with my returning to Kabul, content to have my roots back. Panna said the secret to life was to tend to your own garden on your own earth. I will blossom in this soil."

"The strange thing is that I believe you."

The odds were certainly against Annisa finding that happy ending. Kabul felt like a dying city the minute they entered. The conditions horrendous. "I'll make a pact with you," he said. "I promise not to worry, if you promise to keep in touch."

"We will always know of each other, Matthew."

"Yes." His voice was gruff. "Indian curry will never be the same without you."

She laughed and they parted with a handshake—-both of them secure in their knowledge of each other.

Inside the city Annisa was more appalled by the sights than she had anticipated. More than one third of it had been reduced to rubble in the conflict between Mujahideen Commanders Dostum and Hikmatyar against Rabbani's government. Twenty-five thousand people, mostly civilians had been killed on the streets the year before. Mujahideen supply routes were being cut off by the Taliban Islamic military. Despite this she truly believed the Taliban would never take Kabul even though it was a city being ground to dust. The supply of electricity and water, public transportation, communications and the sanitation systems were all destroyed. Half a million people went to bed at night hungry. The militia camped on the high ground south of the city, hurling rockets daily into Kabul. Children crippled by war played among the ruins. None of them had crutches. She passed a boy on the street without legs. He moved about by lifting his body and scooting on his hands.

On the way to Siddiqa's flat she walked by her father's old house or what was left of it. Part of the roof was gone and the peach tree had not survived this latest assault. Had Fritz Werner? It was rumored he was living in Frankfurt. But like so many people from her past, no one really knew. Uncle Fritz was one of the missing—-missing, like Najib. Najib, her reluctant warrior. She had dreamed the other night that he was suffering from amnesia, triggered by a blow to the head. He was wandering the desert--lost and calling out her name. She reached out her arms to him but he drew back from her-- his eyes locked in a vacant stare. "Who are you?" he said. She awoke, her nightgown bathed in sweat. She had to let it go. All of it. No longer would she let herself be trapped by convention, respectability, or class. Nor would the discipline and self-restraint of Islam be her ultimate goal. She had asked for this new life and there was no looking back.

Siddiqa's apartment was sparsely furnished but with several large rooms--a real treat in Kabul where many people survived in only one. Annisa and Siddiqa would share the space with Siddiqa's five-year-old daughter, Roxanne. Her father had been killed at Gulbahar, north of Kabul, where Siddiqa had once worked at the Afghan Textile Company.

"You must be tired after your long trip," Siddiqa said, offering her a plate of sweets...

"No. I feel very wide-awake. I'm eager to get started."

"How does Kabul look to you after all these years?"

Annisa was honest in her answer, admitting that the landscape had taken on a different perspective and that there was a killing hardness to the land. "But there is poetry in it too."

Siddiqa smiled. "I confess I find it difficult to understand why you would come back to all this."

"I don't understand it myself." She looked at Siddiqa's threadbare dress and the holes in her shoes. Her friend had aged dramatically. There were streaks of grey in her jet-black hair and she was dangerously thin. "What do you live on?"

"I have a meager salary and I sell my belongings but as you can see there is very little left."

"Not to worry. If we are careful I've brought enough to last us for a very long time. You no longer need to feel abandoned." She knew that Siddiqa's parents had died early in the war and that her younger brothers had escaped the dreary conditions inside Afghanistan to study in a *madrassas* in Pakistan. It distressed Siddiqa that her brother's were now fighting with the Taliban.

Annisa commiserated with her. "General Berber is cunning. He knew the *madrassas* would be fertile ground for indoctrinating our young men. My own brother is one of his cutthroats."

"If only the Americans hadn't turned their backs on us. They are indifferent to our sufferings."

"Americans are never indifferent —more like unaware. Besides, it's too easy to blame all the ills of the world on them. They've had their hands full. The Iron Curtain came down. Iraq invaded Kuwait. 'Desert Storm.' Do I dare to say that I think we did it to ourselves? Tribal chieftains and their bickering. On every street corner each group fights for their own little piece of the turf. You just wait. If Kabul falls it will be because of *baksheesh* not bullets. The warlords will sell us out as they always have."

"Let's not dwell on the war. What has life brought you Annisa?"

"Many wonderful things that I did not always appreciate at the time."

"Why did you never marry?"

"I did. One of my uncles in Mazar. But it was a union in name only."

After so many years apart Annisa suddenly felt shy about sharing her past with Siddiqa. After all, Siddiqa had married and had a child. How could she possibly confide she could never be a mother because Russian soldiers had raped her? But Annisa's reticence only lasted a short time. She did confess and was not prepared for Siddiqa's answer.

"It happened to me too. A Mujahideen. Outside Barbar's tomb. There was no law and order here when the Russians first pulled out."

Their shared humiliation soon formed a bridge for them over their long separation. Forgotten memories of childhood came tumbling out. A shared history, accented by giggles and laughs which nourished their souls. It was good to think of happier times as the winter sun dipped lower in the horizon.

Siddiqa's daughter, Roxanne, listened intently to their girlish exploits. The child fascinated Annisa. She had a placid composure and her round rimless glasses gave her face the suggestion of intellectuality.

"Mama, is this the lady who marched with you when the girls of your school shook their fists at the puppets?"

"It is indeed." Siddiqa looked a bit flustered... "It's one of her favorite bedtime stories. Roxanne likes to think of her mother as a hero."

"You were. All of us. That's really why I've come back. I want to reclaim that sense of myself."

"You wish to be heroic?" Roxanne asked.

"No, but I seem to have forgotten how to make a fist." She was thinking of her compromise with Dr. Hammond. She should have stood her ground.

Siddiqa sighed. "I hope you get a chance to make your fist. I don't see how much longer Kabul can hold out against the Taliban. They will take your fist and tie it behind your back."

"That is the risk I have to take. I still believe that men of good will shall prevail."

After dinner they talked of Siddiqa's late husband and of the missing Najib.

"Annisa, you must accept that Najib is dead. Men don't simply vanish for years at a time and then reappear."

"Najib has many times." Then she realized how foolish she sounded. "I admit I have this weakness, I still believe in fairytales. On a moonlight night he will come riding up the streets of Jad-i-Miwand and carry me away."

"And in the morning sun?"

"I will smile at my own foolishness and go off to work in the hospital, into the reality of sickness and the business of healing. I should tell you that Najib was never certain he believed in paradise and said that if it was anywhere it was here on earth. It wasn't until I saw babies delivered that I wondered if perhaps that might be true. I can't tell you the joy I feel when I witness new life."

"I am thrilled you are here, but didn't you see babies born in London?"

"Maybe I've come back because I'm still hoping for that man on the white horse."

"What man?" Siddiqa's daughter asked.

"Never mind," her mother answered. "He's a myth. He doesn't exist."

And Annisa knew that it was true.

It was almost dusk when she left Siddiqa's flat to visit her mother's grave. She was shattered when she could not find it. The hillside where she had been buried had taken several hits from rockets.. But she did find Kassim's. She could have gone there blindfolded. All the things she had planned to say to her mother she had no urge to share with Kassim. She had not really known him very well but had created an image out of a young girl's longings. Her mother was a different story. She carried her blood in her veins. Would her mother forgive her for running away from the family of El-Ham? Or for hating her brother, Rahmin? And had her mother wished for Rahmin to grow up to be a warrior like her brothers or a man of peace like her enlightened husband? But what Annisa had really wanted to ask her mother was had she lived up to what her mother wanted her to be? It was so hard to please a ghost. Panna, Ethan's father — so many had said that all a mother ever really wanted for her children was happiness. So she had come to her mother's grave to report that at last she truly was happy and no longer had to pretend. She finally accepted that it was *her* choice to return to her country—hers alone... She had no illusions about Afghanistan or her role in it. A force blacker than a plague of locusts would soon take the land as it had countless times before. But she felt comfort, secure in the knowledge that the darkness would someday be destroyed.

    A year later in late September that happiness would be sorely tested. The Taliban seized Kabul and imposed strict Islamic code on the city. Women could no longer work and were to be restricted to their homes. Girls' schools were closed and any woman on the streets who wasn't wearing a *chadri* could be stoned. The few women doctors left in the hospitals were being forced to operate while wearing the veil! Soon they would be banned from practicing at all.

    Siddiqa was distraught that her little daughter could no longer go to school.

"I will teach her. Here."

"Annisa, it is forbidden."

"Then we will do it in secret." Annisa felt a mounting excitement. She could no longer work at the hospital, but this was something she could do. "I can teach classes inside our house. And we'll bring other girls to study."

"We could be stoned."

"They will punish us no matter what we do. I saw a woman whipped on the street today because her heels under her *chaderi* made a clicking sound on the pavement. We are living amidst a pack of wild dogs. It's the herd mentality. Afghan men who love their wives are beating them for no reason at all. Do you think these women would betray us? Never. There is not a woman with a child in this city who would do such a thing. Do you know what they said at the hospital? That world health agencies think more than 10% of all Afghans are suffering from mental disorders. No one can cope with the tensions of war year after year."

"Then you are saying it is hopeless?"

"No, our daughters are our hope for a civilized society. Look at our boys. They have never known anything but war. All our young men know how to do is fight. A little boy at the hospital told me, 'War is fun. You get to fight.' Is that anything to build on? I tell you, Siddiqa, this is our calling. We can teach young girls. We can do it!"

Siddiqa threw up her arms. "I feel like a school girl again marching against the palace. You with that battered cane waving our make-shift flag above your head."

"We didn't know the dangers in what we were doing. Now we do." For one brief moment, which she did not share with Siddiqa, Annisa questioned if they were being unwise.

And then, as though to underscore the significance of their cause, a flash of lightening illuminated the room followed by thunder claps.

Annisa jumped back. "That was close!"

"Yes. I think it is an omen. Allah has spoken. He applauds our cause." Siddiqa laughed and clapped her hands together... "It feels so right, Annisa."

"Yes, very right. Najib said that too." Annisa was certain now that death held no sting for her—-paradise or no paradise. It was her choice. Her life. Her task.

1998

CHAPTER 44

FIVE little birdies nesting in a row.
ONE flew out
FOUR more to go.

The younger girls clapped their hands as they recited in unison their lesson in subtraction for the day.

Annisa responded to their eagerness and inwardly rejoiced. The voices of the righteous and deceived — unaware of the wickedness that surrounded them.

Her class consisted of nine girls all under the age of ten. Nine girls who had never known a day of peace.

She checked her watch. Their mothers would be coming for them soon. Time raced. There were never enough hours in the day to keep up with her ambitious plans. She and many others risked their lives to teach the girls and she was going to make sure that the risk was worth it. She was a hard taskmaster but her students thrived on it. Their enthusiasm was remarkable, perhaps born out of eagerness to do what the Taliban had forbidden – to learn. As much as Annisa had loved nursing this was even more satisfying. And she had to admit to herself that the element of risk brought an edge to it.

Most of the time she felt reasonably safe. They had set up a rather elaborate lookout system under the noses of the Taliban. Mothers took turns watching the front of the apartment building from a rooftop across the street. The men of Kabul were not allowed on rooftops out of the Taliban's fear they would look down on their women. This gave the lookout some protection. They were to wave a line of washing hanging on the roof if there was any sign of the religious police force vehicles (labeled the Department for Promoting Virtue and Prohibiting Vice) pulling up in front of the building. This was the signal to the woman who watched from the kitchen of Siddiqa's flat to evacuate the girls. The drill to empty the flat was simple. Each child was assigned to a family on the floors above Annisa and Siddiqa. On the given signal they would disperse immediately scurrying like field mice to safety. By the time the officials arrived up the five flights of stairs they would find Annisa and Siddiqa alone at home with only Roxanne. They had rehearsed their dispersal many times—even down to the time it took Annisa to hide her blackboard under the bed and for Siddiqa to pick up scattered books and papers to hide in the laundry basket. The children loved the drill and treated it as a game, but they also knew it was deadly serious. They failed only one practice run and that was the time when Annisa opened the door with chalk on her nose and on her fingertips. The mother playing the role of an inspector warned this might create suspicion.

In the beginning Annisa thought they were being overly cautious but she soon changed her mind when she learned that two other women in Kabul who were caught teaching girls were whipped and their hands amputated. A friend of Siddiqa's, a sports instructor at the soccer stadium, confided that his team refused to practice one night when they saw a basket full of severed limbs on the field. It was at the sports stadium where the Taliban carried out their grizzly executions.

Annisa checked her watch again and went to the blackboard. "Children, there is time for a *landay* today." This was their favorite time of day. To read or even write a *landay* of their own. Despite the fact that Annisa stressed practical subjects that would be useful to them, such as math and science, she did allow time for poetry and Afghan history. All of her pupils could recite the dates of independence movements. From the first freedom movement in Afghanistan led by Abu Muslim Khorasani to the creation of the People's Democratic Party of Afghanistan in 1965. Annisa was always careful to underline that Afghan women had once served in the parliament and there had been women judges and doctors.

She printed in chalk a *landay* on the blackboard.
Your face is a rose and your eyes are candles;
Faith! I am lost. Should I become a butterfly or a moth?
"Now how many syllables in the first line of the *landay*?"
"Eleven," they chanted in unison.
"And how many the second?"
"Fourteen."
"Now what does it mean, "Should I become a butterfly or a moth?"
Several hands shot up.
She called on Lelah in the first row. "I would like to be a butterfly."
"And why is that?"
"So I could fly around and look pretty. A moth flies into the flame. And burns itself up."

"That's good. Very good. And you Sheila?"

A rap came on the door interrupting Shelia's answer. Annisa put her finger on her lips, signaling that they be quiet. She was hesitant to open the door and went into the kitchen where Siddiqa sat watching out the window. "Any signal from the rooftop?"

"None."

Her hands a bit unsteady, Annisa returned to the door. "Who is it?" she called.

"Kari Gundersen."

A sigh of relief escaped her. Kari was her good Norwegian friend who worked at the UN emergency relief center. Annisa opened the door. "Come in. Come in. We are happy to see you. We thought you might still be in the north working with the earthquake victims."

"No, after the quake, I went back to Norway on home leave. I returned to Kabul late last night. . . Sorry to interrupt."

"It's okay, we were just finishing up."

"What was it like? The earthquake?" one of the girls asked.

"A nightmare. Over 4,000 dead. The aftershocks were horrendous. There is nothing like it when the earth moves under your feet. A very frightening experience."

"Perhaps the earthquake was a sign from Allah. Shaking his fist at the Taliban," Lelah said. The room burst into giggles.

"That's enough," Annisa scolded, trying to keep a straight face.

Kari reached in her bag and held up a tin box of cookies. "I've brought a treat. In Norway we call this *Seterjentas rommedbrod*—Dairymaid's wafers."

A murmur of delight rippled through the room. The girls were very familiar with Kari and her bag of gifts. She was their angel from another land of high mountains. She was a role model to them. They had heard that Kari could ski like a rocket and that she had won medals in skiing for her country. If only Afghan girls were allowed to play sports. At least the boys had soccer.

"I also have two new boxes of crayons and some writing tablets." The girls gathered around her and Roxanne threw her arms around Kari's knees. "I love you," she said. "Do you want to hear me play a new song?"

Last year at Ramadan, Kari had brought musical toys for every girl in the class. Roxanne's was a small harmonica. And it was her greatest sense of joy. The Taliban had smashed her mother's record player and the radio that had belonged to her father was sold to buy food long before Annisa had come to live with them. "I practice every day," she said solemnly.

"Let me hear you."

Kari recognized the tune immediately. *"Frere Jacques."* A French folk song. "Where did you learn that?"

"My father used to sing it."

"He learned it from a French archeologist he worked for one summer." Siddiqa answered from the kitchen. "Come, girls, I've made some tea to go with your cookies."

"I have some interesting news for you," Kari confided to Annisa.

"What is it?"

"Later when the children are gone. . . Oh, and have you heard about the American air strikes against Bin Laden's training camps last night? Near the Pakistan border? They've linked Bin Laden to the bombings of the U.S. embassies in Nairobi and Dar es-Salaam."

Annisa frowned. "I pray that my brother was not involved in this."

"Do you ever hear from him?"

"Never. Nor do I want to."

"It's heartbreaking what war does to families."

One of the mothers who came to pick up her child asked Siddiqa if she and Roxanne would go to the market with her. Women had to go shopping in pairs because a woman was not allowed to walk alone in the bazaars of Kabul. The mother lived on the second floor and never went out. But she needed medicine for the baby.

"You just got here," Siddiqa said to Kari. "Would you mind?"

"Not at all."

The mother stared at Kari with awe. Only foreign women were allowed to work in Kabul and go on the streets without the *chaderi*. Kari wore only a scarf on her head.

Annisa was pleased when all the children had been picked up—happy to be alone with her friend. She went into the kitchen and signaled from the window to the woman on the roof across the street. Her vigil was over. The children were gone for the day.

Kari reached into her bag for yet another treat and proudly removed a cherry cream cake. "I'll have you know I carried this on the plane. My mother made it for you and Siddiqa. We call it *Kirseboerkremkake."*

"Fantastic! Kari, you are a marvel. Only you would do such a thing. . . Now tell me, what is your interesting bit of gossip you promised to tell?"

"It's about a man I met outside Faizabad during the earthquake relief efforts."

"Ah," Annisa smiled. "It's about a man, is it?"

"It's not what you think. He's... well, anyway, when I first met him I thought he was working with a small relief agency—one of those funded by religious groups. He was handing out blankets and cooking oil. You could see everyone loved him. He was so full of fun—cheerful and telling jokes amidst all that desolation. He made the children laugh. People told me he was kind of a modern day Robin Hood-- always on the move from place to place—robbing the rich to give to the poor."

"A benevolent bandit."

"Not exactly. It seems he knows how to get money out of the warlords for his charitable efforts. It turned out he was affiliated to no one—kind of his own one-man band."

"Interesting."

"I thought so. Especially when I found out he is also a very fine artist. He does charcoal sketches in the bazaar."

"He should count his blessing and be grateful he is in Faizabad. The Taliban would have his head in a moment for his cheerfulness and his drawings." Annisa smiled again. "You sound very interested in him. How old is he?"

"Almost 40 I would guess. To add to his mystique he is also incredibly handsome." Kari was watching Annisa intently. "He's an Afghan who speaks beautiful English and he carries himself like a military officer."

Annisa suddenly felt wary, sensing her friend was leading up to something. "And?. . ."

Kari gave her a watchful look. "Annisa, he has gorgeous green eyes and a wicked scar on his cheek."

"And?"

"His charcoal sketches. They all look like you."

"What are you trying to tell me?"

Kari pointed to the framed photo Annisa had on the wall. "I think he might be your Najib."

Annisa leapt to her feet. "Don't say that. It's not possible."

"I wonder."

477

"Did he give you his name?"

"Yes. Sheer. They call him Sheer."

Annisa could feel her neck muscles tighten. "Sheer means Lion. Sheer was Najib's code name in the Resistance." She sank back down in her chair. "Kari, it might really be him."

"What do you think you should do?"

"Do?" Annisa twisted her hands nervously. "I can't even think of doing... I'm going to pretend you never told me."

"Perhaps that is wise. The man had an almost 'other world' look about him. Under his jokes and his laughter he seemed a bit divorced from reality."

"In what way?"

"You know, those men who suffer from shell shock? Who wander the countryside not even knowing who they are? I debated whether I should even mention this to you but I thought you would want to know."

Annisa sighed. "Yes, Kari. I always want to know. I think of him every day even though I am certain he is dead."

"I shouldn't have told you."

"No, no. I'm glad."

But as soon as Kari left, Annisa could no longer pretend she was glad. She reached for the photo of Najib and hurled it across the room. The glass inside the frame shattered into many pieces. And when Siddiqa returned home from the market she found Annisa on her hands and knees picking up shards of glass and moaning softly. "What in the world. What has happened?" Roxanne ran to help Annisa pick up the glass but her mother waved her away. "You'll cut your fingers."

"Did the bad people come, Mama because we have school?"

"No, no. I'm sorry I've made such a mess," Annisa answered. "I'm so sorry, Roxanne, I didn't mean to scare you." She stood up and turned to Sidiqqa. "Kari thinks Najib is still alive. That she saw him in Faziabad."

Siddiqa looked worried as she listened to the details "It has to be a coincidence. They are lots of Afghans with green eyes and the scars of war on their faces. And Sheer is a common name. After all you've been through, Annisa. Surely, you don't believe this. You aren't going to look for him?"

"Of course not."

"I know it's selfish of me to say this, but your home is here."

"Yes, I know that. Kari says this man, Sheer seems to live in his own inner world ... that he seems at peace with himself." Annisa began to choke on her words. "It would be cruel to enter it."

"I think we are making much too much out of this. I don't see how it could be Najib."

Annisa sensed how threatened Siddiqa was by the possibility. "No, probably not," she lied.

Shortly after midnight, Annisa awoke to a full moon streaming in the window. It was full and ripe and beckoning. She felt jumpy and restless. There were demons inside her head that told her to run. To run away. *If this really was Najib.* Her wild crazy thoughts frightened her and she held her fist up to her mouth to keep from shouting. Would she ever feel complete without Najib? It had been so much easier to fill her life when she thought of him as dead. She turned her head away from the light streaming in the window. She must concentrate on the eager faces of her students that looked up to her each day in this very room. Young faces that were full of trust. Invisible strings of duty that tied her to the ground. How could she let her life that had been so full this morning turn to ashes in her mouth? Maybe the man in Faizabad wasn't really Najib. Better to never know the real truth. Or better to think of Najib distributing blankets to the poor instead of rotting in an unmarked grave?

All her life she had been running away from or running to. It had to stop. She had found her niche and it was here. Teaching had become her joy--a true expression of herself. No wonder her father had loved it so. She remembered how curious and eager he was about life and what a sympathetic listener he was.. Her father had been in sympathy with the whole world. And he had mastered the art of letting go.

With a child's eyes she used to watch her father wrestle with his loneliness-- filling that empty space in his heart with his love for all living things. How many times had he told her how fortunate he was to have known that kind of love. He never wanted to marry again. There had been perfection in her mother's arms.

As there had been for her in Najib's.

She was proud that her father was not a warrior and knew how sad it would be for him to witness the sacrifice of Afghanistan's young men. Under that full moon tonight these young warriors slept with their arms embracing their rifles. It would be the Afghan girls who would have to tame the savage beast—a beast unleashed by poverty and pestilence and the arrogance of hunger for revenge. The more she heard abut this Bin Laden the more anxious she became. His money had bought the Taliban victory in Kabul, and very soon men like Najib would no longer be safe in the north. The leaders of al Qaeda were not Afghans but terrorists masquerading as the true interpreters of Islam. Destroyers of the hearts and minds of her land.

"Aunt Annisa, can't you sleep?"

A small hand reached up for hers. It was Roxanne by her side.

"I often can't when the moon is full."

"Mama says the moon pulls the water on the earth. It rules many things."

"Your mother is right."

"Mama says men have walked on the moon?"

"Yes, Americans."

"Is it true you might leave us?"

Annisa could see Roxanne was trembling and put her arms around her waist.

"Never. My place is here... except for tonight."

"Tonight? Auntie Annisa, you scare me."

Annisa reached for her dress hanging on a hook and a money clasp she kept under her pillow. She crossed to the door.

"Wait," Roxanne said as she ran to her side. "You can't go outside without your veil you know. And you are not allowed on the streets at night."

"Shush, you'll wake your mother."

"Where are you going?"

"To ride a horse."

"Oh, Auntie Annisa, why?"

"Don't worry. I will be back before morning. I promise. Tell your mother I'll be back before light."

"But the moon is so bright outside, Auntie Annisa. They will see you."

"No harm will come to me. Back to bed now. Don't speak and don't you dare follow me." Annisa shut the door softly behind her and tiptoed down the hall to the stairway. The full moon illuminated the street. Roxanne was right. There was no way she would not be seen. But the street outside was empty except for an old man asleep on his flat bed truck. She knew exactly where to go. To the house of Mr. P.K Singh, an Indian Sikh who sold fine silks in the bazaar. His *baccha,* Sur Gul, often carried messages for Annisa. He was a smart boy and always eager to earn extra *baksheesh.*

Sur Gul was asleep in the servants quarters when Annisa gently tapped on the window.

A bleary eyed Sur Gul rushed to the door. "*Min-sahib*. Are you crazy? Alone in the night. Without the veil."

"You told me once you could get me a horse?"

"Ah, *min-shaib*. That was before the Taliban came."

"What about the gypsies camped down by the river? They have horses don't they?"

"It is dangerous to go there. Even the Taliban leave them alone. They smuggle drugs for the al Qaeda."

"I will make it worth your while."

He stared at the afghanis she had pressed in his hand. "Where do you go with this horse?"

"I only want to ride it tonight. I can have it back to you before the first light."

He pointed to the moon. "*Dewanna*. This is crazy *min-sahib*. There is light and it is night. The moon makes people crazy."

"Try, Sur Gul. This is very important to me."

"It is so?"

"It is so."

He told her to wait inside his quarters until he returned. "It is darker inside." He was not gone long before she thought of changing her mind—to face up to what a risky thing she was doing. Yet in the very depth of her being she had this sense of knowing. That if she didn't ride tonight to conquer this yearning that she might do something even more foolish in the days ahead.

Much to Annisa's surprise the boy returned sooner than she had anticipated. Her face fell when she saw that he was empty-handed.

"Come with me," he said. "It is tethered to a post at the end of a row of trees in the park. I am afraid if I bring the horse here it will whinny and wake my master."

Annisa followed him, expecting to see a moth eaten nag without a saddle, but an apparition appeared before her eyes. An Arabian stallion with watchful eyes. "He is beautiful." she whispered. "How did you come by him?"

"The gypsy man told me that any woman wild enough to ride alone at night deserved only the best."

"Sur Gul, he is a gift from God. Here, help me up."

"Remember you return before morning. Or I will be in very big trouble. The gypsies carry very large knives."

"I won't let you down," Annisa answered. "Not you. Not anyone."

Annisa patted the horse's neck and whispered in its ear. "Tonight I shall call you Daldal and we will ride across the sky."

She was soon out of town and galloping furiously through moonlit fields—an irresponsible thing to do. These fields were dotted with land minds, but she didn't care. She was daring fate tonight, her mind in the depths of a black depression and, at the same time, intoxicated joy. Never again would she taste such freedom. If only she could change directions and head Daldal towards the north and the man they called Sheer. But to keep her from that temptation she was headed in the other direction. She had no real destination. No goal. She knew it was reckless and wild what she was doing. But she had to have this night. A night of power with the pounding of horse flesh between her thighs. She would race the universe. Free and without any rules. As free as she had been on her own horse as a young girl. Rahmin had hated her taking riding lessons— he had said she didn't know how to be a girl. Rahmin was wrong. She had never suckled a baby at her breast but she would feed the hungry children the honeycomb of knowledge. The hunger in their empty bellies she could do nothing about. She thought again of Najib. Surely, he was the man in Faizabad. If so, how long would he be there? Mazar-i-Sharif had just fallen to the Taliban. Could Massoud stop them in Taloqan?

With her arms around his neck she laid her head on her horses sweating mane. "I push you Daldal," she whispered. "Forgive me. Forgive." Then she righted herself and dug her heels into his side. She fantasized that she could feel Daldal hurtling upwards towards the heavens. They would ride across the sky, galloping, kicking up stardust with his hooves. Annisa shivered and felt the white heat of passion filling her body and making it light. In truth, her horse's hooves were pounding the ground but she had the sensation that she was riding above the minarets of mosques and leaping over the snow-capped mountains that ringed Kabul. She was racing so fast that stars scattered and fell. "Slow, boy, slow," she whispered after she had run Daldal until he could give no more. She eased up on the reins and with great tenderness she patted him gently and slowly brought him to a halt. It was time to go back. Back to the small pleasures-- children reciting their lessons, a cup of sweet green tea. A slice of Norwegian cherry cream cake. Forget the furies-- dust and rubble and pestilence. Forget the four horsemen of the Apocalypse who rode with the Taliban. Would men like her brother be the death of her land or would they finally prove so brutal that the world would somehow rise up against them and smite them down? Had her father not preached that good always triumphed over evil?

As she neared the outskirts of Kabul she dismounted her horse and led him by its reins. Her walk was erect; her head high. Let any man dare to challenge her tonight.

Sur Gul had fallen asleep behind the row of trees where she left him. Once again she startled him out of his sleep. "Merciful Gods. I was in the middle of a wonderful dream. Bombs fell from the sky and destroyed the Taliban. And along with the bombs there were packages of food. Food from the sky!"

"Food from the sky?" Annisa laughed. "That's a very good dream."

"Is your life saved, *min-sahib*? This thing you had to do."

"It is saved. I am no longer tempted to throw it away."

"You talk in riddles, *min-sahib*."

"Not any more."

She left him and headed in the direction of her home. She felt powerful. Invincible. Never again would she be afraid. Nothing could touch the triumph of this night.

Two blocks near her residence a man appeared out of the shadows and blocked her way. The moon lit up his face and she could see in his eyes his wicked intent.

"*Fahesha, fashesa.* You are bold to sell your wares outside the veil."

She glared at him. "I am not a prostitute. Take your money elsewhere."

"Then how will you feed your family?"

His words pierced her heart. Many widows and women without a man in the family to support them had turned to prostitution to survive.

"I am a woman of independent means."

"Independent means." He began to roar with laughter. "I have heard many things from a woman's mouth but never this." He grabbed her arm but she jerked away. "If I had a knife I would cut it off." Then she kicked him in the groin and began to run like the gazelle Ethan had said that she was.

Out of breath, she ducked into the entrance of her apartment complex just as a jeep of Taliban soldiers turned the corner in her direction. She had made it by seconds. Weak with exhaustion but delirious over her triumphant ride, she gently rapped on her door.

Siddiqa answered on the very first knock. "Thank God, you are safe! Just look at you. Your dress is covered with dust and sweat."

"I rode a great horse in the moonlight. It was something I had to do, Siddiqa."

"If I live a million years I will never understand you. Your eyes look like you are possessed. Did anyone not try to stop you on the street?"

"Only a man who thought I was a *kanchini.*"

"Oh, my God. How did you get away?"

"I kicked him and threatened to cut off his penis."

Siddiqa sank onto a chair. "It's a wonder you weren't shot. How could you say such a thing? To cut off his penis!"

"It's possible, you know. A woman in America did this when I was there. She lived in Virginia. It was in all the papers."

"Incredible."

"Even more incredible, they sewed it back on."

Siddiqa put her hand over her mouth to keep from laughing. "Oh, Annisa. The stories you make up. You are funnier than the Mullah Nasruddin."

Annisa couldn't figure out if Siddiqa was laughing from amusement or hysteria. "Believe me it happened."

Siddiqa sighed and shook her head. "I envy you Annisa."

"Why? Because of my stories?"

"Yes, and because I would never have the courage to break the rules. To ride a horse in the moonlight and all by myself."

"It wasn't courage. It was madness."

"Then I love your madness. I was so afraid you might go to look for this man that could be Najib."

"So was I," Annisa sighed. "So was I."

2001

CHAPTER 45

This mild, fair day so prized by most people in New York City was turning out to be a hassle for Matthew Hardcastle. He had just picked up the galleys for his book, "The Unholy War" from his publisher in mid-town and was late for an appointment.

"The World Trade Center," he told the cab driver.

After they had been driving for a few minutes, the cabby turned his head back and said, "That is some kind of blue." He was pointing to the sky. "Remember that old Barbara Streisand song? 'On A Clear Day You Can See Forever.'"

"Yes. Nice." Matthew's tone indicated he didn't want to make further conversation. He could still feel his adrenaline pumping after doing battle with his editor. They were refusing to let him re-write his last chapter. The assassination two days ago of Afghan Commander Akhmed Massoud, the hero of the Panjsher Valley, was crucial to the ending of his book. Only a few weeks before he was killed, Massoud had testified before a European conference that the West could no longer afford to ignore the plans of the Saudi terrorist, Osama Bin Laden. As usual, the Afghan commander's pleas had been politely listened to and then ignored. It was generally agreed among the international community that Massoud was exaggerating the danger in order to raise funds for his dwindling rag-tag army against the Taliban.

"It's too late in the day to be making changes," his editor had argued "It would break the budget. Look, you know what a battle it was to get this into print. They don't expect to make much money on it. They are convinced there is a very limited interest in Afghanistan and who cares about the thoughts of an adolescent girl. Give it up, Matt. The gods have spoken and the answer is, 'no.'"

Dejected, Matt pushed back in his seat in the taxi and stared out the window. His hand edged over and patted his briefcase containing the proofs of his book as though to reassure himself that it was still there. Beneath his fingertips were years of research on the war. Years of sorting out the stories of its victims. He was dedicating his book to Annisa. She would be pleased. It was hard not to worry about her--her infrequent letters smuggled out to him outlined the danger of her every day routine. Yet her letters were uplifting. She confided that she moved without caring for her safety, that she was oblivious as to what was happening in the streets.

He still thought she should leave Afghanistan and wrote to her that she had done her penance for whatever it was that demanded this personal sacrifice. He had truly thought she wouldn't stay that long. She did not reply and he did not hear of her again for almost two years. A member of RAWA, a group of women meeting in secret to promote women's rights in Afghanistan had contacted him to assure him that Annisa was fine. Annisa's good works and unrelenting energy to help others were known throughout Kabul. Men and women alike admired her and wherever she went she was treated with great respect. The woman with RAWA was convinced that the Taliban would not dare touch Annisa. She had become a legendary figure in her own time.

A relief worker with the UN had brought Annisa's most recent letter from Kabul. In the letter Annisa said nothing about herself except to reassure him that she was at peace with her destiny. She wanted to know if he was still working on his Afghan book. She also wanted to know if the West knew that much about the Taliban leader, Mullah Omar. Did Matthew know that the mullah had a piece of shrapnel in his head from the war with the Russians and was subject to seizures? Also, Mullah Omar was becoming more and more irrational. Not only had he outlawed the Afghan custom of kite flying, he was now advocating that the Taliban blow up the 2,000 year old Buddhist statues in Bamiyan—one of the world's great archeological treasures. She was hopeful that Matt could help bring this travesty to the attention of the world. She also enclosed a detailed list of the great prehistoric and pre-Islamic sites in Afghanistan and asked if they would be next. "There are rumors that Mullah Omar is also planning to destroy the Kafir grave effigies brought to Kabul by Amir Abdur Rahman Khan after the defeat and conversion of Nuristani to Islam. This mad man could destroy them all," she wrote. The passion in her letter to save the rich heritage of her land had buoyed him. The old Annisa was back.

Shortly after the Buddhist statues were destroyed he sent her a reprint of an article he had done before the terrible event. The West had made an effort but to no avail. Poor Annisa. She had been so certain the West could stop this desecration. As yet, he had not heard back from her. And the excesses of a Taliban madman in Afghanistan were too bizarre to think about on such a glorious day in Manhattan.

Matthew pitched forward as his cab suddenly swerved to avoid a bicyclist darting in and out of traffic.

"That was close," Matthew said.

"There ought to be a law," the driver responded. "These messenger kids give me the hives."

"Me too."

Matthew began to drum his fingers on his brief case, impatient with the slow moving traffic in lower Manhattan. He had a tight schedule ahead. A 9:30 meeting at the Trade Center and then back to his office at #3 Times Square for Collin Turner's retirement luncheon. He had known Collin before *Reuters* consolidated its jumble of offices and elected to build a new office tower at Times Square. The decision was touted as another milestone in the revitalization of New York City. The politicos were getting their rocks off for having saved 1,200 New York City jobs from the temptations of neighboring New Jersey or Connecticut. Mayor Giuliani had announced that ' the decision to build the new *Reuters* Building confirms New York City's status as the media and information capital of the world.' Matthew had to hand it to them. New York was making a tremendous comeback and particularly Times Square. New York was on a roll -- everything was coming up roses.

He noticed the worry beads hanging from the driver's rear view mirror. Then he checked the driver's license clipped to the sun visor on the front window. The driver's name was Sher Musharaf.

Matthew leaned forward in his seat. "This is a long shot, but did you ever know a cab driver by the name of Rahmin Aziz? He was killed in a robbery in New York years ago."

"No. Why do you ask?"

"I've spent a lot of time in Afghanistan and..."

The driver smiled. "Ah, you speak Farsi."

"A little... Holy shit! What was that?" Matthew shouted as a low flying airline passenger plane roared overhead.

Before the cab driver could answer a ball of flame exploded in the distance and a tornado-like cloud of black smoke billowed upwards. Matthew stuck his head out the window. "Christ, I think that plane hit the Twin Towers! Stop!" He leapt from the cab and tossed a twenty-dollar bill at the driver, "Keep the change."

"Hey, you," the driver shouted after him. "You're going the wrong way. It looks like all hell is breaking out ahead."

Matthew did not even bother to turn around, intent on pushing forward. The sidewalks were full of people who had come out of their shops and were looking upward at the smoke. "What's happened?" a woman wiping her hands on her apron asked him as he hurried past her deli.

"It looks like a plane hit the World Trade Center."

"Jesus, Mary and Joseph."

For some reason he thought he had to explain himself. "I have a meeting there..." He knew he was being foolish, heading towards what looked like a roaring inferno in the middle of the north tower. But instinct drove him. Years of heading into disaster. Somalia. Kosovo. Only to be put out to pasture with a desk job in the financial section of *Reuters*!

He had gone less than a block when he heard the roar of fire engines racing by. A virtual sea of people was rolling towards him; walking briskly but without the appearance of panic. Thick acrid smoke was beginning to sting his eyes but he hurried ahead. He was a block away now, stopping once again to catch his breath. Mesmerized by the sight, he stood transfixed, shielding his eyes with his palm as he watched the fork-tongued flames lick the floors above him. Thank God the towers were built to withstand any catastrophic event. From the corner of his eye he caught a glimpse of what he thought were bodies, twirling downward like falling leaves. Did he really see such a thing or had he imagined that people were jumping out of windows, holding hands on the way down? Bile rose in his throat. So much hell he had covered in a lifetime but he had never seen anything like this. He thought of his friends and competitors at Dow Jones. Thank God they were in the South Tower which hadn't been hit. There shouldn't be a problem. Shit! He had forgotten. There were 6 or 7 television stations above that burning inferno in the North Tower. Most of them on the ll0th floor. Was he witnessing friends of his about to be burned alive?

Suddenly, he felt his knees buckle as the roar of a second plane crashed into the south tower! Fucking Jesus. This was no accident. America was under attack!

Shrill screams of disbelief from horrified on-lookers pierced the air. Determined to get closer, Matthew shoved his way through, following a wave of yellow fire hats into a surrealistic scene: a crisscross of fire hoses dancing in the street amidst screaming people fleeing from the inferno. Rescue workers resolutely heading in and terrified victims streaming out.

A barrier tape was barely visible in the thickening smoke. Undaunted, Matthew crossed the line but was instantly waved back. The march of the walking wounded had begun. Women in blood splattered blouses; a man with a piece of glass sticking out of his leg. None of it seemed real to Matthew even though he could have reached out and touched their wounds. It was like watching an old horror movie as people stumbled zombie-like in a passing parade of disbelief. The sky was raining down ashes and sheets of paper swirled above his head. It was not the joyful bits of confetti from a New York ticker-tape parade. The papers covering the streets were sheets of work undone. He leaned over and picked one up. It was a memo to a field office in Detroit from a brokerage firm. Who had written it? Where were they now? He was transfixed--unable to move from this ghoulish scene. He was also aware that he no longer had any sense of time or space –only a feeling of utter disbelief. He wanted to help, to do something. Anything. But he knew that he was only in the way. He was sleepwalking inside a horrendous nightmare.

"Clear this space," a policeman barked on a bullhorn and he dutifully complied. He was of no use to anyone at the scene and for the first time in his life he walked away from the center of a great news story. Weighted down with an incredible sadness he turned to retrace his steps. He had gone less than a block when the roar of what sounded like a freight train behind him caused him to spin around to face the devastating cloud of concrete and steel in the slow-motion collapse of the north tower.

His instinct for survival took over and he found himself running for his life. Flying feet and flailing arms passed him as workers who had fled the buildings tried to outrun the advancing fire-eating serpent of dust and acrid smoke. His lungs were burning as he ducked into the delicatessen he had passed earlier. "Shut, the door! Shut the door!" a voice inside screamed. He threw himself behind the counter onto the floor just as the giant snowball of hell rolled past them, shattering the storefront window and blanketing them in ashes. Two people were huddled next to him behind the counter—fellow players in this tale of terror choking together in the swirling dust. He had once covered a hurricane. This was worse. There was no eye of calm in the center of the storm. No one moved, the world had lost its sound.

In the carpet of thick white debris near his foot he spied part of a human finger sticking through. Slowly, he reached down and slipped it into his pocket, hoping no one else had seen it. No need to add to their horror. His first thought was to take the finger home and have a proper burial. A ceremony which would be ludicrous since he was a man without a traditional faith. Had he entered into some kind of twilight zone-- that he was thinking about performing a religious ceremony for dead fingers?

"I'd take that down to the police station," a woman curled up next to him whispered in his ear. "They will need every sample of DNA they can get."

He nodded, appalled at his own stupidity that he hadn't thought of this. He prided himself on his logical mind and instead he was being propelled by bizarre thoughts. The woman beside him was covered in ashes, with only her eyes peering out at him. He realized that he must look that way too. And in that moment of their sameness, he felt united with her and all of mankind. 'I do not so much as unite myself as I am united.' A poet's words coming to him in the ashes. He squeezed his eyes to hide the tears inside.

His thoughts were of Annisa and her ardent search for meaning in life and with that memory, grief's bitter tide washed over him.

Four days after the disaster of September 11, Matthew Hardcastle returned the finger he had retrieved to Pier 94 at 54th Street and 12th Avenue. Waiting in a grim line of victim's relatives, which stretched around the block, he felt like an imposter. Their offerings were pitiful- –remnants of a life. A tooth brush. A strand of hair. Dental records were the best… At the New York City Medical Examiner's office, 100 dentists were working in shifts around the clock to assemble the needed X-rays. He found the scene more terrifying to him than Ground Zero. Identifying bits and pieces of a person made it all too personal. They were instructed to give the morgue teams any identifying detail of the missing person they could provide and the examples were macabre. For him, at least. The experts could do just about anything. Peel fingerprints from charred hands and determine your race, age, and sex from the long bone of an arm. Anything but bring back a life.

"Who did you lose?" a woman waiting in line with him asked.

He hesitated. "I found a finger."

"I see."

He had wrapped the finger in aluminum foil and kept it in the refrigerator. But he did not want to confide that. He tapped the cigar box he was carrying. "It's inside here."

"Well, I pray it helps someone. Do you know any of the missing?"

"Yes, yes I do. Friends and colleagues of mine. And other lives it touched." He was thinking of Collin Turner, whose retirement party would never take place. Collin's granddaughter had just started a new job with Fiduciary Trust Company International in the Twin Towers. A bright young girl of 23 with an MBA from Harvard. His old friend, Collin had suffered a stroke when they called him with the news.

The red light on his answering machine was blinking when Matt returned home from Pier 94. His publisher had left a message wanting to know if Matthew had corrected the galleys yet? It was then and only then that Matt remembered his briefcase. In his haste he had left it on the back seat of the taxi with the galleys of his book inside. And in his shock he had been too numb to think about it, retreating instead to spend hours in front of his television set. Watching the plane deliberately crash into the tower over and over and over. Based on the passenger manifest they were saying the terrorists were connected to Bin Laden.

Matthew returned his editor's call and was appalled at the conversation. The prick was actually gloating that the World Trade Center disaster would guarantee them a best seller now that Bin Laden, and the Taliban who harbored him, were all over the tube. His publisher was even going to let him change the ending as Matthew had requested, or did he want to add another chapter about the attack? Of course, they wanted it as soon as possible. There was a rush to get it out now. To strike while the iron was hot. "Lucky for you. Afghanistan is back in the news."

In shock, he placed the receiver on the table and simply walked away from it. Lucky! It had not been so lucky for Collin Turner and thousands like him. His new found faith in the unity of mankind suddenly had been defaced. Bollox! Damn his agent. Damn them all. And damn him for letting his agent's words sink in. The truth was brutal. The tragedy would indeed help his book sell.

With trepidation he dialed the lost-and- found office of New York's central office for cabs. He had left his briefcase in the taxi of a man named Sher Musharf and he was hoping the driver might have turned it in. As he waited on hold he chastised himself for playing such a childish game with his conscience. There were other galley copies of his book—the briefcase was not something that could not be replaced. Rather he was telling himself that if the briefcase had been returned then his faith in the goodness of mankind would be redeemed.

"It's here, Mr. Hardcastle."

"You're joking. Well, hallelujah..." He felt his spirits soar.

"There's a note from the driver who found it. He says he's worried you might be dead. But that if you show up to tell you all Afghans aren't bad."

"I know that."

"You can pick it up between the hours of 2-6 at our office."

"Yes, thank you. And thank Mr. Musharf when you see him. I just hope he can forgive others who may judge him otherwise," he mumbled.

"Excuse me?"

"Oh, nothing. Have a nice day."

But it was not to be.

The phone rang as soon as he hung up. Pierre Logis. A reporter with *Agence France-Presse* was on the line. He had heard that the Brits had lost men in the World Trade Center bombing and he was calling to check up on his old friend, Matt.

"Strangely enough, I was on my way to a meeting there."

Pierre also had some more sad news. He had been in Kabul earlier that summer to do a feature story on the indignities and loss of human rights for Afghan women. At a clandestine meeting with a woman named Siddiqa, he had learned the details of one of RAWA's new martyrs: Annisa Aziz, daughter of the Afghan poet, Suliaman. He knew that Matthew was a friend of hers. Siddiqa reported that Annisa had come upon two women being hassled by the militia in the street and protested their mistreatment. From a single blow to her head, she fell to the ground, never to regain consciousness. She was 32 years old, three months short of her 33rd birthday. He also told Matthew that the death of Annisa Aziz was never reported in the local paper but the tragic circumstances of her death spread like wildfire amidst the women of Kabul. One of the women who were attacked described the man who delivered the blow as an overzealous farmer from the village of Tezeen. She knew he was a veteran Mujahideen who had valiantly fought the Russians in the mountains and that now, he was an eager recruit for the Taliban militia, helping them to impose their strict code of Islam on their women.

"The woman said his name was Ishaq."

"Ishaq. Are you sure? Ishaq from Tezeen?"

"Yes. She said it twice."

It was heart-rending news.

"One other thing. This women, Siddiqa , says that Annisa Aziz had tuberculosis—an advanced stage. There was no medicine for her."

"Bloody hell. That's worse than getting hit in the head."

Long after the phone call Matthew sat slumped in his easy chair twirling an empty scotch glass in his hands. He had gone from wanting to put his fist through the wall into a self-induced stupor. Tuberculosis conjured up scenes out of Charles Dickens. To think of spirited and beautiful Annisa as a frail consumptive, coughing up bits of blood was chilling.. A travesty in this day of modern medicine. Pierre had said the disease was reaching epidemic proportions in Afghanistan. Unconscionable! Perfidy! The ultimate betrayal of a people.

He stared into space, searching for tears for Annisa. None came. All he could think of was that a bright light had gone out—a life well lived. He simply couldn't cry--too anesthetized from his morning at the Family Assistance Center and the pyre he could see still burning outside his window. At least in the end Allah had been merciful to Annisa. She died without knowing of this terrible atrocity in New York. Or that men like her brother might have perpetrated it. She also died without knowing that Ishaq had delivered her deathblow. The same Ishaq from the village of Tezeen who had once, on a moonlit night, ridden a white horse to meet his bride.

The irony of it all left a bitter taste in his mouth.

And on that note Matthew Hardcastle walked to the window of his apartment and looked out onto the haze of the burning skyline of New York. What would Annisa have thought of this sight? The World Trade Center was a smoldering funeral pyre-- a giant crematorium. Inside that billowing smoke non-existence had an image and a world of its own... He thought he could see faces inside the dark clouds, faces that haunted him from the rows of photographs pinned up near Ground Zero by anxious relatives. Certain faces stood out for him. In particular a handsome fireman in his wedding tux. As cynical as he was against anything mystical there were times when he wondered if people crossed your path for a purpose. What would a fireman from engine 33 have to tell him? That America had turned a new leaf? That a new respect was developing for those who serve and risk all as opposed to those who measure success by their paycheck? And what did this dead hero have to do with Afghanistan? Would the missing fireman even have known where it was?

He could not take his eyes off the plumes of smoke. Evil burning along with the good. Those who would save and those who would destroy. It was beyond comprehension how any 19 men on a given day could blow themselves up in order to destroy others. Or that 300 more would sacrifice their lives in an attempt to rescue others. Would the world ever rid itself of its duality? And could he come to grips with his own?

"So be it."

He left the window and went into the kitchen to brew some tea, feeling a sudden lightness. He found himself whistling "I'm a Yankee Doodle Dandy." It amused him that he was doing so. Americans were wrapping themselves in the flag these days and singing songs and giving speeches that he would have at one time considered corny. He had always disdained their overly sentimental nature that he and his fellow Europeans liked to lampoon. But all of that had changed now. He admired the fervor and the fortitude of America's everyday heroes and was amazed at the tenacity of the men he had personally interviewed on Wall Street. They had sworn they would reopen the New York Stock Exchange next week. And they would. Each man a hero in his own way. New York would return-- like a Phoenix rising from the ashes.

His fervent prayer was that someday this also would be true for Afghanistan. But he was far too realistic to believe that peace would come to the land of high flags any time soon. America's smart bombs would fall and topple the Taliban. And after the fighting? The warriors would preach that power deters war and the poets would answer that 'as a man so believes' was the root of it. Both of them would be right.

He knew in his heart that vengeance was never the answer but vengeance would be done. Vengeance, the creator of the vicious circle, would always ensnare man's desire for peace inside.

In his mind's eye he saw the vertical windmills of Herat—those ancient relics of the past which twirled at the time of the '120 days wind.' The time of the harvest. At first his Western eye had not recognized them for what they were because the windmills lacked the familiar huge wheeled arms of the ones with which Don Quixote fenced. The windmills of Herat were all that is simple and strong and they had dotted the landscape of Afghanistan since the seventh century. God willing, they would spin again.

#

About the Author

Kathleen MacArthur's previous book about Afghanistan, *Spies Behind the Pillars, Bandits at the Pass,* was based on a series of articles she wrote for the *Kabul Times* while living and working in Kabul in the late 1960's. In order to gather material for her weekly column, *Afghan Diary*, she traveled extensively in the country. Her book was broadcast in its entirety several times over the *Voice of America.*

Although *Annisa* is fictional, many of the incidents included in the book are true stories of Afghan refugees that Mrs. MacArthur interviewed in Washington D.C. after they had escaped to the West. The University of Nebraska at Omaha has published excerpts from *Annisa* in its *Afghan Studies Journal.*

A former press secretary of the Joint Economic Committee and a speechwriter on Capitol Hill, she worked for Senators John Sherman Cooper, Hubert Humphrey and Lloyd Bentsen. She left the Congress to study English literature at Oxford University in England.

Born in Wichita, Kansas and educated at the University of Kansas, Mrs. MacArthur is the mother of three children and now lives with her husband in Savannah, Georgia and Monpazier, France.